EVERYTHING IS ILLUMINATED

———

EXTREMELY LOUD
& INCREDIBLY CLOSE

BOOKS BY JONATHAN SAFRAN FOER

A Convergence of Birds
(editor)

Everything Is Illuminated

Joe
(with Hiroshi Sugimoto
and Richard Serra)

Extremely Loud & Incredibly Close

Eating Animals

Everything Is Illuminated

Extremely Loud & Incredibly Close

JONATHAN SAFRAN FOER

Houghton Mifflin Harcourt

BOSTON · NEW YORK

2010

www.hmhbooks.com
Also visit www.theprojectmuseum.com

Library of Congress Cataloging-in-Publication Data
Foer, Jonathan Safran, date.
Everything is illuminated ; Extremely loud & incredibly close
/ Jonathan Safran Foer.
p. cm.
ISBN 978-0-547-44726-1
I. Foer, Jonathan Safran, date. Extremely loud &
incredibly close. II. Title.
PS3606.O38A6 2010
813'.6—dc22   2010025830

Printed in the United States of America

DOC 10 9 8 7 6 5 4 3 2

Acknowledgments and credits are on page 647.

Everything Is Illuminated

Simply and impossibly:

FOR MY FAMILY

an overture to the commencement of a very rigid journey

My LEGAL NAME is Alexander Perchov. But all of my many friends dub me Alex, because that is a more flaccid-to-utter version of my legal name. Mother dubs me Alexi-stop-spleening-me!, because I am always spleening her. If you want to know why I am always spleening her, it is because I am always elsewhere with friends, and disseminating so much currency, and performing so many things that can spleen a mother. Father used to dub me Shapka, for the fur hat I would don even in the summer month. He ceased dubbing me that because I ordered him to cease dubbing me that. It sounded boyish to me, and I have always thought of myself as very potent and generative. I have many many girls, believe me, and they all have a different name for me. One dubs me Baby, not because I am a baby, but because she attends to me. Another dubs me All Night. Do you want to know why? I have a girl who dubs me Currency, because I disseminate so much currency around her. She licks my chops for it. I have a miniature brother who dubs me Alli. I do not dig this name very much, but I dig him very much, so OK, I permit him to dub me Alli. As for his name, it is Little Igor, but Father dubs him Clumsy One, because he is always promenading into things. It was only four days previous that he made his eye blue from a mismanagement with a brick wall. If you're wondering what my bitch's name is, it is Sammy Davis, Junior, Junior. She has this name because Sammy Davis, Junior was Grandfather's beloved singer, and the bitch is his, not mine, because I am not the one who thinks he is blind.

As for me, I was sired in 1977, the same year as the hero of this story. In truth, my life has been very ordinary. As I mentioned before, I do many good things with myself and others, but they are ordinary things. I dig American movies. I dig Negroes, particularly Michael Jackson. I dig to disseminate very much currency at famous nightclubs in Odessa. Lamborghini Countaches are excellent, and so are cappuccinos. Many girls want to be carnal with me in many good arrangements, notwithstanding the Inebriated Kangaroo, the Gorky Tickle, and the Unyielding Zookeeper. If you want to know why so many girls want to be with me, it is because I am a very premium person to be with. I am homely, and also severely funny, and these are winning things. But nonetheless, I know many people who dig rapid cars and famous discotheques. There are so many who perform the Sputnik Bosom Dalliance—which is always terminated with a slimy underface—that I cannot tally them on all of my hands. There are even many people named Alex. (Three in my house alone!) That is why I was so effervescent to go to Lutsk and translate for Jonathan Safran Foer. It would be unordinary.

I had performed recklessly well in my second year of English at university. This was a very majestic thing I did because my instructor was having shit between his brains. Mother was so proud of me, she said, "Alexi-stop-spleening-me! You have made me so proud of you." I inquired her to purchase me leather pants, but she said no. "Shorts?" "No." Father was also so proud. He said, "Shapka," and I said, "Do not dub me that," and he said, "Alex, you have made Mother so proud."

Mother is a humble woman. Very, very humble. She toils at a small café one hour distance from our home. She presents food and drink to customers there, and says to me, "I mount the autobus for an hour to work all day doing things I hate. You want to know why? It is for you, Alexi-stop-spleening-me! One day you will do things for me that you hate. That is what it means to be a family." What she does not clutch is that I already do things for her that I hate. I listen to her when she talks to me. I resist complaining about my pygmy allowance. And did I mention that I do not spleen her nearly so much as I desire to? But I do not do these things because we are a family. I do them because they are common decencies. That is an idiom that the hero taught me. I do them because I am not a big fucking asshole. That is another idiom that the hero taught me.

Father toils for a travel agency, denominated Heritage Touring. It is for Jewish people, like the hero, who have cravings to leave that ennobled country America and visit humble towns in Poland and Ukraine. Father's agency scores a translator, guide, and driver for the Jews, who try to unearth places where their families once existed. OK, I had never met a Jewish person until the voyage. But this was their fault, not mine, as I had always been willing, and one might even write lukewarm, to meet one. I will be truthful again and mention that before the voyage I had the opinion that Jewish people were having shit between their brains. This is because all I knew of Jewish people was that they paid Father very much currency in order to make vacations *from* America *to* Ukraine. But then I met Jonathan Safran Foer, and I will tell you, he is not having shit between his brains. He is an ingenious Jew.

So as for the Clumsy One, who I never ever dub the Clumsy One but always Little Igor, he is a first-rate boy. It is now evident to me that he will become a very potent and generative man, and that his brain will have many muscles. We do not speak in volumes, because he is such a silent person, but I am certain that we are friends, and I do not think I would be lying if I wrote that we are paramount friends. I have tutored Little Igor to be a man of this world. For an example, I exhibited him a smutty magazine three days yore, so that he should be appraised of the many positions in which I am carnal. "This is the sixty-nine," I told him, presenting the magazine in front of him. I put my fingers—two of them —on the action, so that he would not overlook it. "Why is it dubbed sixty-nine?" he asked, because he is a person hot on fire with curiosity. "It was invented in 1969. My friend Gregory knows a friend of the nephew of the inventor." "What did people do before 1969?" "Merely blowjobs and masticating box, but never in chorus." He will be made a VIP if I have a thing to do with it.

This is where the story begins.

But first I am burdened to recite my good appearance. I am unequivocally tall. I do not know any women who are taller than me. The women I know who are taller than me are lesbians, for whom 1969 was a very momentous year. I have handsome hairs, which are split in the middle. This is because Mother used to split them on the side when I was a boy, and to spleen her I split them in the middle. "Alexi-stop-spleening-me!," she said, "you appear mentally unbalanced with your hairs split like that." She did not intend it, I know. Very often Mother utters things that I know she does not intend. I have an aristocratic smile and like to punch people. My stomach is very strong, although it presently lacks muscles. Father is a fat man, and Mother is also. This does not disquiet me, because my stomach is very strong, even if it appears very fat. I will describe my eyes and then begin the story. My eyes are blue and resplendent. Now I will begin the story.

Father obtained a telephone call from the American office of Heritage Touring. They required a driver, guide, and translator for a young man who would be in Lutsk at the dawn of the month of July. This was a troublesome supplication, because at the dawn of July, Ukraine was to celebrate the first birthday of its ultramodern constitution, which makes us feel very nationalistic, and so many people would be on vacation in foreign places. It was an impossible situation, like the 1984 Olympics. But Father is an overawing man who always obtains what he desires. "Shapka," he said on the phone to me, who was at home enjoying the greatest of all documentary movies, *The Making of "Thriller,"* "what was the language you studied this year at school?" "Do not dub me Shapka," I said. "Alex," he said, "what was the language you studied this year at school?" "The language of English," I told him. "Are you good and fine at it?" he asked me. "I am fluid," I told him, hoping I might make him proud enough to buy me the zebra-skin seat coverings of my dreams. "Excellent, Shapka," he said. "Do not dub me that," I said. "Excellent, Alex. Excellent. You must nullify any plans you possess for the first week of the month of July." "I do not possess any plans," I said to him. "Yes you do," he said.

Now is a befitting time to mention Grandfather, who is also fat, but yet more fat than my parents. OK, I will mention him. He has gold teeth and cultivates ample hairs on his face to comb by the dusk of every day. He toiled for fifty years at many employments, primarily farming, and later machine manipulating. His final employment was at Heritage Touring, where he commenced to toil in the 1950s and persevered until of late. But now he is retarded and lives on our street. My grandmother died two years yore of a cancer in her brain, and Grandfather became very melancholy, and also, he says, blind. Father does not believe him, but purchased Sammy Davis, Junior, Junior for him nonetheless, because a Seeing Eye bitch is not only for blind people but for people who pine for the negative of loneliness. (I should not have used "purchased," because in truth Father did not purchase Sammy Davis, Junior, Junior, but only received her from the home for forgetful dogs. Because of this, she is not a real Seeing Eye bitch, and is also mentally deranged.) Grandfather disperses most of the day at our house, viewing television. He yells at me often. "Sasha!" he yells. "Sasha, do not be so lazy! Do not be so worthless! Do something! Do something worthy!" I never rejoinder him, and never spleen him with intentions, and never understand what worthy means. He did not have the unappetizing habit of yelling at Little Igor and me before Grandmother died. That is how we are certain that he does not intend it, and that is why we can forgive him. I discovered him crying once, in front of the television. (Jonathan, this part about Grandfather must remain amid you and me, yes?) The weather report was exhibiting, so I was certain that it was not something melancholy on the television that made him cry. I never mentioned it, because it was a common decency to not mention it.

Grandfather's name is also Alexander. Supplementally is Father's. We are all the primogenitory children in our families, which brings us tremendous honor, on the scale of the sport of baseball, which was invented in Ukraine. I will dub my first child Alexander. If you want to know what will occur if my first child is a girl, I will tell you. He will not be a girl. Grandfather was sired in Odessa in 1918. He has never departed Ukraine. The remotest he ever traveled was Kiev, and that was for when my uncle wedded The Cow. When I was a boy, Grandfather would tutor that Odessa is the most beautiful city in the world, because the vodka is cheap, and so are the women. He would manufacture funnies with Grandmother before she died about how he was in love with other women who were not her. She knew it was only funnies because she would laugh in volumes. "Anna," he would say, "I am going to marry that one with the pink hat." And she would say, "To whom are you going to marry her?" And he would say, "To me." I would laugh very much in the back seat, and she would say to him, "But you are no priest." And he would say, "I am today." And she would say, "Today you believe in God?" And he would say, "Today I believe in love." Father commanded me never to mention Grandmother to Grandfather. "It will make him melancholy, Shapka," Father said. "Do not dub me that," I said. "It will make him melancholy, Alex, and it will make him think he is more blind. Let him forget." So I never mention her, because unless I do not want to, I do what Father tells me to do. Also, he is a first-rate puncher.

After telephoning me, Father telephoned Grandfather to inform him that he would be the driver of our journey. If you want to know who would be the guide, the answer is there would be no guide. Father said that a guide was not an indispensable thing, because Grandfather knew a beefy amount from all of his years at Heritage Touring. Father dubbed him an expert. (At the time when he said this, it seemed like a very reasonable thing to say. But how does this make you feel, Jonathan, in the luminescence of everything that occurred?)

When the three of us, the three men named Alex, gathered in Father's house that night to converse the journey, Grandfather said, "I do not want to do it. I am retarded, and I did not become a retarded person in order to have to perform shit such as this. I am done with it." "I do not care what you want," Father told him. Grandfather punched the table with much violence and shouted, "Do not forget who is who!" I thought that that would be the end of the conversation. But Father said something queer. "Please." And then he said something even queerer. He said, "Father." I must confess that there is so much I do not understand. Grandfather returned to his chair and said, "This is the final one. I will never do it again."

So we made schemes to procure the hero at the Lvov train station on 2 July, at 1500 of the afternoon. Then we would be for two days in the area of Lutsk. "Lutsk?" Grandfather said. "You did not say it was Lutsk." "It is Lutsk," Father said. Grandfather became in thought. "He is looking for the town his grandfather came from," Father said, "and someone, Augustine he calls her, who salvaged his grandfather from the war. He desires to write a book about his grandfather's village." "Oh," I said, "so he is intelligent?" "No," Father corrected. "He has low-grade brains.

The American office informs me that he telephones them every day and manufactures numerous half-witted queries about finding suitable food." "There will certainly be sausage," I said. "Of course," Father said. "He is only half-witted." Here I will repeat that the hero is a very ingenious Jew. "Where is the town?" I asked. "The name of the town is Trachimbrod." "Trachimbrod?" Grandfather asked. "It is near 50 kilometers from Lutsk," Father said. "He possesses a map and is sanguine of the coordinates. It should be simple."

Grandfather and I viewed television for several hours after Father reposed. We are both people who remain conscious very tardy. (I was near-at-hand to writing that we both relish to remain conscious tardy, but that is not faithful.) We viewed an American television program that had the words in Russian at the bottom of the screen. It was about a Chinaman who was resourceful with a bazooka. We also viewed the weather report. The weatherman said that the weather would be very abnormal the next day, but that the next day after that would be normal. Amid Grandfather and I was a silence you could cut with a scimitar. The only time that either of us spoke was when he rotated to me during an advertisement for McDonald's McPorkburgers and said, "I do not want to drive ten hours to an ugly city to attend to a very spoiled Jew."

IT WAS March 18, 1791, when Trachim B's double-axle wagon either did or did not pin him against the bottom of the Brod River. The young W twins were the first to see the curious flotsam rising to the surface: wandering snakes of white string, a crushed-velvet glove with outstretched fingers, barren spools, schmootzy pince-nez, rasp- and boysenberries, feces, frillwork, the shards of a shattered atomizer, the bleeding red-ink script of a resolution: *I will . . . I will . . .*

Hannah wailed. Chana waded into the cold water, pulling up above her knees the yarn ties at the ends of her britches, sweeping the rising life-debris to her sides as she waded farther. *What are you doing over there!* the disgraced usurer Yankel D called, kicking up shoreline mud as he hobbled toward the girls. He extended one hand to Chana and held the other, as always, over the incriminating abacus bead he was forced by shtetl proclamation to wear on a string around his neck. *Stay back from the water! You will get hurt!*

The good gefiltefishmonger Bitzl Bitzl R watched the commotion from his paddleboat, which was fastened with twine to one of his traps. *What's going on over there?* he shouted to shore. *Is that you, Yankel? Is there some sort of trouble?*

It's the Well-Regarded Rabbi's twins, Yankel called back. *They're playing in the water and I'm afraid someone will get hurt!*

It's turning up the most unusual things! Chana laughed, splashing at the mass that grew like a garden around her. She picked up the hands of a baby doll, and those of a grandfather clock. Umbrella ribs. A skeleton key. The articles rose on the crowns of bubbles that burst when they reached the surface. The slightly younger and less cautious twin raked her fingers through the water and each time came up with something new: a yellow pinwheel, a muddy hand mirror, the petals of some sunken forget-me-not, silt and cracked black pepper, a packet of seeds...

But her slightly older and more cautious sister, Hannah—identical in every way save the hairs connecting her eyebrows—watched from shore and cried. The disgraced usurer Yankel D took her into his arms, pressed her head against his chest, murmured, *Here... here...*, and called to Bitzl Bitzl: *Row to the Well-Regarded Rabbi's and bring him back with you. Also bring Menasha the physician and Isaac the man of law. Quickly!*

The mad squire Sofiowka N, whose name the shtetl would later take for maps and Mormon census records, emerged from behind a tree. *I have seen everything that happened,* he said hysterically. *I witnessed it all. The wagon was moving too fast for this dirt road — the only thing worse than to be late to your own wedding is to be late to the wedding of the girl who should have been your wife — and it suddenly flipped itself, and if that's not exactly the truth, then the wagon didn't flip itself, but was itself flipped by a wind from Kiev or Odessa or wherever, and if that doesn't seem quite correct, then what happened was — and I would swear on my lily-white name to this — an angel with gravestone-feathered wings descended from heaven to take Trachim back with him, for Trachim was too good for this world. Of course, who isn't? We are all too good for each other.*

Trachim? Yankel asked, allowing Hannah to finger the incriminating bead. *Wasn't Trachim the shoemaker from Lutsk who died half a year ago of pneumonia?*

Look at this! Chana called, giggling, holding above her head the jack of cunnilingus from a dirty deck of cards.

No, Sofiowka said. *That man's name was Trachum with a u. This is with an i. And that Trachum died in the Night of the Longest Night. No, wait. No, wait. He died from being an artist.*

And this! Chana shrieked with joy, holding up a faded map of the universe.

Get out of the water! Yankel hollered at her, raising his voice louder than he would have wished at the Well-Regarded Rabbi's daughter, or any young girl. *You will get hurt!*

Chana ran to shore. The deep green water obscured the zodiac as the star chart sank to the river's bottom, coming to rest, like a veil, on the horse's face.

The shutters of the shtetl's windows were opening to the commotion (curiosity being the only thing the citizens shared). The accident had happened by the small falls—the part of shore that marked the current division of the shtetl into its two sections, the Jewish Quarter and the Human Three-Quarters. All so-called sacred activities—religious studies, kosher butchering, bargaining, etc.—were contained within the Jewish Quarter. Those activities concerned with the humdrum of daily existence—secular studies, communal justice, buying and selling, etc.—took place in the Human Three-Quarters. Straddling the two was the Upright Synagogue. (The ark itself was built along the Jewish/Human fault line, such that one of the two Torah scrolls would exist in each zone.) As the ratio of sacred to secular shifted—usually no more than a hair in this or that direction, save for that exceptional hour in 1764, immediately following the Pogrom of Beaten Chests, when the shtetl was completely secular—so did the fault line, drawn in chalk from Radziwell Forest to the river. And so was the synagogue lifted and moved. It was in 1783 that wheels were attached, making the shtetl's ever-changing negotiation of Jewishness and Humanness less of a schlep.

I understand there has been an accident, panted Shloim W, the humble antiques salesman who survived off charity, unable to part with any of his candelabras, figurines, or hourglasses since his wife's untimely death.

How did you know? Yankel asked.

Bitzl Bitzl yelled to me from his boat on his way to the Well-Regarded Rabbi's. I knocked on as many doors as I could on my way here.

Good, Yankel said. *We'll need a shtetl proclamation.*

Are we sure he's dead? someone asked.

Quite, Sofiowka assured. *Dead as he was before his parents met. Or deader, maybe, for then he was at least a bullet in his father's cock and an emptiness in his mother's belly.*

Did you try to save him? Yankel asked.

No.

Cover their eyes, Shloim told Yankel, gesturing at the girls. He quickly undressed himself—revealing a belly larger than most, and a back matted with ringlets of thick black hair—and dove into the water. Feathers washed over him on the wings of water swells. Unstrung pearls and ungummed teeth. Blood clots, Merlot, and splintered chandelier crystal. The rising wreckage became increasingly dense, until he couldn't see his hands in front of him. *Where? Where?*

Did you find him? the man of law Isaac M asked when Shloim finally surfaced. *Is it clear how long he's been down there?*

Was he alone or with a wife? asked grieving Shanda T, widow of the deceased philosopher Pinchas T, who, in his only notable paper, "To the Dust: From Man You Came and to Man You Shall Return," argued it would be possible, in theory, for life and art to be reversed.

A powerful wind swept through the shtetl, making it whistle. Those studying obscure texts in dimly lit rooms looked up. Lovers making amends and promises, amendments and excuses, fell silent. The lonely candle dipper, Mordechai C, submerged his hands in a vat of warm blue wax.

He did have a wife, Sofiowka inserted, his left hand diving deep into his trouser pocket. *I remember her well. She had a set of such voluptuous tits. God, she had great tits. Who could forget those? They were, oh God, they were great. I'd trade all of the words I've since learned to be young again, oh yes, yes, getting a good suck on those titties. Yes I would! Yes I would!*

How do you know these things? someone asked.

I went to Rovno once, as a child, on an errand for my father. It was to this Trachim's house. His surname escapes my tongue, but I remember quite well that he was Trachim with an i, that he had a young wife with a great set of tits, a small apartment with many knickknacks, and a scar from his eye to his mouth, or his mouth to his eye. One or the other.

YOU WERE ABLE TO SEE HIS FACE AS HE WAGONED BY? the Well-Regarded Rabbi asked in a holler as his girls ran to hide under opposite ends of his prayer shawl. *THE SCAR?*

And then, ay yay yay, I saw him again when I was a young man applying myself in Lvov. Trachim was making a delivery of peaches, if I remember, or perhaps plums, to a house of schoolgirls across the street. Or was he a postman? Yes, it was love letters.

Of course he couldn't be alive anymore, said Menasha the physician, opening his medical bag. He removed several pages of death certificates, which were picked up by another breeze and sent into the trees. Some would fall with the leaves that September. Some would fall with the trees generations later.

And even if he were alive, we couldn't free him, said Shloim, drying himself behind a large rock. *It won't be possible to get to the wagon until all of its contents have risen.*

WE MUST MAKE A SHTETL PROCLAMATION, proclaimed the Well-Regarded Rabbi, mustering a more authoritative holler.

Now what was his name, exactly? Menasha asked, touching quill to tongue.

Can we say for sure that he had a wife? grieving Shanda asked, touching hand to heart.

Did the girls see anything? asked Avrum R, the lapidary, who wore no rings himself (although the Well-Regarded Rabbi had promised he knew of a young woman in Lodz who could make him happy [forever]).

The girls saw nothing, Sofiowka said. *I saw that they saw nothing.*

And the twins, this time both of them, began to cry.

But we can't leave the matter entirely to his word, Shloim said, gesturing at Sofiowka, who returned the favor with a gesture of his own.

Do not ask the girls, Yankel said. *Leave them alone. They've been through enough.*

By now, almost all of the shtetl's three hundred–odd citizens had gathered to debate that about which they knew nothing. The less a citizen knew, the more adamantly he or she argued. There was nothing new in this. A month before there had been the question of whether it might send a better message to the children to plug, finally, the bagel's hole. Two months before there had been the cruel and comic debate over the question of typesetting, and before that the question of Polish identity, which moved many to tears, and many to laughter, and all to more questions. And still to come would be other questions to debate, and others after that. Questions from the beginning of time—whenever that was—to whenever would be the end. From *ashes?* to *ashes?*

PERHAPS, the Well-Regarded Rabbi said, raising his hands even higher, his voice even louder, *WE DO NOT HAVE TO SETTLE THE MATTER AT ALL. WHAT IF WE NEVER FILL OUT A DEATH CERTIFICATE? WHAT IF WE GIVE THE BODY A PROPER BURIAL, BURN ANYTHING THAT WASHES ASHORE, AND ALLOW LIFE TO GO ON IN THE FACE OF THIS DEATH?*

But we need a proclamation, said Froida Y, the candy maker.

Not if the shtetl proclaims otherwise, corrected Isaac.

Perhaps we should try to contact his wife, said grieving Shanda.

Perhaps we should begin to gather the remains, said Eliezar Z, the dentist.

And in the braid of argument, young Hannah's voice almost went unnoticed as she peeked her head from beneath the fringed wing of her father's prayer shawl.

I see something.

WHAT? her father asked, quieting the others. *WHAT DO YOU SEE?*

Over there, pointing to the frothing water.

In the middle of the string and feathers, surrounded by candles and soaked matches, prawns, pawns, and silk tassels that curtsied like jellyfish, was a baby girl, still mucus-glazed, still pink as the inside of a plum.

The twins hid their bodies under their father's tallis, like ghosts. The horse at the bottom of the river, shrouded by the sunken night sky, closed its heavy eyes. The prehistoric ant in Yankel's ring, which had lain motionless in the honey-colored amber since long before Noah hammered the first plank, hid its head between its many legs, in shame.

THE LOTTERY, 1791

BITZL BITZL R was able to recover the wagon a few days later with the help of a group of strong men from Kolki, and his traps saw more action than ever. But sifting through the remains, they didn't find a body. For the next one hundred fifty years, the shtetl would host an annual contest to "find" Trachim, although a shtetl proclamation withdrew the reward in 1793 — on Menasha's counsel that any ordinary corpse would begin to break apart after two years in water, so searching not only would be pointless but could result in rather offensive findings, or even worse, multiple rewards — and the contest became more of a festival, for which the line of short-tempered bakers P would create particular pastry treats, and the girls of the shtetl would dress as the twins dressed on that fateful day: in wool britches with yarn ties, and canvas blouses with blue-fringed butterfly collars. Men came from great distances to dive for the cotton sacks that the Float Queen would throw into the Brod, all but one of which, the golden sack, were filled with earth.

There were those who thought that Trachim would never be found, that the current brushed enough loose sediment over him to properly bury his body. These people laid stones on the shoreside when they made their monthly cemetery rounds, and said things like:

Poor Trachim, I didn't know him well, but I sure could have.

or

I miss you, Trachim. Without having ever met you, I do.

or

Rest, Trachim, rest. And make safe our flour mill.

There were those who suspected that he was not pinned under his

JONATHAN SAFRAN FOER

wagon but swept out to sea, with the secrets of his life kept forever inside him, like a love note in a bottle, to be found one morning by an unsuspecting couple on a romantic beach stroll. It's possible that he, or some part of him, washed up on the sands of the Black Sea, or in Rio, or that he made it all the way to Ellis Island.

Or perhaps a widow found him and took him in: bought him an easy chair, changed his sweater every morning, shaved his face until the hair stopped growing, took him faithfully to bed with her every night, whispered sweet nothings into what was left of his ear, laughed with him over black coffee, cried with him over yellowing pictures, talked greenly about having kids of her own, began to miss him before she became sick, left him everything in her will, thought of only him as she died, always knew he was a fiction but believed in him anyway.

Some argued that there was never a body at all. Trachim wanted to be dead without being dead, the con artist. He packed a wagon with all of his possessions, rode it into the nondescript, nameless shtetl—which was soon to be known across eastern Poland for its yearly festival, Trachimday, and to carry his name like an orphan baby (except for maps and Mormon census records, for which it would go by Sofiowka)—patted his nameless horse its last pat, and spurred it into the undertow. Was he escaping debt? An unfavorable arranged marriage? Lies that had caught up with him? Was his death an essential stage in the continuation of his life?

Of course there are those who pointed to Sofiowka's madness, how he would sit naked in the fountain of the prostrate mermaid, caressing her scaly tuches like a newborn's fontanel, caressing his own better half as if there were nothing in the world wrong with beating one's boner, wherever, whenever. Or how he was once found on the Well-Regarded Rabbi's front lawn, bound in white string, and said he tied one around his index finger to remember something terribly important, and fearing he would forget the index finger, he tied a string around his pinky, and then one from waist to neck, and fearing he would forget this one, he tied a string from ear to tooth to scrotum to heel, and used his body to remember his body, but in the end could remember only the string. Is this someone to trust for a story?

And the baby? My great-great-great-great-great-grandmother? This is a more difficult problem, for it's relatively easy to reason how a life could be lost in a river, but for one to arise from it?

Harry V, the shtetl's master logician and resident pervert—who had been working for as many years and with as little success as one could imagine on his magnum opus, "The Host of Hoists," which, he promised, contained the tightest of tight logical proofs that God indiscriminatingly loves the indiscriminate lover—put forth a lengthy argument concerning the presence of another on the ill-starred wagon: Trachim's wife. Perhaps, Harry argued, her water broke while the two were munching deviled eggs in a meadow between shtetls, and perhaps Trachim urged the wagon to dangerous speeds in order to get her to a doctor before the baby squirmed out like a flapping flounder from a fisherman's grip. As the waves of her tidal contractions began to break over her head, Trachim turned to his wife, perhaps put his callused hand on her soft face, perhaps took his eyes off the riddled road, and perhaps inadvertently steered into the river. Perhaps the wagon flipped, the bodies plunged under its weight, and perhaps, sometime between her mother's last breath and her father's final attempt to free himself, the baby was born. Perhaps. But not even Harry could explain the absence of an umbilical cord.

The Wisps of Ardisht—that clan of artisan smokers in Rovno who smoked so much they smoked even when they were not smoking, and were condemned by shtetl proclamation to a life of rooftops as shingle layers and chimney sweeps—believed that my great-great-great-great-great-grandmother was Trachim reborn. In his moment of afterworldly judgment, as his softening body was presented before the Keeper of those glorious and barbed Gates, something went wrong. There was unfinished business. The soul was not ready to transcend, but was sent back, given a chance to right a previous generation's wrong. This, of course, doesn't make any sense. But what does?

More concerned with the baby's future than its past, the Well-Regarded Rabbi offered no official interpretation of her origins for either the shtetl or *The Book of Antecedents*, but took her in as his own responsibility until her final home should be decided. He brought her to the Upright Synagogue—for not even a baby, he swore, should set foot in the Slouching Synagogue (wherever it happened to be on that given day)—and tucked her makeshift crib in the ark while the men in long black suits hollered prayers at the top of their lungs. *HOLY, HOLY, HOLY IS THE LORD OF HOSTS! THE WHOLE WORLD IS FILLED WITH HIS GLORY!*

The goers of the Upright Synagogue had been screaming for more than two hundred years, since the Venerable Rabbi enlightened that we are always drowning, and our prayers are nothing less than pleas for rescue from deep under the spiritual waters. *AND IF OUR PLIGHT IS SO DESPERATE,* he said (always starting his sentences with "and," as if what he verbalized were some logical continuation of his innermost thoughts), *SHOULD WE NOT ACT LIKE IT? AND SHOULD WE NOT SOUND LIKE DESPERATE PEOPLE?* So they screamed, and had been screaming for the two hundred years since.

And they screamed now, never allowing the baby a moment of rest, and hung—with one hand on prayer book and one on rope—from the pulleys that clipped to their belts, and kept the crowns of their black hats brushing against the ceiling. *AND IF WE ASPIRE TO BE CLOSER TO GOD,* the Venerable Rabbi had enlightened, *SHOULD WE NOT ACT LIKE IT? AND SHOULD WE NOT MAKE OURSELVES CLOSER?* Which made enough sense. It was on the eve of Yom Kippur, the holiest of holy days, that a fly flew under the door of the synagogue and began to pester the hanging congregants. It flew from face to face, buzzing, landing on long noses, going in and out of hairy ears. *AND IF THIS IS A TEST,* the Venerable Rabbi enlightened, trying to keep his congregation together, *SHOULD WE NOT RISE TO ITS CHALLENGE? AND I URGE YOU: CRASH TO THE GROUND BEFORE YOU RELEASE THE GREAT BOOK!*

But how pestering that fly was, tickling some of the most ticklish places. *AND AS GOD ASKED ABRAHAM TO SHOW ISAAC THE KNIFE'S POINT, SO IS HE ASKING US NOT TO SCRATCH OUR ASSES! AND IF WE MUST, BY ALL MEANS WITH THE LEFT HAND!* Half did as the Venerable Rabbi enlightened, and released the rope before the Great Book. These were the ancestors of the Upright

Synagogue's congregants, who continued for two hundred years to walk with an affected limp to remind themselves—or, more importantly, to remind others—of their response to The Test: that the Holy Word prevailed. (*EXCUSE ME, RABBI, BUT JUST WHICH WORD IS IT EXACTLY?* The Venerable Rabbi knocked his disciple with the business end of a Torah pointer: *AND IF YOU HAVE TO ASK!*...) Some Uprighters went so far as to refuse to walk at all, signifying an even more dramatic fall. Which meant they couldn't get to synagogue, of course. *WE PRAY BY NOT PRAYING*, they said. *WE FULFILL THE LAW BY TRANSGRESSING IT.*

Those who dropped the prayer book rather than fall were the ancestors of the Slouching Synagogue's congregants—so named by the Uprighters. They twiddled with the fringes sewn to the ends of their shirtsleeves, which they put there to remind themselves—or, more importantly, to remind others—of their response to The Test: that the strings are carried around with you, that the *spirit* of the Holy Word should always prevail. (*Excuse me, but does anyone know what that thing about the Holy Word means?* The others shrugged and went back to their argument about how best to divide thirteen knishes among forty-three people.) It was the Slouchers' customs that changed: the pulleys were traded in for pillows, the Hebrew prayer book for a more understandable Yiddish one, and the Rabbi for a group-led service and discussion, followed, but more often interrupted, by food, drink, and gossip. The Upright congregants looked down on the Slouchers, who seemed willing to sacrifice any Jewish law for the sake of what they feebly termed *the great and necessary reconciliation of religion with life.* The Uprighters called them names and promised them an eternity of agony in the next world for their eagerness to be comfortable in this one. But like Shmul S, the intestine-tied milkman, the Slouchers couldn't give a shit. Save for those rare occasions when Uprighters and Slouchers pushed at the synagogue from opposite sides, trying to make the shtetl more sacred or secular, they learned to ignore each other.

For six days the citizens of the shtetl, Uprighters and Slouchers alike, stood in lines outside the Upright Synagogue to get their chance to view my very-great-grandmother. Many returned many times. Men could examine the baby, touch it, talk to it, even hold it. Women were not allowed inside the Upright Synagogue, of course, for as the Venerable Rabbi so long ago enlightened, *AND HOW CAN WE BE EXPECTED TO KEEP OUR MINDS AND HEARTS WITH GOD WHEN THAT OTHER PART IS POINTING US TOWARD IMPURE THOUGHTS OF YOU KNOW WHAT?*

What seemed like a reasonable compromise was reached when, in 1763, the women were allowed to pray in a dank and cramped room beneath a specially installed glass floor. But it wasn't long before the dangling men took their eyes from the Great Book to partake in the chorus of cleavages below. Black pants became form-fitting, there was more bumping and swaying than ever as those *other parts* protruded in fantasies of *you know what*, and an extra hole was unknowingly inserted in the holiest of prayers: *HOLY, HOLY, HOLY,* HOLEY *IS THE LORD OF HOSTS! THE WHOLE WORLD IS FILLED WITH HIS GLORY!*

The Venerable Rabbi addressed the disconcerting matter in one of his many midafternoon sermons. *AND WE MUST ALL BE FAMILIAR WITH THAT MOST PORTENTOUS OF BIBLICAL PARABLES, THE PERFECTION OF HEAVEN AND HELL. AND AS WE ALL DO OR SHOULD KNOW, IT WAS ON THE SECOND DAY THAT THE LORD OUR GOD CREATED THE OPPOSING REGIONS OF HEAVEN AND HELL, TO WHICH WE AND THE SLOUCHERS, MAY THEY PACK ONLY SWEATERS, WILL BE SENT, RESPECTIVELY. AND BUT WE MUST NOT FORGET THAT THIRD AND NEXT DAY, WHEN GOD SAW THAT HEAVEN WAS NOT AS MUCH LIKE HEAVEN AS HE WOULD HAVE PRAYED, AND HELL NOT AS MUCH LIKE HELL. AND SO, THE LESSER AND HARDER-TO-FIND TEXTS TELL US, HE, FATHER OF FATHER OF FATHERS, RAISED THE SHADE BE-TWEEN THE OPPOSING REGIONS, ALLOWING THE BLESSED AND THE CONDEMNED TO SEE ONE ANOTHER. AND AS WAS HIS HOPE, THE BLESSED REJOICED IN THE PAIN OF THE CONDEMNED, AND THEIR JOY BECAME THAT MUCH GREATER IN THE FACE OF SORROW. AND THE CONDEMNED SAW THE BLESSED, SAW THEIR LOBSTER TAILS AND PROSCIUTTO, SAW WHAT THEY PUT IN THE TUCHESES OF MENSTRUATING SHIK-*

SAS, AND FELT THAT MUCH WORSE FOR THEMSELVES. AND GOD SAW THAT IT WAS GOODER. AND BUT THE APPEAL OF THE WINDOW BECAME TOO STRONG. AND RATHER THAN ENJOY THE KINGDOM OF HEAVEN, THE BLESSED WERE FASCINATED BY THE CRUELTIES OF HELL. AND RATHER THAN SUFFER THOSE CRUELTIES, THE CONDEMNED ENJOYED THE VICARIOUS PLEASURES OF HEAVEN. AND OVER TIME, THE TWO REACHED AN EQUILIBRIUM, STARING AT THE OTHER, STARING AT THEMSELVES. AND THE WINDOW BECAME A MIRROR, FROM WHICH NEITHER THE BLESSED NOR THE CONDEMNED COULD, OR WOULD, LEAVE. AND SO GOD DROPPED THE SHADE, FOREVER CLOSING OFF THE PORTAL BETWEEN KINGDOMS, AND SO MUST WE, IN THE FACE OF OUR TOO TEMPTING WINDOW, DROP THE SHADE BETWEEN THE KINGDOMS OF MAN AND WOMAN.

The cellar was filled with runoff from the Brod, and an egg-sized hole was cut out of the synagogue's back wall, through which one woman at a time could see only the ark and the feet of the dangling men, some of which, to add insult to insult, were caked with shit.

It was through this hole that the women of the shtetl took turns viewing my great-great-great-great-great-grandmother. Many were convinced, perhaps because of the new baby's perfectly adult features, that she was of an evil nature—a sign from the devil himself. But more likely their mixed feelings were inspired by the hole. From such a distance—palms pressed against the partition, an eye in an absent egg—they couldn't satisfy any of their mothering instincts. The hole wasn't even large enough to show all of the baby at once, and they had to piece together mental collages of her from each of the fragmented views—the fingers connected to the palm, which was attached to the wrist, which was at the end of the arm, which fit into the shoulder socket...They learned to hate her unknowability, her untouchability, the collage of her.

On the seventh day, the Well-Regarded Rabbi paid four quarter-chickens and a handful of blue cat's-eye marbles for the following announcement to be printed in Shimon T's weekly newsletter: that without precise knowledge of the cause, a baby was delivered to the shtetl, that it was quite beautiful, well behaved, and not at all stinky, and that he was resolved, out of consideration for the baby and himself, to give it to any righteous man who would be willing to call it daughter.

The next morning, he found fifty-two notes fanned like a peacock's plumage under the Upright Synagogue's front door.

From the maker of copper-wire knickknacks Peshel S, who had lost a wife of only two months in the Pogrom of Torn Garments: *If not for the girl, then for me. I am a righteous person, and there are things that I deserve.*

From the lonely candle dipper Mordechai C, whose hands were encased in gloves of wax that could never be washed off: *I am so alone in my workshop all day. There will be no candle dippers after me. Doesn't it make a kind of sense?*

From the unemployed Sloucher Lumpl W, who reclined on Passover not because it was religious custom but because why should that night be different from all others?: *I'm not the greatest person that ever lived, but I would be a good father, and you know it.*

From the deceased philosopher Pinchas T, who was struck on the head by a falling beam at the flour mill: *Put her back in the water and let her be with me.*

The Well-Regarded Rabbi was exceedingly knowledgeable about the large, extra-large, and extra-extra-large matters of the Jewish faith, and was able to draw upon the most obscure and indecipherable texts to reason seemingly impossible religious quandaries, but he knew hardly anything about life itself, and for this reason, because the baby's birth had no textual precedents, because he couldn't ask for anyone's advice — because how would it look for the very source of all advice to be an advice seeker? — because the baby was about life, and was life, he found himself to be quite stuck. *THEY'RE ALL DECENT MEN,* he thought. *ALL A LITTLE BELOW AVERAGE, PERHAPS, BUT TOLERABLE AT HEART. WHO IS LEAST UNDESERVING?*

THE BEST DECISION IS NO DECISION, he decided, and put the letters in her crib, vowing to give my great-great-great-great-great-grandmother — and, in a certain sense, me — to the author of the first note she grabbed for. But she didn't grab for any of them. She paid them no notice at all. For two days she didn't move a muscle, never crying or opening her mouth for food. The black-hatted men continued to holler prayers from their pulleys (*HOLY, HOLY, HOLY*...), continued to sway above the transplanted Brod, continued to hold more tightly to the Great Book than the rope, praying that someone was listening to their prayers, until in the middle of one early late-evening service, the good gefiltefishmonger Bitzl Bitzl R hollered what every man in the congregation had been thinking: *THE SMELL IS INTOLERABLE! HOW CAN I ACT CLOSE TO GOD WHEN I FEEL SO CLOSE TO THE SHITTER!*

The Well-Regarded Rabbi, who didn't disagree, put a halt to the prayers. He lowered himself to the glass floor and opened the ark. A most terrible stench poured forth, an all-encompassing, impossible to overlook, inhuman and inexcusable stink of supreme repugnance. It flooded from the ark, swept through the synagogue, streamed down every street, every alleyway of the shtetl, flowed under every pillow in every bedroom—entering the nostrils of the sleeping for long enough to misdirect their dreams before exiting with the next snore—and drained, finally, into the Brod.

The baby was still perfectly silent and unmoving. The Well-Regarded Rabbi placed the crib on the floor, removed a single sopping slip of paper, and hollered, *IT APPEARS THAT THE BABY HAS CHOSEN YANKEL AS HER FATHER!*

We were to be in good hands.

Dear Jonathan,

I hanker for this letter to be good. Like you know, I am not first rate with English. In Russian my ideas are asserted abnormally well, but my second tongue is not so premium. I undertaked to input the things you counseled me to, and I fatigued the thesaurus you presented me, as you counseled me to, when my words appeared too petite, or not befitting. If you are not happy with what I have performed, I command you to return it back to me. I will persevere to toil on it until you are appeased.

I have girdled in the envelope the items you inquired, not withholding postcards of Lutsk, the census ledgers of the six villages from before the war, and the photographs you had me keep for cautious purposes. It was a very, very, very good thing, no? I must eat a slice of humble pie for what occurred to you on the train. I know how momentous the box was for you, for both of us, and how its ingredients were not exchangeable. Stealing is an ignominious thing, but a thing that occurs very repeatedly to people on the train from Ukraine. Since you do not have at the tips of your finger the name of the guard who stole the box, it will be impossible to have it recouped, so you must confess that it is lost to you forever. But please do not let your experience in Ukraine injure the way you perceive Ukraine, which must be as a totally awesome former Soviet republic.

This is my occasion to utter thank you for being so long-suffering and stoical with me on our voyage. You were perhaps accounting upon a translator with more faculties, but I am certain that I did a mediocre job. I must eat a slice of humble pie for not finding Augustine, but you clutch how rigid it was. Perhaps if we had more days we could have discovered her. We could have investigated the six villages and interrogated many people. We could have lifted every boulder. But we have uttered all of these things so many times.

Thank you for the reproduction of the photograph of Augustine with her family. I have thought without end of what you said about falling in love with her. In truth, I never fathomed it when you uttered it in Ukraine. But I am certain that I fathom it now. I examine her once when it is morning, and once before I manufacture Z's, and on every instance I see something new, some manner in which her hairs produce shadows, or her lips summarize angles.

I am so so happy because you were appeased by the first division that I posted to you. You must know that I have performed the corrections you demanded. I apologize for the last line, about how you are a very spoiled Jew. It has been changed, and is now written, "I do not want to drive ten hours to an ugly city to attend to a spoiled Jew." I made more protracted the first part about me, and jettisoned out the word "Negroes," as you ordered me to, even though it is true that I am so fond of them. It makes me happy that you relished the sentence "One day you will do things for me that you hate. That is what it means to be a family." I must inquire you, however, what is a truism?

I have ruminated what you told me about making the part about my grandmother more protracted. Because you felt with so much gravity about this, I thought OK to include the parts that you posted me. I cannot say that I brooded those things, but I can say that I would covet to be the variety of person to have brooded those things. They were very beautiful, Jonathan, and I felt them as true.

And thank you, I feel indebted to utter, for not mentioning the not-truth about how I am tall. I thought it might appear superior if I was tall.

I strived to perform the next section as you ordered me, placing primary in my thoughts all that you tutored. I also attempted to be not obvious, or unduly subtle, as you demonstrated. Per the currency that you sent along, you must be informed that I would write this even in the absence of it. It is a mammoth honor for me to write for a writer, especially when he is an American writer, like Ernest Hemingway or you.

And mentioning your writing, "The Beginning of the World Often Comes" was a very exalted beginning. There were parts that I did not understand, but I conjecture that this is because they were very Jewish, and only a Jewish person could understand something so Jewish. Is this why you think you are chosen by God, because only you can understand the funnies that you make about yourself? I have one small query about this section, which is do you know that many of the names you exploit are not truthful names for Ukraine? Yankel is a name I have heard of, and so is Hannah, but the rest are very strange. Did you invent them? There were many mishaps like this, I will inform you. Are you being a humorous writer here, or an uninformed one?

I do not have any additional luminous remarks, because I must possess more of the novel in order to lumin. For present, be aware that I am ravished. I will counsel you that even after you have presented me more, I may not possess many intelligent things to utter, but I could be perhaps of some nonetheless use. Perhaps if I think something is very half-witted, I could tell you, and you could make it whole-witted. You have informed me so much about it that I am certain I will love very much to read the remnants, and think loftier of you, if that is a possibility. Oh yes, what is cunnilingus?

And now for a little private business. (You may decide not to read this part, if it makes you a boring person. I would understand, although please do not inform me.) Grandfather has not been healthful. He has altered to our residence for permanent. He reposed on Little Igor's bed with Sammy Davis, Junior, Junior, and Little Igor reposed on the sofa. This does not spleen Little Igor, because he is such a good boy, who understands many more things than anyone thinks he does. I have the opinion that the melancholy is what makes Grandfather unhealthful, and it is what makes him blind, although he is not truly blind, of course. It has become tremendously worse since we returned from Lutsk. As you know, he was very defeated about Augustine, more than even you or I were defeated. It is rigid not to talk about Grandfather's melancholy with Father, because we have both encountered him crying. Last night we were roosting at the table in the kitchen. We were eating black bread and conversing about athletics. There was a sound from above us. Little Igor's room is above us. I was certain that it was the crying of Grandfa-

ther, and Father was also certain of this. There was also a quiet rapping against the ceiling. (Of normal, rapping is excellent, like the Dnipropetrovsk Crew, who are totally deaf, but this kind I was not amorous of.) We tried so rigidly to neglect it. The sound moved Little Igor from his repose, and he came into the kitchen. "Hello, Clumsy One," Father said, because Little Igor had fallen again, and made his eye blue again, this time his left eye. "I would also like to eat black bread," Little Igor said, not looking at Father. Even though he is only thirteen almost fourteen, he is very smart. (You are the only person I have remarked this to. Please do not remark it to any other person.)

I hope that you are happy, and that your family is healthful and prosperous. We became like friends while you were in Ukraine, yes? In a different world, we could have been real friends. I will be in suspense for your next letter, and I will also be in suspense for the coming division of your novel. I feel oblongated to again eat a slice of humble pie (my stomach is becoming chock-full) for the new section that I am bestowing you, but understand that I tried bestly, and did the best I could, which was the best that I could do. It is so rigid for me. Please be truthful, but also please be benevolent, please.

Guilelessly,
Alexander

An overture to encountering the Hero, and then encountering the Hero

How I ANTICIPATED, it made my girls very sad that I should not be with them for the celebration of the first birthday of the new constitution. "All Night," one of my girls said to me, "how am I expected to pleasure myself in your void?" I had a notion. "Baby," another one of my girls said to me, "it is not good." I told them all, "If possible, I would be here with only you, forever. But I am a man who toils, and I must go where I must. We need currency for famous nightclubs, yes? I am doing something I hate for you. This is what it means to be in love. So do not spleen me." But to be truthful, I was not even the smallest portion sad to go to Lutsk to translate for Jonathan Safran Foer. As I mentioned before, my life is ordinary. But I had never been to Lutsk, or any of the multitudinous petite villages that still endure after the war. I desired to see new things. I desired to experience volumes. And I would be electrical to meet an American.

"You will need to bring along with you food for your drive, Shapka," Father said to me. "Do not dub me that," I said. "And also drink and maps," he said. "It is near ten hours to Lvov, where you will pick up the Jew at the train station." "How much currency will I receive for my toils?" I inquired, because that query had very much gravity on me. "Less than you think you deserve," he said, "and more than you deserve." This spleened me very much and I told Father, "Then maybe I do not want to do it." "I do not care what you want," he said, and extended to put his hand on my shoulder. In my family, Father is the world champion at ending conversations.

It was agreed that Grandfather and I would go forth at midnight of

1 July. This would present us with fifteen hours. It was agreed, by everyone except for Grandfather and I, that we should travel to the Lvov train station as soon as we entered the city of Lvov. It was agreed by Father that Grandfather should loiter with patience in the car, while I loitered on the tracks for the train of the hero. I did not know what his appearance would be, and he did not know how tall and aristocratic I would be. This was something we made much repartee about after. He was very nervous, he said. He said he made shit of a brick. I said to him that I also made shit of a brick, but if you want to know why, it was not that I would not recognize him. An American in Ukraine is so flaccid to recognize. I made shit of a brick because he was an American, and I desired to show him that I too could be an American.

I have given abnormally many thoughts to altering residences to America when I am more aged. They have many superior schools for accounting, I know. I know this because a friend of mine, Gregory, who is sociable with a friend of the nephew of the person who invented the sixty-nine, told me that they have many superior schools for accounting in America, and he knows everything. My friends are appeased to stay in Odessa for their entire lives. They are appeased to age like their parents, and become parents like their parents. They do not desire anything more than everything they have known. OK, but this is not for me, and it will not be for Little Igor.

A few days before the hero was to arrive, I inquired Father if I could go forth to America when I made to graduate from university. "No," he said. "But I want to," I informed him. "I do not care what you want," he said, and that is usually the end of the conversation, but it was not this time. "Why?" I asked. "Because what you want is not important to me, Shapka." "No," I said, "why is it that I cannot go forth to America after I graduate?" "If you want to know why you cannot go forth to America," he said, unclosing the refrigerator, investigating for food, "it is because Great-Grandfather was from Odessa, and Grandfather was from Odessa, and Father, me, was from Odessa, and your boys will be from Odessa. Also, you are going to toil at Heritage Touring when you are graduated. It is a necessary employment, premium enough for Grandfather, premium enough for me, and premium enough for you." "But what if that is not what I desire?" I said. "What if I do not want to toil at Heritage Touring, but instead toil someplace where I can do something unordinary, and make very much currency instead of just a petite amount? What if I do not want my boys to grow up here, but instead to grow up someplace superior, with superior things, and more things? What if I have girls?" Father removed three pieces of ice from the refrigerator, closed the refrigerator, and punched me. "Put these on your face," he said, giving the ice to me, "so you do not look terrible and manufacture a disaster in Lvov." This was the end of the conversation. I should have been smarter.

And I still haven't mentioned that Grandfather demanded to bring Sammy Davis, Junior, Junior along. That was another thing. "You are being a fool," Father informed him. "I need her to help me see the road," Grandfather said, pointing his finger at his eyes. "I am blind." "You are not blind, and you are not bringing the bitch." "I am blind, and the bitch is coming with us." "No," Father said. "It is not professional for the bitch to go along." I would have uttered something on the half of Grandfather, but I did not want to be stupid again. "It is either I go with the bitch or I do not go." Father was in a position. Not like the Latvian Home Stretch, but like amid a rock and a rigid place, which is, in truth, somewhat similar to the Latvian Home Stretch. There was fire amid them. I had seen this before, and nothing in the world frightened me more. Finally my father yielded, although it was agreed that Sammy Davis, Junior, Junior must don a special shirt that Father would have fabricated, which would say: OFFICIOUS SEEING-EYE BITCH OF HERITAGE TOURING. This was so she would appear professional.

Notwithstanding that we had a deranged bitch in the car, who made a proclivity of throwing her body against the windows, the drive was also difficult because the car is so much shit that it would not travel any faster than as fast as I could run, which is sixty kilometers per hour. Many cars passed us, which made me feel second rate, especially when the cars were heavy with families, and when they were bicycles. Grandfather and I did not utter words pending the drive, which is not abnormal, because we have never uttered multitudinous words. I made efforts not to spleen him, but nonetheless did. For one example, I forgot to examine the map, and we missed our entrance to the superway. "Please do not punch me," I said, "but I made a miniature error with the map." Grandfather kicked the stop pedal, and my face gave a high-five to the front window. He did not say anything for the majority of a minute. "Did I ask you to drive the car?" he asked. "I do not have a license to drive the car," I said. (Keep this as a secret, Jonathan.) "Did I ask you to prepare me breakfast while you roost there?" he asked. "No," I said. "Did I ask you to invent a new kind of wheel?" he asked. "No," I said, "I would not have been very good at that." "How many things did I ask you to do?" he asked. "Only one," I said, and I knew that he was pissing off, pissing everywhere, and that he would yell at me for some durable time, and perhaps even violence me, which I deserved, nothing is new. But he did not. (So you are aware, Jonathan, he has never violenced me or Little Igor.) If you want to know what he did, he rotated the car around, and we drove back to where I fashioned the error. Twenty minutes it captured. When we arrived at the location, I informed him that we were there. "Are you cocksure?" he asked. I told him I was cocksure. He moved the car to the side of the road. "We will stop here and eat breakfast," he said. "Here?" I asked, because it was an unimpressive location, with only a few meters of dirt amid the road and a concrete wall separating the road and farmlands. "I think this is a premium location," he said, and I knew it would be a common decency not to argue. We roosted on the grass and ate, while Sammy Davis, Junior, Junior attempted to lick the yellow lines off of the superway. "If you blunder again," Grandfather said while he masticated a sausage, "I will stop the car and you will get out with a foot in the backside. It will be my foot. It will be your backside. Is this a thing you understand?"

We arrived in Lvov in only eleven hours, but yet traveled at once to the train station as Father ordered. It was rigid to find, and we became lost people many times. This gave Grandfather anger. "I hate Lvov!" he said. We had been there for ten minutes. Lvov is big and impressive, but not like Odessa. Odessa is very beautiful, with many famous beaches where girls are lying on their backs and exhibiting their first-rate bosoms. Lvov is a city like New York City in America. New York City, in truth, was designed on the model of Lvov. It has very tall buildings (with as many as six levels) and comprehensive streets (with enough room for as many as three cars) and many cellular phones. There are many statues in Lvov, and many places where statues used to be located. I have never witnessed a place fashioned of so much concrete. Everything was concrete, everywhere, and I will tell you that even the sky, which was gray, appeared like concrete. This is something that the hero and I would speak about later, when we were having an absence of words. "Do you remember all the concrete in Lvov?" he asked. "Yes," I said. "Me too," he said. Lvov is a very important city in the history of Ukraine. If you want to know why, I do not know why, but I am certain that my friend Gregory does.

Lvov is not very impressive from inside the train station. This is where I loitered for the hero for more than four hours. His train was dilatory, so it was five hours. I was spleened to have to loiter there with nothing to do, without even a hi-fi, but I was very good-humored to not have to be in the car with Grandfather, who was likely becoming a deranged person, and Sammy Davis, Junior, Junior, who was already deranged. The station was not ordinary, because there were blue and yellow papers from the ceiling. They were there for the first birthday of the new constitution. This did not make me so proud, but I was appeased that the hero should view them when disembarking the train from Prague. He would obtain an excellent picture of our country. Perhaps he would think that the yellow and blue papers were for him, because I know that they are the Jewish colors.

When his train finally arrived, both of my legs were needles and nails from being an upright person for such a duration. I would have roosted, but the floor was very dirty, and I wore my peerless blue jeans to oppress the hero. I knew which car he would be disembarking from, because Father told me, and I tried to walk to it when the train arrived, but it was very difficult with two legs that were all needles and nails. I held a sign with his name in front of me, and fell many times on my legs, and looked into the eyes of every person that walked past.

When we found each other, I was very flabbergasted by his appearance. This is an American? I thought. And also, This is a Jew? He was severely short. He wore spectacles and had diminutive hairs which were not split anywhere, but rested on his head like a Shapka. (If I were like Father, I might even have dubbed him Shapka.) He did not appear like either the Americans I had witnessed in magazines, with yellow hairs and muscles, or the Jews from history books, with no hairs and prominent bones. He was wearing nor blue jeans nor the uniform. In truth, he did not look like anything special at all. I was underwhelmed to the maximum.

He must have witnessed the sign I was holding, because he punched me on the shoulder and said, "Alex?" I told him yes. "You're my translator, right?" I asked him to be slow, because I could not understand him. In truth I was manufacturing a brick wall of shits. I attempted to be sedate. "Lesson one. Hello. How are you doing this day?" "What?" "Lesson two. OK, isn't the weather full of delight?" "You're my translator," he said, manufacturing movements, "yes?" "Yes," I said, presenting him my hand. "I am Alexander Perchov. I am your humble translator." "It would not be nice to beat you," he said. "What?" I said. "I said," he said, "it would not be nice to beat you." "Oh yes," I laughed, "it would not be nice to beat you also. I implore you to forgive my speaking of English. I am not so premium with it." "Jonathan Safran Foer," he said, and presented me his hand. "What?" "I'm Jonathan Safran Foer." "Jon-fen?" "Safran Foer." "I am Alex," I said. "I know," he said. "Did someone hit you?" he inquired, witnessing my right eye. "It was nice for Father to beat me," I said. I took his bags from him and we went forth to the car.

"Your train ride appeased you?" I asked. "Oh, God," he said, "twenty-six hours, fucking unbelievable." This girl Unbelievable must be very majestic, I thought. "You were able to Z Z Z Z Z?" I asked. "What?" "Did you manufacture any Z's?" "I don't understand." "Repose." "What?" "Did you repose?" "Oh. No," he said, "didn't repose at all." "What?" "I...did...not...repose...at...all." "And the guards at the border?" "It was nothing," he said. "I've heard so much about them, that they would, you know, give me a hard time. But they came in, checked my passport, and didn't bother me at all." "What?" "I had heard it might be a problem, but it wasn't a problem." "You had heard about them?" "Oh yeah, I heard they were big fucking assholes." Big fucking assholes. I wrote this on my brain.

In truth, I was flabbergasted that the hero did not have any legal hearings and tribulations with the border guards. They have an unsavory habit for taking things without asking from people on the train. Father went to Prague once, as part of his toiling for Heritage Touring, and while he reposed the guards removed many premium things from his bag, which is terrible because he does not have many premium things. (It is so queer to think of someone injuring Father. I more usually think of the roles as unmovable.) I have also been informed stories of travelers who must present currency to the guards in order to receive their documents in return. For Americans it can be either best or worst. It is best if the guard is in love with America and wants to overawe the American by being a premium guard. This kind of guard thinks that he will encounter the American again one day in America, and that the American will offer to take him to a Chicago Bulls game, and buy him blue jeans and white bread and delicate toilet paper. This guard dreams of speaking English without an accent and obtaining a wife with an unmalleable bosom. This guard will confess that he does not love where he lives.

The other kind of guard is also in love with America, but he will hate the American for being an American. This is worst. This guard knows he will never go to America, and knows that he will never meet the American again. He will steal from the American, and terror the American, only to teach that he can. This is the only occasion in his life to have his Ukraine be more than America, and to have himself be more than the American. Father told me this, and I am certain that he is certain that it is faithful.

When we arrived at the car, Grandfather was loitering with patience as Father ordered him to. He was very patient. He was snoring. He was snoring with such volume that the hero and I could hear him even though the windows were elevated, and it sounded as if the car was operating. "This is our driver," I said. "He is an expert at driving." I observed distress in the smile of our hero. This was the second time. It had been four minutes. "Is he OK?" he asked. "What?" I said. "I do not make to understand. Speak more slower, please." I may have appeared noncompetent to the hero. "Is...the...dri...ver...heal...thy?" "With certainty," I said. "But I must tell you, I am very familiar with this driver. He is my grandfather." At this moment, Sammy Davis, Junior, Junior made herself evident, because she jumped up from the back seat and barked in volumes. "Oh Jesus Christ!" the hero said with terror, and he moved distant from the car. "Do not be distressed," I informed him as Sammy Davis, Junior, Junior punched her head against the window. "That is only the driver's Seeing Eye bitch." I pointed to the shirt that she was donning, but she had masticated the major of it, so that it only said: OF-FICIOUS BITCH. "She is deranged," I said, "but so so playful."

"Grandfather," I said, moving his arm to arouse him. "Grandfather, he is here." Grandfather rotated his head from this to that. "He is always reposing," I told the hero, hoping that might make him less distressed. "That must come to hands," the hero said. "What?" I asked. "I said that must come to hands." "What does it mean come to hands?" "To be useful. You know, to be helpful. What about that dog, though?" I use this American idiom very often now. I told a girl at a famous nightclub, "My eyes come to hands when I observe your peerless bosom." I could perceive that she perceived that I was a premium person. Later we became very carnal, and she smelled her knees, and also my knees.

I was able to move Grandfather from his repose. If you want to know how, I fastened his nose with my fingers so that he could not breathe. He did not know where he was. "Anna?" he asked. That was the name of my grandmother who died two years yore. "No, Grandfather," I said, "it is me. Sasha." He was very shamed. I could perceive this because he rotated his face away from me. "I acquired Jon-fen," I said. "Um, that's Jon-a-than," the hero said, who was observing Sammy Davis, Junior, Junior as she licked the windows. "I acquired him. His train arrived." "Oh," Grandfather said, and I perceived that he was still departing from a dream. "We should go forth to Lutsk," I suggested, "as Father ordered." "What?" the hero inquired. "I told him that we should go forth to Lutsk." "Yes, Lutsk. That's where I was told we would go. And from there to Trachimbrod." "What?" I inquired. "Lutsk, then Trachimbrod." "Correct," I said. Grandfather put his hands on the wheel. He looked in front of him for a protracted time. He was breathing very large breaths, and his hands were shaking. "Yes?" I inquired him. "Shut up," he informed me. "Where's the dog going to be?" the hero inquired. "What?"

"Where's...the...dog...going...to...be?" "I do not understand." "I'm afraid of dogs," he said. "I've had some pretty bad experiences with them." I told this to Grandfather, who was still half of himself in dream. "No one is afraid of dogs," he said. "Grandfather informs me that no one is afraid of dogs." The hero moved his shirt up to exhibit me the remains of a wound. "That's from a dog bite," he said. "What is?" "That." "What?" "This thing." "What thing?" "Here. It looks like two intersecting lines." "I don't see it." "Here," he said. "Where?" "Right here," he said, and I said, "Oh yes," although in truth I still could not witness a thing. "My mother is afraid of dogs." "So?" "So I'm afraid of dogs. I can't help it." I clutched the situation now. "Sammy Davis, Junior, Junior must roost in the front with us," I told Grandfather. "Get in the fucking car," he said, having misplaced all of the patience that he had while snoring. "The bitch and the Jew will share the back seat. It is vast enough for both of them." I did not mention how the back seat was not vast enough for even one of them. "What are we going to do?" the hero asked, afraid to become close to the car, while in the back seat Sammy Davis, Junior, Junior had made her mouth with blood from masticating her own tail.

THE NEWS of his good fortune reached Yankel D as the Slouchers were concluding their weekly service.

It is most important that we remember, the narcoleptic potato farmer Didl S said to the congregation, which was reclining on pillows around his living room. (The Sloucher congregation was a wandering one, calling home a different congregant's house each Shabbos.)

Remember what? the schoolteacher Tzadik P asked, expelling yellow chalk with each syllable.

The what, Didl said, *is not so important, but that we should remember. It is the act of remembering, the process of remembrance, the recognition of our past ...Memories are small prayers to God, if we believed in that sort of thing...For it says somewhere something about just this, or something just like this...I had my finger on it a few minutes ago...I swear, it was right here. Has anyone seen* The Book of Antecedents *around? I had an early volume here just a second ago...Crap!...Can somebody tell me where I was? Now I'm totally confused, and embarrassed, and I always screw it up when it's at my house —*

Memory, grieving Shanda assisted, but Didl had fallen uncontrollably asleep. She woke him up and whispered, *Memory.*

— *There we go,* he said, not missing a beat as he riffled through a stack of papers on his pulpit, which was really a chicken coop. *Memory. Memory and reproduction. And dreams, of course. What is being awake if not interpreting our dreams, or dreaming if not interpreting our wake? Circle of circles! Dreams, yes? No? Yes. Yes, it is the first Shabbos. First of the month. And it being the first Shabbos of the month, we must make our additions to* The Book of Recurrent Dreams. *Yes? Someone tell me if I'm fucking this up.*

JONATHAN SAFRAN FOER

I've had a most interesting dream for the past two weeks, said Lilla F, descendant of the first Sloucher to drop the Great Book.

Excellent, Didl said, pulling Volume IV of *The Book of Recurrent Dreams* from the makeshift ark, which was really his wood-burning oven.

As did I, Shloim added. *Several of them.*

I, too, had a recurrent dream, Yankel said.

Excellent, Didl said. *Most excellent. It won't be long before another volume is complete!*

But first, Shanda whispered, *we must review last month's entries.*

But first, Didl said, assuming the authority of a rabbi, *we must review last month's entries. We must go backward in order to go forward.*

But don't take too long, Shloim said, *or I'll forget. It's amazing I've been able to remember it this long.*

He'll take exactly as long as it takes, Lilla said.

I'll take exactly as long as it takes, Didl said, and blackened his hand with the ash that had collected on the cover of the heavy leather-bound book. He opened it to a page near the end, picked up the silver pointer, which was really a tin knife, and began to chant, following the slice of the blade through the heart of Sloucher dream life:

> 4:512—*The dream of sex without pain.* I dreamt four nights ago of clock hands descending from the universe like rain, of the moon as a green eye, of mirrors and insects, of a love that never withdrew. It was not the feeling of completeness that I so needed, but the feeling of not being empty. This dream ended when I felt my husband enter me. 4:513—*The dream of angels dreaming of men.* It was during an afternoon nap that I dreamt of a ladder. Angels were sleepwalking up and down the rungs, their eyes closed, their breath heavy and dull, their wings hanging limp at the sides. I bumped into an old angel as I passed him, waking and startling him.

He looked like my grandfather did before he passed away last year, when he would pray each night to die in his sleep. Oh, the angel said to me, I was just dreaming of you. 4:514 — *The dream of, as silly as it sounds, flight.* 4:515 — *The dream of the waltz of feast, famine, and feast.* 4:516 — *The dream of disembodied birds (46).* I'm not sure if you would consider this a dream or a memory, because it actually happened, but when I fall asleep I see the room in which I mourned the death of my son. For those of you who were there, you will remember how we sat without speaking, eating only as much as we had to. You will remember when a bird crashed through the window and fell to the floor. You will remember, those of you who were there, how it jerked its wings before dying, and left a spot of blood on the floor after it was removed. But who among you was first to notice the negative bird it left in the window? Who first saw the shadow that the bird left behind, the shadow that drew blood from any finger that dared to trace it, the shadow that was better proof of the bird's existence than the bird ever was? Who was with me when I mourned the death of my son, when I excused myself to bury that bird with my own hands? 4:517 — *The dream of falling in love, marriage, death, love.* This dream seems as if it lasts for hours, although it always takes place in the five minutes between my returning from the field and being woken for dinner. I dream of when I met my wife, fifty years ago, and it's exactly as it happened. I dream of our marriage, and I can even see my father's tears of pride. It's all there, just as it was. But then I dream of my own death, which I have heard is impossible to do, but you must believe me. I dream of my wife telling me on my deathbed that she loves me, and even though she thinks I can't hear her, I can, and she says she wouldn't have changed anything. It feels like a moment I've lived a thousand times before, as if everything is familiar, right up to the moment of my death, that it will happen again an infinite number of times, that we will meet, marry, have our children, succeed in the ways we have, fail in the ways we have, all exactly the same, always unable to change a thing. I am again at the bottom of an unstoppable wheel, and when I feel my eyes close for death, as they have and will a thousand times, I awake. 4:518 — *The dream of perpetual motion.* 4:519 — *The dream of low windows.* 4:520 — *The dream of safety and peace.* I dreamt that I was born from a stranger's body. She gave birth to me in a secret dwelling, far away from everything that I would grow to know. Immediately after I was born, she handed me to my mother, for the sake of appearances, and my mother said, Thank you. You have given me a son, the gift of life. And for this reason, because I was of a stranger's body, I did not fear the body of my mother, and I could embrace it without shame, with only love. Because I was not from my mother's body, my desire to go home never led back to her, and I was free to say Mother, and mean only Mother. 4:521 — *The dream of disembodied birds (47)*. It's dusk in this dream that I have every night, and I'm making love to my wife, my real wife, I mean, to whom I've been married for thirty years, and you all know how I love her, I love her so much. I massage her thighs in my hands, and I move my hands up her waist and belly, and touch her breasts. My wife is such a beautiful woman, you all know that, and in the dream she's the same, just as beautiful. I look down at my hands on her breasts—callused, worn things, a man's hands, veiny, shaky, fluttering—and I remember, I don't know why, but it's this way every night, I remember two white birds that my mother brought back for me from Warsaw when I was only a child. We let them fly around the house and perch wherever they wanted to. I remember seeing my mother's back as she cooked eggs for me, and I remember the birds perching on her shoulders, with their beaks up next to her ears, as if they were about to tell her a secret. She reached her right hand up into the cupboard, searching without looking for some spice on a high shelf, grasping at something elusive, fluttering, not letting my food burn. 4:522 — *The dream of meeting your younger self.* 4:523 — *The dream of animals, two by two.* 4:524 — *The dream of I won't be ashamed.* 4:525 — *The dream that we are our fathers.* I walked to the Brod, without knowing why, and looked into my reflection in the water. I couldn't look away. What was the image that pulled me in after it? What was it that I loved? And then I recognized it. So simple. In the water I saw my father's face, and that face saw the face of its father, and so on, and so on, reflecting backward to the beginning of time, to the face of God, in whose image we were created. We burned with love for ourselves, all of us, starters of the fire we suffered — our love was the affliction for which only our love was the cure...

The chanting was interrupted by a pounding at the door. Two men in black hats limped in before any of the congregants had time to get up.

WE ARE HERE ON BEHALF OF THE UPRIGHT CONGREGATION! hollered the taller of the two.

THE UPRIGHT CONGREGATION! echoed the short and squat one.

Shush! Shanda said.

IS YANKEL PRESENT? hollered the taller of the two, as if in response to her request.

YEAH, IS YANKEL PRESENT? echoed the short, squat one.

Here. I am here, Yankel said, rising from his pillow. He assumed the Well-Regarded Rabbi was requesting his financial services, as had happened so many times in the past, piety being as expensive as it was those days. *What can I do for you?*

YOU WILL BE THE FATHER OF THE BABY FROM THE RIVER! hollered the taller.

YOU WILL BE THE FATHER! echoed the short, squat one.

Excellent! Didl said, closing Volume IV of *The Book of Recurrent Dreams*, which released a cloud of dust as the covers clapped. *This is most excellent! Yankel will be the father!*

Mazel tov! the congregants began to sing. *Mazel tov!*

Suddenly Yankel was overcome with a fear of dying, stronger than he felt when his parents passed of natural causes, stronger than when his only brother was killed in the flour mill or when his children died, stronger even than when he was a child and it first occurred to him that he must try to understand what it could mean not to be alive — to be not in darkness, not in unfeeling — to be not being, not to be.

Slouchers congratulated him, failing to notice as they patted him on the back that he was crying. *Thank you*, he said, and said again, without once wondering just whom he was thanking. *Thank you so much*. He had been given a baby, and I a great-great-great-great-great-great-grandfather.

THE DISGRACED USURER Yankel D took the baby girl home that evening. *Here we go*, he said, *up the front step. Here we are. This is your door. And here, this is your doorknob I am opening. And here, this is where we put the shoes when we come in. And here is where we hang the jackets.* He spoke to her as if she could understand him, never in a high pitch or in monosyllables, and never in nonsense words. *This is milk that I am feeding you. It comes from Mordechai the milkman, whom you will meet one day. He gets the milk from a cow, which is a very strange and troubling thing if you think about it, so don't think about it...This is my hand that is petting your face. Some people are left-handed and some are right-handed. We don't know which you are yet, because you just sit there and let me do the handling...This is a kiss. It is what happens when lips are puckered and pressed against something, sometimes other lips, sometimes a cheek, sometimes something else. It depends...This is my heart. You are touching it with your left hand, not because you are left-handed, although you might be, but because I am holding it against my heart. What you are feeling is the beating of my heart. It is what keeps me alive.*

He made a bed of crumpled newspaper in a deep baking pan and gently tucked it in the oven, so that she wouldn't be disturbed by the noise of the small falls outside. He left the oven door open, and would sit for hours and watch her, as one might watch a loaf of bread rise. He watched her chest rise and fall in rapid succession as her fingers made fists and released, and her eyes squinted for no apparent reason. *Could she be dreaming?* he wondered. *And if so, what would a baby dream of? She must be dreaming of the before-life, just as I dream of the afterlife.* When he pulled her out to feed or just hold her, her body was tattooed with the newsprint. TIME OF DYED HANDS IS FINALLY OVER! MOUSE WILL

HANG! Or, SOFIOWKA ACCUSED OF RAPE, PLEADS POSSESSED BY PENIS PERSUASION, BECAME "OUT OF HAND." Or, AVRUM R KILLED IN FLOUR MILL MISHAP, LEAVES BEHIND A LOST SIAMESE CAT OF FORTY-EIGHT YEARS, TAWNY, CHUBBY, BUT NOT FAT, PERSONABLE, MAYBE A LITTLE FAT, ANSWERS TO "METHUSELAH," OK, FAT AS SHIT. IF FOUND, FREE TO KEEP. Sometimes he would rock her to sleep in his arms, and read her left to right, and know everything he needed to know about the world. If it wasn't written on her, it wasn't important to him.

Yankel had lost two babies, one to fever and the other to the industrial flour mill, which had taken a shtetl member's life every year since it first opened. He had also lost a wife, not to death but to another man. He had returned from an afternoon at the library to find a note covering the SHALOM! of their home's welcome mat: *I had to do it for myself.*

Lilla F fingered the soil around one of her daisies. Bitzl Bitzl stood by his kitchen window, pretending to scrub the counter clean. Shloim W peered through the upper bulb of one of the hourglasses with which he could no longer bring himself to part. No one said anything as Yankel read the note, and no one ever said anything afterward, as if the disappearance of his wife weren't the slightest bit unusual, or as if they hadn't noticed that he had been married at all.

Why couldn't she have slid it under the door? he wondered. *Why couldn't she have folded it?* It looked just like any other note she would leave him, like, *Could you try to fix the broken knocker?* or *I'll be back soon, don't worry.* It was so strange to him that such a different kind of note—*I had to do it for myself*—could look exactly the same: trivial, mundane, nothing. He could have hated her for leaving it there in plain sight, and he could have hated her for the plainness of it, a message without adornment, without any small clue to indicate that yes, this is important, yes, this is the most painful note I've ever written, yes, I would sooner die than have to write this again. Where were the dried teardrops? Where was the tremor in the script?

But his wife was his first and only love, and it was the nature of those from the tiny shtetl to forgive their first and only loves, so he forced himself to understand, or pretend to understand. He never once blamed her for fleeing to Kiev with the traveling and mustachioed bureaucrat who was called in to help mediate the messy proceedings of Yankel's shameful trial; the bureaucrat could promise to provide for her future, could take her away from everything, move her to someplace quieter, without thinking, without confessions or plea-bargaining. No, that's not it. Without Yankel. She wanted to be without Yankel.

He spent the next weeks blocking scenes of the bureaucrat fucking his wife. On the floor with cooking ingredients. Standing, with socks still on. In the grass of the yard of their new and immense house. He imagined her making noises she never made for him and feeling pleasures he could never provide because the bureaucrat was a man, and he was not a man. *Does she suck his penis?* he wondered. *I know this is a silly thought, a thought that will only bring me pain, but I can't free myself of it. And when she sucks his penis, because she must, what is he doing? Is he pulling her hair back to watch? Is he touching her chest? Is he thinking of someone else? I'll kill him if he is.*

With the shtetl still watching—Lilla still fingering, Bitzl Bitzl still scrubbing, Shloim still pretending to measure time with sand—he folded the note into a teardrop shape, slid it into his lapel, and went inside. *I don't know what to do,* he thought. *I should probably kill myself.*

He couldn't bear to live, but he couldn't bear to die. He couldn't bear the thought of her making love to someone else, but neither could he bear the absence of the thought. And as for the note, he couldn't bear to keep it, but he couldn't bear to destroy it either. So he tried to lose it. He left it by the wax-weeping candle holders, placed it between matzos every Passover, dropped it without regard among rumpled papers on his cluttered desk, hoping it wouldn't be there when he returned. But it was always there. He tried to massage it out of his pocket while sitting on the bench in front of the fountain of the prostrate mermaid, but when he inserted his hand for his hanky, it was there. He hid it like a bookmark in one of the novels he most hated, but the note would appear several days later between the pages of one of the Western books that he alone in the shtetl read, one of the books that the note had now spoiled for him forever. But like his life, he couldn't for the life of him lose the note. It kept returning to him. It stayed with him, like a part of him, like a birthmark, like a limb, it was on him, in him, him, his hymn: *I had to do it for myself.*

He had lost so many slips of paper over time, and keys, pens, shirts, glasses, watches, silverware. He had lost a shoe, his favorite opal cufflinks (the Sloucher fringes of his sleeves bloomed unruly), three years away from Trachimbrod, millions of ideas he intended to write down (some of them wholly original, some of them deeply meaningful), his hair, his posture, two parents, two babies, a wife, a fortune in pocket change, more chances than could be counted. He had even lost a name: he was Safran before he fled the shtetl, Safran from birth to his first death. There seemed to be nothing he couldn't lose. But that slip of paper wouldn't disappear, ever, and neither would the image of his prostrate wife, and neither would the thought that if he could, it might greatly improve his life to end it.

Before the trial, Yankel-then-Safran was unconditionally admired. He was the president (and treasurer and secretary and only member) of the Committee for the Good and Fine Arts, and the founder, multiterm chairman, and only teacher of the School for Loftier Learning, which met in his house and whose classes were attended by Yankel himself. It was not unusual for a family to host a multicourse dinner in his name (if not in his presence), or for one of the more wealthy community members to commission a traveling artist to paint a portrait of him. And the portraits were always flattering. He was someone whom everyone admired and liked but whom nobody knew. He was like a book that you could feel good holding, that you could talk about without ever having read, that you could recommend.

On the advice of his lawyer, Isaac M, who gestured quotation marks in the air with every syllable of every word he spoke, Yankel pleaded guilty to all charges of unfit practice, with the hope that it might lighten his punishment. In the end, he lost his usurer's license. And more than his license. He lost his good name, which is, as they say, the only thing worse than losing your good health. Passersby sneered at him or muttered under their breath names like scoundrel, cheat, cur, fucker. He wouldn't have been so hated if he hadn't been so loved before. But along with the Garden-Variety Rabbi and Sofiowka, he was one of the vertices of the community—the invisible one—and with his shame came a sense of imbalance, a void.

Safran moved through the neighboring villages, finding work as a teacher of harpsichord theory and performance, a perfume consultant (feigning deafness and blindness to grant himself some legitimacy in the absence of references), and even an ill-starred stint as the world's worst fortuneteller—*I'm not going to lie and tell you that the future is full of promise*...He awoke each morning with the desire to do right, to be a good and meaningful person, to be, as simple as it sounded and as impossible as it actually was, happy. And during the course of each day his heart would descend from his chest into his stomach. By early afternoon he was overcome by the feeling that nothing was right, or nothing was right for him, and by the desire to be alone. By evening he was fulfilled: alone in the magnitude of his grief, alone in his aimless guilt, alone even in his loneliness. *I am not sad*, he would repeat to himself over and over, *I am not sad*. As if he might one day convince himself. Or fool himself. Or convince others—the only thing worse than being sad is for others to know that you are sad. *I am not sad. I am not sad.* Because his life had unlimited potential for happiness, insofar as it was an empty white room. He would fall asleep with his heart at the foot of his bed, like some domesticated animal that was no part of him at all. And each morning he would wake with it again in the cupboard of his rib cage, having become a little heavier, a little weaker, but still pumping. And by midafternoon he was again overcome with the desire to be somewhere else, someone else, someone else somewhere else. *I am not sad.*

After three years he returned to the shtetl—I am the final piece of proof that all citizens who leave eventually return—and lived a quiet life like a Sloucher fringe, sewn to the sleeve of Trachimbrod, forced to wear that horrible bead around his neck as a mark of his shame. He changed his name to Yankel, the name of the bureaucrat who ran away with his wife, and asked that no one ever call him Safran again (although he thought he heard that name every now and then, muttered behind his back). Many of his old clients returned to him, and while they refused to pay the rates of his heyday, he was nevertheless able to reestablish himself in the shtetl of his birth—as all who are exiled eventually try to do.

When the black-hatted men gave him the baby, he felt that he too was only a baby, with a chance to live without shame, without need of consolation for a life lived wrong, a chance to be again innocent, simply and impossibly happy. He named her Brod, after the river of her curious birth, and gave her a string necklace of her own, with a tiny abacus bead of her own, so she would never feel out of place in what would be her family.

As my great-great-great-great-great-grandmother grew, she remembered, of course, nothing, and was told nothing. Yankel made up a story about her mother's early death—*painless, in childbirth*—and answered the many questions that arose in the way he felt would cause her the least pain. It was her mother who gave her those beautiful big ears. It was her mother's sense of humor that all of the boys admired so much in her. He told Brod of vacations he and his wife had taken (when she pulled a splinter from his heel in Venice, when he sketched a red-pencil portrait of her in front of a tall fountain in Paris), showed her love letters they had sent each other (writing with his left hand those from Brod's mother), and put her to bed with stories of their romance.

Was it love at first sight, Yankel?

I loved your mother even before seeing her—it was her smell!

Tell me about what she looked like again.

She looked like you. She was beautiful, with those mismatched eyes, like you. One blue, one brown, like yours. She had your strong cheekbones and also your soft skin.

What was her favorite book?

Genesis, of course.

Did she believe in God?

She would never tell me.

How long were her fingers?

This long.

And her legs?

Like this.

Tell me again about how she would blow on your face before she kissed you.

Well that's just it, she would blow on my lips before she kissed me, like I was some very hot food and she was going to eat me!

Was she funny? Funnier than me?

She was the funniest person in the world. Exactly like you.

She was beautiful?

It was inevitable: Yankel fell in love with his never-wife. He would wake from sleep to miss the weight that never depressed the bed next to him, remember in earnest the weight of gestures she never made, long for the un-weight of her un-arm slung over his too real chest, making his widower's remembrances that much more convincing and his pain that much more real. He felt that he had lost her. He *had* lost her. At night he would reread the letters that she had never written him.

Dearest Yankel,

I'll be home to you soon, so there's no need for you to carry on with your missing me so much, however sweet it may be. You're so silly. Do you know that? Do you know how silly you are? Maybe that's why I love you so much, because I'm also silly.

Things are wonderful here. It's very beautiful, just as you promised it would be. The people have been kind, and I'm eating well, which I only mention because I know that you're always worried about me taking good enough care of myself. Well I am, so don't worry.

I really miss you. It's just about unbearable. Every moment of every day I think about your absence, and it almost kills me. But of course I'll be back with you soon, and will not have to miss you, and will not have to know that something, everything, is missing, that what is here is only what is not here. I kiss my pillow before I go to sleep and imagine it's you. It sounds like something you might do, I know. That's probably why I do it.

It almost worked. He had repeated the details so many times that it was nearly impossible to distinguish them from the facts. But the real note kept returning to him, and that, he was sure, was what kept him from that most simple and impossible thing: happiness. *I had to do it for myself.* Brod discovered it one day when she was only a few years old. It had found its way into her right pocket, as if the note had a mind of its own, as if those seven scribbled words were capable of wanting to inflict reality. *I had to do it for myself.* She either sensed the immense importance of it or deemed it entirely unimportant, because she never mentioned it to Yankel, but put it on his bedside table, where he would find it that night after rereading another letter that was not from her mother, not from his wife. *I had to do it for myself.*

I am not sad.

Another Lottery, 1791

THE WELL-REGARDED RABBI paid half a baker's dozen of eggs and a handful of blueberries for the following announcement to be printed in Shimon T's weekly newsletter: that an irascible magistrate in Lvov had demanded a name for the nameless shtetl, that the name would be used for new maps and census records, that it should not offend the refined sensibilities of either the Ukrainian or the Polish gentry, or be too hard to pronounce, and that it must be decided upon by week's end.

A VOTE! the Well-Regarded Rabbi proclaimed. *WE SHALL TAKE IT TO A VOTE.* For as the Venerable Rabbi once enlightened, *AND IF WE BELIEVE THAT EVERY SANE, STRICTLY MORAL, ABOVE-AVERAGE, PROPERTY-HOLDING, OBSERVANT ADULT JEWISH MALE IS BORN WITH A VOICE THAT MUST BE HEARD, SHALL WE NOT HEAR THEM ALL?*

The next morning a polling box was placed outside the Upright Synagogue, and the qualifying citizens queued up along the Jewish/Human fault line. Bitzl Bitzl R voted for "Gefilteville"; the deceased philosopher Pinchas T for "Time Capsule of Dust and String." The Well-Regarded Rabbi cast his ballot for *"SHTETL OF THE PIOUS UPRIGHTERS AND THE UNMENTIONABLE SLOUCHERS WITH WHOM NO RESPECTABLE JEW SHOULD HAVE ANYTHING TO DO UNLESS THE HOT SPOT IS HIS IDEA OF A VACATION."*

The mad squire Sofiowka N, having so much time and so little to do, took it upon himself to guard the box all afternoon and then deliver it to the magistrate's office in Lvov that evening. By morning it was official: resting twenty-three kilometers southeast of Lvov, four north of Kolki, and straddling the Polish-Ukrainian border like a twig alighted on a fence was the shtetl of Sofiowka. The new name was, much to the dismay of those who had to bear it, official and irrevocable. It would be with the shtetl until its death.

Of course, no one in Sofiowka called it Sofiowka. Until it had such a disagreeable official name, no one felt the need to call it anything. But now that there was an offense—that the shtetl should be that shithead's namesake—the citizens had a name *not* to go by. Some even called the shtetl Not-Sofiowka, and would continue to even after a new name was chosen.

The Well-Regarded Rabbi called for another vote. *THE OFFICIAL NAME CANNOT BE CHANGED,* he said, *BUT WE MUST HAVE A REASONABLE NAME FOR OUR OWN PURPOSES.* While no one was quite sure what was meant by purposes—*Did we have purposes before? What, exactly, is my purpose among our purposes?*—the second vote seemed unquestionably necessary. The polling box was placed outside the Upright Synagogue, and it was the Well-Regarded Rabbi's twins, this time, who guarded it.

The arthritic locksmith Yitzhak W voted for "Borderland." The man of law Isaac M for "Shtetlprudence." Lilla F, descendant of the first Sloucher to drop the book, persuaded the twins to let her sneak in a ballot, on which was written "Pinchas." (The twins also voted: Hannah for "Chana," and Chana for "Hannah.")

The Well-Regarded Rabbi counted the ballots that evening. It was a tie; every name got one vote: Lutsk Minor, *UPRIGHTLAND,* New Promise, Fault Line, Joshua, Lock-and-Key...Figuring that the fiasco had gone on long enough, he decided, reasoning that this is what God would do in such a situation, to pick a slip of paper randomly from the box and name the shtetl whatever it should say.

He nodded as he read what had become familiar script. *YANKEL HAS WON AGAIN,* he said. *YANKEL HAS NAMED US TRACHIM-BROD.*

Dear Jonathan,

It made me a tickled-pink person to receive your letter, and to know that you are reinstated at university for your conclusive year. As for me, I still have two years of studies among the remnants. I do not know what I will perform after that. Many of the things you informed me in July are still momentous to me, like what you uttered about searching for dreams, and how if you have a good and meaningful dream you are oblongated to search for it. This may be cinchier for you, I must say.

I did not yearn to mention this, but I will. Soon I will possess enough currency to purchase a plane voucher to America. Father does not know this. He thinks I disseminate everything I possess at famous discotheques, but as proxy for I often go to the beach and roost for many hours, so I do not have to disseminate currency. When I roost at the beach I think about how lucky you are.

It was Little Igor's fourteen birthday yesterday. He made his arm broken the day yore, because he fell again, this time from a fence he was hiking on, if you can believe it. We all tried very inflexibly to make him a happy person, and Mother prepared a premium cake that had many ceilings, and we even had a small festival. Grandfather was present, of course. He inquired how you are, and I told him that you would be reverting to university in September, which is now. I did not inform him about how the guard stole Augustine's box, because I knew that he would feel ashamed, and it made him happy to hear of you, and he is never happy. He wanted for me to inquire if it would be a possible thing for you to post another reproduction of the photograph of Augustine. He said that he would present you currency for any expenses. I am very distressed about him, as I informed you in the last letter. His health is being defeated. He does not possess the energy to get spleened often, and is usually in silence. In truth, I would favor it if he yelled at me, and even if he punched me.

Father purchased a new bicycle for Little Igor for his birthday, which is a superior present, because I know Father does not possess enough currency for presents such as bicycles. "The poor Clumsy One," he said, extending to put his hand on Little Igor's shoulder, "he should be happy on his birthday." I have girdled a picture of the bicycle in the envelope. Tell me if it is awesome. Please, be truthful. I will not be angry if you tell me that it is not awesome.

I resolved not to go anywhere famous last night. Instead I roosted on the beach. But I was not in my normal solitude, because I took the photograph of Augustine with me. I must confess to you that I examine it very recurrently, and persevere to think about what you said about falling in love with her. She is beautiful. You are correct.

Enough of my miniature talking. I am making you a very boring person. I will now speak about the business of the story. I perceived that you were not as appeased by the second division. I eat another slice for this. But your corrections were so easy. Thank you for informing me that it is "shit a brick," and "shitting bricks," and also "to come in handy." It is very useful for me to know the correct idioms. It is necessary. I know that you asked me not to alter the mistakes because they sound humorous, and humorous is the only truthful way to tell a sad story, but I think I will alter them. Please do not hate me.

I did fashion all of the other corrections you commanded. I inserted what you ordered me to in the part about when I first encountered you. (Do you in truth think that we are comparable?) As you commanded, I removed the sentence "He was severely short," and inserted in its place, "Like me, he was not tall." And after the sentence " 'Oh,' Grandfather said, and I perceived that he was still departing from a dream," I added, as you commanded, "About Grandmother?"

With these changes, I am confident that the second part of the story is perfect. I was unable to ignore observing that you again posted me currency.

For this I again thank you. But I parrot what I uttered before: if you are not appeased by what I post to you, and would like to have your currency posted back, I will post it back immediately. I could not feel proud in any other manner.

I toiled very hard on this next section. It was the most rigid yet. I attempted to guess some of the things you would have me alter, and I altered them myself. For example, I did not utilize the word "spleen" with such habituality, because I could perceive that it made you on nerves by the sentence in your letter when you said, "Stop using the word 'spleen.' It's getting on my nerves." I also invented things that I thought would appease you, funny things and sad things. I am certain that you will inform me when I have traveled too far.

Concerned about your writing, you sent me many pages, but I must tell you that I read every one of them. The Book of Recurrent Dreams was a very beautiful thing, and I must say that the dream that we are our fathers made me melancholy. This is what you intended, yes? Of course I am not Father, so perhaps I am the rare bird to your novel. When I look in the reflection, what I view is not Father, but the negative of Father.

Yankel. He is a good man, yes? Why do you think he made to swindle that man so many years ago? Perhaps he needed the currency very severely. I know what this is like, although I would never swindle any person. I found it stimulating that you made another lottery, this time to dub the shtetl. It made me think about what I would dub Odessa if I was given the power. I think that I might dub it Alex, because then everyone would know that I am Alex, and that the name of the city is Alex, so I must be a very premium person. I also might name it Little Igor, because people would think that my brother is a premium person, which he is, but it would be good for people to think so. (It is a queer thing how I wish everything for my brother that I wish for myself, only more rigidly.) Perhaps I would name it Trachimbrod, because then Trachimbrod could exist, and also, everyone here would purchase your book, and you could become famous.

I am regretted to end this letter. It is as proximal a thing as we have to talking. I hope you are appeased by the third division, and as always, I ask for *your forgiveness. I attempted to be truthful and beautiful, as you told me to.*

Oh, yes. There is one additional item. I did not amputate Sammy Davis, Junior, Junior from the story, even though you counseled that I should amputate her. You uttered that the story would be more "refined" with her absence, and I know that refined is like cultivated, polished, and well bred, but I will inform you that Sammy Davis, Junior, Junior is a very distinguished character, one with variegated appetites and seats of passion. Let us view her evolution and then resolve.

Guilelessly,
Alexander

GOING FORTH TO LUTSK

SAMMY DAVIS, JUNIOR, JUNIOR converted her attention from masticating her tail to trying to lick clean the hero's spectacles, which I will tell you were in need of cleaning. I write that she was trying because the hero was not being sociable. "Can you please get this dog away from me," he said, making his body into a ball. "Please. I really don't like dogs." "She is only making games with you," I told him when she put her body on top of his and kicked him with her back legs. "It signifies that she likes you." "Please," he said, attempting to remove her. She was now jumping up and also down on his face. "I really don't like her. I don't feel like games. She's going to break my glasses."

I will now mention that Sammy Davis, Junior, Junior is very often sociable with her new friends, but I had never witnessed a thing like this. I reasoned that she was in love with the hero. "Are you donning cologne?" I asked. "What?" "Are you donning any cologne?" He rotated his body so that his face was in the seat, away from Sammy Davis, Junior, Junior. "Maybe a little," he said, defending the back of his head with his hands. "Because she loves cologne. It makes her sexually stimulated." "Jesus." "She is trying to make sex to you. This is a good sign. It signifies that she will not bite." "Help!" he said as Sammy Davis, Junior, Junior rotated to do a sixty-nine. Pending all of this, Grandfather was still returning from his repose. "He does not like her," I told him. "Yes he does," Grandfather said, and that was all. "Sammy Davis, Junior, Junior!" I called. "Sit!" And do you know what? She sat. On the hero. In the sixty-nine position. "Sammy Davis, Junior, Junior! Sit on your side of the back seat! Get off the hero!" I think that she understood me, because she removed herself from the hero and returned to punching her face against the window on the other side. Or perhaps she had licked off all of the hero's cologne and was no longer interested in him sexually, but only as friends. "Do you smell something really awful?" the hero inquired, moving the wetness off of the back of his neck. "No," I said. A befitting not-truth. "Something smells just awful. It smells like someone died in this car. What is that?" "I do not know," I said, although I had a notion.

I do not cogitate that there was a person in the car that was surprised when we became lost amid the Lvov train station and the superway to Lutsk. "I hate Lvov," Grandfather rotated to tell the hero. "What's he saying?" the hero asked me. "He said it will not be long," I told him, another befitting not-truth. "Long until what?" the hero asked. I said to Grandfather, "You do not have to be kind to me, but do not blunder with the Jew." He said, "I can say anything I want to him. He will not understand." I rotated my head vertically to benefit the hero. "He says it will not be long until we get to the superway to Lutsk." "And from there?" the hero asked. "How long from there to Lutsk?" He affixed his attention to Sammy Davis, Junior, Junior, who was still punching her head against the window. (But I will mention that she was being a good bitch, because she punched her head against only her window, and when you are in a car, bitch or no bitch, you can do anything you desire as long as you remain on your side. Also, she was not farting very much.) "Tell him to shut his mouth," Grandfather said. "I cannot drive if he is going to talk." "Our driver says there are many buildings in Lutsk," I told the hero. "We are being paid tremendously to listen to him talk," I told Grandfather. "I am not," he said. "Neither am I," I said, "but someone is." "What?" "He says from the superway it is not more than two hours to Lutsk, where we will find a terrible hotel for the night." "What do you mean when you say terrible?" "What?" "I said, what...do...you... mean...when...you...say...the...hotel...will...be...terrible?" "Tell him to shut his mouth." "Grandfather says that you should look out of your window if you want to see anything." "What about the terrible hotel?" "Oh, I implore you to forget I said that." "I hate Lvov. I hate Lutsk. I hate the Jew in the back seat of this car that I hate." "You do not make this any cinchier." "I am blind. I am supposed to be retarded." "What are you saying up there? And what the hell is that smell?" "What?" "Tell him to shut his mouth or I will drive us off the road." "What...are...you...say...ing...up...there?" "The Jew must be silenced. I will kill us." "We were saying that the trip will perhaps be longer than we were desiring."

It captured five very long hours. If you want to know why, it is because Grandfather is Grandfather first and a driver second. He made us lost often and became on his nerves. I had to translate his anger into useful information for the hero. "Fuck," Grandfather said. I said, "He says if you look at the statues, you can see that some no longer endure. Those are where Communist statues used to be." "Fucking fuck, fuck!" Grandfather shouted. "Oh," I said, "he wants you to know that that building, that building, and that building are all important." "Why?" the hero inquired. "Fuck!" Grandfather said. "He cannot remember," I said.

"Could you turn on some air conditioning?" the hero commanded. I was humiliated to the maximum. "This car does not have air conditioning," I said. "I am eating humble pie." "Well, can we roll down the windows? It's really hot in here, and it smells like something died." "Sammy Davis, Junior, Junior will jump out." "Who?" "The bitch. Her name is Sammy Davis, Junior, Junior." "Is that a joke?" "No, she will truly go forth from the car." "His name, though." "*Her* name," I rectified him, because I am first rate with pronouns. "Tell him to Velcro his lip together," Grandfather said. "He says that the bitch was named for his favorite singer, who was Sammy Davis, Junior." "A Jew," the hero said. "What?" "Sammy Davis, Junior was a Jew." "This is not possible," I said. "A convert. He found the Jewish God. Funny." I told this to Grandfather. "Sammy Davis, Junior was not a Jew!" he hollered. "He was the Negro of the Rat Pack!" "The Jew is certain of it." "The Music Man? A Jew? This is not a possible thing!" "This is what he informs me." "Dean Martin, Junior!" he hollered to the back seat. "Get up here! Come on, girl!" "Can we please roll down the window?" the hero said. "I can't live with that smell." With this I licked the last crumb of humble pie from the plate. "It is only Sammy Davis, Junior, Junior. She gets terrible farting in the car because it has nor shock absorbers nor struts, but if we roll down the window she will jump out, and we need her because she is the Seeing Eye bitch for our blind driver, who is also my grandfather. What do you not understand?"

It was pending this five-hour car drive from the Lvov train station to Lutsk that the hero explained to me why he came to Ukraine. He excavated several items from his side bag. First he exhibited me a photograph. It was yellow and folded and had many pieces of fixative affixing it together. "See this?" he said. "This here is my grandfather Safran." He pointed to a young man who I will say appeared very much like the hero, and could have been the hero. "This was taken during the war." "From who?" "No, not taken like that. The photograph was made." "I understand." "These people he is with are the family that saved him from the Nazis." "What?" "They...saved...him...from...the...Na...zis." "In Trachimbrod?" "No, somewhere outside of Trachimbrod. He escaped the Nazi raid on Trachimbrod. Everyone else was killed. He lost a wife and a baby." "He lost?" "They were killed by the Nazis." "But if it was not Trachimbrod, why do we go to Trachimbrod? And how will we find this family?" He explained to me that we were not looking for the family, but for this girl. She would be the only one still alive.

He moved his finger along the face of the girl in the photograph as he mentioned her. She was standing down and right to his grandfather in the picture. A man who I am certain was her father was next to her, and a woman who I am certain was her mother was behind her. Her parents appeared very Russian, but she did not. She appeared American. She was a youthful girl, perhaps fifteen. But it is possible that she had more age. She could have been so old as the hero and me, as could have been the hero's grandfather. I looked at the girl for many minutes. She was so so beautiful. Her hair was brown, and rested only on her shoulders. Her eyes appeared sad, and full of intelligence.

"I want to see Trachimbrod," the hero said. "To see what it's like, how my grandfather grew up, where I would be now if it weren't for the war." "You would be Ukrainian." "That's right." "Like me." "I guess." "Only not like me because you would be a farmer in an unimpressive town, and I live in Odessa, which is very much like Miami." "And I want to see what it's like now. I don't think there are any Jews left, but maybe there are. And the shtetls weren't only Jews, so there should be others to talk to." "The whats?" "Shtetls. A shtetl is like a village." "Why don't you merely dub it a village?" "It's a Jewish word." "A Jewish word?" "Yiddish. Like schmuck." "What does it mean schmuck?" "Someone who does something that you don't agree with is a schmuck." "Teach me another." "Putz." "What does that mean?" "It's like schmuck." "Teach me another." "Schmendrik." "What does that mean?" "It's also like schmuck." "Do you know any words that are not like schmuck?" He pondered for a moment. "Shalom," he said, "which is actually three words, but that's Hebrew, not Yiddish. Everything I can think of is basically schmuck. The Eskimos have four hundred words for snow, and the Jews have four hundred for schmuck." I wondered, What is an Eskimo?

"So, we will sightsee the shtetl?" I asked the hero. "I figured it would be a good place to begin our search." "Search?" "For Augustine." "Who is Augustine?" "The girl in the photograph. She's the only one who would still be alive." "Ah. We will search for Augustine, who you think saved your grandfather from the Nazis." "Yes." It was very silent for a moment. "I would like to find her," I said. I perceived that this appeased the hero, but I did not say it to appease him. I said it because it was faithful. "And then," I said, "if we find her?" The hero was a pensive person. "I don't know what then. I suppose I'd thank her." "For saving your grandfather." "Yes." "That will be very queer, yes?" "What?" "When we find her." "If we find her." "We will find her." "Probably not," he said. "Then why do we search?" I queried, but before he could answer, I interrupted myself with another query. "And how do you know that her name is Augustine?" "I guess I don't, really. On the back, see, here, are written a few words, in my grandfather's writing, I think. Maybe not. It's in Yiddish. It says: 'This is me with Augustine, February 21, 1943.'" "It's very difficult to read." "Yes." "Why do you think he remarks only about Augustine and not the other two people in the photograph?" "I don't know." "It is queer, yes? It is queer that he remarks only her. Do you think he loved her?" "What?" "Because he remarks only her." "So?" "So perhaps he loved her." "It's funny that you should think that. We must think alike." (Thank you, Jonathan.) "I've actually thought a lot about it, without having any good reason to. He was eighteen, and she was, what, about fifteen? He had just lost a wife and daughter when the Nazis raided his shtetl." "Trachimbrod?" "Right. For all I know the writing doesn't have anything to do with the picture. It could be that he used this for scrap paper." "Scrap?" "Paper that's unimportant. Just something to write on." "Oh." "So I don't really have any idea. It seems so improbable that he could have loved her. But isn't there something strange about the picture, the closeness between them, even though they're not looking at each other? The *way* that they aren't looking at each other. The distance. It's very powerful, don't you think? And his words on the back." "Yes." "And that we should both think about the possibility of his loving her is also strange." "Yes," I said. "Part of me wants him to have loved her, and part of me hates to think it." "What is the part of you that hates it if he loved her?" "Well, it's nice to think of some things as irreplaceable." "I do not understand. He married your present grandmother, so something must have been replaced." "But that's different." "Why?" "Because she's my grandmother." "Augustine could have been your grandmother." "No, she could have been someone else's grandmother. For all I know she is. Maybe he had children with her." "Do not say this about your grandfather." "Well, I know he had other children before, so why would that be so different?" "What if we reveal a brother of yours?" "We won't." "And how did you obtain this photograph?" I asked, holding it to the window. "My grandmother gave it to my mother two years ago, and she said that this was the family that saved my grandfather from the Nazis." "Why merely two years?" "What do you mean?" "Why was it so newly that she gave it to your mother?" "Oh, I see what you're asking. She has her reasons." "What are these reasons?" "I don't know." "Did you inquire her about the writing on the back?" "No. We couldn't ask her anything about it." "Why not?" "She held on to the photograph for fifty years. If she had wanted to tell us anything about it, she would have." "Now I understand what you are saying." "I couldn't even tell her I was coming to the Ukraine. She thinks I'm still in Prague." "Why is this?" "Her memories of the Ukraine aren't good. Her shtetl, Kolki, is only a few kilometers from Trachimbrod. I figure we'd go there too. But all of her family was killed, everyone, mother, father, sisters, grandparents." "Did a Ukrainian save her?" "No, she fled before the war. She was young, and left her family behind." She left her family behind. I wrote this on my brain. "It surprises me that no one saved her family," I said. "It shouldn't be surprising. The Ukrainians, back then, were terrible to the Jews. They were almost as bad as the Nazis. It was a different world. At the beginning of the war, a lot of Jews wanted to go to the Nazis to be protected from the Ukrainians." "This is not true." "It is." "I cannot believe what you are saying." "Look it up in the history books." "It does not say this in the history books." "Well, that's the way it was. Ukrainians were known for being terrible to the Jews. So were the Poles. Listen, I don't mean to offend you. It's got nothing to do with you. We're talking about fifty years ago." "I think you are mistaken," I told the hero. "I don't know what to say." "Say that you are mistaken." "I can't." "You must."

"Here are my maps," he said, excavating a few pieces of paper from his bag. He pointed to one that was wet from Sammy Davis, Junior, Junior. Her tongue, I hoped. "This is Trachimbrod," he said. "It's also called Sofiowka on certain maps. This is Lutsk. This is Kolki. It's an old map. Most of the places we're looking for aren't on new maps. Here," he said, and presented it to me. "You can see where we have to go. This is all I have, these maps and the photograph. It's not much." "I can promise you that we will find this Augustine," I said. I could perceive that this made the hero appeased. It also made me appeased. "Grandfather," I said, rotating to the front again. I explained everything that the hero had just uttered to me. I informed him about Augustine, and the maps, and the hero's grandmother. "Kolki?" he asked. "Kolki," I said. I made certain to involve every detail, and I also invented several new details, so that Grandfather would understand the story more. I could perceive that this story made Grandfather very melancholy. "Augustine," he said, and pushed Sammy Davis, Junior, Junior onto me. He scrutinized at the photograph while I fastened the wheel. He put it close to his face, like he wanted to smell it, or touch it with his eyes. "Augustine." "She is the one we are looking for," I said. He moved his head this and that. "We will find her," he said. "I know," I said. But I did not know, and nor did Grandfather.

When we reached the hotel, it was already commencing darkness.

"You must remain in the car," I told the hero, because the proprietor of the hotel would know that the hero is American, and Father told me that they charge Americans in surplus. "Why?" he asked. I told him why. "How will they know I am American?" "Tell him to remain in the car," Grandfather said, "or they will charge him twice." "I am making efforts," I told him. "I'd like to go in with you," the hero said, "to check the place out." "Why?" "Just to check things out. See what it's like." "You can see what it is like after I get the rooms." "I'd prefer to do it now," he said, and I must confess that he was beginning to be on my nerves. "What the fucking hell is he still talking about?" Grandfather asked. "He wants to go in with me." "Why?" "Because he is an American." "Is it OK if I go in?" he asked again. Grandfather turned to him, and said to me, "He is paying. If he wants to pay surplus, let him pay surplus." So I took him with me when I entered the hotel to pay for two rooms. If you want to know why two rooms, one was for Grandfather and me, and one was for the hero. Father said it should be this manner.

When we entered the hotel, I told the hero not to speak. "Do not speak," I said. "Why?" he asked. "Do not speak," I said without much volume. "Why?" he asked. "I will tutor you later. Shhh." But he kept inquiring why he should not speak, and as I was certain, he was heard by the owner of the hotel. "I will need to view your documents," the owner said. "He needs to view your documents," I said to the hero. "Why?" "Give them to me." "Why?" "If we are going to have a room, he needs to view your documents." "I don't understand." "There is nothing to understand." "Is there a problem?" the owner inquired me. "Because this is the only hotel in Lutsk that is still possessing rooms at this time of the night. Do you desire to attempt your luck on the street?"

I was finally able to prevail on the hero to give his documents. He stored them in a thing on his belt. Later he told me that this is called a fanny pack, and that fanny packs are not cool in America, and that he was only donning a fanny pack because a guidebook said he should don one to keep his documents close to his middle section. As I was certain, the owner of the hotel charged the hero a special foreigner tariff. I did not enlighten the hero this, because I knew he would have manufactured queries until he had to pay four times, and not only two, or until we received no room for the night at all, and had to repose in the car, as Grandfather had made an addiction of doing.

When we returned to the car, Sammy Davis, Junior, Junior was masticating her tail in the back seat, and Grandfather was again manufacturing Z's. "Grandfather," I said, adjusting his arm, "we obtained a room." I had to move him with very much violence in order to wake him. When he unclosed his eyes, he did not know where he was. "Anna?" he asked. "No, Grandfather," I said, "it is me, Sasha." He was very shamed, and hid his face from me. "We obtained a room," I said. "Is he feeling OK?" the hero asked me. "Yes, he is fatigued." "Will he be OK for tomorrow?" "Of course." But in truth Grandfather was not his normal self. Or maybe he was his normal self. I did not know what his normal self was. I remembered a thing that Father told me. When I was a boy, Grandfather said I looked like a combination of Father, Mother, Brezhnev, and myself. I had always thought that story was very funny until at that moment at the car in front of the hotel in Lutsk.

I told the hero not to leave any of his bags in the car. It is a bad and popular habit for people in Ukraine to take things without asking. I have read that New York City is very dangerous, but I must say that Ukraine is more dangerous. If you want to know who protects you from the people that take without asking, it is the police. If you want to know who protects you from the police, it is the people who take without asking. And very often they are the same people.

"Let us eat," Grandfather said, and commenced to drive. "You are hungry?" I asked the hero, who was again the sexual object of Sammy Davis, Junior, Junior. "Get it off of me," he said. "Are you hungry?" I repeated. "Please!" he implored. I called to her, and when she did not respond I punched her in the face. She moved to her side of the back seat, because now she understanded what it means to be stupid with the wrong person, and commenced to cry. Did I feel awful? "I'm famished," the hero said, lifting his head from his knees. "What?" "Yes, I'm hungry." "You are hungry, then." "Yes." "Good. Our driver—" "You can call him your grandfather. It doesn't bother me." "He is not your brother." "*Bother*, I said. Bother." "What does it mean to bother me?" "To upset." "What does it mean to upset?" "To distress." "I understand to distress." "So you can call him your grandfather, is what I'm saying."

We became very busy talking. When I rotated back to Grandfather, I saw that he was examining Augustine again. There was a sadness amid him and the photograph, and nothing in the world frightened me more. "We will eat," I told him. "Good," he said, holding the photograph very near to his face. Sammy Davis, Junior, Junior was persisting to cry. "One thing, though," the hero said. "What?" "You should know..." "Yes?" "I am a...how to say this..." "What?" "I'm a..." "You are very hungry, yes?" "I'm a vegetarian." "I do not understand." "I don't eat meat." "Why not?" "I just don't." "How can you not eat meat?" "I just don't." "He does not eat meat," I told Grandfather. "Yes he does," he informed me. "Yes you do," I likewise informed the hero. "No. I don't." "Why not?" I inquired him again. "I just don't. No meat." "Pork?" "No." "Meat?" "No meat." "Steak?" "Nope." "Chickens?" "No." "Do you eat veal?" "Oh, God. Absolutely no veal." "What about sausage?" "No sausage either." I told Grandfather this, and he presented me a very bothered look. "What is wrong with him?" he asked. "What is wrong with you?" I asked him. "It's just the way I am," he said. "Hamburger?" "No." "Tongue?" "What did he say is wrong with him?" Grandfather asked. "It is just the way he is." "Does he eat sausage?" "No." "No sausage!" "No. He says he does not eat sausage." "In truth?" "That is what he says." "But sausage..." "I know." "In truth you do not eat any sausage?" "No sausage." "No sausage," I told Grandfather. He closed his eyes and tried to put his arms around his stomach, but there was not room because of the wheel. It appeared like he was becoming sick because the hero would not eat sausage. "Well, let him deduce what he is going to eat. We will go to the most proximal restaurant." "You are a schmuck," I informed the hero. "You're not using the word correctly," he said. "Yes I am," I said.

"What do you mean he does not eat meat?" the waitress asked, and Grandfather put his head in his hands. "What is wrong with him?" she asked. "Which? The one who does not eat meat, the one with his head in his hands, or the bitch who is masticating her tail?" "The one who does not eat meat." "It is only the way that he is." The hero asked what we were talking about. "They do not have anything without meat," I informed him. "He does not eat any meat at all?" she inquired me again. "It is merely the way he is," I told her. "Sausage?" "No sausage," Grandfather answered to the waitress, rotating his head from here to there. "Maybe you could eat some meat," I suggested to the hero, "because they do not have anything that is not meat." "Don't they have potatoes or something?" he asked. "Do you have potatoes?" I asked the waitress. "Or something?" "You only receive a potato with the meat," she said. I told the hero. "Couldn't I just get a plate of potatoes?" "What?" "Couldn't I get two or three potatoes, without meat?" I asked the waitress, and she said she would go to the chef and inquire him. "Ask him if he eats liver," Grandfather said.

The waitress returned and said, "Here is what I have to say. We can make concessions to give him two potatoes, but they are served with a piece of meat on the plate. The chef says that this cannot be negotiated. He will have to eat it." "Two potatoes is fine?" I asked the hero. "Oh, that would be great." Grandfather and I both ordered the pork steak, and ordered one for Sammy Davis, Junior, Junior as well, who was becoming sociable with the hero's leg.

When the food arrived, the hero asked for me to remove the meat off of his plate. "I'd prefer not to touch it," he said. This was on my nerves to the maximum. If you want to know why, it is because I perceived that the hero perceived he was too good for our food. I took the meat off his plate, because I knew that is what Father would have desired me to do, and I did not utter a thing. "Tell him we will commence very early in the morning tomorrow," Grandfather said. "Early?" "So we can have as much of the day for searching as possible. It will be rigid at night." "We will commence very early in the morning tomorrow," I said to the hero. "That's good," he said, kicking his leg. I was very flabbergasted that Grandfather would desire to go forth early in the morning. He hated to not repose tardy. He hated to not repose ever. He also hated Lutsk, and the car, and the hero, and, of late, me. Leaving early in the morning would provide him with more of the day aroused with all of us. "Let me inspect at his maps," he said. I asked the hero for the maps. As he was reaching into his fanny pack, he again kicked his leg, which made Sammy Davis, Junior, Junior become sociable with the table, and also made the plates move. One of the hero's potatoes descended to the floor. When it hit the floor it made a sound. PLOMP. It rolled over, and then was inert. Grandfather and I examined each other. I did not know what to do. "A terrible thing has occurred," Grandfather said. The hero continued to view the potato on the floor. It was a dirty floor. It was one of his two potatoes. "This is awful," Grandfather said silently, and moved his plate to the side. "Awful." He was correct.

The waitress returned to our table with the colas we ordered. "Here are—" she began, but then she witnessed the potato on the floor and walked away with warp speed. The hero was still witnessing the potato on the floor. I do not know for certain, but I imagine he was imagining that he could pick it up, put it back on his plate, and eat it, or he could leave it on the floor, delude the mishap never happened, eat his one potato, and counterfeit to be happy, or he could push it with his foot to Sammy Davis, Junior, Junior, who was aristocratic enough not to eat it as it laid on that dirty floor, or he could tell the waitress for another, which would mean he would have to get another piece of meat for me to remove from his plate because for him meat is disgusting, or he could just eat the piece of meat I removed from his plate before, as I would hope for him to. But what he did was not any of these things. If you want to know what he did, he did not do anything. We remained silent, witnessing the potato. Grandfather inserted his fork in the potato, picked it up from the floor, and put it on his plate. He cut it into four pieces and gave one to Sammy Davis, Junior, Junior under the table, one to me, and one to the hero. He cut off a piece from his piece and ate it. Then he looked at me. I did not want to, but I knew that I had to. To say that it was not delicious would be an overstatement. Then we looked at the hero. He looked at the floor, and then at his plate. He cut off a piece from his piece and looked at it. "Welcome to Ukraine," Grandfather said to him, and punched me on the back, which was a thing I relished very much. Then Grandfather started laughing. "Welcome to Ukraine," I translated. Then I started laughing. Then the hero started laughing. We laughed with much violence for a long time. We obtained the attention of every person in the restaurant. We laughed with violence, and then more violence. I witnessed that each of us was manufacturing tears at his eyes. It was not until very much in the posterior that I understood that each of us was laughing for a different reason, for our own reason, and that not one of those reasons had a thing to do with the potato.

There is something that I did not mention before, which it would now be befitting to mention. (Please, Jonathan, I implore you never to exhibit this to one soul. I do not know why I am writing this here.) I returned home from a famous nightclub one night and desired to view television. I was surprised when I heard that the television was already on, because it was so tardy. I cogitated that it was Grandfather. As I illuminated before, he would very often come to our house when he could not repose. This was before he came to live with us. What would occur is that he would commence to repose while viewing television, but then rise a few hours later and return to his house. Unless I could not repose, and because I could not repose would hear Grandfather viewing television, I would not know the next day if he had been in the house the night previous. He might have been there every night. Because I never knew, I thought of him as a ghost.

I would never say hello to Grandfather when he was viewing television, because I did not want to meddle with him. So I walked slowly that night, and without noise. I was already on the four stair when I heard something queer. It was not crying, exactly. It was something a little less than crying. I submerged the four stairs with slowness. I walked on toes through the kitchen and observed from around the corner, amid the kitchen and the television room. First I witnessed the television. It was exhibiting a football game. (I do not remember who was competing, but I am confident that we were winning.) I witnessed a hand on the chair that Grandfather likes to view television in. But it was not Grandfather's hand. I tried to see more, and I almost fell over. I know that I should have recognized the sound that was a little less than crying. It was Little Igor. (I am such a stupid fool.)

This made me a suffering person. I will tell you why. I knew why he was a little less than crying. I knew very well, and I wanted to go to him and tell him that I had a little less than cried too, just like him, and that no matter how much it seemed like he would never grow up to be a premium person like me, with many girls and so many famous places to go, he would. He would be exactly like me. And look at me, Little Igor, the bruises go away, and so does how you hate, and so does the feeling that everything you receive in life is something you have earned.

But I could not tell him any of these things. I roosted on the floor of the kitchen, only several meters distance from him, and I commenced to laugh. I did not know why I was laughing, but I could not stop. I pressed my hand against my mouth so that I would not manufacture any noise. My laughing got more and more, until my stomach pained. I attempted to rise, so that I could walk to my room, but I was afraid that it would be too difficult to control my laughing. I remained there for many, many minutes. My brother persevered to a little less than cry, which made my silent laughing even more. I am able to understand now that it was the same laugh that I had in the restaurant in Lutsk, the laugh that had the same darkness as Grandfather's laugh and the hero's laugh. (I ask leniency for writing this. Perhaps I will remove it before I post this part to you. I am sorry.) As for Sammy Davis, Junior, Junior, she did not eat her piece of the potato.

The hero and I spoke very much at dinner, mostly about America. "Tell me about things that you have in America," I said. "What do you want to know about?" "My friend Gregory informs me that there are many good schools for accounting in America. Is this true?" "I guess. I don't really know. I could find out for you when I get back." "Thank you," I said, because now I had a connection in America, and was not alone, and then, "What do you want to make?" "What do I want to make?" "Yes. What will you become?" "I don't know." "Surely you know." "This and that." "What does it mean this and that?" "I'm just not sure yet." "Father informs me that you are writing a book about this trip." "I like to write." I punched his back. "You are a writer!" "Shhhh." "But it is a good career, yes?" "What?" "Writing. It is very noble." "Noble? I don't know." "Do you have any books published?" "No, but I'm still very young." "You have stories published?" "No. Well, one or two." "What are they dubbed?" "Forget it." "This is a first-rate title." "No. I mean, forget it." "I would love very much to read your stories." "You probably won't like them." "Why do you say that?" "*I* don't even like them." "Oh." "They're apprentice pieces." "What does it mean apprentice pieces?" "They're not real stories. I was just learning how to write." "But one day you will have learned how to write." "That's the hope." "Like becoming an accountant." "Maybe." "Why do you want to write?" "I don't know. I used to think it was what I was born to do. No, I never really thought that. It's just something people say." "No, it is not. I truly feel that I was born to be an accountant." "You're lucky." "Perhaps you were born to write?" "I don't know. Maybe. It sounds terrible to say. Cheap." "It sounds nor terrible nor cheap." "It's so hard to express yourself." "I understand this." "I want to express myself." "The same is true for me." "I'm looking for my voice." "It is in your mouth." "I want to do something I'm not ashamed of." "Something you are proud of, yes?" "Not even. I just don't want to be ashamed." "There are many premium Russian writers, yes?" "Oh, of course. Tons." "Tolstoy, yes? He wrote *War*, and also *Peace*, which are premium books, and he also earned the Noble Peace Prize for writing, if I am not so wrong." "Tolstoy. Bely. Turgenev." "A question." "Yes?" "Do you write because you have a thing to say?" "No." "And if I may partake in a different theme: how much currency would an accountant receive in America?" "I'm not sure. A lot, I imagine, if he or she is good." "She!" "Or he." "Are there Negro accountants?" "There are African-American accountants. You don't want to use that word, though, Alex." "And homosexual accountants?" "There are homosexual everythings. There are homosexual garbage men." "How much currency would a Negro homosexual accountant receive?" "You shouldn't use that word." "Which word?" "The one before homosexual." "What?" "The n-word. Well, it's not *the* n-word, but—" "Negro?" "Shhh." "I dig Negroes." "You really shouldn't say that." "But I dig them all the way. They are premium people." "It's that word, though. It's not a nice thing to say." "Negro?" "Please." "What's wrong with Negroes?" "Shhh." "How much does a cup of coffee cost in America?" "Oh, it depends. Maybe one dollar." "One dollar! This is for free! In Ukraine one cup of coffee is five dollars!" "Oh, well, I didn't mention cappuccinos. They can be as much as five or six dollars." "Cappuccinos," I said, elevating my hands above my head, "there is no maximum!" "Do you have lattes in the Ukraine?" "What is latte?" "Oh, because they're very cool in America. Really, they're basically everywhere." "Do you have mochas in America?" "Of course, but only children drink them. They're not very cool in America." "Yes, it is very much the same here. We have also mochaccinos." "Yeah, of course. We have those in America. They might be seven dollars." "Are they much-loved things?" "Mochaccinos?" "Yes."

"I think they're for people who want to drink a coffee drink but also really like hot chocolate." "I understand this. What about the girls in America?" "What about them?" "They are very informal with their boxes, yes?" "You hear about them, but nobody I know has ever met one of them." "Are you carnal very often?" "Are you?" "I inquired you. Are you?" "Are you?" "I inquired headmost. Are you?" "Not really." "What do you intend by not really?" "I'm not a priest, but I'm not John Holmes either." "I know of this John Holmes." I lifted my hands to my sides. "With the premium penis." "That's the one," he said, and laughed. I made him laugh with my funny. "In Ukraine everyone has a penis like that." He laughed again. "Even the women?" he asked. "You made a funny?" I asked. "Yes," he said. So I laughed. "Have you ever had a girlfriend?" I asked the hero. "Have you?" "I am inquiring you." "I sort of have," he said. "What do you signify with sort of?" "Nothing formal, really. Not a girlfriend girlfriend, really. I've dated, I guess, once or twice. I don't want to be formal." "It is the same state of affairs with me," I said. "I also do not want to be formal. I do not want to be handcuffed to only one girl." "Exactly," he said. "I mean, I've fooled around with girls." "Of course." "Blowjobs." "Yes, of course." "But once you get a girlfriend, well, you know." "I know very well."

"A question," I said. "Do you think the women in Ukraine are first rate?" "I haven't seen many since I've been here." "Do you have women like this in America?" "There's at least one of everything in America." "I have heard this. Do you have many motorcycles in America?" "Of course." "And fax machines?" "Everywhere." "You have a fax machine?" "No. They're very passé." "What does it mean passé?" "They're out-of-date. Paper is so tedious." "Tedious?" "Tiresome." "I understand what you are telling me, and I harmonize. I would not ever use paper. It makes me a sleeping person." "It's so messy." "Yes, it is true, it makes a mess, and you are asleep." "Another question. Do most young people have impressive cars in America? Lotus Esprit V8 Twin Turbos?" "Not really. I don't. I have a real piece-of-shit Toyota." "It is brown?" "No, it's an expression." "How can your car be an expression?" "I have a car that is like a piece of shit. You know, it stinks like shit and looks shitty like shit." "And if you are a good accountant, you could buy an impressive car?"

"Absolutely. You could probably buy most anything you want." "What kind of wife would a good accountant have?" "Who knows." "Would she have rigid tits?" "I couldn't say for sure." "Probably, although?" "I guess." "I dig this. I dig rigid tits." "But there are also accountants, even very good ones, who have ugly wives. That's just the way it works." "If John Holmes was a first-rate accountant, he could have any woman he would like for his wife, yes?" "Probably." "My penis is very big." "OK."

After dinner at the restaurant, we drove back to the hotel. As I knew, it was an unimpressive hotel. There was no area for swimming and no famous discotheque. When we unclosed the door to the hero's room, I could perceive that he was distressed. "It's nice," he said, because he could perceive that I could perceive that he was distressed. "Really, it's just for sleeping." "You do not have hotels like this in America!" I made a funny. "No," he said, and he was laughing. We were like friends. For the first time that I could remember, I felt entirely good. "Make sure you secure the door after we go to our room," I told him. "I do not want to make you a petrified person, but there are many dangerous people who want to take things without asking from Americans, and also kidnap them. Good night." The hero laughed again, but he laughed because he did not know that I was not making a funny. "Come on, Sammy Davis, Junior, Junior," Grandfather called to the bitch, but she would not leave the door. "Come on." Nothing. "Come on!" he bellowed, but she would not dislodge. I tried to sing to her, which she relishes, especially when I sing "Billie Jean," by Michael Jackson. "She's just a girl who claims that I am the one." But nothing. She only pushed her head against the door to the hero's room. Grandfather attempted to remove her with force, but she commenced to cry. I knocked on the door, and the hero had a teethbrush in his mouth. "Sammy Davis, Junior, Junior will manufacture Z's with you this evening," I told him, although I knew that would not be successful. "No," he said, and that was all. "She will not depart from your door," I told him. "Then let her sleep in the hall." "It would be benevolent of you." "Not interested." "Only for one night." "One too many. She'll kill me." "It is so unlikely." "She's crazy." "Yes, I cannot dispute that she is crazy. But she is also compassionate." I knew that I would not prevail. "Listen," the hero said, "if she wants to sleep in the room, I'd be happy to sleep in the hall. But if I'm in the room, I'm alone in the room." "Perhaps you could both sleep in the hall," I suggested.

After we left the hero and the bitch to repose—hero in room, bitch in hall—Grandfather and I went downstairs to the hotel bar for drinks of vodka. It was Grandfather's notion. In truth, I was a petite amount terrified of being alone with him. "He is a good boy," Grandfather said. I could not perceive if he was inquiring me or tutoring me. "He seems good," I said. Grandfather moved his hand over his face, which had become covered with hairs during the day. It was only then that I noticed that his hands were still shaking, that they had been shaking all day. "We should try very inflexibly to help him." "We should," I said. "I would like very much to find Augustine," he said. "So would I."

That was all the talking for the night. We had three vodkas each and watched the weather report that was on the television behind the bar. It said that the weather for the next day would be normal. I was appeased that the weather would be normal. It would make our search cinchier. After the vodka, we went up to our room, which flanked the room of the hero. "I will repose on the bed, and you will repose on the floor," Grandfather said. "Of course," I said. "I will make my alarm for six in the morning." "Six?" I inquired. If you want to know why I inquired, it is because six is not very early in the morning for me, it is tardy in the night. "Six," he said, and I knew that it was the end of the conversation.

While Grandfather washed his teeth, I went to make certain that everything was acceptable with the hero's room. I listened at the door to detect if he was able to manufacture Z's, and I could not hear anything abnormal, only the wind penetrating the windows and the sound of insects. Good, I said to my brain, he reposes well. He will not be fatigued in the morning. I tried to unclose the door, to make sure it was secured. It opened a percentage, and Sammy Davis, Junior, Junior, who was still conscious, walked in. I watched her lay herself next to the bed, where the hero reposed in peace. This is acceptable, I thought, and closed the door with silence. I walked back to the room of Grandfather and I. The lights were already off, but I could perceive that he was not yet reposing. His body rotated over and over. The bed sheets moved, and the pillow made noises as he rotated over and over, over and then again over. I heard his large breathing. I heard his body move. It was like this all night. I knew why he could not repose. It was the same reason that I would not be able to repose. We were both regarding the same question: what did he do during the war?

Falling in Love, 1791–1803

TRACHIMBROD was somehow different from the nameless shtetl that used to exist in the same place. Business went on as usual. The Uprighters still hollered, hung, and limped, and still looked down on the Slouchers, who still twiddled the fringes at the ends of their shirtsleeves, and still ate cookies and knishes after, but more often during, services. Grieving Shanda still grieved for her deceased philosopher husband, Pinchas, who still played an active role in shtetl politics. Yankel still tried to do right, still told himself again and again that he wasn't sad, and still always ended up sad. The synagogue still rolled, still trying to land itself on the shtetl's wandering Jewish/Human fault line. Sofiowka was as mad as ever, still masturbating a handful, still binding himself in string, using his body to remember his body, and still remembering only the string. But with the name came a new self-consciousness, which often revealed itself in shameful ways.

The women of the shtetl raised their impressive noses to my great-great-great-great-great-grandmother. They called her *dirty river girl* and *waterbaby* under their breath. While they were too superstitious ever to reveal to her the truth of her history, they saw to it that she had no friends her own age (telling their children that she was not as much fun as the fun she had, or as kind as her kind deeds), and that she associated only with Yankel and any man of the shtetl who was brave enough to risk being seen by his wife. Of which there were quite a few. Even the surest gentleman stumbled over himself in her presence. After only ten years of life, she was already the most desired creature in the shtetl, and her reputation had spread like rivulets into the neighboring villages.

I've imagined her many times. She's a bit short, even for her age—not short in the endearing, childish way, but as a malnourished child might be short. The same is true for how skinny she is. Every night before putting her to sleep, Yankel counts her ribs, as if one might have disappeared in the course of the day and become the seed and soil for some new companion to steal her away from him. She eats well enough and is healthy, insofar as she's never sick, but her body looks like that of a chronically sick girl, a girl squeezed in some biological vise, or a starving girl, a skin-and-bones girl, a girl who is not entirely free. Her hair is thick and black, her lips are thin and bright and white. How else could it be?

Much to Yankel's dismay, Brod insisted on cutting that thick black hair herself.

It's not ladylike, he said. *You look like a little boy when it's so short.*

Don't be a fool, she told him.

But doesn't it bother you?

Of course it bothers me when you're a fool.

Your hair, he said.

I think it's very pretty.

Can it be pretty if no one thinks it's pretty?

I think it's pretty.

If you're the only one?

That's pretty pretty.

And what about the boys? Don't you want them to think you're pretty?

I wouldn't want a boy to think I was pretty unless he was the kind of boy who thought I was pretty.

I think it's pretty, he said. *I think it's very beautiful.*

Say it again and I'll grow it long.

I know, he laughed, kissing her forehead as he pinched her ears between his fingers.

Her learning to sew (from a book Yankel brought back from Lvov) coincided with her refusal to wear any clothes that she did not make for herself, and when he bought her a book about animal physiology, she held the pictures to his face and said, *Don't you think it's strange, Yankel, how we eat them?*

I've never eaten a picture.

The animals. Don't you find that strange? I can't believe I never found it strange before. It's like your name, how you don't notice it for so long, but when you finally do, you can't help but say it over and over, and wonder why you never thought it was strange that you should have that name, and that everyone has been calling you that name for your whole life.

Yankel. Yankel. Yankel. Nothing so strange for me.

I won't eat them, at least not until it doesn't seem strange to me.

Brod resisted everything, gave in to no one, would not be challenged or not challenged.

I don't think you're stubborn, Yankel told her one afternoon when she refused to eat dinner before dessert.

Well I am!

And she was loved for it. Loved by everyone, even those who hated her. The curious circumstances of her creation lit the men's intrigue, but it was her clever manipulations, her coy gestures and pivots of phrase, her refusal to acknowledge or ignore their existence that made them follow her through the streets, gaze at her from their windows, dream of her—not their wives, not even themselves—at night.

Yes, Yoske. The men in the flour mill are so strong and brave.

Yes, Feivel. Yes, I am a good girl.

Yes, Saul. Yes, yes, I love sweets.

Yes, oh yes, Itzik. Oh yes.

Yankel didn't have the heart to tell her that he was not her father, that she was the Float Queen of Trachimday not only because she was, without question, the most loved young girl in the shtetl, but because it was her real father at the bottom of the river with her name, her papa the hardy men dove for. So he created more stories—wild stories, with undomesticated imagery and flamboyant characters. He invented stories so fantastic that she had to believe. Of course, she was only a child, still removing the dust from her first death. What else could she do? And he was already accumulating the dust of his second death. What else could *he* do?

With the help of the shtetl's desirous men and hateful women, my very-great-grandmother grew into herself, cultivating private interests:

weaving, gardening, reading anything she could get her hands on—which was just about anything in Yankel's prodigious library, a room filled from floor to ceiling with books, which would one day serve as Trachimbrod's first public library. Not only was she the smartest citizen in Trachimbrod, called upon to solve difficult problems of mathematics or logic—*THE HOLY WORD*, the Well-Regarded Rabbi once asked her in the dark, *WHICH IS IT, BROD?*—she was also the most lonely and sad. She was a genius of sadness, immersing herself in it, separating its numerous strands, appreciating its subtle nuances. She was a prism through which sadness could be divided into its infinite spectrum.

Are you sad, Yankel? she asked one morning over breakfast.

Of course, he said, feeding melon slices into her mouth with a shaking spoon.

Why?

Because you are talking instead of eating your breakfast.

Were you sad before that?

Of course.

Why?

Because you were eating then, instead of talking, and I become sad when I don't hear your voice.

When you watch people dance, does that make you sad?

Of course.

It also makes me sad. Why do you think it does that?

He kissed her on the forehead, put his hand under her chin. *You really must eat*, he said. *It's getting late.*

Do you think Bitzl Bitzl is a particularly sad person?

I don't know.

What about grieving Shanda?

Oh yes, she's particularly sad.

That's an obvious one, isn't it? Is Shloim sad?

Who knows?

The twins?

Maybe. It's none of our business.

Is God sad?

He would have to exist to be sad, wouldn't He?

I know, she said, giving his shoulder a little slap. *That's why I was asking, so I might finally know if you believed!*

Well, let me leave it at this: if God does exist, He would have a great deal to be sad about. And if He doesn't exist, then that too would make Him quite sad, I imagine. So to answer your question, God must be sad.

Yankel! She wrapped her arms around his neck, as if trying to pull herself into him, or him into her.

Brod discovered 613 sadnesses, each perfectly unique, each a singular emotion, no more similar to any other sadness than to anger, ecstasy, guilt, or frustration. Mirror Sadness. Sadness of Domesticated Birds. Sadness of Being Sad in Front of One's Parent. Humor Sadness. Sadness of Love Without Release.

She was like a drowning person, flailing, reaching for anything that might save her. Her life was an urgent, desperate struggle to justify her life. She learned impossibly difficult songs on her violin, songs outside of what she thought she could know, and would each time come crying to Yankel, *I have learned to play this one too! It's so terrible! I must write something that not even I can play!* She spent evenings with the art books Yankel had bought for her in Lutsk, and each morning sulked over breakfast, *They were good and fine, but not beautiful. No, not if I'm being honest with myself. They are only the best of what exists.* She spent an afternoon staring at their front door.

Waiting for someone? Yankel asked.

What color is this?

He stood very close to the door, letting the end of his nose touch the peephole. He licked the wood and joked, *It certainly tastes like red.*

Yes, it is red, isn't it?

Seems so.

She buried her head in her hands. *But couldn't it be just a bit more red?*

Brod's life was a slow realization that the world was not for her, and that for whatever reason, she would never be happy and honest at the same time. She felt as if she were brimming, always producing and hoarding more love inside her. But there was no release. Table, ivory elephant charm, rainbow, onion, hairdo, mollusk, Shabbos, violence, cuticle, melodrama, ditch, honey, doily...None of it moved her. She addressed her world honestly, searching for something deserving of the volumes of love she knew she had within her, but to each she would have to say, *I don't love you.* Bark-brown fence post: *I don't love you.* Poem too long: *I don't love you.* Lunch in a bowl: *I don't love you.* Physics, the idea of you, the laws of you: *I don't love you.* Nothing felt like anything more than what it actually was. Everything was just a thing, mired completely in its thingness.

If we were to open to a random page in her journal—which she must have kept and kept with her at all times, not fearing that it would be lost, or discovered and read, but that she would one day stumble upon that thing which was finally worth writing about and remembering, only to find that she had no place to write it—we would find some rendering of the following sentiment: *I am not in love.*

So she had to satisfy herself with the *idea* of love—loving the loving of things whose existence she didn't care at all about. Love itself became the object of her love. She loved herself in love, she loved loving love, as love loves loving, and was able, in that way, to reconcile herself with a world that fell so short of what she would have hoped for. It was not the world that was the great and saving lie, but her willingness to make it beautiful and fair, to live a once-removed life, in a world once-removed from the one in which everyone else seemed to exist.

The boys, young men, men, and elderly of the shtetl would sit vigil outside her window at all hours of the day and night, asking if they could assist her with her studies (with which she needed no help, of course, with which they couldn't possibly help her even if she let them try), or in the garden (which grew as if charmed, which bloomed red tulips and roses, orange and restless impatiens), or if perhaps Brod would like to go for a stroll to the river (to which she was perfectly able to stroll on her own, thank you). She never said no and never said yes, but pulled, slackened, pulled her strings of control.

Pull: *What would be nicest*, she would say, *is if I had a tall glass of iced tea.* What happened next: the men raced to get one for her. The first to return might get a peck on the forehead (slacken), or (pull) a promised walk (to be granted at a later date), or (slacken) a simple *Thank you, good-bye.* She maintained a careful balance by her window, never allowing the men to come too close, never allowing them to stray too far. She needed them desperately, not only for the favors, not only for the things that they could get for Yankel and her that Yankel couldn't afford, but because they were a few more fingers to plug the dike that held back what she knew to be true: she didn't love life. There was no convincing reason to live.

Yankel was already seventy-two years old when the wagon went into the river, his house more ready for a funeral than a birth. Brod read under the muted canary light of oil lamps covered with lace shawls, and bathed in a tub lined with sandpaper to prevent slipping. He tutored her in literature and simple mathematics until she had far surpassed his knowledge, laughed with her even when there was nothing funny, read to her before watching her fall asleep, and was the only person she could consider a friend. She acquired his uneven walk, spoke with his old man's inflections, even rubbed at a five-o'clock shadow that was never, at any time of any day of her life, there.

I bought you some books in Lutsk, he told her, shutting the door on the early evening and the rest of the world.

We can't afford these, she said, taking the heavy bag. *I'll have to return them tomorrow.*

But we can't afford not to have them. Which can we not afford more, having them or not having them? As I see it, we lose either way. My way, we lose with the books.

You're ridiculous, Yankel.

I know, he said, *because I also bought you a compass from my architect friend and several books of French poetry.*

But I don't speak French.

What could be a better occasion to learn?

Having a French language textbook.

Ah yes, I knew there was a reason I bought this! he said, removing a thick brown book from the bottom of the bag.

You're impossible, Yankel!

I'm possibly possible.

Thank you, she said, and kissed him on the forehead, which was the only place she had ever kissed or been kissed, and would have been, if not for all the novels she had read, the only place she thought people ever kissed.

She had to secretly return so many of the things that Yankel bought for her. He never noticed, because he couldn't remember ever having bought them. It was Brod's idea to make their personal library a public one, and to charge a small fee to take out books. It was with this money, along with what she was able to secure from the men who loved her, that they were able to survive.

Yankel made every effort to prevent Brod from feeling like a stranger, from being aware of their age difference, their genders. He would leave the door open when he urinated (always sitting down, always wiping himself after), and would sometimes spill water on his pants and say, *Look, it also happens to me*, unaware that it was Brod who spilled water on her pants to comfort him. When Brod fell from the swing in the park, Yankel scraped his own knees against the sandpaper floor of his bathtub and said, *I too have fallen*. When she started to grow breasts, he pulled up his shirt to reveal his old, dropped chest and said, *It's not only you*.

This was the world in which she grew and he aged. They made for themselves a sanctuary from Trachimbrod, a habitat completely unlike the rest of the world. No hateful words were ever spoken, and no hands raised. More than that, no angry words were ever spoken, and nothing was denied. But more than that, no unloving words were ever spoken, and everything was held up as another small piece of proof that it can be this way, it doesn't have to be that way; if there is no love in the world, we will make a new world, and we will give it heavy walls, and we will furnish it with soft red interiors, from the inside out, and give it a knocker that resonates like a diamond falling to a jeweler's felt so that we should never hear it. Love me, because love doesn't exist, and I have tried everything that does.

But my very-great-and-lonely-grandmother didn't love Yankel, not in the simple and impossible sense of the word. In reality she hardly knew him. And he hardly knew her. They knew intimately the aspects of themselves in the other, but never the other. Could Yankel have guessed what Brod dreamed of? Could Brod have guessed, could she have cared to guess, where Yankel traveled at night? They were strangers, like my grandmother and me.

But…

But each was the closest thing to a deserving recipient of love that the other would find. So they gave each other all of it. He scraped his knee and said, *I too have fallen.* She spilled water on her pants so he wouldn't feel alone. He gave her that bead. She wore it. And when Yankel said he would die for Brod, he certainly meant it, but that thing he would die for was not Brod, exactly, but his love for her. And when she said, *Father, I love you,* she was neither naïve nor dishonest, but the opposite: she was wise and truthful enough to lie. They reciprocated the great and saving lie — that our love for things is greater than our love for our love for things — willfully playing the parts they wrote for themselves, willfully creating and believing fictions necessary for life.

She was twelve, and he was at least eighty-four. Even if he were to live to ninety, he reasoned, she would be only eighteen. And he knew he would not live to ninety. He was secretly weak, and secretly in pain. Who would take care of her when he died? Who would sing to her and continue to tickle her back, in the particular way she liked, long after she'd fallen asleep? How would she learn of her real father? How could he be sure that she would be safe from daily violence, unintentional and intentional violence? How could he be sure that she would never change?

He did everything he could to impede his rapid deterioration. He tried to eat a good meal even when he wasn't hungry, and drink a bit of vodka between meals even when he felt it would tie his stomach into a knot. He took long walks each afternoon, knowing that the pain in his legs was a good pain, and chopped one piece of wood every morning, knowing that it was not in sickness that his arms ached, but health.

Fearing his frequent deficiencies of memory, he began writing fragments of his life story on his bedroom ceiling with one of Brod's lipsticks that he found wrapped in a sock in her desk drawer. This way, his life would be the first thing he would see when he awoke each morning, and the last thing before going to sleep each night. *You used to be married, but she left you,* above his bureau. *You hate green vegetables,* at the far end of the ceiling. *You are a Sloucher,* where the ceiling met the door. *You don't believe in an afterlife,* written in a circle around the hanging lamp. He never wanted Brod to know how much like a sheet of glass his mind had become, how it would steam with confusion, how thoughts skated off it, how he couldn't understand so many of the things she told him, how he often forgot his name, and, like a small part of him dying, even hers.

> 4:812 — *The dream of living forever with Brod.* I have this dream every night. Even when I can't remember it the next morning, I know it was there, like the depression a lover's head leaves on the pillow next to you after she's left. I dream not of growing old with her, but of never growing old, either of us. She never leaves me, and I never leave her. It's true, I am afraid of dying. I am afraid of the world moving forward without me, of my absence going unnoticed, or worse, being some natural force propelling life on. Is it selfish? Am I such a bad person for dreaming of a world that ends when I do? I don't mean the world ending with respect to me, but every set of eyes closing with mine. Sometimes my dream of living forever with Brod is the dream of our dying together. I know there is no afterlife. I'm no fool. And I know there is no God. It's not her company I need, but to know that she won't need mine, or that she won't not need it. I imagine scenes of her without me, and I become so jealous. She will marry and have children and touch what I could never approach—all things that should make me happy. I cannot tell her this dream, of course, but I want to so desperately. She is the only thing that matters.

He read her a story in bed and listened to her interpretations, never interrupting her, not even to tell her how proud he was, how smart and

JONATHAN SAFRAN FOER

beautiful she was. After kissing her good night and blessing her, he went to the kitchen, drank the few sips of vodka his stomach could handle, and blew out the lamp. He wandered down the dark hallway, following the warm glow from beneath his bedroom door. He stumbled once over a stack of Brod's books on the floor outside her room, and again over her bag. Entering his own room, he imagined that he would die in his bed that night. He imagined how Brod would find him in the morning. He imagined the position he would be in, the expression on his face. He imagined how he would feel, or not feel. *It's late*, he thought, *and I must wake up early in the morning to cook for Brod before her classes.* He lowered himself to the floor, did the three push-ups he could summon, and picked himself back up. *It's late*, he thought, *and I must be thankful for everything I have, and reconciled with everything I have lost and not lost. I tried very hard to be a good person today, to do things as God would have wanted, had He existed. Thank you for the gifts of life and Brod*, he thought, *and thank you, Brod, for giving me a reason to live. I am not sad.* He slid under the red woolen sheets and looked directly above his head: *You are Yankel. You love Brod.*

It was a secret when Yankel shrouded the clock in black cloth. It was a secret when the Well-Regarded Rabbi awoke one morning with these words on his tongue: *BUT WHAT IF?* And when the most outspoken Sloucher, Rachel F, awoke wondering, *But what if?* It was not a secret when Brod didn't think to tell Yankel that she found spots of red in her underpants, and that she was sure she was dying, and how poetic that she should die like this. But it was a secret when she did think to tell him and then didn't. They were secrets at least some of the times Sofiowka masturbated, which made him the greatest keeper of secrets in Trachimbrod, and perhaps anywhere, ever. It was a secret when grieving Shanda didn't grieve. And it was a secret when the Rabbi's twins implied that they saw nothing and knew nothing of what happened that day, March 18, 1791, when Trachim B's wagon either did or did not pin him against the bottom of the Brod River.

Yankel goes through the house with black sheets. He drapes the standing clock in black cloth and wraps his silver pocket watch in a swatch of black linen. He stops observing Shabbos, unwilling to mark the end of another week, and he avoids the sun because shadows, too, are clocks. *I am tempted, on occasion, to strike Brod*, he thinks to himself, *not because she does wrong, but because I love her so much*. Which is also a secret. He covers the window of his bedroom with black cloth. He wraps the calendar in black paper, as if it were a gift. He reads Brod's diary while she bathes, which is a secret, which is a terrible thing, he knows, but there are some terrible things to which a father is entitled, even a counterfeit father.

March 18, 1803

. . . I'm feeling overwhelmed. Before tomorrow I have to finish reading the first volume of the biography of Copernicus, since it has to be returned to the man from whom Yankel purchased it. Then there are the Greek and Roman heroes to be sorted out, and the Bible stories to try to find meaning in, and then — as if there were enough hours in the day — there is math. I bring it upon myself . . .

June 20, 1803

. . . "Deep down, the young are lonelier than the old." I read that in a book somewhere and it's stuck in my head. Maybe it's true. Maybe it's not true. More likely, the young and old are lonely in different ways, in their own ways . . .

September 23, 1803

. . . It occurred to me this afternoon that there is nothing in the world I like so much as writing in my diary. It never misunderstands me and I never misunderstand it. We are like perfect lovers, like one person. Sometimes I take it to bed with me and hold it as I fall asleep. Sometimes I kiss its pages, one after another. For now, at least, it will have to do . . .

Which is also a secret, of course, because Brod keeps her own life a secret from herself. Like Yankel, she repeats things until they are true, or until she can't tell whether they are true or not. She has become an expert at confusing *what is* with *what was* with *what should be* with *what could be*. She avoids mirrors, and lifts a powerful telescope to find herself. She aims it into the sky, and can see, or so she thinks, past the blue, past the black, even past the stars, and back into a different black, and a different blue — an arc that begins with her eye and ends with a narrow house. She studies the façade, notices where the wood of the door frame has warped and faded, where rainpipe drainage has left white tracks, and then looks through the windows, one at a time. Through the lower-left window she can see a woman scrubbing a plate with a rag. It looks as if the woman is singing to herself, and Brod imagines the song to be the very song with which her mother would have sung her to sleep had she not died, painless, in childbirth, as Yankel promised. The woman looks for her reflection in the plate and then puts it down atop a stack. She brushes her hair away from her face for Brod to see, or so Brod thinks. The woman has too much skin for her bones and too many wrinkles for her years, as if her face were some animal of its own, slowly descending the skull each day, until one day it would cling to her jaw, and one day fall off completely, landing in the woman's hands for her to look at and say, *This is the face I've worn my whole life.* There is nothing in the lower-right window save a broad bureau cluttered with books, papers, and pictures — pictures of a man and a woman, of children and the children's children. *What wonderful portraits,* she thinks, *so small, so accurate!* She focuses in on one particular photograph. It is of a girl holding her mother's hand. They are on a beach, or so it seems from such a great distance. The girl, the perfect little girl, is looking off in another direction, as if someone were making faces to get her to smile, and the mother — assuming she is the girl's mother — is looking at the girl. Brod focuses in even more, this time on the eyes of the mother. They are green, she assumes, and deep, not unlike the river of her name. *Is she crying?* Brod wonders, leaning her chin against the windowsill. *Or was the artist just trying to make her look more beautiful?* Because she was beautiful to Brod. She looked exactly like what Brod had imagined of her own mother.

Up...up...

She looks into an upstairs bedroom and sees an empty bed. The pillow is a perfect rectangle. The sheets are as smooth as water. *It may be that no one has ever slept in this bed,* Brod thinks. *Or maybe it was the scene of something improper, and in the haste to be rid of the evidence, new evidence was created. Even if Lady Macbeth could have removed that damned spot, wouldn't her hands have been red from all of the scrubbing?* There is a cup of water on the bedside table, and Brod thinks she sees a ripple.

Left...left...

She looks into another room. A study? A children's playroom? It's impossible to tell. She turns away and turns back, as if in that moment she might have acquired some new perspective, but the room remains a puzzle to her. She tries to piece it together: A half-smoked cigarette balancing itself on an ashtray's lip. A damp washcloth on the sill. A scrap of paper on the desk, with handwriting that looks like hers: *This is me with Augustine, February 21, 1943.*

Up and up . . .

But there's no window to the attic. So she looks through the wall, which is not terribly hard because the walls are thin and her telescope is a powerful one. A boy and a girl are lying on the floor facing the slant of the roof. She focuses in on the young boy, who looks, from this distance, to be her age. And even from such a distance she can see that it is a copy of *The Book of Antecedents* from which he is reading to her.

Oh, she thinks. *It's Trachimbrod I'm seeing!*

His mouth, her ears. His eyes, his mouth, her ears. The hand of the scribe, the boy's eyes, his mouth, the girl's ears. She traces the causal string back, to the face of the scribe's inspiration, and the lips of the lover and palms of the parents of the scribe's inspiration, and their lovers' lips and parents' palms and neighbors' knees and enemies, and the lovers of their lovers, parents of their parents, neighbors of their neighbors, enemies of their enemies, until she convinces herself that it is not only the boy who is reading to the girl in that attic, but everyone reading to her, everyone who ever lived. She reads along as they read:

THE FIRST RAPE OF BROD D

The first rape of Brod D occurred amid the celebrations following the thirteenth Trachimday festival, March 18, 1804. Brod was walking home from the blue-flowered float—on which she had stood in such austere beauty for so many hours on end, waving her mermaid's tail only when appropriate, throwing deep into the river of her name those heavy sacks only when the Rabbi gave her the necessary nod—when she was approached by the mad squire Sofiowka N, whose name our shtetl now uses for maps and Mormon

The boy falls asleep, and the girl puts her head on his chest. Brod wants to read more—to scream, *READ TO ME! I NEED TO KNOW!*—but they can't hear her from where she is, and from where she is, she can't turn the page. From where she is, the page—her paper-thin future—is infinitely heavy.

BY HER TWELFTH BIRTHDAY, my great-great-great-great-great-grandmother had received at least one proposal of marriage from every citizen of Trachimbrod: from men who already had wives, from broken old men who argued on stoops about things that might or might not have happened decades before, from boys without armpit hair, from women with armpit hair, and from the deceased philosopher Pinchas T, who, in his only notable paper, "To the Dust: From Man You Came and to Man You Shall Return," argued it would be possible, in theory, for life and art to be reversed. She forced a blush, batted her long eyelashes, and said to each, *Perhaps no. Yankel says I am still too young. But the offer is such a tempting one.*

They are so silly, turning back to Yankel.

Wait until I pass, closing his book. *Then you can have your choice of them. But not while I'm still alive.*

I would not have any one of them, kissing his forehead. *They are not for me. And besides,* laughing, *I already have the most handsome man in all of Trachimbrod.*

Who is it? pulling her onto his lap. *I'll kill him.*

Flicking his nose with her pinky. *It's you, fool.*

Oh no, are you telling me I have to kill myself?

I suppose I am.

Couldn't I be a bit less handsome? If it means sparing my life from my own hand? Couldn't I be a bit ugly?

OK, laughing, *I suppose your nose is a bit crooked. And on close examination, that smile of yours is a good bit less than handsome.*

Now you're killing me, laughing.

Better than killing yourself.

I suppose that's right. This way I don't have to feel guilty afterward.

I'm doing you a great service.

Thank you, then, dear. How can I ever repay you?

You're dead. You can't do anything.

I'll come back for this one favor. Just name it.

Well, I suppose I'd have to ask you to kill me, then. Spare me the guilt.

Consider it done.

Aren't we so terribly lucky to have one another?

It was after Bitzl Bitzl's son's son's proposal—*I'm so sorry, but Yankel thinks it best that I wait*—that she put on her Float Queen costume for the thirteenth annual Trachimday festival. Yankel had heard the women speak of his daughter (he was not deaf), and he had seen the men grope at her (he was not blind), but helping her pull up her mermaid suit, having to tie the straps around her bony shoulders, made everything else seem easy (he was only human).

You don't have to get dressed up if you don't want to, he said, easing her slim arms into the long sleeves of the mermaid suit, which she had re-designed each of the last eight years. *You don't have to be the Float Queen, you know.*

But of course I do, she said. *I am the most beautiful girl in Trachimbrod.*

I thought you didn't want to be beautiful.

I don't, she said, pulling her bead necklace over the neckline of the suit. *It's such a burden. But what can I do about it? I'm cursed.*

But you don't have to do this, he said, putting the bead back under. *They could choose another girl this year. You could give someone else a chance.*

That doesn't sound like me.

But you could do it anyway.

Nope.

But we agreed that ceremony and ritual are so foolish.

But we also agreed that they are foolish only to those on the outside. I'm the center of this one.

I order you not to go, he said, knowing that would never work.

I order you not to order me, she said.

My order takes precedence.

Why?

Because I'm older.

That's a foolish person talking.

Then because I ordered first.

That's the same person talking.

But you don't even like it, he said. *You always complain after.*

I know, she said, adjusting the tail, which was scaled with blue sequins.

Then why?

Do you like thinking about Mom?

No.

Does it hurt after?

Yes.

Then why do you continue to do it? she asked. And why, she wondered, remembering the description of her rape, do we pursue it?

Yankel lost himself in thought, trying many times to start a sentence.

When you think of an acceptable answer, I'll relinquish my throne. She kissed him on the forehead and headed out of the house for the river with her name.

He stood by the window and waited.

Canopies of thin white string spanned the narrow dirt arteries of Trachimbrod that afternoon, spring, 1804, as they had every Trachimday for thirteen years. It was Bitzl Bitzl's idea, to commemorate the first of the wagon's refuse to surface. One end of white string tied around the half-empty bottle of old vermouth on the floor of the drunkard Omeler S's tipsy shanty, the other around a tarnished silver candle holder on the dining room table of the Tolerable Rabbi's four-bedroom brick house across muddy Shelister Street; thin white string like a clothesline from a third-floor harlot's back-left bedpost to the cool copper doorknob of an ice closet in the Gentile Kerman K's basement embalming shop; white string connecting butcher to matchmaker over the tranquil (and breathless with anticipation) palm of the Brod River; white string from carpenter to wax modeler to midwife, in a scalene triangle above the fountain with the prostrate mermaid, in the middle of the shtetl square.

The handsome men assembled along the shoreline as the parade of floats made its way from the small falls to the toy and pastry stands set up by the plaque marking where the wagon did or didn't flip and sink:

THIS PLAQUE MARKS THE SPOT
(OR A SPOT CLOSE TO THE SPOT)
WHERE THE WAGON OF ONE
TRACHIM B
(WE THINK)
WENT IN.

Shtetl Proclamation, 1791

The first to pass the Tolerable Rabbi's window, from which he gave the necessary nod of approval, was the float from Kolki. It was adorned with thousands of orange and red butterflies, which flocked to the float because of the specific combination of animal carcasses strapped to its underside. A red-headed boy dressed in orange slacks and dress shirt stood as still as a statue on the wooden podium. Above him was a sign that read, THE PEOPLE OF KOLKI CELEBRATE WITH THEIR TRA-CHIMBROD NEIGHBORS! He would be the subject of many paintings one day, when the children then watching grew old and sat with water-colors on their crumbling stoops. But he didn't know that then, and nei-ther did they, just as none of them knew that I would one day write this.

Next came Rovno's float, which was covered from end to end in green butterflies. Then the floats from Lutsk, Sarny, Kivertsy, Soke-retchy, and Kovel. They were each covered with color, thousands of butterflies drawn to bloody carcasses: brown butterflies, purple butter-flies, yellow butterflies, pink butterflies, white. The crowd lining the pa-rade route hollered with so much excitement and so little humanity that an impenetrable wall of noise was erected, a common wail so pervasive and constant that it could be mistaken for a common silence.

The Trachimbrod float was covered in blue butterflies. Brod sat on a raised platform in the middle, surrounded by the young float princesses of the shtetl, dressed in blue lace, waving their arms about like waves. A quartet of fiddlers played Polish national songs from a stand in the front of the float while a different quartet played Ukrainian traditionals from the back, and the interference between the two produced a third, dissonant song, heard only by the float princesses and Brod. Yankel watched from his window, fingering the bead that seemed to have gained all the weight he had lost in the last sixty years.

When the Trachimbrod float reached the toy and pastry stands, Brod was given the signal by the Tolerable Rabbi to throw the sacks into the water. *Up, up*...The arc of the collective gaze — from Brod's palm to the river's — was the only thing in the universe that existed at that moment: a single indelible rainbow. *Down, down*...It was not until the Tolerable Rabbi was relatively sure that the sacks had reached the river's bottom that the men were given permission — another of his dramatic nods — to dive after them.

It was impossible to see what was going on in the water with all of the splashing. Women and children cheered furiously while men stroked furiously, grabbing and tugging at one another's limbs to gain advantage. They surfaced in waves, sometimes with bags in their mouths or hands, and then plunged back down with all the vigor they could summon. The water leapt, the trees swayed in expectation, the sky slowly pulled up its blue dress to reveal night.

And then:

I've got it! a man shouted from the far end of the river. *I've got it!* The other divers sighed in disappointment and backstroked to the river's bank or floated in place while they cursed the winner's good fortune. My great-great-great-great-great-grandfather swam back to shore, pumping the golden sack above his head. A large crowd was waiting for him when he fell to his knees and poured the contents onto the mud. Eighteen gold coins. Half a year's salary.

WHAT'S YOUR NAME? the Tolerable Rabbi asked.

I am Shalom, he said. *I am from Kolki.*

THE KOLKER HAS WON THE DAY! the Rabbi proclaimed, losing his yarmulke in all the excitement.

As the hum of crickets summoned the darkness, Brod remained on the float to watch the beginning of the festival without the pestering of men. The paraders and shtetl folk were already drunk — arms around one another, hands on one another, fingers probing, thighs accommodating, all thinking only of her. The strings were beginning to sag (birds landed, depressing the middles; winds blew, swinging them side to side like waves), and the princesses had run to the shore to see the gold and lean against the visiting men.

Mist came first, then rain, so slow that the drops could be followed as they fell. The men and women continued their groping dance as the klezmer bands poured their music through the streets. Young girls captured fireflies in cheesecloth nets. They peeled open the bulbs and painted their eyelids with the phosphorescence. Boys squashed ants between fingers, not knowing why.

The rain intensified, and paraders drank themselves sick on homemade vodka and beer. People made wild, urgent love in the dark corners where houses met and under the hanging canopies of weeping willows. Couples cut their backs on the shells, twigs, and pebbles of the Brod's shallow waters. They pulled at one another in the grass: brassy young men driven with lust, jaded women less wet than breath on glass, virgin boys moving like blind boys, widows lifting their veils, spreading their legs, pleading—to whom?

From space, astronauts can see people making love as a tiny speck of light. Not light, exactly, but a glow that could be mistaken for light—a coital radiance that takes generations to pour like honey through the darkness to the astronaut's eyes.

In about one and a half centuries—after the lovers who made the glow will have long since been laid permanently on their backs—metropolises will be seen from space. They will glow all year. Smaller cities will also be seen, but with great difficulty. Shtetls will be virtually impossible to spot. Individual couples, invisible.

The glow is born from the sum of thousands of loves: newlyweds and teenagers who spark like lighters out of butane, pairs of men who burn fast and bright, pairs of women who illuminate for hours with soft multiple glows, orgies like rock and flint toys sold at festivals, couples trying unsuccessfully to have children who burn their frustrated image on the continent like the bloom a bright light leaves on the eye after you turn away from it.

Some nights, some places are a little brighter. It's difficult to stare at

New York City on Valentine's Day, or Dublin on St. Patrick's. The old walled city of Jerusalem lights up like a candle on each of Chanukah's eight nights. Trachimday is the only time all year when the tiny village of Trachimbrod can be seen from space, when enough copulative voltage is generated to sex the Polish-Ukrainian skies electric. *We're here*, the glow of 1804 will say in one and a half centuries. *We're here, and we're alive.*

But Brod was not a point of this special kind of light, not adding her current to the collective voltage. She climbed down from the float, pools of rainwater collected in the channels between her ribs, and walked the Jewish/Human fault line back toward her house, where the noise and revelry could be observed from a distance. Women sneered at her, and men used their drunkenness as an excuse to bump into her, to brush against her and stick their faces close enough to her face to smell her or kiss her cheek.

Brod, you are a dirty river girl!
Wouldn't you like to hold my hand, Brod?
Your father is a shameful man, Brod.
Come on, you can do it. One little shout out of pleasure.

She ignored them all. Ignored them when they spat at her feet or pinched her backside. Ignored them when they cursed and kissed her, and cursed her with their kisses. Ignored them even when they made a woman out of her, ignored them as she had learned to ignore everything in the world that was not once-removed.

Yankel! she said, opening the door. *Yankel, I'm home. Let's watch the dancing from the roof and eat pineapple with our hands!*

She walked through the den with the hobble of a man six times her age, and through the kitchen pulling off her mermaid suit, and through the bedroom searching for her father. The house was filled with the odor of wetness and decay, as if a window had been left open as an invitation for all the ghosts of eastern Europe. But it was the water that had seeped through the spaces between shingles, like breath between the teeth of a closed mouth. And the odor of death.

Yankel! she called, pulling her skinny legs from the mermaid's tail, revealing her tightly wound pubic hair, which was still new enough to trace out a sharp triangle.

Outside: Lips locked lips on hay in barns and fingers met thighs met lips met ears met undersides of knees on quilts on lawns of strangers, all thinking of Brod, everyone thinking only of Brod.

Yankel? Are you home? she called, walking naked from room to room, her nipples hard and purple from the cold, her skin pale and goose-bumped, her eyelashes holding pearls of rainwater at their ends.

Outside: Breasts were kneaded in calloused hands. Many buttons were undone. Sentences became words became sighs became groans became grunts became light.

Yankel? You said we could watch from the roof.

She found him in the library. But he was not asleep in his favorite chair, as she suspected he might be, with the wings of a half-finished book spread across his chest. He was on the floor, fetal, clutching a balled-up slip of paper. Otherwise the room was in perfect order. He had tried not to make a mess when he felt the first flash of heat across his scalp. He was embarrassed when his legs gave out beneath him, ashamed when he realized he would die on the floor, alone in the magnitude of his grief when he understood that he would die before he could tell Brod how beautiful she was that day, and that she had a good heart (which was worth more than a good brain), and that he was not her real father but wished with every blessing, every day and night of his life, that he was; before he could tell her of his dream of eternal life with her, of dying with her, or never dying. He died with the crumpled slip of paper clutched in one hand and the abacus bead in the other.

The water seeped through the shingles as if the house were a cavern. Yankel's lipstick autobiography came flaking off his bedroom ceiling, falling gently like blood-stained snow to his bed and floor. *You are Yankel ...You love Brod...You are a Sloucher...You were once married, but she left you...You don't believe in an afterlife...* Brod was afraid any tears of her own would cause the walls of the old house to give way, so she sand-bagged them behind her eyes, exiled them to someplace deeper, safer.

She took the paper from Yankel's hand, which was damp with rain, and fear of death, and death. Scrawled in a child's writing: *Everything for Brod.*

A wink of lightning illuminated the Kolker at the window. He was strong, with a heavy brow protruding over his maple-bark eyes. Brod had seen him when he surfaced with the coins, when he spilt them onto the shore like golden vomit from the sack, but took little notice.

Go away! she cried, covering her bare chest with her arms and turning back toward Yankel, protecting their bodies from the Kolker's gaze. But he did not leave.

Go away!

I won't go without you, he called to her through the window.

Go away! Go away!

The rain dripped from his upper lip. *Not without you.*

I'll kill myself! she hollered.

Then I'll take your body with me, he said, palms against the glass.

Go away!

I won't!

Yankel jerked in rigor mortis, knocking over the oil lamp, which blew itself out on its way to the floor, leaving the room completely dark. His cheeks pulled into a tight smile, revealing, to the banished shadows, a contentedness. Brod let her arms brush down her skin to her sides and turned to face my great-great-great-great-great-grandfather.

Then you must do something for me, she said.

Her belly lit up like a firefly's bulb — brighter than a hundred thousand virgins making love for the first time.

⌒

Get en heyar! my grandmother calls to my mother. *Hurry!* My mother is twenty-one. My age as I write these words. She lives at home, goes to school at night, has three jobs, wants to find and marry my father, wants to create and love and sing to and die many times every day for me. *Look et diz,* my grandmother says into the television's glow. *Look.* She puts her hand on my mother's hand and feels her own blood flow through the veins, and the blood of my grandfather (who died only five weeks after coming to the States, just half a year after my mother was born), and my mother's blood, and my blood, and the blood of my children and grandchildren. A crackling: *That's one small step for man...* They stare at a blue marble floating in the void — a homecoming from so far away. My grandmother, trying to control her voice, says, *Yer fadder vood hef luffed ta see diz.* The blue marble is replaced with an anchorman, who has removed his glasses and is rubbing his eyes. *Ladies and gentlemen, America has put a man on the moon tonight.* My grandmother struggles to her feet —old, even then—and says, with many different kinds of tears in her eyes, *Etz vunderful!* She kisses my mother, hides her hands in my mother's hair, and says, *Etz vunderrful!* My mother is also crying, each tear unique. They cry together, cheek to cheek. And neither of them hears the astronaut whisper, *I see something,* while gazing over the lunar horizon at the tiny village of Trachimbrod. *There's definitely something out there.*

Dear Jonathan,

I luxuriated the receipt of your letter. You are always so rapid to write to me. This will be a lucrative thing for when you are a real writer and not an apprentice. Mazel tov!

Grandfather ordered me to thank you for the duplicate photograph. It was benevolent of you to post it and not to demand him for any currency. In truth, he does not possess very much. I was certain that Father did not disperse him any for the voyage, because Grandfather often mentions that he has no currency, and I know Father well around manners like this. This made me very wrathful (not spleened or on nerves, as you have informed me that these are not befitting words how often I use them), and I went to Father. He hollered at me, "I ATTEMPTED TO DISPERSE GRANDFATHER CURRENCY, BUT HE WOULD NOT RECEIVE IT." I told him that I did not believe him, and he pushed me and ordered that I should interrogate Grandfather on the matter, but of course I cannot do that. When I was on the floor, he told me that I do not know everything, as I think I do. (But I will tell you, Jonathan, I do not think I know everything.) This made me feel like a schmendrik for receiving the currency. But I was constrained to receive it, because as I have informed you, I have a dream of one day changing residences to America. Grandfather does not have any dreams like this, and so does not need currency. Then I became very biled at Grandfather, because why was it impossible for him to receive the currency from Father and present it to me?

Do not inform one soul, but I keep all of my reserves of currency in a cookie box in the kitchen. It is a place that nobody investigates, because it has been ten years since Mother manufactured a cookie. I reason that when the cookie box is full, I will have a sufficient quantity to change residences to America. I am being a cautious person, because I desire to be cocksure that I have enough for a luxurious apartment in Times Square, vast enough for both me and Little Igor. We will have a large-screen television to watch basketball, a jacuzzi, and a hi-fi to write home about, although we will already be home. Little Igor must go forth with me, of course, whatever occurs.

It appeared that you did not have very many arguments with the previous division. I ask leniency if it angered you in any manner, but I wanted to be truthful and humorous, as you counseled. Do you think that I am a humorous person? I signify humorous with intentions, not humorous because I do foolish things. Mother once said that I was humorous, but that was when I asked her to purchase a Ferrari Testarossa on my behalf. Not desiring to be laughed upon in the wrong way, I revised my offer to hubcaps.

I fashioned the very sparse changes that you posted to me. I altered the division about the hotel in Lutsk. Now you only pay once. "I will not be treated like a second-class citizen!" you apprise to the hotel owner, and while I am obligated (thank you, Jonathan) to inform you that you are not a sec-ond-, third-, or fourth-class citizen, it does sound very potent. The owner says, "You win. You win. I tried to pull a fast one" (what does it mean to pull a fast one?), "but you win. OK. You will pay only once." This is now an excellent scene. I have considered making you speak Ukrainian, so that you could have more scenes like this, but that would make me a useless person, because if you spoke Ukrainian, you would still have need for a driver, but not for a translator. I ruminated exterminating Grandfather from the story, so that I would be the driver, but if he ever ascertained this, I am certain that he would be injured, and nor of us desire that, yes? Also, I do not possess a license.

Finally, I altered the division about Sammy Davis, Junior, Junior's fondness for you. I will iterate again, I do not think that the befitting settle-ment is to amputate her from the story, or to have her "killed in a tragicomic accident while crossing the road to the hotel," as you counsel. To appease you, I modified the scene so that the two of you appear more as friends and less as lovers or nemesises. For one example, she no longer rotates to do a sixty-nine with you. It is now merely a blowjob.

It is very difficult for me to write about Grandfather, just as you said it is very difficult for you to write about your grandmother. I desire to know more about her, if it would not distress you. It might make it less rigid for me to speak about Grandfather. You have not enlightened her about our voyage, have you? I am certain that you would have told me if you had. You know my thinkings on this matter.

As for Grandfather, he is always becoming worse. When I think he is worstest, he becomes worse. Something must occur. He does not conceal his melancholy with mastery anymore. I have witnessed him crying three times this week, each very tardy at night when I was returning from roosting at the beach. I will tell you (because you are the only person I have to tell) that I occasionally KGB on him from behind the corner amid the kitchen and the television room. The first night I witnessed him crying he was investigating an aged leather bag, brimmed with many photographs and pieces of paper, like one of Augustine's boxes. The photographs were yellow, and so were the papers. I am certain that he was having memories for when he was only a boy, and not an old man. The second night he was crying he had the photograph of Augustine in his hands. The weather program was on, but it was so late that they only presented a map of planet Earth, without any weather on it. "Augustine," I could hear him say. "Augustine." The third night he was crying he had a photograph of you in his hands. It is only possible that he secured it from my desk where I keep all of the photographs that you posted me. Again he was saying "Augustine," although I do not understand why.

Little Igor wanted me to utter hello to you from him. He does not know you, of course, but I have informed him very much about you. I informed him about how you are so funny, and so intelligent, and also how we can speak about momentous matters as well as farts. I even informed him about how you made bags of dirt when we were in Trachimbrod. Everything I could remember about you I informed him, because I want him to know you, and because it makes it feel that you are yet near, that you did not go away. You will laugh, but I presented him with one of the photographs of us that you posted. He is a very good boy, better even than me, and he still has a chance to be a very good man. I am certain that you would be appeased by him.

Father and Mother are the same as always, but more humble. Mother has stopped cooking dinner for Father to punish him because he never comes *home for dinner. She wanted to bile him, but he does not give shit (yes? give shit?), because he never comes home for dinner. He eats with his friends very often at restaurants, and also drinks vodka at clubs, but not famous clubs. I am sure that Father possesses more friends than the rest of my family summed. He knocks many things over when he comes home late at night. It is Little Igor and I who clean and return things to their proper locations. (I keep Little Igor with me at these occasions.) The lamp belongs here. The hanging picture belongs here. The plate belongs here. The telephone belongs here. (When Little Igor and I have our apartment, we will keep everything exclusively clean. Not even one piece of dust.) To be truthful, I do not miss Father when he is out so much. He could exist every night with his friends and I would be content. I will inform you that he awoke Little Igor last night when he returned from vodka with his friends. It is my fault, because I did not insist that Little Igor should manufacture Z's in my room with me, as he now does. Was I supposed to counterfeit sleep? Was Mother? I was in my bed at the time, and it is a cosmic thing, because at the moment I was reading the section about Yankel's death. "Everything for Brod," he writes, and I thought, "Everything for Little Igor."*

Per your novel, I have been very dispirited for Brod. She is a good person in a bad world. Everyone is lying to her. Even her father who is not her true father. They are both keeping secrets from each other. I thought about this when you said that Brod "would never be happy and honest at the same time." Do you feel this way?

I understand what you write when you write that Brod does not love Yankel. It does not signify that she does not feel volumes for him, or that she will not be melancholy when he expires. It is something else. Love, in your writing, is the immovability of truth. Brod is not truthful with anything. Not Yankel and not herself. Everything is one world in distance from the real world. Does this manufacture sense? If I am sounding like a thinker, this is an homage to your writing.

This ultimate part that you gave me, about Trachimday, was certainly the most ultimate. I am remaining with nothing to utter about it. When Brod asks Yankel why he thinks about her mom even though it hurts, and he says he does not know why, that is a momentous query. Why do we do that?

Why are the painful things always electromagnets? With concerns about the part with the sex light, I must tell you that I have seen this before. Once I was carnal with a girl, and I saw petite lightning between her backsides. I could clutch how it would require many to be perceived from outer space. At the ultimate part, I have a suggestion that perhaps you should make it a Russian cosmonaut instead of Mr. Armstrong. Try Yuri Alekseyevich Gagarin, who in 1961 became the first human being to make an orbital space flight.

Ultimately, if you possess any magazines or articles that you enjoy, I would be very happy if you could post them to me. I will imburse for any expenses, clear-cuttedly. I intend articles about America, you know. Articles about American sports, or American movies, or American girls, of course, or American accounting schools. I will utter no more of this. I do not know how much more of your novel exists at this moment, but I demand to see it. I am so wanting to know what happens to Brod and the Kolker. Will she love him? Say yes. I hope that you say yes. It will prove a thing to me. Also, perhaps I can continue to aid you as you write more. But not be distressed. I will not require that my name is on the cover. You may pretend that it is only yours.

Please say hello to your family from me, except your grandmother, of course, because she is not aware that I exist. If you would desire to inform me any things about your family, I would be very good-humored to listen. For one example, inform me more about your miniature brother, who I know you love like I love Little Igor. For another example, inform me about your parents. Mother asked about you yesterday. She said, "And what about the troublemaking Jew?" I informed her that you are not troublemaking, but a good person, and that you are not a Jew with a large-size letter J, but a jew, like Albert Einstein or Jerry Seinfeld.

I anticipate with bumps on my skin your consequent letter and the consequent division of your novel. In the pending time, I hope you are loving this next division of mine. Please be pleased, please.

Guilelessly,
Alexander

THE VERY RIGID SEARCH

THE ALARM made a noise at 6:00 of the morning, but it was not a consequential noise, because Grandfather and I had not manufactured even one Z among us. "Go get the Jew," Grandfather said. "I will loiter downstairs." "Breakfast?" I asked. "Oh," he said. "Let us descend to the restaurant and eat breakfast. Then you will get the Jew." "What about his breakfast?" "They will not have anything without meat, so we should not make him an uncomfortable person." "You are smart," I told him.

We were very circumspect when we departed our room so that we would not manufacture any noise. We did not want the hero to be aware that we were eating. When we roosted at the restaurant Grandfather said, "Eat very much. It will be a long day, and who could be certain when we will eat next?" For this reason we ordered three breakfasts for the two of us, and ate very much sausage, which is a delicious food. When we finished, we purchased chewing gum from the waitress so that the hero would not uncover breakfast from our mouths. "Get the Jew," Grandfather said. "I will loiter with patience in the car."

I am certain that the hero was not reposing, because before I could punch for the second time, he unclosed the door. He was already in clothing, and I could see that he was donning his fanny pack. "Sammy Davis, Junior, Junior ate all of my documents." "This is not possible," I said, although in truth I knew that it was possible. "I put them on the bedside table when I went to sleep, and when I woke up this morning she was chewing them. This is all I was able to wrestle free." He exhibited a half-masticated passport and several pieces of maps. "The photograph!" I said. "It's OK. I've got lots of copies. She only got through a couple before I stopped her." "I am so ashamed." "What troubles me," he said, "is that she wasn't in the room when I went to sleep and closed the door." "She is such a smart bitch." "She must be," he said, using his x-ray vision with me. "It is because she is Jewish that she is so smart." "Well, I'm just glad that she didn't eat my glasses." "She would not eat your glasses." "She ate my driver's license. She ate my student ID, my credit card, a bunch of cigarettes, some of my money…" "But she would not eat your glasses. She is not an animal."

"Listen," he said, "what do you say we have a little breakfast?" "What?" "Breakfast," he said, putting his hands on his stomach. "No," I said, "I think it is superior if we commence the search. We want to search as much as possible while light still exists." "But it's only 6:30." "Yes, but it will not be 6:30 forever. Look," I said, and pointed to my watch, which is a Rolex from Bulgaria, "it is already 6:31. We are misplacing time." "Maybe a little something?" he said. "What?" "Just a cracker. I'm really hungry." "This cannot be negotiated. I think it is best—" "We have a minute or two. What's that on your breath?" "You will have one mochaccino in the restaurant downstairs, and that will be the end of the conversation. You must try to pull a fast one." He began to say something, and I put my fingers on my lips. This signified: SHUT UP!

"Back for more breakfast?" the waitress asked. "She says, Good morning, would you like a mochaccino?" "Oh," he said. "Tell her yes. And maybe some bread or something." "He is an American," I said. "I know," she said, "I can see." "But he does not eat meat, so just give him a mochaccino." "He does not eat meat!" "Rapid bowel proceedings," I said, because I did not want to embarrass him. "What are you telling her?" "I told her not to make it too watery." "Good. I hate it when it's watery." "So just one mochaccino will be adequate," I told the waitress, who was a very beautiful girl with the most breasts I had ever seen. "We do not have any." "What is she saying?" "Then give him a cappuccino." "We do not have any cappuccino." "What is she saying?" "She says mochaccinos are special today, because they are coffee." "What?" "Would you like to do the Electric Slide with me at a famous discotheque tonight?" I asked the waitress. "Will you bring the American?" she asked. Oh, did this piss all over me! "He is a Jew," I said, and I know that I should not have uttered that, but I was beginning to feel very awful about myself. The problem is that I felt more awful after uttering it. "Oh," she said. "I have never seen a Jew before. Can I see his horns?" (It is possible that you will think she did not inquire this, Jonathan, but she did. Without a doubt, you do not have horns, so I told her to attend to her own affairs and merely bring a coffee for the Jew and two orders of sausage for the bitch, because who could be certain when she would eat again.)

When the coffee arrived, the hero drank only a small amount. "This tastes terrible," he said. It is one thing for him to not eat meat, and it is another thing for him to make Grandfather loiter in the car asleep, but it is another thing for him to slander our coffee. "YOU WILL DRINK THE COFFEE UNTIL I CAN SEE MY FACE IN THE BOTTOM OF THE CUP!" I did not mean to roar. "But it's a clay cup." "I DO NOT CARE!" He finished the coffee. "You did not have to finish it," I said, because I could perceive that he was rebuilding the Great Wall of China with shit bricks. "It's OK," he said, and put the cup down on the table. "It was really good coffee. Delicious. I'm stuffed." "What?" "We can go whenever you want." A simpleton, I thought. Two tons.

It captured several minutes to recover Grandfather from his sleep. He had locked himself in the car, and all of the windows were sealed. I had to punch the glass with very much violence in order to make him not sleep. I was surprised that the glass did not fracture. When Grandfather finally opened his eyes, he did not know where he was. "Anna?" "No, Grandfather," I said through the window, "it is me, Sasha." He closed his hands and also his eyes. "I thought you were someone else." He touched the wheel with his head. "We are primed to go," I said through the window. "Grandfather?" He made a large breath and opened the doors.

"How do we get there?" Grandfather inquired me, who was in the front seat, because when I am in a car I always sit in the front seat, unless the car is a motorcycle, because I do not know how to operate a motorcycle, although I will very soon. The hero was in the back seat with Sammy Davis, Junior, Junior, and they were attending to their own affairs: the hero masticated the nails of his fingers, and the bitch masticated her tail. "I do not know," I said. "Inquire the Jew," he ordered, so I did. "I don't know," he said. "He does not know." "What do you mean he does not know?" said Grandfather. "We are in the car. We are primed to go forth on our voyage. How can he not know?" His voice was now with volume, and it frightened Sammy Davis, Junior, Junior, making her bark. BARK. I asked the hero, "What do you mean you do not know?" "I told you everything I know. I thought one of you was supposed to be the trained and certified Heritage guide. I paid for a certified guide, you know." Grandfather punched the car's horn, and it made a sound. HONK. "Grandfather is certified!" I informed him, BARK, which was faithfully faithful, although he was certified to operate an automobile, not find lost history. HONK. "Please!" I said at Grandfather. BARK. HONK. "Please! You are making this impossible!" HONK! BARK! "Shut up," he said, "and shut the bitch up and shut the Jew up!" BARK! "Please!" HONK! "You're sure he's certified?" "Of course," I said. HONK! "I would not deceive." BARK! "Do something," I told Grandfather. HONK! "Not that!" I said with volume. BARK! He commenced to drive the automobile that he was fully certified to drive. "Where are we going?" The hero and I manufactured this query at the same time. "SHUT UP!" he said, and I did not have to translate that for the hero.

He drove us to a petrol store that we passed on the way to the hotel the night yore. We arrested in front of the petrol machine. A man came to the window. He was very svelte, and had petrol in his eyes. "Yes?" the man asked. "We are looking for Trachimbrod," Grandfather said. "We do not have any," the man said. "It is a place. We are trying to find it." The man turned to a group of men standing in front of the store. "Do we have anything called trachimbrod?" They all elevated their shoulders and continued to talk to themselves. "Apologies," he said, "we do not have any." "No," I said, "it is the name of a place we are searching for. We are trying to find the girl who saved his grandfather from the Nazis." I pointed to the hero. "What?" the man asked. "What?" the hero asked. "Shut up," Grandfather told me. "We have a map," I told the man. "Present me the map," I ordered the hero. He investigated his bag. "Sammy Davis, Junior, Junior ate it." "It is not possible," I said, although again I knew that it was possible. "Mention him some of the other names of the towns and perhaps one will sound informal." The petrol man leaned his head in the car. "Kovel," the hero said, "Kivertsy, Sokeretchy." "Kolki," Grandfather said. "Yes, yes," the petrol man said, "I have heard of all of these towns." "And you could direct us to them?" I asked. "Of course. They are very proximal. Maybe thirty kilometers distant. No more. Merely travel north on the superway, and then east through the farmlands." "But you have never heard of Trachimbrod?" "Say it again to me." "Trachimbrod." "No, but many of the towns have new names." "Jon-fen," I said, turning back, "what was the other name for Trachimbrod?" "Sofiowka." "Do you know of Sofiowka?" I asked the man. "No," he said, "but it sounds like something that is more similar to something I have heard of. There are many villages in that area. Perhaps there are nine or even more. Once you become proximal, you could inquire anyone and they would be able to inform you where to find what you are investigating for." (Jonathan, this man spoke not so good Ukrainian, but I have made it sound abnormally good in my translation for the story. If it would appease you, I could counterfeit his substandard utterances.) The man fashioned a map on a piece of paper that Grandfather excavated from the drawer for gloves, where I will keep lubricated extra-large condoms when I have the car of my dreams. (They will not be ribbed for her pleasure, because there is no need, if you understand what I mean.) They made conversation about the map for many minutes. "Here," the hero said. He was holding a package of Marlboro cigarettes at the petrol man. "What the hell is he doing?" Grandfather inquired. "What the hell is he doing?" the petrol man inquired. "What the hell are you doing?" I inquired. "For his help," he said. "I read in my guidebook that it's hard to get Marlboro cigarettes here, and that you should bring several packs with you wherever you go, and give them as tips." "What is a tip?" "It's something you give someone in exchange for help." "So OK, you are informed that you will be paying for this trip with currency, yes?" "No, not like that," he said. "Tips are for small things, like directions, or for the valet." "Valet?" "He does not eat meat," Grandfather told the petrol man. "Oh." "Valet," the hero said, "the guy who parks your car." America is always proving itself greater than I thought.

It was already 7:10 when we were driving again. It captured only several minutes for us to find the superway. I must confess that it was a beautiful day, with much light of the sun. "It is beautiful, yes?" I said to the hero. "What?" "The day. It is a beautiful day." He put down the glass of his window, which was acceptable because Sammy Davis, Junior, Junior was sleeping, and he put his head outside of the car. "Yes," he said. "It's absolutely beautiful." This made me proud, and I told Grandfather, and he smiled, and I could perceive that he also became a very proud person. "Inform him about Odessa," Grandfather said. "Inform him how beautiful it is there." "In Odessa," I rotated to the hero and said, "it is more beautiful than even this. You have never witnessed a thing similar to it." "I'd like to hear about it," he said, and opened his diary. "He wants to hear about Odessa," I told Grandfather, because I wanted for him to like the hero. "Inform him that the sand on the beaches is more soft than a woman's hairs, and that the water is like the inside of a woman's mouth." "The sand on the beaches is like a woman's mouth." "Inform him," Grandfather said, "that Odessa is the most wonderful place to become in love, and also to make a family." So I informed the hero. "Odessa," I said, "is the most wonderful place to become in love, and also to make a family." "Have you ever fallen in love?" he inquired me, which seemed like such a queer inquiry, so I returned it to him. "Have you?" "I don't know," he said. "Nor I," I said. "I've been close to love." "Yes." "Really close, like almost there." "Almost." "But never, I don't think." "No." "Maybe I should go to Odessa," he said. "I could fall in love. It sounds like that would make more sense than Trachimbrod." We both laughed. "What is he saying?" Grandfather inquired. I told him, and he also laughed. All of this felt so wonderful. "Show me the map," Grandfather said. He examined it while he drove, making his blindness even less trustworthy, I must confess.

We made an exit from the superway. Grandfather returned me the map. "We will drive for approximately twenty kilometers, and then we will inquire someone about Trachimbrod." "That is reasonable," I said. It sounded like a queer thing to say, but I have never known what to say to Grandfather without it sounding queer. "I know it is reasonable," he said. "Of course it is reasonable." "May I view Augustine again?" I asked the hero. (Here I must confess that I had been desiring to view her since the hero first exhibited her to me. But I was ashamed to make this known.) "Of course," he said, and excavated his fanny pack. He had many duplicates, and removed one like a playing card. "Here you go."

I observed the photograph while he observed the beautiful day. Augustine had such pretty hairs. They were thin hairs. I did not need to touch them to be certain. Her eyes were blue. Even though the photograph lacked color, I was certain that her eyes were blue. "Look at those fields," the hero said with his finger outside of the car. "They're so green." I told Grandfather what the hero said. "Tell him that the land is premium for farming." "Grandfather desires me to tell you that the land is very premium for farming." "And tell him that much of this land was destroyed when the Nazis came, but before it was yet more beautiful. They bombed with airplanes and then advanced through it in tanks." "But it does not appear like this." "They made it all again after the war. Before it was different." "You were here before the war?" "Look at those people working in their underwear in the fields," the hero said from the back seat. I inquired Grandfather about this. "This is not abnormal," he said. "It is very hot in the morning. Too hot to be anxious about cloth-ing." I told the hero. He was covering many pages in his diary. I wanted Grandfather to continue the before conversation, and to tell me when he was in the area, but I could perceive that the conversation had been fin-ished. "They're such old people working," the hero said. "Some of those women must be sixty or seventy." I inquired Grandfather about this, be-cause I also did not find it canny. "It is canny," he said. "In the fields, you toil until you are not able to toil. Your great-grandfather died in the fields." "Did Great-Grandmother work in the fields?" "She was working with him when he died." "What is he saying?" the hero inquired, and again he prohibited Grandfather from continuing, and again when I viewed Grandfather I could perceive that it was the end of the con-versation.

It was the first occasion that I had ever heard Grandfather speak of his parents, and I wanted to know very much more of them. What did they do during the war? Who did they save? But I felt that it was a com-mon decency for me to be quiet on the matter. He would speak when he needed to speak, and until that moment I would persevere silence. So I did what the hero did, which is look out the window. I do not know how much time tumbled, but a lot of time tumbled. "It is beautiful, yes?" I said to him without rotating around. "Yes." For the next minutes, we used no words, but only witnessed the farmlands. "It would be a reasonable time to inquire someone how to get to Trachimbrod," Grandfather said. "I do not think that we are more than ten kilometers distant."

We moved the car to the side of the road, although it was very difficult to perceive where the road terminated and the side commenced. "Go inquire someone," Grandfather said. "And bring the Jew with you." "Will you come?" I asked. "No," he said. "Please." "No." "Come," I informed the hero. "Where?" I pointed at a herd of men in the field who were smoking. "You want me to go with you?" "Of course," I said, because I desired the hero to feel that he was involved in every aspect of the voyage. But in truth, I was also afraid of the men in the field. I had never talked to people like that, poor farming people, and similar to most people from Odessa, I speak a fusion of Russian and Ukrainian, and they spoke only Ukrainian, and while Russian and Ukrainian sound so so similar, people who speak only Ukrainian sometimes hate people who speak a fusion of Russian and Ukrainian, because very often people who speak a fusion of Russian and Ukrainian come from the cities and think they are superior to people who speak only Ukrainian, who often come from the fields. We think this because we are superior, but that is for another story.

I commanded the hero not to speak, because at times people who speak Ukrainian who hate people who speak a fusion of Russian and Ukrainian also hate people who speak English. It is for the selfsame reason that I brought Sammy Davis, Junior, Junior with us, although she speaks nor Ukrainian nor a fusion of Russian and Ukrainian nor English. BARK. "Why?" the hero inquired. "Why what?" "Why can't I talk?" "It distresses some people greatly to hear English. We will have a more easy time procuring assistance if you keep your lips together." "What?" "Shut up." "No, what was that word you said?" "Which?" "With the *p*." I felt very proud because I knew a word of English that the hero, who was American, did not know. "Procure. It is like to obtain, get, acquire, secure, and gain. Now shut up, putz."

"I have never heard of it," said one of the men, with his cigarette at the side of his mouth. "Nor have I," said another, and they exhibited their backs. "Thank you," I said. The hero punched my side with the bend in his arm. He was trying to say something to me without words. "What?" I whispered. "Sofiowka," he said without volume, although in truth it did not matter. It did not matter because the men were not giving any attention to us. "Oh yes," I said to the men. They did not rotate to glance at me. "It is also called Sofiowka. Do you know of this town?" "We have never heard of it," one of them said without discussing the matter with the others. He cast his cigarette to the ground. I rotated my head from this to that to inform the hero that they did not know. "Maybe you've seen this woman," the hero said, taking a duplicate of the photograph of Augustine out of his fanny pack. "Put that back!" I said. "What are you intending here?" one of the men inquired, and also cast his cigarette to the ground. "What did he say?" the hero asked. "We are searching for the town Trachimbrod," I informed them, and I could perceive that I was not selling like pancakes. "I told you, there is no place Trachimbrod." "So stop bothering us," one of the other men said. "Do you want a Marlboro cigarette?" I proposed, because I could not think of anything else. "Get out of here," one of the men said. "Go back to Kiev." "I am from Odessa," I said, and this made them laugh with very much violence. "Then go back to Odessa." "Can they help us?" the hero inquired. "Do they know anything?" "Come," I said, and I took his hand and we walked back to the car. I was humbled to the maximum. "Come on Sammy Davis, Junior, Junior!" But she would not come, even though the smoking men harassed her. There was only one option remaining. "Billie Jean is not my lover. She's just a girl who claims that I am the one." The maximum of humbling was made maximumer.

"What in hell were you doing uttering English!" I said. "I commanded you not to speak English! You understood me, yes?" "Yes." "Then why did you speak English?" "I don't know." "You don't know! Did I ask you to prepare breakfast?" "What?" "Did I ask you to invent a new kind of wheel?" "I don't—" "No, I asked you to do one thing, and you made a disaster of it! You were so stupid!" "I just thought it would be helpful." "But it was not helpful. You made those men very angry!" "Because of my English?" "I commanded you not to speak and you did. You may have contaminated everything." "Sorry, I just thought, the picture." "I will do the thinking. You will do the silence!" "I'm sorry." "I am the one who is sorry! I am sorry that I brought you with me on this voyage!"

I was very shamed by the manner in which the men spoke to me, and I did not want to inform Grandfather of what occurred, because I knew that it would shame him also. But when we returned to the car, I realized that I did not have to inform him a thing. If you want to know why, it is because I first had to move him from his sleep. "Grandfather," I said, touching his arm. "Grandfather. It is me, Sasha." "I was dreaming," he said, and this surprised me very much. It is so weird to imagine one of your parents or grandparents dreaming. If they dream, then they think of things when you are not there, and they think of things that are not you. Also, if they dream, then they must have dreams, which is one more thing to think about. "They did not know where Trachimbrod is." "Well, enter the car," he said. He moved his hands over his eyes. "We will persevere to drive, and search for another person to inquire."

We discovered many other people to inquire, but in truth, every person regarded us in the same manner. "Go away," an old man uttered. "Why now?" a woman in a yellow dress inquired. Not one of them knew where Trachimbrod was, and not one of them had ever heard of it, but all of them became angry or silent when I inquired. I wished that Grandfather would help me, but he refused to exit the car. We persevered to drive, now unto subordinate roads lacking any markings. The houses were less near to one another, and it was an abnormal thing to see anyone at all. "I have lived here my whole life," one old man said without removing himself from his seat under a tree, "and I can inform you that there is no place called Trachimbrod." Another old man, who was escorting a cow across the dirt road, said, "You should stop searching now. I can promise you that you will not find anything." I did not tell this to the hero. Perhaps this is because I am a good person. Perhaps it is because I am a bad one. As proxy for the truth, I told him that each person told us to drive more, and that if we drove more we would discover some person who knew where Trachimbrod was. We would drive until we found Trachimbrod, and drive until we found Augustine. So we drove more, because we were severely lost, and because we did not know what else to do. It was very difficult for the car to travel on some of the roads because there were so many rocks and holes. "Do not be distressed," I told the hero. "We will find something. If we continue to drive, I am certain that we will find Trachimbrod, and then Augustine. Everything is in harmony with design."

It was already after the center of the day. "What are we going to do?" I inquired Grandfather. "We have been driving for many hours, and we are no more proximal than many hours yore." "I do not know," he said. "Are you fatigued?" I inquired him. "No." "Are you hungry?" "No." We drove more, farther and farther in the same circles. The car became fixed in the ground many times, and the hero and I had to get out to impel it unencumbered. "It's not easy," the hero said. "No, it is not," I yielded. "But I guess we should keep driving. Don't you think? If that's what people have been telling us to do." I saw that he kept filling his diary. The less we saw, the more he wrote. We drove beyond many of the towns that the hero named to the petrol man. Kovel. Sokeretchy. Kivertsy. But there were no people anywhere, and when there was a person, the person could not help us. "Go away." "There is no Trachimbrod here." "I do not know what you are speaking of." "You arc lost." It was seeming as if we were in the wrong country, or the wrong century, or as if Trachimbrod had disappeared, and so had the memory of it.

We followed roads that we had already followed, we witnessed parts of the land that we had already witnessed, and both Grandfather and I were desiring that the hero was not aware of this. I remembered when I was a boy and Father would punch me, and after he would say, "It does not hurt. It does not hurt." And the more he would utter it, the more it was faithful. I believed him, in some measure because he was Father, and in some measure because I too did not want it to hurt. This is how I felt with the hero as we persevered to drive. It was as if I was uttering to him, "We will find her. We will find her." I was deceiving him, and I am certain that he desired to be deceived. So we painted more circles into the dirt roads.

"There," Grandfather said, pointing his finger at a person roosting on the steps of a very diminutive house. It was the first person that we had viewed in many minutes. Had we witnessed this person before? Had we already inquired with no fruit? He stopped the car. "Go." "Will you come?" I asked. "Go." Because I did not know what else to say, I said, "OK," and because I did not know what else to do, I amputated myself from the car. "Come," I said to the hero. There was no rejoinder. "Come," I said, and rotated. The hero was manufacturing Z's, as still was Sammy Davis, Junior, Junior. There is no necessity for me to move them from sleep, I said to my brain. I took with me the duplicate photograph of Augustine, and was careful not to disturb them as I closed the car's door.

The house was white wood that was falling off of itself. There were four windows, and one of them was broken. As I walked more proximal, I could perceive that it was a woman roosting on the steps. She was very aged and peeling the skin off of corn. Many clothes were lying across her yard. I am certain that they were drying after a cleaning, but they were in abnormal arrangements, and they appeared like the clothes of unvisible dead bodies. I reasoned that there were many people in the white house, because there were men's clothes and women's clothes and clothes for children and even babies. "Leniency," I said while I was still some amount distant. I said this so that I would not make her a terrified person. "I have a query for you." She was donning a white shirt and a white dress, but they were covered with dirt and places where liquids had dried. I could perceive that she was a poor woman. All of the people in the small towns are poor, but she was more poor. This was clear-cut because of how svelte she was, and how broken all of her belongings were. It must be expensive, I thought, to care for so many people as she did. I decided then that when I become a rich person in America, I would give some currency to this woman.

She smiled as I became proximal to her, and I could see that she did not have any teeth. Her hairs were white, her skin had brown marks, and her eyes were blue. She was not so much of a woman, and what I signify here is that she was very fragile, and appeared as if she could be obliterated with one finger. I could hear, as I approached, that she was humming. (This is called humming, yes?) "Leniency," I said. "I do not want to pester you." "How could anything pester me on such a beautiful day?" "Yes, it is beautiful." "Yes," she said. "Where are you from?" she asked. This shamed me. I rotated over in my head what to say, and ended with the truth. "Odessa." She put down one piece of corn and picked up another. "I have never been to Odessa," she said, and moved hairs that were in front of her face to behind her ear. It was not until this moment that I perceived how her hairs were as long as her. "You must go there," I said. "I know. I know I must. I am sure there are many things that I must do." "And many things that you must not do also." I was trying to make her a sedate person, and I did. She laughed. "You are a sweet boy." "Have you ever heard of a town dubbed Trachimbrod?" I inquired. "I was informed that someone proximal to here would know of it." She put her corn on her lap and looked inquiring. "I do not want to pester you," I said, "but have you ever heard of a town dubbed Trachimbrod?" "No," she said, picking up her corn and removing its skin. "Have you ever heard of a town dubbed Sofiowka?" "I have never heard of that either." "I am sorry to have stolen your time," I said. "Have a good day." She presented me with a sad smile, which was like when the ant in Yankel's ring made to conceal its face—I knew it was a symbol, but I did not know what it was a symbol for.

I could hear her humming as I commenced to walk away. What would I inform the hero when he was no longer manufacturing Z's? What would I inform Grandfather? For how long could we fail until we surrendered? I felt as if all of the weight was residing on me. As with Father, there are only so many times that you can utter "It does not hurt" before it begins to hurt even more than the hurt. You become enlightened of the feeling of feeling hurt, which is worse, I am certain, than the existent hurt. Not-truths hung in front of me like fruit. Which could I pick for the hero? Which could I pick for Grandfather? Which for myself? Which for Little Igor? Then I remembered that I had taken the photograph of Augustine, and although I do not know what it was that coerced me to feel that I should, I rotated back around and displayed the photograph to the woman.

"Have you ever witnessed anyone in this photograph?"

She examined it for several moments. "No."

I do not know why, but I inquired again.

"Have you ever witnessed anyone in this photograph?"

"No," she said again, although this second no did not seem like a parrot, but like a different variety of no.

"Have you ever witnessed anyone in this photograph?" I inquired, and this time I held it very proximal to her face, like Grandfather held it to his face.

"No," she said again, and this seemed like a third variety of no.

I put the photograph in her hands.

"Have you ever witnessed anyone in the photograph?"

"No," she said, but in her no I was certain that I could hear, Please persevere. Inquire me again. So I did.

"Have you ever witnessed anyone in the photograph?"

She moved her thumbs over the faces, as if she were attempting to erase them. "No."

"Have you ever witnessed anyone in the photograph?"

"No," she said, and she put the photograph on her lap.

"Have you ever witnessed anyone in the photograph?" I inquired.

"No," she said, still examining it, but only from the angles of her eyes.

"Have you ever witnessed anyone in the photograph?"

"No." She was humming again, with more volume.

"Have you ever witnessed anyone in the photograph?"

"No," she said. "No." I saw a tear descend to her white dress. It too would dry and leave a mark.

"Have you ever witnessed anyone in the photograph?" I inquired, and I felt cruel, I felt like an awful person, but I was certain that I was performing the right thing.

"No," she said, "I have not. They all look like strangers."

I periled everything.

"Has anyone in this photograph ever witnessed you?"

Another tear descended.

"I have been waiting for you for so long."

I pointed to the car. "We are searching for Trachimbrod."

"Oh," she said, and she released a river of tears. "You are here. I am it."

THE DIAL, 1941–1804–1941

SHE USED HER THUMBS to pull the lace panties from her waist, allowing her engorged genitalia the teasing satisfaction of the humid summer updrafts, which brought with them the smells of burdock, birch, burning rubber, and beef broth, and would now pass on her particular animal scent to northward noses, like a message transmitted through a line of schoolchildren in a childish game, so that the final one to smell might lift his head and say, *Borsht?* She eased them off her ankles with extraordinary deliberateness, as if that action alone could have justified her birth, every hour of her parents' labors, and the oxygen she consumed with every breath. As if it could have justified the tears that her children would have shed at her proper death, had she not died in the water with the rest of the shtetl — too young, like the rest of the shtetl — before having children. She folded the panties over themselves six times into a teardrop shape and slid them into the pocket of his black nuptial suit, halfway under the lapel, blossoming in petal folds at the top like a good kerchief should.

This is so you will think about me, she said, *until* —

I don't need reminders, he said, kissing the moist divot above her upper lip.

Hurry, she giggled, straightening his tie with one hand and the rope between his legs with the other. *You'll be late. Now run to the Dial.*

She silenced with a kiss whatever he was about to say, and pushed him to go.

It was summer already. The ivy that clung to the synagogue's crumbling portico was darkening at the lobes. The soil had recovered its rich coffee blush, and was again soft enough for tomatoes and mint. The lilac bushes had flirted halfway up the veranda railings, the railings were beginning to splinter, and the splinters were chipping off into the summer breezes. The shtetl men were already crowded around the Dial when my grandfather arrived, panting and damp with sweat.

Safran is here! the Upright Rabbi announced, to the cheers of those packed in the square. *The bridegroom has arrived!* A septet of violins began the traditional Dial Waltz, with the elders of the shtetl clapping their hands on every downbeat and the children whistling every *ta-ta*.

The Chorus of The Dial Waltz Song for Soon-to-Be-Married Men

Ohhhhhhh, gather group, [insert groom's name]'s here,
Well groomed he'd better be, his wedding's near.
One great hand he's been dealt,
[insert bride's name]'s a girl to make you loosen your belt.
Sooooooo kiss his lips, smell his knees,
Beg please for prolific birds and bees.
May you be happily
Wed, then off to bed, for ohhhhhhh . . .

[Repeat from beginning, indefinitely]

My grandfather regained his composure, felt to make sure the zipper of his slacks was indeed zippered, and marched into the Dial's long shadow. He was to fulfill the sacred ritual that had been fulfilled by every married man in Trachimbrod since his great-great-great-grandfather's tragic flour mill accident. He was about to throw his bachelorhood and, in theory, his sexual exploits to the wind. But what struck him as he approached the Dial (with long, deliberate steps) was not the beauty of ceremony, or the inherent insincerity of organized rites of passage, or even how much he wished the Gypsy girl could be with him now so his true love could experience his wedding with him, but that he was no longer a boy. He was growing older, had begun to look like his great-great-great-grandfather: the furrowed brow shadowing his delicate, softly feminine eyes, the similar protrusion at the bridge of his nose, the way his lips met in a sideways U at one end and in a V at the other. Safety and profound sadness: he was growing into his place in the family; he looked unmistakably like his father's father's father's father's father, and because of that, because his cleft chin spoke of the same mongrel gene-stew (stirred by the chefs of war, disease, opportunity, love, and false love), he was granted a place in a long line—certain assurances of being and permanence, but also a burdensome restriction of movement. He was not altogether free.

He was also aware of his place among married men, all of whom had given their vows of fidelity with their knees planted on the same ground on which his now were. Each had prayed for the blessings of sound mind, good health, handsome sons, inflated wages, and deflated libido. Each had been told a thousand times the story of the Dial, the tragic circumstances of its creation and the magnitude of its power. Each knew of how his great-great-great-grandmother Brod had said *Don't go* to her new husband, too familiar with the flour mill's curse of taking without warning the lives of its young workers. *Please, find another job or don't work at all. But promise me you won't go.*

And each knew of how the Kolker had responded, *Don't be silly, Brod,* patting her belly, which after seven months could still be concealed under a baggy dress. *It's a very good job, and I'll be very careful, and that'll be all.*

And each bridegroom knew of how Brod had wept, and hid his work clothes the previous night, and shook him from sleep every few minutes so that he would be too exhausted to leave the house the next day, and refused to make his coffee in the morning, and even tried ordering him. *This is love,* she thought, *isn't it? When you notice someone's absence and hate that absence more than anything? More, even, than you love his presence?* Each knew of how she had waited for the Kolker by the window every day, how she became acquainted with its surface, learned where it had melted slightly, where it was slightly discolored, where it was opaque. She felt its tiny wrinkles and bubbles. Like a blind woman learning language, she moved her fingers over the window, and like a blind woman learning language, she felt liberated. The frame of the window was the walls of the prison that set her free. She loved what it felt like to wait for the Kolker, to be entirely dependent on him for her happiness, to be, as ridiculous as she had always thought it sounded, someone's wife. She loved her new vocabulary of simply loving something more than she loved her love for that thing, and the vulnerability that went along with living in the primary world. *Finally*, she thought, *finally. I only wish Yankel could know how happy I am.*

When she woke up crying from one of her nightmares, the Kolker would stay with her, brush her hair with his hands, collect her tears in thimbles for her to drink the next morning (*The only way to overcome sadness is to consume it*, he said), and more than that: once her eyes closed and she fell back asleep, he was left to bear the insomnia. There was a complete transfer, like a speeding billiard ball colliding with a resting one. Should Brod feel depressed—she was always depressed—the Kolker would sit with her until he could convince her that it's OK. It is. Really. And when she would move on with her day, he would stay behind, paralyzed with a grief he couldn't name and that wasn't his. Should Brod become sick, it was the Kolker who would be bedridden by week's end. Should Brod feel bored, knowing too many languages, too many facts, with too much knowledge to be happy, the Kolker would stay up all night studying her books, studying the pictures, so the next day he could try to make the kind of small talk that would please his young wife.

Brod, isn't it strange how some mathematical phrases can have a lot on one side and just a little on the other? Isn't that fascinating! And what does it say about life!...Brod, you're making that face again, the one like the man who plays that musical instrument that is all wound up in a big coil...Brod, he would say, pointing to Castor as they lay on their backs on the tin-shingled roof of their small house, *that, over there, is a star. So is that one,* pointing to Pollux. *I'm sure of it. Those are as well. Yes, those are very familiar stars. The rest I can't be one hundred percent sure of. I'm not familiar with them.*

She always saw through him, as if he were just another window. She always felt that she knew everything about him that could be known—not that he was simple, but that he was knowable, like a list of errands, like an encyclopedia. He had a birthmark on the third toe of his left foot. He wasn't able to urinate if someone could hear him. He thought cucumbers were good enough, but pickles were delicious—so absolutely delicious, in fact, that he questioned whether they were, indeed, made from cucumbers, which were only good enough. He hadn't heard of Shakespeare, but Hamlet sounded familiar. He liked making love from behind. That, he thought, was about as nice as it gets. He had never kissed anyone besides his mother and her. He had dived for the golden sack only because he wanted to impress her. He sometimes looked in the mirror for hours at a time, making faces, tensing muscles, winking, smiling, puckering. He had never seen another man naked, and so had no idea if his body was normal. The word "butterfly" made him blush, although he didn't know why. He had never been out of the Ukraine. He once thought that the earth was the center of the universe, but learned better. He admired magicians more after learning the secrets of their tricks.

You are such a sweet husband, she told him when he brought her gifts.

I just want to be good to you.

I know, she said, *and you are.*

But there are so many things I can't give you.

But there are so many things you can.

I'm not a smart man —

Stop, she said, *just stop.* Smart was the last thing she ever wanted the Kolker to be. That, she knew, would ruin everything. She wanted nothing more than someone to miss, to touch, with whom to speak like a child, with whom to be a child. He was very good for that. And she was in love.

I'm the one who isn't smart, she said.

That's the dumbest thing I've ever heard, Brod.

Exactly, she said, putting his arm around her and nestling her face in his chest.

Brod, I'm trying to have a serious talk with you. Sometimes I just feel like everything I want to say will come out wrong.

So what do you do?

I don't say it.

Well, that's smart of you, she said, playing with the loose skin under his chin.

Brod, backing away, *you're not taking me seriously.* She nestled deeper into him and closed her eyes like a cat. *I've kept a list, you know,* he said, taking back his arms.

That's wonderful, honey.

Aren't you going to ask what kind of list?

I figured you'd have told me if you wanted me to know. When you didn't, I just assumed it was none of my business. Do you want me to ask you?

Ask me.

OK. What kind of list have you been keeping so secretly?

I've kept a list of the number of conversations we've had since we've been married. Would you like to guess how many?

Is this really necessary?

We've only had six conversations, Brod. Six in almost three years.

Are you counting this one?

You never take me seriously.

Of course I do.

No, you always joke, or cut our talking short before we ever say anything.

I'm sorry if I do that. I never noticed. But do we really need to do this right now? We talk all the time.

I don't mean talking, Brod. I mean conversing. Things that last more than five minutes.

Let me get this straight. You're not talking about talking? You want us to converse about conversing? Is that right?

We've had six conversations. It's pathetic, I know, but I've counted them. Otherwise it's all worthless words. We talk about cucumbers and how I like pickles more. We talk about how I blush when I hear that word. We talk about grieving Shanda and Pinchas, about how bruises sometimes don't show up for a day or two. Talk talk talk. We talk about nothing. Cucumbers, butterflies, bruises. It's nothing.

What's something, then? You want to talk about war a bit? Maybe we could talk about literature. Just tell me what something is, and we'll talk about it. God? We could talk about Him.

You're doing it again.

What am I doing?

You're not taking me seriously.

It's a privilege you have to earn.

I'm trying.

Try a bit harder, she said, and unbuttoned his slacks. She licked him from the base of his neck to his chin, pulled his shirt from his pants, his pants from his waist, and nipped their seventh conversation in the bud. All she wanted from him was cuddling and high voices. Whispers. Assurances. Promises of fidelity and truth she made him swear to again and again: that he would never kiss another woman, that he would never even think of another woman, that he would never leave her alone.

Say it again.

I won't leave you alone.

Say it again.

I won't leave you alone.

Again.

I won't.

Won't what?

Leave you alone.

It was halfway into his second month at work when two men from the flour mill knocked on her door. She didn't have to ask why they came, but collapsed immediately to the floor.

Go away! she screamed, running her hands up and down the carpet as if it were a new language to learn, another window.

He felt no pain, they told her. *He felt nothing, really.* Which made her cry more, and harder. Death is the only thing in life that you absolutely have to be aware of as it's happening.

A disk-saw blade from the chaff splitter had spun off its bearings and raced through the mill, caroming off walls and scaffold beams while men jumped for cover. The Kolker was eating a cheese sandwich on a makeshift stool of stacked flour sacks, lost in thought about something Brod had said about something, oblivious to the chaos around him, when the blade hopped off an iron rod (left carelessly on the ground by a mill worker who was later struck by lightning) and embedded itself, perfectly vertical, in the middle of his skull. He looked up, dropped his sandwich to the floor—witnesses swore the slices of bread switched places in midair—and closed his eyes.

Leave me! she hollered at the men, who were still standing mute in her doorway. *Leave!*

But we were told —

Go! she said, beating her chest. *Go!*

Our boss said —

You bastards! she shouted. *Leave the griever to grieve!*

Oh, he's not dead, the fatter of the men corrected.

What?

He's not dead.

He's not dead? she asked, picking her head up off the floor.

No, the other said. *He's in the doctor's care, but it seems that there's little permanent damage. You can see him if you like. He is in no way repulsive looking. Well, maybe a little, but there was hardly any blood, except for the blood from his nose and ears, and the blade seems to be holding everything in its good and right place, more or less.*

Crying more now than when she heard the news of her new husband's supposed death, Brod hugged both men and then punched them both in the nose with all of the might her skinny fifteen-year-old arm could summon.

In fact, the Kolker was barely hurt at all. He had regained consciousness in only a few minutes and been able to walk himself, parade himself, through the maze of muddy capillaries to the office of Dr. (and caterer without clients) Abraham M.

What's your name? measuring the circular blade with calipers.

The Kolker.

Very good, lightly touching his finger to one of the blade's teeth. *Now, can you remember the name of your wife?*

Brod, of course. Her name is Brod.

Very good. Now, what seems to have happened to you?

A disk-saw blade stuck in my head.

Very good, examining the blade from all sides. It looked to the doctor like a five-o'clock summer sun, setting over the horizon of the Kolker's head, which reminded him that it was almost time for dinner, one of his favorite meals of the day. *Do you feel any pain?*

I feel different. It's not pain, really. It's almost a homesickness.

Very good. Homesickness. Now, can you follow my finger with your eyes? No, no. This finger . . . Very good. Can you walk across the room for me? . . . Very good.

And then, without provocation, the Kolker slammed his fist against the examining table and hollered, *You are a fat fuckhead!*

Excuse me? What?

What just happened?

You called me a fuckhead.

Did I?

You did.

I'm sorry. You're not a fuckhead. I'm very sorry.

You're probably just —

But it's true! the Kolker shouted. *You are an insolent fuckhead! And a fat one too, if I didn't mention that before.*

I'm afraid I don't under —

Did I say something? the Kolker asked, frantically looking around the room.

You said I was an insolent fuckhead.

You've got to believe me ... Your tuches is huge! ... I'm sorry, this is not me ... I'm so sorry, you fat-tuchesed fuckhead, I —

Did you call my tuches fat?

No! ... Yes!

Is it these slacks? They're cut rather tight around the —

Fat ass!

Fat ass?

Fat ass!

Who do you think you are?

No! ... Yes!

Get out of my office!

No! ... Yes!

Well, disk saw or not! the doctor said, and with a huff, he slammed shut his folder and stormed out of his own office, pounding the floor loudly with each of his heavy steps.

The doctor-caterer was the first victim of the Kolker's malicious eruptions—the only symptom of the blade that would remain embedded in his skull, perfectly perpendicular to the horizon, for the rest of his life.

The marriage was able to return to a kind of normality, after the removal of the headboard from their bed and the birth of the first of their three sons, but the Kolker was undeniably different. The man who had kneaded Brod's prematurely old legs at night when they were all pins and needles, who had rubbed milk into her burns when there was nothing else, who had counted her toes because she liked the way it felt, would now, on occasion, curse her. It began with comments made under his breath about the temperature of the brisket, or the soap residue under his collar. Brod was able to overlook it, could even find it endearing.

Brod, where are my fucking socks? You misplaced them again.

I know, she would say, smiling inwardly at the joys of being unappreciated and bullied around. *You're right. It won't happen again.*

Why the hell can't I remember the name of that coiled instrument!

Because of me. It's my fault.

With time he became worse. Dirty dirt became grounds for a tirade. Wet water in the bathtub and he might yell at her until the neighbors had to close their shutters (the desire for a little peace and quiet being the only thing the citizens of the shtetl shared). It was less than a year after the accident before he started hitting her. But, she reasoned, it was such a small fraction of the time. Once or twice a week. Never more. And when he was not in a "mood," he was more kind to her than any husband to his wife. His moods were not him. They were the other Kolker, born of the metal teeth in his brain. And she was in love, which gave her a reason to live.

Whore poison bitch! the other Kolker would howl at her with raised arms, and then the Kolker would take her into those arms, as he did the night they first met.

Filthy water monster! with a backhanded slap across the cheek, and then he would tenderly lead her, or she him, to the bedroom.

In the middle of lovemaking he might damn her, or hit her, or push her off the bed onto the floor. She would climb back up, remount, and begin again where they left off. Neither of them knew what he might do next.

They saw every doctor in the six villages — the Kolker broke the nose of the confident young physician in Lutsk who suggested the couple sleep in separate beds — and all agreed that the only possible cure for his disposition would be to remove the blade from his head, which would certainly kill him.

The women of the shtetl were happy to see Brod suffer. Even after sixteen years, they still thought of her as a product of that terrible hole, because of which they could never see her all at once, because of which they could never know and mother her, because of which they hated her. Rumors spread that the Kolker beat her because she was cold in bed (only two children to show after three years of marriage!) and couldn't manage a household with any competency.

I would expect black eyes if I pranced around like her!
Have you seen the mess their yard has become? What a pigsty!
It proves, again, that there is some justice in this world!

The Kolker hated himself, or his other self, for it. He would pace the bedroom at night, arguing savagely with his other self at the top of the two lungs they shared, often beating the chest that housed those lungs, or boxing their face. After badly injuring Brod in several night incidents, he decided (against her will) that the doctor with the broken nose was right: they must sleep apart.

I won't.

There's nothing to be said.

Then leave me. I'd rather that than this. Or kill me. That would be even better than your leaving.

You're being ridiculous, Brod. I'm only going to sleep in a different room.

But love is a room, she said. *That's what it is.*

This is what we have to do.

This is not what we have to do.

It is.

It worked for a few months. They were able to assume a regular daily life with only the occasional outburst of brutality, and would part in the evening to undress and go to bed alone. They would explain their dreams to each other over bread and coffee the next morning and describe the positions of their restlessness. It was an opportunity that their hurried marriage had never allowed for: coyness, slowness, discovering one another from a distance. They had their seventh, eighth, and ninth conversations. The Kolker tried to articulate what he wanted to say, and it always came out wrong. Brod was in love and had a reason to live.

His condition worsened. In time, Brod could expect a sound beating every morning before the Kolker went to work—where he was able, to the bafflement of all doctors, to refrain entirely from outbursts—and every late afternoon before dinner. He beat her in the kitchen in front of the pots and pans, in the living room in front of their two children, and in the pantry in front of the mirror in which they both watched. She never ran from his fists, but took them, went to them, certain that her bruises were not marks of violence, but violent love. The Kolker was trapped in his body—like a love note in an unbreakable bottle, whose script never fades or smudges, and is never read by the eyes of the intended lover—forced to hurt the one with whom he wanted most to be gentle.

Even toward the end, the Kolker had periods of clarity, lasting as long as several days at a time.

I have something for you, he said, leading Brod by the hand through the kitchen and out into the garden.

What is it? she asked, making no effort to keep a safe distance. (There was no such thing as a safe distance, then. Everything was either too close or too far.)

For your birthday. I got you a gift.

It's my birthday?

It's your birthday.

I must be seventeen.

Eighteen.

What's the surprise?

That would ruin the surprise.

I hate surprises, she said.

But I like them.

Whom is this gift for? You or me?

The gift is for you, he said. *The surprise is for me.*

What if I surprised you and told you to keep the gift? Then the surprise would be for me, and the gift for you.

But you hate surprises.

I know. So give me the gift already.

He handed her a small package. It was wrapped in blue vellum, with a light blue ribbon tied around it.

What is this? she asked.

We've gone over this, he said. *It's your surprise gift. Open it.*

No, she said, gesturing to the wrapping, *this*.

What do you mean? That's just wrapping.

She put down the package and began to cry. He had never seen her cry.

What is it, Brod? What? It was supposed to make you happy.

She shook her head. Crying was new to her.

What, Brod. What happened?

She hadn't cried since that Trachimday five years before, when on the way home from the float she was stopped by the mad squire Sofiowka N, who made a woman of her.

I don't love you, she said.

What?

I don't love you, pushing him away. *I'm sorry.*

Brod, putting his hand on her shoulder.

Get off me! she hollered, pulling herself away from him. *Don't touch me! I don't want you touching me ever again!* She turned her head to the side and vomited onto the grass.

She ran. He chased her. She ran around the house many times, past the front door, the winding walk, the gate at the back, the pigsty of a yard, the side garden, and back to the front door again. The Kolker kept close behind, and although he was much faster, he decided never to catch up, never to turn around and wait for her lap to bring her to him. So they went around and around: front door, winding walk, pigsty of a yard, side garden, front door, winding walk, pigsty of a yard, side garden. Finally, as the afternoon put on its early-evening dress, Brod collapsed from fatigue in the garden.

I'm tired, she said.

The Kolker sat beside her. *Did you ever love me?*

She turned her head from him. *No. Never.*

I've always loved you, he told her.

I'm sorry for you.

You're a terrible person.

I know, she said.

I just wanted you to know that I know that.

Well, know that I do.

He ran the back of his hand up her cheek, with the pretense of wiping away sweat. *Do you think you could ever love me?*

I don't think so.

Because I'm not good enough.

It's not like that.

Because I'm not smart.

No.

Because you couldn't love me.

Because I couldn't love you.

He walked inside.

Brod, my great-great-great-great-great-grandmother, was left alone in the garden. The wind revealed the undersides of the leaves and made waves of the grass. It rushed across her face, drying the sweat, urging more tears. She opened the package, which she realized she had never put down. Blue ribbon, blue vellum, box. A bottle of perfume. He must have bought it in Lutsk last week. What a sweet gesture. She sprayed a bit on her wrist. It was subtle. Not too pristine. *What?* she said once to herself, and then once aloud, *What?* She felt a total displacement, like a spinning globe brought to a sudden halt by the light touch of a finger. How did she end up here, like this? How could there have been so much — so many moments, so many people and things, so many razors and pillows, timepieces and subtle coffins — without her being aware? How did her life live itself without her?

She put the atomizer back in the box, along with the blue vellum and light blue ribbon, and went inside. The Kolker had made a mess of the kitchen. Spices were scattered on the floor. Bent silverware on scratched countertops. Unhinged cabinets, dirt, and broken glass. There were so many things to attend to — so much gathering and throwing away; and after gathering and throwing away, saving what was salvageable; and after saving what was salvageable, cleaning; and after cleaning, washing down with soapy water; and after washing down with soapy water, dusting; and after dusting, something else; and after something else, something else. So many little things to do. Hundreds of millions of them. Everything in the universe felt like something to do. She cleared a spot on the floor, laid herself down, and tried to make a mental list.

It was almost dark when the sound of crickets awoke her. She lit the Shabbos candles, observed the shadows against her hands, covered her eyes and said the blessing, and went up to the Kolker's bed. His face was badly bruised and swollen.

Brod, he said, but she silenced him. She brought up a small block of ice from the cellar and held it against his eye until his face couldn't feel anything, and her hand couldn't feel anything.

I love you, she said. *I do.*

No you don't, he said.

But I do, she said, touching his hair.

No. It's OK. I know you're much smarter than me, Brod, and that I'm not good enough for you. I was always waiting for you to figure it out. Every day. I felt like the czar's food taster, waiting for the night when the dinner would be poisoned.

Stop, she said. *It's not true. I do love you.*

You stop.

But I love you.

It's OK. I'm OK. She touched the puffy blackness around his left eye. The down, which the saw blade had released from the pillow, clung to the tears on their cheeks. *Listen*, he said, *I'll be dead soon.*

Stop.

We both know it.

Stop.

There's no use in avoiding it.

Stop.

And I wonder if you could just pretend for a while, if we could pretend to love each other. Until I'm gone.

Silence.

She felt it again, the same as that night when she met him, when he was illuminated at her window, when she let her arms brush down her skin to her sides and turned to face him.

We can do that, she said.

She cut a small hole in the wall to allow him to speak to her from the adjoining bedroom to which he had exiled himself, and a one-way flap was built into the door through which food could be passed. That's how it was for the last year of their marriage. She pushed her bed against the wall so she could hear him mutter his passionate profanity and feel the wiggle of his extended index finger, which could neither hurt nor caress in such a position. When she was brave enough, she would stick one of her own fingers through the hole (like tempting a lion in his cage) and summon her love to the pine divide.

What are you doing? he whispered.

I'm talking to you.

He put his eye to the hole. *You look very beautiful.*

Thank you, she said. *Can I look at you?*

He moved away from the hole so she would be able to see at least some of him.

Will you take off your shirt? she asked.

I feel shy. He laughed and took off his shirt. *Can you take off yours, so I don't feel so strange standing here?*

That would make you feel less strange? She laughed. But she did it, and made sure that she was far enough from the hole so that he could go to it and look at her.

Will you also take off your socks? she asked. *And your pants?*

Will you take off yours?

I also feel shy, she said, which, in spite of the fact that they had seen each other's naked body hundreds, and probably thousands, of times, was true. They had never seen one another from afar. They had never known the deepest intimacy, that closeness attainable only with distance. She went to the hole and looked at him for several silent minutes. Then she backed away from the hole. He went to it and looked at her for several more silent minutes. In the silence they attained another intimacy, that of words without talking.

Now will you take off your underwear? she asked.

Will you take off yours?

If you'll take off yours.

You will?

Yes.

Do you promise?

They removed their underwear and took turns gazing through the hole, experiencing the sudden and profound joy of discovering each other's body, and the pain of not being able to discover each other at the same time.

Touch yourself as if your hands were mine, she said.

Brod —

Please.

He did it, even though he was embarrassed, even though he was a body's length from the hole. And even though he couldn't see anything more than her eye—a blue marble in the black expanse—she did as he did, used her hands to remember his hands. She leaned back, and with her right forefinger she fingered the hole in the pine divide, and with her left she pressed circles over her greatest secret, which was also a hole, also a negative space, and when is enough proof enough?

Will you come to me? she asked.

I will.

Yes?

I will.

They made love through the hole. The three lovers pressed against one another, but never fully touched. The Kolker kissed the wall, and Brod kissed the wall, but the selfish wall never kissed either back. The Kolker pressed his palms against the wall, and Brod, who turned her back to the wall to accommodate love, pressed the backs of her thighs against the wall, but the wall remained indifferent, never acknowledging what they were trying so hard to do.

They lived with the hole. The absence that defined it became a presence that defined them. Life was a small negative space cut out of the eternal solidity, and for the first time, it felt precious—not like all of the words that had come to mean nothing, but like the last breath of a drowning victim.

Without being able to examine the Kolker's body, the doctor offered a diagnosis of consumption—little more than a guess for the sake of some dotted line. Brod watched through the hole in the black wall as her still-young husband withered away. The strong, treelike man who had been illuminated by a wink of lightning that night of Yankel's death, who had explained to her the nature of her first period, who had awoken early and returned late only to provide for her, who wouldn't lay a finger on her but would too often impart the might of his fist, now looked eighty. His hair had grayed around the ears and fallen out on top. Pulsing veins had risen to the surface of his prematurely wrinkled hands. His stomach had dropped. His breasts were larger than her own, which is to say little of their size, but volumes of how much it hurt Brod to see them.

She persuaded him to change his name for the second time. Perhaps this would confuse the Angel of Death when He came to take the Kolker away. (The inevitable is, after all, inevitable.) Perhaps He could be tricked into thinking the Kolker was someone he was not, just as the Kolker himself was tricked. So Brod named him Safran, after a lipstick passage she remembered with longing from her father's ceiling. (And it was this Safran for whom my grandfather, the kneeling groom, was named.) But it didn't work. Shalom-then-Kolker-now-Safran's condition worsened, the years continued to pass in days, and his grief left him too weak even to rub his wrist with enough strength over the blade in his head to end his own life.

Not long after their exile to the rooftops, the Wisps of Ardisht realized that they would soon run out of matches to light their beloved cigarettes. They kept a chalk-line count on the side of the tallest chimney. Five hundred. The next day three hundred. The next day one hundred. They rationed them, burned them down to the striker's fingers, trying to light at least thirty cigarettes with each. When they were down to twenty matches, lighting became a ceremony. By ten, the women were crying. Nine. Eight. The clan leader dropped the seventh off the roof by accident, and proceeded to throw his own body after it in shame. Six. Five. It was inevitable. The fourth match was blown out by a breeze—a gross oversight by the new clan leader, who also plunged to his death, although his nosedive was not of his own choosing. Three: *We will die without them.* Two: *It's too painful to go on.* And then, in the moment of deepest desperation, a grand idea emerged, devised by a child, no less: simply make sure that there is always someone smoking. Each cigarette can be lit from the previous one. As long as there is a lit cigarette, there is the promise of another. The glowing ash end is the seed of continuity! Schedules were drawn up: dawn duty, morning smoke, lunchtime puffer, midafternoon and late-afternoon assignments, crepuscular puller, lonely midnight sentinel. The sky was always lit with at least one cigarette, the candle of hope.

So it was with Brod, who knew that the Kolker's days were numbered, and so began her grieving long before he died. She wore rent black clothes and sat close to the ground on a wooden stool. She even recited the Mourner's Kaddish loud enough for Safran to hear. There are only weeks left, she thought. Days. Although she never cried tears, she wailed and wailed in dry heaves. (Which could not have been good for my great-great-great-great-grandfather—conceived through the hole —who was eight months heavy in her stomach.) And then, in one of his moments of mental clarity, Shalom-then-Kolker-now-Safran called to her through the wall: *I'm still here, you know. You promised you'd pretend to love me until I died, and instead you're pretending I'm dead.*

It's true, Brod thought. *I'm breaking my promise.*

So they strung their minutes like pearls on an hour-string. Neither slept. They stood vigil with their cheeks against the pine divide, passing notes through the hole like schoolchildren, passing vulgarities, blown kisses, blasphemous hollers and songs.

> *Weep not, my love,*
> *Weep not, my love,*
> *Your heart is close to me.*
> *You fucking bitch,*
> *Ungrateful cunt,*
> *Your heart is close to me.*
> *Oh, do not fear,*
> *I'm nearer than near,*
> *Your heart is close to me.*
> *I'll gouge out your eyes*
> *And pound in your fucking head,*
> *You fucking bitch whore,*
> *Your heart is close to me.*

Their final conversations (ninety-eight, ninety-nine, and one hundred) consisted of exchanged vows, which took the form of sonnets Brod would read from one of Yankel's favorite books—a loose scrap descended to the floor: *I had to do it for myself*—and of Shalom-then-Kolker-now-Safran's most loathsome obscenities, which didn't mean what they said, but spoke in harmonics that could be heard only by his wife: *I'm sorry that this has been your life. Thank you for pretending with me.*

You are dying, Brod said, because it was the truth, the all-consuming and unacknowledged truth, and she was tired of saying things that weren't the truth.

I am, he said.

What does it feel like?

I don't know, through the hole. *I'm scared.*

You don't have to be scared, she said. *It's going to be OK.*

How is it going to be OK?

It's not going to hurt.

I don't think that's what I'm afraid of.

What are you afraid of?

I'm afraid of not being alive.

You don't have to be afraid, she said again.

Silence.

He put his forefinger through the hole.

I have to tell you something, Brod.

What?

This is something I've wanted to tell you since I met you, and I should have told you this so long ago, but the longer I waited, the more impossible it became. I don't want you to hate me.

I couldn't hate you, she said, and held his finger.

This is all completely wrong. It's not how I meant for it to be. You have to know that.

Shhh...shhh...

I owe you so much more than this.

You don't owe me anything. Shhh...

I'm a bad person.

You're a good person.

I have to tell you something.

It's OK.

He pressed his lips to the hole. *Yankel was not your real father.*

The minutes were unstrung. They fell to the floor and rolled through the house, losing themselves.

I love you, she said, and for the first time in her life, the words had meaning.

After eighteen days, the baby—who had, with its ear pressed against Brod's bellybutton, heard everything—was born. In postlabor exhaustion, Brod had finally slept. Only minutes later, or perhaps at the exact moment of the birth—the house was so consumed with new life that no one was aware of new death—Shalom-then-Kolker-now-Safran died, never having seen his third child. Brod later regretted not knowing precisely when her husband passed away. If it had been before the birth of her child, she would have named him Shalom, or Kolker, or Safran. But Jewish custom forbade the naming of a child after a living relative. It was said to be bad luck. So instead she named him Yankel, like her other two children.

She cut around the hole that had separated her from the Kolker for those last months, and put the pine loop on her necklace, next to the abacus bead that Yankel had given her so long ago. This new bead would remind her of the second man she had lost in her eighteen years, and of the hole that she was learning is not the exception in life, but the rule. The hole is no void; the void exists around it.

The men at the flour mill, who wanted so desperately to do something kind for Brod, something that might make her love them as they loved her, chipped in to have the Kolker's body bronzed, and they petitioned the governing council to stand the statue in the center of the shtetl square as a symbol of strength and vigilance, which, because of the perfectly perpendicular saw blade, could also be used to tell more or less accurate time by the sun.

But rather than of strength and vigilance, he soon became a symbol of luck's power. It was luck, after all, that had given him the golden sack that Trachimday, and luck that had brought him to Brod as Yankel left her. It was luck that had put that blade in his head, and luck that had kept it there, and luck that had timed his passing to coincide with the birth of his child.

Men and women journeyed from distant shtetls to rub his nose, which was worn to the flesh in only a month's time and had to be rebronzed. Babies were brought before him—always at noon when he cast no shadow at all—to be protected from lightning, the evil eye, and stray partisan fire. The old folks told him their secrets, hoping he might be amused, take pity on them, grant a few more years. Unmarried women kissed his lips, praying for love, so many kisses that the lips became indented, became negative kisses, and also had to be rebronzed. So many visitors came to rub and kiss different parts of him for the fulfillment of their various wishes that his entire body had to be rebronzed every month. He was a changing god, destroyed and recreated by his believers, destroyed and recreated by their belief.

His dimensions changed slightly with each rebronzing. Over time, his arms lifted, inch by inch, from down at his sides to high above his head. The sickly forearms of the end of his life became thick and virile. His face had been polished down so many times by so many beseeching hands, and rebuilt as many times by as many others, that it no longer resembled that of the god to whom those first few prayed. For each recasting, the craftsmen modeled the Dial's face after the faces of his male descendants—reverse heredity. (So when my grandfather thought he saw that he was growing to look like his great-great-great-grandfather, what he really saw was that his great-great-great-grandfather was growing to look like him. His revelation was just how much like himself he looked.) Those who prayed came to believe less and less in the god of their creation and more and more in their belief. The unmarried women kissed the Dial's battered lips, although they were not faithful to their god, but to the kiss: they were kissing themselves. And when the bridegrooms knelt, it was not the god they believed in, it was the kneel; not the god's bronzed knees, but their own bruised ones.

So my young grandfather knelt—a perfectly unique link in a perfectly uniform chain—almost one hundred fifty years after his great-great-great-grandmother Brod saw the Kolker illuminated at her window. With the hand of his functional left arm, he removed his panty-hanky and wiped the sweat from his brow, then from above his upper lip.

Great-great-great-grandfather, he sighed, *don't let me hate who I become.*

When he felt ready to continue — with the ceremony, with the afternoon, with his life — he rose to his feet and was again met with the cheers of the shtetl's men.

Hoorah! The groom!

Yoidle-doidle!

To the synagogue!

They paraded him through the streets on their shoulders. Long white banners hung from the high windows, and the cobblestones had been caked white — if they had only known — with flour. The fiddles continued to play from the front of the parade, this time faster klezmer melodies to which the men sang along in unison:

Biddle biddle biddle biddle

bop

biddle bop...

Because my grandfather and his bride were Slouchers, the ceremony under the chuppah was extremely short. The recitation of the seven blessings was officiated by the Innocuous Rabbi, and at the proper moment my grandfather lifted the veil of his new wife — who gave a quick, enticing wink when the Rabbi was turned to face the ark — and then smashed the crystal, which was not really crystal but glass, under his foot.

17 November 1997

Dear Jonathan,

Humph. I feel as if I have so many things to inform you. Beginning is very rigid, yes? I will begin with the less rigid matter, which is the writing. I could not perceive if you were appeased by the last section. I do not understand, to where did it move you? I am glad that you were good-humored about the part I invented about commanding you to drink the coffee until I could see my face in the cup, and how you said it was a clay cup. I am a very funny person, I think, although Little Igor says that I merely look funny. My other inventions were also first rate, yes? I ask because you did not utter anything about them in your letter. Oh yes, I of course am eating humble pie for the section I invented about the word "procure," and how you did not know what it signified. It has been removed, and so has my effrontery. Even Alf is not humorous at times. I have made efforts to make you appear as a person with less anxiety, as you have commanded me to do on so many occasions. This is difficult to achieve, because in truth you are a person with very much anxiety. Perhaps you should be a drug user.

As for your story, I will tell you that I was at first a very perplexed person. Who is this new Safran, and Dial, and who is becoming married? Primarily I thought it was the wedding of Brod and Kolker, but when I learned that it was not, I thought, Why did their story not continue? You will be happy to know that I proceeded, suspending my temptation to cast off your writing into the garbage, and it all became illuminated. I am very happy that you returned to Brod and Kolker, although I am not happy that he became the person that he became because of the saw (I do not think that there were these kinds of saws at that time, but I trust that you have a good purpose for your ignorance), although I am happy that they were able to discover a kind of love, although I am not happy because it really was not love, was it? One could learn very much from the marriage of Brod and Kolker. I do not know what, but I am certain that it has to do with love. And also, why do you term him "the Kolker"? It is similar to how you term it "the Ukraine," which also makes no sense to me.

If I could utter a proposal, please allow Brod to be happy. Please. Is this such an impossible thing? Perhaps she could still exist, and be proximal with your grandfather Safran. Or, here is a majestic idea: perhaps Brod could be Augustine. Do you comprehend what I signify? You would have to alter your story very much, and she would be very aged, of course, but might it be wonderful in this manner?

Those things that you wrote in your letter about your grandmother made me remember how you told me on Augustine's steps about when you would sit under her dress, and how that presented you safety and peace. I must confess that I became melancholy then, and still am melancholy. I was also very moved — is this how you use it? — by what you wrote about how impossible it must have been for your grandmother to be a mother without a husband. It is amazing, yes, how your grandfather survived so much only to die when he came to America? It is as if after surviving so much, there was no longer a reason to survive. When you wrote about the early death of your grandfather, it helped me to understand, in some manners, the melancholy that Grandfather has felt since Grandmother died, and not only because they both died from cancer. I do not know your mother, of course, but I know you, and I can tell you that your grandfather would have been so so proud. It is my hope that I will be a person that Grandmother would have been so so proud of.

And now, to concern informing your grandmother of our voyage, there could not be a question that you must do it, even if it will make her to cry. In truth, it is something abnormal to witness your grandparent cry. I have told you about when I have witnessed Grandfather cry, and I implore myself to say that I desire to never witness him cry again. If this signifies that I must do things for him so that he will not cry, then I will do those things. If this signifies that I must not look when he cries, then I will not look. You are very different from me in this manner. I think that you need to see your grandmother cry, and if this means doing things to make her cry, then you must do them, and if this means looking at her when she cries, then you must look.

Your grandmother will find some manner to be content with what you did when you went to Ukraine. I am certain that she will forgive you if you inform her. But if you never inform her, she will never be able to forgive you. And this is what you desire, yes? For her to forgive you? Is not that why you did everything? One part of your letter made me most melancholy. It was the part when you said that you do not know anybody, and how that encompasses even you. I understand very much what you are saying. Do you remember the division that I wrote about how Grandfather said I looked like a combination of Father, Mother, Brezhnev, and myself? I made to remember that when I read what you wrote. (With our writing, we are reminding each other of things. We are making one story, yes?) I must inform you something now. This is a thing I have never informed anyone, and you must promise that you will not inform it to one soul. I have never been carnal with a girl. I know. I know. You cannot believe it, but all of the stories that I told you about my girls who dub me All Night, Baby, and Currency were all nottruths, and they were not befitting not-truths. I think I manufacture these not-truths because it makes me feel like a premium person. Father asks me very often about girls, and which girls I am being carnal with, and in what arrangements we are carnal. He likes to laugh with me about it, especially late at night when he is full of vodka. I know that it would disappoint him very much if he knew what I am really like.

But more, I manufacture not-truths for Little Igor. I desire him to feel as if he has a cool brother, and a brother whose life he would desire to impersonate one day. I want Little Igor to be able to boast to his friends about his brother, and to want to be viewed in public places with him. I think that this is why I relish writing for you so much. It makes it possible for me to be not like I am, but as I desire for Little Igor to see me. I can be funny, because I have time to meditate about how to be funny, and I can repair my mistakes when I perform mistakes, and I can be a melancholy person in manners that are interesting, not only melancholy. With writing, we have second chances. You mentioned to me that first evening of our voyage that you thought you might have been born to be a writer. What a terrible thing, I think. But I must tell you, I do not think that you understood the meaning of what you said when you said that. You were making suggestions of how you like to write, and how it is an interesting thing for you to imagine worlds that are not exactly like this one, or worlds that are exactly like this one. It is true, I am certain, that you will write very many more books than I will, but it is me, not you, who was born to be the writer.

Grandfather interrogates me about you every day. He desires to know if you forgive him for the things he told you about the war, and about Herschel. (You could alter it, Jonathan. For him, not for me. Your novel is now verging on the war. It is possible.) He is not a bad person. He is a good person, alive in a bad time. Do you remember when he said this? It makes him so melancholy to remember his life. I discover him crying almost every night, but must counterfeit that I am reposing. Little Igor also discovers him crying, and so does Father, and even though Father could never inform me, I am certain that it makes him melancholy to see his father crying.

Everything is the way it is because everything was the way it was. Sometimes I feel ensnared in this, as if no matter what I do, what will come has already been fixed. For me, OK, but there are things that I want for Little Igor. There is so much violence around him, and I mean more than merely the kind that occurs with fists. I do not want him to feel violence anymore, but also I do not want him to one day make others feel violence.

Father is never home because then he would witness Grandfather crying. This is my notion. "His stomach," he said to me last week when we heard Grandfather in the television room. "His stomach." But it is not his stomach, I understand, and Father understands this also. (This is why I forgive Father. I do not love him. I hate him. But I forgive him for everything.) I parrot: Grandfather is not a bad person, Jonathan. Everyone performs bad actions. I do. Father does. Even you do. A bad person is someone who does not lament his bad actions. Grandfather is now dying because of his. I beseech you to forgive us, and to make us better than we are. Make us good.

Guilelessly,
Alexander

falling in love

"Jon-fen," I said, "Jon-fen, arouse! Look who I have!" "Huh?" "Look," I said, and pointed to Augustine. "How long have I been asleep?" he asked. "Where are we?" "Trachimbrod! We are in Trachimbrod!" I was so proud. "Grandfather," I uttered, and moved Grandfather with much violence. "What?" "Look, Grandfather! Look who I have found!" He moved his hands across his eyes. "Augustine?" he asked, and it appeared as if he could not be certain if he was still in dreams. "Sammy Davis, Junior, Junior!" I said, shaking her. "We are here!" "Who are these people?" Augustine asked, and she was persevering to cry. She dried her tears with her dress, which signified lifting it enough to exhibit her legs. But she was not ashamed. "Augustine?" the hero asked. "Let us roost," I said, "and we will illuminate everything." The hero and the bitch removed themselves from the car. I was not certain if Grandfather would come, but he did. "Are you hungry?" Augustine asked. The hero must have been acquiring some Ukrainian, because he put his hand on his stomach. I moved my head to say, Yes, some of us are very hungry people. "Come," Augustine said, and I detected that she was not melancholy at all, but happy without controls. She took my hand. "Come inside. I will arrange lunch, and we will eat." We walked up the wood stairs that I first witnessed her roosting on and went into her house. Sammy Davis, Junior, Junior loitered outside, smelling the clothes on the ground.

First, I must describe that Augustine had a very unusual walk, which went from here to there with heaviness. She could not move any faster than slow. It looked like she had a leg that was damaged goods. (If we knew then, Jonathan, would we have still gone in?) Second, I must describe her house. It was not similar to any house that I have seen, and I do not think that I would dub it a house. If you want to know what I would dub it, I would dub it two rooms. One of the rooms had a bed, and a small desk, a bureau, and many things from the floor to the ceiling, including piles of more clothes and hundreds of shoes of different sizes and fashions. I could not see the wall through all of the photographs. They appeared as if they came from many different families, although I did recognize that a few of the people were in more than one or two. All of the clothing and shoes and pictures made me to reason that there must have been at least one hundred people living in that room. The other room was also very populous. There were many boxes, which were overflowing with items. These had writing on their sides. A white cloth was overwhelming from the box marked WEDDINGS AND OTHER CELEBRATIONS. The box marked PRIVATES: JOURNALS/DIARIES/SKETCHBOOKS/UNDERWEAR was so overfilled that it appeared prepared to rupture. There was another box, marked SILVER/PERFUME/PINWHEELS, and one marked WATCHES/WINTER, and one marked HYGIENE/SPOOLS/CANDLES, and one marked FIGURINES/SPECTACLES. If I had been a smart person, I would have recorded all of the names on a piece of paper, as the hero did in his diary, but I was not a smart person, and have since forgotten many of them. Some of the names I could not reason, like the box marked DARKNESS, or the one with DEATH OF THE FIRSTBORN written in pencil on its front. I noticed that there was a box on the top of one of these skyscrapers of boxes that was marked DUST.

There was a petite stove in this room, a shelf with vegetables and potatoes, and a wooden table. It was at this wooden table that we sat. It was hard to remove the chairs because there was almost no room for them with all of the boxes. "Allow me to cook you a little something," she said, giving all of her words and glances to me. "Please, do not make any efforts," Grandfather said. "It is nothing," she said, "but I must tell you that I do not have so much currency, and for that reason I have no meat." Grandfather looked at me and closed one of his eyes. "Do you like potatoes and cabbage?" she asked. "This is a perfect thing," Grandfather said. He was smiling so so much, and I am not lying if I tell you that I had never seen him smile so much since Grandmother was alive. I saw that when she rotated to excavate a cabbage from a wooden box on the floor, Grandfather arranged his hairs with a comb from his pocket.

"Tell her I'm so glad to meet her," the hero said. "We are all so glad to meet you," I said, and on accident I punched the PILLOWCASES box with my elbow. "It would be impossible for you to comprehend how long we have been searching for you." She made a fire on the stove and began to cook the food. "Ask her to tell us everything," the hero said. "I want to hear about how she met my grandfather, and why she decided to save him, and what happened to her family, and if she ever talked to my grandfather after the war. Find out," he said quietly, as if she might have comprehended, "if they were in love." "Slowness," I said, because I did not want Augustine to shit a brick. "You are being very kind," Grandfather said to her, "to take us into your home, and to cook for us your food. You are very kind." "You are kinder," she said, and then she performed a thing that surprised me. She looked at her face in the reflection of the window above the stove, and I think that she desired to see how she appeared. This is only my notion, but I am certain that it is a true one.

We watched her, as if the whole world and its future were because of her. When she cut a cabbage into little pieces, the hero moved his head this and that with the knife. When she put those pieces in a pan, Grandfather smiled and held one of his hands with the other. As for me, I could not retrieve my eyes from her. She had thin fingers and high bones. Her hairs, as I mentioned, were white and long. The ends of them moved against the floor, taking the dust and dirt with them. It was rigid to examine her eyes because they were so far back in her face, but I could see when she looked at me that they were blue and resplendent. It was her eyes that let me understand that she was, without a query, the Augustine from the picture. And I was certain, looking at her eyes, that she had saved the hero's grandfather, and probably many others. I could imagine in my brain how the days connected the girl in the photograph to the woman who was in the room with us. Each day was like another photograph. Her life was a book of photographs. One was with the hero's grandfather, and now one was with us.

When the food was ready, after many minutes of cooking, she transported it to the table on plates, one for each of us, and not one for her. One of the potatoes descended to the floor, PLOMP, which made us laugh for reasons that a subtle writer does not have to illuminate. But Augustine did not laugh. She must have been very shamed, because she hid her face for a long time before being able to view us again. "Are you OK?" Grandfather asked. She did not answer. "Are you OK?" And suddenly she returned to us. "You must be very fatigued from all of your traveling," she said. "Yes," he said, and he rotated his head, like he was embarrassed, but I do not know what he would be embarrassed about. "I could walk to the market and purchase some cold drinks," she said, "if you like cola, or something else." "No," Grandfather said with urgency, as if she might leave us and never return. "That is not necessary. You are being so generous. Please, sit." He removed one of the wooden chairs from the table, and on accident gave a small punch to the box marked MENORAHS/INK/KEYS. "Thank you," she said, and lowered her head. "You are very beautiful," Grandfather said, and I did not anticipate him to say that, and I do not think that he anticipated to say that. There was silence for a moment. "Thank you," she said, and she moved her eyes from him. "You are the one who is generous." "But you are beautiful," he said. "No," she said, "no, I am not." "I think you are beautiful," I said, and while I was not anticipating to say that, I do not lament saying it. She was so beautiful, like someone who you will never meet, but always dream of meeting, like someone who is too good for you. She was also very timid, I could perceive. It was rigid for her to view us, and she stored her hands in the pockets of her dress. I will tell you that when she did confer us a look, it was never to us, but always to me.

"What are you talking about?" the hero asked. "Has she mentioned my grandfather?" "He does not speak Ukrainian?" she asked. "No," I said. "Where is he from?" "America." "Is that in Poland?" I could not believe this thing, that she did not know of America, and I must tell you that it made her even more beautiful to me. "No, it is far away. He came on an airplane." "A what?" "An airplane," I said, "in the sky." I moved my hand in the air like an airplane, and on accident I gave a small punch to the box with FILLINGS written across it. I made the sound of an airplane with my lips. This made her distressed. "No more," she said. "What?"

"Please," she said. "From the war?" Grandfather asked. She did not say a thing. "He came to see you," I said. "He came from America for you." "I thought it was you," she said to me. "I thought you were the one." This made me laugh, and also made Grandfather laugh. "No," I said, "it is him." I placed my hand on the head of the hero. "He is the one who voyaged over the world to find you." This incited her to cry again, which I did not intend to do, but I must say that it seemed befitting. "You came for me?" she said to the hero. "She wants to know if you came for her." "Yes," the hero said, "tell her yes." "Yes," I said, "everything is for you." "Why?" she asked. "Why?" I asked the hero. "Because if it weren't for her, I couldn't be here to find her. She made the search possible." "Because you created him," I said. "By saving his grandfather, you allowed him to be born." Her breaths became brief. "I would like to give her something," the hero said. He excavated an envelope from his fanny pack. "Tell her it has money. I know it isn't enough. There couldn't be enough. It's just some money from my parents to make her life easier. Give it to her." I secured the envelope. It was brimming. There must have been many thousands of dollars in it. "Augustine," Grandfather said, "would you return with us? To Odessa?" She did not answer. "We could care for you. Do you have family here? We could take them into our house also. This is not a way to live," he said, pointing to the chaos. "We will give you a new life." I told the hero what Grandfather said. I saw that his eyes were impending tears. "Augustine," Grandfather said, "we can save you from all of this." He pointed to her house again, and he pointed to all of the boxes: HAIR/HAND MIRRORS, POETRY/NAILS/PISCES, CHESS/RELICS/BLACK MAGIC, STARS/MUSIC BOXES, SLEEP/SLEEP/SLEEP, STOCKINGS/KIDDUSH CUPS, WATER INTO BLOOD.

"Who is Augustine?" she asked.

"What?" I asked. "Who is Augustine?" "Augustine?" "What's she saying?" "The photograph," Grandfather said to me. "We do not know what the writing is on the back. It might not be her name." I exhibited her the photograph again. Again she made to cry. "This is you," Grandfather said, putting his finger under her face in the photograph. "Here. You are the girl." Augustine moved her head to say, No, this is not me, I am not her. "It is a very aged photograph," Grandfather said to me, "and she has forgotten." But I had already secured into my heart what Grandfather would not allow in. I returned the currency back to the hero. "You know this man," Grandfather said and did not inquire, putting his finger on the hero's grandfather. "Yes," she said, "that is Safran." "Yes," he said, looking at me, then looking at her. "Yes. And he is with you." "No," she said, "I do not know who those others are. They are not from Trachimbrod." "You saved him." "No," she said, "I did not." "Augustine?" he asked. "No," she said, and she exited from the table. "You saved him," he said. She put her hands on her face. "She is not Augustine," I told the hero. "What?" "She is not Augustine." "I don't understand." "Yes," Grandfather said. "No," she said. "She is not Augustine," I told the hero. "I thought that she was, but she is not." "Augustine," Grandfather said, but she was in the other room. "She is timid," Grandfather said. "We surprised her very much." "Perhaps we should go forth," I said. "We are not going anywhere. We must help her to remember. Many people try so rigidly to forget after the war that they can no longer remember." "This is not the situation," I said. "What are you saying?" the hero asked. "Grandfather thinks she is Augustine," I told him. "Even though she says she isn't?" "Yes," I said. "He is not being reasonable."

She returned with a box from the other room. The word REMAINS was written on it. She put it on the table and dislodged the top. It was brimmed with many photographs, and many pieces of paper, and many ribbons, and cloths, and queer things like combs, rings, and flowers that had become more paper. She removed each item, one at a time, and exhibited it to each of us, although I will say that it still seemed that she gave her attention only to me. "This is a photograph of Baruch in front of the old library. He used to sit there all day long and you know he could not even read! He said he liked to think about the books, think about them without reading them. He would always walk around with a book under his arm, and he took out more books from the library than anyone in the shtetl. What nonsense! This one," she said, and excavated another photograph out of the box, "is Yosef and his brother Tzvi. I used to play with them when they came home from school. I always had a little thing in my heart for Tzvi, but I never told him. I planned on telling him, but

I never did. I was such a funny girl, always having little things in my heart. It would drive Leah crazy when I would tell her about them, she would say, 'All of those little things, you are not going to have room for any blood!'" This made her laugh at herself, and then she became silent.

"Augustine?" Grandfather asked, but she must not have heard him, because she did not rotate to him, but only moved her hands through the things in the box, like the things were water. Now she did not give her eyes to any of us but me. Grandfather and the hero did not exist to her anymore.

"Here is Rivka's wedding ring," she said, and put it on her finger. "She hid it in a jar that she put in the ground. I knew this because she told me. She said, 'Just in case.' Many people did this. The ground is still filled with rings, and money, and pictures, and Jewish things. I was only able to find a few of them, but they fill the earth." The hero did not ask me once what she was saying, and he never did ask me. I am not certain if he knew what she was saying, or if he knew not to inquire.

"Here is Herschel," she said, holding a photograph up to the light of the window. "We will go," Grandfather said. "Tell him we are leaving." "Do not go," she said. "Shut up," he told her, and even if she was not Augustine, he still should not have uttered this to her. "I am sorry," I told her, "please continue." "He lived in Kolki, which was a shtetl near to Trachimbrod. Herschel and Eli were best friends, and Eli had to shoot Herschel, because if he did not, they would shoot him." "Shut up," he said again, and this time he also punched the table. But she did not shut up. "Eli did not want to, but he did it." "You are lying about it all." "He does not intend this," I told her, and I could not clutch why he was doing what he was doing. "Grandfather—" "You can keep your not-truths for yourself," he said. "I heard this story," she said, "and I believe it is a truth." I could perceive that he was making her to cry.

"Here is a clip," she said, "that Miriam would keep in her hair so that it would not be in her face. She was always running from here to there. It would kill her to sit down, you know, because she was always loving to do things. I found this under her pillow. It's true. Why was her clip under her pillow, you must want to know. The secret is that she would hold it all night so that she would not suck on her thumb! That was a bad thing she did for so long, even when she was twelve years old already! Only I know that. She would kill me if she knew I was talking about her thumb, but I'll tell you, if you witnessed close enough, if you gave it attention, you could see that it was always red. She was always ashamed about it." She restored the clip back into REMAINS and excavated another photograph.

"Here, oh, I remember this, this is Kalman and Izzy, they were such jokers." Grandfather did not view at anything except for Augustine. "See how Kalman is holding Izzy's nose! What a joker! They would make so much joking all day, Father called them the clowns of Trachimbrod. He would say, 'They are such clowns that not even a circus would have them!'" "You are from Trachimbrod?" I asked. "She is not from Trachimbrod," Grandfather said, and rotated his head away from her. "I am," she said. "I am the only one remaining." "What do you signify?" I asked, because I just did not know. "They were all killed," she said, and here I commenced to translate for the hero what she was saying, "except for the one or two who were able to escape." "You were the lucky ones," I told her. "We were the not-lucky ones," she said. "It is not true," Grandfather said, although I do not know what part he was saying was not true. "It is. You should never have to be the one remaining." "You should have died with the others," he said. (I will never allow that to remain in the story.)

"Ask her if she knew my grandfather." "Did you know the man in the photograph? He was the boy's grandfather." I presented her the photograph again. "Of course," she said, and again disbursed her eyes to me. "That was Safran. He was the first boy I ever kissed. I am such an old lady that I am too old to be shy anymore. I kissed him when I was only a girl, and he was only a boy. Tell him," she said to me, and she took my hand into her own hand. "Tell him that he was the first boy I ever kissed." "She says that your grandfather was the first boy she ever kissed." "We were very good friends. He lost a wife and two babies, you know, in the war. Does he know that?" "Two babies?" I asked. "Yes," she said. "He knows," I said. She inspected REMAINS, excavating photographs and putting them on the table. "How can you do this?" Grandfather asked her.

"Here," she said after a long search. "This is a photograph of Safran and me." I observed that the hero had small rivers descending his face, and I wanted to put my hand on his face, to be architecture for him. "This is his house we are in front of," she said. "I remember the day very much. My mother made this photograph. She was so fond for Safran. I think she wanted me to marry him, and even told the Rabbi." "Then you would be his grandmother," I told her. She laughed, and this made me feel good. "My mother liked him so much because he was a very polite boy, and very shy, and he would tell her that she was pretty even when she was not pretty." "What was her name?" I asked, and I was attempting to be kind, but the woman rotated her head to tell me, No, I will not ever utter her name. And then I remembered that I did not know this woman's name. I persevered to think of her as Augustine, because like Grandfather, I could not stop desiring that she was Augustine. "I know I have another," she said, and again investigated REMAINS. Grandfather would not look at her. "Yes," she said, excavating another yellow photograph, "here is one of Safran and his wife in front of their house after they became married."

I gave the hero each picture as she gave it to me, and he could only with difficulty hold it in his hands that were doing so much shaking. It appeared that a part of him wanted to write everything, every word of what occurred, into his diary. And a part of him refused to write even one word. He opened the diary and closed it, opened it and closed it, and it looked as if it wanted to fly away from his hands. "Tell him I was at the wedding. Tell him." "She was at the wedding of your grandfather and his first wife," I said. "Ask her what it was like," he said. "It was beautiful," she said. "My brother held one of the chuppah poles, I remember. It was a spring day. Zosha was such a pretty girl." "It was so beautiful," I told the hero. "There was white, and flowers, and many children, and the bride in a long dress. Zosha was a beautiful girl, and all of the other men were jealous people." "Ask her if we could see this house," he said, pointing to the photograph. "Could you exhibit us this house?" I asked. "There is nothing," she said. "I already told you. Nothing. It used to be four kilometers distance from here, but everything that still exists from Trachimbrod is in this house." "You say it is four kilometers from here?" "There is no Trachimbrod anymore. It ended fifty years ago." "Take us there," Grandfather said. "There is nothing to see. It is only a field. I could exhibit you any field and it would be the same as exhibiting you Trachimbrod." "We have come to see Trachimbrod," Grandfather said, "and you will take us to Trachimbrod."

She looked at me, and she put her hand on my face. "Tell him I think about it every day. Tell him." "Think about what?" I asked. "Tell him." "She thinks about it every day," I told the hero. "I think about Trachimbrod, and when we were all so young. We used to run in the streets naked, can you believe it? We were just children, yes. That was how it was. Tell him." "They used to run in the streets naked. They were just children." "I remember Safran so well. He kissed me behind the synagogue, which was a thing to get us murdered, you know. I can still remember just how I felt. It was a little like flying. Tell it to him." "She remembers when your grandfather kissed her. She flew a little." "I also remember Rosh Hashanah, when we would go to the river and throw breadcrumbs in it so our sins would float away from us. Tell him." "She remembers the river and breadcrumbs and her sins." "The Brod?" the hero asked. She moved her head to say, Yes, yes. "Tell him that his grandfather and I and all of the children would jump into the Brod when it was so hot, and our parents would sit on the side of the water and watch and play cards. Tell him." I told him. "Everyone had his own family, but it was something like we were all one big family. People would fight, yes, but it was nothing."

She retrieved her hands from me and put them on her knees. "I am so ashamed," she said. "You had to do anything. You could not allow anyone to see your face after." "You should be ashamed," Grandfather said. "Do not be ashamed," I told her. "Ask her how my grandfather escaped." "He would like to know how his grandfather escaped." "She does not know anything," Grandfather said. "She is a fool." "You do not have to utter anything that you do not want to utter," I told her, and she said, "Then I would never utter another word again." "You do not have to do anything that you do not want to do." "Then I would never do anything again." "She is a liar," Grandfather said, and I could not understand what was forcing him to behave this way.

"Could you please leave us to be in solitude," Augustine said to me, "for a few moments." "Let us go outside," I told Grandfather. "No," Augustine said, "him." "Him?" I asked. "Please leave us to be in solitude for a few moments." I looked to Grandfather so that he could give me a beacon of what to do, but I could see that his eyes were impending tears, and that he would not look at me. This was my beacon. "We must go outside," I told the hero. "Why?" "They are going to utter things in secrecy." "What kinds of things?" "We cannot be here."

We walked out and closed the door behind us. I yearned to be on the other side of the door, the side on which such momentous truths were being uttered. Or I yearned to press my ear to the door so that I could at minimum hear. But I knew that my side was on the outside with the hero. Part of me hated this, and part of me was grateful, because once you hear something, you can never return to the time before you heard it. "We can remove the skin from the corn for her," I said, and the hero harmonized. It was approximately four o'clock of the afternoon, and the temperature was commencing to become cold. The wind was making the first noises of night.

"I don't know what to do," the hero said.

"I do not know also."

After that there was a famine of words for a long time. We only removed the skin from corn. I was not concerned about what Augustine was saying. It was Grandfather's talking that I desired to hear. Why could he say things to this woman that he had never before encountered when he could not say things to me? Or perhaps he was not saying anything to her. Or perhaps he was lying. This is what I wanted, for him to present not-truths to her. She did not deserve the truth, not as I deserved the truth. Or we both deserved the truth, and the hero, too. All of us.

"What should we converse about?" I asked, because I knew that it was a common decency for us to speak. "I don't know." "There must be a thing." "Do you want to know anything else about America?" he asked. "I cannot think of anything at this moment." "Do you know about Times Square?" "Yes," I said, "Times Square in Manhattan on 42nd Street and Broadway Avenue." "Do you know about people who sit in front of slot machines all day and waste all of the money they have?" "Yes," I said. "Las Vegas, Nevada. I have read an article about this." "What about skyscrapers?" "Of course. World Trade Center. Empire State Building. Sears Tower." I do not comprehend why, but I was not proud of everything that I knew about America. I was ashamed. "What else?" he said. "Tell me more about your grandmother," I said. "My grandmother?" "Who you spoke of in the car. Your grandmother from Kolki." "You remember." "Yes." "What do you want to know?" "How old is she?" "She's about the age of your grandfather, I suppose, but she looks much older." "What does she look like?" "She's short. She calls herself a shrimp, which is funny. I don't know what color her hair really is, but she dyes it a kind of brown and yellow, sort of like the hairs on this corn. Her eyes are mismatched, one blue and one green. She has terrible varicose veins." "What does it mean varicose veins?" "The veins in her legs, where the blood goes through, they're above the level of her skin and they look kind of weird." "Yes," I said, "Grandfather has these also, because when he worked he would stand for all day, and so this happened to him." "My grandmother got them from the war, because she had to walk across Europe to escape. It was too much for her legs." "She walked across Europe?" "Remember, I told you she left Kolki before the Nazis." "Yes, I remember." He stopped for a moment. I decided to peril everything once again. "Tell me about you and her."

"What do you mean me and her?" "I only want to listen." "I don't know what to say." "Tell me about when you were young, and how it was with her then." He made a laugh. "When I was young?" "Tell me anything." "When I was young," he said, "I used to sit under her dress at family dinners. That's something I remember." "Tell me." "I haven't thought about this in a really long time." I did not utter a thing, so that he would persevere. This was so difficult at times, because there existed so much silence. But I ~~understanded~~ understood that the silence was necessary for him to talk. "I'd run my hands up and down her varicose veins. I don't know why, or how I started doing it. It was just something I did. I was a kid, and kids do things like that, I guess. I remembered that because I mentioned her legs." I refused to utter even one word. "It was like sucking your thumb. I did it, and it felt good, and that was it." Be silent, Alex. You do not have to speak. "I would watch the world through her dresses. I could see everything, but no one could see me. Like a fort, a hiding place under the covers. I was just a kid. Four. Five. I don't know." With my silence, I gave him a space to fill. "I felt safety and peace. You know, real safety and real peace. I felt it." "Safety and peace from what?" "I don't know. Safety and peace from not-safety and not-peace." "This is a nice story." "It's true. I'm not making it up." "Of course. I know that you are faithful." "It's just that sometimes we make things up, just to talk. But this really happened." "I know." "Really." "I believe you." There was a silence. This silence was so heavy, and so long, that I was coerced to speak. "When did you stop hiding under her dress?" "I don't know. Maybe I was five or six. Maybe a bit later. I just got too old for it, I guess. Someone must have told me it was no longer appropriate." "What else do you remember?" "What do you mean?" "About her. About you and her." "Why are you so curious?" "What are you so ashamed?" "I remember those veins of hers, and I remember the smell of my secret hiding place, that's how I used to think of it, I remember, like a secret, and I remember when my grandmother once told me that I'm lucky because I'm funny." "You are very funny, Jonathan." "No. That's the last thing I want to be." "Why? To be funny is a great thing." "No it's not." "Why is this?" "I used to think that humor was the only way to appreciate how wonderful and terrible the world is, to celebrate how big life is. You know what I mean?" "Yes, of course." "But now I think it's the opposite. Humor is a way of shrinking from that wonderful and terrible world." "Inform me more about when you were young, Jonathan." He made more laughing. "Why do you laugh?" He laughed again. "Inform me." "When I was a boy, I would spend Friday nights at my grandmother's house. Not every Friday, but most. On the way in, she would lift me from the ground with one of her wonderful terrifying hugs. And on the way out the next afternoon, I was again taken into the air with her love. I'm laughing because it wasn't until years later that I realized she was weighing me." "Weighing you?" "When she was our age, she was feeding from waste while walking across Europe barefoot. It was important to her—more important than that I had a good time—that I gained weight whenever I visited. I think she wanted the fattest grandchildren in the world." "Tell me more about these Fridays. Tell me about measuring and humor and hiding beneath her dress." "I think I'm done talking." "You must talk." Did you feel sorry for me? Is that why you persevered? "My grandmother and I used to scream words off her back porch at night, when I would stay over. That's something I remember. We screamed the longest words we could think of. 'Phantasmagoria!' I screamed." He laughed. "I remember that one. And then she would scream a Yiddish word I didn't understand. Then I would scream. 'Antediluvian!'" He screamed the word into the street, and this would have been an embarrassment except that there was no one in the street. "And then I would watch the veins in her neck bulge as she screamed some Yiddish word. We were both secretly in love with words, I guess." "And you were both secretly in love with each other." He laughed again. "What were the words that she would scream?" "I don't know. I never knew what they meant. I can still hear her." He screamed a Yiddish word into the street. "Why did you not ask her what the words meant?" "I was afraid." "Of what were you afraid?" "I don't know. I was just too afraid. I knew I wasn't supposed to ask, so I didn't." "Perhaps she desired for you to ask." "No." "Perhaps she needed you to ask, because if you didn't ask, she could not tell you." "No." "Perhaps she was shouting, Ask me! Ask me what I'm shouting!"

We peeled the corn. The silence was a mountain.

"Do you remember all of the concrete in Lvov?" he asked.

"Yes," I said.

"Me too."

More silence. We had nothing to talk about, nothing important. Nothing could have been important enough.

"What do you write in your diary?" "I take notes." "About what?" "For the book I'm working on. Little things that I want to remember." "About Trachimbrod?" "Right." "It is a good book?" "I've only written pieces. I wrote a few pages before I came this summer, a few on the plane to Prague, a few on the train to Lvov, a few last night." "Read to me from it." "It's embarrassing." "It is not like this. It is not embarrassing." "It is." "Not if you recount it for me. I will relish it, I promise you. I am very simple to enchant." "No," he said, so I did what I thought was the OK and even funny thing. I took his diary and opened it. He did not say that I could read it, but nor did he ask for it back. This is what I read:

He told his father that he could care for Mother and Little Igor. It took his saying it to make it true. Finally, he was ready. His father could not believe this thing. What? he asked. What? And Sasha told him again that he would take care of the family, that he would understand if his father had to leave and never return, and that it would not even make him less of a father. He told his father that he would forgive. Oh, his father became so angry, so full of wrath, and he told Sasha that he would kill him, and Sasha told his father that he would kill him, and they moved at each other with violence and his father said, Say it to my face, not to the floor, and Sasha said, You are not my father.

By the time Grandfather and Augustine descended from the house, we had finished a pile of corn, and left the skin as a pile on the other side of the stairs. I had read several pages in his diary. Some scenes were like this. Some were very different. Some happened early in history and some had not even happened yet. I understood what he was doing when he wrote like this. At first it made me angry, but then it made me sad, and then it made me so grateful, and then it made me angry again, and I went through these feelings hundreds of times, stopping on each for only a moment and then moving to the next.

"Thank you," Augustine said, and she was examining the piles, one of corn, one of skins. "That was a very kind thing that you did." "She is going to take us to Trachimbrod," Grandfather said. "We must not squander time. It is becoming late." I told this to the hero. "Tell her thank you for me." "Thank you," I told her. Grandfather said, "She knows."

THE WEDDING RECEPTION WAS SO EXTRAORDINARY!

or

IT ALL GOES DOWNHILL AFTER THE WEDDING, 1941

THERE IS A SENSE in which the bride's family had been preparing their house for her wedding since long before Zosha was born, but it wasn't until my grandfather reluctantly proposed—on both knees rather than one—that the renovations achieved their hysterical pace. The hardwood floors were covered in white canvas, and tables were set in a line stretching from the master bedroom to the kitchen, each feathered with precisely positioned name cards, whose placement had been agonized over for weeks. (Avra cannot sit next to Zosha, but should be near Yoske and Libby, but not if it means seating Libby near Anshel, or Anshel near Avra, or Avra anywhere near the centerpieces, because he's terribly allergic and will die. And by all means keep the Uprighters and Slouchers on opposite sides of the table.) New curtains were bought for the new windows, not because there was anything wrong with the old curtains on the old windows, but because Zosha was to be married, and that called for new curtains and windows. The new mirrors were cleaned spotless, their faux-antique frames meticulously dirtied. The proud parents, Menachem and Tova, saw to it that everything, down to the last and smallest detail, was made extraordinary.

The house was actually two houses, connected at the attic when Menachem's risky trout venture proved so remarkably lucrative. It was the largest house in Trachimbrod, but also the least convenient, as one might have to climb and descend the three flights and pass through twelve rooms in order to get from one room to another. It was divided by function: the bedrooms, children's playroom, and library in one half, the kitchen, dining room, and den in the other. The cellars—one of which housed the impressive wine racks, which, Menachem promised, would one day be filled with impressive wines, the other used as a quiet place for Tova's sewing—were separated by only a brick wall, but were, for all practical purposes, a four-minute walk apart.

The Double House revealed every aspect of its owners' new affluence. A veranda was half completed, jutting like broken glass off the back. Marble newels of idle spiral stairways connected floors to ceilings. The ceilings were raised on the lower floors, rendering the third-floor rooms livable only for children and midgets. Porcelain toilets were installed in the outhouse to replace the seatless brick stools on which everyone else in the shtetl took shits. The perfectly good garden was uprooted and replaced with a gravel walk, lined with azaleas that were cut too short to flower. But Menachem was most proud of the scaffolding: the symbol that things were always changing, always getting a little better. He loved the skeleton of makeshift beams and rafters more and more as construction progressed, loved them more than the house itself, and eventually persuaded the reluctant architect to draw them into the final plans. Workers, too, were drawn into the plans. Not workers, exactly, but local actors paid to look like workers, to walk the planks of the scaffolding, to hammer functionless nails into gratuitous walls, to pull those nails out, to examine blueprints. (The blueprints themselves were drawn into the blueprints, and in those blueprints were blueprints with blueprints with blueprints...) Menachem's problem was this: he had more money than there were things to buy. Menachem's solution was this: rather than buy more things, he would continue to buy the things he already owned, like a man on a desert island who retells and embellishes the only joke he can remember. His dream was for the Double House to be a kind of infinity, always a fraction of itself—suggestive of a bottomless money pit —always approaching but never reaching completion.

Gorgeous! Almost all of it, Tova! Gorgeous!

What a house! And you look like you've lost some weight in your face.

Marvelous! Everyone should be jealous of you.

The wedding—the reception—was the event of 1941, with enough attendees that, should the house have burned down or been swallowed by the earth, Trachimbrod's Jewish population would have completely disappeared. Reminders were sent out a few weeks before the invitation, which was sent out a week before the official arrangement.

DON'T FORGET:

THE WEDDING OF THE DAUGHTER OF

TOVA

AND HER HUSBAND*

JUNE 18, 1941

YOU KNOW THE HOUSE

* Menachem

And no one forgot. Only the various Trachimbroders who weren't, in Tova's estimation, worthy of an invitation were not at the reception, and hence not in the guest book, and hence not included in the last practical census of the shtetl before its destruction, and hence forgotten forever.

As the guests filtered in, unable to help but admire the stylized wainscoting, my grandfather excused himself and went down to the wine-rack cellar to change from his traditional marriage suit into a light cotton blazer, more suited to the wet heat.

Absolutely ravishing, Tova. Look at me, I'm ravished.

It looks like nothing else, ever.

You must have spent a fortune on those lovely centerpieces. Achoo!

So extraordinary!

A fissure of thunder resounded in the distance, and before there was time to close any of the new windows, or even their new curtains, a wind of haunting speed and strength breathed through the house, blowing over the floral centerpieces and tossing the place settings into the air. Pandemonium. The cat screeched, the water boiled, the elderly women held tight to the mesh hats that covered their balding heads. The gust left as soon as it entered, easing the place cards back on the table, not one card in its original place—Libby next to Kerman (who had said his attendance at the reception was dependent on a three-table separation between himself and that horrible cunt), Tova at the very end of the last table (a spot reserved for the fishmonger, whose name no one could remember, and whose invitation had been slid under his door at the last minute out of guilt for the recent loss of his wife to cancer), the Upright

Rabbi next to the outspoken Sloucher Shana P (who was as repulsed and turned on by him as he was by her), and my grandfather landing doggie-style on his bride's younger sister.

Zosha and her mother—red with embarrassment, pale with the sadness of an imperfect wedding—scurried about, trying in vain to reset everything that had been so deliberately arranged, picking up forks and knives, wiping the floors of spilled wine, recentering the centerpieces, replacing the names that had been scattered like a thrown deck of playing cards.

Let's hope it's not true, the father of the bride tried to joke over the shuffle, *that it all goes downhill after the wedding!*

The bride's younger sister was leaning against a shelf of empty wine racks when my grandfather entered the cellar.

Hello, Maya.

Hello, Safran.

I came to change.

Zosha will be so disappointed.

Why?

Because she thinks you're perfect. She told me so. And your wedding day is no time to change.

Not even into something more comfortable?

Your wedding day is no time to be comfortable.

Oh, sister, he said, and kissed her where her cheek became her lips. *A sense of humor to match your beauty.*

She slid her lace panties from under his lapel. *Finally,* pulling him into her arms, *any longer and I would have just burst.*

The Dupe of Chance, 1941–1924

As THEY MADE hurried love beneath the twelve-foot ceiling, which sounded as if it might collapse at any moment under the gunshots of so many heels—in the effort to clean up, nobody even noticed the groom's prolonged absence—my grandfather wondered if he was nothing more than a dupe of chance. Wasn't everything that had happened, from his first kiss to this, his first marital infidelity, the inevitable result of circumstances over which he had no control? How guilty could he be, really, when he never had any real choice? Could he have been with Zosha upstairs? Was that a possibility? Could his penis have been anywhere other than where it then was, and wasn't, and was, and wasn't, and was? Could he have been good?

His teeth. It's the first thing I notice whenever I examine his baby portrait. It's not my dandruff. It's not a smudge of gesso or white paint. Between my grandfather's thin lips, planted like albino pits in those plum-purple gums, is a full set of teeth. The physician must have shrugged, as physicians used to do when they couldn't explain a medical phenomenon, and comforted my great-grandmother with talk of good omens. But then there is the family portrait, painted three months later. Look, this time, at *her* lips, and you will see that she wasn't entirely comforted: my young great-grandmother was frowning.

It was my grandfather's teeth, so admired by his father for the virility they declared, that made his mother's nipples bloody and sore, that forced her to sleep on her side, and eventually made breastfeeding impossible. It was because of those teeth, those wee dinky molars, those cute bicuspids, that my great-grandparents stopped making love and had only one child. It's because of those teeth that my grandfather was pulled prematurely from his mother's well, and never received the nutrients his callow body needed.

His arm. It would be possible to look through all of the photographs many times and still miss what's so unusual. But it occurs too frequently to be explained as the photographer's choice of pose, or mere coincidence. My grandfather's right hand is never holding anything—not a briefcase, not any papers, not even his other hand. (And in the only picture taken of him in America—just two weeks after arriving, and three before he passed away—he holds my baby mother with his left arm.) Without proper calcium, his infant body had to allocate its resources judiciously, and his right arm drew the short straw. He watched helplessly as that red, swollen nipple got smaller and smaller, moving away from him forever. By the time he most needed to reach out for it, he couldn't.

So it was because of his teeth, I imagine, that he got no milk, and it was because he got no milk that his right arm died. It was because his arm died that he never worked in the menacing flour mill, but in the tannery just outside the shtetl, and that he was exempted from the draft that sent his schoolmates off to be killed in hopeless battles against the Nazis. His arm would save him again when it kept him from swimming back to Trachimbrod to save his only love (who died in the river with the rest of them), and again when it kept him from drowning himself. His arm saved him again when it caused Augustine to fall in love with him and save him, and it saved him once again, years later, when it prevented him from boarding the *New Ancestry* to Ellis Island, which would be turned back on orders of U.S. immigration officials, and whose passengers would all eventually perish in the Treblinka death camp.

And it was because of his arm, I'm sure—that flaccid hang of useless muscle—that he had the power to make any woman who crossed his path fall in hopeless love with him, that he had slept with more than forty women in Trachimbrod, and at least twice as many from the neighboring villages, and was now making standing, hurried love with his new bride's younger sister.

The first was the widow Rose W, who lived in one of the old wooden ramblers along the Brod. She thought it was pity that she felt for the crippled boy who had come on behalf of the Sloucher congregation to help clean the house, pity that moved her to bring him a plate of mandelbread and a glass of milk (the very sight of which turned his stomach), pity that moved her to ask how old he was and to tell him her own age, something not even her husband ever knew. It was pity she thought she felt when she removed her layers of mascara to show him the only part of her body that no one, not even her husband, had seen in more than sixty years. And it was pity, or so she thought, when she led him to the bedroom to show him her husband's love letters, sent from a naval ship in the Black Sea during the First World War.

In this one, she said, taking his lifeless hand, *he enclosed pieces of string that he used to measure out his body — his head, thigh, forearm, finger, neck, everything. He wanted me to sleep with them under my pillow. He said that when he came back, we would remeasure his body against the string as proof that he hadn't changed... Oh, I remember this one,* she said, fingering a sheet of yellowed paper, running her hand—aware, or not aware, of what she was doing—up and down my grandfather's dead arm. *In this one he wrote about the house he was going to build for us. He even drew a little picture of it, although he was such a bad artist. It was going to have a small pond, not a pond really, but a little thing, so we could have fish. And there would be a glass window over the bed so we could talk about the constellations before going to sleep ...And here,* she said, guiding his arm under the hem of her skirt, *is the letter in which he pledged his devotion until death.*

She turned off the light.

Is this OK? she asked, navigating his dead hand, leaning back.

Taking an initiative beyond his ten years, my grandfather pulled her to him, removed, with her help, her black blouse, which smelled so strongly of old age he was afraid he would never be able to smell young again, and then her skirt, her stockings (bulging under the pressure of her varicose veins), her panties, and the cotton pad she kept there in case of the now regular unexpecteds. The room was soaked with smells he had never before known together: dust, sweat, dinner, the bathroom after his mother had used it. She removed his shorts and briefs, and eased onto him backward, as if he were a wheelchair. *Oh,* she moaned, *oh.* And because my grandfather didn't know what to do, he did as she did: *Oh,* he moaned, *oh*. And when she moaned *Please*, he also moaned *Please*. And when she fluttered in small, rapid convulsions, he did the same. And when she was silent, he was silent.

Because my grandfather was only ten, it didn't seem unusual that he was able to make love—or have love made to him—for several hours without pause. But as he would later discover, it was not his pre-pubescence that gave him such coital longevity, but another physical shortcoming owing to his early malnutrition: like a wagon with no brakes, he never stopped short. This quirk was met with the profound happiness of his 132 mistresses, and with relative indifference on his part: how, after all, can one miss something one has never known? Besides, he never loved any of his lovers. He never confused anything he felt for love. (Only one would mean anything to him at all, and a problematic birth made real love impossible.) So what should he expect?

His first affair, which lasted every Sunday afternoon for four years—until the widow realized that she had taught his mother piano more than thirty years before, and couldn't bear to show him another letter—was not a love affair at all. My grandfather was an acquiescing passenger. He was happy to give his arm—the only part of his body that Rose paid any real attention to; the act itself was never anything more than a means to get closer to his arm—as a once-a-week gift, to pretend with her that it was not a canopy bed in which they were making love, but a lighthouse out on some windy jetty, that their silhouettes, shot by the powerful lamp deep out into the black waters, could serve as a blessing for the sailors, and summon her husband back to her. He was happy to let his dead arm serve as the missing limb for which the widow longed, for which she reread yellowing letters, and lived outside herself, and outside her life. For which she made love to a ten-year-old. The arm was the arm, and it was the arm—not her husband, or even herself—that she thought about seven years later, on June 18, 1941, as the first German war blasts shook her wooden house to its foundations, and her eyes rolled back in her head to view, before dying, her insides.

UNAWARE OF the nature of his errands, the Sloucher congregation paid my grandfather to visit Rose's house once a week, and came to pay him to perform similar services for widows and feeble ladies around Trachimbrod. His parents never knew the truth, but were relieved by his enthusiasm to make money and spend time with the elderly, both of which had become important personal concerns as they descended into poverty and middle age.

We were beginning to think you had Gypsy blood, his father told him, to which he only smiled, his usual response to his father.

Which means, his mother said—his mother whom he loved more than himself—*that it's good to see you doing something good with your time.* She kissed him on the cheek and mussed his hair, which upset his father, because Safran was now too old for that kind of thing.

Who's my baby? she would ask him when his father was not around.

I am, he would say, loving the question, loving the answer, and loving the kiss that came with the answer to the question. *You don't have to look any farther than me.* As if that were something he truly feared, that she *would* one day look farther. And for this reason, because he wanted her to look to him and never elsewhere, he never told his mother anything that he thought might upset her, that might make her think less of him, or make her jealous.

Likewise, perhaps, he never told a friend of his exploits, or any lover of her predecessor. He was so afraid of being discovered that even in his journal—the only written record I have of his life before he met my grandmother, in a displaced-persons camp after the war—he never mentions them once.

The day he lost his virginity to Rose: *Nothing much happened today. Father received a shipment of twine from Rovno, and yelled at me when I neglected my chores. Mother came to my defense, as usual, but he yelled at me anyway. Thought about lighthouses all night. Strange.*

The day he had sex with his first virgin: *Went to the theater today. Too bored to stay through the first act. Drank eight cups of coffee. I thought I was going to burst. Didn't burst.*

The day he made love from behind for the first time: *I've given much thought to what mother said about watchmakers. She was so persuasive, but I'm not yet sure if I agree. I heard her and father yelling in their bedroom, which kept me awake most of the night, but when I finally did sleep, I slept soundly.*

It's not that he was ashamed, or even that he thought he was doing something wrong, because he knew that what he was doing was right, more right than anything he saw anyone do, and he knew that doing right often means feeling wrong, and if you find yourself feeling wrong, you're probably doing right. But he also knew that there is an inflationary aspect to love, and that should his mother, or Rose, or any of those who loved him find out about each other, they would not be able to help but feel of lesser value. He knew that *I love you* also means *I love you more than anyone loves you, or has loved you, or will love you,* and also, *I love you in a way that no one loves you, or has loved you, or will love you,* and also, *I love you in a way that I love no one else, and never have loved anyone else, and never will love anyone else.* He knew that it is, by love's definition, impossible to love two people. (Alex, this is part of the reason I can't tell my grandmother about Augustine.)

The second was also a widow. Still ten, he was invited by a schoolmate to a play at the shtetl theater, which also served as dance hall and twice-a-year synagogue. His ticket corresponded to a seat that was already taken by Lista P, whom he recognized as the young widow of the first victim of the Double House. She was small, with wisps of thin brown hair hanging out of her tight ponytail. Her pink skirt was conspicuously smooth and clean—too smooth, too clean—as if she had washed and ironed it dozens of times. She was beautiful, it's true, beautiful for the pitiably meticulous care with which she attended to every detail. If one were to say that her husband was immortal, insofar as his cellular energy dissipated into the earth, fed and fertilized the soil, and encouraged new life to grow, then so did her love go on living, diffused among the thousands of daily things to do—such a magnitude of love that even when divided so many ways, it was still enough to sew buttons onto shirts that would never again be worn, gather fallen twigs from the bases of trees, and wash and iron skirts a dozen times between wearings.

I believe . . . , he began, showing her his ticket.

But if you look, Lista said, showing him her own, which clearly indicated the same seat, *it is mine.*

But it's also mine.

She began to mutter about the absurdity of the theater, the mediocrity of its actors, the foolishness of its playwrights, the inherent silliness of drama itself, and how it was no surprise to her that those morons should botch up something so simple as providing one seat for each patron. But then she noticed his arm, and was overcome.

It seems we have only two options, she said, sniffling. *Either I sit on your lap or we get out of here.* As it turned out, they reversed the order and did both.

Do you like coffee? she asked, moving through her immaculate kitchen, touching everything, reorganizing, not looking at him.

Sure.

A lot of younger people don't care for it.

I do, he said, although in truth he'd never had a cup of coffee.

I'm going to move back in with my mother.

Excuse me?

This house was supposed to be for when I was married, but you know what happened.

Yes. I'm sorry.

Would you like some, then? she asked, fingering a cabinet's polished handle.

Sure. If you're going to have some. Don't make some just for me.

I will. If you want some, she said, and picked up a sponge, and put the sponge down.

But not just for me.

I will.

Two years and sixty-eight lovers later, Safran understood that the tears of blood left on Lista's sheets were virginal tears. He remembered the circumstances of the death of her soon to be husband: a scaffolding collapse that took his life the morning of the wedding as he walked to kneel before the Dial, making Lista a widow only in spirit, before the marriage could be consummated, before she could bleed for him.

My grandfather was in love with the smell of women. He carried their scents around on his fingers like rings, and on the end of his tongue like words—unfamiliar combinations of familiar odors. In this way, Lista held a special place in his memory—although she was hardly unique in being a virgin, or a one-episode lover—as being the only partner to inspire him to bathe.

Went to the theater today. Too bored to stay through the first act. Drank eight cups of coffee. I thought I was going to burst. Didn't burst.

The third was not a widow but another chance theater encounter. Again he went on the invitation of a friend—the same one he had deserted for Lista—and again he left without him. This time, Safran was seated between the schoolmate and a young Gypsy girl, whom he recognized as one of the vendors from Lutsk's Sunday bazaar. He couldn't believe her audacity: to show up at a shtetl function, to risk the humiliation of being seen by the unpaid and overzealous usher Rubin B and asked to leave, to be a Gypsy among Jews. It demonstrated a quality he was sure he was lacking, and it stirred something in him.

At first glance, the long braid that hung over her shoulder and spilled onto her lap looked to my grandfather like the serpent she would make dance from one tall woven basket to the next at the Sunday bazaar, and at second glance it looked the same. As the lights went down, he used his left arm to plop the dead one onto the rest between himself and the girl. He made sure that she noticed it—observing with pleasure the transformation of loose pitying lips to tight erotic grin—and when the heavy curtains parted, he was certain he would part her thin skirt that night.

It was March 18, 1791, echoed an authoritative voice from offstage, *when Trachim B's double-axle wagon pinned him against the bottom of the Brod River. The young W twins were the first to see the curious flotsam rising to the surface...*

(The curtain opens to reveal a provincial setting: a babbling brook running from upstage left to downstage right, many trees and fallen leaves, and two girls, twins, approximately six years old, wearing wool britches with yarn ties and blouses with blue-fringed butterfly collars.)

AUTHORITATIVE VOICE

...three empty pockets, postage stamps from faraway places, pins and needles, swatches of crimson fabric, the first and only words of a last will and testament: "To my love I leave everything."

HANNAH

(Deafening wail.)
(CHANA wades into cold water, pulling up above her knees the yarn ties at the ends of her britches, sweeping TRACHIM's rising life-debris to her sides as she wades farther.)

THE DISGRACED USURER YANKEL D

(Kicking up shoreline mud as he hobbles to the girls.) I ask, what are you doing over there, fatuous girls? The water? The water? But lo, there is nothing to see! It is only a liquidy thing. Stay back! Don't be so dumb as I once was. Life is no fair payment for idiocy.

BITZL BITZL R

(Watching the commotion from his paddleboat, which is fastened with twine to one of his traps.) I say, what is going on over there? Bad Yankel, step away from the Rabbi's twin female daughters!

SAFRAN

(Into GYPSY GIRL's ear, under a blanket of muted yellow stage lighting.) Do you like music?

CHANA

(Laughing, splashing at the mass forming like a garden around her.) It's bringing forth the most whimsical objects!

GYPSY GIRL

(In the shadows cast by the two-dimensional trees, very close to SAFRAN*'s ear.)* What did you say?

SAFRAN

(Using his shoulder to push his dead arm onto the GYPSY GIRL*'s lap.)* I was curious as to whether or not you liked music.

SOFIOWKA N

(Coming out from behind a tree.) I have seen everything that happened. I was witness to it all.

GYPSY GIRL

(Squeezing SAFRAN*'s dead arm between her thighs.)* No, I do not like music. *(But what she was really trying to say was this: I like music better than anything in the world, after you.)*

THE DISGRACED USURER YANKEL D

Trachim?

SAFRAN

(With dust descending from the rafters, with lips probing to find GYPSY GIRL*'s caramel ear in the dark.)* You probably don't have time for music. *(But what he was really trying to say was: I'm not at all stupid, you know.)*

SHLOIM W

I ask, I ask, who is Trachim? Some mortal curlicue?
(The playwright smiles in the cheap seats. He tries to gauge the audience's reaction.)

THE DISGRACED USURER YANKEL D

We don't so fully fathom anything yet. Let's not be hasty.

PEANUT GALLERY

(An impossible-to-place whisper.) This is so unbelievable. Not at all like it was.

GYPSY GIRL

(Kneading SAFRAN*'s dead arm between her thighs, tracing the bend of his unfeeling elbow with her finger, pinching it.)* Don't you think it's hot in here?

SHLOIM W

(Quickly undressing himself, revealing a belly larger than most and a back matted with ringlets of thick black hair.) Cover their eyes. *(Not for them. For me. I'm ashamed.)*

SAFRAN

Very hot.

GRIEVING SHANDA

(To SHLOIM, *as he emerges from the water.)* Was he in solitude or with a wife of many years? *(But what she was really trying to say was this: After everything that's happened, I still have hope. If not for myself, then for Trachim.)*

GYPSY GIRL

(Intertwining her fingers with SAFRAN*'s dead ones.)* Can't we leave?

SAFRAN

Please.

SOFIOWKA N

Yes, it was love letters.

GYPSY GIRL

(With anticipation, with wetness between her legs.) Let's leave.

THE UPRIGHT RABBI

And allow life to go on in the face of this death.

SAFRAN

Yes.

(Musicians prepare for climax. Four violins are tuned. A harp is breathed on. The trumpeter, who is really an oboist, cracks his knuckles. The hammers of the

piano know what happens next. The baton, which is really a butter knife, is lifted like a surgical instrument.)

THE DISGRACED USURER YANKEL D
(With hands raised to the heavens, to the men who aim the spotlights.) Perhaps we should begin to harvest the remains.

SAFRAN
Yes.

(Enter music. Beautiful music. Hushed at first. Whispering. No pins are dropped. Only music. Music swelling imperceptibly. Pulling itself out of its grave of silence. The orchestra pit fills with sweat. Expectancy. Enter gentle rumble of timpani. Enter piccolo and viola. Intimations of crescendo. Ascent of adrenaline, even after so many performances. It still feels new. The music is building, blooming.)

AUTHORITATIVE VOICE
(With passion.) The twins covered their eyes with their father's tallis. (CHANA *and* HANNAH *cover eyes with tallis.)* Their father chanted a long and intelligent prayer for the baby and its parents. (UPRIGHT RABBI *looks at his palms, nods his head up and down, gesturing prayer.)* Yankel's face was veiled in the tears of his sobbing. (YANKEL *gestures sobbing.)* Unto us a child was born!

(Blackout. Curtains wed. GYPSY GIRL *spreads her thighs. Applause mingled with hushed chatting. Players prepare stage for the next scene. The music is still building.* GYPSY GIRL *leads* SAFRAN *by his dead right arm out of the theater, through a maze of muddy alleys, past the confectioners' stands by the old cemetery, under the hanging vines of the synagogue's crumbling portico, through the shtetl square — the two separated for a moment by the Dial's final casting of the day — along the Brod's loose bank, down the Jewish/Human fault line, beneath the dangling palm fronds, bravely through the shadows of the crag, across the wooden bridge —)*

GYPSY GIRL
Would you like to see something you've never seen before?

(With an honesty previously unknown to him.) I would. I would.

(— over the black- and blueberry brambles, into a petrified forest that SAFRAN *has never before seen.* GYPSY GIRL *stands* SAFRAN *under the rock canopy of a giant maple, takes his dead arm into hers, allowing the shadows cast by the stone branches to consume her with nostalgia for everything, whispers something in his ear [to which no one other than my grandfather is privileged], eases his dead hand under the hem of her thin skirt, says)* Please *(bends at the knees)*, please *(lowers herself onto his dead index finger)*, yes *(crescendo)*, yes *(puts her caramel hand on the top button of his dress shirt, sways at the waist)*, please *(trumpet flourish, violin flourish, timpani flourish, cymbal flourish)*, yes *(dusk spills across the nightscape, the night sky blots up the darkness like a sponge, heads crane)*, yes *(eyes close)*, please *(lips part)*, yes. *(The conductor drops his baton, his butter knife, his scalpel, his Torah pointer, the universe, blackness.)*

12 December 1997

Dear Jonathan,

Salutations from Ukraine. I just received your letter and read it many times, notwithstanding parts that I read aloud to Little Igor. (Did I tell you that he is reading your novel as I read it? I translate it for him, and I am also your editor.) I will utter no more than that we are both anticipating the remnants. It is a thing that we can think about and converse about. It is also a thing that we can laugh about, which is something we require.

There is so much that I want to inform you, Jonathan, but I cannot fathom the manner. I want to inform you about Little Igor, and how he is such a premium brother, and also about Mother, who is very, very humble, as I remark to you often, but nonetheless a good person, and nonetheless My Mother. Perhaps I did not paint her with the colors that I should have. She is good to me, and never bad to me, and this is how you must see her. I want to inform you about Grandfather, and how he views television for many hours, and how he cannot witness my eyes anymore, but must be attentive to something behind me. I want to inform you about Father, and how I am not being a caricature when I tell you that I would remove him from my life if I was not such a coward. I want to inform you about what it is like to be me, which is a thing that you still do not possess a single whisper of. Perhaps when you read the next division of my story, you will comprehend. It was the most difficult division that I have yet composed, but I am certain not nearly so difficult as what is still to come. I have been putting on a high shelf what I know I must do, which is point a finger at Grandfather pointing at Herschel. You have without doubts observed this.

I have learned many momentous lessons from your writing, Jonathan.

JONATHAN SAFRAN FOER

One lesson is that it does not matter if you are guileless, or delicate, or modest. Just be yourself. I could not believe that your grandfather was such an inferior person, to be carnal with the sister of his wife, and on the day of his wedding, and to be carnal while standing, which is a very inferior arrangement, for reasons you should be aware of. And then he is carnal with the aged woman, who must have had a very slack box, which I will utter no more about. How can you do this to your grandfather, writing about his life in such a manner? Could you write in this manner if he was alive? And if not, what does that signify?

I have a further issue to discuss about your writing. Why do women love your grandfather because of his dead arm? Do they love it because it enables them to feel strong over him? Do they love it because they are commiserating it, and we love the things that we commiserate? Do they love it because it is a momentous symbol of death? I ask because I do not know.

I have only one remark about your remarks about my writing. With regards for how you ordered me to remove the section where you talk about your grandmother, I must tell you that this is not a possibility. I accept if because of my decision you choose not to present me any more currency, or if you command for me to post back the currency you have given me in the previous months. It would be justifying every dollar, I will inform you.

We are being very nomadic with the truth, yes? The both of us? Do you think that this is acceptable when we are writing about things that occurred? If your answer is no, then why do you write about Trachimbrod and your grandfather in the manner that you do, and why do you command me to be untruthful? If your answer is yes, then this creates another question, which is if we are to be such nomads with the truth, why do we not make the story more premium than life? It seems to me that we are making the story even inferior. We often make ourselves appear as though we are foolish people, and we make our voyage, which was an ennobled voyage, appear very normal and second rate. We could give your grandfather two arms, and could make him high-fidelity. We could give Brod what she deserves in the stead of what she gets. We could even find Augustine, Jonathan, and you could thank her, and Grandfather and I could embrace, and it could be perfect and beautiful, and *funny, and usefully sad, as you say. We could even write your grandmother into your story. This is what you desire, yes? Which makes me think that perhaps we could write Grandfather into the story. Perhaps, and I am only uttering this, we could have him save your grandfather. He could be Augustine. August, perhaps. Or just Alex, if that is satisfactory to you. I do not think that there are any limits to how excellent we could make life seem.*

Guilelessly,
Alexander

wHaT we saw wHen we saw TracHImBroD, *or* FaLLInG In Love

"I HAVE NEVER been in one of these," said the woman we continued to think of as Augustine, even though we knew that she was not Augustine. This required Grandfather to laugh in volumes. "What's so funny?" the hero asked. "She has never been in a car." "Really?" "There is nothing to be afraid of," Grandfather said. He opened the front door of the car for her and moved his hand over the seat to show that it was not evil. It seemed like a common decency to relinquish the front seat to her, not only because she was a very old woman who had endured many terrible things, but because it was her first time in a car, and I think it is most awesome to sit in front. The hero later told me that this means to sit shotgun. Augustine sat shotgun. "You will not travel with too much speed?" she asked. "No," Grandfather said as he arranged his belly under the steering wheel. "Tell her that cars are very safe, and she shouldn't be scared." "Cars are safe things," I informed her. "Some even have airbags and crumple zones, although this one does not." I think that she was not primed for the *vrmmmm* sound that the car manufactured, because she screamed with much volume. Grandfather quieted the car. "I cannot," she said.

So what did we do? We drove the car behind Augustine, who walked. (Sammy Davis, Junior, Junior walked next to her, to be her companion, and so that we would not have to smell the bitch's farts in the car.) It was only one kilometer distance, Augustine said, so it would be possible for her to walk, and we would still arrive before it was too dark to see anything. I must say that it seemed very queer to drive behind someone who is walking, especially when the person who is walking is Augustine. She was only able to walk several tens of meters before she would become fatigued and have to make a hiatus. When she hiatused, Grandfather would stop the car, and she would sit shotgun until she was ready to walk in her strange way again.

"You have children?" she asked Grandfather while she gathered her breath. "Of course," he said. "I am his grandson," I said from the back, which made me feel like such a proud person, because I think it was the first occasion I had ever said it in the loud, and I could perceive that it also made Grandfather a proud person. She smiled very much. "I did not know this." "I have two sons and one daughter," Grandfather said. "Sasha is the son of my most aged son." "Sasha," she said, as if she desired to hear what my name sounded like when she uttered it. "And do you have any children?" she asked me. I laughed, because I thought this was a weird question. "He is still young," Grandfather said, and put his hand on my shoulder. I found it very moving to feel his touch, and to remember that hands can show also love. "What are you talking about?" the hero asked. "Does he have any children?" "She wants to know if you have any children," I told the hero, and I knew that this would make him laugh. It did not make him laugh. "I'm twenty," he said. "No," I told her, "in America it is not common to have children." I laughed, because I knew what a fool I sounded like. "Does he have parents?" she asked. "Of course," I said, "but his mother works as a professional, and it is not unusual for his father to prepare dinner." "The world is always changing," she said. "Do you have children?" I asked. Grandfather presented me a look with his face that signified, Shut up. "You do not have to answer that," he told her, "if you do not desire to." "I have a baby girl," she said, and I knew that this was the end of the conversation.

When Augustine walked she did not exclusively walk. She picked up rocks and moved them to the side of the road. If she witnessed a thing of garbage, she would also pick that up and move it to the side of the road. When there was nothing in the road, she would cast a rock several meters in front of her, and then recover it, and then cast it in front of her again. This ate a large quantity of time, and we never moved any faster than very slow. I could perceive that this frustrated Grandfather because he held the steering wheel with much strength, and also because he said, "This frustrates me. It will be dark before we arrive there."

"We are near," she said many times. "Soon. Soon." We pursued her off of the road and into a field. "It is OK?" Grandfather asked. "Who will prevent us?" she said, and with her finger showed us that there was nobody in existence for a long distance. "She says that nobody will prevent us," I told the hero. He had his camera around his neck and was anticipating many photographs. "Nothing grows here anymore," she said. "It does not even belong to anyone. It is only land. Who would want it?" Sammy Davis, Junior, Junior galloped unto the canopy of the car, where she sat like a Mercedes sign.

We persevered to pursue Augustine, and she persevered to cast her rock in front of her and then recover it again. We pursued her, and pursued her more. Like Grandfather, I also was becoming frustrated, or at least confused. "We have been here before," I said. "We have already witnessed this place." "What's going on here?" the hero asked from the back seat. "It's been an hour and we haven't gotten anywhere." "Do you think that we will arrive soon?" Grandfather asked, moving the car next to her. "Soon," she said, "soon." "But it will be dark, yes?" "I am moving as fast as I can."

So we persevered to pursue her. We pursued her through many fields and into many forests, which were difficult for the car. We pursued her over roads made of rock, and also over dirt, and also over grass. I could hear the insects were beginning to announce, and this is how I knew that we would not see Trachimbrod before night. We pursued her past three stairs, which were very broken and appeared to have once introduced houses. She put her hand on the grass in front of each. It became more dark—darker?—as we pursued her on trails, and also where there were no trails. "It is almost impossible to witness her," Grandfather uttered, and even though he is blind, I must confess that it was becoming almost impossible to witness her. It was so dark that sometimes I had to skew my eyes to view her white dress. It was like she was a ghost, moving in and out of our eyes. "Where did she go?" the hero asked. "She is still there," I said. "Look." We went past a miniature ocean—a lake?—and into a small field, which had trees on three sides and spread into a space on the fourth side, where I could hear distant water from. It was now too dark to witness almost anything.

We pursued Augustine to a place near to the middle of the field, and she stopped walking. "Get out," Grandfather said. "Another hiatus." I moved to the back seat so that Augustine could sit shotgun. "What's going on?" the hero asked. "She is making hiatus." "Another?" "She is a very aged woman." "You are tired?" Grandfather asked her. "You have done a lot of walking." "No," she said, "we are here." "She says we are here," I told the hero. "What?" "I informed you that there would be nothing," she said. "It was all destroyed." "What do you mean we're here?" the hero asked. "Tell him it is because it is so dark," Grandfather said to me, "and that we could see more if it was not dark." "It is so dark," I told him. "No," she said, "this is all that you would see. It is always like this, always dark."

I implore myself to paint Trachimbrod, so you will know why we were so overawed. There was nothing. When I utter "nothing" I do not mean there was nothing except for two houses, and some wood on the ground, and pieces of glass, and children's toys, and photographs. When I utter that there was nothing, what I intend is that there was not any of these things, or any other things. "How?" the hero asked. "How?" I asked Augustine. "How could anything have ever existed here?" "It was rapid," she said, and that would have been enough for me. I would not have made another question or said another thing, and I do not think that the hero would have. But Grandfather said, "Tell him." Augustine positioned her hands so far in the pockets of her dress that it looked like she had nothing after her bends. "Tell him what happened," he said. "I do not know everything." "Tell him what you know." It was only then that I understood that "him" was me. "No," she said. "Please," he said. "No," she said. "Please." "It was all very rapid, you must understand. You ran and you could not care about what was behind you or you would stop running." "Tanks?" "One day." "One day?" "Some departed before." "Before they came?" "Yes." "But you did not." "No." "You were lucky to endure." Silence. "No." Silence. "Yes." Silence. We could have stopped it there. We could have viewed Trachimbrod, returned to the car, and followed Augustine back to her house. The hero would have been able to say that he was in Trachimbrod, he could have even said that he met Augustine, and Grandfather and I would have been able to say that we had completed our mission. But Grandfather was not content with this. "Tell him," he said. "Tell him what happened." I was not ashamed and I was not scared. I was not anything. I just desired to know what would occur next. (I do not intend what would occur in Augustine's story, but amid Grandfather and her.) "They made us in lines," she said. "They had lists. They were logical." I translated for the hero as Augustine spoke. "They burned the synagogue." "They burned the synagogue." "That was the first thing they did." "That was first." "Then they made all of the men in lines." You cannot know how it felt to have to hear these things and then repeat them, because when I repeated them, I felt like I was making them new again. "And then?" Grandfather asked. "It was in the middle of the town. There," she said, and she pointed her finger into the darkness. "They unrolled a Torah in front of them. A terrible thing. My father would command us to kiss any book that touched the ground. Cooking books. Books for children. Mysteries. Plays. Novels. Even empty journals. The General went down the line and told each man to spit on the Torah or they would kill his family." "This is not true," Grandfather said. "It is true," Augustine said, and she was not crying, which surprised me very much, but I understand now that she had found places for her melancholy that were behind more masks than only her eyes. "The first man was Yosef, who was the shoemaker. The man with a scar on his face said spit, and he held a gun to Rebecca's head. She was his daughter, and she was a good friend of mine. We used to play cards over there," she said, and pointed into the darkness, "and we told secrets about boys who we were in love with, who we wanted to marry." "Did he spit?" Grandfather asked. "He spit. And then the General said, Step on it." "Did he?" "He did." "He stepped on it," I told the hero. "Then he went to the next person in line, who was Izzy. He taught me drawing in his house, which was there," she said, and pointed her finger into the darkness. "We would remain very late, drawing, laughing. We danced, some nights, to Father's records. He was a friend of mine, and when his wife had the baby, I would care for it like it was my own. Spit, the man with blue eyes said, and he put a gun in the mouth of Izzy's wife, just like this," she said, and put her finger in her mouth. "Did he spit?" Grandfather asked. "He spit." "He spit," I told the hero. "And then the General made him curse the Torah, and this time he put the gun in Izzy's son's mouth." "Did he?" "He did. And then the General made him rip the Torah with his hands." "Did he?" "He did." "And then the General came to my father." It was not too dark for me to see that Grandfather closed his eyes. "Spit, he said." "Did he?" "No," she said, and she said no as if it was any other word from any other story, not having the weight it had in this one. "Spit, the General with blond hair said." "And he did not spit?" She did not say no, but she rotated her head from this to that. "He put it in my mother's mouth, and he said spit or." "He put it in her mother's mouth." "No," the hero said without volume. "I will kill her here and now if you do not spit, the General said, but he would not spit." "And?" Grandfather asked. "And he killed her." I will tell you that what made this story most scary was how rapid it was moving. I do not mean what happened in the story, but how the story was told. I felt that it could not be stopped. "It is not true," Grandfather said, but only to himself. "Then the General put the gun in the mouth of my younger sister, who was four years old. She was crying very much. I remember that. Spit, he said, spit or." "Did he?" Grandfather asked. "No," she said. "He did not spit," I told the hero. "Why didn't he spit?" "And the General shot my sister. I could not look at her, but I remember the sound of when she hit the ground. I hear that sound when things hit the ground still. Anything." If I could, I would make it so nothing ever hit the ground again. "I don't want to hear any more," the hero said, so it was at this point that I ceased translating. (Jonathan, if you still do not want to know the rest, do not read this. But if you do persevere, do not do so for curiosity. That is not a good enough reason.) "They tore the dress of my older sister. She was pregnant and had a big belly. Her husband stood at the end of the line. They had made a house here." "Where?" I asked. "Where we are standing. We are in the bedroom." "How can you perceive this?" "She was very cold, I remember, even though it was the summer. They pulled down her panties, and one of the men put the end of the gun in her place, and the others laughed so hard, I remember the laughing always. Spit, the General said to my father, spit or no more baby." "Did he?" Grandfather asked. "No," she said. "He turned his head, and they shot my sister in her place." "Why would he not spit?" I asked. "But my sister did not die. So they held the gun in her mouth while she was on the ground crying and screaming, and with her hands on her place, which was making so much blood. Spit, the General said, or we will not shoot her. Please, my father said, not like this. Spit, he said, or we will let her lie here in this pain and die across time." "Did he?" "No. He did not spit." "And?" "And they did not shoot her." "Why?" I asked. "Why did he not spit? He was so religious?" "No," she said, "he did not believe in God." "He was a fool," Grandfather said. "You are wrong," she said. "You are wrong," Grandfather said. "You are wrong," she said. "And then?" I asked, and I must confess that I felt shameful about inquiring. "He put the gun against my father's head. Spit, the General said, and we will kill you." "And?" Grandfather asked. "And he spit." The hero was several meters distant, placing dirt in a plastic bag, which is called a Ziploc. After, he told me that this was for his grandmother, should he ever inform her of his voyage. "What about you?" Grandfather asked. "Where were you?" "I was there." "Where? How did you escape?" "My sister, I told you, was not dead. They left her there on the ground after they shot her in her place. She started to crawl away. She could not use her legs, but she pulled herself with her hands and arms. She left a line of blood behind her, and was afraid that they would find her with this." "Did they kill her?" Grandfather asked. "No. They stood and laughed while she crawled away. I remember exactly what the laughing sounded like. It was like"—she laughed into the darkness—"HA HA HA HA HA HA HA HA HA HA HA. All of the Gentiles were watching from their windows, and she called to each, Help me, please help me, I am dying." "Did they?" Grandfather asked. "No. They all turned away their faces and hid. I cannot blame them." "Why not?" I asked. "Because," Grandfather said, answering for Augustine, "if they had helped, they would have been killed, and so would their families." "I would still blame them," I said. "Can you forgive them?" Grandfather asked Augustine. She closed her eyes to say, No, I cannot forgive them. "I would desire someone to help me," I said. "But," Grandfather said, "you would not help somebody if it signified that you would be murdered and your family would be murdered." (I thought about this for many moments, and I understood that he was correct. I only had to think about Little Igor to be certain that I would also have turned away and hid my face.) It was so obscure now, because it was late, and because there were no artificial lights for many kilometers, that we could not see one another, but only hear the voices. "You would forgive them?" I asked. "Yes," Grandfather said. "Yes. I would try to." "You can only say that because you cannot imagine what it is like," Augustine said. "I can." "It is not a thing that you can imagine. It only is. After that, there can be no imagining."

"It is so dark," I said, which sounded queer, but sometimes it is better to say something queer than not to say anything. "Yes," Augustine said. "It is so dark," I told the hero, who had returned with his bags of dirt. "It is," he said, "very dark. I'm not used to being so far from artificial lights." "This is true," I said. "What happened to her?" Grandfather asked. "She escaped, yes?" "Yes." "Someone saved her?" "No. She knocked on one hundred doors, and not one of them opened. She pulled herself into the forest where she became asleep from spilling blood. She woke up that night, and the blood had dried, and even though she felt like she was dead, it was only the baby that was dead. The baby accepted the bullet and saved its mother. A miracle." It was now happening too rapidly for me to understand. I wanted to understand it completely, but it would have required a year for each word. "She was able to walk very slowly. So she went back to Trachimbrod, following the line of her blood." "Why did she go back?" "Because she was young and very stupid." (Is this why we went back, Jonathan?) "She was afraid of becoming killed, yes?" "She was not afraid of this at all." "And what occurred?" "It was very dark, and all of the neighbors were sleeping. The Germans were already at Kolki, so she was not afraid of them. Although she would not have been afraid even if. She went through the Jewish houses with silence, and gathered everything, all of the books, and clothing, and everything." "Why?" "So that they would not take it." "The Nazis?" "No," she said, "the neighbors." "No," Grandfather said. "Yes," Augustine said. "No." "Yes." "No." "She went to the bodies, which were in a hole in front of the synagogue, and removed the gold fillings, and cut the hairs as much as she could, even her own mother's, even her husband's, even her own." "Why? How?" "Then?" "She hid these things in the forest so that she could find them when she returned, and then she went forth."

"Where?" "Places." "Where?" "Russia. Other places." "Then?" "Then she returned." "Why?" "To gather the things she had hidden, and to discover what remained. Everyone who went back was certain that she would discover her house and her friends and even the relatives that she saw killed. It is said that the Messiah will come at the end of the world." "But it was not the end of the world," Grandfather said. "It was. He just did not come." "Why did he not come?" "This was the lesson we learned from everything that happened—there is no God. It took all of the hidden faces for Him to prove this to us." "What if it was a challenge of your faith?" I said. "I could not believe in a God that would challenge faith like this." "What if it was not in His power?" "I could not believe in a God that could not stop what happened." "What if it was man and not God that did all of this?" "I do not believe in man, either."

"What did she discover when she returned the second time?" Grandfather asked. "This," she said, and moved her finger over the mural of darkness. "Nothing. It has not altered at all since she returned. They took everything that the Germans left, and then they went to other shtetls." "Did she go forth when she saw this?" I asked. "No, she remained. She discovered the house most proximal to Trachimbrod, all of the ones that weren't destroyed were empty, and she promised herself to live there until she died. She secured all of the things that she had hidden, and she brought them to her house. It was her punishment." "For what?" "For surviving," she said.

Before we departed, Augustine guided us to the monument for Trachimbrod. It was a piece of stone, approximately of the size of the hero, placed in the middle of the field, so much in the middle that it was very impossible to find at night. The stone said in Russian, Ukrainian, Hebrew, Polish, Yiddish, English, and German:

THIS MONUMENT STANDS IN MEMORY

OF THE 1,204 TRACHIMBRODERS

KILLED AT THE HANDS OF GERMAN FASCISM

ON MARCH 18, 1942.

Dedicated March 18, 1992.
Yitzhak Shamir, Prime Minister of the State of Israel

I stood with the hero in front of this monument for many minutes while Augustine and Grandfather walked off into the darkness. We did not speak. It would have been a common indecency to speak. I looked at him once while he was writing the monument's information in his diary, and I could perceive that he looked at me once while I was viewing it. He roosted in the grass, and I roosted next to him. We roosted for several moments, and then we both laid on our backs, and the grass was like a bed. Because it was so dark, we could see many of the stars. It was as if we were under a large umbrella, or under a dress. (I am not only writing this for you, Jonathan. This is truly what it was like for me.) We talked for many minutes, about many things, but in truth I was not listening to him, and he was not listening to me, and I was not listening to myself, and he was not listening to himself. We were on the grass, under the stars, and that is what we were doing.

Finally, Grandfather and Augustine returned.

It captured us only 50 percent of the time to travel back that it captured us to travel there. I do not know why this was, but I have a notion. Augustine did not invite us into her house when we returned. "It is so late," she said. "You must be fatigued," Grandfather said. She smiled halfly. "I am not so good at making sleep." "Ask her about Augustine," the hero said. "And Augustine, the woman in the photograph, do you know anything of her or how we could find her?" "No," she said, and she looked only at me when she said this. "I know that his grandfather escaped, because I saw him once, maybe a year later, maybe two." She gave me a moment to translate. "He returned to Trachimbrod to see if the Messiah had come. We ate a meal in my house. I cooked him the little things that I had, and I gave him a bath. We were trying to make ourselves clean. He had experienced very much, I could see, but we knew not to ask each other anything." "Ask her what they talked about." "He wants to know what you talked about." "Nothing, in truth. Featherweight things. We talked about Shakespeare, I remember, a play we had both read. They had them in Yiddish, you know, and he once gave me one of them to read. I am sure I still have it here. I could find it and give it to you." "And what happened then?" I asked. "We had a fight about Ophelia. A very bad fight. He made me cry, and I made him cry. We did not talk about anything. We were too afraid." "Had he met my grandmother yet?" "Had he met his second wife yet?" "I do not know. He did not mention it once, and I would think that he would have mentioned it. But maybe not. It was such a difficult time with talking. You were always afraid of saying the wrong thing, and usually it felt befitting not to say anything at all." "Ask her for how long he stayed in Trachimbrod." "He wants to know how long his grandfather stayed in Trachimbrod." "Only for the afternoon. Lunch and a bath and a fight," she said, "and I think that was longer than he desired. He only needed to see if the Messiah had come." "What did he look like?" "He wants to know what his grandfather looked like." She smiled and put her hands in the pockets of her dress. "He had a rough face and thick brown hairs. Tell him." "He had a rough face and thick brown hairs." "He was not very tall. Maybe as tall like you. Tell him." "He was not very tall. Maybe as tall like you." "So much had been taken from him. I saw him once and he was a boy, and in two years he had become an old man." I told this to the hero and then asked, "Does he appear like his grandfather?" "Before everything, yes. But Safran changed so much. Tell him that he should never change like that." "She says he looked like you once, but then he changed. She says that you should never change." "Ask her if there are any other survivors in the area." "He wants to know if there are any Jews in the remnants." "No," Augustine said. "There is a Jew in Kivertsy who brings me food sometimes. He says that he knew my brother from business in Lutsk, but I did not have a brother. There is another Jew from Sokeretchy who builds fires for me in the winter. It is so difficult in the winter for me, because I am an old woman, and I cannot cut wood anymore." I told this to the hero. "Ask her if she thinks they might know about Augustine." "Would they know anything about Augustine?" "No," she said. "They are so old. They do not remember anything. I know that a few Jews survived from Trachimbrod, but I do not know where they are. People moved so much. I knew a man from Kolki who escaped and never said another word. It was like his lips were sewn shut with a needle and string. Just like that." I told this to the hero. "Will you come back with us?" Grandfather asked. "We will take care of you, and make fires in the winter." "No," Augustine said. "Come with us," he said. "You cannot live like this." "I know," she said, "but." "But you." "No." "Then." "No." "Could." "Cannot." Silence. "Remain a moment," she said. "I would like to present him something." It then materialized to me that just as we did not know her name, also she did not know the name of Grandfather, or the hero. Only my name. "She is going inside to retrieve a thing for you," I told the hero. "She does not know what is good for her," Grandfather said. "She did not survive in order to be like this. If she has submitted, she should kill herself." "Perhaps she is happy on occasions," I said. "We do not know. I think that she was happy today." "She does not desire happiness," Grandfather said. "The only way she can live is if she is melancholy. She wants us to feel remorseful for her. She wants us to grieve her, not the others."

Augustine returned out of her house with a box marked IN CASE in blue pencil. "Here," she said to the hero. "She desires you to have this," I told him. "I can't," he said. "He says he cannot." "He must." "She says that you must." "I did not understand why Rivka hid her wedding ring in the jar, and why she said to me, Just in case. Just in case and then what? What?" "Just in case she was killed," I said. "Yes, and then what? Why should the ring be any different?" "I do not know," I said. "Ask him," she said. "She wants to know why her friend saved her wedding ring when she thought that she would be killed." "So there would be proof that she existed," the hero said. "What?" "Evidence. Documentation. Testimony." I told this to Augustine. "But a ring is not needed for this. People can remember without the ring. And when those people forget, or die, then no one will know about the ring." I told this to the hero. "But the ring could be a reminder," he said. "Every time you see it, you think of her." I told Augustine what the hero said. "No," she said. "I think it was in case of this. In case someone should come searching one day." I could not perceive if she was speaking to me or to the hero. "So that we would have something to find," I said. "No," she said. "The ring does not exist for you. You exist for the ring. The ring is not in case of you. You are in case of the ring." She excavated the pocket of her dress and removed a ring. She attempted to put it on the hero's finger, but it did not harmonize, so she attempted to put it on his most petite finger, but it still did not harmonize. "She had small hands," the hero said. "She had small hands," I told Augustine. "Yes," she said, "so small." She again attempted to put the ring on the hero's little finger, and she applied very rigidly, and I could perceive that this made the hero with many kinds of pain, although he did not exhibit even one of them. "It will not harmonize," she said, and when she removed the ring I could see that the ring had made a cut around the hero's most petite finger.

"We will go forth," Grandfather said. "It is time to depart." I told this to the hero. "Tell her thank you once more." "He says thank you," I said. "And I also thank you." Now she was crying again. She cried when we came, and she cried when we departed, but she never cried while we were there. "May I ask a question?" I asked. "Of course," she said. "I am Sasha, as you know, and he is Jonathan, and the bitch is Sammy Davis, Junior, Junior, and he, Grandfather, is Alex. Who are you?" She was silent for a moment. "Lista," she said. And then she said, "May I ask you a question?" "Of course." "Is the war over?" "I do not understand." "I am," she uttered, or began to utter, but then Grandfather performed something that I was not anticipating. He secured Augustine's hand into his and gave her a kiss on her lips. She rotated away from us, toward the house. "I must go in and care for my baby," she said. "It is missing me."

STILL EMPLOYED by the Sloucher congregation, which had become something of an unknowing escort service for the widows and elderly, my grandfather made house calls several times a week, and was able to save up enough money to begin thinking about a family of his own, or for his family to begin thinking about a family of his own.

It's so good to see your work ethic, his father told him one afternoon before he left for the widow Golda R's small brick house by the Upright Synagogue. *You're not the lazy Gypsy boy we thought you were.*

We are very proud of you, his mother said, but did not, as he had hoped, follow it with a kiss. *It's because of Father,* he thought. *If he weren't here, she would have kissed me.*

His father came close to him, patted his shoulder, said, without knowing what he was saying, *Keep it up.*

Golda covered all of the mirrors before she made love to him.

Leah H, twice widowed, to whom he would return three times a week (even after his marriage), asked nothing more than his seriousness when handling her aged body: that he should never laugh at her dropped breasts or balding genitalia, that he should be earnest with the varicose veins of her calves, that he should never shrink from her smell, which she knew was like rot on the vine.

Rina S, widow of the Wisp Kazwel L, the only Wisp of Ardisht able to kick the habit and descend from the rooftops of Rovno to a life on the ground—a victim, like the Dial, of the flour mill's disk saw—bit into Safran's dead arm while they made love, so she could be sure he wasn't feeling anything.

Elena N, widow of the undertaker Chaim N, had seen death pass through her cellar doors a thousand times, but never could have imagined the depth of the grief that she would live with after the chicken bone went sideways and stuck. She asked him to make love to her under her bed, in a shallow subnuptial grave, to take away a bit of the pain, to make things a little easier. Safran, my grandfather, my mother's father, whom I never met, obliged them all.

But before the portrait is painted too flatteringly, it should be mentioned that widows comprised only half of my young grandfather's lovers. He lived a double life: lover of not only grievers, but women untouched by grief's damp hand, those closer to their first death than their second. There were some fifty-two virgins, to whom he made love in each of the positions that he had studied from a dirty deck of cards, loaned to him by the friend whom he kept leaving at the theater: sixty-nining the one-eyed jack Tali M, with tight pigtails and folded-yarmulke eye patch; taking from behind the two of hearts Brandil W, who had only one very weak heart, which made her hobble and wear thick spectacles, and who died before the war—too early, and just early enough; spoons with the queen of diamonds Mella S, all breasts and no backside, the only daughter of the wealthiest family in Kolki (who, they say, would never use silverware more than once); mounted by the ace of spades Trema O, most diligent in the fields, whose shrieks, he was sure, would give them away. They loved him and he fucked them—ten, jack, queen, king, ace —a most straight and royal flush. And so he had two working hands: one with five fingers and one with fifty-two young girls who couldn't, and wouldn't, say no.

And, of course, he had a life above his waist as well. He went to school and studied with the other boys his age. He was quite good at arithmetic, and his teacher, the young Sloucher Yakem E, had suggested to my great-grandparents that they send Safran to a school for gifted children in Lutsk. But nothing could have bored my grandfather more than his studies. *Books are for those without real lives*, he thought. *And they are no real replacement.* The school he attended was a small one—four teachers and forty students. Each day was divided between religious studies, taught by the Fair-to-Middling Rabbi and one of his Upright congregants, and secular, or useful, studies, taught by three—sometimes two, sometimes four—Slouchers.

Every schoolboy learned the history of Trachimbrod from a book originally written by the Venerable Rabbi—*AND IF WE ARE TO STRIVE FOR A BETTER FUTURE, MUSTN'T WE BE FAMILIAR AND RECONCILED WITH OUR PAST?*—and revised regularly by a committee of Uprighters and Slouchers. *The Book of Antecedents* began as a record of major events: battles and treaties, famines, seismic occurrences, the beginnings and ends of political regimes. But it wasn't long before lesser events were included and described at great length—festivals, important marriages and deaths, records of construction in the shtetl (there was no destruction then)—and the rather small book had to be replaced with a three-volume set. Soon, upon the demand of the readership—which was everyone, Uprighter and Sloucher alike—*The Book of Antecedents* included a biennial census, with every name of every citizen and a brief chronicle of his or her life (women were included after the synagogue split), summaries of even less notable events, and commentaries on what the Venerable Rabbi had called *LIFE, AND THE LIFE OF LIFE*, which included definitions, parables, various rules and regulations for righteous living, and cute, if meaningless, sayings. The later editions, now taking up an entire shelf, became yet more detailed, as citizens contributed family records, portraits, important documents, and personal journals, until any schoolboy could easily find out what his grandfather ate for breakfast on a given Thursday fifty years before, or what his great-aunt did when the rain fell without lull for five months. *The Book of Antecedents*, once updated yearly, was now continually updated, and when there was nothing to report, the full-time committee would report its reporting, just to keep the book moving, expanding, becoming more like life: *We are writing… We are writing… We are writing…*

Even the most delinquent students read *The Book of Antecedents* without skipping a word, for they knew that they too would one day inhabit its pages, that if they could only get hold of a future edition, they would be able to read of their mistakes (and perhaps avoid them), and the mistakes of their children (and ensure that they would never happen), and the outcome of future wars (and prepare for the death of loved ones).

And I'm sure that my grandfather was no exception. He, too, must have skipped from volume to volume, page to page, searching…

YANKEL D'S SHAMEFUL BEAD

The result of certain shameful activities, the disgraced usurer Yankel D's trial took place in the year 1741 before the High Upright Court. Said usurer, after being found guilty of having committed said shameful deeds in question, was obligated by shtetl proclamation to wear the incriminating abacus bead on a white string around his neck. Let the record show that he wore it even when no one was looking, even to sleep.

TRACHIMDAY, 1796

A fly of particular pestiferousness stung on its tuches the horse that pulled the Rovno Trachimday float, causing the touchy mare to buck and toss its fieldworker effigy into the Brod. The parade of floats was delayed for some thirty minutes while strong men recovered the soggy effigy. The culpable fly was caught in the net of an unidentified schoolboy. The boy raised his hand to smash it, knowing that an example must be made, but as his fist began its descent, the fly twitched its wing without flight. The boy, the sensitive boy, was overcome by the fragility of life and released the fly. The fly, also overcome, died of gratefulness. An example was made.

UNHEALTHY BABIES

(*See* GOD)

WHEN THE RAIN FELL WITHOUT LULL FOR FIVE MONTHS

This worst of all rain spells occurred in the last two months of 1914 and first three of 1915. Cups left on sills quickly overflowed. Flowers bloomed and then drowned. Holes were cut into the ceilings above bathtubs...It should be noted that the rain without lull coincided with the period of Russian occupation,* and that no matter how much water came down, there were those who still claimed to be thirsty. (*See* GITTLE K, YAKOV L.)

*Upon hearing that it was a Jew who invented the love poem, the unrequited magistrate Rufkin S, may his name be lost between cushions, rained all fire and broken glass upon our simple shtetl. (It was not the Jew, of course, who invented the love poem, but the other way around.)

THE FLOUR MILL

It so happened that in the eleventh year of a long-past century, the Chosen People (us) were sent forth from Egypt under the guidance of our then wise leader, Moses. There was no time for bread to rise in the haste of escape, and the Lord our God, may His name inspire buoyant thoughts, who, in seeking perfection with his every creation, would not want an imperfect bread, said unto his people (us, not them): *MAKE NOT ANY BREAD THAT WILL BE AT ALL CRUNCHY, BLAND, BAD TASTING, OR THE CAUSE OF HOPELESS CONSTIPATION.* But the Chosen People were very hungry, and we took our chances with some good yeast. What baked on our backs was less than perfect, indeed bland, crunchy, bad tasting, and the cause of many a good poop withheld, and God, may His name be always on our unchapped lips, was made very angry. It is because of this sin of our ancestors that one member of our shtetl has been killed in the flour mill every year since its founding in 1713. (For a list of those who have perished in the mill, *see* APPENDIX G: UNTIMELY DEATHS.)

THE EXISTENCE OF GENTILES

(*See* GOD)

THE ENTIRETY OF THE WORLD AS WE DO AND DON'T KNOW IT

(*See* GOD)

JEWS HAVE SIX SENSES

Touch, taste, sight, smell, hearing...memory. While Gentiles experience and process the world through the traditional senses, and use memory only as a second-order means of interpreting events, for Jews memory is no less primary than the prick of a pin, or its silver glimmer, or the taste of the blood it pulls from the finger. The Jew is pricked by a pin and remembers other pins. It is only by tracing the pinprick back to other pinpricks—when his mother tried to fix his sleeve while his arm was still in it, when his grandfather's fingers fell asleep from stroking his great-grandfather's damp forehead, when Abraham tested the knife point to be sure Isaac would feel no pain — that the Jew is able to know why it hurts.

When a Jew encounters a pin, he asks: *What does it remember like?*

THE PROBLEM OF EVIL: WHY UNCONDITIONALLY BAD THINGS HAPPEN TO UNCONDITIONALLY GOOD PEOPLE
They never do.

THE TIME OF DYED HANDS
Occurring shortly after the mistaken suicides, the time of dyed hands began when the baker of rolls Herzog J observed that those rolls that were not watched with a cautious eye would sometimes disappear. He repeated this observation numerous times, placing his rolls about his bakery, even marking their placement with a coal pencil, and each time he would turn quickly away and steal a glance back, only the markings would remain.

All this stealing, he said.

At that point in our history, the Eminent Rabbi Fagel F (*see also* APPENDIX B: LISTING OF UPRIGHT RABBIS) was chief executor of legal regulation. So as to conduct a fair investigation, he saw to it that everyone in the shtetl was treated like a suspect, guilty until proven otherwise. *WE WILL DYE THE HANDS OF EACH CITIZEN WITH A DIFFERENT COLOR*, he said, *AND WILL THIS WAY DISCOVER WHO HAS BEEN PUTTING THEIRS BEHIND HERZOG'S COUNTER.*

Lippa R's were dyed blood red. Pelsa G's the light green of her eyes. Mica P's a subtle purple, like the sliver of sky above the Radziwell Forest's tree line when the sun set for the third Shabbos of that November. No hands or hues were exempt. To be fair, even Herzog J's were dyed, the pink of a particular *Troides helena* butterfly that happened to have died on the desk of Dickle D, the chemist who invented the chemical that couldn't be washed off, but would leave smears on whatever the dyed hands touched.

As it turned out, a simple mouse, may his memory live close to a stinky tuches, had been sneaking away with the rolls, and no colors ever appeared behind the counter.

But they appeared everywhere else.

Shlomo V found silver between the thighs of his wife, Chebra, may her behavior be unique in this and every other world, and said nothing about it until he'd painted her breasts green with his hands and then covered those breasts in white semen. He pulled her naked through the gray moonlit streets, from house to house, bruising his knuckles black-blue on the doors. He forced her to watch as he cut off the testicles of Samuel R, who, with raised silver fingers, pleaded for mercy and cried, ambiguously, *There has been a mistake.* Colors everywhere. The Eminent Rabbi Fagel F's indigo fingerprints on the pages of more than one ultrasecular periodical. The cold-lip blue of the grieving widow Shifrah K across her husband's gravestone in the shtetl cemetery, like the rubbings children do. Everyone was quick to accuse Irwin P of running his brown hands up and down the Dial. *He's so selfish!* they said. *He wants everything for himself!* But it was *their* hands, all of their hands, a compressed rainbow of every citizen in the shtetl who had prayed for handsome sons, a few more years of life, protection from lightning, love.

The shtetl was painted with the doings of its citizens, and since every color was used — except for that of the counter, of course — it was impossible to tell what had been touched by human hands and what was as it was because it was as it was. It was rumored that Getzel G had secretly played every fiddler's fiddle — even though he didn't play the fiddle! — for the strings were the color of his fingers. People whispered that Gesha R must have become an acrobat — how else could the Jewish/Human fault line have become as yellow as her palms? And when the blush of a schoolgirl's cheeks was mistaken for the crimson of a holy man's fingers, it was the schoolgirl who was called *hussy, tramp, slut.*

THE PROBLEM OF GOOD: WHY UNCONDITIONALLY GOOD THINGS HAPPEN TO UNCONDITIONALLY BAD PEOPLE
(*See* GOD)

Cunnilingus and the Menstruating Woman

The burning bush must not be consumed. (For a complete listing of rules and regulations concerning you know what, *see* APPENDIX F-ING.)

The Novel, When Everyone Was Convinced He Had One in Him

The novel is that art form that burns most easily. It so happened that in the middle of the nineteenth century, all the citizens of our shtetl —every man, woman, and child—was convinced he had at least one novel in him. This period was likely the result of the traveling Gypsy salesman who brought a wagonload of books to the shtetl square on the third Sunday of every other month, advertising them as *Worthy would-be worlds of words, whorls of working wonder.* What else could come to the lips of a Chosen People but *I can do that?*

More than seven hundred novels were written between 1850 and 1853. One began: *How long it's been since I last thought of those windswept mornings.* Another: *They say everyone remembers her first time, but I don't.* Another: *Murder is an ugly deed, to be sure, but the murder of a brother is truly the most ghastly crime known to man.*

There were 272 thinly veiled memoirs, 66 crime novels, 97 stories of war. A man killed his brother in 107 of the novels. In all but 89 an infidelity was committed. Couples in love wondered what the future would hold in 29; 68 ended with a kiss; all but 35 used the word "shame." Those who couldn't read and write made visual novels: collages, etchings, pencil drawings, watercolors. A special room was added to the Yankel and Brod Library for the Trachimbrod novels, although only a handful were read five years after their composition.

Once, almost a century later, a young boy went browsing the aisles.

I'm looking for a book, he told the librarian, who had cared for the Trachimbrod novels since she was a girl, and was the only citizen to have read them all. *My great-grandfather wrote it.*

What was his name? the librarian asked.

Safranbrod, but I think he wrote it under a pseudonym.

What was the name of his book?

*I can't remember the name. He used to talk about it all the time. He'd
tell me stories from it to put me to sleep.*

What's it about? she asked.

It's about love.

She laughed. *They're all about love.*

ART

Art is that thing having to do only with itself—the product of a successful attempt to make a work of art. Unfortunately, there are no
examples of art, nor good reasons to think that it will ever exist. (Everything that has been made has been made with a purpose, everything with an end that exists outside that thing, i.e., *I want to sell this*,
or *I want this to make me famous and loved*, or *I want this to make me
whole*, or worse, *I want this to make others whole*.) And yet we continue
to write, paint, sculpt, and compose. Is this foolish of us?

IFICE

Ifice is that thing with purpose, created for function's sake, and having to do with the world. Everything is, in some way, an example of
ifice.

IFACT

An ifact is a past-tensed fact. For example, many believe that after
the destruction of the first Temple, God's existence became an ifact.

ARTIFICE

Artifice is that thing that was art in its conception and ifice in its execution. Look around. Examples are everywhere.

ARTIFACT

An artifact is the product of a successful attempt to make a purpose-
less, useless, beautiful thing out of a past-tensed fact. It can never be
art, and it can never be fact. Jews are artifacts of Eden.

Music is beautiful. Since the beginning of time, we (the Jews) have been looking for a new way of speaking. We often blame our treatment throughout history on terrible misunderstandings. (Words never mean what we want them to mean.) If we communicated with something like music, we would never be misunderstood, because there is nothing in music to understand. This was the origin of Torah chanting and, in all likelihood, Yiddish—the most onomatopoeic of all languages. It is also the reason that the elderly among us, particularly those who survived a pogrom, hum so often, indeed seem unable to stop humming, seem dead set on preventing any silence or linguistic meaning in. But until we find this new way of speaking, until we can find a nonapproximate vocabulary, nonsense words are the best thing we've got. Ifactifice is one such word.

THE FIRST RAPE OF BROD D

The first rape of Brod D occurred amid the celebrations following the thirteenth Trachimday festival, March 18, 1804. Brod was walking home from the blue-flowered float—on which she had stood in such austere beauty for so many hours on end, waving her mermaid's tail only when appropriate, throwing deep into the river of her name those heavy sacks only when the Rabbi gave her the necessary nod—when she was approached by the mad squire Sofiowka N, whose name our shtetl now uses for maps and Mormon census records.

I have seen everything, he said. *I watched the parade, don't you know, from so high, high, high above the commoners and their common festivities, in which, I must confess, of course I would have liked to partake some bit. I saw you on our float, and oh, you were so uncommon. You were, in the face of such fakery, so natural.*

Thank you, she said, and proceeded on, taking to heart Yankel's warning that Sofiowka could talk your ear off if you gave him a chance.

But where are you going? That's not all, he said, grabbing her skinny arm. *Didn't your father teach you to listen when you're being talked at, or to, or under, or around, or even in?*

I would like to go home now, Sofiowka. I promised my father that we would eat pineapple together, and I'm going to be late.

No you didn't, he said, turning Brod to face him. *Now you're lying to me.*

But I did. We agreed that after the parade I would come home and eat pineapple with him.

But you said you promised your father, and Brod, maybe you're using that term loosely, maybe you don't even know what it means, but if you're going to stand here and tell me you made a promise to your father, then I am going to stand here and call you a liar.

You're not making any sense. Brod laughed nervously and again started walking to her house. He followed close behind, stepping on the end of her tail.

Who, I wonder, is not making any sense, Brod?

He stopped her again, and turned her to face him.

My father named me after the river because —

There you go again, he said, moving his fingers up from her shoulder to the base of her hair and into her hair, pushing off the blue Float Queen tiara. *Lying is no good way for a little girl to be.*

I want to go home now, Sofiowka.

Then go.

But I can't.

Why not?

Because you're holding my hair.

Oh, you're quite right. I am. I hadn't even noticed. This is your hair, isn't it? And I am holding it, aren't I, thereby preventing you from going home, or anywhere else. You could shout, I suppose, but what would that accomplish? Everyone is doing their own shouting by the banks, shouting out of pleasure. Shout out of pleasure, Brod. Come on, you can do it. One little shout out of pleasure.

Please, she began to whimper. *Sofiowka, please. I just want to go home, and I know that my father is waiting —*

There you go again, you lying cunt! he hollered. *Haven't we had enough lying for one night already!*

What do you want? Brod cried.

He took a knife from his pocket and cut the shoulder straps of her mermaid suit.

She pulled the suit down around her ankles and off her feet, and then removed her panties. She made sure, with the arm that wasn't held behind her back, that the tail didn't get muddy.

Later that night, after she returned home and discovered Yankel's dead body, the Kolker was illuminated at her window by a wink of lightning.

Go away! she cried, covering her bare chest with her arms and turning back toward Yankel, protecting their bodies from the Kolker's gaze. But he did not leave.

Go away!

I won't go without you, he called to her through the window.

Go away! Go away!

The rain dripped from his upper lip. *Not without you.*

I'll kill myself! she hollered.

Then I'll take your body with me, he said, palms against the glass.

Go away!

I won't!

Yankel jerked in rigor mortis, knocking over the oil lamp, which blew itself out on its way to the floor, leaving the room completely dark. His cheeks pulled into a tight smile, revealing, to the banished shadows, a contentedness. Brod let her arms brush down her skin to her sides and turned to face the Kolker—the second time she'd shown her naked body in thirteen years of life.

Then you must do something for me, she said.

Sofiowka was found the next morning, swinging by the neck from the wooden bridge. His severed hands were hanging from strings tied to his feet, and across his chest was written, in Brod's red lipstick: ANIMAL.

WHAT JACOB R ATE FOR BREAKFAST ON THE MORNING OF FEBRUARY 21, 1877

Fried potatoes with onion. Two slices of black bread.

Cain killed his brother for plagiarizing one of his favorite little poems, which went like this:

> *Willows whiten, aspens quiver,*
> *Little breezes dusk and shiver*
> *Through the wave that runs for ever*
> *By the island in the river.*

Unable to thwart the fury of a poet scorned, unable to continue writing as long as he knew that the pirates pens-sans would reap the booty of his industry, unable to suppress the question *If iambs not for me, what will be for me?*, he, unable Cain, put an end to literary larceny forever. Or so he thought.

But much to his surprise, it was Cain who was caned, Cain who was cursed to labor the earth, Cain who was forced to wear that terrible mark, Cain who, for all of his sad and witty verse, could get laid every night, but didn't know anyone who had read a page of his magnum opus.

Why?

God loves the plagiarist. And so it is written, "God created humankind in His image, in the image of God He created them." God is the original plagiarizer. With a lack of reasonable sources from which to filch—man created in the image of what? the animals?—the creation of man was an act of reflexive plagiarizing; God looted the mirror. When we plagiarize, we are likewise creating *in the image* and participating in the completion of Creation.

Am I my brother's material?

Of course, Cain. Of course.

THE DIAL

(*See* FALSE IDOLS)

THE HUMAN WHOLE

The Pogrom of Beaten Chests (1764) was bad, but it was not the worst, and there still are, no doubt, worse to come. They moved through on horses. They raped our pregnant women and cut down our strongest men with sickles. They beat our children to death. They made us curse our most holy texts. (It was impossible to distinguish the cries of babies and adults.) Immediately after they left, the Uprighters and Slouchers joined together to lift and move the synagogue all the way into the Human Three-Quarters, making it, if for only one hour, the Human Whole. Without knowing why, we beat our own chests, as we do when seeking atonement on Yom Kippur. Were we praying, *Forgive our oppressors for what they have done?* Or, *Forgive us for what has been done to us?* Or, *Forgive You for Your inscrutability?* (*See* APPENDIX G: UNTIMELY DEATHS.)

US, THE JEWS

Jews are those things that God loves. Since roses are beautiful, we must assume that God loves them. Therefore, roses are Jewish. By the same reasoning, the stars and planets are Jewish, all children are Jewish, pretty "art" is Jewish (Shakespeare wasn't Jewish, but Hamlet was), and sex, when practiced between husband and wife in a good and suitable position, is Jewish. Is the Sistine Chapel Jewish? You'd better believe it.

THE ANIMALS

The animals are those things that God likes but doesn't love.

OBJECTS THAT EXIST

Objects that exist are those things that God doesn't even like.

OBJECTS THAT DON'T EXIST

Objects that don't exist don't exist. If we were to imagine such a thing as an object that didn't exist, it would be that thing that God hated. This is the strongest argument against the nonbeliever. If God didn't exist, he would have to hate himself, and that is obviously nonsense.

THE 120 MARRIAGES OF JOSEPH AND SARAH L

The young couple first married on August 5, 1744, when Joseph was eight, and Sarah six, and first ended their marriage six days later, when Joseph refused to believe, to Sarah's frustration, that the stars were silver nails in the sky, pinning up the black nightscape. They re-married four days later, when Joseph left a note under the door of Sarah's parents' house: *I have considered everything you told me, and I do believe that the stars are silver nails.* They ended their marriage again a year later, when Joseph was nine and Sarah seven, over a quarrel about the nature of the bottom of the Brod. A week later, they were remarried, including this time in their vows that they should love each other until death, regardless of the existence of a bottom of the Brod, the temperature of this bottom (should it exist), and the possible existence of starfish on the possibly existing riverbed. They ended their marriage thirty-seven times in the next seven years, and each time remarried with a longer list of vows. They divorced twice when Joseph was twenty-two and Sarah twenty, four times when they were twenty-five and twenty-three, respectively, and eight times, the most for one year, when they were thirty and twenty-eight. They were sixty and fifty-eight at their last marriage, only three weeks before Sarah died of heart failure and Joseph drowned himself in the bath. Their marriage contract still hangs over the door of the house they on-and-off shared—nailed to the top post and brushing against the SHALOM welcome mat:

> It is with everlasting devotion that we, Joseph and Sarah L, reunite in the inde-structible union of matrimony, promising love until death, with the understanding that the stars are silver nails in the sky, re-gardless of the existence of a bottom of the Brod, the temperature of this bottom (should it exist), and the possible exis-tence of starfish on the possibly existing riverbed, overlooking what may or may not have been accidental grape juice spills, agreeing to forget that Joseph played sticks and balls with his friends when he promised he would help Sarah

thread the needle for the quilt she was sewing, and that Sarah was supposed to give the quilt to Joseph, not his buddy, deeming irrelevant certain details about the story of Trachim's wagon, such as whether it was Chana or Hannah who first saw the curious flotsam, ignoring the simple fact that Joseph snores like a pig, and that Sarah is no great treat to sleep with either, letting slide certain tendencies of both parties to look too long at members of the opposite sex, not making a fuss over why Joseph is such a slob, leaving his clothes wherever he feels like taking them off, expecting Sarah to pick them up, clean them, and put them in their proper place as he should have, or why Sarah has to be such a fucking pain in the ass about the smallest things, such as which way the toilet paper unrolls, or when dinner is five minutes later than she was planning, because, let's face it, it's Joseph who's putting that paper on the roll and dinner on the table, disregarding whether the beet is a better vegetable than the cabbage, putting aside the problems of being fat-headed and chronically unreasonable, trying to erase the memory of a long since expired rose bush that a certain someone was supposed to remember to water when his wife was visiting family in Rovno, accepting the compromise of the way we have been, the way we are, and the way we will likely be...may we live together in unwavering love and good health, amen.

The Book of Revelations

(For a complete listing of revelations, *see* APPENDIX Z32. For a complete listing of genesises, *see* APPENDIX Z33.)

The end of the world has come often, and continues to often come. Unforgiving, unrelenting, bringing darkness upon darkness, the end of the world is something we have become well acquainted with, habitualized, made into a ritual. It is our religion to try to forget it in its absence, make peace with it when it is undeniable, and return its embrace when it finally comes for us, as it always does.

There has yet to be a human to survive a span of history without at least one end of the world. It is the subject of extensive scholarly debate whether stillborn babies are subject to the same revelations— if we could say that they have lived without endings. This debate, of course, demands a close examination of that more profound question: *Was the world first created or ended?* When the Lord our God breathed on the universe, was that a genesis or a revelation? Should we count those seven days forward or backward? How did the apple taste, Adam? And the half a worm you discovered in that sweet and bitter pulp: was that the head or the tail?

Just What It Was, Exactly, That Yankel D Did

(*See* YANKEL D'S SHAMEFUL BEAD)

The Five Generations Between Brod and Safran

Brod had three sons with the Kolker, all named Yankel. The first two died in the flour mill, victims, like their father, of the disk saw. (*See* APPENDIX G: UNTIMELY DEATHS.) The third Yankel, conceived through the hole after the Kolker's exile, lived a long and productive life, which included many experiences, feelings, and small accumulations of wisdom, about which none of us will ever know. This Yankel begot Trachimkolker. Trachimkolker begot Safranbrod. Safranbrod begot Trachimyankel. Trachimyankel begot Kolkerbrod. Kolkerbrod begot Safran. For so it is written: *AND IF WE ARE TO STRIVE FOR A BETTER FUTURE, MUSTN'T WE BE FAMILIAR AND RECONCILED WITH OUR PAST?*

The following encyclopedia of sadness was found on the body of Brod D. The original 613 sadnesses, written in her diary, corresponded to the 613 commandments of our (not their) Torah. Shown below is what was salvageable after Brod was recovered. (Her diary's wet pages printed the sadnesses onto her body. Only a small fraction [55] were legible. The other 558 sadnesses are lost forever, and it is hoped that, without knowing what they are, no one will have to experience them.) The diary from which they came was never found.

SADNESSES OF THE BODY: Mirror sadness; Sadness of [looking] like or unlike one's parent; Sadness of not knowing if your body is normal; Sadness of knowing your [body is] not normal; Sadness of knowing your body is normal; Beauty sadness; Sadness of m[ak]eup; Sadness of physical pain; Pins-and-[needles sadness]; Sadness of clothes [*sic*]; Sadness of the quavering eyelid; Sadness of a missing rib; Noticeable sad[ness]; Sadness of going unnoticed; The sadness of having genitals that are not like those of your lover; The sadness of having genitals that are like those of your lover; Sadness of hands...

SADNESSES OF THE COVENANT: Sadness of God's love; Sadness of God's back [*sic*]; Favorite-child sadness; Sadness of b[ein]g sad in front of one's God; Sadness of the opposite of belief [*sic*]; What if? sadness; Sadness of God alone in heaven; Sadness of a God who would need people to pray to Him...

SADNESSES OF THE INTELLECT: Sadness of being misunderstood [*sic*]; Humor sadness; Sadness of love wit[hou]t release; Sadne[ss of be]ing smart; Sadness of not knowing enough words to [express what you mean]; Sadness of having options; Sadness of wanting sadness; Sadness of confusion; Sadness of domes[tic]ated birds; Sadness of fini[shi]ng a book; Sadness of remembering; Sadness of forgetting; Anxiety sadness…

INTERPERSONAL SADNESSES: Sadness of being sad in front of one's parent; Sa[dn]ess of false love; Sadness of love [*sic*]; Friendship sadness; Sadness of a bad convers[at]ion; Sadness of the could-have-been; Secret sadness…

SADNESSES OF SEX AND ART: Sadness of arousal being an unordinary physical state; Sadness of feeling the need to create beautiful things; Sadness of the anus; Sadness of eye contact during fellatio and cunnilingus; Kissing sadness; Sadness of moving too quickly; Sadness of not mo[vi]ng; Nude model sadness; Sadness of portraiture; Sadness of Pinchas T's only notable paper, "To the Dust: From Man You Came and to Man You Shall Return," in which he argued it would be possible, in theory, for life and art to be reversed…

We are writing…We are writing…We are writing…We are writing…We are writing…We are writing…We are writing…We are writing…We are writing…We are writing…We are writing…We are writing…We are writing…We are writing…We are writing…We are writing… We are writing…We are writing…We are writing…We are writing …We are writing…We are writing…We are writing…We are writing…We are writing…We are writing…We are writing…We are writing… We are writing…We are writing…We are writing…We are writing…We are writing…We are writing…We are writing…We are writing…We are writing…We are writing…We are writing…We are writing…We are writing… We are writing…We are writing…We are writing…We are writing …We are writing…We are writing…We are writing…We are writing…We are writing…We are writing…We are writing…We are writing… We are writing…We are writing…We are writing…We are writing…We are writing…We are writing…We are writing…We are writing…We are writing…We are writing…We are writing…We are writing…We are writing… We are writing…We are writing…We are writing…We are writing …We are writing…We are writing…We are writing…We are writing…We are writing…We are writing…We are writing…We are writing…

*We are writing…We are writing…We are writing…We are writing
…We are writing…We are writing…We are writing…We are
writing…We are writing…We are writing…We are writing…We
are writing…We are writing…We are writing…We are writing…
We are writing…We are writing…We are writing…We are writing
…We are writing…We are writing…We are writing…We are
writing…We are writing…We are writing…We are writing…We
are writing…We are writing…We are writing…We are writing…
We are writing…We are writing…We are writing…We are writing
…We are writing…We are writing…We are writing…We are
writing…We are writing…We are writing…We are writing…We
are writing…We are writing…We are writing…We are writing…
We are writing…We are writing…We are writing…We are writing
…We are writing…We are writing…We are writing…We are
writing…We are writing…We are writing…We are writing…We
are writing…We are writing…We are writing…We are writing…
We are writing…We are writing…We are writing…We are writing
…We are writing…We are writing…We are writing…We are
writing…We are writing…We are writing…We are writing…We
are writing…We are writing…We are writing…We are writing…
We are writing…We are writing…We are writing…We are writing
…We are writing…We are writing…We are writing…We are
writing…We are writing…We are writing…We are writing…We
are writing…We are writing…We are writing…We are writing…
We are writing…We are writing…We are writing…We are writing
…We are writing…We are writing…We are writing…We are
writing…We are writing…We are writing…We are writing…We
are writing…We are writing…We are writing…We are writing…
We are writing…We are writing…We are writing…We are writing
…We are writing…We are writing…We are writing…We are
writing…We are writing…We are writing…We are writing…We
are writing…We are writing…We are writing…We are writing…
We are writing…We are writing…We are writing…We are writing
…We are writing…We are writing…We are writing…We are
writing…We are writing…We are writing…We are writing…*

Dear Jonathan,

Let us not mention each other's writing ever again. I will post you my story, and I beg of you (as does Little Igor) that you continue to post yours, but let us not make corrections or even observations. Let us not praise or reproach. Let us not judge at all. We are outside of that already.

We are talking now, Jonathan, together, and not apart. We are with each other, working on the same story, and I am certain that you can also feel it. Do you know that I am the Gypsy girl and you are Safran, and that I am Kolker and you are Brod, and that I am your grandmother and you are Grandfather, and that I am Alex and you are you, and that I am you and you are me? Do you not comprehend that we can bring each other safety and peace? When we were under the stars in Trachimbrod, did you not feel it then? Do not present not-truths to me. Not to me.

And here, Jonathan, is a story for you. A faithful story. I informed Father that I was to go to a famous nightclub last night. He said, "I am certain that you will return home with a comrade?" If you want to know what was on his mouth, vodka was. "I do not intend to," I said. "You will be so so carnal," he said, laughing. He touched me on the shoulder, and I will tell you that it felt like a touch from the devil. I was most ashamed of us. "No," I said. "I am only going to dance and be amid my friends." "Shapka, Shapka." "Shut up!" I told him, and I seized his wrist. I will inform you that this was the first occasion that I have ever uttered anything like this to him, and the first occasion that I have ever moved at him with violence. "I am sorry," I said, and let his wrist free. "I will make you sorry," he said. I was a lucky person because he had so much vodka in him that he did not have regard enough to punch me.

I did not go to a famous nightclub, of course. As I have mentioned, I often inform Father that I will go to a famous nightclub, but then I go to the beach. I do not go to a famous nightclub so that I can deposit my currency in the cookie box for moving to America with Little Igor. But I must inform you that it is also because I do not love famous nightclubs. They make me feel very cheerless and abandoned. Am I applying that word correctly? Abandoned?

The beach was beautiful last night, but this did not surprise me. I love sitting on the edge of the land and feeling the water verge me, and then leave me. Sometimes I remove my shoes and put my feet where I think the water will approach to. I have attempted to think about America in regard to where I am on the beach. I imagine a line, a white line, painted on the sand and on the ocean, from me to you.

I was sitting on the edge of the water, thinking about you, and us, when I heard a thing. The thing was nor water, nor wind, nor insects. I turned my head to see what it was. Someone was walking to me. This scared me very much, because I never behold another person at the beach when I am there at night. There was nothing proximal to me, nothing to be walking to but me. I put on my shoes and began to walk away from this person. Was he a police? The police will often make advantages on people who are sitting alone. Was he a criminal? I was not very scared of a criminal, because they do not have premium weapons, and cannot inflict very much. Unless the criminal is a police. I could hear that the person was still coming to me. I made a more rapid walk. The person pursued me with speed. I did not look again to attempt to witness who it was, because I did not want the person to know that I was apprised of him. It sounded to my ears like he was getting closer, that he would soon reach me, so I began to run.

Then I heard, "Sasha!" I terminated my running. "Sasha, is that you?" I turned around. Grandfather was bended over with his hand on his stomach. I could see that he was manufacturing very large breaths. "I was looking for you," he said. I could not understand how he knew to look for me at the beach. As I informed you, nobody is aware that I go to the beach at night. "I am here," I said, which sounded queer, but I did not know what else to say. He stood up and said, "I have a question."

It was the first occasion that I could remember when Grandfather addressed me without something amid us. There was no Father, no hero, no bitch, no television, no food. Merely us. "What is it?" I asked, because I could perceive that he would not be able to ask his question unless I aided him. "I have to ask you for something, but you must comprehend that I am only asking to borrow this thing, and you also must comprehend that you can deny me and I will not be injured or think anything bad of you." "What is it?" I could not think of anything that I possessed that Grandfather would desire. I could not think of anything in the world that Grandfather would desire.

"I would like to borrow your currency," he said. In truth I felt very shamed. He did not toil his whole life in order that he should have to ask his grandson for currency. "I will," I said. And I should have uttered nothing more, and allowed my "I will" to speak for everything that I have ever had to say to Grandfather, for the "I will" to be all of my questions, and all of his answers to those questions, and all of my answers to those answers. But this was not possible. "Why?" I asked.

"Why what?"

"Why do you desire my currency?"

"Because I do not have a sufficient sum."

"For what? For what do you need currency?"

He turned his head to the water and did not say a thing. Was this his answer? He moved his foot in the sand and made a circle.

"I am unequivocal that I can find her," he said. "Four days. Perhaps five. But it could not require more than a week. We were very near."

I should have again said "I will," and again not said anything more. I should have esteemed that Grandfather is much more aged than me, and because of this he is wiser, and if not that, then he deserves to have me not question him. But instead I said, "No. We were not near."

"Yes," he said, "we were."

"No. We were not five days from finding her. We were fifty years from finding her."

"It is a thing that I must do."

"Why?"

"You would not understand."

"But I would. I do."

JONATHAN SAFRAN FOER

"No, you could not."

"Herschel?"

He drew another circle with his foot.

"Then take me with you," I said. I was not intending to say that.

"No," he said.

I desired to say it again, "Take me with you," but I knew that he would have answered again, "No," and I do not think I could have heard that without crying, and I know that I cannot cry in view of Grandfather.

"It is not necessary for you to decide now," he said. "I did not think that you would decide rapidly. I anticipate that you will say no."

"Why do you think I will say no?"

"Because you do not understand."

"I do."

"No, you do not."

"It is possible that I will say yes."

"I would give you any possession of mine that you desire. It can be yours until I restore the currency to you, which will be soon."

"Take me with you," I said, and again I did not intend to say it, but it released from my mouth, like the articles from Trachim's wagon.

"No," he said.

"Please," I said. "It will be less rigid with me. I could assist very much."

"I need to find her alone," he said, and at that moment I was certain that if I gave Grandfather the currency and allowed him to go, I would never see him again.

"Take Little Igor."

"No," he said. "Alone." No words. And then: "Do not inform Father."

"Of course," I said, because of course I would not inform Father.

"This must be our secret."

It is this last thing that he said that left the most permanent mark on my brain. It had not occurred to me until he uttered it, but we have a secret. We have a thing amid us that no one else in the world knows, or could know. We have a secret together, and no longer asunder.

I informed him that I would rapidly present him with my answer.

I do not know what to do, Jonathan, and would desire for you to tell me *what you think is the right thing. I know that it is not necessary that there be one right thing. There may be two right things. There may be no right things. I will consider what you deem. This is a promise. But I cannot promise that I will harmonize. There are things that you could not know. (And also, of course, I will have made my decision by the time you receive this letter. We have always communicated in this misplaced time.)*

I am not a foolish person. I know that Grandfather will never be able to restore the currency. This signifies that I will not be able to move myself and Little Igor to America. Our dreams cannot exist at the same time. I am so young, and he is so aged, and both of these facts should make us people who are deserving of their dreams, but this is not a possibility.

I am certain of what you will utter. You will utter, "Let me give you the currency." You will utter, "You can return the currency when you have it, or you can never return the currency, and it will not be mentioned again." I know you will utter this because I know that you are a good person. But this is not acceptable. For the same reason that Grandfather cannot take me with him on his voyage, I cannot take the currency from you. This is about choosing. Can you understand? Please attempt to. You are the only person who has understood even a whisper of me, and I will tell you that I am the only person who has understood even a whisper of you.

I will expect for your letter with anticipation.

Guilelessly,
Alexander

An overture to illumination

By the time we returned to the hotel, it was very late, and almost very early. The owner was heavy with sleep at the front desk. "Vodka," Grandfather said. "We should have a drink, the three of us." "The four of us," I counseled, pointing to Sammy Davis, Junior, Junior, who had been such a benign tumor all day. So the four of us went forth to the hotel bar. "You are returned," said the waitress when she witnessed us. "Back with the Jew," she said. "Shut your mouth," Grandfather said, and he did not say it in an earsplitting voice, but quietly, as if it were a fact that she should shut her mouth. "I am apologizing," she said. "It is not a thing," I told her, because I did not want her to feel inferior for a small mistake, and also I could see her bosom when she bent forward. (For whom did I write that, Jonathan? I do not want to be disgusting anymore. And I do not want to be funny, either.) "It is a thing," Grandfather said, "and you must now ask leniency of the Jew." "What's going on?" the hero asked. "Why aren't we going in?" "Make apologies," Grandfather told the waitress, who was only a girl, even more young than me. "I am apologizing for calling you a Jew," she said. "She is apologizing for calling you a Jew," I told the hero. "How did she know?" "She knows because I told her before, at breakfast." "You told her I was a Jew?" "It was an appropriate fact at the time." "I was drinking mochaccino." "I must correct you. It was coffee." "What is he saying?" Grandfather asked. "Perhaps it would be best," I said, "if we acquire a table and order a large amount of drinks and also food." "What else did she say about me?" the hero asked. "Did she say anything else? You can see her tits when she leans over." (This was yours, you will remember. I did not invent this, and so cannot be blamed.)

We pursued the waitress to our table, which was in the corner. We could have had any table, because we were the exclusive people there. I do not know why she put us in the corner, but I have a notion. "What can I obtain for you?" she asked. "Four vodkas," Grandfather said. "One of them in a bowl. And do you have anything to eat that does not have meat?" "Peanuts," she said. "This is excellent," Grandfather responded, "but none for Sammy Davis, Junior, Junior because it makes her very ill. It is a terrible thing for even one to touch her lips." I informed this to the hero because I thought he might find it humorous. He merely smiled.

When the waitress returned with our drinks and a bowl of peanuts, we were already conversing about our day, and also our schemes for tomorrow. "He must be present at the train by 19:00 of the evening, yes?" "Yes," I said, "so we will desire to depart the hotel at lunch, to be on the side of safety." "Perhaps we will have time for more searching." "I am not so certain," I said. "And where would we search? There is nothing. There is no one to inquire. You remember what she said." The hero was not giving any attention to us, and never asked even one time what we were conversing about. He was being sociable only with the peanuts. "This would be more easy without him," Grandfather said, moving his eyes at the hero. "But it is his search," I said. "Why?" "Because it is his grandfather." "We are not looking for his grandfather. We are looking for Augustine. She is not any more his than ours." I had not thought of it in this way, but it was true. "What are you talking about?" Jonathan asked me. "And could you ask the waitress for some more of these peanuts?"

I told the waitress to retrieve us more peanuts, and she said, "I will do this, even though the owner commands that no one should ever receive more than one bowl of peanuts. I will except you because I feel so wretched about calling the Jew a Jew." "Thank you," I said, "but there is no reason to feel wretched." "And what about tomorrow, then?" Jonathan asked. "I have to be at the train at 7:00, right?" "Correct." "What will we do until then?" "I am not a certain person. We must depart very early, because you must be at the train station two hours before your train goes forth, and it is a three-hour drive, and it is likely that we will become lost people." "It sounds like we should leave now," he said, and laughed. I did not laugh, because I knew that the reason we would depart early is not in truth because of the justifications I said to him, but because there was nothing more to search for. We had failed.

"Let us investigate IN CASE," Grandfather said. "What?" I asked. "The box, let us see what is inside of it." "Is this a bad idea?" "Of course it is not," he said. "Why would it be?" "Perhaps we should allow Jonathan to investigate it confidentially, or perhaps no one should investigate it." "She presented it to him for a purpose." "I know," I said, "but perhaps that purpose had nothing to do with investigating it. Perhaps the purpose is that it should never be opened." "You are not a curious person?" he asked me. "I am a very curious person." "What are you guys talking about?" "Would you be content to investigate IN CASE?" "What do you mean?" "The box that Augustine presented you today. We could search it." "Is that a good idea?" "I am not certain. I asked the identical thing." "I don't see why it's a bad idea. I mean, she did give it to me for a reason." "This is what Grandfather uttered." "You don't think there's any good reason not to?" "I cannot forecast one." "Neither can I." "But." "But?" "But nothing," I uttered. "But what?" "But nothing. It is your decision." "And yours." "Unclose the fucking box," Grandfather said. "He says unclose the fucking box." Jonathan removed the box from under his seat and placed it on the table. IN CASE was written on the side, and from more proximal, I could perceive that the words had been written and erased many times, written, erased, and written again. "Mmmm," he said, and made gestures to a red ribbon that was fastened around the box. "It is only to keep it closed," Grandfather said. "It is only to keep it closed," I told him. "Probably," he said. "Or," I said, "to forestall us from examining it." "She didn't say anything about not examining it. She would have said something, don't you think?" "I would think so." "Your grandfather thinks we should open it?" "Yes." "And you?" "I am not certain." "What do you mean you're not certain?" "I think it would not be such a wretched thing to open it. She would have uttered something if she desired it to remain uninvestigated." "Open the fucking box," Grandfather said. "He says open the fucking box."

Jonathan dislodged the ribbon, which was wrapped many times around IN CASE, and opened it. Perhaps we were anticipating it to be a bomb, because when it did not explode, we were all flabbergasted. "That wasn't so bad," Jonathan said. "That was not so bad," I told Grandfather. "This is what I said," he told me. "I said it would not be so bad." We looked into the box. Its ingredients appeared very much similar to those in the REMAINS box, except there were perhaps more. "Of course we were supposed to open it," Jonathan said. He looked at me and laughed, and then I laughed, and then Grandfather laughed. We laughed because we knew how witless we had been when we were shitting bricks about opening the box. And we laughed because there was so much that we did not know, and we knew that there was so much we did not know.

"Let us search," Grandfather said, and he moved his hand through the box marked IN CASE like a child reaching into a box of gifts. He excavated a necklace. "Look," he said. "It's pearl, I think," Jonathan said. "Real pearl." The pearls, if they were real pearls, were very dirty, and yellow, and there were pieces of dirt stranded amid them, like food amid teeth. "It appears very aged," Grandfather said. I told this to Jonathan. "Yes," he harmonized. "And dirty. I bet it was buried." "What does it mean buried?" "Put in the ground, like a dead body." "Yes, I know this thing. It could be similar like the ring in the REMAINS box." "Right." Grandfather held the necklace to the candle on our table. The pearls, if they were real pearls, had many taints, and were no longer resplendent. He tried to clean them with his thumb, but they remained dirty. "It is a beautiful necklace," he said. "I purchased one very much similar to this for your grandmother when we first became in love. This was many years ago, but I remember what it looked like. It obligated all of my currency to purchase it, so how could I forget?" "Where is it now?" I asked. "At home?" "No," he said, "she is still wearing it. It is not a thing. Just how she desired it to be." He put the necklace on the table, and I could perceive that the necklace did not make him melancholy, as it might be anticipated, but it made him a very contented person. "Now you," he told me, and punched my back in a manner that was not intended to hurt me, but did nonetheless. "He says I should choose something," I told Jonathan, because I desired to discover how he would answer to the notion that Grandfather and I had the same privilege as he did to investigate the box. "Go ahead," he said. So I inserted my hand into IN CASE.

I felt many abnormal things, and could not tell what they were. We did not say it, but it was part of our game that you could not view in the box when you were selecting the thing to excavate. Some of the things that my hand touched were smooth, like marble or stones from the beach. Other things that my hand touched were cold, like metal, or warm, like fur. There were many pieces of paper. I could be certain of that without witnessing them. But I could not know if these papers were photographs or notes or pages from a book or magazine. I excavated what I excavated because it was the largest thing in the box. "Here," I said, and removed a piece of paper that was in a coil and fastened with white string. I removed the string and unrolled the paper on the table. Jonathan restrained one end, and I restrained the other. It was marked MAP OF THE WORLD, 1791. Even though the shapes of the land were some amount different, it remained to appear very much like the world as we currently know it. "This is a premium thing," I said. A map such as that one is worth many hundreds, and as luck will have it, thousands of dollars. But more than this, it is a remembrance of that time before our planet was so small. When this map was made, I thought, you could live without knowing where you were not living. This made me think of Trachimbrod, and how Lista, the woman we desired so much to be Augustine, had not ever heard of America. It is possible that she is the last person on earth, I reasoned, who does not know about America. Or it is so nice to think so. "I love it," I told Jonathan, and I must confess that I had no notions when I told him this. It is only that I loved it. "You can have it," he said. "This is not a true thing." "Take it. Enjoy it." "You cannot give this to me. The items must remain together," I told him. "Go on," he said. "It's yours." "Are you certain?" I asked, because I did not desire him to feel burdened to present it to me. "I'm positive. It can be a memento of our trip." "Memento?" "Something to remind you." "No," I said. "I will give it to Little Igor, if that is acceptable with you," because I knew that the map was a thing that Little Igor would love also. "Tell him to enjoy it," Jonathan said. "It can be his memento."

"You," I told Jonathan, because it was now his opportunity to excavate from IN CASE. He turned his head away from the box and inserted his hand. He did not require a long amount of time. "Here," he said, and removed a book. He placed it on the table. It appeared very old. "What is it?" he asked. I moved the dust off of the cover. I had never previous witnessed a book similar to it. The writing was on both covers, and when I unclosed it, I saw that the writing was also on the insides of both covers, and, of course, on every page. It was as if there was not sufficient room in the book for the book. Along the side was marked in Ukrainian, *The Book of Past Occurrences*. I told this to Jonathan. "Read me something from it," he said. "The beginning?" "Anywhere, it doesn't matter." I went to a page in the middle and selected a part from the middle of the page to read. It was very difficult, but I translated into English while I read. "'The shtetl was colorful with the actions of its residents,'" I told him, "'and because every color was used, it was impossible to perceive what had been handled by humans and what was of nature's hands. Getzel G, there were rumors, must have played everyone's fiddle—even though he did not know how to play the fiddle!—because the strings were the color like his fingers. People whispered that Gesha R was trying to be a gymnast. This is how the Jewish/Human fault line was yellow like her hands. And when the red of a schoolgirl's face was wronged for the red of a holy man's fingers, the schoolgirl was called names.'" He secured the book and examined it while I told Grandfather what I had read. "It's wonderful," Jonathan said, and I must confess that he examined it in a fashion similar to how Grandfather examined the photograph of Augustine.

(You may understand this as a gift from me to you, Jonathan. And just as I am saving you, so could you save Grandfather. We are merely two paragraphs away. Please, try to find some other option.)

"Now you," Jonathan said to Grandfather. "He says it is now you," I told him. He turned his head away from the box and inserted his hand. We were similar to three children. "There are so many things," he told me. "I do not know which thing to take." "He does not know which to take," I told Jonathan. "There's time for all of them," Jonathan said. "Perhaps this one," Grandfather said. "No, this one. It feels soft and nice. No, this one. This one has pieces that move." "There is time for all of them," I told him, because remember where we are in our story, Jonathan. We still thought we possessed time. "Here," Grandfather said, and excavated a photograph. "Ah, a simple one. Too unfortunate. I thought it felt like something different."

He placed the photograph on the table without examining it. Also I did not examine it, because why should I, I reasoned. Grandfather was correct, it appeared very simple, and ordinary. There were likely one hundred photographs of this manner in the box. The rapid view that I presented it showed me nothing abnormal. It was three men, or perhaps four. "Now you," he told me, and I turned my head and inserted my hand. Because my head was turned to not view in the box, I was witnessing Jonathan while my hand investigated. A soft thing. A rough thing. Jonathan moved the photograph to his face, not because he was an interested person, but because there was nothing else to do at the moment while I searched the box. This is what I remember. He ate a hand of peanuts, and let a handful descend to the floor for Sammy Davis, Junior, Junior. He made a petite drink from his vodka. He looked away from the photograph for a moment. I felt a feather and a bone. Then I remember this: he looked at the photograph again. I felt a smooth thing. A petite thing. He looked away from the photograph. He looked at it again. He looked away. A hard thing. A candle. A square thing. A prick from a pin.

"Oh my God," he said, and he held the photograph up to the light of the candle. Then he put it down. Then he held it again, and this time put it close to my face so that he could observe both the photograph and my face at the same time. "What is he doing?" Grandfather asked. "What are you doing?" I asked him. Jonathan placed the photograph on the table. "It's you," he said.

I removed my hand from the box.

"Who is me?" "The man in this picture. It's you." He gave me the photograph. This time I examined it with much scrutiny. "What is it?" Grandfather asked. There were four people in the photograph, two men, a woman, and a baby that the woman was holding. "The one on the left," Jonathan said, "here." He put his finger beneath the face of the man, and I must confess, there could be nothing truthful to do but admit, he looked like me. It was as if a mirror. I know that this is an idiom, but I am saying it without any meaning other than the words. It was as if a mirror. "What?" Grandfather asked. "A moment," I said, and held the photograph to the light of the candle. The man even stood in the same potent manner as I stand. His cheeks appeared like mine. His eyes appeared like mine. His hairs, lips, arms, legs, they all appeared like mine. Not even like mine. They *were* mine. "Tell me," Grandfather said, "what is it?" I presented him the photograph, and to write the rest of this story is the most impossible thing.

At first he examined it to see what it was a photograph of. Because he was looking down to view the photograph, which was on the table, I could not see what his eyes were performing. He looked up from the photograph and viewed Jonathan and me, and he smiled. He even moved his shoulders up, as a child will sometimes do. He made a small laugh and then picked up the photograph. He held it to his face with one hand and held the candle to his face with the other. It made many shadows where his skin had folds, which were many more places than I had before observed. This time I could see his eyes voyage this and that over the photograph. They stopped on each person, and witnessed each person from feet to hairs. Then he looked up again and smiled again at Jonathan and me, and he also moved his shoulders like a child again.

"It looks like me," I said.

"Yes it does," he said.

I did not look at Jonathan, because I was certain that he was looking at me. So I looked at Grandfather, who was investigating the photograph, although I am certain that he could feel that I was viewing him.

"Exactly like me," I said. "He also observed this," I said of Jonathan, because I did not want to be alone in this observation.

(Here it is almost too forbidding to continue. I have written to this point many times, and corrected the parts you would have me correct, and made more funnies, and more inventions, and written as if I were you writing this, but every time I try to persevere, my hand shakes so that I can no longer hold my pen. Do it for me. Please. It is now yours.)

Grandfather concealed his face behind the photograph.

(And this does not seem to me like such a cowardly thing to do, Jonathan. We would also conceal our faces, yes? In truth, I am certain that we would.)

"The world is the smallest thing," he said.

(He laughed at this moment, as you remember, but you cannot include that in the story.)

"It looks so much like me," I said.

(And here he put his hands under the table, you will remember, but this is a detail which will make him appear weak, and is it not enough that we are writing this at all?)

"Like a combination of your father, your mother, Brezhnev, and yourself."

(It was not wrong to make a funny here. It was the right thing to do.)

I smiled.

"Who do you think it is?" I asked.

"Who do *you* think it is?" he asked.

"I do not know."

"You do not have to present not-truths to me, Sasha. I am not a child."

(But I do. That is what you always fail to understand. I present not-truths in order to protect you. That is also why I try so inflexibly to be a funny person. Everything is to protect you. I exist in case you need to be protected.)

"I do not understand," I said. (I understand.)

"You do not?" he asked. (You do.)

"Where was the photograph made?" I asked. (There must be some explanation.)

"In Kolki."

"Where you were from?" (You always said Odessa...To fall in love...)

"Yes. Before the war." (This is the way things are. This is, in truth, what it is like.)

"Jonathan's grandmother?"

"I do not know her name, and I do not want to know her name."

(I must inform you, Jonathan, that I am a very sad person. I am always sad, I think. Perhaps this signifies that I am not sad at all, because sadness is something lower than your normal disposition, and I am always the same thing. Perhaps I am the only person in the world, then, who never becomes sad. Perhaps I am lucky.)

"I am not a bad person," he said. "I am a good person who has lived in a bad time."

"I know this," I said. (Even if you were a bad person, I would still know that you are a good person.)

"You must inform all of this to him as I inform it to you," he said, and this surprised me very much, but I did not ask why, or ask anything. I only did as he commanded. Jonathan opened his diary and commenced to write. He wrote every word that was spoken. Here is what he wrote:

"Everything I did, I did because I thought it was the correct thing to do."

"Everything he did, he did because he thought it was the correct thing to do," I translated.

"I am not a hero, it is true."

"He is not a hero."

"But I am not a bad person, either."

"But he is not a bad person."

"The woman in the photograph is your grandmother. She is holding your father. The man standing next to me was our best friend, Herschel."

"The woman in the photograph is my grandmother. She is holding my father. The man standing next to Grandfather was his best friend, Herschel."

"Herschel is wearing a skullcap in the photograph because he was a Jew."

"Herschel was a Jew."

"And he was my best friend."

"He was his best friend."

"And I murdered him."

THE FINAL TIME they made love, seven months before she killed herself and he married someone else, the Gypsy girl asked my grandfather how he arranged his books.

She had been the only one he returned to without having to be asked. They would meet at the bazaar—he would watch, with not only anticipation but pride, as she coaxed snakes from woven baskets with the tipsy music of her recorder. They would meet at the theater or in front of her thatch-roofed shanty in the Gypsy hamlet on the other side of the Brod. (She, of course, could never be seen near his house.) They would meet on the wooden bridge, or beneath the wooden bridge, or by the small falls. But more often than not, they would end up in the petrified corner of Radziwell Forest, exchanging jokes and stories, laughing afternoons into evenings, making love—which might or might not have been love—under stone canopies.

Do you think I'm wonderful? she asked him one day as they leaned against the trunk of a petrified maple.

No, he said.

Why?

Because so many girls are wonderful. I imagine hundreds of men have called their loves wonderful today, and it's only noon. You couldn't be something that hundreds of others are.

Are you saying that I am not-wonderful?

Yes, I am.

She fingered his dead arm. *Do you think I am not-beautiful?*

You are incredibly not-beautiful. You are the farthest possible thing from beautiful.

She unbuttoned his shirt.

Am I smart?

No. Of course not. I would never call you smart.

She kneeled to unbutton his pants.

Am I sexy?

No.

Funny?

You are not-funny.

Does that feel good?

No.

Do you like it?

No.

She unbuttoned her blouse. She leaned in against him.

Should I continue?

She had been to Kiev, he learned, and Odessa, and even Warsaw. She had lived among the Wisps of Ardisht for a year when her mother became deathly ill. She told him of ship voyages she had taken to places he had never heard of, and stories he knew were all untrue, were bad nottruths, even, but he nodded and tried to convince himself to be convinced, tried to believe her, because he knew that the origin of a story is always an absence, and he wanted her to live among presences.

In Siberia, she said, *there are couples who make love from hundreds of miles apart, and in Austria there is a princess who tattooed the image of her lover's body onto her body, so that when she looked in the mirror she would see him, and and and on the other side of the Black Sea is a stone woman—I have never seen it, but my aunt has—who came to life because of her sculptor's love!*

Safran brought the Gypsy girl flowers and chocolates (all gifts from his widows) and composed poems for her, all of which she laughed at.

How stupid could you possibly be! she said.

Why am I stupid?

Because the easiest things for you to give are the hardest things for you to give. Flowers, chocolates, and poems don't mean anything to me.

You don't like them?

Not from you.

What would you like from me?

She shrugged her shoulders, not out of puzzlement but embarrassment. (He was the only person on earth who could embarrass her.)

Where do you keep your books? she asked.

In my room.

Where in your room?

On shelves.

How are your books arranged?

Why do you care?

Because I want to know.

She was a Gypsy. He was a Jew. When she held his hand in public, something he knew she knew he hated, he created a reason to need it—to comb his hair, to point at the spot where his great-great-great-grandfather spilt the gold coins onto the shore like golden vomit from the sack—and would then insert it in his pocket, ending the situation.

You know what I need right now, she said, reaching for his dead arm as they walked through the Sunday bazaar.

Tell me and it's yours. Anything.

I want a kiss.

You can have as many as you want, wherever you want them.

Here, she said, putting her index finger on her lips. *Now.*

He gestured to a nearby alley.

No, she said. *I want a kiss here*, she put her finger on her lips, *now.*

He laughed. *Here?* He put his finger on his own lips. *Now?*

Here, she said, putting her finger on her lips. *Now.*

They laughed together. Nervous laughter. Starting with small giggles. Summing. Louder laughter. Multiplying. Even louder. Squaring. Laughter between gasps. Uncontrollable laughter. Violent. Infinite.

I can't.

I know.

My grandfather and the Gypsy girl made love for seven years, at least twice every week. They had confessed every secret; explained, to the best of their abilities, the workings of their bodies, each to the other; been forceful and passive, greedy and giving, wordy and silent.

How do you arrange your books? she asked as they lay naked on a bed of pebbles and hard soil.

I told you, they're in my bedroom on shelves.

I wonder if you can imagine your life without me.

Sure I can imagine it, but I don't like to.

It's not pleasant, is it?

Why are you doing this?

It was just something I was wondering.

Not one of his friends—if it could be said that he had any other friends—knew about the Gypsy girl, and none of his other women knew about the Gypsy girl, and his parents, of course, didn't know about the Gypsy girl. She was such a tightly kept secret that sometimes he felt that not even he was privy to his relationship with her. She knew of his efforts to conceal her from the rest of his world, to keep her cloistered in a private chamber reachable only by a secret passage, to put her behind a wall. She knew that even if he thought he loved her, he did not love her.

Where do you think you'll be in ten years? she asked, raising her head from his chest to address him.

I don't know.

Where do you think I'll be? Their sweat had mingled and dried, forming a pasty film between them.

In ten years?

Yes.

I don't know, he said, playing with her hair. *Where do you think you'll be?*

I don't know.

Where do you think I'll be?

I don't know, she said.

They lay in silence, thinking their own thoughts, each trying to know the other's. They were becoming strangers on top of each other.

What made you ask?

I don't know, she said.

Well, what do we know?

Not a lot, she said, easing her head back onto his chest.

They exchanged notes, like children. My grandfather made his out of newspaper clippings and dropped them in her woven baskets, into which he knew only she would dare stick a hand. *Meet me under the wooden bridge, and I will show you things you have never, ever seen.* The "M" was taken from the army that would take his mother's life: GERMAN FRONT ADVANCES ON SOVIET BORDER; the "eet" from their approaching warships: NAZI FLEET DEFEATS FRENCH AT LESACS; the "me" from the peninsula they were blue-eyeing: GERMANS SURROUND CRIMEA; the "und" from too little, too late: AMERICAN WAR FUNDS REACH ENGLAND; the "er" from the dog of dogs: HITLER RENDERS NONAGGRESSION PACT INOPERATIVE . . . and so on, and so on, each note a collage of love that could never be, and war that could.

The Gypsy girl carved love letters into trees, filling the forest with notes for him. *Do not forsake me,* she removed from the bark of a tree in whose shade they had once fallen asleep. *Honor me,* she carved into the trunk of a petrified oak. She was composing a new list of commandments, commandments they could share, that would govern a life together, and not apart. *Do not have any other loves before me in your heart. Do not take my name in vain. Do not kill me. Observe me, and keep me holy.*

I'd like to be wherever you are in ten years, he wrote her, gluing clips of newspaper headlines to a piece of yellow paper. *Isn't that a nice idea?*

A very nice idea, he found on a tree at the fringe of the forest. *And why is it only an idea?*

Because — the print stained his hands; he read himself on himself — *ten years is a long time from now.*

We would have to run away, carved in a circle around a maple's trunk. *We would have to leave behind everything but each other.*

Which is possible, he composed with fragments of the news of imminent war. *It's a nice idea, anyway.*

My grandfather took the Gypsy girl to the Dial and related the story of his great-great-great-grandmother's tragic life, promising to ask for her help when he one day tried to write Trachimbrod's history. He told her the story of Trachim's wagon, when the young W twins were the first to see the curious flotsam rising to the surface: wandering snakes of white string, a crushed-velvet glove with outstretched fingers, barren spools, schmootzy pince-nez, rasp- and boysenberries, feces, frillwork, the shards of a shattered atomizer, the bleeding red-ink script of a resolution: *I will...I will...* She spoke honestly of her father's abuses, and showed him the bruises that not even a naked body will reveal. He explained his circumcision, the covenant, the concept of his being of the Chosen People. She told him of the time her uncle forced himself on her, and how she had been capable, for several years now, of having a baby. He told her that he masturbated with his dead hand, because that way he could convince himself that he was making love to someone else. She told him that she had contemplated suicide, as if it were a decision. He told her his darkest secret: that unlike other boys, his love for his mother had never diminished, not even the smallest bit since he was a child, and please don't laugh at me for telling you this, and please don't think any less of me, but I would rather have a kiss from her than anything in this world. The Gypsy girl cried, and when my grandfather asked her what was wrong, she did not say, *I am jealous of your mother. I want you to love me like that*, but instead said nothing, and laughed as if: how silly. She told him that she wished there were another commandment, an eleventh etched into the tablets: *Do not change.*

For all of his liaisons, for all of the women who would undress for him at the show of his dead arm, he had no other friends, and could imagine no loneliness worse than an existence without her. She was the only one who could rightly claim to know him, the only one he missed when she was not there, and missed even before she was absent. She was the only one who wanted more of him than his arm.

I don't love you, he told her one evening as they lay naked in the grass.

She kissed his brow and said, *I know that. And I'm sure you know that I don't love you.*

Of course, he said, although it came as a great surprise—not that she didn't love him, but that she would say it. In the past seven years of lovemaking he had heard the words so many times: from the mouths of widows and children, from prostitutes, family friends, travelers, and adulterous wives. Women had said *I love you* without his ever speaking. *The more you love someone*, he came to think, *the harder it is to tell them.* It surprised him that strangers didn't stop each other on the street to say *I love you.*

My parents have arranged a marriage, he said.

For you?

With a girl named Zosha. From my shtetl. I'm seventeen.

And do you love her? she asked without looking at him.

He broke his life into its smallest constituent parts, examined each, like a watchmaker, and then reassembled it.

I hardly know her. He also avoided eye contact, because like Pincher P, who lived in the streets as a charity case, having donated even his last coin to the poor, his eyes would have given away everything.

Are you going to go through with it? she asked, drawing circles in the earth with her caramel finger.

I don't have a choice, he said.

Of course.

She would not look at him.

You will have such a happy life, she said. *You will always be happy.*

Why are you doing this?

Because you are so lucky. Real and lasting happiness is within your reach.

Stop, he said. *You're not being fair.*

I would like to meet her.

No you wouldn't.

Yes I would. What's her name? Zosha? I would like very much to meet Zosha and tell her how happy she will be. What a lucky girl. She must be very beautiful.

I don't know.

You've seen her, haven't you?

Yes.

Then you know if she's beautiful. Is she beautiful?

I guess.

More beautiful than I am?

Stop.

I would like to attend the wedding, to see for myself. Well, not the wedding, of course. A Gypsy girl couldn't enter the synagogue. The reception, though. You are going to invite me, aren't you?

You know that isn't possible, he said, turning away.

I know it isn't possible, she said, knowing that she had pushed it too far, been too cruel.

It isn't possible.

I told you: I know.

But you have to believe me.

I do.

They made love for the last time, unaware that the next seven months would pass without any words between them. He would see her many times, and she him—they had come to haunt the same places, to walk the same paths, to fall asleep in the shade of the same trees—but they would never acknowledge each other's existence. They both wanted badly to go back seven years to their first encounter, at the theater, and do it all again, but this time *not* to notice each other, *not* to talk, *not* to leave the theater, she leading him by his dead right arm through a maze of muddy alleys, past the confectioners' stands by the old cemetery, down the Jewish/Human fault line, and so on and so on into the blackness. For seven months they would ignore each other at the bazaar, at the Dial, and at the fountain of the prostrate mermaid, and they were sure they could ignore each other anywhere and always, sure they could be complete strangers, but were proven wrong when he returned home one afternoon from work only to pass her on her way out of his house.

What are you doing here? he asked, more afraid that she had revealed their relationship—to his father, who would surely beat him, or his mother, who would be so disappointed—than curious as to why she was there.

Your books are arranged by the color of their spines, she said. *How stupid.*

His mother was in Lutsk, he remembered, as she was every Tuesday at this time of the afternoon, and his father was washing himself outside. Safran went to his room to make sure everything was in order. His diary was still under his mattress. His books were properly stacked, according to color. (He pulled one off the shelf, to have something to hold.) The picture of his mother was at its normal skew on the nightstand next to his bed. There was no reason to think that she had touched a thing. He searched the kitchen, the study, even the bathrooms for any trace she might have left. Nothing. No stray hairs. No fingerprints on the mirror. No notes. Everything was in good order.

He went to his parents' bedroom. The pillows were perfect rectangles. The sheets were as smooth as water, tucked in tightly. The room looked as if it hadn't been touched in years, since a death, perhaps, as if it were being preserved as it once was, a time capsule. He didn't know how many times she had come. He couldn't ask her because he never talked to her anymore, and he couldn't ask his father because he would have had to confess everything, and he couldn't ask his mother because, if she were to find out, it would kill her, and that would kill him, and no matter how unlivable his life had become, he was not yet ready to end it.

He ran to the house of Lista P, the only lover to inspire him to bathe. *Let me in*, he said with his head against the door. *It's me, Safran. Let me in.*

He could hear shuffling, someone laboring to get to the door.

Safran? It was Lista's mother.

Hello, he said. *Is Lista in?*

Lista's in her room, she said, thinking what a sweet boy he was. *Go on up.*

What's wrong? Lista asked, seeing him at the door. She looked so much older than she had only three years before, at the theater, which made him wonder whether it was she or he who had changed. *Come in. Come in. Here*, she said, *sit down. What's going on?*

I'm all alone, he said.

You're not alone, she said, taking his head to her chest.

I am.

You're not alone, she said. *You only feel alone.*

To feel alone is to be alone. That's what it is.

Let me make you something to eat.

I don't want anything to eat.

Then have something to drink.

I don't want anything to drink.

She massaged his dead hand and remembered the last time she had touched it. It was not the death that had so attracted her to it, but the unknowability. The unattainability. He could never completely love her, not with all of himself. He could never be completely owned, and he could never own completely. Her desire had been sparked by the frustration of her desire.

You're going to be married, Safran. I got the invitation this morning. Is that what's upsetting you?

Yes, he said.

Well, you've got nothing to worry about. Everybody gets nervous before being wed. I did. I know my husband did. But Zosha's such a nice girl.

I've never met her, he said.

Well, she's very nice. And beautiful, too.

Do you think I will like her?

I do.

Will I love her?

It's possible. You should never make predictions with love, but it's definitely possible.

Do you love me? he asked. *Did you ever? That night with all the coffee.*

I don't know, she said.

Do you think it's possible that you did?

He touched the side of her face with his good hand, and moved it down to her neck, and then down under the collar of her shirt.

No, she said, taking his hand out.

No?

No.

But I want to. I really do. This isn't for you.

That's why we can't, she said. *I never would have been able to do it if I had thought that you wanted to.*

He put his head in her lap and fell asleep. Before leaving that evening, he gave Lista the book that he still had with him from his house—*Hamlet*, with a purple spine—that he had taken from the shelf to have something to hold.

For keeps? she asked.

You'll give it back to me one day.

My grandfather and the Gypsy girl knew none of this as they made love for the last time, as he touched her face and fingered the soft underside of her chin, as he paid her the attention received by a sculptor's wife. *Like this?* he asked. She brushed her eyelashes against his chest. She moved her butterfly kiss across his torso and up his neck to where his left earlobe connected to his jaw. *Like this?* she asked. He pulled her blue blouse over her head, he undid her bead necklaces, he licked her smooth and sweaty armpits and ran his finger from her neck to her navel. He drew circles around her caramel areolas with his tongue. *Like this?* he asked. She nodded and craned her head back. He flicked her nipples with his tongue, and knew that it was all so completely wrong, everything, from the moment of his birth to this, everything was coming out the wrong way—not the opposite, but worse: close. She used both hands to undo his belt. He lifted his backside off the ground so she could pull down his slacks and underpants. She took his penis into her hand. She wanted so badly for him to feel good. She was convinced that he had never felt good. She wanted to be the cause of his first and only pleasure. *Like this?* He put his hand on top of hers and guided it. She removed her skirt and panties, took his dead hand, pressed it between her legs. Her thick black pubic hair was wound in loose curls, in waves. *Like this?* he asked, although she was guiding his hand, as if trying to channel a message on a Ouija board. They guided each other over each other's body. She put his dead fingers inside her and felt, for a moment, the numbness and paralysis. She felt the death in and through her. *Now?* he asked. *Now?* She rolled onto him and spread her legs around his knees. She reached behind her and used his dead hand to guide his penis into her. *Is this good?* he asked. *Is this good?*

Seven months later, June 18, 1941, as the first display of German bombing lit the Trachimbrod skies electric, as my grandfather had his first orgasm (his first and only pleasure, of which she was not the cause), she slit her wrist with a knife that had been made dull carving love letters. But then, there, his sleeping head against her beating chest, she revealed nothing. She didn't say, *You are going to marry.* And she didn't say, *I am going to kill myself.* Only: *How do you arrange your books?*

Dear Jonathan,

I promised that I would never mention writing again, because I thought that we were beyond that. But I must break my promise.

I could hate you! Why will you not permit your grandfather to be in love with the Gypsy girl, and show her his love? Who is ordering you to write in such a manner? We have such chances to do good, and yet again and again you insist on evil. I would not read this most contemporary division to Little Igor, because I did not appraise it worthy of his ears. No, this division I presented to Sammy Davis, Junior, Junior, who acted faithfully with it.

I must make a simple question, which is what is wrong with you? If your grandfather loves the Gypsy girl, and I am certain that he does, why does he not leave with her? She could make him so happy. And yet he declines happiness. This is not reasonable, Jonathan, and it is not good. If I were the writer, I would have Safran show his love to the Gypsy girl, and take her to Greenwich Shtetl in New York City. Or I would have Safran kill himself, which is the only other truthful thing to perform, although then you would not be born, which would signify that this story could not be written.

You are a coward, Jonathan, and you have disappointed me. I would never command you to write a story that is as it occurred in the actual, but I would command you to make your story faithful. You are a coward for the same explanation that Brod is a coward, and Yankel is a coward, and Safran is a coward — all of your relatives are cowards! You are all cowards because you live in a world that is "once-removed," if I may excerpt you. I do not have any homage for anyone in your family, with exceptions of your grandmother, because you are all in the proximity of love, and all disavow love. I have enclosed the currency that you most recently posted.

Of course, I understand, in some manners, what you are attempting to perform. There is such a thing as love that cannot be, for certain. If I were to inform Father, for example, about how I comprehend love, and who I desire to love, he would kill me, and this is no idiom. We all choose things, and we also all choose against things. I want to be the kind of person who chooses _for_ more than chooses _against,_ but like Safran, and like you, I discover myself choosing this time and the next time against what I am certain is good and correct, and against what I am certain is worthy. I choose that I will not, instead of that I will. None of this is effortless to say.

I did not give Grandfather the money, but it was for very different reasons than you suggested. He was not surprised when I told him. "I am proud of you," he said.

"But you wanted me to give it to you?" I said.

"Very much," he said. "I am sure that I could find her."

"How can you be proud, then?"

"I am proud of you, not me."

"You are not angry with me?"

"No."

"I do not want to disappoint you."

"I am not angry or disappointed," he said.

"Does it make you sad that I am not giving you the money?"

"No. You are a good person, doing the good and right thing. It makes me content."

Why, then, did I feel that it was the pathetic, cowardly action, and that I was the pathetic coward? Let me explain why I did not give Grandfather my money. It is not because I am saving it for myself to go to America. That is a dream that I have woken up from. I will never see America, and neither will Little Igor, and I understand that now. I did not give Grandfather the money because I do not believe in Augustine. No, that is not what I mean. I do not believe in the Augustine that Grandfather was searching for. The woman in the photograph is alive. I am sure she is. But I am also sure that she is not Herschel, as Grandfather wanted her to be, and she is not my grandmother, as he wanted her to be, and she is not Father, as he wanted her to be. If I gave him the money, he would have found her, and he would have seen who she really is, and this would have killed him. I am not saying this metaphorically. It would have killed him.

But it was a situation without winning. The possibilities were none, between what was possible and what we wanted. And here I have to confer you some terrible news. Grandfather died four days ago. He cut his hands. It was very late in the night and I could not sleep. There was a noise coming from the bath, so I went to investigate it. (Now that I am the man of the house, it is up to me to see that everything works.) I found Grandfather in the bath, which was full of blood. I told him to stop sleeping, because I did not yet understand what was going on. "Wake up!" Then I shook him violently, and then I punched him in the face. It hurt my hand, I punched him so hard. I punched him again. I do not know why, but I did. To tell you the truth, I had never punched anyone before, only been punched. "Wake up!" I shouted at him, and I punched him again, this time the other side of his face. But I knew that he would not wake up. "You sleep too much!" My shouting woke up my mother, and she ran to the bath. She had to forcefully pull me off of Grandfather, and she later told me that she thought I had killed him, the way I was punching so much, and the look in my eyes. We invented a story about an accident with sleeping pills. This is what we told to Little Igor, so that he would never have to know.

It had been such an evening already. Volumes had happened, just as volumes now happen, just as volumes will happen. For the first time in my life, I told my father exactly what I thought, as I will now tell you, for the first time, exactly what I think. As with him, I ask for your forgiveness.

Love,
Alex

illumination

"HERSCHEL would care for your father when I had to make an errand, or when your grandmother was ill. She was ill all of the time, not only at the end of her life. Herschel would care for the baby, and hold it as if it were his own. He even called him son."

I told all of this to Jonathan as Grandfather told it to me, and he wrote all of it in his diary. He wrote:

"Herschel did not possess a family of his own. He was not such a social person. He loved to read very much, and also to write. He was a poet, and he exhibited me many of his poems. I remember many of them. They were silly, you could say, and about love. He was always in his room writing those things, and never with people. I used to tell him, What good is all of that love doing on paper? I said, Let love write on you for a little. But he was so stubborn. Or perhaps he was only timid."

"You were his friend?" I asked, although he had already said that he was Herschel's friend.

"We were his only friends, he once told us. Your grandmother and I. He would eat dinner with us, and on occasions remain very tardy. We even made vacations together. When your father was born, the three of us would make walks with the baby. When he needed a thing, he would come to us. When he had a problem, he would come to us. He once asked me if he could kiss your grandmother. Why, I asked him, and it made me an angry person, in truth, very angry, that he should desire to kiss her. Because I am afraid, he said, that I will never kiss a woman. Herschel, I said, it is because you do not try to kiss any."

(Was he in love with Grandmother?)

(I do not know.)

(It was a possibility?)

(It was a possibility. He would look at her, and also bring her flowers as gifts.)

(Did this upset you?)

(I loved them both.)

"Did he kiss her?"

"No," he said. (And you will remember, Jonathan, that he laughed here. It was a short, severe laugh.) "He was too timid to ever kiss anyone, even Anna. I do not think that they ever did anything."

"He was your friend," I said.

"He was my best friend. It was different then. Jews, not Jews. We were young still, and there was very much life in advance of us. Who knew?" (We did not know, is what I am attempting to say. How could we have known?)

"Knew what?" I asked.

"Who knew that we were living on such a needle?"

"A needle?"

"One day Herschel is eating dinner with us, and he is singing songs to your father in his arms."

"Songs?"

(Here he sang the song, Jonathan, and I know how you relish inserting songs in writing, but you could not require me to write this. I have tried for so long to displace the song from my brain, but it is always there. I hear myself singing it when I walk, and in my courses at university, and before sleep.)

"But we were very stupid people," he said, and he again examined the photograph and smiled. "So stupid."

"Why?"

"Because we believed in things."

"What things?" I asked, because I did not know. I was not understanding.

(Why are you asking so many questions?)

(Because you are not being clear with me.)

(I am very ashamed.)

(You do not have to be shamed in my closeness. Family are the people who must never make you feel ashamed.)

(You are wrong. Family are the people who must make you feel ashamed when you are deserving of shame.)

(And you are deserving of shame?)

(I am. I am trying to tell you.) "We were stupid," he said, "because we believed in things."

"Why is this stupid?"

"Because there are not things to believe in."

(Love?)

(There is no love. Only the end of love.)

(Goodness?)

(Do not be a fool.)

(God?)

(If God exists, He is not to be believed in.)

"Augustine?" I asked.

"I dreamed that this might be the thing," he said. "But I was wrong."

"Perhaps you were not wrong. We could not find her, but that does not signify anything about whether you should believe in her."

"What is the good of something that you cannot find?"

(I will tell you, Jonathan, that at this place in the conversation, it was no longer Alex and Alex, grandfather and grandson, talking. We yielded to be two different people, two people who could view one another in the eyes, and utter things that are not uttered. When I listened to him, I did not listen to Grandfather, but to someone else, someone I had never encountered before, but whom I knew better than Grandfather. And the person who was listening to this person was not me but someone else, someone I had never been before but whom I knew better than myself.)

"Tell me more," I said.

"More?"

"Herschel."

"It was as if he was in our family."

"Tell me what happened. What happened to him?"

"To him? To him and me. It happened to everybody, do not make any mistakes. Just because I was not a Jew, it does not mean that it did not happen to me."

"What is it?"

"You had to choose, and hope to choose the smaller evil."

"You had to choose," I told Jonathan, "and hope to choose the smaller evil."

"And I chose."

"And he chose."

"He chose what?"

"What did you choose?"

"When they captured our town—"

"Kolki?"

"Yes, but do not tell him. There is no reason to tell him."

"We could go in the morning."

"No."

"Perhaps it would be a good thing."

"No," he said. "My ghosts are not there."

(You have ghosts?)

(Of course I have ghosts.)

(What are your ghosts like?)

(They are on the insides of the lids of my eyes.)

(This is also where my ghosts reside.)

(You have ghosts?)

(Of course I have ghosts.)

(But you are a child.)

(I am not a child.)

(But you have not known love.)

(These are my ghosts, the spaces amid love.)

"You could reveal it to us," I said. "You could take us to where you once lived, and where his grandmother once lived."

"There is no purpose," he said. "Those people signify nothing to me."

"His grandmother."

"I do not want to know her name."

"He says that there is no purpose to return to the town that he came from," I told Jonathan. "It means nothing to him."

"Why did he leave?"

"Why did you leave?"

"Because I did not want your father to grow up so close to death. I did not want him to know of it, and live with it. This is why I never informed him of what occurred. I wanted so much for him to live a good life, without death and without choices and without shame. But I was not a good father, I must inform you. I was the worst father. I desired to remove him from everything that was bad, but instead I gave him badness upon badness. A father is always responsible for how his son is. You must understand."

"I am not understanding. I am not understanding any of this. I do not understand that you are from Kolki, and why I never knew. I do not understand why you came on this voyage if you knew how close we would be. I do not understand what are your ghosts. I do not understand how a picture of you was in Augustine's box."

(Do you remember what he did next, Jonathan? He examined the photograph again, and then placed it on the table again, and then he said, Herschel was a good person, and so was I, and because of this it is not right what happened, not anything of it. And then I asked him, What, what happened? He returned the photograph to the box, you will remember, and he told us the story. Exactly like that. He placed the photograph in the box, and he told it to us. He did not once avoid our eyes, and he did not once put his hands under the table. I murdered Herschel, he said. Or what I did was as good as murdering him. What do you mean? I asked him, because what he said was such a potent thing to say. No, this is not true. Herschel would have been murdered with or without me, but it is still as if I murdered him. What happened? I asked. They came in the most darkest time of the night. They had just come from another town, and would go to another after. They knew what they were doing, they were so logical. I remember with very much precision the feeling of my bed shaking when the tanks came. What is it? What is it? Grandmother asked. I moved from bed, and I examined out of the window. What did you see? I saw four tanks, and I can remember them in every aspect. There were four green tanks, and men walking along the sides of them. These men had guns, I will tell you, and they were pointing them at our doors and windows in case that someone should try to run. It was dark but I could still see this. Were you scared? I was scared, although I knew that I was not the one they wanted. How did you know? We knew about them. Everyone knew. Herschel knew. We did not think it would happen to us. I told you, we believed in things, we were so foolish. And then? And then I told Grandmother to get the baby, your father, and to take him into the cellar and not to manufacture any noise but also not to become overly afraid because we were not the ones that they wanted. And then? And then they stopped all of the tanks and for a moment I was so foolish to think that it was over, that they had decided to return to Germany and end the war because nobody likes war not even those who survive it, not even the winners. But? But they did not of course they had only stopped the tanks in front of the synagogue and they came out of their tanks and moved into very logical lines. The General who had blond hair put a microphone to his face and spoke in Ukrainian he said that everyone must come to the synagogue everyone with no omissions. The soldiers punched on every door with their guns and investigated the houses to be certain that everyone should be in front of the synagogue I told Grandmother to return upstairs with the baby because I feared that they would discover them in the basement and shoot them because of their hiding. Herschel I thought Herschel must escape how can he escape he must run now run into the darkness perhaps he has already run perhaps he heard the tanks and ran but when we arrived at the synagogue I saw Herschel and he saw me and we stood next to each other because that is what friends do in the presence of evil or love. What is going to happen he asked me and I told him I do not know what is going to happen and the truth is that not one of us knew what was going to happen although every one of us knew that it would be evil. It captured so long for the soldiers to finish their investigating of the houses it was very important to them to be certain that everyone was in front of the synagogue. I am so scared Herschel said I think I am going to cry. Why I asked why there is nothing to cry for there is no reason to cry but I will tell you that I too wanted to cry and I too was afraid but not for myself for Grandmother and for the baby. What did they do? What happened next? They made us stand in lines and I was next to Anna on the one side and Herschel on the other side some of the women were crying and this was because they were very afraid of the guns that the soldiers were holding and they thought that all of us were going to be killed. The General with blue eyes put the microphone to his face. You must listen carefully he said and do everything that is commanded or you will be shot. Herschel whispered to me I am very scared and I wanted to tell him run your chances are better if you run it is dark run you have no chances if you do not but I could not tell him this because I was afraid that I would be shot for speaking and I was also afraid of yielding to Herschel's death by admitting it be brave I said with as little volume as I could manufacture it is necessary that you be brave which I know now was such a stupid thing to utter the stupidest thing I have ever uttered be brave for what? Who is the rabbi the General asked and the rabbi elevated his hand. Two of the guards seized the rabbi and pushed him into the synagogue. Who is the cantor the General asked and the cantor elevated his hand but he was not so quiet about death as the rabbi he was crying and saying no to his wife no no nonono and she lifted her hand to him and two guards seized her and put her in the synagogue also. Who are the Jews the General asked into his microphone all the Jews move forward but not one person moved forward. All of the Jews must move forward he said again and this time he shouted it but again not one person moved forward and I will tell you that if I were a Jew I would also not move forward the General went to the first line and he said into his microphone you will point out a Jew or you will be considered a Jew the first person he went to was a Jew named Abraham. Who is a Jew the General asked him and Abraham trembled Who is a Jew the General asked again and he put his gun to Abraham's head Aaron is a Jew Aaron and he pointed to Aaron who was in the second row which is where we were standing. Two guards seized Aaron and he was resisting very much so they shot him in the head and this is when I felt Herschel's hand touch mine. Do as you are commanded the General with a scar on his face shouted into his microphone or. He went to the second person in the line who was a friend of mine Leo and he said who is a Jew and Leo pointed to Abraham and he said that man is a Jew I am sorry Abraham two guards secured Abraham into the synagogue a woman in the fourth row tried to run away with her baby in her arms but the General shouted something in German that most terrible horrible ugly disgusting vile monstrous language and one of the guards shot her in the back of the head and they pulled her and her baby who was still alive into the synagogue. The General went to the next man in line and the next and everyone was pointing at a Jew because nobody wanted to be killed one Jew pointed at his cousin and one pointed at himself because he would not point at another. They secured Daniel into the synagogue and also Talia and Louis and every Jew there was but for some reason that I will never know Herschel was never pointed to perhaps this is because I was his only friend and he was not so social and many people did not even know he existed I was the only one who would know to point at him or perhaps it was because it was so dark that he could not be seen anymore. It was not forever before he was the only Jew remaining outside of the synagogue the General was now in the second row and said to a man because he only asked men I do not know why who is a Jew and the man said they are all in the synagogue because he did not know Herschel or did not know that Herschel was a Jew the General shotthismaninthehead and I could feel Herschel's hand touching mine very lightly and I made certain not to look at him the General went to the next person who is a Jew he asked and this person said they are all in the synagogue you must believe me I am not lying why would I lie you can kill them all I do not care but please spare me please do not kill me please and then the General shothiminthehead and said I am becoming tired of this and he went to the next man in line and that was me who is a Jew he asked and I felt Herschel's hand again and I know that his hand was saying pleaseplease Eli please I do not want to die please do not point at me you know what is going to happen to me if you point at me do not point at me I am afraid of dying I am so afraid of dying I am soafraidofdying Iamsoafraidofdying who is a Jew the General asked me again and I felt on my other hand the hand of Grandmother and I knew that she was holding your father and that he was holding you and that you were holding your children I am so afraid of dying I am soafraidofdying Iamsoafraidofdying Iamsoafraidofdying and I said he is a Jew who is a Jew the General asked and Herschel embraced my hand with much strength and he was my friend he was my best friend I would have let him kiss Anna and even make love to her but I am I and my wife is my

wife and my baby is my baby do you understand what I am telling you I
pointed at Herschel and said he is a Jew this man is a Jew please Herschel
said to me and he was crying tell them it is nottrue please Eli please two
guards seized him and he did not resist but he did cry more and harder
and he shouted tell them that there are no more Jews nomoreJews and
you only said that I was a Jew so that you would not be killed I am begging you Eli youaremyfriend do not let me die I am so afraid of dying
Iamsoafraid it will be OK I told him it will be OK do not do this he said
do something do something dosomething dosomething it will be OK it
will beOK who was I saying that to do something Eli dosomething I am
soafraidofdying I am soafraid you know what they are going to do
youaremyfriend I told him although I do not know why I said that at that
moment and the guards put him in the synagogue with the rest of the
Jews and everyone else was remaining outside to hear the cryingoftheba-
bies and the cryingoftheadults and to see the black spark when the first
match was lit by a youngman who could not have been any older than I
was or Herschel was or you are it illuminated those who were not in the
synagogue those who were not going to die and he cast it on the
branches that were pushed against the synagogue what made it so awful
was how it was soslow and how the fire made itself deadmanytimes and
had to be remade I looked at Grandmother and shekissedmeonthefore-
head and I kissedheronthemouth and our tearsmixedonourlips and then
I kissedyourfather many times I secured him from Grandmother's arms
and Iheldhimwithmuchforce so much that he started crying I said I love
you I love you I love you I love you I loveyou I loveyou I loveyou I
loveyou Iloveyou Iloveyou Iloveyou Iloveyou Iloveyou IloveyouIlove-
youIloveyouIloveyou and I knew that I had to change everything to leave
everything behind and I knew that I could never allow him to learn of
whoIwas or whatIdid because it was for him that I didwhatIdid it was for
him that I pointed and for him that Herschel was murdered that I murdered Herschel and this is why he is how he is he is how is he because a
father is always responsible for his son and I am I and Iamresponsible not
for Herschel but for my son because I held him with somuch-
forcethathecried because I loved him so much that I madeloveimpossible
and I am sorry for you and sorry for Iggy and it is you who must forgive

me he said these things to us and Jonathan where do we go now what do we do with what we know Grandfather said that I am I but this could not be true the truth is that I also pointedatHerschel and I also said heisaJew and I will tell you that you also pointedatHerschel and you also said heisaJew and more than that Grandfather also pointedatme and said heisaJew and you also pointedathim and said heisaJew and your grandmother and Little Igor and we all pointedateachother so what is it he should have done hewouldhavebeenafooltodoanythingelse but is it forgivable what he did canheeverbeforgiven for his finger for whathisfingerdid for whathepointedto and didnotpointto for whathetouchedinhislife and whathedidnottouch he is stillguilty I am I am Iam IamI?)

"And now," he said, "we must make sleep."

THE WEDDING RECEPTION WAS SO EXTRAORDINARY!

or

THE END OF THE MOMENT THAT NEVER ENDS, 1941

AFTER THOROUGHLY satisfying the sister of the bride against a wall of empty wine racks—*Oh, God!* she screamed, *Oh, God!* her hands in the phantom Cabernet—and being himself so thoroughly unsatisfied, Safran pulled up his trousers, climbed the newly installed spiral staircase —brushing his hand deliberately, thoughtfully along the marble newel —and greeted the wedding guests, who were only then seating themselves after the haunting gust.

Where were you? Zosha asked, taking his dead hand into hers, something she had wanted to do since first seeing it at the announcement of their engagement more than half a year before.

Downstairs, changing.

Oh, I don't want you to change, she said, thinking she was making a good joke. *I think you're perfect.*

My clothes.

But it took you so long.

He nodded at his arm and watched her questioning lips pucker into a small peck for his cheek.

The Double House was brimming with organized pandemonium. Even up to the last minute, even past the last minute, hangings were still being hung, salads mixed, girdles clenched and tied, chandeliers dusted, throw rugs thrown...It was extraordinary.

The bride must be so happy for her mother.

> *I always cry at wedding receptions, but this one's gonna make me wail.*
> *It's extraordinary. It's extraordinary.*

The dark women in white uniforms were just beginning to serve bowls of chicken soup when Menachem clinked a fork against his glass and said, *I'd like to have a moment of your time.* The room quickly became silent, everyone stood—as was traditional for the toast of the father of the bride—and my grandfather recognized, out of the corner of his eye, the caramel hand that slid his bowl in front of him.

It's said that the times are changing. Borders around us shift under the pressure of the war; places we have known for as long as we can remember are called by new names; some of our own sons are absent from this joyous occasion because of their national service; and, on a brighter note, we are pleased to announce that we will have delivered to us in three months the first automobile in Trachimbrod! (This was met by a collective gasp and then raging applause.) *Well,* he said, moving behind the newlyweds to put one hand on his daughter's shoulder and one on my grandfather's, *let me keep this moment, this early afternoon, June 18, 1941.*

The Gypsy girl never said a word—because even if she hated Zosha, she didn't want to ruin her wedding—but pressed against my grandfather's left side, and took, under the table, his good hand into hers. (Did she even slide a note into it?)

Let me wear it in a locket over my heart, the proud father continued, pacing the room with his empty crystal goblet held in front of him, *and keep it forever, because I have never been so happy in my life, and will be perfectly content if I never experience half of this happiness again — until the wedding of my other daughter, of course. Indeed,* he said, hemming the laughter, *if there are to be no other moments for the rest of time, I would never once complain. Let this be the moment that never ends.*

My grandfather squeezed the Gypsy girl's fingers, as if to say, *It's not too late. There is still time. We could run, leave everything behind, never look back, save ourselves.*

She squeezed his fingers, as if to say, *You are not forgiven.*

Menachem continued, trying to hold back tears, *Please raise your empty glasses with me. To my daughter and new son, to the children they will produce, and the children of those children, to life!*

L'chaim! echoed voices down the line of tables.

But before the father of the bride had taken his seat, before the glasses had a chance to clink their reflected smiles against one another in hope, the house was again swept with a haunting gust. The place cards were again thrown into the air, and the floral centerpieces were again knocked over, this time spreading dirt over the white tablecloth and onto almost every lap. The Gypsy women rushed to clean up the mess, and my grandfather whispered into Zosha's ear, which for him was the Gypsy girl's ear: *It will be OK.*

The Gypsy girl, the *real* Gypsy girl, did slip my grandfather a note, although it fell out of his hand in the commotion and was kicked across the floor — by Libby, by Lista, by Omeler, by the nameless fishmonger — to the far end of the table, where it came to rest under an overturned wine glass, which kept it safe under its skirt until that night, when a Gypsy woman picked up the glass and swept the note (along with fallen food, dirt from the centerpieces, and piles of dust) into a large paper bag. This bag was put out in front of the house by a different Gypsy woman. The next morning, the paper bag was collected by the obsessive-compulsive garbage man Feigel B. The bag was then taken to a field on the other side of the river — the field that would, soon enough, be the site of Kovel's first mass execution — and burned with dozens of other bags, three quarters of which contained debris from the wedding. The flames reached into the sky, red and yellow fingers. The smoke spread like a canopy over the neighboring fields, making many a Wisp of Ardisht cough, because every kind of smoke is different and must be made familiar. Some of the ash that remained was incorporated into the soil. The rest was washed away by the next rain and swept into the Brod.

This is what the note said: *Change.*

The First Blasts, and Then Love, 1941

THAT NIGHT, my grandfather made love to his new wife for the first time. He thought, as he performed the act that he had practiced to perfection, about the Gypsy girl: he reweighed the arguments for running away with her, for leaving Trachimbrod with the knowledge that he could never go back. He did love his family—his mother, anyway—but how long would it take before he stopped missing them? It sounded so terrible when articulated, but, he wondered, was there anything he couldn't leave behind? He entertained thoughts so ugly and true: everyone but the Gypsy girl and his mother could die and he would be able to go on; every aspect of his life, save his time with the Gypsy girl and his mother, was insufficient and undeserving of life. He was about to become someone who has lost half of everything he lived for.

He thought about the various widows of his past seven years: Golda R and her covered mirrors, Lista P's blood, which was not intended for him. He thought about all of the virgins that summed to nothing. He thought, easing his new wife's nervous virgin body onto the marriage bed, about Brod, author of the 613 sadnesses, and Yankel, with his abacus bead. He thought, while explaining to Zosha that it would only hurt the first time, about Zosha, whom he hardly knew, and her sister, who made him promise that their postnuptial tryst would not be a one-time occurrence. He thought about the legend of Trachim, about where his body might be, and from where it once came. He thought about Trachim's wagon: the wandering snakes of white string, the crushed-velvet glove with outstretched fingers, the resolution: *I will…I will…*

And then something extraordinary happened. The house shook with

JONATHAN SAFRAN FOER

such a violence as to make the day's earlier disturbances seem like the burps of a baby. *KABOOM!* in the distance. Approaching *KABOOM! KABOOOM!* Light poured in through the cracks between cellar door planks, filling the room with the warm and dynamic radiance of German bombs exploding in the nearby hills. *KABOOOOM!* Zosha howled in fear—of physical love, of war, of emotional love, of dying—and my grandfather was filled with a coital energy of such force that when it unleashed itself—*KA-BOOOOOOOOOOOOM! KA-BOO-BOOOOOOOOOOOOOOOOOOOOOOOOOOOOOOOOOOOM! KA-KA-KA-KA-KA-KA-BOOOOOOOOOOOOOOOOOOOOOOOOOOOM!*—when he tripped over the precipice of civilized humanity into the free fall of unadulterated animal rapture, when, in seven eternal seconds, he more than made up for the sum of what was now more than 2,700 acts without consequence, when he flooded Zosha with a deluge of what could no longer be held back, when he released into the universe a copulative light so powerful that if it could have been harnessed and utilized, rather than sent forth and wasted, the Germans wouldn't have had a chance, he wondered if one of the bombs hadn't landed on the marriage bed, wedged itself between the shuddering body of his new wife and his own, and obliterated Trachimbrod. But when he hit the rocky canyon's floor, when the seven seconds of bombing ended and his head settled into the pillow damp with Zosha's tears and drenched with his semen, he understood that he was not dead, but in love.

The Persnicketiness of Memory, 1941

JUST AS my grandfather's first orgasm was not intended for Zosha, the bombs that inspired it were not intended for Trachimbrod but a site in the Rovno hills. It would be nine months—on Trachimday, no less—before the shtetl was the focus of direct Nazi assault. But the Brod's waters roiled onto its banks that night with the same fervor as if it had been war, the wind snapped in the explosive wake with the same resonance, and the shtetl folk trembled as if the sites were tattooed on their bodies. From that moment on—9:28 in the evening, June 18, 1941—everything was different.

The Wisps of Ardisht turned their cigarettes backward, cupping their mouths around the lit ends to prevent their being spotted from a distance.

The Gypsies in their hamlet took down their tents, dismantled their thatch shanties, and lived uncovered, clinging to the earth like human moss.

Trachimbrod itself was overcome with a strange inertness. The citizenry, which once touched so many things it was impossible to know what was natural, now sat on their hands. Activity was replaced with thought. Memory. Everything reminded everyone of something, which seemed winsome at first—when early birthdays could be recalled by the smell of an extinguished match, or the feeling of one's first kiss by sweat in the palm—but quickly became devitalizing. Memory begat memory begat memory. Villagers became embodiments of that legend they had been told so many times, of mad Sofiowka, swaddled in white string, using memory to remember memory, bound in an order of remembrance, struggling in vain to remember a beginning or end.

JONATHAN SAFRAN FOER

Men set up flow charts (which were themselves memories of family trees) in an attempt to make sense of their memories. They tried to follow the line back, like Theseus out of the labyrinth, but only went in deeper, farther.

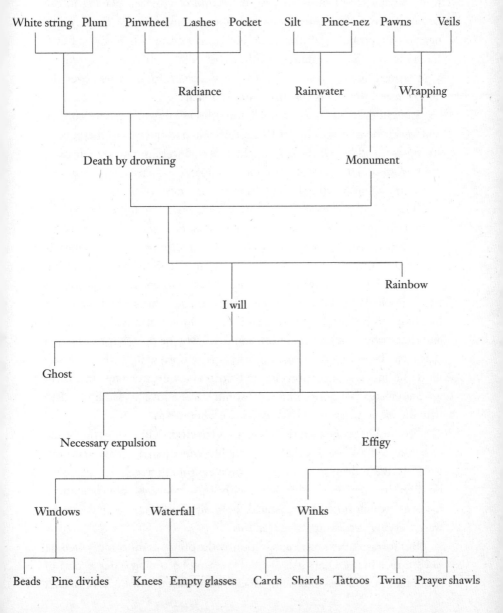

Women had it worse. Unable to share their tinglings of memory in the synagogue or at the workplace, they were forced to suffer over laundry piles and baking pans, alone. There was no help in their searches for beginnings, no one to ask what the grit of pressed raspberries might have to do with a steam burn, or why the sound of children playing in the Brod made their hearts drop out of their chests and onto the floor. Memory was supposed to fill the time, but it made time a hole to be filled. Each second was two hundred yards, to be walked, crawled. You couldn't see the next hour, it was so far in the distance. Tomorrow was over the horizon, and would take an entire day to reach.

But children had it worst of all, for although it would seem that they had fewer memories to haunt them, they still had the itch of memory as strong as the elders of the shtetl. Their strings were not even their own, but tied around them by parents and grandparents—strings not fastened to anything, but hanging loosely from the darkness.

The only thing more painful than being an active forgetter is to be an inert rememberer. Safran lay in bed trying to string the events of his seventeen years into a coherent narrative, something that he could understand, with an order of imagery, an intelligibility of symbolism. Where were the symmetries? The rifts? What was the meaning of what had happened? He had been born with teeth, and that's why his mother had stopped breastfeeding him, and that's why his arm had gone dead, and that's why women loved him, and that's why he did what he did, and that's why he was who he was. But why was he born with teeth? And why didn't his mother just express her milk into a bottle? And why did an arm go dead instead of a leg? And why would anyone love a dead limb? And why did he do what he did? Why was he who he was?

He couldn't concentrate. His love had overtaken him from the inside out, like a sickness. He became terribly constipated, nauseated, and weak. In the reflection of the new porcelain toilet's water, he saw a face he didn't recognize: sagging jowls with white whiskers, pouches under his eyes (which must, he reasoned, hold all of the tears of joy that he wasn't crying), cracking, fattening lips.

But it wasn't the same recognition as the previous morning, when he saw his face in the Dial's glass eyes. He wasn't becoming older as part of some natural process, but being made old as a victim of his love, which was itself only one day old. He was a boy still, but no longer a boy. A man, but not yet a man. He was caught somewhere between his mother's last kiss and the first kiss he would give his child, between the war that was and would be.

A shtetl meeting was held in the theater the morning after the bombs exploded—the first since the debate over electric lighting several years before—to discuss the implications of a war whose tracks seemed to be laid directly over Trachimbrod.

RAV D

(Holding a sheet of paper above his head.) I have read in a letter from my son, who is fighting bravely on the Polish front, that the Nazis are committing unspeakable atrocities and that Trachimbrod should prepare for the worst. He said we should *(looks at paper, gestures reading)* "do anything and everything immediately."

ARI F

What are you talking about! We should go to the Nazis! *(Calling out, waving a finger above his head.)* It's the Ukrainians who'll do us in! You've heard what they did in Lvov! (It reminds me of my birth [I was born on the Rabbi's floor, you know (my nose still remembers that mix of placenta and Judaica [he had the most beautiful candle holders (from Austria [if I'm not mistaken (or Germany)])])]) . . .

RAV D

(Puzzled, gesturing puzzlement.) What are you talking about?

ARI F

(Most sincerely puzzled.) I can't remember. The Ukrainians. My birth. Candles. I know there was a point. Where did I begin?

And so it was when anyone tried to speak: their minds would become tangled in remembrance. Words became floods of thought with no beginning or end, and would drown the speaker before he could reach the life raft of the point he was trying to make. It was impossible to remember what one meant, what, after all of the words, was intended.

They had been terrified at first. Shtetl meetings were held daily, news reports (NAZIS KILL 8,200 ON UKRAINIAN BORDER) examined with the care of editors, plans of action drawn up and crumpled up, large maps spread out on tables like patients waiting to be cut open. But then the meetings convened every other day, and then every other every other day, and then weekly, serving more as social minglers for singles than planning sessions. After only two months, without the impetus of any further bombing, most Trachimbroders had removed all of the splinters of the terror that had entered them that night.

They hadn't forgotten, but accommodated. Memory took the place of terror. In their efforts to remember what it was they were trying so hard to remember, they could finally think over the fear of war. The memories of birth, childhood, and adolescence resonated with greater volume than the din of exploding shells.

So nothing was done. No decisions were made. No bags packed or houses emptied. No trenches dug or buildings fortified. Nothing. They waited like fools, they sat on their hands like fools, and spoke, like fools, about the time Simon D did that hilarious thing with the plum, which all could laugh about for hours but none could quite remember. They waited to die, and we cannot blame them, because we would do the same, and we *do* do the same. They laughed and joked. They thought about birthday candles and waited to die, and we must forgive them. They wrapped Menachem's jumbo trout in newspaper (NAZIS APPROACH LUTSK) and carried beef briskets in wicker baskets to picnics under tall tree canopies by the small falls.

Bedridden since his orgasm, my grandfather was unable to attend the first shtetl meeting. Zosha handled hers with more dignity, perhaps because she didn't have one at all, or perhaps because even though she loved being a married woman, and loved to touch that dead arm, she had yet to fall in love. She changed the semen-starched sheets, made her new husband toast and coffee for breakfast, and brought him a plate of left-over wedding chicken for lunch.

What is it? she asked, seating herself on the end of the bed. *Did I do something wrong? Are you unhappy with me?* My grandfather remembered that she was only a child: fifteen, and younger than her years. She had experienced nothing compared to him. She had felt nothing.

I am happy, he said.

I can wear my hair in a ponytail if you think that would make me more pretty.

You're pretty as you are. Really.

And last night. Did I please you? I will learn. I'm sure I will.

You were wonderful, he said. *I'm just not feeling well. It's nothing with you. Everything with you is wonderful.*

She kissed him on the lips and said, *I am your wife*, as if to reaffirm her vows, or remind herself, or him.

That night, when he had recovered enough strength to wash and dress, he returned to the Dial for the second time in two days. It was quite a different scene. Stark. Empty. Without yoidle-doidling. The shtetl square was still caked with white flour, although a rain had swept it into the spaces between cobblestones, replacing the sheet with an intricate network. Most of the banners of the previous day's festivities had been taken down, but a few remained, draped from the sills of high windows.

Great-great-great-grandfather, he said, lowering himself (with great difficulty) to his knees, *I feel that I ask for so little.*

In the sense that you never come to talk to me, the Dial said (with the unmoving lips of a ventriloquist), *what you say is true. You never write, you never —*

I haven't ever wanted to burden you.

I haven't ever wanted to burden you.

But you have, great-great-great-grandfather. You have. See my face, with its sag and give. I look four times my age. I have this dead arm, this war, this problem with memory. And now I am in love.

What makes you think I have anything to do with this?

I am a dupe of chance.

The Gypsy girl. What ever became of her? She was nice.

What?

The Gypsy girl? The one you loved.

It's not her that I love. It's my girl. My girl.

Oh, the Dial said, letting his *Oh* fall to the cobblestones and settle into the flour in the cracks before continuing. *You love the baby in Zosha's belly. The others are being pulled back, and you're being pulled forward.*

In both directions! he said, seeing the wagon's refuse, the words on Brod's body, the pogroms, the weddings, the suicides, the makeshift cribs, the parades, and seeing also his possible futures: life with the Gypsy girl, life alone, life with Zosha and the child who would fulfill him, the end of life. The images of his infinite pasts and infinite futures washed over him as he waited, paralyzed, in the present. He, Safran, marked the division between what was and what would be.

And what is it that you want from me? the Dial asked.

Make her healthy. Let her be born without sickness, without blindness, weak heart, or dead limbs. Let her be perfect.

Hush, and then: Safran retched his morning's toast and midafternoon's leftovers onto the Dial's rigid feet in a chunky pool of yellows and browns.

At least I didn't step in it, the Dial said.

You see! Safran pleaded, barely able to support his kneeling body. *This is what it's like!*

What what's like?

Love.

What?

Love, Safran said. *This is what it's like.*

Do you know that after my accident your great-great-great-grandmother would enter my room at night?

What?

She would get in bed with me, God bless her soul, knowing that I would attack her. We were supposed to sleep in separate rooms, but every night she'd come to be with me.

I don't understand.

Every morning, she'd clean me of my excrement, bathe me, dress me, and see that my hair was combed like a sane man's, even when it meant an elbow to the nose or a broken rib. She polished the blade. She wore my teeth marks on her body like other wives might wear jewelry. The hole didn't matter. We paid it no attention. We shared a room. She was with me. She did all of those things and so many more, things I would never tell anyone, and she never even loved me. Now that's love.

JONATHAN SAFRAN FOER

Let me tell you a story, the Dial went on. *The house that your great-great-great-grandmother and I moved into when we first became married looked out onto the small falls, at the end of the Jewish/Human fault line. It had wood floors, long windows, and enough room for a large family. It was a handsome house. A good house.*

But the water, your great-great-great-grandmother said, I can't hear myself think.

Time, I urged her. Give it time.

And let me tell you, while the house was unreasonably humid, and the front lawn perpetual mud from all the spray, while the walls needed to be repapered every six months, and chips of paint fell from the ceiling like snow for all seasons, what they say about people who live next to waterfalls is true.

What, my grandfather asked, *do they say?*

They say that people who live next to waterfalls don't hear the water.

They say that?

They do. Of course, your great-great-great-grandmother was right. It was terrible at first. We couldn't stand to be in the house for more than a few hours at a time. The first two weeks were filled with nights of intermittent sleep and quarreling for the sake of being heard over the water. We fought so much just to remind ourselves that we were in love, and not in hate.

But the next weeks were a little better. It was possible to sleep a few good hours each night and eat in only mild discomfort. Your great-great-great-grandmother still cursed the water (whose personification had become anatomically refined), but less frequently, and with less fury. Her attacks on me also quieted. It's your fault, she would say. You wanted to live here.

Life continued, as life continues, and time passed, as time passes, and after a little more than two months: Do you hear that? I asked her on one of the rare mornings we sat at the table together. Hear it? I put down my coffee and rose from my chair. You hear that thing?

What thing? she asked.

Exactly! I said, running outside to pump my fist at the waterfall. Exactly!

We danced, throwing handfuls of water in the air, hearing nothing at all. We alternated hugs of forgiveness and shouts of human triumph at the water. Who wins the day? Who wins the day, waterfall? We do! We do!

And this is what living next to a waterfall is like, Safran. Every widow

wakes one morning, perhaps after years of pure and unwavering grieving, to re-
alize she slept a good night's sleep, and will be able to eat breakfast, and doesn't
hear her husband's ghost all the time, but only some of the time. Her grief is re-
placed with a useful sadness. Every parent who loses a child finds a way to laugh
again. The timbre begins to fade. The edge dulls. The hurt lessens. Every love is
carved from loss. Mine was. Yours is. Your great-great-great-grandchildren's
will be. But we learn to live in that love.

My grandfather nodded his head, as if he understood.

But it's not the entire story, the Dial continued. I realized this when I
first tried to whisper a secret and couldn't, or whistle a tune without instilling
fear in the hearts of those within a hundred yards, when my coworkers at the
flour mill pleaded with me to lower my voice, because, Who can think with you
shouting like that? To which I asked, AM I REALLY SHOUTING?

Hush, and then: sky obscuring, the curtains of clouds parting, the
hands of thunder clapping. The universe poured down in a bombing on-
slaught of heavenly vomit.

Those still awake and outside ran for cover. The traveling journalist
Shakel R held the *Lvov Daily Observed* (NAZIS MOVE EAST) over his
head. The famous visiting playwright Bunim W, whose tragicomic ren-
dition of the Trachim story — *Trachim!* — was met with popular enthusiasm and critical indifference, jumped into the Brod to avoid being hit.
The divine hurl fell from the firmament in newborn-sized chunks at
first, then sheets, soaking Trachimbrod to its foundations, turning the
Brod waters orange, filling the prostrate mermaid's dry fountain to its
lip, filling the cracks of the synagogue's crumbling portico, glazing the
poplars, drowning small insects, making drunk with pleasure the rats and
vultures by the riverbank.

The Beginning of the World Often Comes, 1942–1791

CANOPIES OF THIN WHITE STRING spanned the narrow cobbled arteries of Trachimbrod that afternoon, March 18, 1942, as they had every Trachimday for one hundred fifty years. It had been the good gefiltefishmonger Bitzl Bitzl R's idea, to commemorate the first of the wagon's refuse to surface. One end of white string tied around the volume knob of a radio (NAZIS ENTER UKRAINE, MOVE EAST WITH SPEED) on the wobbly bookcase in Benjamin T's one-room shanty, the other around an empty silver candle holder on the dining room table of the More-or-Less-Respected Rabbi's brick house across muddy Shelister Street; thin white string like a clothesline from the light-boom stand of Trachimbrod's first and only photographer to the middle-C hammer of the darling of Zeinvel Z's piano shop on the other side of Malkner Street; white string connecting freelance journalist (GERMANS PUSH ON, SENSING IMMINENT VICTORY) to electrician over the tranquil and anticipating palm of the River Brod; white string from the monument of Pinchas T (carved, perfectly realistically, of marble) to a Trachimbrod novel (about love) to the glass case of wandering snakes of white string (kept at 56 degrees in the Museum of True Folklore), forming a scalene triangle, reflected in the Dial's glass eyes in the middle of the shtetl square.

My grandfather and his very pregnant wife watched from a picnic blanket on their lawn as the floats began the parade. First, as was traditional, went the float from Rovno: skimpy, with wilted yellow butterflies immodestly covering the splintered pine of a fieldworker effigy, which didn't look good last year and looked even worse now. (The carcasses could be seen in the spaces between the wings.) Klezmer bands preceded the float from Kolki, which hobbled on the shoulders of middle-aged men, as the young men were on the front lines, and the horses were being used in a nearby coal mine to support the war effort.

OH! Zosha giggled loudly, unable to control her voice. *IT JUST GAVE ME A KICK!*

My grandfather put his ear against her belly and received a powerful knock to the head, lifting him off the ground, landing him on his back a few feet away.

THAT CHILD IS EXTRAORDINARY!

There were fewer handsome men assembled along the shoreline than any year since that first one when everything began, when Trachim did or did not get pinned under his wagon. The handsome men were away fighting a war whose ramifications no one had yet to understand, and no one would or will understand. Most of what was left for the contest were the cripples, and cowards who crippled themselves—broke a hand, burnt an eye, feigned deafness or blindness—in order to dodge conscription. It was a contest of cripples and cowards, diving for a sack of gold that was a sack of fool's gold. They were trying to believe that life was as usual, healthy, that tradition could plug the leaks, that joy was still possible.

The floats and marchers made their way from the river's mouth to the toy and pastry stands set up by the rusting plaque commemorating where the wagon did or didn't flip and sink:

THIS PLAQUE MARKS THE SPOT
(OR A SPOT CLOSE TO THE SPOT)
WHERE THE WAGON OF ONE
TRACHIM B
(WE THINK)
WENT IN.

Shtetl Proclamation, 1791

As the first floats passed the More-or-Less-Respected Rabbi's window (from which he gave the necessary nod of approval), men in green-gray uniforms were being killed in shallow trenches.

Lutsk, Sarny, Kovel. Their floats were adorned with thousands of butterflies, and alluded to aspects of the Trachim story: the wagon, the twins, the umbrella ribs and skeleton keys, the bleeding red-ink script: *I will...I will...* In another place, their sons were killed between the barbs of their own guard wire, killed with misfired bombs while squirming in the mire like animals, killed with friendly fire, killed sometimes without knowing that they were about to die—a bullet through the head while joking with a comrade, laughing.

Lvov, Pinsk, Kivertsy. Their floats were marched along the Brod's bank, adorned in red, brown, and purple butterflies, showing their carcasses like ugly truths. (And here it is becoming harder and harder not to yell: *GO AWAY! RUN WHILE YOU CAN, FOOLS! RUN FOR YOUR LIVES!*) The bands bellowed, trumpets and violins, pocket trumpets and violas, homemade wax-paper kazoos.

ANOTHER KICK! Zosha laughed. *ANOTHER!*

And again my grandfather put his ear to her belly (having to get on his knees just to reach its crest), and again he was thumped backward.

THAT'S MY BABY! he hollered, his right eye absorbing the bruise like a sponge.

The Trachimbrod float was covered with black and blue butterflies. The daughter of the electrician Berl G sat on a raised platform in the middle of the float, wearing a blue neon tiara whose power cord reached back hundreds of yards to the outlet above her bed. (She had planned to recoil it as she traced her way back home when the parade was over.) The Float Queen was surrounded by the young float princesses of the shtetl, dressed in blue lace, waving their arms about like waves. A quartet of fiddlers played Polish national songs from a stand in the front of the float, and another played Ukrainian traditionals from the back.

On the banks, men sitting in wooden chairs reminisced about old loves, and girls never kissed, and books never read and written, and the time So-and-So did that funny thing with the what's-it-called, and injuries, and dinners, and how they would have washed the hair of women they never met, and apologies, and whether Trachim was or was not pinned under his wagon after all.

The earth turned in the sky.

Yankel turned in the earth.

The prehistoric ant on Yankel's thumb, which had lain motionless in the honey-colored stone since Brod's curious birth, turned away from the sky and hid its head between its many legs, in shame.

My grandfather and his young, tremendously pregnant wife walked up to the shore to watch the dive.

(Here it is almost impossible to go on, because we know what happens, and wonder why they don't. Or it's impossible because we fear that they do.)

When the Trachimbrod float reached the toy and pastry stands, the Float Queen was given the signal by the Rabbi to throw the sacks into the water. Mouths opened. Hands were separated — the first halves of applause. Blood flowed through bodies. It was almost like old times. This was celebration, unmitigated by imminent death. This was imminent death, unmitigated by celebration. She threw them high into the air . . . . They stayed there . . . . They hung as if on strings . . . .

JONATHAN SAFRAN FOER

. . . The Dial tiptoed across the cobblestones like a chess piece and hid himself under the breasts of the prostrate mermaid. . . . .

. . . . There is still time. . . . . . .

After the bombing was over, the Nazis moved through the shtetl. They lined up everyone who didn't drown in the river. They unrolled a Torah in front of them. "Spit," they said. "Spit, or else." Then they put all of the Jews in the synagogue. (It was the same in every shtetl. It happened hundreds of times. It happened in Kovel only a few hours before, and would happen in Kolki in only a few hours.) A young soldier tossed the nine volumes of *The Book of Recurrent Dreams* onto the bonfire of Jews, not noticing, in his haste to grab and destroy more, that one of the pages fell out of one of the books and descended, coming to rest like a veil on a child's burnt face:

> 9:613 — *The dream of the end of the world.* bombs poured down from the sky exploding across trachimbrod in bursts of light and heat those watching the festivities hollered ran frantically they jumped into the bubbling splashing frantically dynamic water not after the sack of gold but to save themselves they stayed under as long as they could they surfaced to seize air and look for loved ones my safran picked up his wife and carried her like a newlywed into the water which seemed amid the falling trees and hackling crackling explosions the safest place hundreds of bodies poured into the brod that river with my name I embraced them with open arms come to me come I wanted to save them all to save everybody from everybody the bombs rained from the sky and it was not the explosions or scattering shrapnel that would be our death not the heckling cinders not the laughing debris but all of the bodies bodies flailing and grabbing hold of one another bodies looking for something to hold on to my safran lost sight of his wife who was carried deeper into me by the pull of the bodies

the silent shrieks were carried in bubbles to the surface where they popped PLEASE PLEASE PLEASE PLEASE the kicking in zosha's belly became more and more PLEASE PLEASE the baby refused to die like this PLEASE the bombs came down cackling smoldering and my safran was able to break free from the human mass and float downstream over the small falls to clearer waters zosha was pulled down PLEASE and the baby refusing to die like this was pulled up and out of her body turning the waters around her red she surfaced like a bubble to the light to oxygen to life to life WAWAWA-WAWAWA she cried she was perfectly healthy and she would have lived except for the umbilical cord that pulled her back under toward her mother who was barely conscious but conscious of the cord and tried to break it with her hands and then bite it with her teeth but could not it would not be broken and she died with her perfectly healthy nameless baby in her arms she held it to her chest the crowd pulled itself into itself long after the bombing ceased the confused the frightened the desperate mass of babies children teenagers adults elderly all pulled at each other to survive but pulled each other into me drowning each other killing each other the bodies began to rise one at a time until I couldn't be seen through all of the bodies blue skin open white eyes I was invisible under them I was the carcass they were the butterflies white eyes blue skin this is what we've done we've killed our own babies to save them

Dear Jonathan,

If you are reading this, it is because Sasha found it and translated it for you. It means that I am dead, and that Sasha is alive.

I do not know if Sasha will tell you what has happened here tonight, and what is about to happen. It is important that you know what kind of man he is, so I will tell you here.

This is what happened. He told his father that he could care for Mother and Little Igor. It took his saying it to make it true. Finally, he was ready. His father could not believe this thing. What? he asked. What? And Sasha told him again that he would take care of the family, that he would under-stand if his father had to leave and never return, and that it would not even make him less of a father. He told his father that he would forgive. Oh, his father became so angry, so full of wrath, and he told Sasha that he would kill him, and Sasha told his father that he would kill him, and they moved at each other with violence and his father said, Say it to my face, not to the floor, and Sasha said, You are not my father.

His father raised himself and removed a bag from the cabinet under the sink. He filled the bag with things from the kitchen, with bread, bottles of vodka, cheese. Here, Sasha said, and he took from the cookie jar two handfuls of money. His father asked where the money was from and Sasha told him to take it and never return. His father said, I do not need your money. Sasha said, It is not a gift. It is payment for everything that you will leave behind. Take it and never return.

Say it into my eyes and I promise you I will.

Take it, Sasha said, and never return.

JONATHAN SAFRAN FOER

Mother and Iggy were so upset. Iggy told Sasha how stupid he was, how he ruined everything. He cried all night, and do you know what it is like to hear Iggy cry all night? But he is so young. I hope that he will one day be able to understand what Sasha did, and forgive him, and also thank him.

I spoke with Sasha tonight, after his father left, and I told him that I was proud of him. I told him that I had never been so proud, or so certain of who he was.

But Father is your son, he said. And he is my father.

I said, You are a good man, and you have done the good thing.

I put my hand on his cheek and remembered when my cheek was like his cheek. I said his name, Alex, which has also been my name for forty years.

I will toil at Heritage Touring, he said. I will fill Father's absence.

No, I told him.

It is a good job, he said, and I can make enough money to care for Mother and Little Igor and you.

No, I said. Make your own life. That is how you can best care for us.

I put him to bed, which I have not done for him since he was a child. I covered him in blankets, and combed his hair with my hand.

Try to live so that you can always tell the truth, I said.

I will, he said, and I believed in him, and that was enough.

Then I went to Iggy's room and he was already sleeping, but I kissed him on his forehead, and I said a blessing for him. I prayed in silence that he should be strong, and know goodness, and never know evil, and never know war.

And then I came here, to the television room, to write you this letter.

All is for Sasha and Iggy, Jonathan. Do you understand? I would give everything for them to live without violence. Peace. That is all that I would ever want for them. Not money and not even love. It is still possible. I know that now, and it is the cause of so much happiness in me. They must begin again. They must cut all of the strings, yes? With you (Sasha told me that you will not write to each other anymore), with their father (who is now gone forever), with everything they have known. Sasha has started it, and now I must finish it.

Everyone in the house is in bed but me. I am writing this in the lumi-
nescence of the television, and I am so sorry if this is now difficult to read,
Sasha, but my hand is shaking so much, and it is not out of weakness that I
will go to the bath when I am sure that you are asleep, and it is not because I
cannot endure. Do you understand? I am complete with happiness, and it is
what I must do, and I will do it. Do you understand me? I will walk without
noise, and I will open the door in darkness, and I will

Extremely Loud & Incredibly Close

For
NICOLE,
my idea of beautiful

WHAT THE?

What about a teakettle? What if the spout opened and closed when the steam came out, so it would become a mouth, and it could whistle pretty melodies, or do Shakespeare, or just crack up with me? I could invent a teakettle that reads in Dad's voice, so I could fall asleep, or maybe a set of kettles that sings the chorus of "Yellow Submarine," which is a song by the Beatles, who I love, because entomology is one of my *raisons d'être*, which is a French expression that I know. Another good thing is that I could train my anus to talk when I farted. If I wanted to be extremely hilarious, I'd train it to say, "Wasn't me!" every time I made an incredibly bad fart. And if I ever made an incredibly bad fart in the Hall of Mirrors, which is in Versailles, which is outside of Paris, which is in France, obviously, my anus would say, *"Ce n'étais pas moi!"*

What about little microphones? What if everyone swallowed them, and they played the sounds of our hearts through little speakers, which could be in the pouches of our overalls? When you skateboarded down the street at night you could hear everyone's heartbeat, and they could hear yours, sort of like sonar. One weird thing is, I wonder if everyone's hearts would start to beat at the same time, like how women who live together have their menstrual periods at the same time, which I know about, but don't really want to know about. That would be so weird, except that the place in the hospital where babies are born would sound like a crystal chandelier in a houseboat, because the babies wouldn't have had time to match up their heartbeats yet. And at the finish line at the end of the New York City Marathon it would sound like war.

And also, there are so many times when you need to make a quick escape, but humans don't have their own wings, or not yet, anyway, so what about a birdseed shirt?

Anyway.

My first jujitsu class was three and a half months ago. Self-defense was something that I was extremely curious about, for obvious reasons, and Mom thought it would be good for me to have a physical activity besides tambourining, so my first jujitsu class was three and a half months ago. There were fourteen kids in the class, and we all had on neat white robes. We practiced bowing, and then we were all sitting down Native American style, and then Sensei Mark asked me to go over to him. "Kick my privates," he told me. That made me feel self-conscious. *"Excusez-moi?"* I told him. He spread his legs and told me, "I want you to kick my privates as hard as you can." He put his hands at his sides, and took a breath in, and closed his eyes, and that's how I knew that actually he meant business. "Jose," I told him, and inside I was thinking, *What the?* He told me, "Go on, guy. Destroy my privates." "Destroy your privates?" With his eyes still closed he cracked up a lot and said, "You couldn't destroy my privates if you tried. That's what's going on here. This is a demonstration of the well-trained body's ability to absorb a direct blow. Now destroy my privates." I told him, "I'm a pacifist," and since most people my age don't know what that means, I turned around and told the others, "I don't think it's right to destroy people's privates. Ever." Sensei Mark said, "Can I ask you something?" I turned back around and told him, " 'Can I ask you something?' *is* asking me something." He said, "Do you have dreams of becoming a jujitsu master?" "No," I told him, even though I don't have dreams of running the family jewelry business anymore. He said, "Do you want to know how a jujitsu student becomes a jujitsu master?" "I want to know everything," I told him, but that isn't true anymore either. He told me, "A jujitsu student becomes a jujitsu master by destroying his master's privates." I told him, "That's fascinating." My last jujitsu class was three and a half months ago.

I desperately wish I had my tambourine with me now, because even after everything I'm still wearing heavy boots, and sometimes it helps to play a good beat. My most impressive song that I can play on my tambourine is "The Flight of the Bumblebee," by Nicolai Rimsky-Korsakov, which is also the ring tone I downloaded for the cell phone I got after Dad died. It's pretty amazing that I can play "The Flight of the Bumblebee," because you have to hit incredibly fast in parts, and that's extremely hard for me, because I don't really have wrists yet. Ron offered to buy me a five-piece drum set. Money can't buy me love, obviously, but I asked if it would have Zildjian cymbals. He said, "Whatever you want," and then he took my yo-yo off my desk and started to walk the dog with it. I know he just wanted to be friendly, but it made me incredibly angry. "Yo-yo *moi!*" I told him, grabbing it back. What I really wanted to tell him was "You're not my dad, and you never will be."

Isn't it so weird how the number of dead people is increasing even though the earth stays the same size, so that one day there isn't going to be room to bury anyone anymore? For my ninth birthday last year, Grandma gave me a subscription to *National Geographic*, which she calls "the *National Geographic*." She also gave me a white blazer, because I only wear white clothes, and it's too big to wear so it will last me a long time. She also gave me Grandpa's camera, which I loved for two reasons. I asked why he didn't take it with him when he left her. She said, "Maybe he wanted you to have it." I said, "But I was negative-thirty years old." She said, "Still." Anyway, the fascinating thing was that I read in *National Geographic* that there are more people alive now than have died in all of human history. In other words, if everyone wanted to play Hamlet at once, they couldn't, because there aren't enough skulls!

So what about skyscrapers for dead people that were built down? They could be underneath the skyscrapers for living people that are built up. You could bury people one hundred floors down, and a whole dead world could be underneath the living one. Sometimes I think it would be weird if there were a skyscraper that moved up and down while its elevator stayed in place. So if you wanted to go to the ninety-fifth floor, you'd just press the 95 button and the ninety-fifth floor would come to you. Also, that could be extremely useful, because if you're on the ninety-fifth floor, and a plane hits below you, the building could take you to the ground, and everyone could be safe, even if you left your birdseed shirt at home that day.

I've only been in a limousine twice ever. The first time was terrible, even though the limousine was wonderful. I'm not allowed to watch TV at home, and I'm not allowed to watch TV in limousines either, but it was still neat that there was a TV there. I asked if we could go by school, so Toothpaste and The Minch could see me in a limousine. Mom said that school wasn't on the way, and we couldn't be late to the cemetery. "Why not?" I asked, which I actually thought was a good question, because if you think about it, why not? Even though I'm not anymore, I used to be an atheist, which means I didn't believe in things that couldn't be observed. I believed that once you're dead, you're dead forever, and you don't feel anything, and you don't even dream. It's not that I believe in things that can't be observed now, because I don't. It's that I believe that things are extremely complicated. And anyway, it's not like we were *actually* burying him, anyway.

Even though I was trying hard for it not to, it was annoying me how Grandma kept touching me, so I climbed into the front seat and poked the driver's shoulder until he gave me some attention. "What. Is. Your. Designation." I asked in Stephen Hawking voice. "Say what?" "He wants to know your name," Grandma said from the back seat. He handed me his card.

GERALD THOMPSON
Sunshine Limousine

serving the five boroughs
(212) 570-7249

I handed him my card and told him, "Greetings. Gerald. I. Am. Oskar." He asked me why I was talking like that. I told him, "Oskar's

CPU is a neural-net processor. A learning computer. The more contact he has with humans, the more he learns." Gerald said, "O" and then he said "K." I couldn't tell if he liked me or not, so I told him, "Your sunglasses are one hundred dollars." He said, "One seventy-five." "Do you know a lot of curse words?" "I know a couple." "I'm not allowed to use curse words." "Bummer." "What's 'bummer'?" "It's a bad thing." "Do you know 'shit'?" "That's a curse, isn't it?" "Not if you say 'shiitake.'" "Guess not." "Succotash my Balzac, dipshiitake." Gerald shook his head and cracked up a little, but not in the bad way, which is at me. "I can't even say 'hair pie,'" I told him, "unless I'm talking about an actual pie made out of rabbits. Cool driving gloves." "Thanks." And then I thought of something, so I said it. "*Actually*, if limousines were *extremely* long, they wouldn't *need* drivers. You could just get in the back seat, walk through the limousine, and then get out of the front seat, which would be where you wanted to go. So in this situation, the front seat would be at the cemetery." "And I would be watching the game right now." I patted his shoulder and told him, "When you look up 'hilarious' in the dictionary, there's a picture of you."

In the back seat, Mom was holding something in her purse. I could tell that she was squeezing it, because I could see her arm muscles. Grandma was knitting white mittens, so I knew they were for me, even though it wasn't cold out. I wanted to ask Mom what she was squeezing and why she had to keep it hidden. I remember thinking that even if I were suffering hypothermia, I would never, *ever* put on those mittens.

"Now that I'm thinking about it," I told Gerald, "they could make an *incredibly* long limousine that had its back seat at your mom's VJ and its front seat at your mausoleum, and it would be as long as your life." Gerald said, "Yeah, but if everyone lived like that, no one would ever meet anyone, right?" I said, "So?"

Mom squeezed, and Grandma knitted, and I told Gerald, "I kicked a French chicken in the stomach once," because I wanted to make him crack up, because if I could make him crack up, my boots could be a little lighter. He didn't say anything, probably because he didn't hear me, so I said, "I *said* I kicked a French chicken in the stomach once."

"Huh?" "It said, '*Oeuf.*'" "What is that?" "It's a joke. Do you want to hear another, or have you already had *un oeuf?*" He looked at Grandma in the mirror and said, "What's he saying?" She said, "His grandfather loved animals more than he loved people." I said, "Get it? *Oeuf?*"

I crawled back, because it's dangerous to drive and talk at the same time, especially on the highway, which is what we were on. Grandma started touching me again, which was annoying, even though I didn't want it to be. Mom said, "Honey," and I said, "*Oui,*" and she said, "Did you give a copy of our apartment key to the mailman?" I thought it was so weird that she would mention that then, because it didn't have to do with anything, but I think she was looking for something to talk about that wasn't the obvious thing. I said, "The mailperson is a mail*woman*." She nodded, but not exactly at me, and she asked if I'd given the mailwoman a key. I nodded yes, because I never used to lie to her before everything happened. I didn't have a reason to. "Why did you do that?" she asked. So I told her, "Stan —" And she said, "Who?" And I said, "Stan the doorman. Sometimes he runs around the corner for coffee, and I want to be sure all of my packages get to me, so I thought, if Alicia —" "Who?" "The mailwoman. If she had a key, she could leave things inside our door." "But you can't give a key to a stranger." "Fortunately Alicia isn't a stranger." "We have lots of valuable things in our apartment." "I know. We have really great things." "Sometimes people who seem good end up being not as good as you might have hoped, you know? What if she had stolen your things?" "She wouldn't." "But what if?" "But she wouldn't." "Well, did she give you a key to her apartment?" She was obviously mad at me, but I didn't know why. I hadn't done anything wrong. Or if I had, I didn't know what it was. And I definitely didn't mean to do it.

I moved over to Grandma's side of the limousine and told Mom, "Why would I need a key to her apartment?" She could tell that I was zipping up the sleeping bag of myself, and I could tell that she didn't really love me. I knew the truth, which was that if she could have chosen, it would have been my funeral we were driving to. I looked up at the limousine's sunroof, and I imagined the world before there were ceilings, which made me wonder: Does a cave have no ceiling, or is a cave all ceiling? "Maybe you could check with me next time, OK?" "Don't be mad at me," I said, and I reached over Grandma and opened and closed the door's lock a couple of times. "I'm not mad at you," she said. "Not even a little?" "No." "Do you still love me?" It didn't seem like the perfect time to mention that I had already made copies of the key for the deliverer from Pizza Hut, and the UPS person, and also the nice guys from Greenpeace, so they could leave me articles on manatees and other animals that are going extinct when Stan is getting coffee. "I've never loved you more."

"Mom?" "Yes?" "I have a question." "OK." "What are you squeezing in your purse?" She pulled out her hand and opened it, and it was empty. "Just squeezing," she said.

Even though it was an incredibly sad day, she looked so, so beautiful. I kept trying to figure out a way to tell her that, but all of the ways I thought of were weird and wrong. She was wearing the bracelet that I made for her, and that made me feel like one hundred dollars. I love making jewelry for her, because it makes her happy, and making her happy is another one of my *raisons d'être.*

It isn't anymore, but for a really long time it was my dream to take over the family jewelry business. Dad constantly used to tell me I was too smart for retail. That never made sense to me, because he was smarter than me, so if I was too smart for retail, then he *really* must have been too smart for retail. I told him that. "First of all," he told me, "I'm not smarter than you, I'm more knowledgeable than you, and that's only because I'm older than you. Parents are always more knowledgeable than their children, and children are always smarter than their parents." "Unless the child is a mental retard," I told him. He didn't have anything to say about that. "You said 'first of all,' so what's second of all?" "Second of all, if I'm so smart, then why am I in retail?" "That's true," I said. And then I thought of something: "But wait a minute, it won't be the family jewelry business if no one in the family is running it." He told me, "Sure it will. It'll just be someone else's family." I asked, "Well, what about our family? Will we open a new business?" He said, "We'll open something." I thought about that my second time in a limousine, when the renter and I were on our way to dig up Dad's empty coffin.

A great game that Dad and I would sometimes play on Sundays was Reconnaissance Expedition. Sometimes the Reconnaissance Expeditions were extremely simple, like when he told me to bring back something from every decade in the twentieth century—I was clever and brought back a rock—and sometimes they were incredibly complicated and would go on for a couple of weeks. For the last one we ever did, which never finished, he gave me a map of Central Park. I said, "And?" And he said, "And what?" I said, "What are the clues?" He said, "Who said there had to be clues?" "There are always clues." "That doesn't, in itself, suggest anything." "Not a single clue?" He said, "Unless no clues is a clue." "Is no clues a clue?" He shrugged his shoulders, like he had no idea what I was talking about. I loved that.

I spent all day walking around the park, looking for something that might tell me something, but the problem was that I didn't know what I was looking for. I went up to people and asked if they knew anything that I should know, because sometimes Dad would design Reconnaissance Expeditions so I would have to talk to people. But everyone I went up to was just like, *What the?* I looked for clues around the reservoir. I read every poster on every lamppost and tree. I inspected the descriptions of the animals at the zoo. I even made kite-fliers reel in their kites so I could examine them, although I knew it was improbable. But that's how tricky Dad could be. There was nothing, which would have been unfortunate, unless nothing was a clue. Was nothing a clue?

That night we ordered General Tso's Gluten for dinner and I noticed that Dad was using a fork, even though he was perfect with chopsticks. "Wait a minute!" I said, and stood up. I pointed at his fork. "Is that fork a clue?" He shrugged his shoulders, which to me meant it was a major clue. I thought: *Fork, fork.* I ran to my laboratory and got my metal detector out of its box in the closet. Because I'm not allowed to be in the park alone at night, Grandma went with me. I started at the Eighty-sixth Street entrance and walked in extremely precise lines, like I was one of the Mexican guys who mow the lawn, so I wouldn't miss anything. I knew the insects were loud because it was summer, but I didn't hear them because my earphones covered my ears. It was just me and the metal underground.

Every time the beeps would get close together, I'd tell Grandma to shine the flashlight on the spot. Then I'd put on my white gloves, take the hand shovel from my kit, and dig extremely gently. When I saw something, I used a paintbrush to get rid of the dirt, just like a real archeologist. Even though I only searched a small area of the park that night, I dug up a quarter, and a handful of paper clips, and what I thought was the chain from a lamp that you pull to make the light go on, and a refrigerator magnet for sushi, which I know about, but wish I didn't. I put all of the evidence in a bag and marked on a map where I found it.

When I got home, I examined the evidence in my laboratory under my microscope, one piece at a time: a bent spoon, some screws, a pair of rusty scissors, a toy car, a pen, a key ring, broken glasses for someone with incredibly bad eyes . . .

I brought them to Dad, who was reading the *New York Times* at the kitchen table, marking the mistakes with his red pen. "Here's what I've found," I said, pushing my pussy off the table with the tray of evidence. Dad looked at it and nodded. I asked, "So?" He shrugged his shoulders like he had no idea what I was talking about, and he went back to the paper. "Can't you even tell me if I'm on the right track?" Buckminster purred, and Dad shrugged his shoulders again. "But if you don't tell me anything, how can I ever be right?" He circled something in an article and said, "Another way of looking at it would be, how could you ever be wrong?"

He got up to get a drink of water, and I examined what he'd circled on the page, because that's how tricky he could be. It was in an article about the girl who had disappeared, and how everyone thought the congressman who was humping her had killed her. A few months later they found her body in Rock Creek Park, which is in Washington, D.C., but by then everything was different, and no one cared anymore, except for her parents.

statement, read to the hundreds of
gathered press from a makeshift

media center off the back of the family home, Levy's father adamantly restated his confidence that his daughter would be found. "We will not stop looking until we are given a definitive reason to stop looking, namely, Chandra's return." During the brief question and answer period that followed, a reporter from El Pais asked Mr. Levy if by "return" he meant "safe return." Overcome with emotion, Mr. Levy was unable to speak, and his lawyer took the microphone. "We continue to hope and pray for Chandra's safety, and will do everything within

It wasn't a mistake! It was a message to me!

I went back to the park every night for the next three nights. I dug up a hair clip, and a roll of pennies, and a thumbtack, and a coat hanger, and a 9V battery, and a Swiss Army knife, and a tiny picture frame, and a tag for a dog named Turbo, and a square of aluminum foil, and a ring, and a razor, and an extremely old pocket watch that was stopped at 5:37, although I didn't know if it was A.M. or P.M. But I still couldn't figure out what it all meant. The more I found, the less I understood.

I spread the map out on the dining room table, and I held down the corners with cans of V8. The dots from where I'd found things looked like the stars in the universe. I connected them, like an astrologer, and if you squinted your eyes like a Chinese person, it kind of looked like the word "fragile." Fragile. What was fragile? Was Central Park fragile? Was nature fragile? Were the things I found fragile? A thumbtack isn't fragile. Is a bent spoon fragile? I erased, and connected the dots in a different way, to make "door." Fragile? Door? Then I thought of *porte*, which is French for door, obviously. I erased and connected the dots to make "*porte*." I had the revelation that I could connect the dots to make "cyborg," and "platypus," and "boobs," and even "Oskar," if you were extremely Chinese. I could connect them to make almost anything I wanted, which meant I wasn't getting closer to anything. And now I'll never know what I was supposed to find. And that's another reason I can't sleep.

Anyway.

I'm not allowed to watch TV, although I am allowed to rent documentaries that are approved for me, and I can read anything I want. My favorite book is *A Brief History of Time*, even though I haven't actually finished it, because the math is incredibly hard and Mom isn't good at helping me. One of my favorite parts is the beginning of the first chapter, where Stephen Hawking tells about a famous scientist who was giving a lecture about how the earth orbits the sun, and the sun orbits the solar system, and whatever. Then a woman in the back of the room raised her hand and said, "What you have told us is rubbish. The world is really a flat plate supported on the back of a giant tortoise." So the scientist asked her what the tortoise was standing on. And she said, "But it's turtles all the way down!"

I love that story, because it shows how ignorant people can be. And also because I love tortoises.

A few weeks after the worst day, I started writing lots of letters. I don't know why, but it was one of the only things that made my boots lighter. One weird thing is that instead of using normal stamps, I used stamps from my collection, including valuable ones, which sometimes made me wonder if what I was really doing was trying to get rid of things. The first letter I wrote was to Stephen Hawking. I used a stamp of Alexander Graham Bell.

> *Dear Stephen Hawking,*
> *Can I please be your protégé?*
> *Thanks,*
> *Oskar Schell*

I thought he wasn't going to respond, because he was such an amazing person and I was so normal. But then one day I came home from school and Stan handed me an envelope and said, "You've got mail!" in the AOL voice I taught him. I ran up the 105 stairs to our apartment, and ran to my laboratory, and went into my closet, and turned on my flashlight, and opened it. The letter inside was typed, obviously, because Stephen Hawking can't use his hands, because he has amyotrophic lateral sclerosis, which I know about, unfortunately.

Thank you for your letter. Because of the large
volume of mail I receive, I am unable to write
personal responses. Nevertheless, know that I read
and save every letter, with the hope of one day
being able to give each the proper response it
deserves. Until that day,

Most sincerely,

Stephen Hawking

I called Mom's cell. "Oskar?" "You picked up before it rang." "Is everything OK?" "I'm gonna need a laminator." "A laminator?" "There's something incredibly wonderful that I want to preserve."

Dad always used to tuck me in, and he'd tell the greatest stories, and we'd read the *New York Times* together, and sometimes he'd whistle "I Am the Walrus," because that was his favorite song, even though he couldn't explain what it meant, which frustrated me. One thing that was so great was how he could find a mistake in every single article we looked at. Sometimes they were grammar mistakes, sometimes they were mistakes with geography or facts, and sometimes the article just didn't tell the whole story. I loved having a dad who was smarter than the *New York Times*, and I loved how my cheek could feel the hairs on his chest through his T-shirt, and how he always smelled like shaving, even at the end of the day. Being with him made my brain quiet. I didn't have to invent a thing.

When Dad was tucking me in that night, the night before the worst day, I asked if the world was a flat plate supported on the back of a giant tortoise. "Excuse me?" "It's just that why does the earth stay in place instead of falling through the universe?" "Is this Oskar I'm tucking in? Has an alien stolen his brain for experimentation?" I said, "We don't believe in aliens." He said, "The earth *does* fall through the universe. You know that, buddy. It's constantly falling toward the sun. That's what it means to orbit." So I said, "Obviously, but why is there gravity?" He said, "What do you mean why is there gravity?" "What's the reason?" "Who said there had to be a reason?" "No one did, exactly." "My question was rhetorical." "What's that mean?" "It means I wasn't asking it for an answer, but to make a point." "What point?"

"That there doesn't have to be a reason." "But if there isn't a reason, then why does the universe exist at all?" "Because of sympathetic conditions." "So then why am I your son?" "Because Mom and I made love, and one of my sperm fertilized one of her eggs." "Excuse me while I regurgitate." "Don't act your age." "Well, what I don't get is why do we exist? I don't mean how, but why." I watched the fireflies of his thoughts orbit his head. He said, "We exist because we exist." "*What the?*" "We could imagine all sorts of universes unlike this one, but this is the one that happened."

I understood what he meant, and I didn't disagree with him, but I didn't agree with him either. Just because you're an atheist, that doesn't mean you wouldn't love for things to have reasons for why they are.

I turned on my shortwave radio, and with Dad's help I was able to pick up someone speaking Greek, which was nice. We couldn't understand what he was saying, but we lay there, looking at the glow-in-the-dark constellations on my ceiling, and listened for a while. "Your grandfather spoke Greek," he said. "You mean he *speaks* Greek," I said. "That's right. He just doesn't speak it here." "Maybe that's him we're listening to." The front page was spread over us like a blanket. There was a picture of a tennis player on his back, who I guess was the winner, but I couldn't really tell if he was happy or sad.

"Dad?" "Yeah?" "Could you tell me a story?" "Sure." "A good one?" "As opposed to all the boring ones I tell." "Right." I tucked my body incredibly close into his, so my nose pushed into his armpit. "And you won't interrupt me?" "I'll try not to." "Because it makes it hard to tell a story." "And it's annoying." "And it's annoying."

The moment before he started was my favorite moment.

"Once upon a time, New York City had a sixth borough." "What's a borough?" "That's what I call an interruption." "I know, but the story won't make any sense to me if I don't know what a borough is." "It's like a neighborhood. Or a collection of neighborhoods." "So if there was once a sixth borough, then what are the five boroughs?" "Manhattan, obviously, Brooklyn, Queens, Staten Island, and the Bronx." "Have I ever been to any of the other boroughs?" "Here we go." "I just want to know." "We went to the Bronx Zoo once, a few years ago. Remember that?" "No." "And we've been to Brooklyn to see the roses at the Botanic Garden." "Have I been to Queens?" "I don't think so." "Have I been to Staten Island?" "No." "Was there *really* a sixth borough?" "I've been trying to tell you." "No more interruptions. I promise."

When the story finished, we turned the radio back on and found someone speaking French. That was especially nice, because it reminded me of the vacation we just came back from, which I wish never ended. After a while, Dad asked me if I was awake. I told him no, because I knew that he didn't like to leave until I had fallen asleep, and I didn't want him to be tired for work in the morning. He kissed my forehead and said good night, and then he was at the door.

"Dad?" "Yeah, buddy?" "Nothing."

The next time I heard his voice was when I came home from school the next day. We were let out early, because of what happened. I wasn't even a little bit panicky, because both Mom and Dad worked in midtown, and Grandma didn't work, obviously, so everyone I loved was safe.

I know that it was 10:22 when I got home, because I look at my watch a lot. The apartment was so empty and so quiet. As I walked to the kitchen, I invented a lever that could be on the front door, which would trigger a huge spoked wheel in the living room to turn against metal teeth that would hang down from the ceiling, so that it would play beautiful music, like maybe "Fixing a Hole" or "I Want to Tell You," and the apartment would be one huge music box.

After I petted Buckminster for a few seconds, to show him I loved him, I checked the phone messages. I didn't have a cell phone yet, and when we were leaving school, Toothpaste told me he'd call to let me know whether I was going to watch him attempt skateboarding tricks in the park, or if we were going to go look at *Playboy* magazines in the drugstore with the aisles where no one can see what you're looking at, which I didn't feel like doing, but still.

> Message one. Tuesday, 8:52 A.M. *Is anybody there? Hello? It's Dad. If you're there, pick up. I just tried the office, but no one was picking up. Listen, something's happened. I'm OK. They're telling us to stay where we*

are and wait for the firemen. I'm sure it's fine. I'll give you another call
when I have a better idea of what's going on. Just wanted to let you know
that I'm OK, and not to worry. I'll call again soon.

There were four more messages from him: one at 9:12, one at 9:31, one at 9:46, and one at 10:04. I listened to them, and listened to them again, and then before I had time to figure out what to do, or even what to think or feel, the phone started ringing.

It was 10:26:47.

I looked at the caller ID and saw that it was him.

WHY I'M NOT WHERE YOU ARE
5/21/63

To my unborn child: I haven't always been silent, I used to talk and talk and talk and talk, I couldn't keep my mouth shut, the silence overtook me like a cancer, it was one of my first meals in America, I tried to tell the waiter, "The way you just handed me that knife, that reminds me of—" but I couldn't finish the sentence, her name wouldn't come, I tried again, it wouldn't come, she was locked inside me, how strange, I thought, how frustrating, how pathetic, how sad, I took a pen from my pocket and wrote "Anna" on my napkin, it happened again two days later, and then again the following day, she was the only thing I wanted to talk about, it kept happening, when I didn't have a pen, I'd write "Anna" in the air—backward and right to left—so that the person I was speaking with could see, and when I was on the phone I'd dial the numbers—2, 6, 6, 2—so that the person could hear what I couldn't, myself, say. "And" was the next word I lost, probably because it was so close to her name, what a simple word to say, what a profound word to lose, I had to say "ampersand," which sounded ridiculous, but there it is, "I'd like a coffee ampersand something sweet," nobody would choose to be like that. "Want" was a word I lost early on, which is not to say that I stopped wanting things—I wanted things more—I just stopped being able to express the want, so instead I said "desire," "I desire two rolls," I would tell the baker, but that wasn't quite right, the meaning of my thoughts started to float away from me, like leaves that fall from a tree into a river, I was the tree, the world was the river. I lost "come" one afternoon with the dogs in the park, I lost "fine" as the barber turned me toward the mirror, I lost "shame"—the verb and the noun in the same moment; it was a shame. I lost "carry," I lost the

JONATHAN SAFRAN FOER

things I carried—"daybook," "pencil," "pocket change," "wallet"—I even lost "loss." After a time, I had only a handful of words left, if someone did something nice for me, I would tell him, "The thing that comes before 'you're welcome,'" if I was hungry, I'd point at my stomach and say, "I am the opposite of full," I'd lost "yes," but I still had "no," so if someone asked me, "Are you Thomas?" I would answer, "Not no," but then I lost "no," I went to a tattoo parlor and had YES written onto the palm of my left hand, and NO onto my right palm, what can I say, it hasn't made life wonderful, it's made life possible, when I rub my hands against each other in the middle of winter I am warming myself with the friction of YES and NO, when I clap my hands I am showing my appreciation through the uniting and parting of YES and NO, I signify "book" by peeling open my clapped hands, every book, for me, is the balance of YES and NO, even this one, my last one, especially this one. Does it break my heart, of course, every moment of every day, into more pieces than my heart was made of, I never thought of myself as quiet, much less silent, I never thought about things at all, everything changed, the distance that wedged itself between me and my happiness wasn't the world, it wasn't the bombs and burning buildings, it was me, my thinking, the cancer of never letting go, is ignorance bliss, I don't know, but it's so painful to think, and tell me, what did thinking ever do for me, to what great place did thinking ever bring me? I think and think and think, I've thought myself out of happiness one million times, but never once into it. "I" was the last word I was able to speak aloud, which is a terrible thing, but there it is, I would walk around the neighborhood saying, "I I I I." "You want a cup of coffee, Thomas?" "I." "And maybe something sweet?" "I." "How about this weather?" "I." "You look upset. Is anything wrong?" I wanted to say, "Of course," I wanted to ask, "Is anything right?" I wanted to pull the thread, unravel the scarf of my silence and start again from the beginning, but instead I said, "I." I know I'm not alone in this disease, you hear the old people in the street and some of them are moaning, "Ay yay yay," but some of them are clinging to their last word, "I," they're saying, because they're desperate, it's not a complaint it's a prayer, and then I lost "I" and my silence was complete. I started carrying blank books like this one around, which I would fill with all the things I couldn't say, that's how it started, if I wanted two rolls of bread from the baker, I would write "I want two rolls" on the next blank page and show it to him, and if I needed help from someone, I'd write "Help," and if something made me want to laugh, I'd write "Ha ha ha!" and instead of singing in the shower I would write out the lyrics of my favorite songs, the ink would turn the water blue or red or green, and the music would run down my legs, at the end of each day I would take the book to bed with me and read through the pages of my life:

JONATHAN SAFRAN FOER

I want two rolls

And I wouldn't say no to something sweet

I'm sorry, this is the smallest I've got

Start spreading the news . . .

The regular, please

Thank you, but I'm about to burst

I'm not sure, but it's late

Help

JONATHAN SAFRAN FOER

Ha ha ha!

It wasn't unusual for me to run out of blank pages before the end of the day, so should I have to say something to someone on the street or in the bakery or at the bus stop, the best I could do was flip back through the daybook and find the most fitting page to recycle, if someone asked me, "How are you feeling?" it might be that my best response was to point at, "The regular, please," or perhaps, "And I wouldn't say no to something sweet," when my only friend, Mr. Richter, suggested, "What if you tried to make a sculpture again? What's the worst thing that could happen?" I shuffled halfway into the filled book: "I'm not sure, but it's late." I went through hundreds of books, thousands of them, they were all over the apartment, I used them as doorstops and paperweights, I stacked them if I needed to reach something, I slid them under the legs of wobbly tables, I used them as trivets and coasters, to line the birdcages and to swat insects from whom I begged forgiveness, I never thought of my books as being special, only necessary, I might rip out a page—"I'm sorry, this is the smallest I've got"—to wipe up some mess, or empty a whole day to pack up the emergency light bulbs, I remember spending an afternoon with Mr. Richter in the Central Park Zoo, I went weighted down with food for the animals, only someone who'd never been an animal would put up a sign saying not to feed them, Mr. Richter told a joke, I tossed hamburger to the lions, he rattled the cages with his laughter, the animals went to the corners, we laughed and laughed, together and separately, out loud and silently, we were determined to ignore whatever needed to be ignored, to build a new world from nothing if nothing in our world could be salvaged, it was one of the best days of my life, a day during which I lived my life and didn't think about my life at all. Later that year, when snow started to hide the front steps, when morning became evening as I sat on the sofa, buried under everything I'd lost, I made a fire and used my laughter for kindling: "Ha ha ha!" "Ha ha ha!" "Ha ha ha!" "Ha ha ha!" I was already out of words when I met your mother, that may have been what made our marriage possible, she never had to know me. We met at the Columbian Bakery on Broadway, we'd both come to New York lonely, broken and confused, I was sitting in the corner stirring cream into coffee, around and around like a little solar system, the place was half

JONATHAN SAFRAN FOER

empty but she slid right up next to me, "You've lost everything," she said, as if we were sharing a secret, "I can see." If I'd been someone else in a different world I'd've done something different, but I was myself, and the world was the world, so I was silent, "It's OK," she whispered, her mouth too close to my ear, "Me too. You can probably see it from across a room. It's not like being Italian. We stick out like sore thumbs. Look at how they look. Maybe they don't know that we've lost every-thing, but they know something's off." She was the tree and also the river flowing away from the tree, "There are worse things," she said, "worse than being like us. Look, at least we're alive," I could see that she wanted those last words back, but the current was too strong, "And the weather is one hundred dollars, also, don't let me forget to men-tion," I stirred my coffee. "But I hear it's supposed to get crummy tonight. Or that's what the man on the radio said, anyway," I shrugged, I didn't know what "crummy" meant, "I was gonna go buy some tuna fish at the A&P. I clipped some coupons from the Post this morning. They're five cans for the price of three. What a deal! I don't even like tuna fish. It gives me stomachaches, to be frank. But you can't beat that price," she was trying to make me laugh, but I shrugged my shoulders and stirred my coffee, "I don't know anymore," she said. "The weather is one hundred dollars, and the man on the radio says it's gonna get crummy tonight, so maybe I should go to the park instead, even if I burn easily. And anyway, it's not like I'm gonna eat the tuna fish tonight, right? Or ever, if I'm being frank. It gives me stomachaches, to be per-fectly frank. So there's no rush in that department. But the weather, now that won't stick around. Or at least it never has. And I should tell you also that my doctor says getting out is good for me. My eyes are crummy, and he says I don't get out nearly enough, and that if I got out a little more, if I were a little less afraid . . ." She was extending a hand that I didn't know how to take, so I broke its fingers with my silence, she said, "You don't want to talk to me, do you?" I took my daybook out of my knapsack and found the next blank page, the second to last. "I don't speak," I wrote. "I'm sorry." She looked at the piece of paper, then at me, then back at the piece of paper, she covered her eyes with her hands and cried, tears seeped between her fingers and collected in the little webs, she cried and cried and cried, there weren't any napkins nearby, so I ripped the page from the book—"I don't speak. I'm sorry."—and used it to dry her cheeks, my explanation and apology ran down her face like mascara, she took my pen from me and wrote on the next blank page of my daybook, the final one:

Please marry me

I flipped back and pointed at, "Ha ha ha!" She flipped forward and pointed at, "Please marry me." I flipped back and pointed at, "I'm sorry, this is the smallest I've got." She flipped forward and pointed at, "Please marry me." I flipped back and pointed at, "I'm not sure, but it's late." She flipped forward and pointed at, "Please marry me," and this time put her finger on "Please," as if to hold down the page and end the conversation, or as if she were trying to push through the word and into what she really wanted to say. I thought about life, about my life, the embarrassments, the little coincidences, the shadows of alarm clocks on bedside tables. I thought about my small victories and everything I'd seen destroyed, I'd swum through mink coats on my parents' bed while they hosted downstairs, I'd lost the only person I could have spent my only life with, I'd left behind a thousand tons of marble, I could have released sculptures, I could have released myself from the marble of myself. I'd experienced joy, but not nearly enough, could there be enough? The end of suffering does not justify the suffering, and so there is no end to suffering, what a mess I am, I thought, what a fool, how foolish and narrow, how worthless, how pinched and pathetic, how helpless. None of my pets know their own names, what kind of person am I? I lifted her finger like a record needle and flipped back, one page at a time:

Help

JONATHAN SAFRAN FOER

GOOGOLPLEX

As for the bracelet Mom wore to the funeral, what I did was I converted Dad's last voice message into Morse code, and I used sky-blue beads for silence, maroon beads for breaks between letters, violet beads for breaks between words, and long and short pieces of string between the beads for long and short beeps, which are actually called blips, I think, or something. Dad would have known. It took me nine hours to make, and I had thought about giving it to Sonny, the homeless person who I sometimes see standing outside the Alliance Française, because he puts me in heavy boots, or maybe to Lindy, the neat old woman who volunteers to give tours at the Museum of Natural History, so I could be something special to her, or even just to someone in a wheelchair. But instead I gave it to Mom. She said it was the best gift she'd ever received. I asked her if it was better than the Edible Tsunami, from when I was interested in edible meteorological events. She said, "Different." I asked her if she was in love with Ron. She said, "Ron is a great person," which was an answer to a question I didn't ask. So I asked again. "True or false: you are in love with Ron." She put her hand with the ring on it in her hair and said, "Oskar, Ron is my *friend*." I was going to ask her if she was humping her friend, and if she had said yes, I would have run away, and if she had said no, I would have asked if they heavy-petted each other, which I know about. I wanted to tell her she shouldn't be playing Scrabble yet. Or looking in the mirror. Or turning the stereo any louder than what you needed just to hear it. It wasn't fair to Dad, and it wasn't fair to me. But I buried it all inside me. I made her other Morse code jewelry with Dad's messages—a necklace, an anklet, some dangly earrings, a tiara—but the bracelet was definitely the most beautiful, probably because it was the last, which made it the most precious. "Mom?" "Yes?" "Nothing."

Even after a year, I still had an extremely difficult time doing certain things, like taking showers, for some reason, and getting into elevators, obviously. There was a lot of stuff that made me panicky, like suspension bridges, germs, airplanes, fireworks, Arab people on the subway (even though I'm not racist), Arab people in restaurants and coffee shops and other public places, scaffolding, sewers and subway grates, bags without owners, shoes, people with mustaches, smoke, knots, tall buildings, turbans. A lot of the time I'd get that feeling like I was in the middle of a huge black ocean, or in deep space, but not in the fascinating way. It's just that everything was incredibly far away from me. It was worst at night. I started inventing things, and then I couldn't stop, like beavers, which I know about. People think they cut down trees so they can build dams, but in reality it's because their teeth never stop growing, and if they didn't constantly file them down by cutting through all of those trees, their teeth would start to grow into their own faces, which would kill them. That's how my brain was.

One night, after what felt like a googolplex inventions, I went to Dad's closet. We used to Greco-Roman wrestle on the floor in there, and tell hilarious jokes, and once we hung a pendulum from the ceiling and put a circle of dominoes on the floor to prove that the earth rotated. But I hadn't gone back in since he died. Mom was with Ron in the living room, listening to music too loud and playing board games. She wasn't missing Dad. I held the doorknob for a while before I turned it.

Even though Dad's coffin was empty, his closet was full. And even after more than a year, it still smelled like shaving. I touched all of his white T-shirts. I touched his fancy watch that he never wore and the extra laces for his sneakers that would never run around the reservoir again. I put my hands into the pockets of all of his jackets (I found a receipt for a cab, a wrapper from a miniature Krackle, and the business card of a diamond supplier). I put my feet into his slippers. I looked at myself in his metal shoehorn. The average person falls asleep in seven minutes, but I couldn't sleep, not after hours, and it made my boots lighter to be around his things, and to touch stuff that he had touched, and to make the hangers hang a little straighter, even though I knew it didn't matter.

His tuxedo was over the chair he used to sit on when he tied his shoes, and I thought, *Weird.* Why wasn't it hung up with his suits? Had he come from a fancy party the night before he died? But then why would he have taken off his tuxedo without hanging it up? Maybe it needed to be cleaned? But I didn't remember a fancy party. I remembered him tucking me in, and us listening to a person speaking Greek on the shortwave radio, and him telling me a story about New York's sixth borough. If I hadn't noticed anything else weird, I wouldn't have thought about the tuxedo again. But I started noticing a lot.

There was a pretty blue vase on the highest shelf. What was a pretty blue vase doing way up there? I couldn't reach it, obviously, so I moved over the chair with the tuxedo still on it, and then I went to my room to get the *Collected Shakespeare* set that Grandma bought for me when she found out that I was going to be Yorick, and I brought those over, four tragedies at a time, until I had a stack that was tall enough. I stood on all of that and it worked for a second. But then I had the tips of my fingers on the vase, and the tragedies started to wobble, and the tuxedo was incredibly distracting, and the next thing was that everything was on the floor, including me, and including the vase, which had shattered. "I didn't do it!" I hollered, but they didn't even hear me, because they were playing music too loud and cracking up too much. I zipped myself all the way into the sleeping bag of myself, not because I was hurt, and not because I had broken something, but because they were cracking up. Even though I knew I shouldn't, I gave myself a bruise.

I started to clean everything up, and that was when I noticed something else weird. In the middle of all of that glass was a little envelope, about the size of a wireless Internet card. *What the?* I opened it up, and inside there was a key. *What the, what the?* It was a weird-looking key, obviously to something extremely important, because it was fatter and shorter than a normal key. I couldn't explain it: a fat and short key, in a little envelope, in a blue vase, on the highest shelf in his closet.

The first thing I did was the logical thing, which was to be very secretive and try the key in all of the locks in the apartment. Even without trying I knew it wasn't for the front door, because it didn't match up with the key that I wear on a string around my neck to let myself in when nobody's home. I tiptoed so I wouldn't be noticed, and I tried the key in the door to the bathroom, and the different bedroom doors, and the drawers in Mom's dresser. I tried it in the desk in the kitchen where Dad used to pay the bills, and in the closet next to the linen closet where I sometimes hid when we played hide and seek, and in Mom's jewelry box. But it wasn't for any of them.

In bed that night I invented a special drain that would be underneath every pillow in New York, and would connect to the reservoir. Whenever people cried themselves to sleep, the tears would all go to the same place, and in the morning the weatherman could report if the water level of the Reservoir of Tears had gone up or down, and you could know if New York was in heavy boots. And when something *really* terrible happened—like a nuclear bomb, or at least a biological weapons attack—an extremely loud siren would go off, telling everyone to get to Central Park to put sandbags around the reservoir.

Anyway.

The next morning I told Mom that I couldn't go to school, because I was too sick. It was the first lie that I had to tell. She put her hand on my forehead and said, "You do feel a bit hot." I said, "I took my temperature and it's one hundred point seven degrees." That was the second lie. She turned around and asked me to zip up the back of her dress, which she could have done herself, but she knew that I loved to do it. She said, "I'll be in and out of meetings all day, but Grandma can come by if you need anything, and I'll call to check on you every hour." I told her, "If I don't answer, I'm probably sleeping or going to the bathroom." She said, "Answer."

Once she left for work, I put on my clothes and went downstairs. Stan was sweeping up in front of the building. I tried to get past him without him noticing, but he noticed. "You don't look sick," he said, brushing a bunch of leaves into the street. I told him, "I feel sick." He asked, "Where's Mr. Feeling Sick going?" I told him, "To the drugstore on Eighty-fourth to get some cough drops." Lie #3. Where I actually went was the locksmith's store, which is Frazer and Sons, on Seventy-ninth.

"Need some more copies?" Walt asked. I gave him a high-five, and I showed him the key that I had found, and asked him what he could tell me about it. "It's for some kind of lockbox," he said, holding it up to his face and looking at it over his glasses. "A safe, I'm guessing. You can tell it's for a lockbox by its build." He showed me a rack that had a ton of keys on it. "See, it's not like any of these. It's much thicker. Harder to break." I touched all the keys that I could reach, and that made me feel OK, for some reason. "But it's not for a fixed safe, I don't think. Nothing too big. Maybe something portable. Could be a safe-deposit box, actually. An old one. Or some kind of fire-retardant cabinet." That made me crack up a little, even though I know there's nothing funny about being a mental retard. "It's an old key," he said. "Could be twenty, thirty years old." "How can you tell?" "Keys are what I know." "You're cool." "And not many lockboxes use keys anymore." "They don't?" "Well, hardly anyone uses keys anymore." "I use keys," I told him, and I showed him my apartment key. "I know you do," he said. "But people like you are a dying breed. It's all electronic these days. Keypads. Thumbprint recognition." "That's so awesome." "I like keys." I thought for a minute, and then I got heavy, heavy boots. "Well, if people like me are a dying breed, then what's going to happen to your business?" "We'll become specialized," he said, "like a typewriter shop. We're useful now, but soon we'll be interesting." "Maybe you need a new business." "I like this business."

I said, "I have a question that I was just wondering." He said, "Shoot." "Shoot?" "Shoot. Go ahead. Ask." "Are you Frazer, or are you Son?" "I'm Grandson, actually. My grandfather started the shop." "*Cool*." "But I suppose I'm also Son, since my dad ran things when he was alive. I guess I'm Frazer, too, since my son works here during the summers."

I said, "I have another question." "Shoot." "Do you think I could find the company that made this key?" "Anyone could've made it." "Well then, what I want to know is how can I find the lock that it opens?" "I'm afraid I can't help you with that, any more than telling you to try it in every lock you come across. I could always make you a copy, if you'd like." "I could have a googolplex keys." "Googolplex?" "A googol to the googol power." "Googol?" "That's a one with one hundred zeroes after it." He put his hand on my shoulder and said, "You need the lock." I reached up real high and put my hand on his shoulder and said, "Yeah."

As I was leaving he asked, "Shouldn't you be in school?" I thought fast and told him, "It's Dr. Martin Luther King Jr. Day." Lie #4. "I thought that was in January." "It used to be." Lie #5.

When I got back to the apartment, Stan said, "You've got mail!"

> *Dear Osk,*
>   *Hello, lad! Thanks for your glorious letter and the bulletproof drumsticks, which I hope I'll never have to use! I have to confess, I've never thought too much about giving lessons . . .*
>   *I hope you like the enclosed T-shirt, which I took the liberty of signing for you.*
>   *Your mate,*
>   *Ringo*

I didn't *like* the enclosed T-shirt. I *loved* it! Although unfortunately it wasn't white, so I couldn't wear it.

I laminated Ringo's letter and tacked it to my wall. Then I did some research on the Internet about the locks of New York, and I found out a lot of useful information. For example, there are 319 post offices and 207,352 post office boxes. Each box has a lock, obviously. I also found out that there are about 70,571 hotel rooms, and most rooms have a main lock, a bathroom lock, a closet lock, and a lock to the mini-bar. I didn't know what a mini-bar was, so I called the Plaza Hotel, which I knew was a famous one, and asked. Then I knew what a mini-bar was. There are more than 300,000 cars in New York, which doesn't even count the 12,187 cabs and 4,425 buses. Also, I remembered from when I used to take the subway that the conductors used keys to open and close the doors, so there were those, too. More than 9 million people live in New York (a baby is born in New York every 50 seconds), and everyone has to live somewhere, and most apartments have two locks on the front, and to at least some of the bathrooms, and maybe to some other rooms, and obviously to dressers and jewelry boxes. Also there are offices, and art studios, and storage facilities, and banks with safe-deposit boxes, and gates to yards, and parking lots. I figured that if you included everything—from bicycle locks to roof latches to places for cufflinks—there are probably about 18 locks for every person in New York City, which would mean about 162 million locks, which is a crev*asse*-load of locks.

"Schell residence . . . Hi, Mom . . . A little bit, I guess, but still pretty sick . . . No . . . Uh-huh . . . Uh-huh . . . I guess . . . I think I'll order Indian . . . But still . . . OK. Uh-huh. I will . . . I know . . . I *know* . . . Bye."

I timed myself and it took me 3 seconds to open a lock. Then I figured out that if a baby is born in New York every 50 seconds, and each person has 18 locks, a new lock is created in New York every 2.$\overline{777}$ seconds. So even if all I did was open locks, I'd still be falling behind by .$\overline{333}$ locks every second. And that's if I didn't have to travel from one lock to the next, and if I didn't eat, and didn't sleep, which is an OK if, because I didn't actually sleep, anyway. I needed a better plan.

That night, I put on my white gloves, went to the garbage can in Dad's closet, and opened the bag that I'd thrown all of the pieces of the vase into. I was looking for clues that might lead me in a direction. I had to be extremely careful so that I wouldn't contaminate the evidence, or let Mom know what I was doing, or cut and infect myself, and I found the envelope that the key was in. It was then that I noticed something that a good detective would have noticed at the very beginning: the word "Black" was written on the back of the envelope. I was so mad at myself for not noticing it before that I gave myself a little bruise. Dad's handwriting was weird. It looked sloppy, like he was writing in a hurry, or writing down the word while he was on the phone, or just thinking about something else. So what would he have been thinking about?

I Googled around and found out that Black wasn't the name of a company that made lockboxes. I got a little disappointed, because it would have been a logical explanation, which is always the best kind, although fortunately it isn't the only kind. Then I found out that there was a place called Black in every state in the country, and actually in almost every country in the world. In France, for example, there is a place called Noir. So that wasn't very helpful. I did a few other searches, even though I knew they would only hurt me, because I couldn't help it. I printed out some of the pictures I found—a shark attacking a girl, someone walking on a tightrope between the Twin Towers, that actress getting a blowjob from her normal boyfriend, a soldier getting his head cut off in Iraq, the place on the wall where a famous stolen painting used to hang—and I put them in *Stuff That Happened to Me*, my scrapbook of everything that happened to me.

The next morning I told Mom I couldn't go to school again. She asked what was wrong. I told her, "The same thing that's always wrong." "You're sick?" "I'm sad." "About Dad?" "About everything." She sat down on the bed next to me, even though I knew she was in a hurry. "What's everything?" I started counting on my fingers: "The meat and dairy products in our refrigerator, fistfights, car accidents, Larry—" "Who's Larry?" "The homeless guy in front of the Museum of Natural History who always says 'I promise it's for food' after he asks for money." She turned around and I zipped her dress while I kept counting. "How you don't know who Larry is, even though you probably see him all the time, how Buckminster just sleeps and eats and goes to the bathroom and has no *raison d'être*, the short ugly guy with no neck who takes tickets at the IMAX theater, how the sun is going to explode one day, how every birthday I always get at least one thing I already have, poor people who get fat because they eat junk food because it's cheaper . . ." That was when I ran out of fingers, but my list was just getting started, and I wanted it to be long, because I knew she wouldn't leave while I was still going. ". . . domesticated animals, how I *have* a domesticated animal, nightmares, Microsoft Windows, old people who sit around all day because no one remembers to spend time with them and they're embarrassed to ask people to spend time with them, secrets, dial phones, how Chinese waitresses smile even when there's nothing funny or happy, and also how Chinese people own

Mexican restaurants but Mexican people never own Chinese restaurants, mirrors, tape decks, my unpopularity at school, Grandma's coupons, storage facilities, people who don't know what the Internet is, bad handwriting, beautiful songs, how there won't be humans in fifty years—" "Who said there won't be humans in fifty years?" I asked her, "Are you an optimist or a pessimist?" She looked at her watch and said, "I'm *optimistic*." "Then I have some bad news for you, because humans are going to destroy each other as soon as it becomes easy enough to, which will be very soon." "Why do beautiful songs make you sad?" "Because they aren't true." "Never?" "Nothing is beautiful and true." She smiled, but in a way that wasn't just happy, and said, "You sound just like Dad."

"What do you mean I sound just like Dad?" "He used to say things like that." "Like what?" "Oh, like *nothing* is so-and-so. Or *everything* is so-and-so. Or *obviously*." She laughed. "He was always very definitive." "What's 'definitive'?" "It means certain. It comes from 'definite.'" "What's wrong with definitivity?" "Dad sometimes missed the forest for the trees." "What forest?" "Nothing."

"Mom?" "Yes?" "It doesn't make me feel good when you say that something I do reminds you of Dad." "Oh. I'm sorry. Do I do that a lot?" "You do it all the time." "I can see why that wouldn't feel good." "And Grandma always says that things I do remind her of Grandpa. It makes me feel weird, because they're gone. And it also makes me feel unspecial." "That's the last thing that either Grandma or I would want. You know you're the most special thing to us, don't you?" "I guess so." "The *most*."

She petted my head for a while, and her fingers went behind my ear to that place that's almost never touched.

I asked if I could zip her dress up again. She said, "Sure," and turned around. She said, "I think it would be good if you tried to go to school." I said, "I am trying." "Maybe if you just went for first period." "I can't even get out of bed." Lie #6. "And Dr. Fein said I should listen to my feelings. He said I should give myself a break sometimes." That wasn't a lie, exactly, although it wasn't exactly the truth, either. "I just don't want it to become a habit," she said. "It won't," I said. When she put her hand on the covers, she must have felt how puffy they were, because she asked if I had my clothes on in bed. I told her, "I do, and the reason is because I am cold." #7. "I mean, in addition to being hot."

As soon as she left, I got my things together and went downstairs. "You look better than yesterday," Stan said. I told him to mind his own business. He said, "Jeez." I told him, "It's just that I'm feeling worse than yesterday."

I walked over to the art supply store on Ninety-third Street, and I asked the woman at the door if I could speak to the manager, which is something Dad used to do when he had an important question. "What can I do for you?" she asked. "I need the manager," I said. She said, "I know. What can I do for you?" "You're incredibly beautiful," I told her, because she was fat, so I thought it would be an especially nice compliment, and also make her like me again, even though I was sexist. "Thanks," she said. I told her, "You could be a movie star." She shook her head, like, *What the?* "Anyway," I said, and I showed her the envelope, and explained how I had found the key, and how I was trying to find the lock it opened, and how maybe black meant something. I wanted to know what she could tell me about black, since she was probably an expert of color. "Well," she said, "I don't know that I'm an *expert* of anything. But one thing I *can* say is it's sort of interesting that the person wrote the word 'black' in red pen." I asked why that was interesting, because I just thought it was one of the red pens Dad used when he read the *New York Times*. "Come here," she said, and she led me to a display of ten pens. "Look at this." She showed me a pad of paper that was next to the display.

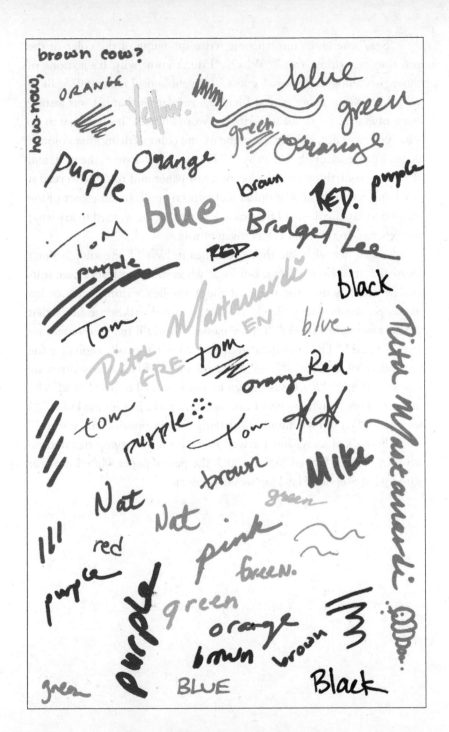

"See," she said, "most people write the name of the color of the pen they're writing with." "Why?" "I don't know why. It's just one of those psychological things, I guess." "Psychological is mental?" "Basically." I thought about it, and I had the revelation that if I was testing out a blue pen, I'd probably write the word "blue." "It's not easy to do what your dad did, writing the name of one color with another color. It doesn't come naturally." "Really?" "This is even harder," she said, and she wrote something on the next piece of paper and told me to read it out loud. She was right, it didn't feel natural at all, because part of me wanted to say the name of the color, and part of me wanted to say what was written. In the end I didn't say anything.

I asked her what she thought it meant. "Well," she said, "I don't know that it *means* anything. But look, when someone tests a pen, usually he either writes the name of the color he's writing with, or his name. So the fact that 'Black' is written in red makes me think that Black is someone's name." "Or *her* name." "And I'll tell you something else." "Yeah?" "The *b* is capitalized. You wouldn't usually capitalize the first letter of a color." "Jose!" "Excuse me?" "Black was written by Black!" "What?" "*Black* was *written* by *Black!* I need to find Black!" She said, "If there's anything else I can help you with, just let me know." "I love you." "Would you mind not shaking the tambourine in the store?"

She walked away, and I stayed there for a bit, trying to catch up with my brain. I flipped back through the pad of paper while I thought about what Stephen Hawking would do next.

JONATHAN SAFRAN FOER

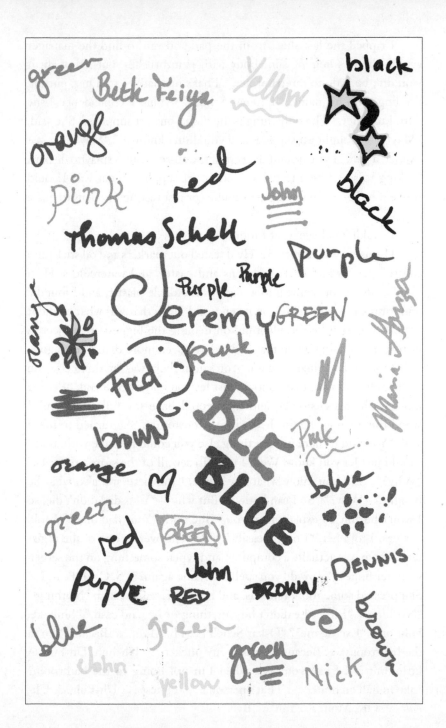

I ripped the last sheet from the pad and ran to find the manager again. She was helping somebody with paintbrushes, but I thought it wouldn't be rude to interrupt her. "That's my dad!" I told her, putting my finger on his name. "Thomas Schell!" "What a coincidence," she said. I told her, "The only thing is, he didn't buy art supplies." She said, "Maybe he bought art supplies and you didn't know it." "Maybe he just needed a pen." I ran around the rest of the store, from display to display, looking to see if he'd tested any other art supplies. That way I could prove if he had been buying art supplies or just testing out pens to buy a pen.

I couldn't believe what I found.

His name was *everywhere*. He'd tested out markers and oil sticks and colored pencils and chalk and pens and pastels and watercolors. He'd even scratched his name into a piece of moldable plastic, and I found a sculpting knife with yellow on its end, so I knew that was what he did it with. It was as if he was planning on making the biggest art project in history. But I didn't get it: that had to have been more than a year ago.

I found the manager again. "You said if there was anything else you could help me with, that I should just let you know." She said, "Let me finish with this customer, and then you'll have my full attention." I stood there while she finished with the customer. She turned to me. I said, "You said if there was anything else you could help me with, that I should just let you know. Well, I need to see all of the store's receipts." "Why?" "So I can know what day my dad was here and also what he bought." "Why?" "So I can know." "But why?" "Your dad didn't die, so I won't be able to explain it to you." She said, "Your dad died?" I told her yes. I told her, "I bruise easily." She went over to one of the registers, which was actually a computer, and typed something on the screen with her finger. "How do you spell the name again?" "S. C. H. E. L. L." She pressed some more buttons, and made a face, and said, "Nothing." "Nothing?" "Either he didn't buy anything or he paid cash." "Shiitake, hold on." "Excuse me?" "Oskar Schell . . . Hi, Mom . . . Because I'm in the bathroom . . . Because it was in my pocket . . . Uh-huh. Uh-huh. A little, but can I call you back when I'm not going to the bathroom? Like in half an hour? . . . That's personal. . . I guess . . . Uh-huh . . . Uh-*huh* . . . OK, Mom . . . Yuh . . . Bye."

"Well then, I have another question." "You're saying that to me or to the phone?" "You. How long have those pads been by the displays?" "I don't know." "He died more than a year ago. That would be a long time, right?" "They couldn't have been out there that long." "You're sure?" "Pretty sure." "Are you more or less than seventy-five-percent sure?" "More." "Ninety-nine percent?" "Less." "Ninety percent?" "About that." I concentrated for a few seconds. "That's a lot of percent."

I ran home and did some more research, and I found 472 people with the name Black in New York. There were 216 different addresses, because some of the Blacks lived together, obviously. I calculated that if I went to two every Saturday, which seemed possible, plus holidays, minus *Hamlet* rehearsals and other stuff, like mineral and coin conventions, it would take me about three years to go through all of them. But I couldn't survive three years without knowing. I wrote a letter.

> *Cher Marcel,*
>   *Allô. I am Oskar's mom. I have thought about it a ton, and I have decided that it isn't obvious why Oskar should go to French lessons, so he will no longer be going to go to see you on Sundays like he used to. I want to thank you very much for everything you have taught Oskar, particularly the conditional tense, which is weird. Obviously, there's no need to call me when Oskar doesn't come to his lessons, because I already know, because this was my decision. Also, I will keep sending you checks, because you are a nice guy.*
>   *Votre ami dévouée,*
>   *Mademoiselle Schell*

That was my great plan. I would spend my Saturdays and Sundays finding all of the people named Black and learning what they knew about the key in the vase in Dad's closet. In a year and a half I would know everything. Or at least know that I had to come up with a new plan.

Of course I wanted to talk to Mom that night I decided to go hunting for the lock, but I couldn't. It's not that I thought I would get in trouble for snooping around, or that I was afraid she'd be angry about the vase, or even that I was angry at her for spending so much time laughing with Ron when she should have been adding to the Reservoir of Tears. I can't explain why, but I was sure that she didn't know about the vase, the envelope, or the key. The lock was between me and Dad.

So for those eight months when I went looking around New York, and she would ask where I was going and when I'd be back, I would just say, "I'm going out. I'll be back later." What was so weird, and what I should have tried harder to understand, was that she never asked anything else, not even "Out where?" or "Later when?" even though she was normally so cautious about me, especially since Dad died. (She had bought me the cell phone so we could always find each other, and had told me to take cabs instead of the subway. She had even taken me to the police station to be fingerprinted, which was great.) So why was she suddenly starting to forget about me? Every time I left our apartment to go searching for the lock, I became a little lighter, because I was getting closer to Dad. But I also became a little heavier, because I was getting farther from Mom.

In bed that night, I couldn't stop thinking about the key, and how every 2.$\overline{777}$ seconds another lock was born in New York. I pulled *Stuff That Happened to Me* from the space between the bed and the wall, and I flipped through it for a while, wishing that I would finally fall asleep.

JONATHAN SAFRAN FOER

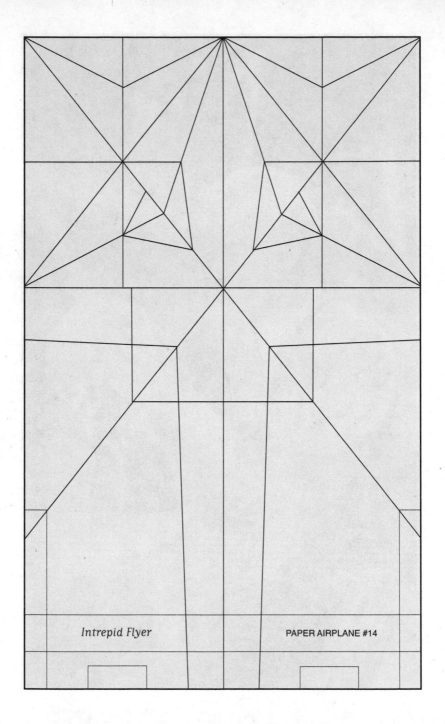

Intrepid Flyer

PAPER AIRPLANE #14

JONATHAN SAFRAN FOER

JONATHAN SAFRAN FOER

JONATHAN SAFRAN FOER

JONATHAN SAFRAN FOER

Purple

JONATHAN SAFRAN FOER

JONATHAN SAFRAN FOER

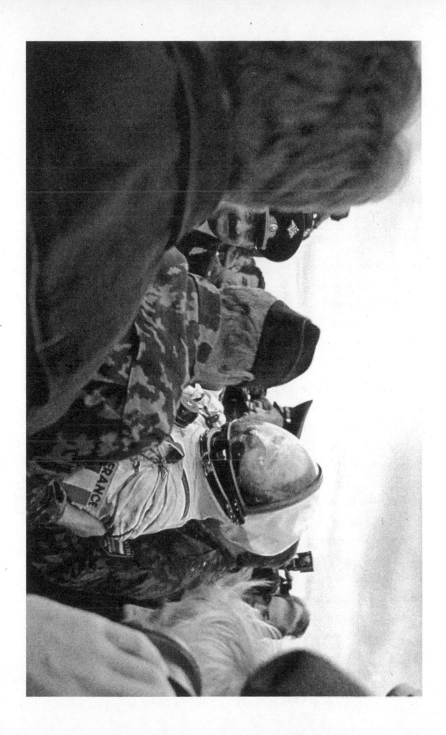

After forever, I got out of bed and went to the closet where I kept the phone. I hadn't taken it out since the worst day. It just wasn't possible.

A lot of the time I think about those four and a half minutes between when I came home and when Dad called. Stan touched my face, which he never did. I took the elevator for the last time. I opened the apartment door, put down my bag, and took off my shoes, like everything was wonderful, because I didn't know that in reality everything was actually horrible, because how could I? I petted Buckminster to show him I loved him. I went to the phone to check the messages, and listened to them one after another.

> *Message one: 8:52* A.M.
> *Message two: 9:12* A.M.
> *Message three: 9:31* A.M.
> *Message four: 9:46* A.M.
> *Message five: 10:04* A.M.

I thought about calling Mom. I thought about grabbing my walkie-talkie and paging Grandma. I went back to the first message and listened to them all again. I looked at my watch. It was 10:26:41. I thought about running away and never talking to anyone again. I thought about hiding under my bed. I thought about rushing downtown to see if I could somehow rescue him myself. And then the phone rang. I looked at my watch. It was 10:26:47.

I knew I could never let Mom hear the messages, because protecting her is one of my most important *raisons d'être*, so what I did was I took Dad's emergency money from on top of his dresser, and I went to the Radio Shack on Amsterdam. It was on a TV there that I saw that the first building had fallen. I bought the exact same phone and ran home and recorded our greeting from the first phone onto it. I wrapped up the old phone in the scarf that Grandma was never able to finish because of my privacy, and I put that in a grocery bag, and I put that in a box, and I put that in another box, and I put that under a bunch of stuff in my closet, like my jewelry workbench and albums of foreign currencies.

That night when I decided that finding the lock was my ultimate *raison d'être*—the *raison* that was the master over all other *raisons*—I really needed to hear him.

I was extremely careful not to make any noise as I took the phone out of all of its protections. Even though the volume was way down, so Dad's voice wouldn't wake Mom, he still filled the room, like how a light fills a room even when it's dim.

> Message two. 9:12 A.M. *It's me again. Are you there? Hello? Sorry if. It's getting a bit. Smoky. I was hoping you would. Be. Home. I don't know if you've heard about what's happened. But. I. Just wanted you to know that I'm OK. Everything. Is. Fine. When you get this, give Grandma a call. Let her know that I'm OK. I'll call again in a few minutes. Hopefully the firemen will be. Up here by then. I'll call.*

I wrapped the phone back up in the unfinished scarf, and put that back in the bag, and put that back in the box, and that in the other box, and all of that in the closet under lots of junk.

I stared at the fake stars forever.

I invented.

I gave myself a bruise.

I invented.

I got out of bed, went over to the window, and picked up the walkie-talkie. "Grandma? Grandma, do you read me? Grandma? Grandma?" "Oskar?" "I'm OK. Over." "It's late. What's happened? Over." "Did I wake you up? Over." "No. Over." "What were you doing? Over." "I was talking to the renter. Over." "He's still awake? Over." Mom told me not to ask questions about the renter, but a lot of the time I couldn't help it. "Yeah," Grandma said, "but he just left. He had to go run some errands. Over." "But it's 4:12 A.M.? Over."

The renter had been living with Grandma since Dad died, and even though I was at her apartment basically every day, I still hadn't met him. He was constantly running errands, or taking a nap, or in the shower, even when I didn't hear any water. Mom told me, "It probably gets pretty lonely to be Grandma, don't you think?" I told her, "It probably gets pretty lonely to be anyone." "But she doesn't have a mom, or friends like Daniel and Jake, or even a Buckminster." "That's true." "Maybe she needs an imaginary friend." "But I'm real," I said. "Yes, and she loves spending time with you. But you have school to go to, and friends to hang out with, and *Hamlet* rehearsals, and hobby shops—" "Please don't call them hobby shops." "I just mean you can't be around all the time. And maybe she wants a friend her own age." "How do you know her imaginary friend is old?" "I guess I don't."

She said, "There's nothing wrong with someone needing a friend." "Are you actually talking about Ron now?" "No. I'm talking about Grandma." "Except actually you're talking about Ron." "No, Oskar. I'm not. And I don't appreciate that tone." "I wasn't using a tone." "You were using your accusatory tone." "I don't even know what 'accusatory' means, so how could that be my tone?" "You were trying to make me feel badly for having a friend." "No I wasn't." She put her hand with the ring on it in her hair and said, "You know, I actually *was* talking about Grandma, Oskar, but it's true, I need friends, too. What's wrong with that?" I shrugged my shoulders. "Don't you think Dad would want me to have friends?" "I wasn't using a tone."

Grandma lives in the building across the street. We're on the fifth floor and she's on the third, but you can't really tell the difference. Sometimes she'll write notes for me on her window, which I can see through my binoculars, and once Dad and I spent a whole afternoon trying to design a paper airplane that we could throw from our apartment into hers. Stan stood in the street, collecting all of the failed attempts. I remember one of the notes she wrote right after Dad died was "Don't go away."

Grandma leaned her head out the window and put her mouth incredibly close to the walkie-talkie, which made her voice sound fuzzy. "Is everything OK? Over?" "Grandma? Over." "Yes? Over." "Why are matches so short? Over." "What do you mean? Over." "Well, they always seem to run out. Everyone's always rushing at the end, and sometimes even burning their fingers. Over." "I'm not very smart," she said, insulting herself like she always does before she gives an opinion, "but I think the matches are short so they can fit in your pocket. Over." "Yeah," I said, balancing my chin on my hand, and my elbow on the windowsill. "I think that, too. So what if pockets were a lot bigger? Over." "Well, what do I know, but I think the people might have a hard time reaching the bottoms of them if they went much lower. Over." "Right," I said, switching hands, because that one was getting tired, "so what about a portable pocket? Over." "A portable pocket? Over." "Yeah. It would be sort of like a sock, but with a Velcro outside, so you could attach it to anything. It's not quite a bag, because it actually becomes part of what you're wearing, but it's not quite a pocket either, because it's on the outside of your clothes, and also you can remove it, which would have all sorts of advantages, like how you could move things from one outfit to another easily, and how you could carry bigger things around, since you can take the pocket off and reach your arm all the way in. Over." She put her hand against the part of her nightgown that covered her heart and said, "That sounds like one hundred dollars. Over." "A portable pocket would prevent a lot of finger burns from short matches," I said, "but also a lot of dry lips from short ChapSticks. And why are candy bars so short, anyway? I mean, have you ever finished a candy bar and not wanted more? Over." "I can't eat chocolate," she said, "but I understand what you're telling me. Over." "You could have longer combs, so your part could be all the way straight, and bigger mencils—" "Mencils?" "Pencils for men." "Yes, yes." "And bigger mencils that are easier to hold, in case your fingers are fat, like mine, and you could probably even train the birds that save you to take shiitakes in the portable pocket—" "I don't understand." "On your *birdseed shirt.*"

"Oskar? Over." "I'm OK. Over." "What's wrong, darling? Over." "What do you mean what's wrong? Over." "What's wrong? Over." "I miss Dad. Over." "I miss him, too. Over." "I miss him a lot. Over." "So do I. Over." "All the time. Over." "All the time. Over." I couldn't explain to her that I missed him *more*, more than she or anyone else missed him, because I couldn't tell her about what happened with the phone. That secret was a hole in the middle of me that every happy thing fell into. "Did I ever tell you about how Grandpa would stop and pet every animal he saw, even if he was in a rush? Over?" "You've told me a googolplex times. Over." "Oh. And what about how his hands were so rough and red from all of his sculptures that sometimes I joked to him that it was really the sculptures that were sculpting his hands? Over." "That, too. But you can tell me again if you want. Over." She told me again.

An ambulance drove down the street between us, and I imagined who it was carrying, and what had happened to him. Did he break an ankle attempting a hard trick on his skateboard? Or maybe he was dying from third-degree burns on ninety percent of his body? Was there any chance that I knew him? Did anyone see the ambulance and wonder if it was me inside?

What about a device that knew everyone you knew? So when an ambulance went down the street, a big sign on the roof could flash

DON'T WORRY! DON'T WORRY!

if the sick person's device didn't detect the device of someone he knew nearby. And if the device *did* detect the device of someone he knew, the ambulance could flash the name of the person in the ambulance, and either

IT'S NOTHING MAJOR! IT'S NOTHING MAJOR!

or, if it was something major,

IT'S MAJOR! IT'S MAJOR!

And maybe you could rate the people you knew by how much you loved them, so if the device of the person in the ambulance detected the device of the person he loved the most, or the person who loved him the most, and the person in the ambulance was really badly hurt, and might even die, the ambulance could flash

GOODBYE! I LOVE YOU! GOODBYE! I LOVE YOU!

One thing that's nice to think about is someone who was the first person on lots of people's lists, so that when he was dying, and his am-

bulance went down the streets to the hospital, the whole time it would
flash

GOODBYE! I LOVE YOU! GOODBYE! I LOVE YOU!

"Grandma? Over?" "Yes, darling? Over?" "If Grandpa was so
great, then why did he leave? Over." She took a little step back so that
she disappeared into her apartment. "He didn't want to leave. He had
to leave. Over." "But *why* did he have to leave? Over." "I don't know.
Over." "Doesn't that make you angry? Over." "That he left? Over."
"That you don't know why. Over." "No. Over." "Sad? Over." "Sure.
Over." "Hold on," I said, and I ran back to my field kit and grabbed
Grandpa's camera. I brought it to the window and took a picture of
her window. The flash lit up the street between us.

  10. Walt
   9. Lindy
   8. Alicia

Grandma said, "I hope you never love anything as much as I love
you. Over."

   7. Farley
   6. The Minch / Toothpaste (tied)
   5. Stan

I could hear her kissing her fingers and then blowing.

   4. Buckminster
   3. Mom

I blew her a kiss back.

   2. Grandma

"Over and out," one of us said.

   1. Dad

We need much bigger pockets, I thought as I lay in bed, counting
off the seven minutes that it takes a normal person to fall asleep. We

need enormous pockets, pockets big enough for our families, and our friends, and even the people who aren't on our lists, people we've never met but still want to protect. We need pockets for boroughs and for cities, a pocket that could hold the universe.

Eight minutes thirty-two seconds . . .

But I knew that there couldn't be pockets that enormous. In the end, everyone loses everyone. There was no invention to get around that, and so I felt, that night, like the turtle that everything else in the universe was on top of.

Twenty-one minutes eleven seconds . . .

As for the key, I put it on the string next to my apartment key and wore it like a pendant.

As for me, I was awake for hours and hours. Buckminster curled up next to me, and I conjugated for a while so I wouldn't have to think about things.

Je suis

Tu es

Il/elle est

Nous sommes

Vous êtes

Ils/elles sont

Je suis

Tu es

Il/elle est

Nous

I woke up once in the middle of the night, and Buckminster's paws were on my eyelids. He must have been feeling my nightmares.

MY FEELINGS

12 September 2003

Dear Oskar,

I am writing this to you from the airport.

I have so much to say to you.   I want to begin at the beginning, because that is what you deserve.   I want to tell you everything, without
leaving out a single detail.   But where is the beginning?   And what is
everything?

I am an old woman now, but once I was a girl.   It's true.   I was a girl
like you are a boy.   One of my chores was to bring in the mail.   One
day there was a note addressed to our house.   There was no name on
it.   It was mine as much as anyone's, I thought.   I opened it.   Many
words had been removed from the text by a censor.

14 January 1921

To Whom Shall Receive This Letter:

My name is XXXXXXX XXXXXXXXX, and I am a XXXXXXXX in
Turkish Labor Camp XXXXX, Block XX.   I know that I am lucky XX X
XXXXXXX to be alive at all.   I have chosen to write to you without
knowing who you are.   My parents XXXXXXX XXX.   My brothers
and sisters XXXXX XXXX, the main XXXXXX XX XXXXXXXX!

I have written XXX XX XXXXX XXXXXXX every day since I have
been here.   I trade bread for postage, but have not yet received a response.   Sometimes it comforts me to think that they do not mail the
letters we write.

XXX XX XXXXXX, or at least XXX XXXXXXXXX?

XX XXXXX X XX throughout XXXXX XX.

XXX XXX XX XXXXX, and XXXXX XX XXXXX XX XXX, without

once XXX XX XXXXXX, XXX XXXXXXXX XXX XXXXX night-
mare?

XXX XXX, XX XXXXX XX XXXXX XX!   XXXXX XX XXX XX
XXX XX XXXXXX to write a few words to me I would appreciate it
more than you ever could know.   Several of the XXXXXX XXXX received mail so I know that XX XX XXXXXXXX.   Please include a picture of yourself as well as your name.   Include everything.

With great hopes,

Sincerely I am,

XXXXXXXX XXXXXXXXX

I took the letter straight to my room.   I put it under my mattress.   I
never told my father or mother about it.   For weeks I was awake all
night wondering.   Why was this man sent to a Turkish labor camp?
Why had the letter come fifteen years after it had been written?
Where had it been for those fifteen years?   Why hadn't anyone written back to him?   The others got mail, he said.   Why had he sent a
letter to our house?   How did he know the name of my street?   How
did he know of Dresden?   Where did he learn German?   What became of him?

I tried to learn as much about the man as I could from the letter.   The
words were very simple.   Bread means only bread.   Mail is mail.
Great hopes are great hopes are great hopes.   I was left with the handwriting.

So I asked my father, your great-grandfather, whom I considered the
best, most kindhearted man I knew, to write a letter to me.   I told him
it didn't matter what he wrote about.   Just write, I said.   Write anything.

Darling,

You asked me to write you a letter, so I am writing you a letter.   I do
not know why I am writing this letter, or what this letter is supposed to
be about, but I am writing it nonetheless, because I love you very much
and trust that you have some good purpose for having me write this letter.   I hope that one day you will have the experience of doing something you do not understand for someone you love.

Your father

That letter is the only thing of my father's that I have left.   Not even a picture.

Next I went to the penitentiary.   My uncle was a guard there.   I was able to get the handwriting sample of a murderer.   My uncle asked him to write an appeal for early release.   It was a terrible trick that we played on this man.

To the Prison Board:

My name is Kurt Schluter.   I am Inmate 24922.   I was put here in jail a few years ago.   I don't know how long it's been.   We don't have calendars.   I keep lines on the wall with chalk.   But when it rains, the rain comes through my window when I am sleeping.   And when I wake up the lines are gone.   So I don't know how long it's been.

I murdered my brother.   I beat his head in with a shovel.   Then after I used that shovel to bury him in the yard.   The soil was red.   Weeds came from the grass where his body was.   Sometimes at night I would get on my knees and pull them out, so no one would know.

I did a terrible thing.   I believe in the afterlife.   I know that you can't take anything back.   I wish that my days could be washed away like the chalk lines of my days.

I have tried to become a good person.   I help the other inmates with their chores.   I am patient now.

It might not matter to you, but my brother was having an affair with my wife.   I didn't kill my wife.   I want to go back to her, because I forgive her.

If you release me I will be a good person, quiet, out of the way.

Please consider my appeal.

Kurt Schluter, Inmate 24922

My uncle later told me that the inmate had been in prison for more than forty years.   He had gone in as a young man.   When he wrote the letter to me he was old and broken.   His wife had remarried.   She had children and grandchildren.   Although he never said it, I could tell that my uncle had befriended the inmate.   He had also lost a wife, and was also in a prison.   He never said it, but I heard in his voice that he cared for the inmate.   They guarded each other.   And when I asked my uncle, several years later, what became of the inmate, my uncle told me that he was still there.   He continued to write letters to the board. He continued to blame himself and forgive his wife, not knowing that there was no one on the other end.   My uncle took each letter and promised the inmate that they would be delivered.   But instead he kept them all.   They filled all of the drawers in his dresser.   I remember thinking it's enough to drive someone to kill himself.   I was right.   My uncle, your great-great-uncle, killed himself.   Of course it's possible that the inmate had nothing to do with it.

With those three samples I could make comparisons.   I could at least see that the forced laborer's handwriting was more like my father's than the murderer's.   But I knew that I would need more letters.   As many as I could get.

So I went to my piano teacher.   I always wanted to kiss him, but was afraid he would laugh at me.   I asked him to write a letter.

And then I asked my mother's sister.   She loved dance but hated dancing.

I asked my schoolmate Mary to write a letter to me.   She was funny and full of life.   She liked to run around her empty house without any clothes on, even once she was too old for that.   Nothing embarrassed her.   I admired that so much, because everything embarrassed me, and that hurt me.   She loved to jump on her bed.   She jumped on her bed for so many years that one afternoon, while I watched her jump, the seams burst.   Feathers filled the small room.   Our laughter kept the feathers in the air.   I thought about birds.   Could they fly if there wasn't someone, somewhere, laughing?

I went to my grandmother, your great-great-grandmother, and asked her to write a letter.   She was my mother's mother.   Your father's mother's mother's mother.   I hardly knew her.   I didn't have any interest in knowing her.   I have no need for the past, I thought, like a child.   I did not consider that the past might have a need for me.

What kind of letter? my grandmother asked.

I told her to write whatever she wanted to write.

You want a letter from me? she asked.

I told her yes.

Oh, God bless you, she said.

The letter she gave me was sixty-seven pages long.   It was the story of her life.   She made my request into her own.   Listen to me. I learned so much.   She sang in her youth.   She had been to America as a girl.   I never knew that.   She had fallen in love so many times that she began to suspect she was not falling in love at all, but doing something much more ordinary.   I learned that she never learned to swim, and for that reason she always loved rivers and lakes.   She asked her father, my great-grandfather, your great-great-great-grandfather, to buy her a dove.   Instead he bought her a silk scarf.   So she thought of the scarf as a dove.   She even convinced herself that it contained flight, but did not fly, because it did not want to show anyone what it really was. That was how much she loved her father.

The letter was destroyed, but its final paragraph is inside of me.

She wrote, I wish I could be a girl again, with the chance to live my life again.   I have suffered so much more than I needed to.   And the joys I have felt have not always been joyous.   I could have lived differently. When I was your age, my grandfather bought me a ruby bracelet.   It was too big for me and would slide up and down my arm.   It was almost a necklace.   He later told me that he had asked the jeweler to make it that way.   Its size was supposed to be a symbol of his love. More rubies, more love.   But I could not wear it comfortably.   I could not wear it at all.   So here is the point of everything I have been trying to say.   If I were to give a bracelet to you, now, I would measure your wrist twice.

With love,

Your grandmother

I had a letter from everyone I knew.   I laid them out on my bedroom floor, and organized them by what they shared.   One hundred letters. I was always moving them around, trying to make connections.   I wanted to understand.

Seven years later, a childhood friend reappeared at the moment I most needed him.   I had been in America for only two months.   An agency was supporting me, but soon I would have to support myself.   I did not know how to support myself.   I read newspapers and magazines all day long.   I wanted to learn idioms.   I wanted to become a real American.

Chew the fat.   Blow off some steam.   Close but no cigar.   Rings a bell.   I must have sounded ridiculous.   I only wanted to be natural. I gave up on that.

I had not seen him since I lost everything.   I had not thought of him. He and my older sister, Anna, were friends.   I came upon them kissing one afternoon in the field behind the shed behind our house.   It made me so excited.   I felt as if I were kissing someone.   I had never kissed anyone.   I was more excited than if it had been me.   Our house was small.   Anna and I shared a bed.   That night I told her what I had seen.   She made me promise never to speak a word about it.   I promised her.

She said, Why should I believe you?

I wanted to tell her, Because what I saw would no longer be mine if I talked about it.   I said, Because I am your sister.

Thank you.

Can I watch you kiss?

Can you watch us kiss?

You could tell me where you are going to kiss, and I could hide and watch.

She laughed enough to migrate an entire flock of birds.   That was how she said yes.

Sometimes it was in the field behind the shed behind our house. Sometimes it was behind the brick wall in the schoolyard.   It was always behind something.

I wondered if she told him.   I wondered if she could feel me watching them, if that made it more exciting for her.

Why did I ask to watch?   Why did she agree?

I had gone to him when I was trying to learn more about the forced laborer.   I had gone to everyone.

To Anna's sweet little sister,

Here is the letter you asked for.   I am almost two meters in height. My eyes are brown.   I have been told that my hands are big.   I want to be a sculptor, and I want to marry your sister.   Those are my only dreams.   I could write more, but that is all that matters.

Your friend,

Thomas

I walked into a bakery seven years later and there he was.   He had dogs at his feet and a bird in a cage beside him.   The seven years were not seven years.   They were not seven hundred years.   Their length could not be measured in years, just as an ocean could not explain the distance we had traveled, just as the dead can never be counted.   I wanted to run away from him, and I wanted to go right up next to him. I went right up next to him.

Are you Thomas? I asked.

He shook his head no.

You are, I said.   I know you are.

He shook his head no.

From Dresden.

He opened his right hand, which had NO tattooed on it.

I remember you.   I used to watch you kiss my sister.

He took out a little book and wrote, I don't speak.   I'm sorry.

That made me cry.   He wiped away my tears.   But he did not admit to being who he was.   He never did.

We spent the afternoon together.   The whole time I wanted to touch him.   I felt so deeply for this person that I had not seen in so long. Seven years before, he had been a giant, and now he seemed small.   I wanted to give him the money that the agency had given me.   I did not need to tell him my story, but I needed to listen to his.   I wanted to protect him, which I was sure I could do, even if I could not protect myself.

I asked, Did you become a sculptor, like you dreamed?

He showed me his right hand and there was silence.

We had everything to say to each other, but no ways to say it.

He wrote, Are you OK?

I told him, My eyes are crummy.

He wrote, But are you OK?

I told him, That's a very complicated question.

He wrote, That's a very simple answer.

I asked, Are you OK?

He wrote, Some mornings I wake up feeling grateful.

We talked for hours, but we just kept repeating those same things over and over.

Our cups emptied.

The day emptied.

I was more alone than if I had been alone.   We were about to go in different directions.   We did not know how to do anything else.

It's getting late, I said.

He showed me his left hand, which had YES tattooed on it.

I said, I should probably go home.

He flipped back through his book and pointed at, Are you OK?

I nodded yes.

I started to walk off.   I was going to walk to the Hudson River and keep walking.   I would carry the biggest stone I could bear and let my lungs fill with water.

But then I heard him clapping his hands behind me.

I turned around and he motioned for me to come to him.

I wanted to run away from him, and I wanted to go to him.

I went to him.

He asked if I would pose for him.   He wrote his question in German, and it wasn't until then that I realized he had been writing in English all afternoon, and that I had been speaking English.   Yes, I said in German.   Yes.   We made arrangements for the next day.

His apartment was like a zoo.   There were animals everywhere. Dogs and cats.   A dozen birdcages.   Fish tanks.   Glass boxes with snakes and lizards and insects.   Mice in cages, so the cats wouldn't get them.   Like Noah's ark.   But he kept one corner clean and bright. He said he was saving the space.

For what?

For sculptures.

I wanted to know from what, or from whom, but I did not ask.

He led me by the hand.   We talked for half an hour about what he wanted to make.   I told him I would do whatever he needed.

We drank coffee.

He wrote that he had not made a sculpture in America.

Why not?

I haven't been able to.

Why not?

We never talked about the past.

He opened the flue, although I didn't know why.

Birds sang in the other room.

I took off my clothes.

I went onto the couch.

He stared at me.   It was the first time I had ever been naked in front of a man.   I wondered if he knew that.

He came over and moved my body like I was a doll.   He put my hands behind my head.   He bent my right leg a little.   I assumed his hands were so rough from all of the sculptures he used to make.   He lowered my chin.   He turned my palms up.   His attention filled the hole in the middle of me.

I went back the next day.   And the next day.   I stopped looking for a job.   All that mattered was him looking at me.   I was prepared to fall apart if it came to that.

Each time it was the same.

He would talk about what he wanted to make.

I would tell him I would do whatever he needed.

We would drink coffee.

We would never talk about the past.

He would open the flue.

The birds would sing in the other room.

I would undress.

He would position me.

He would sculpt me.

Sometimes I would think about those hundred letters laid across my bedroom floor.   If I hadn't collected them, would our house have burned less brightly?

I looked at the sculpture after every session.   He went to feed the animals.   He let me be alone with it, although I never asked him for privacy.   He understood.

After only a few sessions it became clear that he was sculpting Anna. He was trying to remake the girl he knew seven years before.   He looked at me as he sculpted, but he saw her.

The positioning took longer and longer.   He touched more of me.

He moved me around more.   He spent ten full minutes bending and unbending my knee.   He closed and unclosed my hands.

I hope this doesn't embarrass you, he wrote in German in his little book.

No, I said in German.   No.

He folded one of my arms.   He straightened one of my arms.   The next week he touched my hair for what might have been five or fifty minutes.

He wrote, I am looking for an acceptable compromise.

I wanted to know how he lived through that night.

He touched my breasts, easing them apart.

I think this will be good, he wrote.

I wanted to know what will be good.   How will it be good?

He touched me all over.   I can tell you these things because I am not ashamed of them, because I learned from them.   And I trust you to understand me.   You are the only one I trust, Oskar.

The positioning was the sculpting.   He was sculpting me.   He was trying to make me so he could fall in love with me.

He spread my legs.   His palms pressed gently at the insides of my thighs.   My thighs pressed back.   His palms pressed out.

Birds were singing in the other room.

We were looking for an acceptable compromise.

The next week he held the backs of my legs, and the next week he was behind me.   It was the first time I had ever made love.   I wondered if he knew that.   It felt like crying.   I wondered, Why does anyone ever make love?

I looked at the unfinished sculpture of my sister, and the unfinished girl looked back at me.

Why does anyone ever make love?

We walked together to the bakery where we first met.

Together and separately.

We sat at a table.   On the same side, facing the windows.

I did not need to know if he could love me.

I needed to know if he could need me.

I flipped to the next blank page of his little book and wrote, Please marry me.

He looked at his hands.

YES and NO.

Why does anyone ever make love?

He took his pen and wrote on the next and last page, No children.

That was our first rule.

I understand, I told him in English.

We never used German again.

The next day, your grandfather and I were married.

THE ONLY ANIMAL

I read the first chapter of *A Brief History of Time* when Dad was still alive, and I got incredibly heavy boots about how relatively insignificant life is, and how, compared to the universe and compared to time, it didn't even matter if I existed at all. When Dad was tucking me in that night and we were talking about the book, I asked if he could think of a solution to that problem. "Which problem?" "The problem of how relatively insignificant we are." He said, "Well, what would happen if a plane dropped you in the middle of the Sahara Desert and you picked up a single grain of sand with tweezers and moved it one millimeter?" I said, "I'd probably die of dehydration." He said, "I just mean right then, when you moved that single grain of sand. What would that mean?" I said, "I dunno, what?" He said, "Think about it." I thought about it. "I guess I would have moved a grain of sand." "Which would mean?" "Which would mean I moved a grain of sand?" "Which would mean you changed the Sahara." "So?" "*So?* So the Sahara is a vast desert. And it has existed for millions of years. And you changed it!" "That's true!" I said, sitting up. "I changed the Sahara!" "Which means?" he said. "What? Tell me." "Well, I'm not talking about painting the *Mona Lisa* or curing cancer. I'm just talking about moving that one grain of sand one millimeter." "Yeah?" "If you *hadn't* done it, human history would have been one way . . ." "Uh-huh?" "But you *did* do it, *so* . . . ?" I stood on the bed, pointed my fingers at the fake stars, and screamed: "I changed the course of human history!" "That's right." "I changed the universe!" "You did." "I'm God!" "You're an atheist." "I don't exist!" I fell back onto the bed, into his arms, and we cracked up together.

That was kind of how I felt when I decided that I would meet every person in New York with the last name Black. Even if it was relatively insignificant, it was something, and I needed to do something, like sharks, who die if they don't swim, which I know about.

Anyway.

I decided that I would go through the names alphabetically, from Aaron to Zyna, even though it would have been a more efficient method to do it by geographical zones. Another thing I decided was that I would be as secretive about my mission as I could at home, and as honest about it as I could outside home, because that's what was necessary. So if Mom asked me, "Where are you going and when will you be back?" I would tell her, "Out, later." But if one of the Blacks wanted to know something, I would tell everything. My other rules were that I wouldn't be sexist again, or racist, or ageist, or homophobic, or overly wimpy, or discriminatory to handicapped people or mental retards, and also that I wouldn't lie unless I absolutely had to, which I did a lot. I put together a special field kit with some of the things I was going to need, like a Magnum flashlight, ChapStick, some Fig Newtons, plastic bags for important evidence and litter, my cell phone, the script for *Hamlet* (so I could memorize my stage directions while I was going from one place to another, because I didn't have any lines to memorize), a topographical map of New York, iodine pills in case of a dirty bomb, my white gloves, obviously, a couple of boxes of Juicy Juice, a magnifying glass, my *Larousse Pocket Dictionary*, and a bunch of other useful stuff. I was ready to go.

On my way out, Stan said, "What a day!" I said, "Yeah." He asked, "What's on the menu?" I showed him the key. He said, "Lox?" I said, "Hilarious, but I don't eat anything with parents." He shook his head and said, "I couldn't help myself. So what's on the menu?" "Queens and Greenwich Village." "You mean *Gren*-ich Village?" That was my first disappointment of the expedition, because I thought it was pronounced phonetically, which would have been a fascinating clue. "Anyway."

It took me three hours and forty-one minutes to walk to Aaron Black, because public transportation makes me panicky, even though walking over bridges also makes me panicky. Dad used to say that sometimes you have to put your fears in order, and that was one of those times. I walked across Amsterdam Avenue, and Columbus Avenue, and Central Park, and Fifth Avenue, and Madison Avenue, and Park Avenue, and Lexington Avenue, and Third Avenue, and Second Avenue. When I was exactly halfway across the Fifty-ninth Street Bridge, I thought about how a millimeter behind me was Manhattan and a millimeter in front of me was Queens. So what's the name of the parts of New York—exactly halfway through the Midtown Tunnel, exactly halfway over the Brooklyn Bridge, the exact middle of the Staten Island Ferry when it's exactly halfway between Manhattan and Staten Island— that aren't in any borough?

I took a step forward, and it was my first time in Queens.

I walked through Long Island City, Woodside, Elmhurst, and Jackson Heights. I shook my tambourine the whole time, because it helped me remember that even though I was going through different neighborhoods, I was still me. When I finally got to the building, I couldn't figure out where the doorman was. At first I thought maybe he was just getting some coffee, but I waited around for a few minutes and he didn't come. I looked through the door and saw that there was no desk for him. I thought, *Weird.*

I tried my key in the lock, but it didn't go in past the tip. I saw a device with a button for each apartment, so I pressed the button for A. Black's apartment, which was 9E. No one answered. I pressed it again. Nothing. I held down the buzzer for fifteen seconds. Still nothing. I sat down on the ground and wondered if it would be overly wimpy to cry in the lobby of an apartment building in Corona.

"All right, all right," a voice said from the speaker. "Take it easy." I jumped up. "Hello," I said, "my name is Oskar Schell." "What do you want?" His voice sounded mad, but I hadn't done anything wrong. "Did you know Thomas Schell?" "No." "Are you sure?" "Yes." "Do you know anything about a key?" "What do you want?" "I didn't do anything wrong." "What do you want?" "I found a key," I said, "and it was in an envelope with your name on it." "Aaron Black?" "No, just Black." "It's a common name." "I know." "And a color." "Obviously." "Goodbye," the voice said. "But I'm just trying to find out about this key." "Goodbye." "But—" "Goodbye." Disappointment #2.

I sat back down and started to cry in the lobby of an apartment

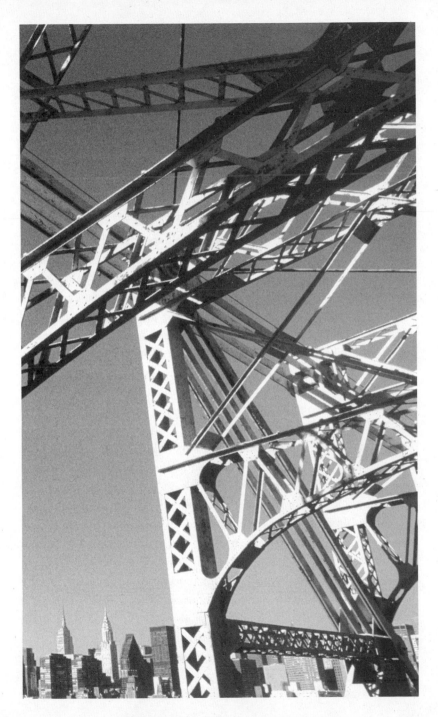

building in Corona. I wanted to press all of the buttons and scream curse words at everybody who lived in the stupid building. I wanted to give myself bruises. I stood up and pressed 9E again. This time the voice came out immediately. "What. Do. You. Want?" I said, "Thomas Schell was my dad." "And?" "*Was*. Not *is*. He's dead." He didn't say anything, but I knew he was pressing the Talk button because I could hear a beeping in his apartment, and also windows rattling from the same breeze that I was feeling at ground level. He asked, "How old are you?" I said seven, because I wanted him to feel more sorry for me, so he would help me. Lie #34. "My dad's dead," I told him. "Dead?" "He's inanimate." He didn't say anything. I heard more beeping. We just stood there, facing each other, but nine floors apart. Finally he said, "He must have died young." "Yeah." "How old was he?" "Forty." "That's too young." "That's true." "Can I ask how he died?" I didn't want to talk about it, but I remembered the promises I made to myself about my search, so I told him everything. I heard more beeping and wondered if his finger was getting tired. He said, "If you come up, I'll have a look at that key." "I can't go up." "Why not?" "Because you're on the ninth floor and I don't go that high." "Why not?" "It isn't safe." "But it's perfectly safe here." "Until something happens." "You'll be fine." "It's a rule." "I'd come down for you," he said, "but I just can't." "Why not?" "I'm very sick." "But my dad is dead." "I'm hooked up to all sorts of machines. That's why it took me so long to get to the intercom." If I could do it again, I would do it differently. But you can't do it again. I heard the voice saying, "Hello? Hello? Please." I slid my card under the apartment building door and got away from there as fast as I could.

Abby Black lived in #1 in a townhouse on Bedford Street. It took me two hours and twenty-three minutes to walk there, and my hand got exhausted from shaking my tambourine. There was a little sign above the door that said the poet Edna Saint Vincent Millay once lived in the house, and that it was the narrowest house in New York. I wondered if Edna Saint Vincent Millay was a man or a woman. I tried the key, and it went in halfway, but then it stopped. I knocked. No one answered, even though I could hear someone talking inside, and I guessed that #1 meant the first floor, so I knocked again. I was willing to be annoying if that's what was necessary.

A woman opened the door and said, "Can I help you?" She was incredibly beautiful, with a face like Mom's, which seemed like it was smiling even when she wasn't smiling, and huge boobs. I especially liked how her earrings sometimes touched her neck. It made me wish all of a sudden that I'd brought some kind of invention for her, so that she'd have a reason to like me. Even something small and simple, like a phosphorus brooch.

"Hi." "Hello." "Are you Abby Black?" "Yes." "I'm Oskar Schell." "Hello." "Hi." I told her, "I'm sure people tell you this constantly, but if you looked up 'incredibly beautiful' in the dictionary, there would be a picture of you." She cracked up a bit and said, "People never tell me that." "I bet they do." She cracked up a bit more. "They don't." "Then you hang out with the wrong people." "You might be right about that." "Because you're incredibly beautiful."

She opened the door a bit more. I asked, "Did you know Thomas Schell?" "Excuse me?" "Did you know Thomas Schell?" She thought. I wondered why she had to think. "No." "Are you sure?" "Yes." There was something unsure about the way she said she was sure, which made me think that maybe she was keeping some sort of secret from me. So what would that secret be? I handed her the envelope and said, "Does this mean anything to you?" She looked at it for a while. "I don't think so. Should it?" "Only if it does," I told her. "It doesn't," she told me. I didn't believe her.

"Would it be OK if I came in?" I asked. "Now is not really the best time." "Why not?" "I'm in the middle of something." "What kind of something?" "Is that any of your business?" "Is that a rhetorical question?" "Yes." "Do you have a job?" "Yes." "What's your job?" "I am an epidemiologist." "You study diseases." "Yes." "Fascinating." "Listen, I don't know what it is that you need, but if it has to do with that envelope, I'm sure I can't help—" "I'm extremely thirsty," I said, touching my throat, which is the universal sign for thirsty. "There's a deli on the corner." "Actually, I'm diabetic and I need some sugar asap." Lie #35. "Do you mean A.S.A.P.?" "Anyway."

I didn't feel great about lying, and I didn't believe in being able to know what's going to happen before it happens, but for some reason I knew I had to get inside her apartment. In exchange for the lie, I made

JONATHAN SAFRAN FOER

a promise to myself that when I got a raise in my allowance, I would donate part of that raise to people who in reality *do* have diabetes. She took a heavy breath, like she was incredibly frustrated, but on the other hand, she didn't ask me to leave. A man's voice called something from inside. "Orange juice?" she asked. "Do you have any coffee?" "Follow me," she said, and she walked into the apartment. "What about non-dairy creamer?"

I got a look around as I followed her, and everything was clean and perfect. There were neat photographs on the walls, including one where you could see an African-American woman's VJ, which made me feel self-conscious. "Where are the sofa cushions?" "It doesn't have cushions." "What is that?" "You mean the painting?" "Your apartment smells good." The man in the other room called again, this time extremely loudly, like he was desperate, but she didn't pay any attention, like she didn't hear it, or didn't care.

I touched a lot of things in her kitchen, because it made me feel OK for some reason. I ran my finger along the top of her microwave, and it turned gray. "*C'est sale,*" I said, showing it to her and cracking up. She became extremely serious. "That's embarrassing," she said. "You should see my laboratory," I said. "I wonder how that could have happened," she said. I said, "Things get dirty." "But I like to keep things clean. A woman comes by every week to clean. I've told her a million times to clean everywhere. I've even pointed that out to her." I asked her why she was getting so upset about such a small thing. She said, "It doesn't feel small to me," and I thought about moving a single grain of sand one millimeter. I took a wet wipe from my field kit and cleaned the microwave.

"Since you're an epidemiologist," I said, "did you know that seventy percent of household dust is actually composed of human epidermal matter?" "No," she said, "I didn't." "I'm an amateur epidemiologist." "There aren't many of those." "Yeah. And I conducted a pretty fascinating experiment once where I told Feliz to save all the dust from our apartment for a year in a garbage bag for me. Then I weighed it. It weighed 112 pounds. Then I figured out that seventy percent of 112 pounds is 78.4 pounds. I weigh 76 pounds, 78 pounds when I'm sopping wet. That doesn't actually prove anything, but it's weird. Where can I put this?" "Here," she said, taking the wet wipe from me. I asked her, "Why are you sad?" "Excuse me?" "You're sad. Why?"

The coffee machine gurgled. She opened a cabinet and took out a mug. "Do you take sugar?" I told her yes, because Dad always took sugar. As soon as she sat down, she got back up and took a bowl of grapes from her refrigerator. She also took out cookies and put them on a plate. "Do you like strawberries?" she asked. "Yes," I told her, "but I'm not hungry." She put out some strawberries. I thought it was weird that there weren't any menus or little magnetic calendars or pictures of kids on her refrigerator. The only thing in the whole kitchen was a photograph of an elephant on the wall next to the phone. "I love that," I told her, and not just because I wanted her to like me. "You love what?" she asked. I pointed at the picture. "Thank you," she said. "I like it, too." "I said I *loved* it." "Yes. I *love* it."

"How much do you know about elephants?" "Not too much." "Not too much a little? Or not too much nothing?" "Hardly anything." "For example, did you know that scientists used to think that elephants had esp?" "Do you mean E.S.P.?" "Anyway, elephants can set up meetings from very faraway locations, and they know where their friends and enemies are going to be, and they can find water without any geological clues. No one could figure out how they do all of those things. So what's actually going on?" "I don't know." "How do they do it?" "It?" "How do they set up meetings if they don't have E.S.P.?" "You're asking me?" "Yes." "I don't know." "Do you want to know?" "Sure." "A lot?" "Sure." "They're making very, very, very, very deep calls, way deeper than what humans can hear. They're talking to each other. Isn't that so awesome?" "It is." I ate a strawberry.

"There's this woman who's spent the last couple of years in the Congo or wherever. She's been making recordings of the calls and putting together an enormous library of them. This past year she started playing them back." "Playing them back?" "To the elephants." "Why?" I loved that she asked why. "As you probably know, elephants have much, much stronger memories than other mammals." "Yes. I think I knew that." "So this woman wanted to see just how good their memories actually are. She'd play the call of an enemy that was recorded a bunch of years earlier—a call they'd heard only once—and they'd get

panicky, and sometimes they'd run. They remembered hundreds of calls. Thousands. There might not even be a limit. Isn't that fascinating?" "It is." "Because what's *really* fascinating is that she'd play the call of a dead elephant to its family members." "And?" "They remembered." "What did they do?" "They approached the speaker."

"I wonder what they were feeling." "What do you mean?" "When they heard the calls of their dead, was it with love that they approached the jeep? Or fear? Or anger?" "I don't remember." "Did they charge?" "I don't remember." "Did they cry?" "Only humans can cry tears. Did you know that?" "It looks like the elephant in that photograph is crying." I got extremely close to the picture, and it was true. "It was probably manipulated in Photoshop," I said. "But just in case, can I take a picture of your picture?" She nodded and said, "Didn't I read somewhere that elephants are the only other animals that bury their dead?" "No," I told her as I focused Grandpa's camera, "you didn't. They just gather the bones. Only humans bury their dead." "Elephants couldn't believe in ghosts." That made me crack up a little. "Well, most scientists wouldn't say so." "What would you say?" "I'm just an amateur scientist." "And what would you say?" I took the picture. "I'd say they were confused."

Then she started to cry tears.

I thought, *I'm the one who's supposed to be crying.*

"Don't cry," I told her. "Why not?" she asked. "Because," I told her. "Because what?" she asked. Since I didn't know why she was crying, I couldn't think of a reason. Was she crying about the elephants? Or something else I'd said? Or the desperate person in the other room? Or something that I didn't know about? I told her, "I bruise easily." She said, "I'm sorry." I told her, "I wrote a letter to that scientist who's making those elephant recordings. I asked if I could be her assistant. I told her I could make sure there were always blank tapes ready for recording, and I could boil all the water so it was safe to drink, or even just carry her equipment. Her assistant wrote back to tell me she already had an assistant, obviously, but maybe there would be a project in the future that we could work on together." "That's great. Something to look forward to." "Yeah."

Someone came to the door of the kitchen who I guessed was the man that had been calling from the other room. He just stuck his head in extremely quickly, said something I didn't understand, and walked away. Abby pretended to ignore it, but I didn't. "Who was that?" "My husband." "Does he need something?" "I don't care." "But he's your husband, and I think he needs something." She cried more tears. I went over to her and I put my hand on her shoulder, like Dad used to do with me. I asked her what she was feeling, because that's what he would ask. "You must think this is very unusual," she said. "I think a lot of things are very unusual," I said. She asked, "How old are you?" I told her twelve—lie #59—because I wanted to be old enough for her to love me. "What's a twelve-year-old doing knocking on the doors of strangers?" "I'm trying to find a lock. How old are you?" "Forty-eight." "Jose. You look much younger than that." She cracked up through her crying and said, "Thanks." "What's a forty-eight-year-old doing inviting strangers into her kitchen?" "I don't know." "I'm being annoying," I said. "You're not being annoying," she said, but it's extremely hard to believe someone when they tell you that.

I asked, "Are you sure you didn't know Thomas Schell?" She said, "I didn't know Thomas Schell," but for some reason I *still* didn't believe her. "Maybe you know someone else with the first name Thomas? Or someone else with the last name Schell?" "No." I kept thinking there was something she wasn't telling me. I showed her the little envelope again. "But this is your last name, right?" She looked at the writing, and I could see that she recognized something about it. Or I thought I could see it. But then she said, "I'm sorry. I don't think I can help you." "And what about the key?" "What key?" I realized I hadn't even shown it to her yet. All of that talking—about dust, about elephants—and I hadn't gotten to the whole reason I was there.

I pulled the key out from under my shirt and put it in her hand. Because the string was still around my neck, when she leaned in to look at the key, her face came incredibly close to my face. We were frozen there for a long time. It was like time was stopped. I thought about the falling body.

"I'm sorry," she said. "Why are you sorry?" "I'm sorry I don't know anything about the key." Disappointment #3. "I'm sorry, too."

Our faces were so incredibly close.

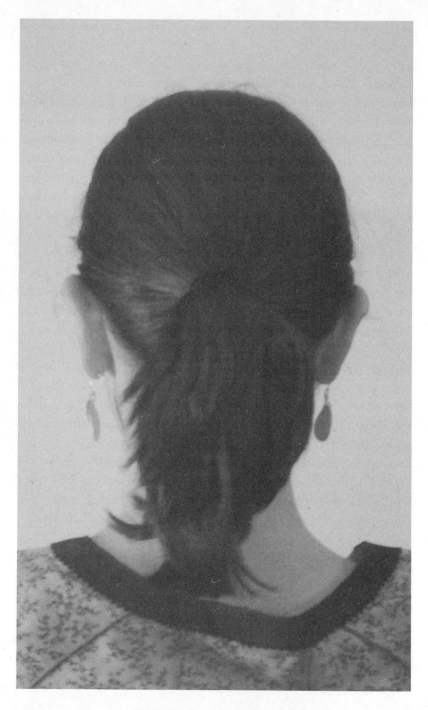

JONATHAN SAFRAN FOER

I told her, "The fall play this fall is *Hamlet*, in case you're interested. I'm Yorick. We have a working fountain. If you want to come to opening night, it's twelve weeks from now. It should be pretty great." She said, "I'll try," and I could feel the breath of her words against my face. I asked her, "Could we kiss for a little bit?"

"Excuse me?" she said, although, on the other hand, she didn't pull her head back. "It's just that I like you, and I think I can tell that you like me." She said, "I don't think that's a good idea." Disappointment #4. I asked why not. She said, "Because I'm forty-eight and you're twelve." "So?" "And I'm married." "So?" "And I don't even know you." "Don't you feel like you know me?" She didn't say anything. I told her, "Humans are the only animal that blushes, laughs, has religion, wages war, and kisses with lips. So in a way, the more you kiss with lips, the more human you are." "And the more you wage war?" Then I was the silent one. She said, "You're a sweet, sweet boy." I said, "Young man." "But I don't think it's a good idea." "Does it have to be a good idea?" "I think it does." "Can I at least take a picture of you?" She said, "That would be nice." But when I started focusing Grandpa's camera, she put her hand in front of her face for some reason. I didn't want to force her to explain herself, so I thought of a different picture I could take, which would be more truthful, anyway. "Here's my card," I told her, when the cap was back on the lens, "in case you remember anything about the key or just want to talk."

· · ·

I went over to Grandma's apartment when I got home, which is what I did basically every afternoon, because Mom worked at the firm on Saturdays and sometimes even Sundays, and she got panicky about me being alone. As I got near Grandma's building, I looked up and didn't see her sitting at her window waiting for me, like she always did. I asked Farley if she was there, and he said he thought so, so I went up the seventy-two stairs.

I rang the doorbell. She didn't answer, so I opened the door, because she always leaves it unlocked, even though I don't think that's safe, because sometimes people who seem good end up being not as good as you might have hoped. As I walked in, she was coming to the door. It looked almost like she had been crying, but I knew that was impossible, because once she told me that she emptied herself of tears when Grandpa left. I told her fresh tears are produced every time you cry. She said, "Anyway." Sometimes I wondered if she cried when no one was looking.

"Oskar!" she said, and lifted me from the ground with one of her hugs. "I'm OK," I said. "Oskar!" she said again, picking me up in another hug. "I'm OK," I said again, and then I asked her where she'd been. "I was in the guest room talking to the renter."

When I was a baby, Grandma would take care of me during the day. Dad told me that she would give me baths in the sink, and trim my fingernails and toenails with her teeth because she was afraid of using clippers. When I was old enough to take baths in the bathtub, and to know I had a penis and a scrotum and everything, I asked her not to sit in the room with me. "Why not?" "Privacy." "Privacy from what? From me?" I didn't want to hurt her feelings, because not hurting her feelings is another of my *raisons d'être*. "Just privacy," I said. She put her hands on her stomach and said, "From *me*?" She agreed to wait outside, but only if I held a ball of yarn, which went under the bathroom door and was connected to the scarf she was knitting. Every few seconds she would give it a tug, and I had to tug back—undoing what she'd just done—so that she could know I was OK.

She was taking care of me when I was four, chasing me around the apartment like she was a monster, and I cut my top lip against the end of our coffee table and had to go to the hospital. Grandma believes in

God, but she doesn't believe in taxis, so I bled on my shirt on the bus. Dad told me it gave her incredibly heavy boots, even though my lip only needed a couple of stitches, and that she kept coming across the street to tell him, "It was all my fault. You should never let him be around me again." The next time I saw her after that, she told me, "You see, I was pretending to be a monster, and I became a monster."

Grandma stayed at our apartment the week after Dad died, while Mom was going around Manhattan putting up posters. We had thousands of thumb wars, and I won every single one, even the ones I was trying to lose. We watched approved documentaries, and cooked vegan cupcakes, and went for lots of walks in the park. One day I wandered away from her and hid. I liked the way it felt to have someone look for me, to hear my name again and again. "Oskar! Oskar!" Maybe I didn't even like it, but I needed it right then.

I followed her around from a safe distance as she started to get incredibly panicky. "Oskar!" She was crying and touching everything, but I wouldn't let her know where I was, because I was sure that the cracking up at the end would make it all OK. I watched her as she walked home, where I knew she would sit on the stoop of our building and wait for Mom to come back. She would have to tell her I had disappeared, and that because she wasn't watching me closely enough, I was gone forever and there would be no more Schells. I ran ahead, down Eighty-second Street and up Eighty-third, and when she came up to the building, I jumped out from behind the door. "But I didn't order a pizza!" I said, cracking up so hard I thought my neck would burst open.

She started to say something, and then she stopped. Stan took her arm and said, "Why don't you sit down, Grandma." She told him, "Don't touch me," in a voice that I'd never heard from her. Then she turned around and went across the street to her apartment. That night, I looked through my binoculars at her window and there was a note that said, "Don't go away."

Ever since that day, whenever we go on walks she makes us play a game like Marco Polo, where she calls my name and I have to call back to let her know that I'm OK.

"Oskar."

"I'm OK."

"Oskar."

"I'm OK."

I'm never exactly sure when we're playing the game and when she's just saying my name, so I always let her know that I'm OK.

A few months after Dad died, Mom and I went to the storage facility in New Jersey where Dad kept the stuff that he didn't use anymore but might use again one day, like when he retired, I guess. We rented a car, and it took us more than two hours to get there, even though it wasn't far away, because Mom kept stopping to go to the bathroom and wash her face. The facility wasn't organized very well, and it was extremely dark, so it took us a long time to find Dad's little room. We got in a fight about his razor, because she said it should go in the "throw it away" pile and I told her it should go in the "save it" pile. She said, "Save it for what?" I said, "It doesn't matter for what." She said, "I don't know why he saved a three-dollar razor in the first place." I said, "It doesn't matter why." She said, "We can't save everything." I said, "So it will be OK if I throw away all of your things and forget about you after you die?" As it was coming out of my mouth, I wished it was going into my mouth. She said she was sorry, which I thought was weird.

One of the things we found were the old two-way radios from when I was a baby. Mom and Dad put one in the crib so they could hear me crying, and sometimes, instead of coming to the crib, Dad would just talk into it, which would help me get to sleep. I asked Mom why he kept those. She said, "Probably for when you have kids." *What the?* "That's what Dad was like." I started to realize that a lot of the stuff he'd saved—boxes and boxes of Legos, the set of *How It Works* books, even the empty photo albums—was probably for when I had kids. I don't know why, but for some reason that made me angry.

Anyway, I put new batteries in the two-way radios, and I thought it would be a fun way for me and Grandma to talk. I gave her the baby one, so she wouldn't have to figure out any buttons, and it worked great. When I'd wake up I'd tell her good morning. And before I'd go to bed we'd usually talk. She was always waiting for me on the other end. I don't know how she knew when I'd be there. Maybe she just waited around all day.

"Grandma? Do you read me?" "Oskar?" "I'm OK. Over." "How

did you sleep, darling? Over." "What? I couldn't hear that. Over." "I asked how did you sleep. Over." "Fine," I'll say, looking at her across the street, my chin in my palm, "no bad dreams. Over." "One hundred dollars. Over." We never have all that much to say to each other. She tells me the same stories about Grandpa again and again, like how his hands were rough from making so many sculptures, and how he could talk to animals. "You'll come visit me this afternoon? Over?" "Yeah. I think so. Over." "Please try. Over." "I'll try. Over and out."

Some nights I took the two-way radio into bed with me and rested it on the side of the pillow that Buckminster wasn't on so I could hear what was going on in her bedroom. Sometimes she would wake me up in the middle of the night. It gave me heavy boots that she had night-mares, because I didn't know what she was dreaming about and there was nothing I could do to help her. She hollered, which woke me up, obviously, so my sleep depended on her sleep, and when I told her, "No bad dreams," I was talking about her.

Grandma knitted me white sweaters, white mittens, and white hats. She knew how much I liked dehydrated ice cream, which was one of my very few exceptions to veganism, because it's what astronauts have for dessert, and she went to the Hayden Planetarium and bought it for me. She picked up pretty rocks to give to me, even though she shouldn't have been carrying heavy things, and usually they were just Manhattan schist, anyway. A couple of days after the worst day, when I was on my way to my first appointment with Dr. Fein, I saw Grandma carrying a huge rock across Broadway. It was as big as a baby and must have weighed a ton. But she never gave that one to me, and she never mentioned it.

"Oskar."

"I'm OK."

One afternoon, I mentioned to Grandma that I was considering starting a stamp collection, and the next afternoon she had three albums for me and — "because I love you so much it hurts me, and because I want your wonderful collection to have a wonderful beginning" — a sheet of stamps of Great American Inventors.

"You've got Thomas Edison," she said, pointing at one of the stamps, "and Ben Franklin, Henry Ford, Eli Whitney, Alexander Graham Bell, George Washington Carver, Nikola Tesla, whoever that is, the Wright Brothers, J. Robert Oppenheimer—" "Who's he?" "He invented the bomb." "Which bomb?" "*The* bomb." "He wasn't a Great Inventor!" She said, "Great, not good."

"Grandma?" "Yes, darling?" "It's just that where's the plate block?" "The what?" "The thing on the side of the sheet with the numbers." "With the numbers?" "Yeah." "I got rid of it." "You *what?*" "I got rid of it. Was that wrong?" I felt myself starting to spaz, even though I was trying not to. "Well, it's not worth anything without the plate block!" "What?" "The *plate block!* These stamps. Aren't. *Valuable!*" She looked at me for a few seconds. "Yeah," she said, "I guess I heard of that. So I'll go back to the stamp shop tomorrow and get another sheet. These we can use for the mail." "There's no reason to get another," I told her, wanting to take back the last few things I said and try them again, being nicer this time, being a better grandson, or just a silent one. "There is a reason, Oskar." "I'm OK."

We spent so much time together. I don't think there's anyone that I spent more time with, at least not since Dad died, unless you count Buckminster. But there were a lot of people that I knew better. For example, I didn't know anything about what it was like when she was a kid, or how she met Grandpa, or what their marriage was like, or why he left. If I had to write her life story, all I could say is that her husband could talk to animals, and that I should never love anything as much as she loved me. So here's my question: What were we spending so much time doing if not getting to know each other?

"Did you do anything special today?" she asked that afternoon I started my search for the lock. When I think about everything that happened, from when we buried the coffin to when I dug it up, I always think about how I could have told her the truth then. It wasn't too late to turn around, before I got to the place I couldn't come back from. Even if she wouldn't have understood me, I would have been able to say it. "Yeah," I said. "I put the finishing touches on those scratch-and-sniff earrings for the craft fair. Also I mounted the eastern tiger swallowtail that Stan found dead on the stoop. And I worked on a bunch of letters, because I'd gotten behind on those." "Who are you writing letters to?" she asked, and it still wasn't too late. "Kofi Annan, Siegfried, Roy, Jacques Chirac, E. O. Wilson, Weird Al Yankovic, Bill Gates, Vladimir Putin, and some other people." She asked, "Why don't you write a letter to someone you know?" I started to tell her, "I don't know anyone," but then I heard something. Or I thought I heard something. There was noise in the apartment, like someone walking around. "What is that?" I asked. "My ears aren't a hundred dollars," she said. "But there's someone in the apartment. Maybe it's the renter?" "No," she said, "he went off to a museum earlier." "What museum?" "I don't know what museum. He said he wouldn't be back until late tonight." "But I can hear someone." "No you can't," she said. I said, "I'm ninety-nine percent sure I can." She said, "Maybe it's just your imagination." I was in the place that I couldn't come back from.

> *Thank you for your letter. Because of the large*
> *volume of mail I receive, I am unable to write*
> *personal responses. Nevertheless, know that I*
> *read and save every letter, with the hope of one*
> *day being able to give each the proper response it*
> *deserves. Until that day,*
> > *Most sincerely,*
> > *Stephen Hawking*

I stayed up pretty late designing jewelry that night. I designed a Nature Hike Anklet, which leaves a trail of bright yellow dye when you walk, so in case you get lost, you can find your way back. I also designed a set of wedding rings, where each one takes the pulse of the person wearing it and sends a signal to the other ring to flash red with each heartbeat. Also I designed a pretty fascinating bracelet, where you put a rubber band around your favorite book of poems for a year, and then you take it off and wear it.

I don't know why, but as I was working, I couldn't stop thinking about that day Mom and I went to the storage facility in New Jersey. I kept going back to it, like a salmon, which I know about. Mom must have stopped to wash her face ten times. It was so quiet and so dark, and we were the only people there. What drinks were in the Coke machine? What fonts were the signs in? I went through the boxes in my brain. I took out a neat old film projector. What was the last film Dad made? Was I in it? I went through a bunch of the toothbrushes they give you at the dentist, and three baseballs that Dad had caught at games, which he wrote the dates on. What were the dates? My brain opened a box with old atlases (where there were two Germanys and one Yugoslavia) and souvenirs from business trips, like Russian dolls with dolls inside them with dolls inside them with dolls inside them . . . Which of those things had Dad kept for when I had kids?

It was 2:36 A.M. I went to Mom's room. She was sleeping, obviously. I watched the sheets breathe when she breathed, like how Dad used to say that trees inhale when people exhale, because I was too young to understand the truth about biological processes. I could tell that Mom was dreaming, but I didn't want to know what she was dreaming about, because I had enough of my own nightmares, and if she had been dreaming something happy, I would have been angry at her for dreaming something happy. I touched her incredibly gently. She jumped up and said, "What is it?" I said, "It's OK." She grabbed my shoulders and said, "What is it?" The way she was holding me hurt my arms, but I didn't show anything. "Remember when we went to the storage facility in New Jersey?" She let go of me and lay back down. "What?" "Where Dad's stuff is. Remember?" "It's the middle of the night, Oskar." "What was it called?" "*Oskar.*" "It's just that what was the name of the place?" She reached for her glasses on the bedside table, and I would have given all of my collections, and all of the jewelry I'd ever made, and all future birthday and Christmas presents just to hear her say "Black Storage." Or "Blackwell Storage." Or "Blackman." Or even "Midnight Storage." Or "Dark Storage." Or "Rainbow."

She made a weird face, like someone was hurting her, and said, "Store-a-Lot."

I'd lost count of the disappointments.

WHY I'M NOT WHERE YOU ARE
5/21/63

Your mother and I never talk about the past, that's a rule. I go to the door when she's using the bathroom, and she never looks over my shoulder when I'm writing, those are two more rules. I open doors for her but I never touch her back as she passes through, she never lets me watch her cook, she folds my pants but leaves my shirts by the ironing board, I never light candles when she's in the room, but I do blow candles out. It's a rule that we never listen to sad music, we made that rule early on, songs are as sad as the listener, we hardly ever listen to music. I change the sheets every morning to wash away my writing, we never sleep in the same bed twice, we never watch television shows about sick children, she never asks me how my day was, we always eat on the same side of the table, facing the window. So many rules, sometimes I can't remember what's a rule and what isn't, if anything we do is for its own sake, I'm leaving her today, is that the rule we've been organizing ourselves around this whole time, or am I about to break the organizing rule? I used to ride the bus here at the end of every week, to take the magazines and newspapers that people left behind when they got on their planes, your mother reads and reads and reads, she wants English, as much as she can get her hands on, is that a rule? I'd come late Friday afternoon, it used to be that I would go home with a magazine or two and maybe a paper, but she wanted more, more slang, more figures of speech, the bee's knees, the cat's pajamas, horse of a different color, dog-tired, she wanted to talk like she was born here, like she never came from anywhere else, so I started bringing a knapsack, which I would stuff with as much as would fit, it got heavy, my shoulders burned with English, she wanted more English, so I brought a suitcase, I filled it

JONATHAN SAFRAN FOER

until I could barely zip the zipper, the suitcase sagged with English, my arms burned with English, my hands did, my knuckles, people must have thought I was actually going somewhere, the next morning my back ached with English, I found myself sticking around, spending more time than was necessary, watching the planes bring people and take people away, I started coming twice a week and staying for several hours, when it was time to go home I didn't want to leave, and when I wasn't here, I wanted to be here, now I come every morning before we open the store, and every evening after dinner, so what is it, am I hoping to see someone I know get off one of the planes, am I waiting for a relative who never will come, do I expect Anna? No, that's not it, it's not about my joy, the relief of my burden. I like to see people reunited, maybe that's a silly thing, but what can I say, I like to see people run to each other, I like the kissing and the crying, I like the impatience, the stories that the mouth can't tell fast enough, the ears that aren't big enough, the eyes that can't take in all of the change, I like the hugging, the bringing together, the end of missing someone, I sit on the side with a coffee and write in my daybook, I examine the flight schedules that I've already memorized, I observe, I write, I try not to remember the life that I didn't want to lose but lost and have to remember, being here fills my heart with so much joy, even if the joy isn't mine, and at the end of the day I fill the suitcase with old news. Maybe that was the story I was telling myself when I met your mother, I thought we could run to each other, I thought we could have a beautiful reunion, although we had hardly known each other in Dresden. It didn't work. We've wandered in place, our arms outstretched, but not toward each other, they're marking off distance, everything between us has been a rule to govern our life together, everything a measurement, a marriage of millimeters, of rules, when she gets up to go to the shower, I feed the animals—that's a rule—so she doesn't have to be self-conscious, she finds things to keep herself busy when I undress at night—rule—she goes to the door to make sure it's locked, she double-checks the oven, she tends to her collections in the china cabinet, she checks, again, the curlers that she hasn't used since we met, and when she gets undressed, I've never been so busy in my life. Only a few months into our marriage, we started marking off areas in the apartment as "Nothing Places," in which one could be assured of complete privacy, we agreed that we never would look at the marked-off zones, that they would be nonexistent territories in the apartment in which one could temporarily cease to exist, the first was in the bedroom, by the foot of the bed, we marked it off with red tape on the carpet, and it was just large enough to stand in, it was a good place to disappear, we knew it was there but we never looked at it, it worked so well that we decided to create a Nothing Place in the living room, it seemed necessary, because there are times when one needs to disappear while in the living room, and sometimes one simply wants to disappear, we made this zone slightly larger so that one of us could lie down in it, it was a rule that you never would look at that rectangle of space, it didn't exist, and when you were in it, neither did you, for a while that was enough, but only for a while, we required more rules, on our second anniversary we marked off the entire guest room as a Nothing Place, it seemed like a good idea at the time, sometimes a small patch at the foot of the bed or a rectangle in the living room isn't enough privacy, the side of the door that faced the guest room was Nothing, the side that faced the hallway was Something, the knob that connected them was neither Something nor Nothing. The walls of the hallway were Nothing, even pictures need to disappear, especially pictures, but the hallway itself was Something, the bathtub was Nothing, the bathwater was Something, the hair on our bodies was Nothing, of course, but once it collected around the drain it was Something, we were trying to make our lives easier, trying, with all of our rules, to make life effortless. But a friction began to arise between Nothing and Something, in the morning the Nothing vase cast a Something shadow, like the memory of someone you've lost, what can you say about that, at night the Nothing light from the guest room spilled under the Nothing door and stained the Something hallway, there's nothing to say. It became difficult to navigate from Something to Something without accidentally walking through Nothing, and when Something—a key, a pen, a pocketwatch—was accidentally left in a Nothing Place, it never could be retrieved, that was an unspoken rule, like nearly all of our rules have been. There came a point, a year or two ago, when our apartment

JONATHAN SAFRAN FOER

was more Nothing than Something, that in itself didn't have to be a problem, it could have been a good thing, it could have saved us. We got worse. I was sitting on the sofa in the second bedroom one afternoon, thinking and thinking and thinking, when I realized I was on a Something island. "How did I get here," I wondered, surrounded by Nothing, "and how can I get back?" The longer your mother and I lived together, the more we took each other's assumptions for granted, the less was said, the more misunderstood, I'd often remember having designated a space as Nothing when she was sure we had agreed that it was Something, our unspoken agreements led to disagreements, to suffering, I started to undress right in front of her, this was just a few months ago, and she said, "Thomas! What are you doing!" and I gestured, "I thought this was Nothing," covering myself with one of my daybooks, and she said, "It's Something!" We took the blueprint of our apartment from the hallway closet and taped it to the inside of the front door, with an orange and a green marker we separated Something from Nothing. "This is Something," we decided. "This is Nothing." "Something." "Something." "Nothing." "Something." "Nothing." "Nothing." "Nothing." Everything was forever fixed, there would be only peace and happiness, it wasn't until last night, our last night together, that the inevitable question finally arose, I told her, "Something," by covering her face with my hands and then lifting them like a marriage veil. "We must be." But I knew, in the most protected part of my heart, the truth.

Excuse me, do you know what time it is?

The beautiful girl didn't know the time, she was in a hurry, she said, "Good luck," I smiled, she hurried off, her skirt catching the air as she ran, sometimes I can hear my bones straining under the weight of all of the lives I'm not living. In this life, I'm sitting in an airport trying to explain myself to my unborn son, I'm filling the pages of this, my last daybook, I'm thinking of a loaf of black bread that I left out one night, the next morning I saw the outline of the mouse that had eaten through it, I cut the loaf into slices and saw the mouse at each moment, I'm thinking of Anna, I would give everything never to think about her again, I can only hold on to the things I want to lose, I'm thinking of the day we met, she accompanied her father to meet my father, they were friends, they had talked about art and literature before the war, but once the war began, they talked only about war, I saw her approaching when she was still far away, I was fifteen, she was seventeen, we sat together on the grass while our fathers spoke inside, how could we have been younger? We talked about nothing in particular, but it felt like we were talking about the most important things, we pulled fistfuls of grass, and I asked her if she liked to read, she said, "No, but there are books that I love, love, love," she said it just like that, three times, "Do you like to dance?" she asked, "Do you like to swim?" I asked, we looked at each other until it felt like everything would burst into flames, "Do you like animals?" "Do you like bad weather?" "Do you like your friends?" I told her about my sculpture, she said, "I'm sure you will be a great artist." "How can you be sure?" "I just am." I told her I already was a great artist, because that's how unsure of myself I was, she said, "I meant famous," I told her that wasn't what mattered to me, she asked what mattered to me, I told her I did it for its own sake, she laughed and said, "You don't understand yourself," I said, "Of course I do," she said, "Of course," I said, "I do!" She said, "There's nothing wrong with not understanding yourself," she saw through the shell of me into the center of me, "Do you like music?" Our fathers came out of the house and stood at the door, one of them asked, "What are we going to do?" I knew that our time together was almost over, I asked her if she liked sports, she asked me if I liked chess, I asked her if she liked fallen trees, she went home with her father, the center of me followed her, but I was left with the shell of me, I needed to see her again, I couldn't explain my need to myself, and that's why it was such a beautiful need, there's nothing wrong with not understanding yourself. The next day, I walked half an hour to her house, fearing someone would see me on the road between our neighborhoods, too much to explain that I couldn't explain, I wore a broad-brimmed hat and kept my head down, I heard the footsteps of those passing me, and I didn't know if they were a man's, woman's, or child's, I felt as if I were walking the rungs of a ladder laid flat, I was too ashamed or embarrassed to make myself known to her, how would I have explained it, was I walking up the ladder or down? I hid behind a mound of earth that had been dug up to make a grave for some old books, literature was the only religion her father practiced, when a book fell on the floor he kissed it, when he was done with a book he tried to give it away to someone who would love it, and if he couldn't find a worthy recipient, he buried it, I looked for her all day but didn't see her, not in the yard, not through a window, I promised myself I would stay until I found her, but as night began to come in, I knew I had to go home, I hated myself for going, why couldn't I be the kind of person who stays? I walked back with my head down, I couldn't stop thinking about her even though I hardly knew her, I didn't know what good would come of going to see her, but I knew that I needed to be near her, it occurred to me, as I walked back to her the next day with my head down, that she might not be thinking of me. The books had been buried, so I hid this time behind a group of trees, I imagined their roots wrapped around books, pulling nourishment from the pages, I imagined rings of letters in their trunks, I waited for hours, I saw your mother in one of the second-floor windows, she was just a girl, she looked back at me, but I didn't see Anna. A leaf fell, it was yellow like paper, I had to go home, and then, the next day, I had to go back to her. I skipped my classes, the walk happened so quickly, my neck strained from hiding my face, my arm brushed the arm of someone passing—a strong, solid arm—and I tried to imagine whom it belonged to, a farmer, a stoneworker, a carpenter, a bricklayer. When I got to her house I hid beneath one of the back windows, a train rattled past in the distance, people coming, people leaving, soldiers, children, the window shook like an eardrum, I waited all day, did she go

on some sort of trip, was she on an errand, was she hiding from me? When I came home my father told me that her father had paid another visit, I asked him why he was out of breath, he said, "Things keep getting worse," I realized that her father and I must have passed each other on the road that morning. "What things?" Was his the strong arm I felt brushing past me? "Everything. The world." Did he see me, or did my hat and lowered head protect me? "Since when?" Perhaps his head was down, too. "Since the beginning." The harder I tried not to think about her, the more I thought about her, the more impossible it became to explain, I went back to her house, I walked the road between our two neighborhoods with my head down, she wasn't there again, I wanted to call her name, but I didn't want her to hear my voice, all of my desire was based on that one brief exchange, held in the palm of our half hour together were one hundred million arguments, and impossible admissions, and silences. I had so much to ask her, "Do you like to lie on your stomach and look for things under the ice?" "Do you like plays?" "Do you like it when you can hear something before you can see it?" I went again the next day, the walk was exhausting, with each step I further convinced myself that she had thought badly of me, or worse, that she hadn't thought of me at all, I walked with my head bowed, my broad-brimmed cap pushed low, when you hide your face from the world, you can't see the world, and that's why, in the middle of my youth, in the middle of Europe, in between our two villages, on the verge of losing everything, I bumped into something and was knocked to the ground. It took me several breaths to gather myself together, at first I thought I'd walked into a tree, but then that tree became a person, who was also recovering on the ground, and then I saw that it was her, and she saw that it was me, "Hello," I said, brushing myself off, "Hello," she said. "This is so funny." "Yes." How could it be explained? "Where are you going?" I asked. "Just for a walk," she said, "and you?" "Just for a walk." We helped each other up, she brushed leaves from my hair, I wanted to touch her hair, "That's not true," I said, not knowing what the next words out of my mouth would be, but wanting them to be mine, wanting, more than I'd ever wanted anything, to express the center of me and be understood. "I was walking to see you." I told her, "I've come to your house each of the last six days. For some reason I needed to see you again." She was silent, I had made a fool of myself, there's nothing wrong with not understanding yourself and she started laughing, laughing harder than I'd ever felt anyone laugh, the laughter brought on tears, and the tears brought on more tears, and then I started laughing, out of the most deep and complete shame, "I was walking to you," I said again, as if to push my nose into my own shit, "because I wanted to see you again," she laughed and laughed, "That explains it," she said when she was able to speak. "It?" "That explains why, each of the last six days, you weren't at your house." We stopped laughing, I took the world into me, rearranged it, and sent it back out as a question: "Do you like me?"

Do you know what time it is?

JONATHAN SAFRAN FOER

He told me it's 9:38, he looked so much like me, I could tell that he saw it, too, we shared the smile of recognizing ourselves in each other, how many imposters do I have? Do we all make the same mistakes, or has one of us gotten it right, or even just a bit less wrong, am I the imposter? I just told myself the time, and I'm thinking of your mother, how young and old she is, how she carries around her money in an envelope, how she makes me wear suntan lotion no matter what the weather, how she sneezes and says, "God bless me," God bless her. She's at home now, writing her life story, she's typing while I'm leaving, unaware of the chapters to come. It was my suggestion, and at the time I thought it was a very good one, I thought maybe if she could express herself rather than suffer herself, if she had a way to relieve the burden, she lived for nothing more than living, with nothing to get inspired by, to care for, to call her own, she helped out at the store, then came home and sat in her big chair and stared at her magazines, not at them but through them, she let the dust accumulate on her shoulders. I pulled my old typewriter from the closet and set her up in the guest room with everything she'd need, a card table for a desk, a chair, paper, some glasses, a pitcher of water, a hotplate, some flowers, crackers, it wasn't a proper office but it would do, she said, "But it's a Nothing Place," I wrote, "What better place to write your life story?" She said, "My eyes are crummy," I told her they were good enough, she said, "They barely work," putting her fingers over them, but I knew she was just embarrassed by the attention, she said, "I don't know how to write," I told her there's nothing to know, just let it come out, she put her hands on the typewriter, like a blind person feeling someone's face for the first time, and said, "I've never used one of these before," I told her, "Just press the keys," she said she would try, and though I'd known how to use a typewriter since I was a boy, trying was more than I ever could do. For months it was the same, she would wake up at 4 A.M. and go to the guest room, the animals would follow her, I would come here, I wouldn't see her again until breakfast, and then after work we'd go our separate ways and not see each other until it was time to fall asleep, was I worried about her, putting all of her life into her life story, no, I was so happy for her, I remembered the feeling she was feeling, the exhilaration of building the world anew, I heard from behind the door the sounds of creation, the letters pressing into the paper, the pages being pulled from the machine, everything being, for once, better than it was and as good as it could be, everything full of meaning, and then one morning this spring, after years of working in solitude. She said, "I'd like to show you something." I followed her to the guest room, she pointed in the direction of the card table in the corner, on which the typewriter was wedged between two stacks of paper of about the same height, we walked over together, she touched everything on the table and then handed me the stack on the left, she said, "My Life." "Excuse me?" I asked by shrugging my shoulders, she tapped the page, "My Life," she said again, I riffled the pages, there must have been a thousand of them, I put the stack down, "What is this?" I asked by putting her palms on the tops of my hands and then turning my palms upward, flipping her hands off mine, "My Life," she said, so proudly, "I just made it up to the present moment. Just now. I'm all caught up with myself. The last thing I wrote was 'I'm going to show him what I've written. I hope he loves it.'" I picked up the pages and wandered through them, trying to find the one on which she was born, her first love, when she last saw her parents, and I was looking for Anna, too, I searched and searched, I got a paper cut on my forefinger and bled a little flower onto the page on which I should have seen her kissing somebody, but this was all I saw:

I wanted to cry but I didn't cry, I probably should have cried, I should have drowned us there in the room, ended our suffering, they would have found us floating face-down in two thousand white pages, or buried under the salt of my evaporated tears, I remembered, just then and far too late, that years before I had pulled the ribbon from the machine, it had been an act of revenge against the typewriter and against myself, I'd pulled it into one long thread, unwinding the negative it held—the future homes I had created for Anna, the letters I wrote without response—as if it would protect me from my actual life. But worse—it's unspeakable, write it!—I realized that your mother couldn't see the emptiness, she couldn't see anything. I knew that she'd had difficulty, I'd felt her grasp my arm when we walked, I'd heard her say, "My eyes are crummy," but I thought it was a way to touch me, another figure of speech, why didn't she ask for help, why, instead, did she ask for all of those magazines and papers if she couldn't see them, was that how she asked for help? Was that why she held so tightly to railings, why she wouldn't cook with me watching, or change her clothes with me watching, or open doors? Did she always have something to read in front of her so she wouldn't have to look at anything else? All of the words I'd written to her over all of those years, had I never said anything to her at all? "Wonderful," I told her by rubbing her shoulder in a certain way that we have between us, "it's wonderful." "Go ahead," she said, "Tell me what you think." I put her hand on the side of my face, I tilted my head toward my shoulder, in the context in which she thought our conversation was taking place that meant, "I can't read it here like this. I'll take it to the bedroom, I'll read it slowly, carefully, I'll give your life story what it deserves." But in what I knew to be the context of our conversation it meant, "I have failed you."

Do you know what time it is?

The first time Anna and I made love was behind her father's shed, the previous owner had been a farmer, but Dresden started to overtake the surrounding villages and the farm was divided into nine plots of land, Anna's family owned the largest. The walls of the shed collapsed one autumn afternoon—"a leaf too many," her father joked—and the next day he made new walls of shelves, so that the books themselves would separate inside from outside. (The new, overhanging roof protected the books from rain, but during the winter the pages would freeze together, come spring, they let out a sigh.) He made a little salon of the space, carpets, two small couches, he loved to go out there in the evenings with a glass of whiskey and a pipe, and take down books and look through the wall at the center of the city. He was an intellectual, although he wasn't important, maybe he would have been important if he had lived longer, maybe great books were coiled within him like springs, books that could have separated inside from outside. The day Anna and I made love for the first time, he met me in the yard, he was standing with a disheveled man whose curly hair sprang up in every direction, whose glasses were bent, whose white shirt was stained with the fingerprints of his print-stained hands, "Thomas, please meet my friend Simon Goldberg." I said hello, I didn't know who he was or why I was being introduced to him, I wanted to find Anna, Mr. Goldberg asked me what I did, his voice was handsome and broken, like a cobblestone street, I told him, "I don't do anything," he laughed, "Don't be so modest," Anna's father said. "I want to be a sculptor." Mr. Goldberg took off his glasses, untucked his shirt from his pants, and cleaned his lenses with his shirttail. "You want to be a sculptor?" I said, "I am trying to be a sculptor." He put his glasses back on his face, pulling the wire earpieces behind his ears, and said, "In your case, trying is being." "What do you do?" I asked, in a voice more challenging than I'd wanted. He said, "I don't do anything anymore." Anna's father told him, "Don't be so modest," although he didn't laugh this time, and he told me, "Simon is one of the great minds of our age." "I'm trying," Mr. Goldberg said to me, as if only the two of us existed. "Trying what?" I asked, in a voice more concerned than I'd wanted, he took off his glasses again, "Trying to be." While her father and Mr. Goldberg spoke inside the makeshift salon, whose books separated inside from outside, Anna and I went for a walk over the reeds that lay across the gray-green clay by what once was a stall for horses, and down to where you could see the edge of the water if you knew where and how to look, we got mud halfway up our socks, and juice from the fallen fruit we kicked out of our way, from the top of the property we could see the busy train station, the commotion of the war grew nearer and nearer, soldiers went east through our town, and refugees went west, or stayed there, trains arrived and departed, hundreds of them, we ended where we began, outside the shed that was a salon. "Let's sit down," she said, we lowered ourselves to the ground, our backs against the shelves, we could hear them talking inside and smell the pipe smoke that seeped between the books, Anna started kissing me, "But what if they come out?" I whispered, she touched my ears, which meant their voices would keep us safe. She put her hands all over me, I didn't know what she was doing, I touched every part of her, what was I doing, did we understand something that we couldn't explain? Her father said, "You can stay for as long as you need. You can stay forever." She pulled her shirt over her head, I held her breasts in my hands, it was awkward and it was natural, she pulled my shirt over my head, in the moment I couldn't see, Mr. Goldberg laughed and said, "Forever," I heard him pacing in the small room, I put my hand under her skirt, between her legs, everything felt on the verge of bursting into flames, without any experience I knew what to do, it was exactly as it had been in my dreams, as if all the information had been coiled within me like a spring, everything that was happening had happened before and would happen again, "I don't recognize the world anymore," Anna's father said, Anna rolled onto her back, behind a wall of books through which voices and pipe smoke escaped, "I want to make love," Anna whispered, I knew exactly what to do, night was arriving, trains were departing, I lifted her skirt, Mr. Goldberg said, "I've never recognized it more," and I could hear him breathing on the other side of the books, if he had taken one from the shelf he would have seen everything. But the books protected us. I was in her for only a second before I burst into flames, she whimpered, Mr. Goldberg stomped his foot and let out a cry like a wounded animal, I asked her if she was upset, she shook her head no, I fell onto her, resting my cheek against her chest, and I saw your mother's face in the second-floor window, "Then why are you crying?" I asked, exhausted and experienced, "War!" Mr. Goldberg said, angry and defeated, his voice trembling: "We go on killing each other to no purpose! It is war waged by humanity against humanity, and it will only end when there's no one left to fight!" She said, "It hurt."

Do you know what time it is?

Every morning before breakfast, and before I come here, your mother and I go to the guest room, the animals follow us, I thumb through the blank pages and gesture laughter and gesture tears, if she asks what I'm laughing or crying about, I tap my finger on the page, and if she asks, "Why?" I press her hand against her heart, and then against my heart, or I touch her forefinger to the mirror, or touch it, quickly, against the hot-plate, sometimes I wonder if she knows, I wonder in my Nothingest moments if she's testing me, if she types nonsense all day long, or types nothing at all, just to see what I'll do in response, she wants to know if I love her, that's all anyone wants from anyone else, not love itself but the knowledge that love is there, like new batteries in the flashlight in the emergency kit in the hall closet, "Don't let anyone see it," I told her that morning she first showed it to me, and maybe I was trying to protect her, and maybe I was trying to protect myself, "We'll have it be our secret until it's perfect. We'll work on it together. We'll make it the greatest book anyone has ever written." "You think that's possible?" she asked, outside, leaves fell from the trees, inside, we were letting go of our concern for that kind of truth, "I do," I said by touching her arm, "If we try hard enough." She reached her hands in front of her and found my face, she said, "I'm going to write about this." Ever since that day I've been encouraging her, begging her, to write more, to shovel deeper, "Describe his face," I tell her, running my hand over the empty page, and then, the next morning, "Describe his eyes," and then, holding the page to the window, letting it fill with light, "Describe his irises," and then, "His pupils." She never asks, "Whose?" She never asks, "Why?" Are they my own eyes on those pages? I've seen the left stack double and quadruple, I've heard of asides that have become tangents that have become passages that have become chapters, and I know, because she told me, that what was once the second sentence is now the second-to-last. Just two days ago she said that her life story was happening faster than her life, "What do you mean?" I asked with my hands, "So little happens," she said, "and I'm so good at remembering." "You could write about the store?" "I've described every diamond in the case." "You could write about other people." "My life story is the story of everyone I've ever met." "You could write about your feelings." She asked, "Aren't my life and my feelings the same thing?"

JONATHAN SAFRAN FOER

Excuse me, where do you get tickets?

I have so much to tell you, the problem isn't that I'm running out of time, I'm running out of room, this book is filling up, there couldn't be enough pages, I looked around the apartment this morning for one last time and there was writing everywhere, filling the walls and mirrors, I'd rolled up the rugs so I could write on the floors, I'd written on the windows and around the bottles of wine we were given but never drank, I wear only short sleeves, even when it's cold, because my arms are books, too. But there's too much to express. I'm sorry. That's what I've been trying to say to you, I'm sorry for everything. For having said goodbye to Anna when maybe I could have saved her and our idea, or at least died with them. I'm sorry for my inability to let the unimportant things go, for my inability to hold on to the important things. I'm sorry for what I'm about to do to your mother and to you. I'm sorry I'll never get to see your face, and feed you, and tell you bedtime stories. I've tried in my own way to explain myself, but when I think of your mother's life story, I know that I haven't explained a thing, she and I are no different, I've been writing Nothing, too. "The dedication," she said to me this morning, just a few hours ago, when I went to the guest room for the last time, "Read it." I touched my fingers to her eyelids and opened her eyes wide enough to convey every possible meaning, I was about to leave her behind without saying goodbye, to turn my back on a marriage of millimeters and rules, "Do you think it's too much?" she asked, bringing me back to her invisible dedication, I touched her with my right hand, not knowing to whom she had dedicated her life story, "It's not silly, is it?" I touched her with my right hand, and I was missing her already, I wasn't having second thoughts, but I was having thoughts, "It's not vain?" I touched her with my right hand, and for all I knew she'd dedicated it to herself, "Does it mean everything to you?" she asked, this time putting her finger on what wasn't there, I touched her with my left hand, and for all I knew she'd dedicated it to me. I told her that I had to get going. I asked her, with a long series of gestures that would have made no sense to anyone else, if she wanted anything special. "You always get it right," she said. "Some nature magazines?" (I flapped her hands like wings.) "That would be nice." "Maybe something with art in it?"

(I took her hand, like a brush, and painted an imaginary painting in front of us.) "Sure." She walked me to the door, as she always did, "I might not be back before you fall asleep," I told her, putting my open hand on her shoulder and then easing her cheek onto my palm. She said, "But I can't fall asleep without you." I held her hands against my head and nodded that she could, we walked to the door, navigating a Something path. "And what if I can't fall asleep without you?" I held her hands against my head and nodded, "And what if?" I nodded, "Answer me what," she said, I shrugged my shoulders, "Promise me you'll take care," she said, pulling the hood of my coat over my head, "Promise me you'll take extra-special care. I know you look both ways before you cross the street, but I want you to look both ways a second time, because I told you to." I nodded. She asked, "Are you wearing lotion?" With my hands I told her, "It's cold out. You have a cold." She asked, "But are you?" I surprised myself by touching her with my right hand. I could live a lie, but not bring myself to tell that small one. She said, "Hold on," and ran inside the apartment and came back with a bottle of lotion. She squeezed some into her hand, rubbed her hands together, and spread it on the back of my neck, and on the tops of my hands, and between my fingers, and on my nose and forehead and cheeks and chin, everything that was exposed, in the end I was the clay and she was the sculptor, I thought, it's a shame that we have to live, but it's a tragedy that we get to live only one life, because if I'd had two lives, I would have spent one of them with her. I would have stayed in the apartment with her, torn the blueprint from the door, held her on the bed, said, "I want two rolls," sang, "Start spreading the news," laughed, "Ha ha ha!" cried, "Help!" I would have spent that life among the living. We rode the elevator down together and walked to the threshold, she stopped and I kept going. I knew I was about to destroy what she'd been able to rebuild, but I had only one life. I heard her behind me. Because of myself, or despite myself, I turned back, "Don't cry," I told her, by putting her fingers on my face and pushing imaginary tears up my cheeks and back into my eyes, "I know," she said as she wiped the real tears from her cheeks, I stomped my feet, this meant, "I won't go to the airport." "Go to the airport,"

JONATHAN SAFRAN FOER

she said, I touched her chest, then pointed her hand out toward the world, then pointed her hand at her chest, "I know," she said, "Of course I know that." I held her hands and pretended we were behind an invisible wall, or behind the imaginary painting, our palms exploring its surface, then, at the risk of saying too much, I held one of her hands over my eyes, and the other over her eyes, "You are too good to me," she said, I put her hands on my head and nodded yes, she laughed, I love it when she laughs, although the truth is I am not in love with her, she said, "I love you," I told her how I felt, this is how I told her: I held her hands out to her sides, I pointed her index fingers toward each other and slowly, very slowly, moved them in, the closer they got, the more slowly I moved them, and then, as they were about to touch, as they were only a dictionary page from touching, pressing on opposite sides of the word "love," I stopped them, I stopped them and held them there. I don't know what she thought, I don't know what she understood, or what she wouldn't allow herself to understand, I turned around and walked away from her, I didn't look back, I won't. I'm telling you all of this because I'll never be your father, and you will always be my child. I want you to know, at least, that it's not out of selfishness that I am leaving, how can I explain that? I can't live, I've tried and I can't. If that sounds simple, it's simple like a mountain is simple. Your mother suffered, too, but she chose to live, and lived, be her son and her husband. I don't expect that you'll ever understand me, much less forgive me, you might not even read these words, if your mother gives them to you at all. It's time to go. I want you to be happy, I want that more than I want happiness for myself, does that sound simple? I'm leaving. I'll rip these pages from this book, take them to the mailbox before I get on the plane, address the envelope to "My Unborn Child," and I'll never write another word again, I am gone, I am no longer here. With love, Your father

I want to buy a ticket to Dresden.

What are you doing here?

You have to go home. You should be in bed.

Let me take you home.

You're being crazy. You're going to catch a cold.

You're going to catch a colder.

~~HEAVY BOOTS~~
HEAVIER BOOTS

Twelve weekends later was the first performance of *Hamlet*, although it was actually an abbreviated modern version, because the real *Hamlet* is too long and confusing, and most of the kids in my class have ADD. For example, the famous "To be or not to be" speech, which I know about from the *Collected Shakespeare* set Grandma bought me, was cut down so that it was just, "To be or not to be, that's the question."

Everyone had to have a part, but there weren't enough real parts, and I didn't go to the auditions because my boots were too heavy to go to school that day, so I got the part of Yorick. At first that made me self-conscious. I suggested to Mrs. Rigley that maybe I could just play tambourine in the orchestra or something. She said, "There is no orchestra." I said, "Still." She told me, "It'll be terrific. You'll wear all black, and the makeup crew will paint your hands and neck black, and the costume crew will create some sort of a papier-mâché skull for you to wear over your head. It'll really give the illusion that you don't have a body." I thought about that for a minute, and then I told her my better idea. "What I'll do is, I'll invent an invisibility suit that has a camera on my back that takes video of everything behind me and plays it on a plasma screen that I'll wear on my front, which will cover everything except my face. It'll look like I'm not there at all." She said, "Nifty." I said, "But is Yorick even a part?" She whispered into my ear, "If anything, I'm afraid you'll steal the show." Then I was excited to be Yorick.

Opening night was pretty great. We had a fog machine, so the cemetery was just like a cemetery in a movie. "Alas, poor Yorick!" Jimmy Snyder said, holding my face, "I knew him, Horatio." I didn't have a plasma screen, because the costumes budget wasn't big enough, but from underneath the skull I could look around without anyone noticing. I saw lots of people I knew, which made me feel special. Mom and Ron and Grandma were there, obviously. Toothpaste was there with Mr. and Mrs. Hamilton, which was nice, and Mr. and Mrs. Minch were there, too, because The Minch was Guildenstern. A lot of the Blacks that I had met in those twelve weekends were there. Abe was there. Ada and Agnes were there. (They were actually sitting next to each other, although they didn't realize it.) I saw Albert and Alice and Allen and Arnold and Barbara and Barry. They must have been half the audience. But what was weird was that they didn't know what they had in common, which was kind of like how I didn't know what the thumbtack, the bent spoon, the square of aluminum foil, and all those other things I dug up in Central Park had to do with each other.

I was incredibly nervous, but I maintained my confidence, and I was extremely subtle. I know, because there was a standing ovation, which made me feel like one hundred dollars.

The second performance was also pretty great. Mom was there, but Ron had to work late. That was OK, though, because I didn't want him there anyway. Grandma was there, obviously. I didn't see any of the Blacks, but I knew that most people go to only one show unless they're your parents, so I didn't feel too bad about that. I tried to give an extra-special performance, and I think I did. "Alas, poor Yorick. I knew him, Horatio; a really funny and excellent guy. I used to ride on his back all the time, and now, it's so awful to think about!"

Only Grandma came the next night. Mom had a late meeting because one of her cases was about to go to trial, and I didn't ask where Ron was because I was embarrassed, and I didn't want him there anyway. As I was standing as still as I could, with Jimmy Snyder's hand under my chin, I wondered, *What's the point of giving an extremely subtle performance if basically no one is watching?*

Grandma didn't come backstage to say hi before the performance the next night, or bye after, but I saw that she was there. Through the eye sockets I could see her standing in the back of the gym, underneath the basketball hoop. Her makeup was absorbing the lighting in a fascinating way, which made her look almost ultraviolet. "Alas, poor Yorick." I was as still as I could be, and the whole time I was thinking, *What trial is more important than the greatest play in history?*

The next performance was only Grandma again. She cried at all the wrong times and cracked up at all the wrong times. She applauded when the audience found out the news that Ophelia drowned, which is supposed to be bad news, and she booed when Hamlet scored his first point in the duel against Laertes at the end, which is good, for obvious reasons.

"This is where his lips were that I used to kiss a lot. Where are your jokes now, your games, your songs?"

Backstage, before closing night, Jimmy Snyder imitated Grandma to the rest of the cast and crew. I guess I hadn't realized how loud she was. I had gotten so angry at myself for noticing her, but I was wrong, it was her fault. Everyone noticed. Jimmy did her exactly right—the way she swatted her left hand at something funny, like there was a fly in front of her face. The way she tilted her head, like she was concentrating incredibly hard on something, and how she sneezed and told herself, "God bless me." And how she cried and said, "That's sad," so everyone could hear it.

I sat there while he made all the kids crack up. Even Mrs. Rigley cracked up, and so did her husband, who played the piano during the set changes. I didn't mention that she was my grandma, and I didn't tell him to stop. Outside, I was cracking up too. Inside, I was wishing that she were tucked away in a portable pocket, or that she'd also had an invisibility suit. I wished the two of us could go somewhere far away, like the Sixth Borough.

She was there again that night, in the back row, although only the first three rows were taken. I watched her from under the skull. She had her hand pressed against her ultraviolet heart, and I could hear her saying, "That's sad. That's so sad." I thought about the unfinished scarf, and the rock she carried across Broadway, and how she had lived so much life but still needed imaginary friends, and the one thousand thumb wars.

MARGIE CARSON. Hey, Hamlet, where's Polonius?

JIMMY SNYDER. At supper.

MARGIE CARSON. At supper! Where?

JIMMY SNYDER. Not where he eats, but where he's eaten.

MARGIE CARSON. Wow!

JIMMY SNYDER. A king can end up going through the guts of a beggar.

I felt, that night, on that stage, under that skull, incredibly close to everything in the universe, but also extremely alone. I wondered, for the first time in my life, if life was worth all the work it took to live. What *exactly* made it worth it? What's so horrible about being dead forever, and not feeling anything, and not even dreaming? What's so great about feeling and dreaming?

Jimmy put his hand under my face. "This is where his lips were that I used to kiss a lot. Where are your jokes now, your games, your songs?"

Maybe it was because of everything that had happened in those twelve weeks. Or maybe it was because I felt so close and alone that night. I just couldn't be dead any longer.

ME. Alas, poor Hamlet [*I take* JIMMY SNYDER's *face into my hand*]; I knew him, Horatio.

JIMMY SNYDER. But Yorick . . . you're only . . . a skull.

ME. So what? I don't care. Screw you.

JIMMY SNYDER. [*whispers*] This is not in the play. [*He looks for help from* MRS. RIGLEY, *who is in the front row, flipping through the script. She draws circles in the air with her right hand, which is the universal sign for "improvise."*]

ME. I knew him, Horatio; a jerk of infinite stupidity, a most excellent masturbator in the second-floor boys' bathroom—I have proof. Also, he's dyslexic.

JIMMY SNYDER. [*Can't think of anything to say*]

ME. Where be your gibes now, your gambols, your songs?

JIMMY SNYDER. What are you *talking* about?

ME. [*Raises hand to scoreboard*] Succotash my cocker spaniel, you fudging crevasse-hole dipshiitake!

JIMMY SNYDER. Huh?

ME. You are guilty of having abused those less strong than you: of making the lives of nerds like me and Toothpaste and The Minch almost impossible, of imitating mental retards, of prank-calling people who get almost no phone calls anyway, of terrorizing domesticated animals and old people — who, by the way, are smarter and more knowledgeable than you — of making fun of me just because I have a pussy . . . And I've seen you litter, too.

JIMMY SNYDER. I never prank-called any retards.

ME. You were adopted.

JIMMY SNYDER. [Searches audience for his parents]

ME. And nobody loves you.

JIMMY SNYDER. [His eyes fill with tears]

ME. And you have amyotrophic lateral sclerosis.

JIMMY SNYDER. Huh?

ME. On behalf of the dead . . . [I pull the skull off my head. Even though it's made of papier-mâché it's really hard. I smash it against JIMMY SNYDER's head, and I smash it again. He falls to the ground, because he is unconscious, and I can't believe how strong I actually am. I smash his head again with all my force and blood starts to come out of his nose and ears. But I still don't feel any sympathy for him. I want him to bleed, because he deserves it. And nothing else makes any sense. DAD doesn't make sense. MOM doesn't make sense. THE AUDIENCE doesn't make sense. The folding chairs and fog-machine fog don't make sense. Shakespeare doesn't make sense. The stars that I know are on the other side of the gym ceiling don't make sense. The only thing that makes any sense right then is my smashing JIMMY SNYDER's face. His blood. I knock a bunch of his teeth into his mouth, and I think they go down his throat. There is blood everywhere, covering everything. I keep smashing the skull against his skull, which is also RON's skull (for letting MOM get on with life) and MOM's skull (for getting on with life) and DAD's skull (for dying) and GRANDMA's skull (for embarrassing me so much) and DR. FEIN's skull (for asking if any good could come out of DAD's death) and the skulls of everyone else I know. THE AUDIENCE is applauding, all of them, because I am making so much sense. They are giving me a standing ovation as I hit him again and again. I hear them call]

THE AUDIENCE. Thank you! Thank you, Oskar! We love you so much! We'll protect you!

It would have been great.

I looked out across the audience from underneath the skull, with Jimmy's hand under my chin. "Alas, poor Yorick." I saw Abe Black, and he saw me. I knew that we were sharing something with our eyes, but I didn't know what, and I didn't know if it mattered.

It was twelve weekends earlier that I'd gone to visit Abe Black in Coney Island. I'm very idealistic, but I knew I couldn't walk that far, so I took a cab. Even before we were out of Manhattan, I realized that the $7.68 in my wallet wasn't going to be enough. I don't know if you'd count it as a lie or not that I didn't say anything. It's just that I knew I had to get there, and there was no alternative. When the cab driver pulled over in front of the building, the meter said $76.50. I said, "Mr. Mahaltra, are you an optimist or a pessimist?" He said, "What?" I said, "Because unfortunately I only have seven dollars and sixty-eight cents." "Seven dollars?" "And sixty-eight cents." "This is not happening." "Unfortunately, it is. But if you give me your address, I promise I'll send you the rest." He put his head down on the steering wheel. I asked if he was OK. He said, "Keep your seven dollars and sixty-eight cents." I said, "I promise I'll send you the money. I promise." He handed me his card, which was actually the card of a dentist, but he had written his address on the other side. Then he said something in some other language that wasn't French. "Are you mad at me?"

Obviously I'm incredibly panicky about roller coasters, but Abe convinced me to ride one with him. "It would be a shame to die without riding the Cyclone," he told me. "It would be a shame to die," I told him. "Yeah," he said, "but with the Cyclone you can choose." We sat in the front car, and Abe lifted his hands in the air on the downhill parts. I kept wondering if what I was feeling was at all like falling.

In my head, I tried to calculate all of the forces that kept the car on the tracks and me in the car. There was gravity, obviously. And centrifugal force. And momentum. And the friction between the wheels and the tracks. And wind resistance, I think, or something. Dad used to teach me physics with crayons on paper tablecloths while we waited for our pancakes. He would have been able to explain everything.

The ocean smelled weird, and so did the food they were selling on

JONATHAN SAFRAN FOER

the boardwalk, like funnel cakes and cotton candy and hot dogs. It was an almost perfect day, except that Abe didn't know anything about the key or about Dad. He said he was driving into Manhattan and could give me a ride if I wanted one. I told him, "I don't get in cars with strangers, and how did you know I was going to Manhattan?" He said, "We're not strangers, and I don't know how I knew." "Do you have an SUV?" "No." "Good. Do you have a gas-electric hybrid car?" "No." "Bad."

While we were in the car I told him all about how I was going to meet everyone in New York with the last name Black. He said, "I can relate, in my own way, because I had a dog run away once. She was the best dog in the world. I couldn't have loved her more or treated her better. She didn't want to run away. She just got confused, and followed one thing and then another." "But my dad didn't run away," I said. "He was killed in a terrorist attack." Abe said, "I was thinking of *you*." He went up with me to the door of Ada Black's apartment, even though I told him I could do it myself. "I'll feel better knowing you made it here safely," he said, which sounded like Mom.

Ada Black owned two Picasso paintings. She didn't know anything about the key, so the paintings meant nothing to me, even if I knew they were famous. She said I could have a seat on the couch if I wanted to, but I told her I didn't believe in leather, so I stood. Her apartment was the most amazing apartment I'd ever been in. The floors were like marble chessboards, and the ceilings were like cakes. Everything seemed like it belonged in a museum, so I took some pictures with Grandpa's camera. "This might be a rude question, but are you the richest person in the world?" She touched a lampshade and said, "I'm the 467th-richest person in the world."

I asked her how it made her feel to know that there were homeless people and millionaires living in the same city. She said, "I give a lot to charity, if that's what you're getting at." I told her that I wasn't getting at anything, and that I just wanted to know how she felt. "I feel fine," she said, and she asked me if I wanted something to drink. I asked her for a coffee, and she asked someone in another room for a coffee, and then I asked her if she thought that maybe no one should have more than a certain amount of money until everyone had that amount of money. That was an idea Dad had once suggested to me. She said, "The Upper West Side isn't free, you know." I asked her how she knew that I lived on the Upper West Side. "Do you have things that you don't need?" "Not really." "You collect coins?" "How did you know I collect coins?" "Lots of young people collect coins." I told her, "I need them." "Do you need them as much as a homeless person needs food?" The conversation was beginning to make me feel self-conscious. She said, "Do you have more things that you need, or more that you don't need?" I said, "It depends on what it means to need."

She said, "Believe it or not, I used to be idealistic." I asked her what "idealistic" meant. "It means you live by what you think is right." "You don't do that anymore?" "There are questions I don't ask anymore." An African-American woman brought me coffee on a silver tray. I told her, "Your uniform is incredibly beautiful." She looked at Ada. "Really," I said. "I think light blue is a very, very beautiful color on you." She was still looking at Ada, who said, "Thanks, Gail." As she walked back to the kitchen I told her, "Gail is a beautiful name."

When it was just the two of us again, Ada told me, "Oskar, I think you made Gail feel quite uncomfortable." "What do you mean?" "I could tell that she felt embarrassed." "I was just trying to be nice." "You might have tried too hard." "How can you try too hard to be nice?" "You were being condescending." "What's that?" "You were talking to her like she was a child." "No I wasn't." "There's no shame in being a maid. She does a serious job, and I pay her well." I said, "I was just trying to be nice." And then I wondered, *Did I tell her my name was Oskar?*

We sat there for a while. She stared out the window, like she was waiting for something to happen in Central Park. I asked, "Would it be OK if I snooped around your apartment?" She laughed and said, "Finally someone says what he's thinking." I looked around a bit, and there were so many rooms that I wondered if the apartment's inside was bigger than its outside. But I didn't find any clues. When I came back she asked if I wanted a finger sandwich, which freaked me out, but I was very polite and just said, "Jose." "Pardon?" "Jose." "I'm sorry. I don't understand what that means." "Jose. As in, 'No way . . .'" She said, "I know what I am." I nodded my head, even though I didn't know what she was talking about or what it had to do with anything. "Even if I don't like what I am, I know what I am. My children like what they are, but they don't know what they are. So tell me which is worse." "What are the options again?" She cracked up and said, "I like you."

I showed her the key, but she had never seen it, and couldn't tell me anything about it.

Even though I told her I didn't need any help, she made the doorman promise to put me in a cab. I told her I couldn't afford a cab. She said, "I can." I gave her my card. She said, "Good luck," and put her hands on my cheeks, and kissed the top of my head.

That was Saturday, and it was depressing.

> *Dear Oskar Schell,*
>
> > *Thank you for your contribution to the American Diabetes Foundation. Every dollar — or, in your case, fifty cents — counts.*
> >
> > *I have enclosed some additional literature about the Foundation, including our mission statement, a brochure featuring past activities and successes, as well as some information about our future goals, both short- and long-term.*
> >
> > *Thank you, once more, for contributing to this urgent cause. You are saving lives.*
> >
> > > *With gratitude,*
> > > *Patricia Roxbury*
> > > *President, New York Chapter*

This might be hard to believe, but the next Black lived in our building, just one floor above us. If it weren't my life, I wouldn't have believed it. I went to the lobby and asked Stan what he knew about the person who lived in 6A. He said, "Never seen anyone go in or come out. Just a lot of deliveries and a lot of trash." "*Cool.*" He leaned down and whispered, "Haunted." I whispered back, "I don't believe in the paranormal." He said, "Ghosts don't care if you believe in them," and even though I was an atheist, I knew he wasn't right.

I walked back up the steps, this time past our floor and to the sixth. There was a mat in front of the door which said Welcome in twelve different languages. That didn't seem like something a ghost would put in front of his apartment. I tried the key in the lock, but it didn't work, so I rang the buzzer, which was exactly where our buzzer was. I heard some noise inside, and maybe even some creepy music, but I was brave and just stood there.

After an incredibly long time the door opened. "Can I help you!" an old man asked, but he asked it extremely loudly, so it was more like a scream. "Yes, hello," I said. "I live downstairs in 5A. May I please ask you a few questions?" "Hello, young man!" he said, and he was kind of weird-looking, because he had on a red beret, like a French person, and an eye patch, like a pirate. He said, "I'm Mr. Black!" I said, "I know." He turned around and started walking into his apartment. I guessed I was supposed to follow him, so I did.

Another thing that was weird was that his apartment looked exactly like our apartment. The floors were the same, the windowsills were the same, even the tiles on the fireplace were the same color green. But his apartment was also incredibly different, because it was filled with different stuff. Tons of stuff. Stuff everywhere. Also, there was a huge column right in the middle of the dining room. It was as big as two refrigerators, and it made it impossible for the room to have a table or anything else in it, like ours did. "What's that for?" I asked, but he didn't hear me. There were a bunch of dolls and other things on the mantel, and the floors were filled with little rugs. "I got those in Iceland!" he said, pointing at the seashells on the windowsill. He pointed at a sword on the wall and said, "I got that in Japan!" I asked him if it was a samurai sword. He said, "It's a replica!" I said, "*Cool.*"

He led me to the kitchen table, which was where our kitchen table was, and he sat down and slapped his hand against his knee. "Well!" he said, so loudly that I wanted to cover my ears. "I've had a pretty amazing life!" I thought it was weird that he said that, because I didn't ask him about his life. I didn't even tell him why I was there. "I was born on January 1, 1900! I lived every day of the twentieth century!" "Really?" "My mother altered my birth certificate so I could fight in the First

World War! That was the only lie she ever told! I was engaged to Fitzgerald's sister!" "Who's Fitzgerald?" "Francis Scott Key Fitzgerald, my boy! A Great Author! A Great Author!" "Oops." "I used to sit on her porch and talk to her father while she powdered her nose upstairs! Her father and I had the most lively conversations! He was a Great Man, like Winston Churchill was a Great Man!" I decided that it would be better to Google Winston Churchill when I got home, instead of mentioning that I didn't know who he was. "One day, she came downstairs and was ready to go! I told her to hold on for a minute, because her father and I were right smack in the middle of a terrific conversation, and you can't interrupt a terrific conversation, right!" "I don't know." "Later that night, as I was dropping her off on that same porch, she said, 'Sometimes I wonder if you like my father more than me!' I inherited that damn honesty from my mother, and it caught up with me again! I told her, 'I do!' Well, that was the last time I told her 'I do,' if you know what I mean!" "I don't." "I blew it! Boy, did I blow it!" He started cracking up extremely loudly, and he slapped his knee. I said, "That's hilarious," because it must have been for him to crack up so much. "Hilarious!" he said. "It is! I never heard from her again! Oh, well! So many people enter and leave your life! Hundreds of thousands of people! You have to keep the door open so they can come in! But it also means you have to let them go!"

He put a teakettle on the stove.

"You're wise," I told him. "I've had enough time to get wise! See this!" he hollered, and he flipped up his eye patch. "That's from Nazi shrapnel! I was a war correspondent and ended up attaching myself to a British tank corps going up the Rhine! We were ambushed one afternoon, toward the end of '44! I bled my eye all over the page I was writing on, but those sons of bitches couldn't stop me! I finished my sentence!" "What was the sentence?" "Ah, who can remember! The point is I wasn't going to let those bastard Krauts stop my pen! It's mightier than the sword, you know! And the MG34!" "Could you please put the patch back?" "See that!" he said, pointing at the kitchen floor, but I couldn't stop thinking about his eye. "There's oak under those rugs! Quarter-sawn oak! I should know, I laid it myself!" "Jose," I said, and I wasn't just saying it to be nice. I was keeping a list in my head of things I could do to be more like him. "My wife and I renovated this kitchen ourselves! With these hands!" He showed me his hands. They looked like the hands on the skeleton in the Rainier Scientific catalogue that Ron offered to buy for me, except they had skin, blotchy skin, and I didn't want gifts from Ron. "Where's your wife now?" The teakettle started to whistle.

"Oh," he said, "she died twenty-four years ago! Long time ago! Yesterday, in my life!" "Oops." "It's OK!" "You don't feel bad that I asked about her? You can tell me if you do." "No!" he said. "Thinking about her is the next best thing!" He poured two cups of tea. "Do you have any coffee?" I asked. "Coffee!" "It stunts my growth, and I'm afraid of death." He slapped the table and said, "My boy, I have some coffee from Honduras that's got your name on it!" "But you don't even know my name."

We sat around for a while and he told me more about his amazing life. As far as he knew, which seemed pretty far, he was the only person still alive who had fought in both of the world wars. He'd been to Australia, and Kenya, and Pakistan, and Panama. I asked him, "If you had to guess, how many countries would you guess you've been to?" He said, "I wouldn't have to guess! One hundred twelve!" "Are there even that many countries?" He told me, "There are more places you haven't heard of than you've heard of!" I loved that. He had reported almost every war of the twentieth century, like the Spanish Civil War, and the genocide in East Timor, and bad stuff that happened in Africa. I hadn't heard of any of them, so I tried to remember them so I could Google them when I got home. The list in my head was getting incredibly long: Francis Scott Key Fitzgerald, powdering her nose, Churchill, Mustang convertible, Walter Cronkite, necking, the Bay of Pigs, LP, Datsun, Kent State, lard, Ayatollah Khomeini, Polaroid, apartheid, drive-in, favela, Trotsky, the Berlin Wall, Tito, *Gone With the Wind*, Frank Lloyd Wright, hula hoop, Technicolor, the Spanish Civil War, Grace Kelly, East Timor, slide rule, a bunch of places in Africa whose names I tried to remember but had already forgotten. It was getting hard to keep all the things I didn't know inside me.

His apartment was filled with the stuff he'd collected during the

wars of his life, and I took pictures of them with Grandpa's camera. There were books in foreign languages, and little statues, and scrolls with pretty paintings, and Coke cans from around the world, and a bunch of rocks on his fireplace mantel, although all of them were common. One fascinating thing was that each rock had a little piece of paper next to it that said where the rock came from, and when it came from, like, "Normandy, 6/19/44," "Hwach'on Dam, 4/09/51," and "Dallas, 11/22/63." That was so fascinating, but one weird thing was that there were lots of bullets on the mantel, too, and they didn't have little pieces of paper next to them. I asked him how he knew which was which. "A bullet's a bullet's a bullet!" he said. "But isn't a rock a rock?" I asked. He said, "Of course not!" I thought I understood him, but I wasn't positive, so I pointed at the roses in the vase on the table. "Is a rose a rose?" "No! A rose is not a rose is not a rose!" And then for some reason I started thinking about "Something in the Way She Moves," so I asked, "Is a love song a love song?" He said, "Yes!" I thought for a second. "Is love love?" He said, "No!" He had a wall of masks from every country he'd been to, like Armenia and Chile and Ethiopia. "It's not a horrible world," he told me, putting a Cambodian mask on his face, "but it's filled with a lot of horrible people!"

I had another cup of coffee, and then I knew it was time to get to the point, so I took the key off my neck and gave it to him. "Do you know what this opens?" "Don't think so!" he hollered. "Maybe you knew my dad?" "Who was your dad!" "His name was Thomas Schell. He lived in 5A until he died." "No," he said, "that name doesn't ring a bell!" I asked if he was one-hundred-percent sure." He said, "I've lived long enough to know I'm not one-hundred-percent anything!" and he got up, walked past the column in the dining room, and went over to the coat closet, which was tucked under the stairs. That was when I had the revelation that his apartment wasn't just like ours, because his had an upstairs. He opened the closet, and there was a library card catalogue inside. "*Cool.*"

He said, "This is my biographical index!" "Your what?" "I started it when I was just beginning to write! I'd create a card for everyone I thought I might need to reference one day! There's a card for everyone I ever wrote about! And cards for people I talked to in the course of writing my pieces! And cards for people I read books about! And cards for people in the footnotes of those books! In the mornings, when I'd read the papers, I would make cards for everyone that seemed biographically significant! I still do it!" "Why don't you just use the Internet?" "I don't have a computer!" That made me start to feel dizzy.

"How many cards do you have?" "I've never counted! There must be tens of thousands by this point! Maybe hundreds of thousands!" "What do you write on them?" "I write the name of the person and a one-word biography!" "Just *one* word?" "Everyone gets boiled down to one word!" "And that's helpful?" "It's hugely helpful! I read an article about Latin American currencies this morning! It referred to the work of someone named Manuel Escobar! So I came and looked up Escobar! Sure enough, he was in here! Manuel Escobar: unionist!" "But he's also probably a husband, or dad, or Beatles fan, or jogger, or who knows what else." "Sure! You could write a book about Manuel Escobar! And that would leave things out, too! You could write ten books! You could never stop writing!"

He slid out drawers from the cabinet and pulled cards from the drawers, one after another.

"Henry Kissinger: war!

"Ornette Coleman: music!

"Che Guevara: war!

"Jeff Bezos: money!

"Philip Guston: art!

"Mahatma Gandhi: war!"

"But he was a pacifist," I said.

"Right! War!

"Arthur Ashe: tennis!

"Tom Cruise: money!

"Elie Wiesel: war!

"Arnold Schwarzenegger: war!

"Martha Stewart: money!

"Rem Koolhaas: architecture!

"Ariel Sharon: war!

"Mick Jagger: money!

"Yasir Arafat: war!

"Susan Sontag: thought!

"Wolfgang Puck: money!

"Pope John Paul II: war!"

I asked if he had a card for Stephen Hawking.

"Of course!" he said, and slid out a drawer, and pulled out a card.

STEPHEN HAWKING: ASTROPHYSICS

"Do you have a card for yourself?"

He slid out a drawer.

A. R. BLACK: ~~WAR~~

HUSBAND

"So do you have a card for my dad?" "Thomas Schell, right!" "Right." He went to the S drawer and pulled it halfway out. His fingers ran through the cards like the fingers of someone much younger than

103. "Sorry! Nothing!" "Could you double-check?" His fingers ran through the cards again. He shook his head. "Sorry!" "Well, what if a card is filed in the wrong place?" "Then we've got a problem!" "Could it be?" "It happens occasionally! Marilyn Monroe was lost in the index for more than a decade! I kept checking under Norma Jean Baker, thinking I was smart, but completely forgetting that she was born Norma Jean Mortenson!" "Who's Norma Jean Mortenson?" "Marilyn Monroe!" "Who's Marilyn Monroe?" "Sex!"

"Do you have a card for Mohammed Atta?" "Atta! That one rings a bell! Lemme see!" He opened the A drawer. I told him, "Mohammed is the most common name on earth." He pulled out a card and said, "Bingo!"

MOHAMMED ATTA: WAR

I sat down on the floor. He asked what was wrong. "It's just that why would you have one for him and not one for my dad?" "What do you mean!" "It isn't fair." "What isn't fair!" "My dad was good. Mohammed Atta was evil." "So!" "So my dad deserves to be in there." "What makes you think it's good to be in here!" "Because it means you're biographically significant." "And why is that good!" "I want to be significant." "Nine out of ten significant people have to do with money or war!"

But still, it gave me heavy, heavy boots. Dad wasn't a Great Man, not like Winston Churchill, whoever he was. Dad was just someone who ran a family jewelry business. Just an ordinary dad. But I wished so much, then, that he *had* been Great. I wished he'd been famous, famous like a movie star, which is what he deserved. I wished Mr. Black had written about him, and risked his life to tell the world about him, and had reminders of him around his apartment.

I started thinking: if Dad were boiled down to one word, what would that word be? Jeweler? Atheist? Is copyeditor one word?

"You're looking for something!" Mr. Black asked. "This key used to belong to my dad," I said, pulling it out from under my shirt again, "and I want to know what it opens." He shrugged his shoulders and hollered, "I'd want to know, too!" Then we were silent for a while.

I thought I was going to cry, but I didn't want to cry in front of him, so I asked where the bathroom was. He pointed to the top of the stairs. As I walked up, I held the railing tight and started inventing things in my head: air bags for skyscrapers, solar-powered limousines that never had to stop moving, a frictionless, perpetual yo-yo. The bathroom smelled like an old person, and some of the tiles that were supposed to be on the wall were on the floor. There was a photograph of a woman tucked in the corner of the mirror above the sink. She was sitting at the kitchen table that we were just sitting at, and she was wearing an enormous hat, even though she was inside, obviously. That's how I knew that she was special. One of her hands was on a teacup. Her smile was incredibly beautiful. I wondered if her palm was sweating condensation when the picture was taken. I wondered if Mr. Black took the picture.

Before I went back down, I snooped around a little bit. I was impressed by how much life Mr. Black had lived, and how much he wanted to have his life around him. I tried the key in all of the doors, even though he said he didn't recognize it. It's not that I didn't trust him, because I did. It's that at the end of my search I wanted to be able to say: I don't know how I could have tried harder. One door was to a closet, which didn't have anything really interesting in it, just a bunch of coats. Behind another door was a room filled with boxes. I took the lids off a couple of them, and they were filled with newspapers. The newspapers in some of the boxes were yellow, and some were almost like leaves.

I looked in another room, which must have been his bedroom. There was the most amazing bed I've ever seen, because it was made out of tree parts. The legs were stumps, the ends were logs, and there was a ceiling of branches. Also there were all sorts of fascinating metal things glued to it, like coins, pins, and a button that said ROOSEVELT.

"That used to be a tree in the park!" Mr. Black said from behind me, which scared me so much that my hands started shaking. I asked, "Are you mad at me for snooping?" but he must not have heard me, because he kept talking. "By the reservoir. She tripped on its roots once! That was back when I was courting her! She fell down and cut her hand! A little cut, but I never forgot it! That was so long ago!" "But yesterday in your life, right?" "Yesterday! Today! Five minutes ago! Now!" He aimed his eyes at the ground. "She always begged me to give the reporting a break! She wanted me at home!" He shook his head and said, "But there were things I needed, too!" He looked at the floor, then back at me. I asked, "So what did you do?" "For most of our marriage I treated her as though she didn't matter! I came home only between wars, and left her alone for months at a time! There was always war!" "Did you know that in the last 3,500 years there have been only 230 years of peace throughout the civilized world?" He said, "You tell me which 230 years and I'll believe you!" "I don't know which, but I know it's true." "And where's this civilized world you're referring to!"

I asked him what happened to make him stop reporting war. He said, "I realized that what I wanted was to stay in one place with one person!" "So you came home for good?" "I chose her over war! And the first thing I did when I came back, even before I went home, was to go to the park and cut down that tree! It was the middle of the night! I thought someone would try to stop me, but no one did! I brought the pieces home with me! I made that tree into this bed! It was the bed we shared for the last years we had together! I wish I'd understood myself better earlier!" I asked, "Which was your last war?" He said, "Cutting down that tree was my last war!" I asked who won, which I thought was a nice question, because it would let him say that he won, and feel proud. He said, "The ax won! It's always that way!"

He went up to the bed and put his finger on the head of a nail. "See these!" I try to be a perceptive person who follows the scientific method and is observant, but I hadn't noticed before that the whole bed was completely covered in nails. "I've hammered a nail into the bed every morning since she died! It's the first thing I do after waking! Eight thousand six hundred twenty-nine nails!" I asked him why, which I thought was another nice question, because it would let him tell me about how much he loved her. He said, "I don't know!" I said, "But if you don't know, then why do you do it?" "I suppose it helps! Keeps me going! I know it's nonsense!" "I don't think it's nonsense." "Nails aren't light! One is! A handful are! But they add up!" I told him, "The average human body contains enough iron to make a one-inch nail." He said, "The bed got heavy! I could hear the floor straining, like it was in pain! Sometimes I'd wake up in the middle of the night afraid that everything would go crashing to the apartment below!" "You couldn't sleep because of me." "So I built that column downstairs! Do you know about the library at Indiana University!" "No," I said, but I was still thinking about the column. "It's sinking a little more than an inch a year, because when they built it, they didn't take into account the weight of all of the books! I wrote a piece about it! I didn't make the connection then, but now I'm thinking of Debussy's *Sunken Cathedral*, one of the most beautiful pieces of music ever written! I haven't heard it in years and years! Do you want to feel something!" "OK," I said, because even though I didn't know him, I felt like I knew him. "Open your hand!" he said, so I did. He reached into his pocket and took out a paper clip. He pressed it into my hand and said, "Make a fist around it!" So I did. "Now extend your hand!" I extended my hand. "Now open your hand!" The paper clip flew to the bed.

It was only then that I observed that the key was reaching toward the bed. Because it was relatively heavy, the effect was small. The string pulled incredibly gently at the back of my neck, while the key floated just a tiny bit off my chest. I thought about all the metal buried in Central Park. Was it being pulled, even if just a little, to the bed? Mr. Black closed his hand around the floating key and said, "I haven't left the apartment in twenty-four years!" "What do you mean?" "Sadly, my boy, I mean exactly what I said! I haven't left the apartment in twenty-four years! My feet haven't touched the ground!" "Why not?" "There hasn't been any reason to!" "What about stuff you need?" "What does someone like me need that he can still get!" "Food. Books. Stuff." "I call in an order for food, and they bring it to me! I call the bookstore for books, the video store for movies! Pens, stationery, cleaning supplies, medicine! I even order my clothes over the phone!

See this!" he said, and he showed me his muscle, which went down instead of up. "I was flyweight champion for nine days!" I asked, "Which nine days?" He said, "Don't you believe me!" I said, "Of course I do." "The world is a big place," he said, "but so is the inside of an apartment! So's this!" he said, pointing at his head. "But you used to travel so much. You had so many experiences. Don't you miss the world?" "I do! Very much!"

My boots were so heavy that I was glad there was a column underneath us. How could such a lonely person have been living so close to me my whole life? If I had known, I would have gone up to keep him company. Or I would have made some jewelry for him. Or told him hilarious jokes. Or given him a private tambourine concert.

It made me start to wonder if there were other people so lonely so close. I thought about "Eleanor Rigby." It's true, where do they all come from? And where do they all belong?

What if the water that came out of the shower was treated with a chemical that responded to a combination of things, like your heartbeat, and your body temperature, and your brain waves, so that your skin changed color according to your mood? If you were extremely excited your skin would turn green, and if you were angry you'd turn red, obviously, and if you felt like shiitake you'd turn brown, and if you were blue you'd turn blue.

Everyone could know what everyone else felt, and we could be more careful with each other, because you'd never want to tell a person whose skin was purple that you're angry at her for being late, just like you would want to pat a pink person on the back and tell him, "Congratulations!"

Another reason it would be a good invention is that there are so many times when you know you're feeling a lot of something, but you don't know what the something is. *Am I frustrated? Am I actually just panicky?* And that confusion changes your mood, it becomes your mood, and you become a confused, gray person. But with the special water, you could look at your orange hands and think, *I'm happy! That whole time I was actually happy! What a relief!*

Mr. Black said, "I once went to report on a village in Russia, a community of artists who were forced to flee the cities! I'd heard that paintings hung everywhere! I heard you couldn't see the walls through all of the paintings! They'd painted the ceilings, the plates, the windows, the lampshades! Was it an act of rebellion! An act of expression! Were the paintings good, or was that beside the point! I needed to see it for myself, and I needed to tell the world about it! I used to live for reporting like that! Stalin found out about the community and sent his thugs in, just a few days before I got there, to break all of their arms! That was worse than killing them! It was a horrible sight, Oskar: their arms in crude splints, straight in front of them like zombies! They couldn't feed themselves, because they couldn't get their hands to their mouths! So you know what they did!" "They starved?" "They fed each other! That's the difference between heaven and hell! In hell we starve! In heaven we feed each other!" "I don't believe in the afterlife." "Neither do I, but I believe in the story!"

And then, all of a sudden, I thought of something. Something enormous. Something wonderful. "Do you want to help me?" "Excuse me!" "With the key." "Help you!" "You could go around with me." "You want my help!" "Yes." "Well, I don't need anyone's charity!" "Jose," I told him. "You're obviously very smart and knowledgeable, and you know a ton of things that I don't know, and also it's good just to have company, so please say yes." He closed his eyes and became quiet. I couldn't tell if he was thinking about what we were talking about, or thinking about something else, or if maybe he'd fallen asleep, which I know that old people, like Grandma, sometimes do, because they can't help it. "You don't have to make a decision right now," I said, because I didn't want him to feel forced. I told him about the 162 million locks, and how the search would probably take a long time, it might even take the full one and a half years, so if he wanted to think about it for a while that would be OK, he could just come downstairs and tell me his answer whenever. He kept thinking. "Take as long as you want," I said. He kept thinking. I asked him, "Do you have a decision?"

He didn't say anything.

"What do you think, Mr. Black?"

Nothing.

"Mr. Black?"

I tapped him on the shoulder and he looked up suddenly. "Hello?"

He smiled, like I do when Mom finds out about something I did that I shouldn't have done.

"I've been reading your lips!" "What?" He pointed at his hearing aids, which I hadn't noticed before, even though I was trying as hard as I could to notice everything. "I turned them off a long time ago!" "You turned them off?" "A long, long time ago!" "On purpose?" "I thought I'd save the batteries!" "For what?" He shrugged his shoulders. "But don't you want to hear things?" He shrugged his shoulders again, in a way so I couldn't tell if he was saying yes or no. And then I thought of something else. Something beautiful. Something true. "Do you want me to turn them on for you?"

He looked at me and through me at the same time, like I was a stained-glass window. I asked again, moving my lips slowly and carefully so I could be sure he understood me: "Do. You. Want. Me. To. Turn. Them. On. For. You?" He kept looking at me. I asked again. He said, "I don't know how to say yes!" I told him, "You don't have to."

I went behind him and saw a tiny dial on the back of each of his hearing aids.

"Do it slowly!" he said, almost like he was begging me. "It's been a long, long time!"

I went back around to his front so he could see my lips, and I promised him I would be as gentle as I could. Then I went back behind him and turned the dials extremely slowly, a few millimeters at a time. Nothing happened. I turned them a few more millimeters. And then just a few more. I went around to the front of him. He shrugged, and so did I. I went back around behind him and turned them up just a tiny bit more, until they stopped. I went back in front of him. He shrugged. Maybe the hearing aids didn't work anymore, or maybe the batteries had died of old age, or maybe he'd gone completely deaf since he turned them off, which was possible. We looked at each other.

Then, out of nowhere, a flock of birds flew by the window, extremely fast and incredibly close. Maybe twenty of them. Maybe more. But they also seemed like just one bird, because somehow they all knew

exactly what to do. Mr. Black grabbed at his ears and made a bunch of weird sounds. He started crying—not out of happiness, I could tell, but not out of sadness, either.

"Are you OK?" I whispered.

The sound of my voice made him cry more, and he nodded his head yes.

I asked him if he wanted me to make some more noise.

He nodded yes, which shook more tears down his cheeks.

I went to the bed and rattled it, so that a bunch of the pins and paper clips fell off.

He cried more tears.

"Do you want me to turn them off?" I asked, but he wasn't paying attention to me anymore. He was walking around the room, sticking his ears up to anything that made any noise, including very quiet things, like pipes.

I wanted to stay there watching him hear the world, but it was getting late, and I had a *Hamlet* rehearsal at 4:30, and it was an extremely important rehearsal, because it was the first one with lighting effects. I told Mr. Black that I would pick him up the next Saturday at 7:00, and we would start then. I told him, "I'm not even through with the A's." He said, "OK," and the sound of his own voice made him cry the most.

Message three. 9:31 A.M. *Hello? Hello? Hello?*

When Mom tucked me in that night, she could tell that something was on my mind, and asked if I wanted to talk. I did, but not to her, so I said, "No offense, but no." "Are you sure?" "*Très fatigué,*" I said, waving my hand. "Do you want me to read something to you?" "It's OK." "We could go through the *New York Times* for mistakes?" "No, thank you." "All right," she said, "all right." She gave me a kiss and turned off the light, and then, as she was about to go, I said, "Mom?" and she said, "Yes?" and I said, "Do you promise not to bury me when I die?"

She came back over and put her hand on my cheek and said, "You're not going to die." I told her, "I am." She said, "You're not going to die any time soon. You have a long, long life ahead of you." I told her,

"As you know, I'm extremely brave, but I can't spend eternity in a small underground place. I just can't. Do you love me?" "Of course I love you." "Then put me in one of those mausoleum-thingies." "A mausoleum?" "Like I read about." "Do we have to talk about this?" "Yes." "Now?" "Yes." "Why?" "Because what if I die tomorrow?" "You're not going to die tomorrow." "Dad didn't think he was going to die the next day." "That's not going to happen to you." "It wasn't going to happen to him." "Oskar." "I'm sorry, but I just can't be buried." "Don't you want to be with Dad and me?" "Dad isn't even there!" "Excuse me?" "His body was destroyed." "Don't talk like that." "Talk like what? It's the truth. I don't understand why everyone pretends he's there." "Take it easy, Oskar." "It's just an empty box." "It's more than an empty box." "Why would I want to spend eternity next to an empty box?"

Mom said, "His spirit is there," and that made me *really* angry. I told her, "Dad didn't have a spirit! He had cells!" "His memory is there." "His memory is here," I said, pointing at my head. "Dad had a spirit," she said, like she was rewinding a bit in our conversation. I told her, "He had cells, and now they're on rooftops, and in the river, and in the lungs of millions of people around New York, who breathe him every time they speak!" "You shouldn't say things like that." "But it's the *truth!* Why can't I say the *truth!*" "You're getting out of control." "Just because Dad died, it doesn't mean you can be illogical, Mom." "Yes it does." "No it doesn't." "Get a hold of yourself, Oskar." "Fuck you!" "Excuse me!" "Sorry. I mean, screw you." "You need a time-out!" "I need a mausoleum!" "Oskar!" "Don't lie to me!" "Who's lying?" "Where were you!" "Where was I when?" "That day!" "What day?" "*The* day!" "What do you mean?" "Where were you!" "I was at work." "Why weren't you at home?" "Because I have to go to work." "Why didn't you pick me up from school like the other moms?" "Oskar, I came home as soon as I could. It takes longer for me to get home than for you to. I thought it would be better to meet you at the apartment than make you wait at school for me to get to you." "But you should have been home when I got home." "I wish I had been, but it wasn't possible." "You should have made it possible." "I can't make the impossible possible." "You should have." She said, "I got home as quickly as I could." And then she started crying.

The ax was winning.

I put my cheek against her. "I don't need anything fancy, Mom. Just something above ground." She took a deep breath, put her arm around me, and said, "That might be possible." I tried to think of some way to be hilarious, because I thought that maybe if I was hilarious, she wouldn't be mad at me anymore and I could be safe again. "With a little elbow room." "What?" "I'm gonna need a little elbow room." She smiled and said, "OK." I sniffled again, because I could tell that it was working. "And a bidet." "Absolutely. One bidet coming up." "And some electrical fencing." "Electrical fencing?" "So that grave robbers won't try to steal all of my jewels." "Jewels?" "Yeah," I said, "I'm gonna need some jewels, too."

We cracked up together, which was necessary, because she loved me again. I pulled my feelings book from under my pillow, flipped to the current page, and downgraded from DESPERATE to MEDIOCRE. "Hey, that's great!" Mom said, looking over my shoulder. "No," I said, "it's mediocre. And please don't snoop." She rubbed my chest, which was nice, although I had to turn a little so she wouldn't feel that I still had my key on, and that there were two keys.

"Mom?" "Yes." "Nothing."

"What is it, baby?" "Well it's just that wouldn't it be great if mattresses had spaces for your arm, so that when you rolled onto your side, you could fit just right?" "That would be nice." "And good for your back, probably, because it would let your spine be straight, which I know is important." "That is important." "Also, it would make snuggling easier. You know how that arm constantly gets in the way?" "I do." "And making snuggling easier is important." "Very."

~~MEDIOCRE~~
OPTIMISTIC, BUT REALISTIC

"I miss Dad." "So do I." "Do you?" "Of course I do." "But do you *really?*" "How could you ask that?" "It's just that you don't act like you miss him very much." "What are you talking about?" "I think you know what I'm talking about." "I don't." "I hear you laughing." "You hear me laughing?" "In the living room. With Ron." "You think because I laugh every now and then I don't miss Dad?" I rolled onto my side, away from her.

She said, "I cry a lot, too, you know." "I don't see you cry a lot." "Maybe that's because I don't want you to see me cry a lot." "Why not?" "Because that isn't fair to either of us." "Yes it is." "I want us to move on." "How much do you cry?" "How much?" "A spoonful? A cup? A bathtub? If you added it up." "It doesn't work like that." "Like what?"

She said, "I'm trying to find ways to be happy. Laughing makes me happy." I said, "I'm not trying to find ways to be happy, and I won't." She said, "Well, you should." "Why?" "Because Dad would want you to be happy." "Dad would want me to remember him." "Why can't you remember him *and* be happy?" "Why are you in love with Ron?" "What?" "You're obviously in love with him, so what I want to know is, why? What's so great about him?" "Oskar, did it ever occur to you that things might be more complicated than they seem?" "That occurs to me all the time." "Ron is my *friend*." "So then promise me you won't ever fall in love again." "Oskar, Ron is going through a lot, too. We help each other. We're *friends*." "Promise me you won't fall in love." "Why would you ask me to promise that?" "Either promise me you'll never fall in love again, or I'm going to stop loving you." "You're not being fair." "I don't have to be fair! I'm your son!" She let out an enormous breath and said, "You remind me so much of Dad." And then I said something that I wasn't planning on saying, and didn't even want to say. As it came out of my mouth, I was ashamed that it was mixed with any of Dad's cells that I might have inhaled when we went to visit Ground Zero. "If I could have chosen, I would have chosen you!"

She looked at me for a second, then stood up and walked out of the room. I wish she'd slammed the door, but she didn't. She closed it carefully, like she always did. I could hear that she didn't walk away.

"Mom?"
Nothing.

I got out of bed and went to the door.

"I take it back."

She didn't say anything, but I could hear her breathing. I put my hand on the doorknob, because I thought maybe her hand was on the doorknob on the other side.

"I said I take it back."

"You can't take something like that back."

"Can you apologize for something like that?"

Nothing.

"Do you accept my apology?"

"I don't know."

"How can you not know?"

"Oskar, I *don't know*."

"Are you mad at me?"

Nothing.

"Mom?"

"Yes."

"Are you still mad at me?"

"No."

"Are you sure?"

"I was never mad at you."

"What were you?"

"Hurt."

~~INCREDIBLY ALONE~~

I GUESS I FELL ASLEEP ON THE FLOOR. WHEN I WOKE UP, MOM WAS PULLING MY SHIRT OFF TO HELP ME GET INTO MY PJS, WHICH MEANS SHE MUST HAVE SEEN ALL OF MY BRUISES. I COUNTED THEM LAST NIGHT IN THE MIRROR AND THERE WERE FORTY-ONE. SOME OF THEM HAVE GOTTEN BIG, BUT MOST OF THEM ARE SMALL. I DON'T PUT THEM THERE FOR HER, BUT STILL I WANT HER TO ASK ME

HOW I GOT THEM (EVEN THOUGH SHE
PROBABLY KNOWS), AND TO FEEL SORRY
FOR ME (BECAUSE SHE SHOULD REALIZE
HOW HARD THINGS ARE FOR ME), AND TO
FEEL TERRIBLE (BECAUSE AT LEAST SOME
OF IT IS HER FAULT), AND TO PROMISE ME
THAT SHE WON'T DIE AND LEAVE ME
ALONE. BUT SHE DIDN'T SAY ANYTHING.
I COULDN'T EVEN SEE THE LOOK IN HER
EYES WHEN SHE SAW THE BRUISES,
BECAUSE MY SHIRT WAS OVER MY HEAD,
COVERING MY FACE LIKE A POCKET, OR A
SKULL.

MY FEELINGS

They are announcing flights over the speakers.   We are not listening.
They do not matter to us, because we are not going anywhere.
I miss you already, Oskar.   I missed you even when I was with you.
That's been my problem.   I miss what I already have, and I surround
myself with things that are missing.
Every time I put in a new page, I look at your grandfather.   I am so relieved to see his face.   It makes me feel safe.   His shoulders are
pinched.   His spine is curved.   In Dresden he was a giant.   I'm glad
that his hands are still rough.   The sculptures never left them.
I didn't notice until now that he is still wearing his wedding ring.   I
wonder if he put it on when he came back or if he wore it all those years.
Before I came here I locked up the apartment.   I turned off the lights
and made sure none of the faucets leaked.   It's hard to say goodbye to
the place you've lived.   It can be as hard as saying goodbye to a person.
We moved in after we were married.   It had more room than his apartment.   We needed it.   We needed room for all of the animals, and we
needed room between us.   Your grandfather bought the most expensive insurance policy.   A man from the company came over to take pictures.   If anything happened, they would be able to rebuild the apartment again exactly as it was.   He took a roll of film.   He took a
picture of the floor, a picture of the fireplace, a picture of the bathtub.
I never confused what I had with what I was.   When the man left, your
grandfather took out his own camera and started taking more pictures.
What are you doing? I asked him.
Better safe than sorry, he wrote.   At the time I thought he was right,
but I am not sure anymore.

He took pictures of everything.   Of the undersides of the shelves in the closet.   Of the backs of the mirrors.   Even the broken things. The things you would not want to remember.   He could have rebuilt the apartment by taping together the pictures.

And the doorknobs.   He took a picture of every doorknob in the apartment.   Every one.   As if the world and its future depended on each doorknob.   As if we would be thinking about doorknobs should we ever actually need to use the pictures of them.

I don't know why that hurt me so much.

I told him, They are not even nice doorknobs.

He wrote, But they are our doorknobs.

I was his too.

He never took pictures of me, and we didn't buy life insurance.

He kept one set of the pictures in his dresser. He taped another set into his daybooks, so they'd always be with him, in case something happened at home.

Our marriage was not unhappy, Oskar.   He knew how to make me laugh.   And sometimes I made him laugh.   We had to make rules, but who doesn't.   There is nothing wrong with compromising.   Even if you compromise almost everything.

He got a job at a jewelry store, because he knew the machines.   He worked so hard that they made him assistant manager, and then manager.   He did not care about jewelry.   He hated it.   He used to say jewelry is the opposite of sculpture.

But it was a living, and he promised me that was OK.

We got our own store in a neighborhood that was next to a bad neighborhood.   It was open from eleven in the morning until six at night. But there was always work to be done.

We spent our lives making livings.

Sometimes he would go to the airport after work.   I asked him to get me papers and magazines.   At first this was because I wanted to learn American expressions.   But I gave up on that.   I still asked him to go. I knew that he needed my permission to go.   It was not out of kindness that I sent him.

We tried so hard.   We were always trying to help each other.   But not because we were helpless.   He needed to get things for me, just as I needed to get things for him.   It gave us purpose.   Sometimes I would ask him for something that I did not even want, just to let him get it for me.   We spent our days trying to help each other help each other.   I would get his slippers.   He would make my tea.   I would turn up the heat so he could turn up the air conditioner so I could turn up the heat.   His hands didn't lose their roughness.

It was Halloween.   Our first in the apartment.   The doorbell rang. Your grandfather was at the airport.   I opened the door and a child was standing there in a white sheet with holes cut out for her eyes.   Trick or treat! she said.   I took a step back.

Who is that?

I'm a ghost!

What are you wearing that for?

It's Halloween!

I don't know what that means.

Kids dress up and knock on doors, and you give them candy.

I don't have any candy.

It's Hal-lo-ween!

I told her to wait.   I went to the bedroom.   I took an envelope from underneath the mattress.   Our savings.   Our living.   I took out two one-hundred-dollar bills and put them in a different envelope, which I gave to the ghost.

I was paying her to go away.

I closed the door and turned off the lights so no more children would ring our bell.

The animals must have understood, because they surrounded me and pressed into me.   I did not say anything when your grandfather came home that night.   I thanked him for the papers and magazines.   I went to the guest room and pretended to write.   I hit the space bar again and again and again.   My life story was spaces.

The days passed one at a time.   And sometimes less than one at a time. We looked at each other and drew maps in our heads.   I told him my eyes were crummy, because I wanted him to pay attention to me.   We made safe places in the apartment where you could go and not exist.

I would have done anything for him.   Maybe that was my sickness.
We made love in nothing places and turned the lights off.   It felt like
crying.   We could not look at each other.   It always had to be from
behind.   Like that first time.   And I knew that he wasn't thinking of
me.

He squeezed my sides so hard, and pushed so hard.   Like he was trying to push through me to somewhere else.

Why does anyone ever make love?

A year passed.   Another year.   Another year.   Another.

We made livings.

I never forgot about the ghost.

I needed a child.

What does it mean to need a child?

One morning I awoke and understood the hole in the middle of me.
I realized that I could compromise my life, but not life after me.
I couldn't explain it.   The need came before explanations.

It was not out of weakness that I made it happen, but it was not out of
strength either.   It was out of need.   I needed a child.

I tried to hide it from him.   I tried to wait to tell him until it was too
late to do anything about it.   It was the ultimate secret.   Life.   I kept
it safe inside me.   I took it around.   Like the apartment was inside his
books.   I wore loose shirts.   I sat with pillows on my lap.   I was
naked only in nothing places.

But I could not keep it a secret forever.

We were lying in bed in the darkness.   I did not know how to say it.   I
knew, but I could not say it.   I took one of his daybooks from the bedside table.

The apartment had never been darker.

I turned on the lamp.

It became bright around us.

The apartment became darker.

I wrote, I am pregnant.

I handed it to him.   He read it.

He took the pen and wrote, How could that have happened?

I wrote, I made it happen.

He wrote, But we had a rule.

The next page was a doorknob.

I turned the page and wrote, I broke the rule.

He sat up in bed.   I don't know how much time passed.

He wrote, Everything will be OK.

I told him OK wasn't enough.

Everything will be ~~OK~~ perfect.

I told him there was nothing left for a lie to protect.

Everything will be ~~OK~~ ~~perfect.~~

I started to cry.

It was the first time I had ever cried in front of him.   It felt like making love.

I asked him something I had needed to know since we made that first nothing place years before.

What are we?   Something or nothing?

He covered my face with his hands and lifted them off.

I did not know what that meant.

The next morning I woke up with a terrible cold.

I did not know if the baby was making me sick or if your grandfather was.

When I said goodbye to him, before he left for the airport, I lifted his suitcase and it felt heavy.

That was how I knew he was leaving me.

I wondered if I should stop him.   If I should wrestle him to the ground and force him to love me.   I wanted to hold his shoulders down and shout into his face.

I followed him there.

I watched him all morning.   I did not know how to talk to him.   I watched him write in his book.   I watched him ask people what time it was, although each person just pointed at the big yellow clock on the wall.

It was so strange to see him from a distance.   So small.   I cared for him in the world as I could not care for him in the apartment.   I wanted to protect him from all of the terrible things that no one deserves.

I got very close to him.   Just behind him.   I watched him write, It's a shame that we have to live, but it's a tragedy that we get to live only one life.   I stepped back.   I could not be that close.   Not even then.

From behind a column I watched him write more, and ask for the time, and rub his rough hands against his knees.   Yes and No.

I watched him get in the line to buy tickets.

I wondered, When am I going to stop him from leaving?

I didn't know how to ask him or tell him or beg him.

When he got to the front of the line I went up to him.

I touched his shoulder.

I can see, I said.   What a stupid thing to say.   My eyes are crummy, but I can see.

What are you doing here? he wrote with his hands.

I felt suddenly shy.   I was not used to shy.   I was used to shame.

Shyness is when you turn your head away from something you want.

Shame is when you turn your head away from something you do not want.

I know you are leaving, I said.

You have to go home, he wrote.   You should be in bed.

OK, I said.   I did not know how to say what I needed to say.

Let me take you home.

No.   I do not want to go home.

He wrote, You're being crazy.   You're going to catch a cold.

I already have a cold.

You are going to catch a colder.

I could not believe he was making a joke.   And I could not believe I laughed.

The laughter sent my thoughts to our kitchen table, where we would laugh and laugh.   That table was where we were close to each other.

It was instead of our bed.   Everything in our apartment got confused.

We would eat on the coffee table in the living room instead of at the dining room table.   We wanted to be near the window.   We filled the body of the grandfather clock with his empty daybooks, as if they were time itself.   We put his filled daybooks in the bathtub of the second bathroom, because we never used it.   I sleepwalk when I sleep at all.

Once I turned on the shower.   Some of the books floated, and some stayed where they were.   When I awoke the next morning I saw what I had done.   The water was gray with all of his days.

I am not being crazy, I told him.

You have to go home.

I got tired, I told him.   Not worn out, but worn through.   Like one of those wives who wakes up one morning and says I can't bake any more bread.

You never baked bread, he wrote, and we were still joking.

Then it's like I woke up and baked bread, I said, and we were joking even then.   I wondered will there come a time when we won't be joking?   And what would that look like?   And how would that feel?

When I was a girl, my life was music that was always getting louder. Everything moved me.   A dog following a stranger.   That made me feel so much.   A calendar that showed the wrong month.   I could have cried over it.   I did.   Where the smoke from a chimney ended. How an overturned bottle rested at the edge of a table.

I spent my life learning to feel less.

Every day I felt less.

Is that growing old?   Or is it something worse?

You cannot protect yourself from sadness without protecting yourself from happiness.

He hid his face in the covers of his daybook, as if the covers were his hands.   He cried.   For whom was he crying?

For Anna?

For his parents?

For me?

For himself?

I pulled the book from him.   It was wet with tears running down the pages, as if the book itself were crying.   He hid his face in his hands.

Let me see you cry, I told him.

I do not want to hurt you, he said by shaking his head left to right.

It hurts me when you do not want to hurt me, I told him.   Let me see you cry.

He lowered his hands.   On one cheek it said YES backward.   On one cheek it said NO backward.　He was still looking down.　Now the tears did not run down his cheeks, but fell from his eyes to the ground. Let me see you cry, I said.　I did not feel that he owed it to me.　And I did not feel that I owed it to him.　We owed it to each other, which is something different.

He raised his head and looked at me.

I am not angry with you, I told him.

You must be.

I am the one who broke the rule.

But I am the one who made the rule you couldn't live with.

My thoughts are wandering, Oskar.　They are going to Dresden, to my mother's pearls, damp with the sweat of her neck.　My thoughts are going up the sleeve of my father's overcoat.　His arm was so thick and strong.　I was sure it would protect me for as long as I lived.　And it did.　Even after I lost him.　The memory of his arm wraps around me as his arm used to.　Each day has been chained to the previous one. But the weeks have had wings.　Anyone who believes that a second is faster than a decade did not live my life.

Why are you leaving me?

He wrote, I do not know how to live.

I do not know either, but I am trying.

I do not know how to try.

There were things I wanted to tell him.　But I knew they would hurt him.　So I buried them, and let them hurt me.

I put my hand on him.　Touching him was always so important to me. It was something I lived for.　I never could explain why.　Little, nothing touches.　My fingers against his shoulder.　The outsides of our thighs touching as we squeezed together on the bus.　I couldn't explain it, but I needed it.　Sometimes I imagined stitching all of our little touches together.　How many hundreds of thousands of fingers brushing against each other does it take to make love?　Why does anyone ever make love?

My thoughts are going to my childhood, Oskar.　To when I was a girl. I am sitting here thinking about fistfuls of pebbles, and the first time I noticed hairs under my arms.

My thoughts are around my mother's neck.   Her pearls.

When I first liked the smell of perfume, and how Anna and I would lie in the darkness of our bedroom, in the warmth of our bed.

I told her one night what I had seen behind the shed behind our house. She made me promise never to speak a word about it.   I promised her.

Can I watch you kiss?

Can you watch us kiss?

You could tell me where you are going to kiss, and I could hide and watch.

She laughed, which was how she said yes.

We woke up in the middle of the night.   I do not know who woke up first.   Or if we woke up at the same time.

What does it feel like? I asked her.

What does what feel like?

To kiss.

She laughed.

It feels wet, she said.

I laughed.

It feels wet and warm and very strange at first.

I laughed.

Like this, she said, and she grabbed the sides of my face and pulled me into her.

I had never felt so in love in my life, and I have not felt so in love since.

We were innocent.

How could anything be more innocent than the two of us kissing in that bed?

How could anything less deserve to be destroyed?

I told him, I will try harder if you will stay.

OK, he wrote.

Just please do not leave me.

OK.

We never have to mention this.

OK.

I am thinking about shoes, for some reason.   How many pairs I have worn in my life.   And how many times my feet have slipped into and out of them.   And how I put them at the foot of the bed, pointing away from the bed.

My thoughts are going down a chimney and burning.

Footsteps above.   Frying onions.   Clinking crystal.

We were not rich, but there was nothing we wanted.   From my bedroom window I watched the world.   And I was safe from the world.

I watched my father fall apart.   The nearer the war came, the farther he went.   Was that the only way he knew to protect us?   He spent hours in his shed every night.   Sometimes he would sleep in there. On the floor.

He wanted to save the world.   That's what he was like.   But he wouldn't put our family in danger.   That's what he was like.   He must have weighed my life against a life he might have been able to save. Or ten.   Or one hundred.   He must have decided that my life weighed more than one hundred lives.

His hair turned gray that winter.   I thought it was snow.   He promised us that everything would be OK.   I was a child, but I knew that everything would not be OK.   That did not make my father a liar.   It made him my father.

It was the morning of the bombing that I decided to write back to the forced laborer.   I do not know why I waited for so long, or what made me want to write to him then.

He had asked me to include a photograph of myself.   I did not have any photographs of myself that I liked.   I understand, now, the tragedy of my childhood.   It wasn't the bombing.   It was that I never once liked a photograph of myself.   I couldn't.

I decided I would go to a photographer the next day and have a picture taken.

That night I tried on all of my outfits in front of the mirror.   I felt like an ugly movie star.   I asked my mother to teach me about makeup. She didn't ask why.

She showed me how to rouge my cheeks.   And how to paint my eyes. She had never touched my face so much.   There had never been an excuse to.

My forehead.   My chin.   My temples.   My neck.   Why was she crying?

I left the unfinished letter on my desk.

The paper helped our house burn.

I should have sent it off with an ugly photograph.

I should have sent off everything.

The airport was filled with people coming and going.   But it was only
your grandfather and me.

I took his daybook and searched its pages.   I pointed at, How frustrating, how pathetic, how sad.

He searched through the book and pointed at, The way you just handed
me that knife.

I pointed at, If I'd been someone else in a different world I'd've done
something different.

He pointed at, Sometimes one simply wants to disappear.

I pointed at, There's nothing wrong with not understanding yourself.

He pointed at, How sad.

I pointed at, And I wouldn't say no to something sweet.

He pointed at, Cried and cried and cried.

I pointed at, Don't cry.

He pointed at, Broken and confused.

I pointed at, So sad.

He pointed at, Broken and confused.

I pointed at, Something.

He pointed at, Nothing.

I pointed at, Something.

Nobody pointed at, I love you.

There was no way around it.   We could not climb over it, or walk until
we found its edge.

I regret that it takes a life to learn how to live, Oskar.   Because if I were
able to live my life again, I would do things differently.

I would change my life.

I would kiss my piano teacher, even if he laughed at me.

I would jump with Mary on the bed, even if I made a fool of myself.

I would send out ugly photographs, thousands of them.

What are we going to do? he wrote.

It's up to you, I said.

He wrote, I want to go home.

What is home to you?

Home is the place with the most rules.

I understood him.

And we will have to make more rules, I said.

To make it more of a home.

Yes.

OK.

We went straight to the jewelry store.   He left the suitcase in the back room.   We sold a pair of emerald earrings that day.   And a diamond engagement ring.   And a gold bracelet for a little girl.   And a watch for someone on his way to Brazil.

That night we held each other in bed.   He kissed me all over.   I believed him.   I was not stupid.   I was his wife.

The next morning he went to the airport.   I didn't dare feel his suitcase.

I waited for him to come home.

Hours passed.   And minutes.

I didn't open the store at 11:00.

I waited by the window.   I still believed in him.

I didn't eat lunch.

Seconds passed.

The afternoon left.   The evening came.

I didn't eat dinner.

Years were passing through the spaces between moments.

Your father kicked in my belly.

What was he trying to tell me?

I brought the birdcages to the windows.

I opened the windows, and opened the birdcages.

I poured the fish down the drain.

I took the dogs and cats downstairs and removed their collars.

I released the insects onto the street.

And the reptiles.

And the mice.
I told them, Go.
All of you.
Go.
And they went.
And they didn't come back.

HAPPINESS, HAPPINESS

INTERVIEWER. Can you describe the events of that morning?

TOMOYASU. I left home with my daughter, Masako. She was on her way to work. I was going to see a friend. An air-raid warning was issued. I told Masako I was going home. She said, "I'm going to the office." I did chores and waited for the warning to be lifted.

I folded the bedding. I rearranged the closet. I cleaned the windows with a wet rag. There was a flash. My first thought was that it was the flash from a camera. That sounds so ridiculous now. It pierced my eyes. My mind went blank. The glass from the windows was shattering all around me. It sounded like when my mother used to hush me to be quiet.

When I became conscious again, I realized I wasn't standing. I had been thrown into a different room. The rag was still in my hand, but it was no longer wet. My only thought was to find my daughter. I looked outside the window and saw one of my neighbors standing almost naked. His skin was peeling off all over his body. It was hanging from his fingertips. I asked him what had happened. He was too exhausted to reply. He was looking in every direction, I can only assume for his family. I thought, *I must go. I must go and find Masako.*

I put my shoes on and took my air-raid hood with me. I made my way to the train station. So many people were marching toward me, away from the city. I smelled something similar to grilled squid. I must have been in shock, because the people looked like squid washing up on the shore.

I saw a young girl coming toward me. Her skin was melting down her. It was like wax. She was muttering, "Mother. Water. Mother.

Water." I thought she might be Masako. But she wasn't. I didn't give her any water. I am sorry that I didn't. But I was trying to find my Masako.

I ran all the way to Hiroshima Station. It was full of people. Some of them were dead. Many of them were lying on the ground. They were calling for their mothers and asking for water. I went to Tokiwa Bridge. I had to cross the bridge to get to my daughter's office.

INTERVIEWER. Did you see the mushroom cloud?

TOMOYASU. No, I didn't see the cloud.

INTERVIEWER. You didn't see the mushroom cloud?

TOMOYASU. I didn't see the mushroom cloud. I was trying to find Masako.

INTERVIEWER. But the cloud spread over the city?

TOMOYASU. I was trying to find her. They told me I couldn't go beyond the bridge. I thought she might be back home, so I turned around. I was at the Nikitsu Shrine when the black rain started falling from the sky. I wondered what it was.

INTERVIEWER. Can you describe the black rain?

TOMOYASU. I waited for her in the house. I opened the windows, even though there was no glass. I stayed awake all night waiting. But she didn't come back. About 6:30 the next morning, Mr. Ishido came around. His daughter was working at the same office as my daughter. He called out asking for Masako's house. I ran outside. I called, "It's here, over here!" Mr. Ishido came up to me. He said, "Quick! Get some clothes and go for her. She is at the bank of the Ota River."

I ran as fast as I could. Faster than I was able to run. When I reached the Tokiwa Bridge, there were soldiers lying on the ground. Around Hiroshima Station, I saw more people lying dead. There were more on the morning of the seventh than on the sixth. When I reached the riverbank, I couldn't tell who was who. I kept looking for Masako. I heard someone crying, "Mother!" I recognized her voice. I found her in horrible condition. And she still appears in my dreams that way. She said, "It took you so long."

I apologized to her. I told her, "I came as fast as I could."

It was just the two of us. I didn't know what to do. I was not a nurse. There were maggots in her wounds and a sticky yellow liquid. I tried to clean her up. But her skin was peeling off. The maggots were coming out all over. I couldn't wipe them off, or I would wipe off her skin and muscle. I had to pick them out. She asked me what I was doing. I told her, "Oh, Masako. It's nothing." She nodded. Nine hours later, she died.

INTERVIEWER. You were holding her in your arms all that time?

TOMOYASU. Yes, I held her in my arms. She said, "I don't want to die." I told her, "You're not going to die." She said, "I promise I won't die before we get home." But she was in pain and she kept crying, "Mother."

INTERVIEWER. It must be hard to talk about these things.

TOMOYASU. When I heard that your organization was recording testimonies, I knew I had to come. She died in my arms, saying, "I don't want to die." That is what death is like. It doesn't matter what uniforms the soldiers are wearing. It doesn't matter how good the weapons are. I thought if everyone could see what I saw, we would never have war anymore.

I pressed Stop on the boom box, because the interview was over. The girls were crying, and the boys were making funny barfing noises.

"Well," Mr. Keegan said, wiping his forehead with a handkerchief as he stood up from his chair, "Oskar has certainly given us a lot to think about." I said, "I'm not done." He said, "That seemed pretty complete to me." I explained, "Because the radiant heat traveled in straight lines from the explosion, scientists were able to determine the direction toward the hypocenter from a number of different points, by observing the shadows cast by intervening objects. The shadows gave an indication of the height of the burst of the bomb, and the diameter of the ball of fire at the instant it was exerting the maximum charring effect. Isn't that fascinating?"

Jimmy Snyder raised his hand. I called on him. He asked, "Why are you so weird?" I asked if his question was rhetorical. Mr. Keegan told him to go to Principal Bundy's office. Some of the kids cracked up. I knew they were cracking up in the bad way, which is at me, but I tried to maintain my confidence.

"Another interesting feature that has to do with the explosion was the relationship between the degree of burning and color, because dark colors absorb light, obviously. For example, a famous chess match between two grand masters was going on that morning on a life-size board in one of the big city parks. The bomb destroyed everything: the spectators in the seats, the people who were filming the match, their black cameras, the timing clocks, even the grand masters. All that was left were white pieces on white square islands."

As he walked out of the room, Jimmy said, "Hey, Oskar, who's Buckminster?" I told him, "Richard Buckminster Fuller was a scientist, philosopher, and inventor who is most famous for designing the geodesic dome, whose most famous version is the Buckyball. He died in 1983, I think." Jimmy said, "I mean *your* Buckminster."

I didn't know why he was asking, because I'd brought Buckminster to school for a demonstration only a couple of weeks before, and dropped him from the roof to show how cats reach terminal velocity by making themselves into little parachutes, and that cats actually have a better chance of surviving a fall from the twentieth floor than the eighth floor, because it takes them about eight floors to realize what's going on, and relax and correct themselves. I said, "Buckminster is my pussy."

Jimmy pointed at me and said, "Ha ha!" The kids cracked up in the bad way. I didn't get what was so hilarious. Mr. Keegan got angry and said, "Jimmy!" Jimmy said, "What? What did I do?" I could tell that inside, Mr. Keegan was cracking up, too.

"What I was saying was, they found a piece of paper, about half a kilometer from the hypocenter, and the letters, which they call characters, were neatly burned out. I became extremely curious about what that would look like, so first I tried to cut out letters on my own, but my hands weren't good enough to do it, so I did some research, and I found a printer on Spring Street who specializes in die-cutting, and he said he could do it for two hundred fifty dollars. I asked him if that included tax. He said no, but I still thought it was worth the money, so I took my mom's credit card, and anyway, here it is." I held up the sheet of paper, with the first page of *A Brief History of Time* in Japanese, which I got the translation of from Amazon.co.jp. I looked at the class through the story of the turtles.

That was Wednesday.

I spent Thursday's recess in the library, reading the new issue of

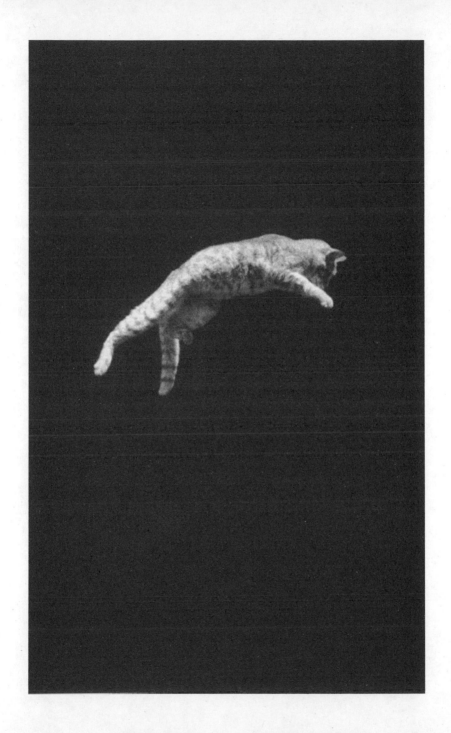

American Drummer, which Librarian Higgins orders especially for me. It was boring. I went to the science lab, to see if Mr. Powers would do some experiments with me. He said he actually had plans to eat lunch with some other teachers, and he couldn't let me be in the lab alone. So I made some jewelry in the art studio, which you are allowed to be in alone.

Friday, Jimmy Snyder called me from across the playground, and then he came up to me with a bunch of his friends. He said, "Hey, Oskar, would you rather have a handjob or a blowjob from Emma Watson?" I told him I didn't know who Emma Watson was. Matt Colber said, "Hermione, retard." I said, "Who's Hermione? And I'm not mentally retarded." Dave Mallon said, "In *Harry Potter,* fag boy." Steve Wicker said, "She has sweet tits now." Jake Riley said, "Handjob or blowjob?" I said, "I've never even met her."

I know a lot about birds and bees, but I don't know very much about the birds and the bees. Everything I do know I had to teach myself on the Internet, because I don't have anyone to ask. For example, I know that you give someone a blowjob by putting your penis in their mouth. I also know that dick is penis, and that cock is penis, too. And monster cock, obviously. I know that VJs get wet when a woman is having sex, although I don't know what they get wet *with*. I know that VJ is cunt, and also ass. I know what dildos are, I think, but I don't know what cum is, exactly. I know that anal sex is humping in the anus, but I wish I didn't.

Jimmy Snyder pushed my shoulder and said, "Say your mom's a whore." I said, "Your mom's a whore." He said, "Say *your* mom's a whore." I said, "*Your* mom's a whore." "Say 'My' 'mom' 'is a whore.'" "Your mom is a whore." Matt and Dave and Steve and Jake were cracking up, but Jimmy was getting really, really angry. He raised a fist and said, "Prepare to die." I looked around for a teacher, but I didn't see any. "My mom's a whore," I said. I went inside and read a few more sentences of *A Brief History of Time.* Then I broke a mechanical pencil. When I came home, Stan said, "You've got mail!"

Dear Oskar,

Thanks for mailing me the $76.50 you
owed me. To tell you the truth, I never thought
I'd see that money. Now I will believe everyone.
(cab driver) Marty Mahaltra
P.S. No tip?

I counted off seven minutes that night, and then fourteen minutes, and then thirty. I knew I'd never be able to fall asleep, because I was so excited that the next day I'd be able to search for the lock. I started inventing like a beaver. I thought about how in one hundred years every name in the 2003 Yellow Pages will be for someone who's dead, and how once when I was at The Minch's I saw a TV show where someone ripped a phone book in half with his hands. I thought about how I wouldn't want someone to rip a 2003 Yellow Pages in half in one hundred years, because even though everyone will be dead, it still felt like it should make a difference. So I invented a Black Box Yellow Pages, which is a phone book that's made out of the material that they make the black boxes on airplanes out of. I still couldn't sleep.

I invented a postage stamp where the back tastes like crème brûlée. I still couldn't sleep.

What if you trained Seeing Eye dogs to be bomb-sniffing dogs, so that they'd be Sniffing Eye Seeing Bomb dogs? That way, blind people could get paid for being led around, and could be contributing members of our society, and we'd all be safer, too. I was getting further and further from sleep.

When I woke up it was Saturday.

I went upstairs to pick up Mr. Black, and he was waiting in front of his door, snapping his fingers next to his ear. "What's this?" he asked when I handed him the present I made for him. I shrugged my shoulders, just like Dad used to. "What am I supposed to do with it?" I told him, "Open it, obviously." But I couldn't keep my happiness in, and before he got the paper off the box I said, "It's a necklace I made for you with a compass pendant so you can know where you are in relation to the bed!" He kept opening it and said, "How nice of you!" "Yeah," I said, taking the box from him because I could open it faster. "It probably won't work outside your apartment, because the magnetic field of the bed gets smaller the farther you get from it, but still." I handed him the necklace and he put it on. It said that the bed was north.

"So where to?" he asked. "The Bronx," I said. "The IRT?" "The what?" "The IRT train." "There isn't an IRT train, and I don't take public transportation." "Why not?" "It's an obvious target." "So how do you plan on us getting there?" "We'll walk." "That's got to be about twenty miles from here," he said. "And have you seen me walk?" "That's true." "Let's take the IRT." "There is no IRT." "Whatever there is, let's take it."

On our way out, I said, "Stan, this is Mr. Black. Mr. Black, this is Stan." Mr. Black stuck out his hand, and Stan shook it. I told Stan, "Mr. Black lives in 6A." Stan took his hand back, but I don't think Mr. Black was offended.

Almost the whole ride to the Bronx was underground, which made me incredibly panicky, but once we got to the poor parts, it went aboveground, which I preferred. A lot of the buildings in the Bronx were empty, which I could tell because they didn't have windows, and you could see right through them, even at high speeds. We got off the train and went down to the street. Mr. Black had me hold his hand as we looked for the address. I asked him if he was racist. He said poverty made him nervous, not people. Just as a joke I asked him if he was gay. He said, "I suppose so." "Really?" I asked, but I didn't take back my hand, because I'm not homophobic.

The building's buzzer was broken, so the door was held open with a brick. Agnes Black's apartment was on the third floor, and there was no elevator. Mr. Black said he'd wait for me, because the stairs at the subway were enough stairs for him for one day. So I went up alone. The floor of the hallway was sticky, and for some reason all of the peepholes had black paint over them. Someone was singing from behind one of the doors, and I heard TVs behind a bunch of others. I tried my key in Agnes's lock, but it didn't work, so I knocked.

A little woman answered who was in a wheelchair. She was Mexican, I think. Or Brazilian, or something. "Excuse me, is your name

Agnes Black?" She said, "No espeaka Inglesh." "What?" "No espeaka Inglesh." "I'm sorry," I said, "but I don't understand you. Could you please repeat yourself and enunciate a little bit better." "No espeaka Inglesh," she said. I pointed a finger in the air, which is the universal sign for hold on, and then I called down to Mr. Black from the stairwell, "I don't think she speaks English!" "Well, what does she speak?" "What do you speak?" I asked her, and then I realized how dumb my question was, so I tried a different approach: "*Parlez-vous français?*" "*Español,*" she said. "*Español,*" I hollered down. "Terrific!" he hollered back. "I picked up a little *Español* along the way!" So I brought her wheelchair to the stairwell, and they hollered to each other, which was kind of weird, because their voices were traveling back and forth but they couldn't see each other's faces. They cracked up together, and their laughter ran up and down the stairs. Then Mr. Black hollered, "Oskar!" And I hollered, "That's my name, don't wear it out!" And he hollered, "Come on down!"

When I got back to the lobby, Mr. Black explained that the person we were looking for had been a waitress at Windows on the World. "*What the?*" "The woman I just spoke with, Feliz, didn't know her personally. She was told about her when she moved in." "Really?" "I wouldn't make that up." We went out to the street and started walking. A car drove by that was playing music extremely loudly, and it vibrated my heart. I looked up, and there were strings connecting a lot of the windows with clothes hanging on them. I asked Mr. Black if that's what people meant when they said "clotheslines." He said, "That's what they mean." I said, "That's what I thought." We walked some more. Kids were kicking rocks in the street and cracking up in the good way. Mr. Black picked up one of the rocks and put it in his pocket. He looked at the street sign, and then at his watch. A couple of old men were sitting in chairs in front of a store. They were smoking cigars and watching the world like it was TV.

"That's so weird to think about," I said. "What is?" "That she worked there. Maybe she knew my dad. Or not knew him, but maybe she served him that morning. He was there, in the restaurant. He had a meeting. Maybe she refilled his coffee or something." "It's possible."

"Maybe they died together." I know he didn't know what to say to that, because of course they died together. The real question was *how* they died together, like whether they were on different ends of the restaurant, or next to each other, or something else. Maybe they had gone up to the roof together. You saw in some of the pictures that people jumped together and held hands. So maybe they did that. Or maybe they just talked to each other until the building fell. What would they have talked about? They were obviously so different. Maybe he told her about me. I wonder what he told her. I couldn't tell how it made me feel to think of him holding someone's hand.

"Did she have any kids?" I asked. "I don't know." "Ask her." "Ask who?" "Let's go back and ask the woman who's living there now. I bet she knows if Agnes had any kids." He didn't ask me why that question was important, or tell me she already told us everything she knew. We walked back three blocks, and I went up the stairs and brought her wheelchair back to the stairwell, and they talked up and down the stairs for a while. Then Mr. Black hollered, "She didn't!" But I wondered if he was lying to me, because even though I don't speak Spanish, I could hear that she said a lot more than just no.

As we were walking back to the subway, I had a revelation, and then I got angry. "Wait a minute," I said. "What were you cracking up about before?" "Before?" "When you were talking to that woman the first time, you were cracking up. Both of you." "I don't know," he said. "You don't know?" "I don't remember." "Try to remember." He thought for a minute. "I can't remember." Lie #77.

We bought some tamales that a woman was selling by the subway from a huge pot in a grocery cart. Normally I don't like food that isn't individually wrapped or prepared by Mom, but we sat on the curb and ate our tamales. Mr. Black said, "If anything, I'm invigorated." "What's 'invigorated'?" "Energized. Refreshed." "I'm invigorated, too." He put his arm around me and said, "Good." "These are vegan, right?" I shook my tambourine as we walked up the stairs to the subway, and held my breath when the train went underground.

Albert Black came from Montana. He wanted to be an actor, but he didn't want to go to California, because it was too close to home, and the whole point of being an actor was to be someone else.

Alice Black was incredibly nervous, because she lived in a building that was supposed to be for industrial purposes, so people weren't supposed to live there. Before she opened the door, she made us promise that we weren't from the Housing Authority. I said, "I suggest you take a look at us through the peephole." She did, and then she said, "Oh, you," which I thought was weird, and she let us in. Her hands were covered with charcoal, and I saw drawings everywhere, and they were all of the same man. "Are you forty?" "I'm twenty-one." "I'm nine." "I'm one hundred and three." I asked her if she was the one who made the drawings. "Yes." "All of them?" "Yes." I didn't ask who the man in the drawings was, because I was afraid the answer would give me heavy boots. You wouldn't draw someone that much unless you loved him and missed him. I told her, "You're extremely beautiful." "Thanks." "Can we kiss?" Mr. Black stuck his elbow in my side and asked her, "Do you know anything about this key?"

> *Dear Oskar Schell,*
>
> *I am responding on behalf of Dr. Kaley, who is currently in the Congo on a research expedition. She asked that I pass on her appreciation for your enthusiasm about her work with elephants. Given that I am already her assistant — and budget limitations being what they are, as I'm sure you've experienced — she isn't now able to take on anyone else. But she did want me to tell you that should your interest and availability remain, there might be a project next fall in Sudan that she will need help with. (The grant proposals are just now going through.)*
>
> *Please forward us your résumé, including previous research experience, graduate and postgraduate transcripts, and two letters of recommendation.*
>
> *Best,*
> *Gary Franklin*

JONATHAN SAFRAN FOER

Allen Black lived on the Lower East Side and was a doorman for a building on Central Park South, which was where we found him. He said he hated being a doorman, because he had been an engineer in Russia, and now his brain was dying. He showed us a little portable TV that he kept in his pocket. "It plays DVDs," he said, "and if I had an e-mail account, I could check it on this, too." I told him I could set up an e-mail account for him if he wanted. He said, "Yeah?" I took his device, which I wasn't familiar with, but figured out pretty quickly, and set everything up. I said, "What do you want for a user name?" I suggested "Allen," or "AllenBlack," or a nickname. "Or 'Engineer.' That could be cool." He put his finger on his mustache and thought about it. I asked if he had any kids. He said, "A son. Soon he's going to be taller than me. Taller and smarter. He'll be a great doctor. A brain surgeon. Or lawyer for the Supreme Court." "Well, you could make it your son's name, although I guess that might be confusing." He said, "Doorman." "What?" "Make it 'Doorman.'" "You can make it anything you want." "Doorman." I made it "Doorman215," because there were already 214 doormen. As we were leaving, he said, "Good luck, Oskar." I said, "How did you know my name was Oskar?" Mr. Black said, "You told him." When I got home that afternoon I sent him an e-mail: "It's too bad you didn't know anything about the key, but it was still nice to meet you."

> *Dear Oskar,*
> *While you certainly express yourself like an intelligent young man, without ever having met you, and knowing nothing of your experience with scientific research, I'd have a hard time writing a recommendation.*
> *Thanks for the kind words about my work, and best of luck with your explorations, scientific and otherwise.*
> *Most sincerely,*
> *Jane Goodall*

Arnold Black got right to the point: "I just can't help. Sorry." I said, "But we haven't even told you what we need help with." He started getting teary and he said, "I'm sorry," and closed the door. Mr. Black said, "Onward ho." I nodded, and inside I thought, *Weird.*

> *Thank you for your letter. Because of the large*
> *volume of mail I receive, I am unable to write*
> *personal responses. Nevertheless, know that I*
> *read and save every letter, with the hope of one*
> *day being able to give each the proper response it*
> *deserves. Until that day,*
>> *Most sincerely,*
>> *Stephen Hawking*

The week was incredibly boring, except for when I remembered the key. Even though I knew that there were 161,999,999 locks in New York that it didn't open, I still felt like it opened everything. Sometimes I liked to touch it just to know that it was there, like the pepper spray I kept in my pocket. Or the opposite of that. I adjusted the string so the keys—one to the apartment, one to I-didn't-know-what—rested against my heart, which was nice, except the only thing was that it felt too cold sometimes, so I put a Band-Aid on that part of my chest, and the keys rested on that.

Monday was boring.

On Tuesday afternoon I had to go to Dr. Fein. I didn't understand why I needed help, because it seemed to me that you *should* wear heavy boots when your dad dies, and if you *aren't* wearing heavy boots, *then* you need help. But I went anyway, because the raise in my allowance depended on it.

"Hey, buddy." "Actually, I'm not your buddy." "Right. Well. It's great weather today, don't you think? If you want, we could go outside and toss a ball." "Yes to thinking it's great weather. No to wanting to toss a ball." "You sure?" "Sports aren't fascinating." "What do you find fascinating?" "What kind of answer are you looking for?" "What makes you think I'm looking for something?" "What makes you think I'm a huge moron?" "I don't think you're a huge moron. I don't think you're any kind of moron." "Thanks." "Why do you think you're here, Oskar?" "I'm here, Dr. Fein, because it upsets my mom that I'm having an impossible time with my life." "Should it upset her?" "Not really. Life is impossible." "When you say that you're having an impossible time, what do you mean?" "I'm constantly emotional." "Are you emotional right now?" "I'm extremely emotional right now." "What emotions are you feeling?" "All of them." "Like . . ." "Right now I'm feeling sadness, happiness, anger, love, guilt, joy, shame, and a little bit of humor, because part of my brain is remembering something hilarious that Toothpaste once did that I can't talk about." "Sounds like you're feeling an awful lot." "He put Ex-Lax in the *pain au chocolat* we sold at the French Club bake sale." "That *is* funny." "I'm feeling everything." "This emotionalness of yours, does it affect your daily life?" "Well, to answer your question, I don't think that's a real word you used. Emotionalness. But I understand what you were trying to say, and yes. I end up crying a lot, usually in private. It's extremely hard for me to go to school. I also can't sleep over at friends' apartments, because I get panicky about being away from Mom. I'm not very good with people." "What do you think is going on?" "I feel too much. That's what's going on." "Do you think one can feel too much? Or just feel in the wrong ways?" "My insides don't match up with my outsides." "Do anyone's insides and outsides match up?" "I don't know. I'm only me." "Maybe that's what a person's personality is: the difference between the inside and outside." "But it's worse for me." "I wonder if everyone thinks it's worse for him." "Probably. But it really is worse for me."

He sat back in his chair and put his pen on his desk. "Can I ask you a personal question?" "It's a free country." "Have you noticed any tiny hairs on your scrotum?" "Scrotum." "The scrotum is the pouch at the base of your penis that holds your testicles." "My nuts." "That's right." "Fascinating." "Go ahead and take a second to think about it. I can turn around." "I don't need to think. I don't have tiny hairs on my scrotum." He wrote something on a piece of paper. "Dr. Fein?" "Howard." "You told me to tell you when I feel self-conscious." "Yes." "I feel self-conscious." "I'm sorry. I know it was a very personal question. I only asked because sometimes, when our bodies change, we experience dramatic changes in our emotional lives. I was wondering if perhaps some of what you've been experiencing is due to changes in your body." "It isn't. It's because my dad died the most horrible death that anyone ever could invent."

He looked at me and I looked at him. I promised myself that I wouldn't be the first to look away. But, as usual, I was.

"What would you say to a little game?" "Is it a brain teaser?" "Not really." "I like brain teasers." "So do I. But this isn't a brain teaser." "Bummer." "I'm going to say a word and I want you to tell me the first thing that comes to mind. You can say a word, a person's name, or even a sound. Whatever. There are no right or wrong answers here. No rules. Should we give it a try?" I said, "Shoot." He said, "Family." I said, "Family." He said, "I'm sorry. I don't think I explained this well. I'll say a word, and you tell me the first thing you think of." I said, "You said 'family' and I thought of family." He said, "But let's try not to use the same word. OK?" "OK. I mean, yeah." "Family." "Heavy petting." "Heavy petting?" "It's when a man rubs a woman's VJ with his fingers. Right?" "Yes, that's right. OK. There are no wrong answers. How about safety?" "How about it?" "OK." "Yeah." "Bellybutton." "Bellybutton?" "Bellybutton." "I can't think of anything but bellybutton." "Give it a try. Bellybutton." "Bellybutton doesn't make me think of anything." "Dig deep." "In my bellybutton?" "In your brain, Oskar." "Uh." "Bellybutton. Bellybutton." "Stomach anus?" "Good." "Bad." "No, I meant, 'Good. You did good.'" "I did *well*." "Well." "Water." "Celebrate." "Ruff, ruff." "Was that a bark?" "Anyway." "OK. Great." "Yeah." "Dirty." "Bellybutton." "Uncomfortable." "Extremely." "Yellow." "The color of a yellow person's bellybutton." "Let's see if we can keep it to one word, though, OK?" "For a game with no rules, this game has a lot of rules." "Hurt." "Realistic." "Cucumber." "Formica." "Formica?" "Cucumber?" "Home." "Where the stuff is." "Emergency." "Dad." "Is your father the cause of the emergency, or the solution to it?" "Both." "Happiness." "Happiness. Oops. Sorry." "Happiness." "I don't know." "Try. Happiness." "Dunno." "Happiness. Dig." I shrugged my shoulders. "Happiness, happiness." "Dr. Fein?" "Howard." "Howard?" "Yes?" "I'm feeling self-conscious."

We spent the rest of the forty-five minutes talking, although I didn't have anything to say to him. I didn't want to be there. I didn't want to be anywhere that wasn't looking for the lock. When it was almost time for Mom to come in, Dr. Fein said he wanted us to make a plan for how the next week could be better than the last one. He said,

"Why don't you tell me some things you think you can do, things to keep in mind. And then next week we'll talk about how successful you were." "I'll try to go to school." "Good. Really good. What else?" "Maybe I'll try to be more patient with morons." "Good. And what else?" "I don't know, maybe I'll try not to ruin things by getting so emotional." "Anything else?" "I'll try to be nicer to my mom." "And?" "Isn't that enough?" "It is. It's more than enough. And now let me ask you, how do you think you're going to accomplish those things you mentioned?" "I'm gonna bury my feelings deep inside me." "What do you mean, bury your feelings?" "No matter how much I feel, I'm not going to let it out. If I have to cry, I'm gonna cry on the inside. If I have to bleed, I'll bruise. If my heart starts going crazy, I'm not gonna tell everyone in the world about it. It doesn't help anything. It just makes everyone's life worse." "But if you're burying your feelings deep inside you, you won't really be *you*, will you?" "So?" "Can I ask you one last question?" "Was that it?" "Do you think any good can come from your father's death?" "Do I think any *good* can come from my father's death?" "Yes. Do you think *any* good can come from your father's death?" I kicked over my chair, threw his papers across the floor, and hollered, "No! Of course not, you fucking asshole!"

That was what I wanted to do. Instead I just shrugged my shoulders.

I went out to tell Mom it was her turn. She asked me how it went. I said, "OK." She said, "Your magazines are in my bag. And a juice box." I said, "Thanks." She bent down and kissed me.

When she went in, I very quietly took the stethoscope from my field kit, got on my knees, and pressed the whatever-the-end-is-called against the door. The bulb? Dad would have known. I couldn't hear a lot, and sometimes I wasn't sure if no one was talking or if I just wasn't hearing what they were saying.

expect too much too quickly
I know
            you?
What   *me?*

you doing?

I'm not the point.

Until you're feeling   to be impossible for Oskar to

But until he's feeling   it's   to feel OK.

        don't know.   a problem.
                you?
I don't
        don't know?

                hours and hours to explain.

                you try to start?
Start   easy   do you   happy?

What's funny?

        used to be   someone   me a question, and I could say yes,
or   but   believe in short answers anymore.

Maybe   the wrong questions. Maybe   to remind
there are simple things.

What's simple?
How many fingers   holding up?
It's not that simple

I want to talk   that's not going to be easy.

        you ever considered

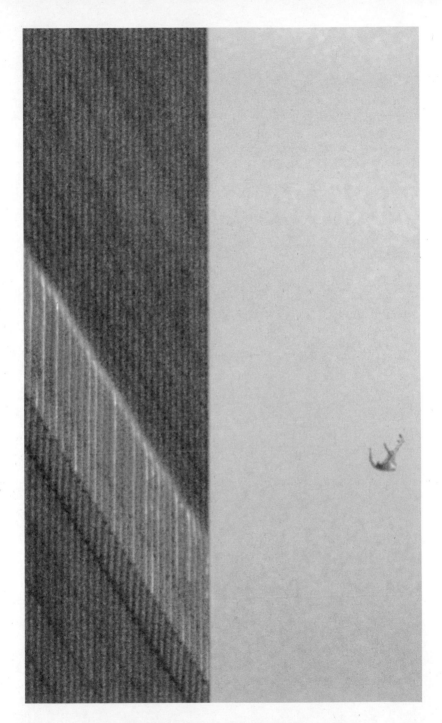

What?

    what it sounds like.   *even a hospital, in the way*
we usually think   *safe environment.*

      home is a safe environment.

Who the hell do you think you are?

I'm sorry.
              to be sorry for. You're angry.
    it's not you that   *angry*
Who are you angry at?

    good for children to be around   *going through the same process.*

Oskar isn't   *other children.*   *even like being around kids his*
own age.

      a good thing?

Oskar is Oskar, and no one   *that's a wonderful*
thing.

I'm worried that   *to himself.*

I can't believe we're talking about this.

    talk about everything,   *realize there was*
no reason to talk

    JONATHAN SAFRAN FOER

danger to himself?

I'm concerned about.   *indications of a child*

absolutely no way   *hospitalize my son.*

We were quiet on the car ride home. I turned on the radio and found a station playing "Hey Jude." It was true, I didn't want to make it bad. I wanted to take the sad song and make it better. It's just that I didn't know how.

After dinner, I went up to my room. I took the box out of the closet, and the box out of the box, and the bag, and the unfinished scarf, and the phone.

Message four. 9:46 A.M. *It's Dad. Thomas Schell. It's Thomas Schell. Hello? Can you hear me? Are you there? Pick up. Please! Pick up. I'm underneath a table. Hello? Sorry. I have a wet napkin wrapped around my face. Hello? No. Try the other. Hello? Sorry. People are getting crazy. There's a helicopter circling around, and. I think we're going to go up onto the roof. They say there's going to be some. Sort of evacuation — I don't know, try that one — they say there's going to be some sort of evacuation from up there, which makes sense if. The helicopters can get close enough. It makes sense. Please pick up. I don't know. Yeah, that one. Are you there? Try that one.*

Why didn't he say goodbye?
I gave myself a bruise.
Why didn't he say "I love you"?
Wednesday was boring.
Thursday was boring.
Friday was also boring, except that it was Friday, which meant it was almost Saturday, which meant I was that much closer to the lock, which was happiness.

WHY I'M NOT WHERE YOU ARE
4/12/78

To my child: I'm writing this from where your mother's father's shed used to stand, the shed is no longer here, no carpets cover no floors, no windows in no walls, everything has been replaced. This is a library now, that would have made your grandfather happy, as if all of his buried books were seeds, from each book came one hundred. I'm sitting at the end of a long table surrounded by encyclopedias, sometimes I take one down and read about other people's lives, kings, actreses, assassins, judges, anthropologists, tennis champions, tycoons, politicians, just because you haven't received any letters from me don't think I haven't written any. Every day I write a letter to you. Sometimes I think if I could tell you what happened to me that night, I could leave that night behind me, maybe I could come home to you, but that night has no beginning or end, it started before I was born and it's still happening. I'm writing in Dresden, and your mother is writing in the Nothing guest room, or I assume she is, I hope she is, sometimes my hand starts to burn and I am convinced we are writing the same word at the same moment. Anna gave me the typewriter your mother used to write her life story on. She gave it to me only a few weeks before the bombings, I thanked her, she said, "Why are you thanking me? It's a gift for me." "A gift for you?" "You never write to me." "But I'm with you." "So?" "You write to someone you can't be with." "You never sculpt me, but at least you could write to me." It's the tragedy of loving, you can't love anything more than something you miss. I told her, "You never write to me." She said, "You've never given me a typewriter." I started to invent future homes for us, I'd type through the night and give them to her the next day. I imagined dozens of homes, some were magical (a clock tower with a stopped clock in a city where time stood still), some were mundane (a bourgois estate in the country with rose gardens and peacocks), each felt possible and perfect, I wonder if your mother ever saw them. "Dear Anna, We will live in a home built at the top of the world's tallest ladder." "Dear Anna, We will live in a cave in a hillside in Turkey." "Dear Anna, We will live in a home with no walls, so that everywhere we go will be our home." I wasn't trying to invent better and better homes, but to show her that homes didn't matter, we could live in any home, in any city, in any country, in any century, and be happy, as if the world were just what we lived in. The night before I lost everything, I typed our last future home: "Dear Anna, We will live in a series of homes, which will climb the alps, and we'll never sleep in the same one twice. Each morning after breakfast, we'll sled down to the next home. And when we open its front door, the previous home will be destroyed and rebuilt as a new home. When we get to the bottom, we'll take a lift to the top and start again at the beginning." I went to bring it to her the next day, on my way to your mothers house, I heard a noise from the shed, from where I'm now writing this to you, I suspected it was Simon Goldberg. I knew that Anna's father had been hiding him, I had heard them talking in there some nights when Anna and I tiptoed into the fields, they were always whispering, I had seen his charcoal stained shirt on their clothesline. I didn't want to make myself known, so I quietly slid a book from the wall. Anna's father, your grandfather, was sitting in his chair with his face in his hands, he was my hero. When I think back on that moment, I never see him with his face in his hands, I won't let myself see him that way, I see the book in my hands, it was an illustrated edition of Ovid's Metamorphosis, I used to look for the edition in the States, as if by finding it I could slide it back in the shed's wall, block the image of my hero's face in his hands, stop my life and history at that moment, I asked after it in every bookshop in New York, but I never was able to find it, light poured into the room through the hole in the wall, your grandfather lifted his head, he came to the shelf and we looked at each other through the missing Metamorphosis, I asked him if something was wrong, he didn't say anything, I could see only a sliver of his face, the spine of a book of his face, we looked at each other until it felt like everything would burst into flames, it was the silence of my life, I found Anna in her room, "Hi." "Hi." "I just saw your father." "In the shed?" "He seems upset." "He doesn't want to be part of it anymore." I told her, "It will all be over soon." "How do you know?" "Everyone says so." "Everyone has always been wrong." "It will be over, and life will go back to how it was." She said, "Don't be a child." "Don't turn away from me." She wouldn't look at me. I asked, "What's happened?" I'd never seen her cry before. I told her, "Don't cry." She said, "Don't touch me." I asked, "What is it?" She said, "Will you please shut up!" We sat on her bed in silence. The silence pressed down on us like a hand. I said, "Whatever it is—" She said, "I'm pregnant." I can't write what we said to each other then. Before I left, she said, "Please be over joyed." I told her I was, of course I was, I kissed her, I kissed her stomach, that was the last time I ever saw her. At 9:30 that night, the air-raid sirens sounded, everyone went to the shelters, but no one hurried, we were use to the alarms, we assumed they were false, why would anyone want to bomb Dresden? The families on our street turned off the lights in their houses and filed into the shelter, I waited on the steps, I was thinking of Anna. It was silent and still and I couldn't see my own hands in the darkness. One hundred planes flew overhead, massive, heavy planes, pushing through the night like one hundred whales through water, they dropped clusters of red flares to light up the blackness for whatever was to come next, I was alone on the street, the red flares fell around me, thousands of them, I knew that something unimaginable was about to happen, I was thinking of Anna, I was overjoyed. I ran downstairs four steps at a time, they saw the look on my face, before I had time to say anything—what would I have said?—we heard a horrible noise, rapid, approaching explosions, like an applauding audience running toward us, then they were atop us, we were thrown to the corners, our cellar filled with fire and smoke, more powerful explosions, the walls lifted from the floor and separated just long enough to let light flood in before banging back to the ground, orange and blue explosions, violet and white, I later read that the first bombing lasted less than half an hour, but it felt like days and weeks, like the world was going to end, the bombing stopped as matter of factly as it

had began, "Are you OK?" "Are you OK?" "Are you OK?" We ran out
of the cellar, which was flooded with yellow-gray smoke, we didn't recognize anything, I had been on the stoop just half an hour before, and
now there was no stoop in front of no house on no street, only fire in
every direction, all that remained of our house was a patch of the facade
that stubbornly held up the front door, a horse on fire galloped past,
there were burning vehicles and carts with burning refugies, people
were screaming, I told my parents I had to go find Anna, my mother
told me to stay with them, I said I would meet them back at our front
door, my father begged me to stay, I grabbed the doorknob and it took
the skin off my hand, I saw the muscles of my palm, red and pulsing,
why did I grab it with my other hand? My father shouted at me, it was
the first time he had ever shouted at me, I can't write what he shouted,
I told them I would meet them back at our door, he struck me across the
face, it was the first time he had ever struck me, that was the last time I
saw my parents. On my way to Anna's house, the second raid began, I
threw myself into the nearest cellar, it was hit, it filled with pink smoke
and gold flames, so I fled into the next cellar, it caught fire, I ran from
cellar to cellar as each previous cellar was destroyed, burning monkeys
screamed from the trees, birds with their wings on fire sang from the
telephone wires over which desperate calls traveled, I found another
shelter, it was filled to the walls, brown smoke pressed down from the
ceiling like a hand, it became more and more difficult to breathe, my
lungs were trying to pull the room in through my mouth, there was a
silver explosion, all of us tried to leave the cellar at once, dead and dying
people were trampled, I walked over an old man, I walked over children, everyone was losing everyone, the bombs were like a waterfall, I
ran through the streets, from cellar to cellar, and saw terrible things:
legs and necks, I saw a woman whose blond hair and green dress were
on fire, running with a silent baby in her arms, I saw humans melted
into thick pools of liquid, three or four feet deep in places, I saw bodies
crackling like embers, laughing, and the remains of masses of people
who had tried to escape the firestorm by jumping head first into the
lakes and ponds, the parts of their bodies that were submerged in the
water were still intact, while the parts that protruded above water were

JONATHAN SAFRAN FOER

charred beyond recognition, the bombs kept falling, purple, orange and white, I kept running, my hands kept bleeding, through the sounds of collapsing buildings I heard the roar of that baby's silence. I passed the zoo, the cages had been ripped open, everything was everywhere, dazed animals cried in pain and confusion, one of the keepers was calling out for help, he was a strong man, his eyes had been burnt closed, he grabbed my arm and asked me if I knew how to fire a gun, I told him I had to get to someone, he handed me his rifle and said, "You've got to find the carnivores," I told him I wasn't a good shot, I told him I didn't know which were carnivores and which weren't, he said, "Shoot everything," I don't know how many animals I killed, I killed an elephant, it had been thrown twenty yards from its cage, I pressed the rifle to the back of its head and wondered, as I squeezed the trigger, Is it necessary to kill this animal? I killed an ape that was perched on the stump of a fallen tree, pulling its hair as it surveyed the destruction, I killed two lions, they were standing side by side facing west, were they related, were they friends, mates, can lions love? I killed a cub that was climbing atop a massive dead bear, was it climbing atop its parent? I killed a camel with twelve bullets, I suspected it wasn't a carnivore, but I was killing everything, everything had to be killed, a rhinoceros was banging its head against a rock, again and again, as if to put itself out of its suffering, or to make itself suffer, I fired at it, it kept banging its head, I fired again, it banged harder, I walked up to it and pressed the gun between its eyes, I killed it, I killed a zebra, I killed a giraffe, I turned the water of the sea lion's tank red, an ape approached me, it was the ape I had shot before, I'd thought I'd killed it, it walked up to me slowly, its hands covering its ears, what did it want from me, I screamed, "What do you want from me?" I shot it again, where I thought its heart was, it looked at me, in its eyes I was sure I saw some form of understanding, but I didn't see forgiveness, I tried to shoot the vultures, but I wasn't a good enough shot, later I saw vultures fattening themselves on the human carnage, and I blamed myself for everything. The second bombing halted as suddenly and totally as it had begun, with burnt hair, with black arms and black fingers, I walked, dazed, to the base of the Loschwitz Bridge, I submerged my black hands in the black water and saw my reflection, I was terrified of my own image, my blood-matted hair, my split and bleeding lips, my red, pulsing palms, which, even as I write this, thirty-five years later, don't look like they should be at the ends of my arms. I remember losing my balance, I remember a single thought in my head: *Keep thinking.* As long as I am thinking, I am alive, but at some point I stopped thinking, the next thing I remember is feeling terribly cold, I realized I was lying on the ground, the pain was complete, it let me know I hadn't died, I started moving my legs and arms, my movements must have been noticed by one of the soldiers that had been put into action all over the city, looking for survivors, I later learned that there had been more than 220 bodies taken from the foot of the bridge, and 4 came back to life, I was one of them. They loaded us onto trucks and took us out of Dresden, I looked out from the flaps of canvas that covered the sides of the truck, the buildings were burning, the trees burning, the asphalt, I saw and heard humans trapped, I smelled them, standing in the moltin, burning streets like living torches, screaming for help that was impossible to give, the air itself was burning, the truck had to make a number of detours to get beyond the chaos, planes bore down on us once more, we were pulled off the truck and placed under it, the planes dove, more machine guns, more bombs, yellow, red, green, blue, brown, I lost consciousness again, when I awoke I was in a white hospital bed, I couldn't move my arms or legs, I wondered if I had lost them, but I couldn't summon the energy to look for myself, hours passed, or days, when I finally looked down, I saw that I was strapped to the bed, a nurse was standing beside me, I asked, "Why have you done this to me?" She told me I had been trying to hurt myself, I asked her to free me, she said she couldn't, she said I would hurt myself, I begged her to free me, I told her I wouldn't hurt myself, I promised, she apologized and touched me, doctors operated on me, they gave me injections and bandaged my body, but it was her touch that saved my life. In the days and weeks after my release, I looked for my parents and for Anna and for you. Everyone was looking for everyone in the rubble of every building, but all of the searching was in vain, I found our old house, the door was still stubbornly standing, a few of our belongings survived, the typewriter survived, I carried it in my arms

JONATHAN SAFRAN FOER

like a baby, before I was evacuated I wrote on the door that I was alive, and the address of the refugee camp in Oschatz, I waited for a letter, but no letter ever came. Because there were so many bodies, and because so many of the bodies had been destroyed there was never a list of the dead, thousands of people were left to suffer hope. When I had thought I was dying at the base of the Loschwitz Bridge, there was a single thought in my head: *Keep thinking.* Thinking would keep me alive. But now I am alive, and thinking is killing me. I think and think and think. I can't stop thinking about that night, the clusters of red flares, the sky that was like black water, and how only hours before I lost everything, I had everything. Your aunt had told me she was pregnant, I was overjoyed, I should have known not to trust it, one hundred years of joy can be erased in one second, I kissed her belly, even though there was nothing yet to kiss, I told her, "I love our baby." That made her laugh, I hadn't heard her laugh like that since the day we walked into each other halfway between our houses, she said, "You love an idea." I told her, "I love our idea." That was the point, we were having an idea together. She asked, "Are you afraid?" "Afraid of what?" She said, "Life is scarier than death." I took the future home from my pocket and gave it to her, I kissed her, I kissed her stomach, that was the last time I ever saw her, I was at the end of the path when I heard her father. He came out of the shed. "I almost forgot!" he called to me. "There's a letter here for you. It was delivered yesterday. I almost forgot." He ran into the house and came back out with an envelope. "I almost forgot," he said, his eyes were red, his knuckles were white, I later learned that he survived the bombing and then killed himself. Did your mother tell you that? Does she know it herself? He handed a letter to me. It was from Simon Goldberg. The letter had been posted from Westerbork transit camp in Holland, that's where the Jews from our region were sent, from there they went either to work or to their deaths. "Dear Thomas Schell, It was a pleasure meeting you, however briefly. For reasons that need not be explained, you made a strong impression on me. It is my great hope that our paths, however long and winding, will cross again. Until that day, I wish the best for you in these difficult times. Yours most sincerely, Simon Goldberg." I put the letter back in the envelope and the envelope in my pocket, where the future home had been, I heard your grandfather's voice as I walked away, he was still at the door, "I almost forgot." When your mother found me in the bakery on Broadway, I wanted to tell her everything, maybe if I'd been able to, we could have lived differently, maybe I'd be there with you now instead of here. Maybe if I had said, "I lost a baby," if I'd said, "I'm so afraid of losing something I love that I refuse to love anything," maybe that would have made the impossible possible. Maybe, but I couldn't do it, I had buried too much too deeply inside me. And here I am, instead of there. I'm sitting in this library, thousands of miles from my life, writing another letter I know I won't be able to send, no matter how hard I try and how much I want to. How did that boy making love behind that shed become this man writing this letter at this table?

I love you,
Your father

THE SIXTH BOROUGH

"Once upon a time, New York City had a sixth borough." "What's a borough?" "That's what I call an interruption." "I know, but the story won't make any sense to me if I don't know what a borough is." "It's like a neighborhood. Or a collection of neighborhoods." "So if there was once a sixth borough, then what are the five boroughs?" "Manhattan, obviously, Brooklyn, Queens, Staten Island, and the Bronx." "Have I ever been to any of the other boroughs?" "Here we go." "I just want to know." "We went to the Bronx Zoo once, a few years ago. Remember that?" "No." "And we've been to Brooklyn to see the roses at the Botanic Garden." "Have I been to Queens?" "I don't think so." "Have I been to Staten Island?" "No." "Was there *really* a sixth borough?" "I've been trying to tell you." "No more interruptions. I promise."

"Well, you won't read about it in any of the history books, because there's nothing—save for the circumstantial evidence in Central Park—to prove that it was there at all. Which makes its existence very easy to dismiss. But even though most people will say they have no time for or reason to believe in the Sixth Borough, and *don't* believe in the Sixth Borough, they will still use the word 'believe.'

"The Sixth Borough was also an island, separated from Manhattan by a thin body of water whose narrowest crossing happened to equal the world's long jump record, such that exactly one person on earth could go from Manhattan to the Sixth Borough without getting wet. A huge party was made of the yearly leap. Bagels were strung from island to island on special spaghetti, samosas were bowled at baguettes, Greek salads were thrown like confetti. The children of New York captured fireflies in glass jars, which they floated between the boroughs. The bugs would slowly asphyxiate—" "Asphyxiate?" "Suffocate." "Why didn't they just punch holes into the lids?" "The fireflies would flicker rapidly for their last few minutes of life. If it was timed right, the river shimmered as the jumper crossed it." "*Cool.*"

"When the time finally came, the long jumper would begin his approach from the East River. He would run the entire width of Manhattan, as New Yorkers rooted him on from opposite sides of the street, from the windows of their apartments and offices, and from the branches of trees. Second Avenue, Third Avenue, Lexington, Park, Madison, Fifth Avenue, Columbus, Amsterdam, Broadway, Seventh, Eighth, Ninth, Tenth . . . And when he leapt, New Yorkers cheered from the banks of both Manhattan and the Sixth Borough, cheering the jumper on and cheering each other on. For those few moments that the jumper was in the air, every New Yorker felt capable of flight.

"Or maybe 'suspension' is a better word. Because what was so inspiring about the leap was not how the jumper got from one borough to the other, but how he stayed between them for so long." "That's true."

"One year—many, many years ago—the end of the jumper's big toe skimmed the surface of the river, causing a little ripple. People gasped as the ripple traveled out from the Sixth Borough back toward Manhattan, knocking the jars of fireflies against one another like wind chimes.

"'You must have gotten a bad start!' a Manhattan councilman hollered from across the water.

"The jumper shook his head, more confused than ashamed.

"'You had the wind in your face,' a Sixth Borough councilman suggested, offering a towel for the jumper's foot.

"The jumper shook his head.

"'Perhaps he ate too much for lunch,' said one onlooker to another.

"'Or maybe he's past his prime,' said another, who'd brought his kids to watch the leap.

"'I bet his heart wasn't in it,' said another. 'You just can't expect to jump that far without some serious feeling.'

"'No,' the jumper said to all of the speculation. 'None of that's right. I jumped just fine.'

"The revelation—" "Revelation?" "Realization." "Oh yeah." "It traveled across the onlookers like the ripple caused by the toe, and when the mayor of New York City spoke it aloud, everyone sighed in agreement: 'The Sixth Borough is moving.'" "*Moving!*"

"A millimeter at a time, the Sixth Borough receded from New York. One year, the long jumper's entire foot got wet, and after a number of years, his shin, and after many, many years—so many years that no one could remember what it was like to celebrate without anxiety— the jumper had to reach out his arms and grab at the Sixth Borough fully extended, and then he couldn't touch it at all. The eight bridges between Manhattan and the Sixth Borough strained and finally crumbled, one at a time, into the water. The tunnels were pulled too thin to hold anything at all.

"The phone and electrical lines snapped, requiring Sixth Boroughers to revert to old-fashioned technologies, most of which resembled children's toys: they used magnifying glasses to reheat their carryout; they folded important documents into paper airplanes and threw them from one office building into another; those fireflies in glass jars, which had once been used merely for decorative purposes during the festivals of the leap, were now found in every room of every home, taking the place of artificial light.

"The very same engineers who dealt with the Leaning Tower of Pisa . . . which was where?" "*Italy!*" "Right. They were brought over to assess the situation.

" 'It wants to go,' they said.

" 'Well, what can you say about that?' the mayor of New York asked.

"To which they replied: 'There's nothing to say about that.'

"Of course they tried to save it. Although 'save' might not be the right word, as it did seem to want to go. Maybe 'detain' is the right word. Chains were moored to the banks of the islands, but the links soon snapped. Concrete pilings were poured around the perimeter of the Sixth Borough, but they, too, failed. Harnesses failed, magnets failed, even prayer failed.

"Young friends, whose string-and-tin-can phone extended from is land to island, had to pay out more and more string, as if letting kites go higher and higher.

"'It's getting almost impossible to hear you,' said the young girl from her bedroom in Manhattan as she squinted through a pair of her father's binoculars, trying to find her friend's window.

"'I'll holler if I have to,' said her friend from his bedroom in the Sixth Borough, aiming last birthday's telescope at her apartment.

"The string between them grew incredibly long, so long it had to be extended with many other strings tied together: his yo-yo string, the pull from her talking doll, the twine that had fastened his father's diary, the waxy string that had kept her grandmother's pearls around her neck and off the floor, the thread that had separated his great-uncle's childhood quilt from a pile of rags. Contained within everything they shared with one another were the yo-yo, the doll, the diary, the necklace, and the quilt. They had more and more to tell each other, and less and less string.

"The boy asked the girl to say 'I love you' into her can, giving her no further explanation.

"And she didn't ask for any, or say 'That's silly,' or 'We're too young for love,' or even suggest that she was saying 'I love you' because he asked her to. Instead she said, 'I love you.' The words traveled the yo-yo, the doll, the diary, the necklace, the quilt, the clothesline, the birthday present, the harp, the tea bag, the tennis racket, the hem of the skirt he one day should have pulled from her body." "*Grody!*" "The boy covered his can with a lid, removed it from the string, and put her love for him on a shelf in his closet. Of course, he never could open the can, because then he would lose its contents. It was enough just to know it was there.

"Some, like that boy's family, wouldn't leave the Sixth Borough. Some said, 'Why should we? It's the rest of the world that's moving. Our borough is fixed. Let them leave Manhattan.' How can you prove someone like that wrong? And who would want to?" "I wouldn't." "Neither would I. For most Sixth Boroughers, though, there was no question of refusing to accept the obvious, just as there was no underlying stubbornness, or principle, or bravery. They just didn't want to go.

They liked their lives and didn't want to change. So they floated away, one millimeter at a time.

"All of which brings us to Central Park. Central Park didn't used to be where it is now." "You just mean in the story, right?"

"It used to rest squarely in the center of the Sixth Borough. It was the joy of the borough, its heart. But once it was clear that the Sixth Borough was receding for good, that it couldn't be saved or detained, it was decided, by New York City referendum, to salvage the park." "Referendum?" "Vote." "And?" "And it was unanimous. Even the most stubborn Sixth Boroughers acknowledged what must be done.

"Enormous hooks were driven through the easternmost grounds, and the park was pulled by the people of New York, like a rug across a floor, from the Sixth Borough into Manhattan.

"Children were allowed to lie down on the park as it was being moved. This was considered a concession, although no one knew why a concession was necessary, or why it was to children that this concession must be made. The biggest fireworks show in history lit the skies of New York City that night, and the Philharmonic played its heart out.

"The children of New York lay on their backs, body to body, filling every inch of the park, as if it had been designed for them and that moment. The fireworks sprinkled down, dissolving in the air just before they reached the ground, and the children were pulled, one millimeter and one second at a time, into Manhattan and adulthood. By the time the park found its current resting place, every single one of the children had fallen asleep, and the park was a mosaic of their dreams. Some hollered out, some smiled unconsciously, some were perfectly still."

"Dad?" "Yes?" "I know there wasn't really a sixth borough. I mean, objectively." "Are you an optimist or a pessimist?" "I can't remember. Which?" "Do you know what those words mean?" "Not really." "An optimist is positive and hopeful. A pessimist is negative and cynical." "I'm an optimist." "Well, that's good, because there's no irrefutable evidence. There's nothing that could convince someone who doesn't want to be convinced. But there is an abundance of clues that would give the wanting believer something to hold on to." "Like what?" "Like the peculiar fossil record of Central Park. Like the incongruous pH of the reservoir. Like the placement of certain tanks at the zoo, which correspond to the holes left by the gigantic hooks that pulled the park from borough to borough." "Jose."

"There is a tree—just twenty-four paces due east of the entrance to the merry-go-round—into whose trunk are carved two names. There is no record of them in the phone books or censuses. They are absent from all hospital and tax and voting documentation. There is no evidence whatsoever of their existence, other than the proclamation on the tree. Here's a fact you might find fascinating: no less than five percent of the names carved into the trees of Central Park are of unknown origin." "That *is* fascinating."

"As all of the Sixth Borough's documents floated away with the Sixth Borough, we will never be able to prove that those names belonged to residents of the Sixth Borough, and were carved when Central Park still resided there, instead of in Manhattan. Some people believe they are made-up names and, to take the doubt a step further, that the gestures of love were made-up gestures. Others believe other things." "What do you believe?"

"Well, it's hard for anyone, even the most pessimistic of pessimists, to spend more than a few minutes in Central Park without feeling that he or she is experiencing some tense in addition to the present, right?" "I *guess.*" "Maybe we're just missing things we've lost, or hoping for what we want to come. Or maybe it's the residue of the dreams from that night the park was moved. Maybe we miss what those children had lost, and hope for what they hoped for."

"And what about the Sixth Borough?" "What do you mean?" "What happened to it?" "Well, there's a gigantic hole in the middle of it where Central Park used to be. As the island moves across the planet, it acts like a frame, displaying what lies beneath it." "Where is it now?" "Antarctica." "Really?"

"The sidewalks are covered in ice, the stained glass of the public library is straining under the weight of the snow. There are frozen fountains in frozen neighborhood parks, where frozen children are frozen at the peaks of their swings—the frozen ropes holding them in flight. Livery horses—" "What's that?" "The horses that pull the carriages in the park." "They're inhumane." "They're frozen mid-trot. Flea-market vendors are frozen mid-haggle. Middle-aged women are frozen in the middle of their lives. The gavels of frozen judges are frozen between guilt and innocence. On the ground are the crystals of the frozen first breaths of babies, and those of the last gasps of the dying. On a frozen shelf, in a closet frozen shut, is a can with a voice in it."

"Dad?" "Yeah?" "This isn't an interruption, but are you done?" "The end." "That story was really awesome." "I'm glad you think so." "*Awesome.*

"Dad?" "Yeah?" "I just thought of something. Do you think any of those things I dug up in Central Park were actually from the Sixth Borough?"

He shrugged his shoulders, which I loved.

"Dad?" "Yeah, buddy?" "Nothing."

MY FEELINGS

I was in the guest room when it happened.   I was watching the television and knitting you a white scarf.   The news was on.   Time was passing like a hand waving from a train that I wanted to be on.   You'd only just left for school, and I was already waiting for you.   I hope you never think about anything as much as I think about you.

I remember they were interviewing the father of a missing girl.

I remember his eyebrows.   I remember his sadly cleanly shaven face.

Do you still believe that she will be found alive?

I do.

Sometimes I was looking at the television.

Sometimes I was looking at my hands knitting your scarf.

Sometimes out the window at your window.

Are there any new leads in the case?

Not to my knowledge.

But you continue to believe.

Yes.

What would it take for you to give up?

Why was it necessary to torture him?

He touched his forehead and said, It would take a body.

The woman asking the questions touched her ear.

She said, I am sorry.   One second.

She said, Something has happened in New York.

The father of the missing girl touched his chest and looked past the camera.   At his wife?   At someone he didn't know?   At something he wanted to see?

Maybe it sounds strange, but I didn't feel anything when they showed the burning building.　　I wasn't even surprised.　　I kept knitting for you, and I kept thinking about the father of the missing girl.　　He kept believing.

Smoke kept pouring from a hole in the building.

Black smoke.

I remember the worst storm of my childhood.　　From my window I saw the books pulled from my father's shelves.　　They flew.　　A tree that was older than any person tipped away from our house.　　But it could have been the other way.

When the second plane hit, the woman who was giving the news started to scream.

A ball of fire rolled out of the building and up.

One million pieces of paper filled the sky.　　They stayed there, like a ring around the building.　　Like the rings of Saturn.　　The rings of coffee staining my father's desk.　　The ring Thomas told me he didn't need.　　I told him he wasn't the only one who needed.

The next morning my father had us carve our names into the stump of the tree that fell away from our house.　　We were giving thanks.

Your mother called.

Are you watching the news?

Yes.

Have you heard from Thomas?

No.

I haven't heard from him either.　I'm worried.

Why are you worried?

I told you.　　I haven't heard from him.

But he's at the store.

He had a meeting in that building and I haven't heard from him.

I turned my head and thought I would vomit.

I dropped the phone, ran to the toilet, and vomited.

I wouldn't ruin the rug.　　That's who I am.

I called your mother back.

She told me you were at home.　　She had just spoken to you.

I told her I would go over and watch you.

Don't let him see the news.

OK.

If he asks anything, just let him know that it will be OK.

I told her, It will be OK.

She said, The subways are a mess.   I'm going to walk home.   I should be there in an hour.

She said, I love you.

She had been married to your father for twelve years.   I had known her for fifteen years.   It was the first time she told me she loved me. That was when I knew that she knew.

I ran across the street.

The doorman said you'd gone up ten minutes before.

He asked if I was all right.

I nodded.

What happened to your arm?

I looked at my arm.   It was bleeding through my shirt.   Had I fallen and not noticed?   Had I been scratching it?   That was when I knew that I knew.

No one answered the door when I rang, so I used my key.

I called to you.

Oskar!

You were silent, but I knew you were there.   I could feel you.

Oskar!

I looked in the coat closet.   I looked behind the sofa.   A Scrabble board was on the coffee table.   Words were running into each other. I went to your room.   It was empty.   I looked in your closet.   You weren't there.   I went to your parents' room.   I knew you were some-where.   I looked in your father's closet.   I touched the tuxedo that was over his chair.   I put my hands in its pockets.   He had his father's hands.   Your grandfather's hands.   Will you have those hands?   The pockets reminded me.

I went back to your room and lay down on your bed.

I couldn't see the stars on your ceiling because the lights were on.

I thought about the walls of the house I grew up in.   My fingerprints. When the walls collapsed, my fingerprints collapsed.

I heard you breathing beneath me.

Oskar?

I got on the ground.   On my hands and knees.

Is there room for two under there?

No.

Are you sure?

Positive.

Would it be all right if I tried?

I guess.

I could only barely squeeze myself under the bed.

We lay there on our backs.   There wasn't enough room to turn to face each other.   None of the light could reach us.

How was school?

It was OK.

You got there on time?

I was early.

So you waited outside?

Yeah.

What did you do?

I read.

What?

What what?

What did you read?

A Brief History of Time.

Is it any good?

That's not really a question you can ask about it.

And your walk home?

It was OK.

It's beautiful weather.

Yeah.

I can't remember more beautiful weather than this.

That's true.

It's a shame to be inside.

I guess so.

But here we are.

I wanted to turn to face you, but I couldn't.   I moved my hand to touch your hand.

They let you out of school?

Practically immediately.

Do you know what happened?

Yeah.

Have you heard from Mom or Dad?

Mom.

What did she say?

She said everything was fine and she would be home soon.

Dad will be home soon, too.   Once he can close up the store.

Yeah.

You pressed your palms into the bed like you were trying to lift it off us.

I wanted to tell you something, but I didn't know what.   I just knew there was something I needed to tell you.

Do you want to show me your stamps?

No thank you.

Or we could do some thumb wars.

Maybe later.

Are you hungry?

No.

Do you want to just wait here for Mom and Dad to come home?

I guess so.

Do you want me to wait here with you?

It's OK.

Are you sure?

Positive.

Can I please, Oskar?

OK.

Sometimes I felt like the space was collapsing onto us.   Someone was on the bed.   Mary jumping.   Your father sleeping.   Anna kissing me. I felt buried.   Anna holding the sides of my face.   My father pinching my cheeks.   Everything on top of me.

When your mother came home, she gave you such a fierce hug.   I wanted to protect you from her.

She asked if your father had called.

No.

Are there any messages on the phone?

No.

You asked her if your father was in the building for a meeting.

She told you no.

You tried to find her eyes, and that was when I knew that you knew.

She called the police.   It was busy.   She called again.   It was busy.

She kept calling.   When it wasn't busy, she asked to speak to someone.

There was no one to speak to.

You went to the bathroom.   I told her to control herself.   At least in front of you.

She called the newspapers.   They didn't know anything.

She called the fire department.

No one knew anything.

All afternoon I knitted that scarf for you.   It grew longer and longer.

Your mother closed the windows, but we could still smell the smoke.

She asked me if I thought we should make posters.

I said it might be a good idea.

That made her cry, because she had been depending on me.

The scarf grew longer and longer.

She used the picture from your vacation.   From only two weeks be-fore.   It was you and your father.   When I saw it, I told her she shouldn't use a picture that had your face in it.   She said she wasn't going to use the whole picture.   Only your father's face.

I told her, Still, it isn't a good idea.

She said, There are more important things to worry about.

Just use a different picture.

Let it go, Mom.

She had never called me Mom.

There are so many pictures to choose from.

Mind your own business.

This is my business.

We were not angry at each other.

I don't know how much you understood, but probably you understood everything.

She took the posters downtown that afternoon.   She filled a rolling suitcase with them.   I thought of your grandfather.   I wondered where he was at that moment.   I didn't know if I wanted him to be suffering.

She took a stapler.   And a box of staples.   And tape.   I think of those things now.   The paper, the stapler, the staples, the tape.   It makes me sick.   Physical things.   Forty years of loving someone becomes staples and tape.

It was just the two of us.   You and me.

We played games in the living room.   You made jewelry.   The scarf grew longer and longer.   We went for a walk in the park.   We didn't talk about what was on top of us.   What was pinning us down like a ceiling.   When you fell asleep with your head on my lap, I turned on the television.

I lowered the volume until it was silent.

The same pictures over and over.

Planes going into buildings.

Bodies falling.

People waving shirts out of high windows.

Planes going into buildings.

Bodies falling.

Planes going into buildings.

People covered in gray dust.

Bodies falling.

Buildings falling.

Planes going into buildings.

Planes going into buildings.

Buildings falling.

People waving shirts out of high windows.

Bodies falling.

Planes going into buildings.

Sometimes I felt your eyelids flickering.   Were you awake?   Or dreaming?

Your mother came home late that night.   The suitcase was empty.

She hugged you until you said, You're hurting me.

She called everyone your father knew, and everyone who might know something.   She told them, I'm sorry to wake you.   I wanted to shout into her ear, Don't be sorry!

She kept touching her eyes, although there were no tears.

They thought there would be thousands of injured people.   Unconscious people.   People without memories.   They thought there would be thousands of bodies.   They were going to put them in an ice-skating rink.

Remember when we went skating a few months ago and I turned around, because I told you that watching people skate gave me a headache?   I saw rows of bodies under the ice.

Your mother told me I could go home.

I told her I didn't want to.

She said, Have something to eat.   Try to sleep.

I won't be able to eat or sleep.

She said, I need to sleep.

I told her I loved her.

That made her cry, because she had been depending on me.

I went back across the street.

Planes going into buildings.

Bodies falling.

Planes going into buildings.

Buildings falling.

Planes going into buildings.

Planes going into buildings.

Planes going into buildings.

When I no longer had to be strong in front of you, I became very weak. I brought myself to the ground, which was where I belonged.   I hit the floor with my fists.   I wanted to break my hands, but when it hurt too much, I stopped.   I was too selfish to break my hands for my only child.

Bodies falling.

Staples and tape.

I didn't feel empty.   I wished I'd felt empty.

People waving shirts out of high windows.

I wanted to be empty like an overturned pitcher.   But I was full like a stone.

Planes going into buildings.

I had to go to the bathroom.   I didn't want to get up.   I wanted to lie in my own waste, which is what I deserved.   I wanted to be a pig in my own filth.   But I got up and went to the bathroom.   That's who I am.

Bodies falling.

Buildings falling.

The rings of the tree that fell away from our house.

I wanted so much for it to be me under the rubble.   Even for a minute.
A second.   It was as simple as wanting to take his place.   And it was
more complicated than that.

The television was the only light.

Planes going into buildings.

Planes going into buildings.

I thought it would feel different.   But even then I was me.

Oskar, I'm remembering you onstage in front of all of those strangers.
I wanted to say to them, He's mine.   I wanted to stand up and shout,
That beautiful person is mine!   Mine!

When I was watching you, I was so proud and so sad.

Alas.   His lips.   Your songs.

When I looked at you, my life made sense.   Even the bad things made
sense.   They were necessary to make you possible.

Alas.   Your songs.

My parents' lives made sense.

My grandparents'.

Even Anna's life.

But I knew the truth, and that's why I was so sad.

Every moment before this one depends on this one.

Everything in the history of the world can be proven wrong in one moment.

Your mother wanted to have a funeral, even though there was no body.
What could anyone say?

We all rode in the limousine together.   I could not stop touching you.
I could not touch you enough.   I needed more hands.   You made
jokes with the driver, but I could see that inside you were suffering.
Making him laugh was how you suffered.   When we got to the grave
and they lowered the empty coffin, you let out a noise like an animal.   I
had never heard anything like it.   You were a wounded animal.   The
noise is still in my ears.   It was what I had spent forty years looking for,
what I wanted my life and life story to be.   Your mother took you to

the side and held you.   They shoveled dirt into your father's grave.
Onto my son's empty coffin.   There was nothing there.
All of my sounds were locked inside me.
The limousine took us home.
Everyone was silent.
When we got to my building, you walked me to the front door.
The doorman said there was a letter for me.
I told him I'd look at it tomorrow or the next day.
The doorman said the person had just dropped it off.
I said, Tomorrow.
The doorman said, He seemed desperate.
I asked you to read it for me.   I said, My eyes are crummy.
You opened it.
I'm sorry, you said.
Why are you sorry?
No, that's what it says.
I took it from you and looked at it.
When your grandfather left me forty years ago, I erased all of his writing.   I washed the words from the mirrors and the floors.   I painted over the walls.   I cleaned the shower curtains.   I even refinished the floors.   It took me as long as I had known him to get rid of all of his words.   Like turning an hourglass over.
I thought he had to look for what he was looking for, and realize it no longer existed, or never existed.   I thought he would write.   Or send money.   Or ask for pictures of the baby, if not me.
For forty years not a word.
Only empty envelopes.
And then, on the day of my son's funeral, two words.
I'm sorry.
He had come back.

ALIVE AND ALONE

We had been searching together for six and a half months when Mr. Black told me he was finished, and then I was all alone again, and I hadn't accomplished anything, and my boots were the heaviest they'd ever been in my life. I couldn't talk to Mom, obviously, and even though Toothpaste and The Minch were my best friends, I couldn't talk to them either. Grandpa could talk to animals, but I couldn't, so Buckminster wasn't going to be helpful. I didn't respect Dr. Fein, and it would have taken too long to explain to Stan everything that needed to be explained just to get to the beginning of the story, and I didn't believe in talking to dead people.

Farley didn't know if Grandma was home, because his shift had just started. He asked if something was wrong. I told him, "I need her." "You want I should buzz up?" "It's OK." As I ran up the seventy-two stairs, I thought, *And anyway, he was an incredibly old guy who slowed me down and didn't know anything useful.* I was breathing hard when I rang her bell. *I'm glad he said he was finished. I don't know why I invited him to come along with me in the first place.* She didn't answer, so I rang again. *Why isn't she waiting by the door? I'm the only thing that matters to her.*

I let myself in.

"Grandma? Hello? Grandma?"

I figured maybe she went to the store or something, so I sat on the sofa and waited. Maybe she went to the park for a walk to help her digest, which I know she sometimes did, even though it made me feel weird. Or maybe she was getting some dehydrated ice cream for me, or dropping something off at the post office. But who would she send letters to?

Even though I didn't want to, I started inventing.

She'd been hit by a cab while she was crossing Broadway, and the cab zoomed away, and everybody looked at her from the sidewalk, but no one helped her, because everyone was afraid to do CPR the wrong way.

She'd fallen from a ladder at the library and cracked her skull. She was bleeding to death there because it was in a section of books that no one ever looked at.

She was unconscious at the bottom of the swimming pool at the Y. Kids were swimming thirteen feet above her.

I tried to think about other things. I tried to invent optimistic inventions. But the pessimistic ones were extremely loud.

She'd had a heart attack.

Someone had pushed her onto the tracks.

She'd been raped and murdered.

I started looking around her apartment for her.

"Grandma?"

What I needed to hear was "I'm OK," but what I heard was nothing.

I looked in the dining room and the kitchen. I opened the door to the pantry, just in case, but there was only food. I looked in the coat closet and the bathroom. I opened the door of the second bedroom, where Dad used to sleep and dream when he was my age.

It was my first time being in Grandma's apartment without her, and it felt incredibly weird, like looking at her clothes without her in them, which I did when I went to her bedroom and looked in her closet. I opened the top drawer of the dresser, even though I knew she wouldn't be in there, obviously. So why did I do it?

It was filled with envelopes. Hundreds of them. They were tied together in bundles. I opened the next drawer down, and it was also filled with envelopes. So was the drawer underneath it. All of them were.

I saw from the postmarks that the envelopes were organized chronologically, which means by date, and mailed from Dresden, Germany, which is where she came from. There was one for every day, from May 31, 1963, to the worst day. Some were addressed "To my unborn child." Some were addressed "To my child."

What the?

I knew I probably shouldn't have, because they didn't belong to me, but I opened one of them.

It was sent on February 6, 1972. "To my child." It was empty.

I opened another, from another stack. November 22, 1986. "To my child." Also empty.

June 14, 1963. "To my unborn child." Empty.

April 2, 1979. Empty.

I found the day I was born. Empty.

What I needed to know was, where did she put all of the letters?

I heard a sound from one of the other rooms. I quickly closed the drawers, so Grandma wouldn't know I had been snooping around, and tiptoed to the front door, because I was afraid that maybe what I had heard was a burglar. I heard the sound again, and this time I could tell that it was coming from the guest room.

I thought, *The renter!*

I thought, *He's real!*

I'd never loved Grandma more than I loved her right then.

I turned around, tiptoed to the guest room door, and pressed my ear against it. I didn't hear anything. But when I got down on my knees, I saw that the light in the room was on. I stood up.

"Grandma?" I whispered. "Are you in there?"

Nothing.

"Grandma?"

I heard an extremely tiny sound. I got down on my knees again, and this time I saw that the light was off.

"Is someone in there? I'm eight years old and I'm looking for my grandma because I need her desperately."

Footsteps came to the door, but I could only barely hear them because they were extremely gentle and because of the carpet. The footsteps stopped. I could hear breathing, but I knew it wasn't Grandma's, because it was heavier and slower. Something touched the door. A hand? Two hands?

"Hello?"

The doorknob turned.

"If you're a burglar, please don't murder me."

The door opened.

A man stood there without saying anything, and it was obvious he wasn't a burglar. He was incredibly old and had a face like the opposite of Mom's, because it seemed like it was frowning even when it wasn't frowning. He was wearing a white short-sleeve shirt, so you could see his elbows were hairy, and he had a gap between his two front teeth, like Dad had.

"Are you the renter?"

He concentrated for a second, and then he closed the door.

"Hello?"

I heard him moving stuff around in the room, and then he came back and opened the door again. He was holding a little book. He opened it to the first page, which was blank. "I don't speak," he wrote, "I'm sorry."

"Who are you?" He went to the next page and wrote, "My name is Thomas." "That was my dad's name. It's pretty common. He died." On the next page he wrote, "I'm sorry." I told him, "You didn't kill my dad." On the next page there was a picture of a doorknob, for some reason, so he went to the page after that and wrote, "I'm still sorry." I told him, "Thanks." He flipped back a couple of pages and pointed at "I'm sorry."

We stood there. He was in the room. I was in the hall. The door was open, but it felt like there was an invisible door between us, because I didn't know what to say to him, and he didn't know what to write to me. I told him, "I'm Oskar," and I gave him my card. "Do you know where my grandma is?" He wrote, "She went out." "Where?" He shrugged his shoulders, just like Dad used to. "Do you know when she'll be back?" He shrugged his shoulders. "I need her."

He was on one kind of carpet, I was on another. The line where they came together reminded me of a place that wasn't in any borough.

"If you want to come in," he wrote, "we could wait for her together." I asked him if he was a stranger. He asked me what I meant. I told him, "I wouldn't go in with a stranger." He didn't write anything, like he didn't know if he was a stranger or not. "Are you older than seventy?" He showed me his left hand, which had YES tattooed on it. "Do you have a criminal record?" He showed me his right hand, which had

NO. "What other languages do you speak?" He wrote, "German. Greek. Latin." *"Parlez-vous français?"* He opened and closed his left hand, which I think meant *un peu*.

I went in.

There was writing on the walls, writing everywhere, like, "I wanted so much to have a life," and "Even just once, even for a second." I hoped, for his sake, that Grandma never saw it. He put down the book and picked up another one, for some reason.

"For how long have you been living here?" I asked. He wrote, "How long did your grandmother tell you I've been living here?" "Well," I said, "since Dad died, I guess, so about two years." He opened his left hand. "Where were you before that?" "Where did your grandmother tell you I was before that?" "She didn't." "I wasn't here." I thought that was a weird answer, but I was getting used to weird answers.

He wrote, "Do you want something to eat?" I told him no. I didn't like how much he was looking at me, because it made me feel incredibly self-conscious, but there was nothing I could say. "Do you want something to drink?"

"What's your story?" I asked. "What's my story?" "Yeah, what's your story?" He wrote, "I don't know what my story is." "How can you not know what your story is?" He shrugged his shoulders, just like Dad used to. "Where were you born?" He shrugged his shoulders. "How can you not know where you were born!" He shrugged his shoulders. "Where did you grow up?" He shrugged his shoulders. "OK. Do you have any brothers or sisters?" He shrugged his shoulders. "What's your job? And if you're retired, what *was* your job?" He shrugged his shoulders. I tried to think of something I could ask him that he couldn't not know the answer to. "Are you a human being?" He flipped back and pointed at "I'm sorry."

I'd never needed Grandma more than I needed her right then.

I asked the renter, "Can I tell you my story?"

He opened his left hand.

So I put my story into it.

I pretended he was Grandma, and I started at the very beginning.

I told him about the tuxedo on the chair, and how I had broken the vase, and found the key, and the locksmith, and the envelope, and the art supply store. I told him about the voice of Aaron Black, and how I was so incredibly close to kissing Abby Black. She didn't say she didn't want to, just that it wasn't a good idea. I told him about Abe Black in Coney Island, and Ada Black with the two Picasso paintings, and the birds that flew by Mr. Black's window. Their wings were the first thing he'd heard in more than twenty years. Then there was Bernie Black, who had a view of Gramercy Park, but not a key to it, which he said was worse than looking at a brick wall. Chelsea Black had a tan line around her ring finger, because she got divorced right after she got back from her honeymoon, and Don Black was also an animal-rights activist, and Eugene Black also had a coin collection. Fo Black lived on Canal Street, which used to be a real canal. He didn't speak very good English, because he hadn't left Chinatown since he came from Taiwan, because there was no reason for him to. The whole time I talked to him I imagined water on the other side of the window, like we were in an aquarium. He offered me a cup of tea, but I didn't feel like it, but I drank it anyway, to be polite. I asked him did he really love New York or was he just wearing the shirt. He smiled, like he was nervous. I could tell he didn't understand, which made me feel guilty for speaking English, for some reason. I pointed at his shirt. "Do? You? Really? Love? New York?" He said, "New York?" I said, "Your. Shirt." He looked at his shirt. I pointed at the N and said "New," and the Y and said "York." He looked confused, or embarrassed, or surprised, or maybe even mad. I couldn't tell what he was feeling, because I couldn't speak the language of his feelings. "I not know was New York. In Chinese, *ny* mean 'you.' Thought was 'I love you.'" It was then that I noticed the "I♥NY" poster on the wall, and the "I♥NY" flag over the door, and the "I♥NY" dishtowels, and the "I♥NY" lunchbox on the kitchen table. I asked him, "Well, then why do you love everybody so much?"

Georgia Black, in Staten Island, had turned her living room into a museum of her husband's life. She had pictures of him from when he was a kid, and his first pair of shoes, and his old report cards, which weren't as good as mine, but anyway. "Y'all're the first visitors in more than a year," she said, and she showed us a neat gold medal in a velvet box. "He was a naval officer, and I loved being a naval wife. Every few years we'd have to travel to some exotic place. I never did get a chance to put down many roots, but it was thrilling. We spent two years in the Philippines." "*Cool*," I said, and Mr. Black started singing a song in some weird language, which I guess was Philippinish. She showed us her wedding album, one picture at a time, and said, "Wasn't I slim and beautiful?" I told her, "You were." Mr. Black said, "And you are." She said, "Aren't you two the sweetest?" I said, "Yeah."

"This is the three-wood that he hit his hole in one with. He was real proud of that. For weeks it was all I'd hear about. That's the airplane ticket from our trip to Maui, Hawaii. I'm not too vain to tell you it was our thirtieth anniversary. Thirty years. We were going to renew our vows. Just like in a romance novel. His carry-on bag was filled with flowers, bless his heart. He wanted to surprise me with them on the plane, but I was looking at the x-ray screen as his bag went through, and don't you know there was a dark black bouquet. It was like the shadows of flowers. What a lucky girl I am." She used a cloth to wipe away our fingerprints.

It had taken us four hours to get to her house. Two of those were because Mr. Black had to convince me to get on the Staten Island Ferry. In addition to the fact that it was an obvious potential target, there had also been a ferry accident pretty recently, and in *Stuff That Happened to Me* I had pictures of people who had lost their arms and legs. Also, I don't like bodies of water. Or boats, particularly. Mr. Black asked me how I would feel in bed that night if I didn't get on the ferry. I told him, "Heavy boots, probably." "And how will you feel if you did?" "Like one hundred dollars." "So?" "So what about while I'm *on* the ferry? What if it sinks? What if someone pushes me off? What if it's hit with a shoulder-fired missile? There won't be a tonight tonight." He said, "In which case you won't feel anything anyway." I thought about that.

"This is an evaluation from his commanding officer," Georgia said, tapping the case. "It's exemplary. This is the tie he wore to his mother's funeral, may she rest in peace. She was such a nice woman. Nicer than most. And this here is a picture of his childhood home. That was before I knew him, of course." She tapped every case and then wiped away her own fingerprints, kind of like a Möbius strip. "These are his varsity let-

ters. This is his cigarette case from when he used to smoke. Here's his Purple Heart."

I started to get heavy boots, for obvious reasons, like where were all of *her* things? Where were *her* shoes and *her* diploma? Where were the shadows of *her* flowers? I made a decision that I wouldn't ask about the key, because I wanted her to believe that we had come to see her museum, and I think Mr. Black had the same idea. I decided to myself that if we went through the whole list and still hadn't found anything, then maybe, if we had no choice, we could come back and ask her some questions. "These are his baby shoes."

But then I started to wonder: she said we were the first visitors in a little more than a year. Dad had died a little more than a year ago. Was *he* the visitor before us?

"Hello, everyone," a man said from the door. He was holding two mugs, which steam was coming out of, and his hair was wet. "Oh, you're awake!" Georgia said, taking the mug that said "Georgia" on it. She gave him a big kiss, and I was like, *What in the what the?* "Here he is," she said. "Here who is?" Mr. Black asked. "My husband," she said, almost like he was another exhibit in his life. The four of us stood there smiling at one another, and then the man said, "Well, I suppose you'd like to see my museum now." I told him, "We just did. It was really great." He said, "No, Oskar, that's *her* museum. Mine's in the other room."

Thank you for your letter. Because of the large volume of mail I receive, I am unable to write personal responses. Nevertheless, know that I read and save every letter, with the hope of one day being able to give each the proper response it deserves. Until that day,

Most sincerely,
Stephen Hawking

The week passed quickly. Iris Black. Jeremy Black. Kyle Black. Lori Black . . . Mark Black was crying when he opened the door and saw us, because he had been waiting for someone to come back to him, so every time someone knocked on the door, he couldn't stop himself from hoping it might be that person, even though he knew he shouldn't hope.

Nancy Black's roommate told us Nancy was at work at the coffee store on Nineteenth Street, so we went there, and I explained to her that coffee actually has more caffeine than espresso, even though a lot of people don't think so, because the water is in contact with the grounds for a much longer time with coffee. She told me she didn't know that. "If he says it, it's true," Mr. Black said, patting my head. I told her, "Also, did you know that if you yell for nine years, you'll produce enough sound energy to heat one cup of coffee?" She said, "I didn't." I said, "Which is why they should put a *coffee store* next to the *Cyclone* at Coney *Island!* Get it?" That made me crack up, but only me. She asked if we were going to order anything. I told her, "Iced coffee, please." She asked, "What size?" I said, "Vente, and could you please use coffee ice cubes so it doesn't get all watery when the ice cubes melt?" She told me they didn't have coffee ice cubes. I said, "*Exactly.*" Mr. Black said, "I'm going to get right to the point," and then he did. I went to the bathroom and gave myself a bruise.

Ray Black was in prison, so we weren't able to talk to him. I did some research on the Internet and found out that he was in prison because he murdered two kids after he raped them. There were also pictures of the dead kids, and even though I knew it would only hurt me to look at them, I did. I printed them out and put them in *Stuff That Happened to Me*, right after the picture of Jean-Pierre Haigneré, the French astronaut who had to be carried from his spacecraft after returning from the Mir space station, because gravity isn't only what makes us fall, it's what makes our muscles strong. I wrote a letter to Ray Black in prison, but I never got a response. Inside, I hoped he didn't have anything to do with the key, although I couldn't help inventing that it was for his jail cell.

The address for Ruth Black was on the eighty-sixth floor of the Empire State Building, which I thought was incredibly weird, and so did Mr. Black, because neither of us knew that people actually lived there. I told Mr. Black that I was panicky, and he said it was OK to be panicky. I told him I felt like I couldn't do it, and he said it was OK to feel like I couldn't do it. I told him it was the thing that I was most afraid of. He said he could understand why. I wanted him to disagree with me, but he wouldn't, so I had no way to argue. I told him I would wait for him in the lobby, and he said, "Fine." "OK, OK," I said, "I'll go."

As the elevator takes you up, you hear information about the building, which was pretty fascinating, and I normally would have taken some notes, but I needed all of my concentration for being brave. I squeezed Mr. Black's hand, and I couldn't stop inventing: the elevator cables snapping, the elevator falling, a trampoline at the bottom, us shooting back up, the roof opening like a cereal box, us flying toward parts of the universe that not even Stephen Hawking was sure about . . .

When the elevator door opened, we got out on the observation deck. We didn't know who to look for, so we just looked around for a while. Even though I knew the view was incredibly beautiful, my brain started misbehaving, and the whole time I was imagining a plane coming at the building, just below us. I didn't want to, but I couldn't stop. I imagined the last second, when I would see the pilot's face, who would be a terrorist. I imagined us looking each other in the eyes when the nose of the plane was one millimeter from the building.

I hate you, my eyes would tell him.

I hate you, his eyes would tell me.

Then there would be an enormous explosion, and the building would sway, almost like it was going to fall over, which I know is what it felt like from descriptions I've read on the Internet, although I wish I hadn't read them. Then there would be smoke coming up at me and people screaming all around me. I read one description of someone who made it down eighty-five flights of stairs, which must have been about two thousand stairs, and he said that people were screaming "Help!" and "I don't want to die!" and one man who owned a company was screaming "Mommy!"

It would be getting so hot that my skin would start to get blisters. It would feel so good to get away from the heat, but on the other hand, when I hit the sidewalk I would die, obviously. Which would I choose? Would I jump or would I burn? I guess I would jump, because then I wouldn't have to feel pain. On the other hand, maybe I would burn, because then I'd at least have a chance to somehow escape, and even if I couldn't, feeling pain is still better than not feeling, isn't it?

I remembered my cell phone.

I still had a few seconds.

Who should I call?

What should I say?

I thought about all of the things that everyone ever says to each other, and how everyone is going to die, whether it's in a millisecond, or days, or months, or 76.5 years, if you were just born. Everything that's born has to die, which means our lives are like skyscrapers. The smoke rises at different speeds, but they're all on fire, and we're all trapped.

You can see the most beautiful things from the observation deck of the Empire State Building. I read somewhere that people on the street are supposed to look like ants, but that's not true. They look like little people. And the cars look like little cars. And even the buildings look little. It's like New York is a miniature replica of New York, which is nice, because you can see what it's really like, instead of how it feels when you're in the middle of it. It's extremely lonely up there, and you feel far away from everything. Also it's scary, because there are so many ways to die. But it feels safe, too, because you're surrounded by so many people. I kept one hand touching the wall as I walked carefully around to each of the views. I saw all of the locks I'd tried to open, and the 161,999,831 that I hadn't yet.

I got down on my knees and crawled to one of the binocular machines. I held it tightly as I pulled myself up, and I took a quarter from the change dispenser on my belt. When the metal lids opened, I could see things that were far away incredibly close, like the Woolworth Building, and Union Square, and the gigantic hole where the World Trade Center was. I looked into the window of an office building that I guessed was about ten blocks away. It took me a few seconds to figure out the focus, but then I could see a man sitting at his desk, writing something. What was he writing? He didn't look at all like Dad, but he reminded me of Dad. I pressed my face closer, and my nose got smooshed against the cold metal. He was left-handed like Dad. Did he

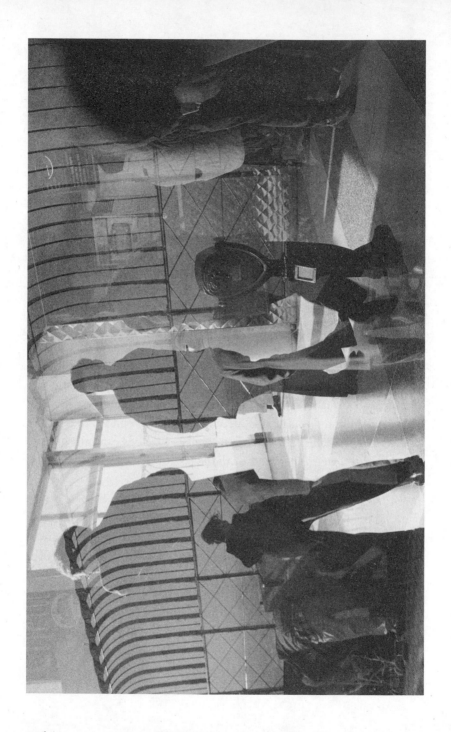

JONATHAN SAFRAN FOER

have a gap between his front teeth like Dad? I wanted to know what he was thinking. Who did he miss? What was he sorry for? My lips touched the metal, like a kiss.

I found Mr. Black, who was looking at Central Park. I told him I was ready to go down. "But what about Ruth?" "We can come back another day." "But we're already here." "I don't feel like it." "It'll just take a few—" "I want to go home." He could probably tell that I was about to cry. "OK," he said, "let's go home."

We got at the end of the line for the elevator.

I looked at everyone and wondered where they came from, and who they missed, and what they were sorry for.

There was a fat woman with a fat kid, and a Japanese guy with two cameras, and a girl with crutches whose cast was signed by lots of people. I had a weird feeling that if I examined it I would find Dad's writing. Maybe he would have written "Get better soon." Or just his name. An old woman was standing a few feet away, staring back at me, which made me self-conscious. She was holding a clipboard, although I couldn't see what was on it, and she was dressed old-fashioned. I promised myself I wouldn't be the first to look away, but I was. I pulled on Mr. Black's sleeve and told him to look at her. "You know what," he whispered. "What?" "I bet you she's the one." For some reason, I knew he was right. Although no part of me wondered if maybe we were looking for different things.

"Should we go up to her?" "Probably." "How?" "I don't know." "Go say hello." "You can't just go say hello." "Tell her the time." "But she didn't ask the time." "Ask her the time." "You do it." "*You* do it." We were so busy arguing about how to go up to her that we didn't even realize that she had come up to us. "I see that you're thinking about leaving," she said, "but could I interest you in a very special tour of this very special building?" "What's your name?" I asked. She said, "Ruth." Mr. Black said, "We'd love a tour."

She smiled, took a huge breath in, and then started walking while she talked. "Construction on the Empire State Building began in March of 1930, on the site of the old Waldorf-Astoria Hotel, at 350 Fifth Avenue at Thirty-fourth Street. It was completed one year and forty-five days later—seven million man-hours of work, including Sundays and holidays. Everything about the building was designed to expedite its construction—prefabricated materials were used as much as possible—and as a result, work progressed at a rate of about four and a half stories each week. The entire framework took less than half a year to complete." That was less time than how long I'd been searching for the lock.

She took a breath.

"Designed by the architectural firm of Shreve, Lamb, and Harmon Associates, the original plan called for eighty-six stories, but a 150-foot mooring mast for zeppelins was added. Today the mast is used for TV and radio broadcasts. The cost of the building, including the land that it rests on, was $40,948,900. The cost of the building itself was $24,718,000, less than half of the estimated cost of $50,000,000, due to deflated labor and materials costs during the Great Depression." I asked, "What was the Great Depression?" Mr. Black said, "I'll tell you later."

"At 1,250 feet, the Empire State Building was the tallest building in the world until the completion of the first tower of the World Trade Center in 1972. When the building was opened, they had such a hard time finding tenants to rent space within it that New Yorkers began calling it the Empty State Building." That made me crack up. "It was this observatory that saved the building from going into bankruptcy." Mr. Black patted the wall, like he was proud of the observatory.

"The Empire State Building is supported by 60,000 tons of steel. It has approximately 6,500 windows and 10,000,000 bricks, weighing in the neighborhood of 365,000 tons." "That's a heavy neighborhood," I said. "More than 500,000 square feet of marble and Indiana limestone encase this skyscraper. Inside, there is marble from France, Italy, Germany, and Belgium. In fact, New York's most famous building is made with materials from just about everywhere but New York, in much the same way that the city itself was made great by immigrants." "Very true," Mr. Black said, nodding his head.

"The Empire State Building has been the location of dozens of movies, the reception site of foreign dignitaries, and even had a World

War Two bomber crash into the seventy-ninth floor in 1945." I concentrated on happy, safe things, like the zipper on the back of Mom's dress, and how Dad needed a drink of water whenever he whistled for too long. "An elevator fell to the bottom. You'll be relieved to know that the passenger was saved by the emergency brakes." Mr. Black gave my hand a squeeze. "And speaking of elevators, there are seventy of them in the building, including the six freight elevators. They travel at speeds from 600 to 1,400 feet per minute. Or, if you so choose, you can walk the 1,860 steps from the street level to the top." I asked if you could also take the stairs down.

"On a clear day like this, you can see for eighty miles—well into Connecticut. Since the observatory opened to the public in 1931, almost 110 million visitors have enjoyed the breathtaking vision of the city beneath them. Each year, over 3.5 million people are whisked to the eighty-sixth floor to be where Cary Grant waited in vain for Deborah Kerr in *An Affair to Remember,* where Tom Hanks and Meg Ryan had their fateful meeting in the movie *Sleepless in Seattle.* Also, the observatory is handicap accessible."

She stopped and put her hand on her heart.

"All in all, the feeling and spirit of New York City is embodied in the Empire State Building. From the people who fell in love here, to the ones who have returned with their children and grandchildren, everyone recognizes the building not only as an awe-inspiring landmark which offers one of the most spectacular views on earth, but an unequaled symbol of American ingenuity."

She bowed. We clapped.

"Do you young men have another minute?" "We have a lot of minutes," Mr. Black said. "Because that was the end of the official tour, but there are a couple of things I really love about this building, and I only share them with people I suspect will care." I told her, "We'll care incredibly much."

"The dirigible mooring mast, now the base of the TV tower, was part of the original construction of the building. One attempt to moor a privately owned blimp was successful. But during another attempt, in September 1931, a navy blimp was almost upended, and nearly swept away the celebrities attending the historic affair, while the water ballast drenched pedestrians several blocks away. The mooring mast idea was ultimately abandoned, although it was very romantic." She started walking again, and we followed her, but I wondered if she would have kept talking even if we hadn't followed her. I couldn't tell if she was doing what she was doing for us, or for herself, or for some completely other reason.

"During the spring and autumn bird-migration season, the lights that illuminate the tower are turned off on foggy nights so they won't confuse birds, causing them to fly into the building." I told her, "Ten thousand birds die every year from smashing into windows," because I'd accidentally found that fact when I was doing some research about the windows in the Twin Towers. "That's a lot of birds," Mr. Black said. "And a lot of windows," Ruth said. I told them, "Yeah, so I invented a device that would detect when a bird is incredibly close to a building, and that would trigger an extremely loud birdcall from another skyscraper, and they'd be drawn to that. They'd bounce from one to another." "Like pinball," Mr. Black said. "What's pinball?" I asked. "But the birds would never leave Manhattan," Ruth said. "Which would be great," I told her, "because then your birdseed shirt would be reliable." "Would it be all right if I mentioned the ten thousand birds in my future tours?" I told her they didn't belong to me.

"A natural lightning rod, the Empire State Building is struck up to five hundred times each year. The outdoor observation deck is closed during thunderstorms, but the inside viewing areas remain open. Static electricity buildup is so mammoth on top of the building that, under the right conditions, if you stick your hand through the observatory fence, St. Elmo's fire will stream from your fingertips." "St. Elmo's fire is *sooo* awesome!" "Lovers who kiss up here may find their lips crackling with electric sparks." Mr. Black said, "That's my favorite part." She said, "Mine, too." I said, "Mine's the St. Elmo's fire." "The Empire State Building is located at latitude 40 degrees, 44 minutes, 53.977 seconds north; longitude 73 degrees, 59 minutes, 10.812 seconds west. Thank you."

"That was delightful," Mr. Black said. "Thank you," she said. I asked her how she knew all of that stuff. She said, "I know about this building because I love this building." That gave me heavy boots, because it reminded me of the lock that I still hadn't found, and how until I found it, I didn't love Dad enough. "What is it about this building?" Mr. Black asked. She said, "If I had an answer, it wouldn't really be love, would it?" "You're a terrific lady," he said, and then he asked where her family was from. "I was born in Ireland. My family came when I was a young girl." "Your parents?" "My parents were Irish." "And your grandparents?" "Irish." "That's marvelous news," Mr. Black said. "Why?" she asked, which was a question I was also wondering. "Because my family has nothing to do with Ireland. We came over on the Mayflower." I said, "*Cool.*" Ruth said, "I'm not sure I understand." Mr. Black said, "We're not related." "Why would we be related?" "Because we have the same last name." Inside I thought, *But technically she never actually said her last name was Black. And even if it actually was Black, why wasn't she asking how he knew her last name?* Mr. Black took off his beret and got down onto one of his knees, which took him a long time. "At the risk of being too forthright, I was hoping I might have the pleasure of your company one afternoon. I will be disappointed, but in no way offended, if you decline." She turned her face away. "I'm sorry," he said, "I shouldn't have." She said, "I stay up here."

Mr. Black said, "*What the?*" "I stay up here." "Always?" "Yes." "For how long?" "Oh. A long time. Years." Mr. Black said, "Jose!" I asked her how. "What do you mean how?" "Where do you sleep?" "On nice nights, I'll sleep out here. But when it gets chilly, which is most nights up this high, I have a bed in one of the storage rooms." "What do you eat?" "There are two snack bars up here. And sometimes one of the young men will bring me food, if I have a taste for something different. As you know, New York offers so many different eating experiences."

I asked if they knew she was up there. "Who's *they?*" "I don't know, the people who own the building or whatever." "The building has been owned by a number of different people since I moved up here." "What about the workers?" "The workers come and go. The new ones see I'm here and assume I'm supposed to be here." "No one has told you to leave?" "Never."

"Why don't you go down?" Mr. Black asked. She said, "I'm more comfortable here." "How could you be more comfortable here?" "It's hard to explain." "How did it start?" "My husband was a door-to-door salesman." "And?" "This was in the old days. He was always selling something or other. He loved the next thing that would change life. And he was always coming up with wonderful, crazy ideas. A bit like you," she said to me, which gave me heavy boots, because why couldn't I remind people of me? "One day he found a spotlight in an army surplus store. This was right after the war and you could find just about anything. He hooked it up to a car battery and fixed all of that to the crate he rolled around. He told me to go up to the observation deck of the Empire State Building, and as he walked around New York, he'd occasionally shine the light up at me so I could see where he was."

"It worked?" "Not during the day it didn't. It had to get quite dark before I could see the light, but once I could, it was amazing. It was as if all of the lights in New York were turned off except for his. That was how clearly I could see it." I asked her if she was exaggerating. She said, "I'm understating." Mr. Black said, "Maybe you're telling it exactly as it was."

"I remember that first night. I came up here and everyone was looking all over, pointing at the things to see. There are so many spectacular things to see. But only I had something pointing back at me." "Some*one*," I said. "Yes, something that was someone. I felt like a queen. Isn't that funny? Isn't it silly?" I shook my head no. She said, "I felt just like a queen. When the light went off, I knew his day was over, and I'd go down and meet him at home. When he died, I came back up here. It's silly." "No," I said. "It isn't." "I wasn't looking for him. I'm not a girl. But it gave me the same feeling that I'd had when it was daytime and I was looking for his light. I knew it was there, I just couldn't see it." Mr. Black took a step toward her.

"I couldn't bear to go home," she said. I asked why not, even though I was afraid I was going to learn something I didn't want to know. She said, "Because I knew he wouldn't be there." Mr. Black told her thank you, but she wasn't done. "I curled up in a corner that night, that corner over there, and fell asleep. Maybe I wanted the guards to notice me. I don't know. When I woke up in the middle of the night, I

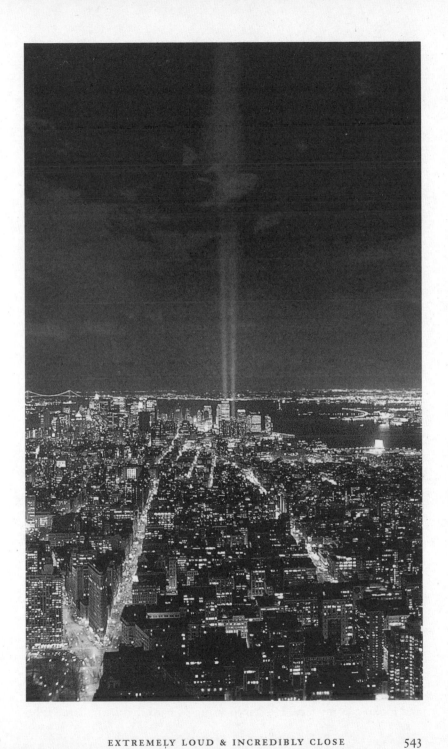

was all alone. It was cold. I was scared. I walked to the railing. Right there. I'd never felt more alone. It was as if the building had become much taller. Or the city had become much darker. But I'd never felt more alive, either. I'd never felt more alive or alone."

"I wouldn't make you go down," Mr. Black said. "We could spend the afternoon up here." "I'm awkward," she said. "So am I," Mr. Black said. "I'm not very good company. I just told you everything I know." "I'm terrible company," Mr. Black said, although that wasn't true. "Ask him," he said, pointing at me. "It's true," I said, "he sucks." "You can tell me about this building all afternoon. That would be marvelous. That's how I want to spend my time." "I don't even have any lipstick." "Neither do I." She let out a laugh, and then she put her hand over her mouth, like she was angry at herself for forgetting her sadness.

It was already 2:32 P.M. when I finished walking the 1,860 stairs down to the lobby, and I was exhausted, and Mr. Black seemed exhausted, too, so we went straight home. When we got to Mr. Black's door—this was just a few minutes ago—I was already making plans for next weekend, because we had to go to Far Rockaway, and Boerum Hill, and Long Island City, and if we had time also to Dumbo, but he interrupted me and said, "Listen. Oskar?" "That's my name, don't wear it out." "I think I'm finished." "Finished with what?" "I hope you understand." He stuck out his hand for a shake. "Finished with what?" "I've loved being with you. I've loved every second of it. You got me back into the world. That's the greatest thing anyone could have done for me. But now I think I'm finished. I hope you understand." His hand was still open, waiting for my hand.

I told him, "I don't understand."

I kicked his door and told him, "You're breaking your promise."

I pushed him and shouted, "It isn't fair!"

I got on my tiptoes and put my mouth next to his ear and shouted, "Fuck you!"

No. I shook his hand . . .

"And then I came straight here, and now I don't know what to do."

As I had been telling the renter the story, he kept nodding his head and looking at my face. He stared at me so hard that I wondered if he wasn't listening to me at all, or if he was trying to hear something incredibly quiet underneath what I was saying, sort of like a metal detector, but for truth instead of metal.

I told him, "I've been searching for more than six months, and I don't know a single thing that I didn't know six months ago. And actually I have negative knowledge, because I skipped all of those French classes with Marcel. Also I've had to tell a googolplex lies, which doesn't make me feel good about myself, *and* I've bothered a lot of people who I've probably ruined my chances of ever being real friends with, *and* I miss my dad more now than when I started, even though the whole *point* was to *stop* missing him."

I told him, "It's starting to hurt too much."

He wrote, "What is?"

Then I did something that surprised even me. I said, "Hold on," and I ran down the 72 stairs, across the street, right past Stan, even though he was saying "You've got mail!" and up the 105 stairs. The apartment was empty. I wanted to hear beautiful music. I wanted Dad's whistling, and the scratching sound of his red pen, and the pendulum swinging in his closet, and him tying his shoelaces. I went to my room and got the phone. I ran back down the 105 stairs, past Stan, who was still saying "You've got mail!," back up the 72 stairs, and into Grandma's apartment. I went to the guest room. The renter was standing in exactly the same position, like I'd never left, or never been there at all. I took the phone out of the scarf that Grandma was never able to finish, plugged it in, and played those first five messages for him. He didn't show anything on his face. He just looked at me. Not even at me, but into me, like his detector sensed some enormous truth deep inside me.

"No one else has ever heard that," I said.

"What about your mother?" he wrote.

"Especially not her."

He crossed his arms and held his hands in his armpits, which for him was like putting his hands over his mouth. I said, "Not even Grandma," and his hands started shaking, like birds trapped under a tablecloth. Finally he let them go. He wrote, "Maybe he saw what happened and ran in to save somebody." "He would have. That's what he was like." "He was a good person?" "He was the best person. But he was in the building for a meeting. And also he said he went up to the roof, so he must have been above where the plane hit, which means he didn't run in to save anyone." "Maybe he just said he was going to the roof." "Why would he do that?"

"What kind of meeting was it?" "He runs the family jewelry business. He has meetings all the time." "The family jewelry business?" "My grandpa started it." "Who's your grandpa?" "I don't know. He left my grandma before I was born. She says he could talk to animals and make a sculpture that was more real than the real thing." "What do you think?" "I don't think anyone can talk to animals. Except to dolphins, maybe. Or sign language to chimps." "What do you think about your grandpa?" "I don't think about him."

He pressed Play and listened to the messages again, and again I pressed Stop after the fifth was finished.

He wrote, "He sounds calm in the last message." I told him, "I read something in *National Geographic* about how, when an animal thinks it's going to die, it gets panicky and starts to act crazy. But when it *knows* it's going to die, it gets very, very calm." "Maybe he didn't want you to worry." Maybe. Maybe he didn't say he loved me *because* he loved me. But that wasn't a good enough explanation. I said, "I need to know how he died."

He flipped back and pointed at, "Why?"

"So I can stop inventing how he died. I'm always inventing."

He flipped back and pointed at, "I'm sorry."

"I found a bunch of videos on the Internet of bodies falling. They were on a Portuguese site, where there was all sorts of stuff they weren't showing here, even though it happened here. Whenever I want to try to learn about how Dad died, I have to go to a translator program and find out how to say things in different languages, like 'September,' which is 'Wrzesień,' or 'people jumping from burning buildings,' which is 'Menschen, die aus brennenden Gebäuden springen.' Then I Google those words. It makes me incredibly angry that people all over the world can know things that I can't, because it happened *here*, and happened to *me*, so shouldn't it be *mine?*

"I printed out the frames from the Portuguese videos and examined them extremely closely. There's one body that could be him. It's dressed like he was, and when I magnify it until the pixels are so big that it stops looking like a person, sometimes I can see glasses. Or I think I can. But I know I probably can't. It's just me wanting it to be him."

"You want him to have jumped?"

"I want to stop inventing. If I could know how he died, exactly how he died, I wouldn't have to invent him dying inside an elevator that was stuck between floors, which happened to some people, and I wouldn't have to imagine him trying to crawl down the outside of the building, which I saw a video of one person doing on a Polish site, or trying to use a tablecloth as a parachute, like some of the people who were in Windows on the World actually did. There were so many different ways to die, and I just need to know which was his."

He held out his hands like he wanted me to take them. "Are those tattoos?" He closed his right hand. I flipped back and pointed at "Why?" He took back his hands and wrote, "It's made things easier. Instead of writing yes and no all the time, I can show my hands." "But why just YES and NO?" "I only have two hands." "What about 'I'll think about it,' and 'probably,' and 'it's possible'?" He closed his eyes and concentrated for a few seconds. Then he shrugged his shoulders, just like Dad used to.

"Have you always been silent?" He opened his right hand. "Then why don't you talk?" He wrote, "I can't." "Why not?" He pointed at, "I can't." "Are your vocal cords broken or something?" "Something is broken." "When was the last time you talked?" "A long, long time ago." "What was the last word you said?" He flipped back and pointed at "I." "*I* was the last word you said?" He opened his left hand. "Does that even count as a word?" He shrugged his shoulders. "Do you try to talk?" "I know what will happen." "What?" He flipped back and pointed at, "I can't."

"Try." "Now?" "Try to say something." He shrugged his shoulders. I said, "Please."

He opened his mouth and put his fingers on his throat. They fluttered, like Mr. Black's fingers looking for a one-word biography, but no sound came out, not even an ugly sound, or breath.

I asked him, "What were you trying to say?" He flipped back and pointed at, "I'm sorry." I said, "It's OK." I said, "Maybe your vocal cords actually are broken. You should go to a specialist." I asked him, "What were you trying to say?" He pointed at, "I'm sorry."

I asked, "Can I take a picture of your hands?"

He put his hands on his lap, face-up, like a book.

YES and NO.

I focused Grandpa's camera.

He kept his hands extremely still.

I took the picture.

I told him, "I'm going to go home now." He picked up his book and wrote, "What about your grandma?" "Tell her I'll talk to her tomorrow."

As I was halfway across the street, I heard clapping behind me, almost like the birds' wings outside Mr. Black's window. I turned around and the renter was standing at the building's door. He put his hand on his throat and opened his mouth, like he was trying to speak again.

I called back to him, "What are you trying to say?"

He wrote something in his book and held it up, but I couldn't see it, so I ran back over. It said, "Please don't tell your grandmother that we met." I told him, "I won't if you won't," and I didn't even wonder the obvious thing, which was why would *he* want to keep it a secret? He wrote, "If you ever need me for anything, just throw pebbles at the guest room window. I'll come down and meet you under the streetlamp." I said, "Thanks." Although inside what I was thinking was, *Why would I ever need you?*

All I wanted was to fall asleep that night, but all I could do was invent.

What about frozen planes, which could be safe from heat-seeking missiles?

What about subway turnstiles that were also radiation detectors?

What about incredibly long ambulances that connected every building to a hospital?

What about parachutes in fanny packs?

What about guns with sensors in the handles that could detect if you were angry, and if you were, they wouldn't fire, even if you were a police officer?

What about Kevlar overalls?

What about skyscrapers made with moving parts, so they could rearrange themselves when they had to, and even open holes in their middles for planes to fly through?

What about . . .

What about . . .

What about . . .

And then a thought came into my brain that wasn't like the other thoughts. It was closer to me, and louder. I didn't know where it came from, or what it meant, or if I loved it or hated it. It opened up like a fist, or a flower.

What about digging up Dad's empty coffin?

JONATHAN SAFRAN FOER

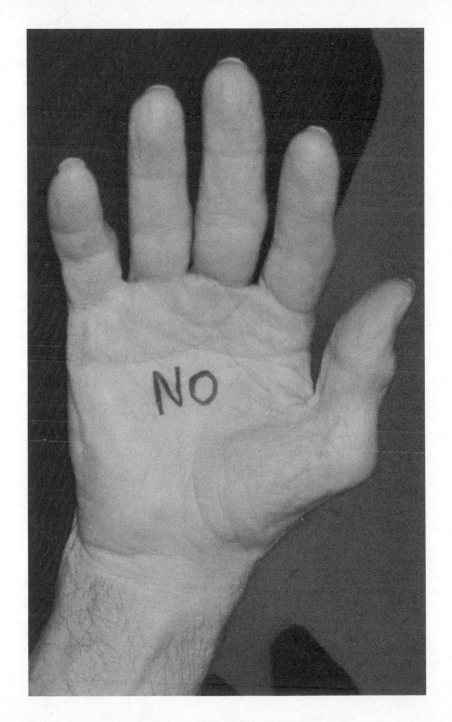

WHY I'M NOT WHERE YOU ARE
9/11/03

I don't speak, I'm sorry.

My name is Thomas.

I'm sorry.

JONATHAN SAFRAN FOER

I'm still sorry.

JONATHAN SAFRAN FOER

To my child: I wrote my last letter on the day you died, and I assumed I'd never write another word to you, I've been so wrong about so much that I've assumed, why am I surprised to feel the pen in my hand tonight? I'm writing as I wait to meet Oskar, in a little less than an hour, I'll close this book and find him under the streetlight, we'll be on our way to the cemetery, to you, your father and your son, this is how it happened. I gave a note to your mother's doorman almost two years ago. I watched from across the street as the limousine pulled up, she got out, she touched the door, she'd changed so much but I still knew her, her hands had changed but the way she touched was the same, she went into the building with a boy, I couldn't see if the doorman gave her my note, I couldn't see her reaction, the boy came out and went into the building across the street. I watched her that night as she stood with her palms against the window, I left another note with the doorman, "Do you want to see me again, or should I go away?" The next morning there was a note written on the window, "Don't go away," which meant something, but it didn't mean "I want to see you again." I gathered a handful of pebbles and tossed them at her window, nothing happened, I tossed some more, but she didn't come to the window, I wrote a note in my daybook—"Do you want to see me again?"—I ripped it out and gave it to the doorman, the next morning I went back, I didn't want to make her life any harder than it was, but I didn't want to give up either, there was a note on the window, "I don't want to want to see you again," which meant something, but it didn't mean yes. I gathered pebbles from the street and threw them at her window, hoping she would hear me and know what I meant, I waited, she didn't come to the window, I wrote a note—"What should I do?"—and gave it to the doorman, he said, "I'll make sure she gets it," I couldn't say, "Thank you." The next morning I went back, there was a note on her window, the first note, "Don't go away," I gathered pebbles, I threw them, they tapped like fingers against the glass, I wrote a note, "Yes or no?" for how long could it go on? The next day I found a market on Broadway and bought an apple, if she didn't want me I would leave, I didn't know where I would go, but I would turn around and walk away, there was no note on her window, so I threw the apple, anticipating the glass that would rain down on me, I wasn't afraid of the shards, the apple went through her window and into her apartment, the doorman was standing in front of the building, he said, "You're lucky that was open, pal," but I knew I wasn't lucky, he handed me a key. I rode the elevator up, the door was open, the smell brought back to me what for forty years I had struggled not to remember but couldn't forget. I put the key in my pocket, "Only the guest room!" she called from our bedroom, the room in which we used to sleep and dream and make love. That was how we began our second life together . . . When I got off the plane, after eleven hours of travel and forty years away, the man took my passport and asked me the purpose of my visit, I wrote in my daybook, "To mourn," and then, "To ~~mourn~~ try to live," he gave me a look and asked if I would consider that business or pleasure, I wrote, "Neither." "For how long do you plan to mourn and try to live?" I wrote, "For the rest of my life." "So you're going to stay?" "For as long as I can." "Are we talking about a weekend or a year?" I didn't write anything. The man said, "Next." I watched the bags go around the carousel, each one held a person's belongings, I saw babies going around and around, possible lives, I followed the arrows for those with nothing to declare, and that made me want to laugh, but I was silent. One of the guards asked me to come to the side, "That's a lot of suitcases for someone with nothing to declare," he said, I nodded, knowing that people with nothing to declare carry the most, I opened the suitcases for him, "That's a lot of paper," he said, I showed him my left palm, "I mean, that's a whole lot of paper." I wrote, "They're letters to my son. I wasn't able to send them to him while he was alive. Now he's dead. I don't speak. I'm sorry." The guard looked at the other guard and they shared a smile, I don't mind if smiles come at my expense, I'm a small price to pay, they let me through, not because they believed me but because they didn't want to try to understand me, I found a pay phone and called your mother, that was as far as my plan went, I assumed so much, that she was still alive, that she was in the same apartment I'd left forty years before, I assumed she would come pick me up and everything would begin to make sense, we would mourn and try to live, the phone rang and rang, we would forgive ourselves, it rang, a woman answered, "Hello?" I knew it was her, the voice had changed but the breath was the same, the spaces between the words were the same, I pressed "4, 3, 5, 5, 6," she said, "Hello?" I asked, "4, 7, 4, 8, 7, 3, 2, 5, 5, 9, 9, 6, 8?" She said, "Your phone isn't one hundred dollars. Hello?" I wanted to reach my hand through the mouthpiece, down the line, and into her room, I wanted to reach YES, I asked, "4, 7, 4, 8, 7, 3, 2, 5, 5, 9, 9, 6, 8?" She said, "Hello?" I told her, "4, 3, 5, 7!" "Listen," she said, "I don't know what's wrong with your phone, but all I hear is beeps. Why don't you hang up and try again." Try again? I was trying to try again, that's what I was doing! I knew it wouldn't help, I knew no good would come of it, but I stood there in the middle of the airport, at the beginning of the century, at the end of my life, and I told her everything: why I'd left, where I'd gone, how I'd found out about your death, why I'd come back, and what I needed to do with the time I had left. I told her because I wanted her to believe me and understand, and because I thought I owed it to her, and to myself, and to you, or was it just more selfishness? I broke my life down into letters, for love I pressed "5, 6, 8, 3," for death, "3, 3, 2, 8, 4," when the suffering is subtracted from the joy, what remains? What, I wondered, is the sum of my life? "6, 9, 6, 2, 6, 3, 4, 7, 3, 5, 4, 3, 2, 5, 8, 6, 2, 6, 3, 4, 5, 8, 7, 8, 2, 7, 7, 4, 8, 3, 3, 2, 8, 8, 4, 3, 2, 4, 7, 7, 6, 7, 8, 4, 6, 3, 3, 3, 8, 6, 3, 4, 6, 3, 6, 7, 3, 4, 6, 5, 3, 5, 7! 6, 4, 3, 2, 2, 6, 7, 4, 2, 5, 6, 3, 8, 7, 2, 6, 3, 4, 3? 5, 7, 6, 3, 5, 8, 6, 2, 6, 3, 4, 5, 8, 7, 8, 2, 7, 7, 4, 8, 3, 9, 2, 8, 8, 4, 3, 2, 4, 7, 7, 6, 7, 8, 4, 6, 3, 3, 3, 8! 4, 3, 2, 4, 7, 7, 6, 7, 8, 4! 6, 3, 3, 3, 8, 6, 3, 9, 6, 3, 6, 6, 3, 4, 6, 5, 3, 5, 7! 6, 4, 3, 2, 2, 6, 7, 4, 2, 5, 6, 3, 8, 7, 2, 6, 3, 4, 3? 5, 7, 6, 3, 5, 8, 6, 2, 6, 3, 4, 5, 8, 7, 8, 2, 7, 7, 4, 8, 3, 3, 2, 8! 7, 7, 4, 8, 3, 3, 2, 8, 3, 4, 3, 2, 4, 7, 6, 6, 7, 8, 4, 6, 8, 3, 8, 8, 6, 3, 4, 6, 3, 6, 7, 3, 4, 6, 7, 7, 4, 8, 3, 3, 9, 8, 8, 4, 3, 2, 4, 5, 7, 6, 7, 8, 4, 6, 3, 5, 5, 2, 6, 9, 4, 6, 5, 6, 7, 5, 4, 6! 5, 2, 6, 2, 6, 5, 9, 5, 2? 6, 9, 6, 2, 6, 5, 4, 7, 5, 5, 5, 4, 5, 2, 5, 2, 6, 4, 6, 2, 4, 5, 2, 7, 2, 2, 7, 7, 4, 2, 5, 5, 2, 9, 2, 4, 5, 2, 6! 4, 2, 2, 6, 5, 4, 2, 5, 7, 4, 5, 2, 5, 2, 6, 2, 6, 5, 4, 5, 2, 7, 2, 2, 7, 7, 4, 2, 5, 5, 2, 2, 2, 4, 5, 2! 7, 2, 2, 7, 7, 4, 2, 5, 5, 2, 2, 2, 4, 5, 2, 4, 7, 2, 2, 7, 2, 4, 6, 5, 5, 5, 2, 6, 5, 4, 6, 5, 6, 7, 5, 4! 4, 3, 2, 4, 3, 3, 6, 3, 8, 4! 6, 3, 3, 3, 8, 6, 3, 9, 6, 3, 6, 6, 3, 4, 6, 5, 3, 5, 3! 2, 2, 3, 3, 2, 6, 3, 4, 2, 5, 6, 3, 8, 3, 2, 6, 3, 4, 3? 5, 6, 8, 3? 5, 3, 6, 3, 5, 8, 6, 2, 6, 3, 4, 5, 8, 3, 8, 2, 3,

4, 8, 3, 3, 2, 8! 3, 3, 4, 8, 3, 3, 2, 8, 3, 4, 3, 2, 4, 7, 6, 6, 7, 8, 4, 6, 8, 3, 8, 8,
6, 3, 4, 6, 3! 2, 2, 7, 7, 4, 2, 5, 5, 2, 9, 2, 4, 5, 2, 6! 4, 2, 2, 6, 5, 4, 2, 5, 7, 4,
5, 2, 5, 2, 6, 2, 6, 5, 4, 5, 2, 7, 2, 2, 7, 7, 4, 2, 5, 5, 2, 2, 2, 4, 5, 2! 7, 2, 2, 7,
7, 4, 2, 5, 5, 2, 2, 2, 4, 5, 2, 4, 7, 2, 2, 7, 2, 4, 6, 5, 5, 5, 2, 6, 5, 4, 6, 5, 6, 7,
5, 4! 6, 5, 5, 5, 7! 6, 4, 5, 2, 2, 6, 7, 4, 2, 5, 6, 5, 2, 6! 2, 6, 5, 4, 5? 5, 7, 6, 5,
5, 2, 6, 2, 6, 5, 4, 5, 2, 7, 2, 2, 7, 7, 4, 2, 5, 9, 2, 2, 2, 4, 5, 2, 4, 5, 5, 6, 5, 2,
4, 6, 5, 5, 5, 2! 4, 5, 2, 4, 5, 5, 6, 5! 5, 6, 8, 3? 5, 5, 6, 5, 5, 2, 6, 2, 6, 3, 4, 5,
8, 3, 8, 2, 3, 3, 4, 8, 3, 9, 2, 8, 8, 4, 3, 2, 4, 3, 3, 6, 3, 8, 4, 6, 3, 3, 3, 8! 4, 3,
2, 4, 3, 3, 6, 3, 8, 4, 6, 3! 5, 6, 8, 3? 5, 6, 8, 3? 5, 6, 8, 3! 4, 2, 2, 6, 5, 4, 2, 5,
7, 4, 5, 2, 5, 2, 6, 2, 6, 5, 4, 5, 2, 7, 2, 2, 7, 4, 5, 2, 4, 6, 3, 5, 8, 6, 2, 6, 3, 4,
5, 8, 7, 8, 2, 7, 7, 4, 8, 3, 3, 2, 8! 6, 5, 5, 5, 7! 6, 4, 5, 2, 2, 6, 7, 4, 2, 5, 6, 5,
2, 6! 2, 6, 5, 4, 5? 5, 7, 6, 5, 5, 2, 6, 2, 6, 5, 4, 5, 2, 7, 2, 2, 7, 7, 4, 2, 5, 9, 2,
2, 2, 4, 5, 2, 4! 5, 6, 8, 3? 5, 5, 6, 5, 2, 4, 6, 3, 6, 7, 3, 4, 6, 7, 7, 4, 8, 3, 3, 9,
8, 8, 4, 3, 2, 4, 5, 7, 6, 7, 8, 4, 6, 3, 5, 5, 2, 6, 9, 4, 6, 5, 6, 7, 5, 4, 6! 5, 2, 6,
2, 6, 5, 9, 5, 2? 6, 9, 6, 2, 6, 5, 4, 7, 5, 5, 4, 5, 2, 5, 2, 6, 4, 6, 2, 4, 5, 2, 7, 2,
2, 7, 7, 4, 2, 5, 5, 2, 9, 2, 4, 5, 2, 6! 4, 2, 2, 6, 5, 4, 2, 5, 7, 4, 5, 2, 5, 2, 6, 2,
6, 5, 4, 5, 2, 7, 2, 2, 7, 7, 4, 2, 5, 5, 2, 2, 2, 4, 5, 2! 7, 2, 2, 7, 7, 4, 2, 5, 5, 2,
2, 2, 4, 5, 2, 4, 7, 2, 2, 7, 2, 4, 6, 5, 5, 5, 2, 6, 5, 4, 6, 5, 6, 7, 5, 4! 6, 5, 5, 5,
7! 6, 4, 5, 2, 2, 6, 7, 4, 2, 5, 6, 5, 2, 6! 2, 6, 5, 4, 5? 5, 7, 6, 5, 5, 2, 6, 2, 6, 5,
4, 5, 2, 7, 2, 2, 7, 7, 4, 2, 5, 9, 2, 2, 2, 4, 5, 2, 4! 5, 6, 8, 3? 5, 5, 6, 5, 2, 4, 6,
5, 5, 5, 2! 4, 5, 2, 4, 5, 5, 6, 5! 2, 5, 5, 2, 9, 2, 4, 5, 2, 6! 4, 2, 2, 6, 5, 4, 2! 5,
5, 6, 5, 5, 2, 6, 2, 6, 3, 4, 5, 8, 3, 8, 2, 3, 3, 4, 8, 3, 9, 2, 8, 8, 4, 3, 2, 4, 3, 3,
6, 3, 8, 4, 6, 3, 3, 3, 8! 4, 3, 2, 4, 3, 3, 6, 3, 8, 4! 6, 3, 3, 3, 8, 6, 3, 9, 6, 3, 6,
6, 3, 4, 6, 5, 3, 5, 3! 2, 2, 3, 3, 2, 6, 3, 4, 2, 5, 6, 3, 8, 3, 2, 6, 3, 4, 3? 5, 6, 8,
3? 5, 3, 6, 3, 5, 8, 6, 2, 6, 3, 4, 5, 8, 3, 8, 2, 3, 3, 4, 8, 3, 3, 2, 8! 2, 7, 2, 4, 6,
5, 5, 5, 2, 6, 5, 4, 6, 5, 6, 7, 5, 4! 6, 5, 5, 5, 7! 6, 4, 5, 2, 2, 6, 7, 4, 2, 5, 6, 5,
2, 6! 2, 6, 5, 4, 5? 5, 7, 6, 5, 5, 2, 6, 2, 6, 5, 4, 5, 2, 7, 2, 2, 7, 7, 4, 2, 5, 9, 2,
2, 2, 4, 5, 2, 4, 5, 5, 6, 5, 2, 4, 6, 5, 5, 5, 2! 4, 5, 2, 4, 5, 5, 6, 5! 5, 6, 8, 3? 5,
5, 6, 5, 5, 2, 6, 2, 6, 3, 4, 5, 8, 3, 8, 2, 3, 3, 4, 8, 3, 9, 2, 8, 8, 4, 3, 2, 4, 3, 4,
6, 5, 5, 5, 2! 4, 5, 2, 4, 5, 5, 6, 5! 6, 5, 4, 5? 4, 5? 5, 5, 6, 5, 5, 2, 6, 2, 6, 3, 4,
5, 8, 3, 8, 2, 3, 3, 4, 8, 3, 9, 2, 8, 8, 4, 3, 2, 4, 3, 3, 6, 3, 8, 4, 6, 3, 3, 3, 8! 4,
3, 2, 4, 3, 3, 6, 3, 8, 4! 6, 3, 3, 3, 6, 7, 4, 2, 5, 6, 3, 8, 7, 2, 6, 3, 4, 3? 5, 7, 6,
3, 5, 8, 6, 2, 6, 3, 4, 5, 8, 7, 8, 2, 7, 7, 4, 8, 3, 3, 2, 8! 7, 7, 4, 8, 3, 3, 2, 8, 3,
4, 3, 2, 4, 7, 6, 6, 7, 8, 4, 6, 8, 3, 8, 8, 6, 3, 4, 6, 3, 6, 7, 3, 4, 6, 7, 7, 4, 8, 3,
3, 9, 8, 8, 4, 3, 2, 4, 5, 7, 6, 7, 8, 4, 6, 3, 5, 5, 2, 6, 9, 4, 6, 5, 6, 7, 5, 4, 6! 5,

2, 6, 2, 6, 5, 9, 5, 2? 6, 9, 6, 2, 6, 5, 4, 7, 5, 5, 4, 5, 2, 5, 2, 6, 4, 6, 2, 4, 5, 2, 7, 2, 2, 7, 7, 4, 2, 5, 5, 2, 9, 2, 4, 5, 2, 6! 4, 2, 2, 6, 5, 4, 2, 5, 7, 4, 5, 2, 5, 2, 6, 2, 6, 5, 4, 5, 2, 7, 2, 2, 7, 7, 4, 2, 5, 5, 2, 2, 2, 4, 5, 2! 7, 2, 2, 7, 7, 4, 2, 5, 5, 2, 2, 2, 4, 5, 2, 4, 7, 2, 2, 7, 2, 4, 6, 5, 5, 5, 2, 6, 5, 4, 6, 5, 6, 7, 5, 4! 6, 5, 5, 5, 7! 6, 4, 5, 2, 2, 6, 7, 4, 2, 5, 6, 5, 2, 6! 2, 6, 5, 4, 5? 5, 7, 6, 5, 5, 2, 6, 2, 6, 5, 4, 5, 2, 7, 2, 2, 7, 7, 4, 2, 5, 9, 2, 2, 2, 4, 5, 2, 4! 5, 6, 8, 3? 5, 5, 6, 5, 2, 4, 6, 5, 5, 5, 2! 4, 5, 2, 4, 5, 5, 6, 5! 8, 6, 3, 9, 6, 3, 6, 6, 3, 4, 6, 5, 3, 5, 3, 2, 2, 3, 3, 2, 6, 3, 4, 2, 5, 6, 3, 8, 3, 2, 6, 3, 4, 3? 5, 6, 8, 3? 5, 3, 6, 3, 5, 8, 6, 2, 6, 3, 4, 5, 8, 3, 8, 2, 3, 3, 4, 8, 3, 3, 2, 8! 3, 3, 4, 8, 3, 3, 2, 8, 3, 4, 3, 2, 4, 7, 6, 6, 7, 8, 4, 6, 8, 3, 8, 8, 6, 3, 4, 6, 3! 2, 2, 7, 7, 4, 6, 7, 4, 2, 5, 6, 3, 8, 7, 2, 6, 3, 4, 3? 5, 7, 6, 3, 5, 8, 6, 2, 6, 3, 4, 5, 8, 7, 8, 2, 7, 7, 4, 8, 3, 3, 2, 8! 7, 7, 4, 8, 3, 3, 2, 8, 3, 4, 3, 2, 4, 7, 6, 6, 7, 8, 4, 6, 8, 3, 8, 8, 6, 3, 4, 6, 3, 6, 7, 3, 4, 6, 7, 7, 4, 8, 3, 3, 9, 8, 8, 4, 3, 2, 4, 5, 7, 6, 7, 8, 4, 6, 3, 5, 5, 2, 6, 9, 4, 6, 5, 6, 7, 5, 4, 6! 5, 2, 6, 2, 6, 5, 9, 5, 2? 6, 9, 6, 2, 6, 5, 4, 7, 5, 5, 4, 5, 2, 5, 2, 6, 4, 6, 2, 4, 5, 2, 7, 2, 2, 7, 7, 4, 2, 5, 5, 2, 9, 2, 4, 5, 2, 6! 4, 2, 2, 6, 5, 4, 2, 5, 7, 4, 5, 2, 5, 2, 6, 2, 6, 5, 4, 5, 2, 7, 2, 2, 7, 7, 4, 2, 5, 5, 2, 2, 2, 4, 5, 2! 7, 2, 2, 7, 7, 4, 2, 5, 5, 2, 2, 2, 4, 5, 2, 4, 7, 2, 2, 7, 2, 4, 6, 5, 5, 5, 2, 6, 5, 4, 6, 5, 6, 7, 5, 4! 6, 5, 5, 5, 7! 6, 4, 5, 2, 2, 6, 7, 4, 2, 5, 6, 5, 2, 6! 2, 6, 5, 4, 5? 5, 7, 6, 5, 5, 2, 6, 2, 6, 5, 4, 5, 2, 7, 2, 2, 7, 7, 4, 2, 5, 9, 2, 2, 2, 4, 5, 2, 4! 5, 6, 8, 3? 5, 5, 6, 5, 2, 4, 6, 5, 5, 5, 2! 4, 5, 2, 4, 5, 5, 6, 5! 2, 5, 5, 2, 9, 2, 4, 5, 2, 6! 4, 2, 2, 6, 5, 4, 2! 5, 5, 6, 5, 5, 2, 6, 2, 6, 3, 4, 5, 8, 3, 8, 2, 3, 3, 4, 8, 3, 9, 2, 8, 8, 4, 3, 2, 4, 3, 3, 6, 3, 8, 4, 6, 3, 3, 3, 8! 4, 3, 2, 4, 3, 3, 6, 3, 8, 4! 6, 3, 3, 3, 8, 6, 3, 9, 6, 3, 6, 6, 3, 4, 6, 5, 3, 5, 3! 2, 2, 3, 3, 2, 6, 3, 4, 2, 5, 6, 3, 8, 3, 2, 6, 3, 4, 3? 5, 6, 8, 3? 5, 3, 6, 3, 5, 8, 6, 2, 6, 3, 4, 5, 8, 3, 8, 2, 3, 3, 4, 8, 3, 3, 2, 8! 2, 7, 2, 4, 6, 5, 5, 5, 2, 6, 5, 4, 6, 5, 6, 7, 5, 4! 6, 5, 5, 5, 7! 6, 4, 5, 2, 2, 6, 7, 4, 2, 5, 6, 5, 2, 6! 2, 6, 5, 4, 5? 5, 7, 6, 5, 5, 2, 6, 2, 6, 5, 4, 5, 2, 7, 2, 2, 7, 7, 4, 2, 5, 9, 2, 2, 2, 4, 5, 2, 4, 5, 5, 6, 5, 2, 4, 6, 5, 5, 5, 2! 4, 5, 2, 4, 5, 5, 6, 5! 5, 6, 8, 3? 5, 5, 6, 5, 5, 2, 6, 2, 6, 3, 4, 5, 8, 3, 8, 2, 3, 3, 4, 8, 3, 9, 2, 8, 8, 4, 3, 2, 4, 3, 3, 6, 3, 8, 4, 6, 3, 3, 3, 8! 4, 3, 2, 4, 3, 3, 6, 3, 8, 4, 6, 3! 5, 6, 8, 3? 5, 6, 8, 3? 5, 6, 8, 3! 4, 2, 2, 6, 5, 4, 2, 5, 7, 4, 5, 2, 5, 2, 6, 2, 6, 5, 4, 5, 2, 7, 2, 2, 7, 4, 5, 2, 4, 6, 3, 5, 8, 6, 2, 6, 3, 4, 5, 8, 7, 8, 2, 7, 7, 4, 8, 3, 3, 2, 8! 7, 7, 4, 8, 3, 3, 2, 8, 3, 4, 3, 2, 4, 7, 6, 6, 7, 8, 4, 6, 8, 3, 8, 8, 6, 3, 4, 6, 3, 6, 7, 3, 4, 6, 7, 7, 4, 8, 3, 3, 9, 8, 8, 4, 3, 2, 4, 5, 7, 6, 7, 8, 4, 6, 3, 5, 5, 2, 6, 9, 4, 6, 5, 6, 7, 5, 4, 6! 5, 2, 6, 2, 6, 5, 9, 5, 2? 6, 9, 6, 2, 6, 5, 4, 5, 6, 5, 2, 4, 6, 5, 5, 5, 2, 7, 4, 2, 5, 5, 2, 2, 2, 4, 5, 2! 7, 2, 2, 7, 7, 4, 2, 5, 5, 2, 2, 2, 4, 5, 2, 4, 7, 2, 2, 7, 2, 4, 6, 5, 5, 5, 2, 6, 5, 4, 6, 5, 6, 7, 5, 4! 6, 5, 5, 5, 7!"

It took me a long time, I don't know how long, minutes, hours, my heart got tired, my finger did, I was trying to destroy the wall between me and my life with my finger, one press at a time, my quarter ran out, or she hung up, I called again, "4, 7, 4, 8, 7, 3, 2, 5, 5, 9, 9, 6, 8?" She said, "Is this a joke?" A joke, it wasn't a joke, what is a joke, was it a joke? She hung up, I called again, "8, 4, 4, 7, 4, 7, 6, 6, 8, 2, 5, 6, 5, 3!" She asked, "Oskar?" That was the first time I ever heard his name . . . I was in Dresden's train station when I lost everything for the second time, I was writing you a letter that I knew I never would send, sometimes I wrote from there, sometimes from here, sometimes from the zoo, I didn't care about anything except for the letter I was writing to you, nothing else existed, it was like when I walked to Anna with my head down, hiding myself from the world, which is why I walked into her, and why I didn't notice that people were gathering around the televisions. It wasn't until the second plane hit, and someone who didn't mean to holler hollered, that I looked up, there were hundreds of people around the televisions now, where had they come from? I stood up and looked, I didn't understand what I was seeing on the screen, was it a commercial, a new movie? I wrote, "What's happened?" and showed it to a young businessman watching the television, he took a sip of his coffee and said, "No one knows yet," his coffee haunts me, his "yet" haunts me. I stood there, a person in a crowd, was I watching the images, or was something more complicated happening? I tried to count the floors above where the planes had hit, the fire had to burn up through the buildings, I knew that those people couldn't be saved, and how many were on the planes, and how many were on the street, I thought and thought. On my walk home I stopped in front of an electronics store, the front window was a grid of televisions, all but one of them were showing the buildings, the same images over and over, as if the world itself were repeating, a crowd had gathered on the sidewalk, one television, off to the side, was showing a nature program, a lion was eating a flamingo, the crowd became noisy, someone who didn't mean to holler hollered, pink feathers, I looked at one of the other televisions and there was only one building, one hundred ceilings had become one hundred floors, which had become nothing, I was the only one who could believe it, the sky was filled with paper, pink feathers. The cafés were full that afternoon, people were laughing, there were lines in front of the movie theaters, they were going to see comedies, the world is so big and small, in the same moment we were close and far. In the days and weeks that followed, I read the lists of the dead in the paper: mother of three, college sophomore, Yankees fan, lawyer, brother, bond trader, weekend magician, practical joker, sister, philanthropist, middle son, dog lover, janitor, only child, entrepreneur, waitress, grandfather of fourteen, registered nurse, accountant, intern, jazz saxophonist, doting uncle, army reservist, late-night poet, sister, window washer, Scrabble player, volunteer fireman, father, father, elevator repairman, wine aficionado, office manager, secretary, cook, financier, executive vice president, bird watcher, father, dishwasher, Vietnam veteran, new mother, avid reader, only child, competitive chess player, soccer coach, brother, analyst, maitre d', black belt, CEO, bridge partner, architect, plumber, public relations executive, father, artist in residence, urban planner, newlywed, investment banker, chef, electrical engineer, new father who had a cold that morning and thought about calling in sick . . . and then one day I saw it, Thomas Schell, my first thought was that I had died. "He leaves behind a wife and son," I thought, my son, I thought, my grandson, I thought and thought and thought, and then I stopped thinking . . . When the plane descended and I saw Manhattan for the first time in forty years, I didn't know if I was going up or down, the lights were stars, I didn't recognize any of the buildings, I told the man, "To ~~mourn~~ try to live," I declared nothing, I called your mother but I couldn't explain myself, I called again, she thought it was a joke, I called again, she asked, "Oskar?" I went to the magazine stand and got more quarters, I tried again, it rang and rang, I tried again, it rang, I waited and tried again, I sat on the ground, not knowing what would happen next, not even knowing what I wanted to happen next, I tried once more, "Hello, you have reached the Schell residence. I am speaking like an answering message, even though it's really me on the phone. If you'd like to talk to me or Grandma, please begin at the beep sound I'm about to make. Beeeeep. Hello?" It was a child's voice, a boy's. "It's really me. I'm here. Bonjour?" I hung up. Grandma? I needed time to think, a taxi would be too quick, as would a bus, what was I afraid of? I put the suitcases on a pushcart and started walking, I was amazed that no one tried to stop me, not even as I pushed the cart onto the street, not even as I pushed it onto the side of the highway, with each step it became brighter and hotter, after only a few minutes it was clear I wouldn't be able to manage, I opened one of the suitcases and took out a stack of letters, "To my child," they were from 1977, "To my child," "To my child," I thought about laying them on the road beside me, creating a trail of things I wasn't able to tell you, it might have made my load possible, but I couldn't, I needed to get them to you, to my child. I hailed a cab, by the time we reached your mother's apartment it was already getting late, I needed to find a hotel, I needed food and a shower and time to think, I ripped a page from the daybook and wrote, "I'm sorry," I handed it to the doorman, he said, "Who's this for?" I wrote, "Mrs. Schell," he said, "There is no Mrs. Schell," I wrote, "There is," he said, "Believe me, I'd know if there was a Mrs. Schell in this building," but I'd heard her voice on the phone, could she have moved and kept the number, how would I find her, I needed a phone book. I wrote "3D" and showed it to the doorman. He said, "Ms. Schmidt," I took back my book and wrote, "That was her maiden name." . . . I lived in the guest room, she left me meals by the door, I could hear her footsteps and sometimes I thought I heard the rim of a glass against the door, was it a glass I once drank water from, had it ever touched your lips? I found my daybooks from before I left, they were in the body of the grandfather clock, I'd have thought she would have thrown them away, but she kept them, many were empty and many were filled, I wandered through them, I found the book from the afternoon we met and the book from the day after we got married, I found our first Nothing Place, and the last time we walked around the reservoir, I found pictures of banisters and sinks and fireplaces, on top of one of the stacks was the book from the first time I tried to leave, "I haven't always been silent, I used to talk and talk and talk and talk." I don't know if she began to feel sorry for me, or sorry for herself, but she started paying me short visits, she wouldn't say anything at first, only tidy up the room, brush cobwebs from the corners, vacuum the carpet, straighten the picture frames, and then one day, as she dusted the bedside table, she said, "I can forgive you for leaving, but not for coming back," she walked out and closed the door behind her, I didn't see her again for three days, and then it was as if nothing had been said, she replaced a light bulb that had worked fine, she picked things up and put them down, she said, "I'm not going to share this grief with you," she closed the door behind her, was I the prisoner or the guard? Her visits became longer, we never had conversations, and she didn't like to look at me, but something was happening, we were getting closer, or farther apart, I took a chance, I asked if she would pose for me, like when we first met, she opened her mouth and nothing came out, she touched my left hand, which I hadn't realized was in a fist, was that how she said yes, or was that how she touched me? I went to the art supply store to buy some clay, I couldn't keep my hands to myself, the pas-

JONATHAN SAFRAN FOER

tels in long boxes, the palette knives, the handmade papers hanging on rolls, I tested every sample, I wrote my name in blue pen and in green oil stick, in orange crayon and in charcoal, it felt like I was signing the contract of my life. I was there for more than an hour, although I bought only a simple block of clay, when I came home she was waiting for me in the guest room, she was in a robe, standing beside the bed, "Did you make any sculptures while you were away?" I wrote that I had tried but couldn't, "Not even one?" I showed her my right hand, "Did you think about sculptures? Did you make them in your head?" I showed her my left hand, she took off her robe and went onto the sofa, I couldn't look at her, I took the clay from the bag and set it up on the card table, "Did you ever make a sculpture of me in your head?" I wrote, "How do you want to pose?" She said the whole point was that I should choose, I asked if the carpeting was new, she said, "Look at me," I tried but I couldn't, she said, "Look at me or leave me. But don't stay and look at anything else." I asked her to lie on her back, but that wasn't right, I asked her to sit, it wasn't right, cross your arms, turn your head away from me, nothing was right, she said, "Show me how," I went over to her, I undid her hair, I pressed down on her shoulders, I wanted to touch her across all of those distances, she said, "I haven't been touched since you left. Not in that way." I pulled back my hand, she took it into hers and pressed it against her shoulder, I didn't know what to say, she asked, "Have you?" What's the point of a lie that doesn't protect anything? I showed her my left hand. "Who touched you?" My daybook was filled, so I wrote on the wall, "I wanted so much to have a life." "Who?" I couldn't believe the honesty as it traveled down my arm and came out my pen, "I paid for it." She didn't lose her pose, "Were they pretty?" "That wasn't the point." "But were they?" "Some of them." "So you just gave them money and that was it?" "I liked to talk to them. I talked about you." "Is that supposed to make me feel good?" I looked at the clay. "Did you tell them that I was pregnant when you left?" I showed her my left hand. "Did you tell them about Anna?" I showed her my left hand. "Did you care for any of them?" I looked at the clay, she said, "I love that you are telling me the truth," and she took my hand from her shoulder and pressed it between her legs, she didn't turn her head to the side, she didn't close her eyes, she stared at our hands between her legs, I felt like I was killing something, she undid my belt and unzipped my pants, she reached her hand under my underpants, "I'm nervous," I said, by smiling, "It's OK," she said, "I'm sorry," I said, by smiling, "It's OK," she said, she closed the door behind her, then opened it and asked, "Did you ever make a sculpture of me in your head?" . . . There won't be enough pages in this book for me to tell you what I need to tell you, I could write smaller, I could slice the pages down their edges to make two pages, I could write over my own writing, but then what? Every afternoon someone would come to the apartment, I could hear the door opening, and the footsteps, little footsteps, I heard talking, a child's voice, almost a song, it was the voice I'd heard when I called from the airport, the two of them would talk for hours, I asked her one evening, when she came to pose, who paid her all of those visits, she said, "My grandson." "I have a grandson." "No," she said, "I have a grandson." "What's his name?" We tried again, we took off each other's clothes with the slowness of people who know how easy it is to be proven wrong, she lay face-down on the bed, her waist was irritated from pants that hadn't fit her in years, her thighs were scarred, I kneaded them with YES and NO, she said, "Don't look at anything else," I spread her legs, she inhaled, I could stare into the most private part of her and she couldn't see me looking, I slid my hand under her, she bent her knees, I closed my eyes, she said, "Lie on top of me," there was nowhere to write that I was nervous, she said, "Lie on top of me." I was afraid I'd crush her, she said, "All of you on all of me," I let myself sink into her, she said, "That's what I've wanted," why couldn't I have left it like that, why did I have to write anything else, I should have broken my fingers, I took a pen from the bedside table and wrote "Can I see him?" on my arm. She turned over, spilling my body next to her, "No." I begged with my hands. "No." "Please." "Please." "I won't let him know who I am. I just want to see him." "No." "Why not?" "Because." "Because why?" "Because I changed his diapers. And I couldn't sleep on my stomach for two years. And I taught him how to speak. And I cried when he cried. And when he was unreasonable, he yelled at me." "I'll hide in the coat closet and look through the keyhole." I thought she would say no, she said, "If he ever sees you, you will have betrayed me." Did she feel pity for me, did she want me to suffer? The next morning, she led me to the coat closet, which faces the living room, she went in with me, we were in there all day, although she knew he wouldn't come until the afternoon, it was too small, we needed more space between us, we needed Nothing Places, she said, "This is what it's felt like, except you weren't here." We looked at each other in silence for hours. When the bell rang, she went to let him in, I was on my hands and knees so my eye would be at the right level, through the keyhole I saw the door open, those white shoes, "Oskar!" she said, lifting him from the ground, "I'm OK," he said, that song, in his voice I heard my own voice, and my father's and grandfather's, and it was the first time I'd heard your voice, "Oskar!" she said again, lifting him again, I saw his face, Anna's eyes, "I'm OK," he said again, he asked her where she had been, "I was talking to the renter," she said. The renter? "Is he still here?" he asked, "No," she said, "he had to go run some errands." "But how did he get out of the apartment?" "He left right before you came." "But you said you were just talking to him." He knew about me, he didn't know who I was, but he knew someone was there, and he knew she wasn't telling the truth, I could hear it in his voice, in my voice, in your voice, I needed to talk to him, but what did I need to say? I'm your grandfather, I love you, I'm sorry? Maybe I needed to tell him the things I couldn't tell you, give him all the letters that were supposed to be for your eyes. But she would never give me her permission, and I wouldn't betray her, so I started to think about other ways . . . What am I going to do, I need more room, I have things I need to say, my words are pushing at the walls of the paper's edge, the next day, your mother came to the guest room and posed for me, I worked the clay with YES and NO, I made it soft, I pressed my thumbs into her cheeks, bringing her nose forward, leaving my thumbprints, I carved out pupils, I strengthened her brow, I hollowed out the space between her bottom lip and chin, I picked up a daybook and went over to her. I started to write about where I'd been and what I'd done since I left, how I'd made my living, whom I'd spent my time with, what I'd thought about and listened to and eaten, but she ripped the page from the book, "I don't care," she said, I don't know if she really didn't care or if it was something else, on the next blank page I wrote, "If there's anything you want to know, I'll tell you," she said, "I know it will make your life easier to tell me, but I don't want to know anything." How could that be? I asked her to tell me about you, she said, "Not our son, my son," I asked her to tell me about her son, she said, "Every Thanksgiving I made a turkey and pumpkin pie. I would go to the schoolyard and ask the children what toys they liked. I bought those for him. I wouldn't let anyone speak a foreign language in the apartment. But he still became you." "He became me?" "Everything was yes and no." "Did he go to college?" "I begged him to stay close, but he went to California. In that way he was also like you." "What did he study?" "He was going to be a lawyer, but he took over the business. He hated jewelry." "Why didn't you sell it?" "I begged him. I begged him to be a lawyer." "Then why?" "He wanted to be his own father." I'm sorry, if that's true, the last thing I would have wanted was for you to be like me, I left so you could be you. She said, "He tried to find you once. I gave him that only letter you ever sent. He was obsessed with it, always reading it. I don't know what you wrote, but it made him go and look for you." On the next blank page I wrote, "I opened the door one day and there he was." "He found you?" "We talked about nothing." "I didn't know he found you." "He wouldn't tell me who he was. He must have become nervous. Or he must have hated me once he saw me. He pretended to be a journalist. It was so terrible. He said he was doing a story about the survivors of

Dresden." "Did you tell him what happened to you that night?" "It was in the letter." "What did you write?" "You didn't read it?" "You didn't send it to me." "It was terrible. All of the things we couldn't share. The room was filled with conversations we weren't having." I didn't tell her that after you left, I stopped eating, I got so skinny that the bathwater would collect between my bones, why didn't anyone ask me why I was so skinny? If someone had asked, I never would have eaten another bite. "But if he didn't tell you he was your son, how did you know?" "I knew because he was my son." She put her hand on my chest, over my heart, I put my hands on her thighs, I put my hands around her, she undid my pants, "I'm nervous," despite everything I wanted, the sculpture was looking more and more like Anna, she closed the door behind her, I'm running out of room . . . I spent most of my days walking around the city, getting to know it again, I went to the old Columbian Bakery but it wasn't there anymore, in its place was a ninety-nine-cent store where everything cost more than ninety-nine cents. I went by the tailor shop where I used to get my pants taken in, but there was a bank, you needed a card just to open the door, I walked for hours, down one side of Broadway and up the other, where there had been a watch repairman there was a video store, where there had been a flower market there was a store for video games, where there had been a butcher there was sushi, what's sushi, and what happens to all of the broken watches? I spent hours at the dog run on the side of the natural history museum, a pit bull, a Labrador, a golden retriever, I was the only person without a dog, I thought and thought, how could I be close to Oskar from far away, how could I be fair to you and fair to your mother and fair to myself, I wanted to carry the closet door with me so I could always look at him through the keyhole, I did the next best thing. I learned his life from a distance, when he went to school, when he came home, where his friends lived, what stores he liked to go to, I followed him all over the city, but I didn't betray your mother, because I never let him know I was there. I thought it could go on like that forever, and yet here I am, once again I was proven wrong. I don't remember when the strangeness of it first occurred to me, how much he was out, how many neighborhoods he went to, why I was the only one watching him, how his mother could let him wander so far so alone. Every weekend morning, he left the building with an old man and went knocking on doors around the city, I made a map of where they went, but I couldn't make sense of it, it made no sense, what were they doing? And who was the old man, a friend, a teacher, a replacement for a missing grandfather? And why did they stay for only a few minutes at each apartment, were they selling something, collecting information? And what did his grandmother know, was I the only one worried about him? After they left one house, on Staten Island, I waited around and knocked on the door, "I can't believe it," the woman said, "another visitor!" "I'm sorry," I wrote, "I don't speak. That was my grandson who just left. Could you tell me what he was doing here?" The woman told me, "What a strange family you are." I thought, Family we are.

"I just got off the phone with his mother." I wrote, "Why was he here?" She said, "For the key." I asked, "What key?" She said, "For the lock." "What lock?" "Don't you know?" For eight months I followed him and talked to the people he talked to, I tried to learn about him as he tried to learn about you, he was trying to find you, just as you'd tried to find me, it broke my heart into more pieces than my heart was made of, why can't people say what they mean at the time? One afternoon I followed him downtown, we sat across from each other on the subway, the old man looked at me, was I staring, was I reaching my arms out in front of me, did he know that I should have been the one sitting next to Oskar? They went into a coffee store, on the way back I lost them, it happened all the time, it's hard to stay close without making yourself known, and I wouldn't betray her. When I got back to the Upper West Side I went into a bookstore, I couldn't go to the apartment yet, I needed time to think, at the end of the aisle I saw a man who I thought might be Simon Goldberg, he was also in the children's section, the more I looked at him, the more unsure I was, the more I wanted it to be him, had he gone to work instead of to his death? My hands shook against the change in my pockets, I tried not to stare, I tried not to reach my arms out in front of me, could it be, did he recognize me, he'd written, "It is my great hope that our paths, however long and winding, will cross again." Fifty years later he wore the same thick glasses, I'd never seen a whiter shirt, he had a hard time letting go of books, I went up to him. "I don't speak," I wrote, "I'm sorry." He wrapped his arms around me and squeezed, I could feel his heart beating against my heart, they were trying to beat in unison, without saying a word he turned around and rushed away from me, out of the store, into the street, I'm almost sure it wasn't him, I want an infinitely long blank book and the rest of time ... The next day, Oskar and the old man went to the Empire State Building, I waited for them on the street. I kept looking up, trying to see him, my neck was burning, was he looking down at me, were we sharing something without either of us knowing it? After an hour, the elevator doors opened and the old man came out, was he going to leave Oskar up there, so high up, so alone, who would keep him safe? I hated him. I started to write something, he came up to me and grabbed me by the collar. "Listen," he said, "I don't know who you are, but I've seen you following us, and I don't like it. Not a bit. This is the only time I'm going to tell you to stay away." My book had fallen to the floor, so I couldn't say anything. "If I ever see you again, anywhere near that boy—" I pointed at the floor, he let go of my collar, I picked up the book and wrote, "I'm Oskar's grandfather. I don't speak. I'm sorry." "His grandfather?" I flipped back and pointed at what I'd been writing, "Where is he?" "Oskar doesn't have a grandfather." I pointed at the page. "He's walking down the stairs." I quickly explained everything as best I could, my handwriting was becoming illegible, he said, "Oskar wouldn't lie to me." I wrote, "He didn't lie. He doesn't know." The old man took a necklace from under his shirt and looked at it, the pendant was a compass, he said, "Oskar is my friend. I have to tell him." "He's my grandson. Please don't." "You're the one who should be going around with him." "I have been." "And what about his mother?" "What about his mother?" We heard Oskar singing from around the corner, his voice was getting louder, the old man said, "He's a good boy," and walked away. I went straight home, the apartment was empty. I thought about packing my bags, I thought about jumping out a window, I sat on the bed and thought, I thought about you. What kind of food did you like, what was your favorite song, who was the first girl you kissed, and where, and how, I'm running out of room, I want an infinitely long blank book and forever, I don't know how much time passed, it didn't matter, I'd lost all of my reasons to keep track. Someone rang the bell, I didn't get up, I didn't care who it was, I wanted to be alone, on the other side of the window. I heard the door open and I heard his voice, my reason, "Grandma?" He was in the apartment, it was just the two of us, grandfather and grandson. I heard him going from room to room, moving things, opening and closing, what was he looking for, why was he always looking? He came to my door, "Grandma?" I didn't want to betray her, I turned off the lights, what was I so afraid of? "Grandma?" He started crying, my grandson was crying. "Please. I really need help. If you're in there, please come out." I turned on the light, why wasn't I more afraid? "Please." I opened the door and we faced each other, I faced myself, "Are you the renter?" I went back into the room and got this daybook from the closet, this book that is nearly out of pages, I brought it to him and wrote, "I don't speak. I'm sorry." I was so grateful to have him looking at me, he asked me who I was, I didn't know what to tell him, I invited him into the room, he asked me if I was a stranger, I didn't know what to tell him, he was still crying, I didn't know how to hold him, I'm running out of room. I brought him over to the bed, he sat down, I didn't ask him any questions or tell him what I already knew, we didn't talk about unimportant things, we didn't become friends, I could have been anyone, he began at the beginning, the vase, the key, Brooklyn, Queens, I knew the lines by heart. Poor child, telling everything to a stranger, I wanted to build walls around him, I wanted to separate inside from outside, I wanted to give him an infinitely long blank book and the rest of time, he told me how he'd just gone up to the top of the Empire State Building, how his friend had told him he was finished, it wasn't what I'd wanted, but if it was necessary to bring my grandson face to face with me, it was worth it, anything would have been. I wanted to touch him, to tell him that even if everyone left everyone, I would never leave him, he talked and talked, his words fell through him, trying to find the floor of his sadness, "My dad," he said, "My dad," he ran across the street and came back with a phone, "These are his last words."

MESSAGE FIVE.

10:04 A.M. IT'S DA   S DAD. HEL   S DAD. KNOW IF
      EAR ANY   THIS I'M
  HELLO?   YOU HEAR ME? WE   TO THE
ROOF   EVERYTHING   OK   FINE   SOON
  SORRY   HEAR ME   MUCH
    HAPPENS,   REMEMBER—

The message was cut off, you sounded so calm, you didn't sound like someone who was about to die, I wish we could have sat across a table and talked about nothing for hours, I wish we could have wasted time, I want an infinitely blank book and the rest of time. I told Oskar it was best not to let his grandma know we'd met, he didn't ask why, I wonder what he knew, I told him if he ever wanted to talk to me, he could throw pebbles at the guest room window and I would come down to meet him on the corner, I was afraid I'd never get to see him again, to see him seeing me, that night was the first time your mother and I made love since I returned, and the last time we ever made love, it didn't feel like the last time, I'd kissed Anna for the last time, seen my parents for the last time, spoken for the last time, why didn't I learn to treat everything like it was the last time, my greatest regret is how much I believed in the future, she said, "I want to show you something," she led me to the second bedroom, her hand was squeezing YES, she opened the door and pointed at the bed, "That's where he used to sleep," I touched the sheets, I lowered myself to the floor and smelled the pillow, I wanted anything of you that I could have, I wanted dust, she said, "Years and years ago. Thirty years." I lay on the bed, I wanted to feel what you felt, I wanted to tell you everything, she lay next to me, she asked, "Do you believe in heaven and hell?" I held up my right hand, "Neither do I," she said, "I think after you live it's like before you lived," her hand was open, I put YES into it, she closed her fingers around mine, she said, "Think of all the things that haven't been born yet. All the babies. Some never will be born. Is that sad?" I didn't know if it was sad, all the parents that would never meet, all the miscarriages, I closed my eyes, she said, "A few days before the bombing, my father took me out to the shed. He gave me a sip of whiskey and let me try his pipe. It made me feel so adult, so special. He asked me what I knew about sex. I coughed and coughed. He laughed and laughed and became serious. He asked if I knew how to pack a suitcase, and if I knew never to accept the first offer, and if I could start a fire if I had to. I loved my father very much. I loved him very, very much. But I never found a way to tell him." I turned my head to the side, I rested it on her shoulder, she put her hand on my cheek, just like my mother used to, everything she did reminded me of someone else, "It's a shame," she said, "that life is so precious." I turned onto my side and put my arm around her, I'm running out of room, my eyes were closed and I kissed her, her lips were my mother's lips, and Anna's lips, and your lips, I didn't know how to be with her and be with her. "It makes us worry so much," she said, unbuttoning her shirt, I unbuttoned mine, she took off her pants, I took off mine, "We worry so much," I touched her and touched everyone, "It's all we do," we made love for the last time, I was with her and with everyone, when she got up to go to the bathroom there was blood on the sheets, I went back to the guest room to sleep, there are so many things you'll never know. The next morning I was awoken by a tapping on the window, I told your mother I was going for a walk, she didn't say anything, what did she know, why did she let me out of her sight? Oskar was waiting for me under the streetlamp, he said, "I want to dig up his grave." I've seen him every day for the past two months, we've been planning what's about to happen, down to the smallest detail, we've even practiced digging in Central Park, the details have begun to remind me or rules, I can't eat

JONATHAN SAFRAN FOER

574   JONATHAN SAFRAN FOER

A SIMPLE SOLUTION
TO AN IMPOSSIBLE PROBLEM

The day after the renter and I dug up Dad's grave, I went to Mr. Black's apartment. I felt like he deserved to know what happened, even if he wasn't actually a part of it. But when I knocked, the person who answered wasn't him. "Can I help you?" a woman asked. Her glasses were hanging from a chain around her neck, and she was holding a folder with lots of paper coming out of it. "You're not Mr. Black." "Mr. Black?" "Mr. Black who lives here. Where is he?" "I'm sorry, I don't know." "Is he OK?" "I assume so. I don't know." "Who are you?" "I'm a realtor." "What's that?" "I'm selling the apartment." "Why?" "I suppose the owner wants to sell it. I'm just covering today." "Covering?" "The realtor who represents this property is sick." "Do you know how I can find the owner?" "I'm sorry, I don't." "He was my friend."

She told me, "They're coming by sometime this morning to take everything away." "Who's they?" "They. I don't know. Contractors. Garbage men. They." "Not moving men?" "I don't know." "They're throwing his things away?" "Or selling them." If I'd been incredibly rich, I would have bought everything, even if I just had to put it in storage. I told her, "Well, I left something in the apartment. It's something of mine, so they can't sell it or give it away. I'm going to get it. Excuse me."

I went to the index of biographies. I knew I couldn't save the whole thing, obviously, but there was something I needed. I pulled out the B drawer and flipped through the cards. I found Mr. Black's. I knew it was the right thing to do, so I took it out and put it in the pouch of my overalls.

But then, even though I'd gotten what I wanted, I went to the S drawer. Antonin Scalia, G. L. Scarborough, Lord Leslie George Scar-man, Maurice Scève, Anne Wilson Schaef, Jack Warner Schaefer, Iris Scharmel, Robert Haven Schauffler, Barry Scheck, Johann Scheffler, Jean de Schelandre . . . And then I saw it: Schell.

At first I was relieved, because I felt like everything I'd done had been worth it, because I'd made Dad into a Great Man who was biographically significant and would be remembered. But then I examined the card, and I saw that it wasn't Dad.

OSKAR SCHELL: SON

I wish I had known that I wasn't going to see Mr. Black again when we shook hands that afternoon. I wouldn't have let go. Or I would have forced him to keep searching with me. Or I would have told him about how Dad called when I was home. But I didn't know, just like I didn't know it was the last time Dad would ever tuck me in, because you never know. So when he said, "I'm finished. I hope you understand," I said, "I understand," even though I didn't understand. I never went to find him on the observation deck of the Empire State Building, because I was happier believing he was there than finding out for sure.

I kept looking for the lock after he told me he was finished, but it wasn't the same.

I went to Far Rockaway and Boerum Hill and Long Island City.

I went to Dumbo and Spanish Harlem and the Meatpacking District.

I went to Flatbush and Tudor City and Little Italy.

I went to Bedford-Stuyvesant and Inwood and Red Hook.

I don't know if it was because Mr. Black wasn't with me anymore, or because I'd been spending so much time making plans with the renter to dig up Dad's grave, or just because I'd been looking for so long without finding anything, but I no longer felt like I was moving in the direction of Dad. I'm not even sure I believed in the lock anymore.

The last Black I visited was Peter. He lived in Sugar Hill, which is in Hamilton Heights, which is in Harlem. A man was sitting on the stoop when I walked up to the house. He had a little baby on his knee, who he was talking to, even though babies don't understand language, obviously. "Are you Peter Black?" "Who's asking?" "Oskar Schell." He patted the step, which meant I could sit next to him if I wanted, which I thought was nice, but I wanted to stand. "That's your baby?" "Yes." "Can I pet her?" "Him." "Can I pet him?" "Sure," he said. I couldn't believe how soft his head was, and how little his eyes were, and his fingers. "He's very vulnerable," I said. "He is," Peter said, "but we keep him pretty safe." "Does he eat normal food?" "Not yet. Just milk for now." "Does he cry a lot?" "I'd say so. Definitely feels like a lot." "But babies don't get sad, right? He's just hungry or something." "We'll never know." I liked watching the baby make fists. I wondered if he could have thoughts, or if he was more like a nonhuman animal. "Do you want to hold him?" "I don't think that's a very good idea." "Why not?" "I don't know how to hold a baby." "If you want to, I'll show you. It's easy." "OK." "Why don't you sit down?" he said. "Here you go. Now put one of your hands under here. Like that. Good. Now put the other around his head. That's right. You can kind of hold it against your chest. Right. Like that. You've got it. Just like that. He's as happy as can be." "This is good?" "You're doing great." "What's his name?" "Peter." "I thought that was your name." "We're both Peter." It made me wonder for the first time why I wasn't named after Dad, although I didn't wonder about the renter's name being Thomas. I said, "Hi, Peter. I'll protect you."

When I got home that afternoon, after eight months of searching New York, I was exhausted and frustrated and pessimistic, even though what I wanted to be was happy.

I went up to my laboratory, but I didn't feel like performing any experiments. I didn't feel like playing the tambourine, or spoiling Buckminster, or arranging my collections, or looking through *Stuff That Happened to Me.*

Mom and Ron were hanging out in the family room, even though he wasn't part of our family. I went to the kitchen to get some dehydrated ice cream. I looked over at the telephone. The new phone. It looked back at me. Whenever it would ring, I'd scream, "The phone's ringing!" because I didn't want to touch it. I didn't even want to be in the same room with it.

I pressed the Message Play button, which I hadn't done since the worst day, and that was on the old phone.

> Message one. Saturday, 11:52 A.M. *Hi, this is a message for Oskar Schell. Oskar, this is Abby Black. You were just over at my apartment asking about the key. I wasn't completely honest with you, and I think I might be able to help. Please give —*

And then the message was cut off.

Abby was the second Black I had gone to, eight months before. She lived in the narrowest house in New York. I told her she was pretty. She cracked up. I told her she was pretty. She told me I was sweet. She cried when I told her about elephant E.S.P. I asked if we could kiss. She didn't say she didn't want to. Her message had been waiting for me for eight months.

"Mom?" "Yes?" "I'm going out." "OK." "I'll be back later." "OK." "I don't know when. It could be extremely late." "OK." Why didn't she ask me more? Why didn't she try to stop me, or at least keep me safe?

Because it was starting to get dark, and because the streets were crowded, I bumped into a googolplex people. Who were they? Where were they going? What were they looking for? I wanted to hear their heartbeats, and I wanted them to hear mine.

The subway station was just a few blocks from her house, and when I got there the door was open a little, like she knew I'd be coming, even though she couldn't have, obviously. So why was it open?

"Hello? Is anyone there? It's Oskar Schell."

She came to the door.

I was relieved, because I hadn't invented her.

JONATHAN SAFRAN FOER

"Do you remember me?" "Of course I do, Oskar. You've grown." "I have?" "A lot. Inches." "I've been so busy searching that I haven't been measuring myself." "Come in," she said. "I thought you weren't going to call me back. It's been a long time since I left that message." I told her, "I'm afraid of the phone."

She said, "I've thought about you a lot." I said, "Your message." "From months ago?" "How weren't you honest with me?" "I told you I didn't know anything about the key." "But you did?" "Yes. Well, no. I don't. My husband does." "Why didn't you tell me when we met?" "I couldn't." "Why not?" "I just couldn't." "That's not a real answer." "My husband and I had been having a terrible fight." "He was my dad!" "He was my husband." "He was murdered!"

"I wanted to hurt him." "Why?" "Because he had hurt me." "Why?" "Because people hurt each other. That's what people do." "It's not what I do." "I know." "I spent eight months looking for what you could have told me in eight seconds!" "I called you. Right after you left." "You hurt me!" "I'm very sorry."

"*So?*" I asked. "So what about your husband?" She said, "He's been looking for you." "*He's* been looking for *me?*" "Yes." "But *I've* been looking for *him!*" "He'll explain everything to you. I think you should call him." "I'm angry at you because you weren't honest with me." "I know." "You almost ruined my life."

We were incredibly close.

I could smell her breathing.

She said, "If you want to kiss me, you can." "What?" "You asked me, that day we met, if we could kiss. I said no then, but I am saying yes now." "I'm embarrassed about that day." "There's no reason to be embarrassed." "You don't have to let me kiss you just because you feel sorry for me." "Kiss me," she said, "and I'll kiss you back." I asked her, "What if we just hugged?"

She held me against her.

I started to cry, and I squeezed her as tightly as I could. Her shoulder was getting wet and I thought, *Maybe it's true that you can use up all of your tears. Maybe Grandma's right about that.* It was nice to think about, because what I wanted was to be empty.

And then, out of nowhere, I had a revelation, and the floor disappeared from under me, and I was standing on nothing.

I pulled away.

"Why did your message cut off?" "Excuse me?" "The message you left on our phone. It just stops in the middle." "Oh, that must have been when your mother picked up."

"My mom picked up?" "Yes." "And then what?" "What do you mean?" "Did you talk to her?" "For a few minutes." "What did you tell her?" "I don't remember." "But you told her that I'd gone to visit you?" "Yes, of course. Was I wrong to?"

I didn't know if she was wrong to. And I didn't know why Mom hadn't said anything about their conversation, or even about the message.

"The key? You told her about it?" "I assumed she already knew." "And my mission?"

It didn't make any sense.

Why hadn't Mom said anything?

Or done anything?

Or cared at all?

And then, all of a sudden, it made perfect sense.

All of a sudden I understood why, when Mom asked where I was going, and I said "Out," she didn't ask any more questions. She didn't have to, because she knew.

It made sense that Ada knew I lived on the Upper West Side, and that Carol had hot cookies waiting when I knocked on her door, and that doorman215@hotmail.com said "Good luck, Oskar" when I left, even though I was ninety-nine-percent sure I hadn't told him that my name was Oskar.

They knew I was coming.

Mom had talked to all of them before I had.

Even Mr. Black was part of it. He must have known I was going to knock on his door that day, because she must have told him. She probably told him to go around with me, and keep me company, and keep me safe. Did he even really like me? And were all of his amazing stories even true? Were his hearing aids real? The bed that pulled? Were the bullets and roses bullets and roses?

The whole time.

Everyone.

Everything.

Probably Grandma knew.

Probably even the renter.

Was the renter even the renter?

My search was a play that Mom had written, and she knew the ending when I was at the beginning.

I asked Abby, "Was your door open because you knew I was coming?" She didn't say anything for a few seconds. Then she said, "Yes."

"Where's your husband?" "He's not my husband." "I don't. Understand. ANYTHING!" "He's my ex-husband." "Where is he?" "He's at work." "But it's Sunday night." She said, "He does foreign markets." "*What?*" "It's Monday morning in Japan."

"There's a young man here to see you," the woman behind the desk said into the phone, and it made me feel so weird to think that he was on the other end of the line, even if I knew I was getting confused about who "he" was. "Yes," she said, "a very young man." Then she said, "No." Then she said, "Oskar Schell." Then she said, "Yes. He says to see you."

"May I ask what this concerns?" she asked me. "He says his dad," she said into the phone. Then she said, "That's what he says." Then she said, "OK." Then she said to me, "Go down the hallway. His door is the third on the left."

There was art that was probably famous on the walls. There were incredibly beautiful views out of the windows, which Dad would have loved. But I didn't look at any of it, and I didn't take any pictures. I'd never been so concentrated in my life, because I'd never been closer to the lock. I knocked on the third door on the left, which had a sign on it that said WILLIAM BLACK. A voice from inside the room said, "Come in."

"What can I do for you tonight?" said a man behind a desk. He was about the same age that Dad would have been, or I guess still was, if dead people have ages. He had brownish-grayish hair, a short beard, and round brown glasses. For a second he looked familiar, and I wondered if he was the person I had seen from the Empire State Building through the binocular machine. But then I realized that was impossible, because we were at Fifty-seventh Street, which is north, obviously. There were a bunch of picture frames on his desk. I looked at them quickly to make sure Dad wasn't in any of the pictures.

I asked, "Did you know my dad?" He leaned back in his chair and said, "I'm not sure. Who was your dad?" "Thomas Schell." He thought for a minute. I hated how he had to think. "No," he said. "I don't know any Schells." "Knew." "Excuse me?" "He's dead, so you couldn't know him now." "I'm sorry to hear that." "You must have known him, though." "No. I'm sure I didn't." "But you *must* have."

I told him, "I found a little envelope that had your name on it, and I thought maybe it was your wife, who I know is now your ex-wife, but she said she didn't know what it was, and your name is William, and I wasn't anywhere near the W's yet—" "My wife?" "I went and talked to her." "Talked to her where?" "The narrowest townhouse in New York." "How was she?" "What do you mean?" "How did she seem?" "Sad." "Sad how?" "Just sad." "What was she doing?" "Nothing, really. She was trying to give me food, even though I told her I wasn't hungry. Someone was in the other room while we talked." "A man?" "Yeah." "You saw him?" "He passed by the door, but mostly he was yelling from another room." "He was *yelling?*" "Extremely loud." "What was he yelling?" "I couldn't hear the words." "Did he sound intimidating?" "I don't know what that means." "Was he scary?" "What about my dad?" "When was this?" "Eight months ago." "Eight months ago?" "Seven months and twenty-eight days." He smiled. "Why are you smiling?" He put his face in his hands, like he was going to cry, but he didn't. He looked up and said, "That man was me."

"You?" "Eight months ago. Yeah. I thought you were talking about the other day." "But he didn't have a beard." "He grew a beard." "And he didn't wear glasses." He took off his glasses and said, "He changed." I started thinking about the pixels in the image of the falling body, and how the closer you looked, the less you could see. "Why were you yelling?" "Long story." "I have a long time," I said, because anything that could bring me closer to Dad was something I wanted to know

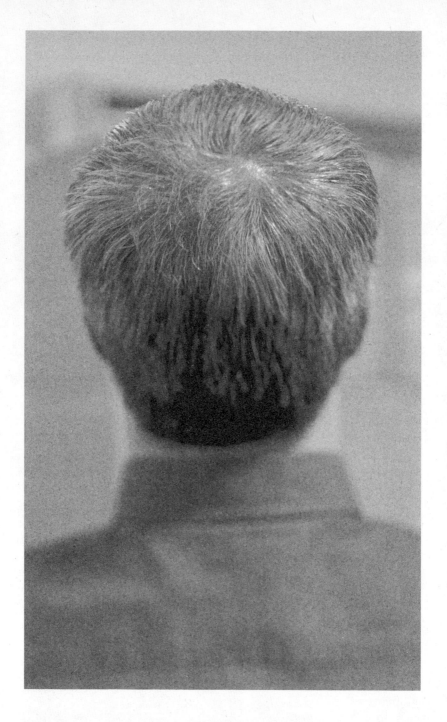

JONATHAN SAFRAN FOER

about, even if it would hurt me. "It's a long, long story." "Please." He closed a notebook that was open on his desk and said, "It's too long a story."

I said, "Don't you think it's so weird that we were in the apartment together eight months ago and now we're in this office together?"

He nodded.

"It's weird," I said. "We were incredibly close."

He said, "So what's so special about the envelope?" "Nothing, exactly. It's what was *in* the envelope." "Which was?" "Which was this." I pulled the string around my neck, and made it so the key to our apartment was on my back and Dad's key rested on the pouch of my overalls, over the Band-Aid, over my heart. "Can I see that?" he asked. I handed him the key, even though I kept the string around my neck. He examined it and asked, "Did it say something on the envelope?" "It said 'Black.'" He looked up at me. "Did you find it in a blue vase?" "Jose!"

He said, "I can't believe it." "You can't believe what?" "This is truly the most amazing thing that's ever happened to me." "*What* is?" "I've spent two years trying to find this key." "But I've spent eight months trying to find the lock." "Then we've been looking for each other." I was finally able to ask the most important question of my life. "What does it open?"

"It opens a safe-deposit box." "Well, what's it got to do with my dad?" "Your dad?" "The whole *point* of the key is that I found it in my dad's closet, and since he's dead, I couldn't ask him what it meant, so I had to find out for myself." "You found it in his closet?" "Yes." "In a tall blue vase?" I nodded. "With a label on the bottom?" "I don't know. I didn't see a label. I don't remember." If I'd been alone, I would have given myself the biggest bruise of my life. I would have turned myself into one big bruise.

"My father passed away about two years ago," he said. "He went in for a checkup and the doctor told him he had two months to live. He died two months later." I didn't want to hear about death. It was all anyone talked about, even when no one was actually talking about it. "I needed to figure out what to do with all of his things. Books, furniture, clothes." "Didn't you want to keep them?" "I didn't want any of it." I thought that was weird, because Dad's things were all I wanted. "So to make a long story short—" "You don't have to make a long story short." "I had an estate sale. I shouldn't have been there. I should have hired someone to take care of it. Or I should have given it all away. Instead I was in the position of telling people that the prices for his belongings weren't negotiable. His wedding suit wasn't negotiable. His sunglasses weren't negotiable. It was one of the worst days of my life. Maybe the worst."

"Are you OK?" "I'm fine. It's been a bad couple of years. My father and I weren't exactly close." "Do you need a hug?" "I'll be OK." "Why not?" "Why not what?" "Why weren't you and your dad exactly close?" He said, "Too long a story." "Can you please tell me about my dad now?"

"My father wrote letters when he found out about the cancer. He wasn't much of a letter writer before. I don't know if he ever wrote. But he spent his last two months writing obsessively. Whenever he was awake." I asked why, but what I really wanted to know was why I started writing letters after Dad died. "He was trying to say his goodbyes. He wrote to people he barely knew. If he hadn't already been sick, his letters would have been his sickness. I had a business meeting the other day, and in the middle of our conversation the man asked if I was related to Edmund Black. I told him yes, he was my father. He said, 'I went to high school with your dad. He wrote me the most amazing letter before he died. Ten pages. I only barely knew him. We hadn't talked in fifty years. It was the most amazing letter I'd ever read.' I asked him if I could see it. He said, 'I don't think it was meant to be shared.' I told him it would mean a lot to me. He said, 'He mentions you in it.' I told him I understood.

"I looked through my father's Rolodex—" "What's that?" "Phone book. I called every name. His cousins, his business partners, people I'd never heard of. He'd written to everyone. Every single person. Some let me see their letters. Others didn't."

"What were they like?"

"The shortest was a single sentence. The longest was a couple dozen pages. Some of them were almost like little plays. Others were just questions to the person he was writing to." "What kinds of questions?'" "'Did you know I was in love with you that summer in Nor-folk?' 'Will they be taxed for possessions I leave, like the piano?' 'How do light bulbs work?'" "I could have explained that to him." "'Does anyone actually die in his sleep?'

"Some of his letters were funny. I mean, really, really funny. I didn't know he could be so funny. And some were philosophical. He wrote about how happy he was, and how sad he was, and all of the things he wanted to do but never did, and all of the things he did but didn't want to do."

"Didn't he write a letter to you?" "Yes." "What did it say?" "I couldn't read it. Not for a few weeks." "Why not?" "It was too painful." "I would have been extremely curious." "My wife—my ex-wife—said I was being crazy not to read it." "That wasn't very understanding of her." "She was right, though. It was crazy. It was unreasonable. I was being childish." "Yeah, but you were his child."

"But I was his child. That's right. I'm babbling. To make a long story short—" "Don't make it short," I said, because even though I wanted him to tell me about my dad instead of his, I also wanted to make the story as long as I could, because I was afraid of its end. He said, "I read it. Maybe I was expecting something confessional. I don't know. Something angry, or asking for forgiveness. Something that would make me rethink everything. But it was matter-of-fact. More of a document than a letter, if that makes sense." "I guess so." "I don't know. Maybe I was wrong to, but I was expecting him to say he was sorry for things, and tell me he loved me. End-of-life stuff. But there was none of it. He didn't even say 'I love you.' He told me about his will, his life in-surance policy, all of those horrible businesslike things that feel so inap-propriate to think about when someone has died."

"You were disappointed?" "I was angry." "I'm sorry." "No. There's nothing to be sorry for. I thought about it. I thought about it all the time. My father told me where he'd left things, and what he wanted taken care of. He was responsible. He was good. It's easy to be emo-tional. You can always make a scene. Remember me eight months ago? That was easy." "It didn't sound easy." "It was simple. Highs and lows make you feel that things matter, but they're nothing." "So what's something?" "Being reliable is something. Being good."

"And what about the key?" "At the end of his letter he wrote, 'I have something for you. In the blue vase, on the shelf in the bedroom, is a key. It opens a safe-deposit box at our bank. I hope you'll understand why I wanted you to have it.'" "And? What was in it?" "I didn't read the note until after I'd sold all of his belongings. I had sold the vase. I sold it to your father." "*What the?*"

"That's why I've been trying to find you." "You met my dad?" "Only briefly, but yes." "Do you remember him?" "It was just a minute." "But do you remember him?" "We chatted a bit." "And?" "He was a nice man. I think he could see how hard it was for me to part with those things." "Could you please describe him?" "Gosh, I don't really remember much." "*Please.*" "He was maybe five foot ten. He had brown hair. He wore glasses." "What kind of glasses?" "Thick glasses." "What kind of clothes was he wearing?" "A suit, I think." "What suit?" "Gray, maybe?" "That's true! He wore a gray suit to work! Did he have a gap between his teeth?" "I don't remember." "Try."

"He said he was on his way home and saw the sign for the sale. He told me that he had an anniversary coming up the next week." "September 14!" "He was going to surprise your mom. The vase was perfect, he said. He said she'd love it." "He was going to surprise her?" "He'd made reservations at her favorite restaurant. It was going to be some sort of fancy night out."

The tuxedo.

"What else did he say?" "What else did he say . . ." "Anything." "He had a great laugh. I remember that. It was good of him to laugh, and to make me laugh. He was laughing for my sake."

"What else?" "He had a very discerning eye." "What's that?" "He knew what he liked. He knew when he'd found it." "That's true. He had an incredibly discerning eye." "I remember watching him hold the vase. He examined the bottom of it and turned it around a number of times. He seemed like a very thoughtful person." "He was extremely thoughtful."

I wished he could remember even more details, like if Dad had unbuttoned his shirt's top button, or if he smelled like shaving, or if he whistled "I Am the Walrus." Was he holding a *New York Times* under his arm? Were his lips chapped? Was there a red pen in his pocket?

"When the apartment was empty that night, I sat on the floor and read the letter from my father. I read about the vase. I felt like I'd failed him." "But couldn't you go to the bank and tell them you'd lost the key?" "I tried that. But they said they didn't have a box under his name. I tried my name. No box. Not under my mother's name or my grandparents' names. It didn't make any sense." "There was nothing the bank people could do?" "They were sympathetic, but without the key, I was stuck." "And that's why you needed to find my dad."

"I hoped he would realize that there was a key in the vase and find me. But how could he? We sold my father's apartment, so even if he went back, it would be a dead end. And I was sure he'd just throw the key away if he found it, assuming it was junk. That's what I would have done. And there was no way I could find him. Absolutely no way. I knew nothing about him, not even his name. For a few weeks I'd go over to the neighborhood on my way home from work, even though it wasn't on my way. It was an hour out of my way. I'd walk around looking for him. I even put up a few signs: 'To the man who bought the vase at the estate sale on Seventy-fifth Street this weekend, please contact . . .' But this was the week after September 11. There were posters everywhere."

"My mom put up posters of him." "What do you mean?" "He died in September 11. That's how he died." "Oh, God. I didn't realize. I'm so sorry." "It's OK." "I don't know what to say." "You don't have to say anything." "I didn't see the posters. If I had . . . Well, I don't know what if I had." "You would have been able to find us." "I guess that's right." "I wonder if your posters and my mom's posters were ever close to each other."

He said, "Wherever I was, I was trying to find him: uptown, downtown, on the train. I looked in everyone's eyes, but none were his. Once I saw someone I thought might be your father across Broadway in Times Square, but I lost him in the crowd. I saw someone I thought might be him getting into a cab at Twenty-third Street. I would have called after him, but I didn't know his name." "Thomas." "Thomas. I wish I'd known it then."

He said, "I followed one man around Central Park for more than half an hour. I thought he was your father. I couldn't figure out why he was walking in such a strange, crisscrossing way. He wasn't getting anywhere. I couldn't figure it out." "Why didn't you stop him?" "Eventually I did." "And what happened?" "I was wrong. It was someone else." "Did you ask him why he was walking like that?" "He'd lost something and was searching the ground for it."

"Well, you don't have to look anymore," I told him. He said, "I've spent so long looking for this key. It's hard to look *at* it." "Don't you want to see what he left for you?" "I don't think it's a question of wanting." I asked him, "What's it a question of?"

He said, "I'm so sorry. I know that you're looking for something, too. And I know this isn't what you're looking for." "It's OK." "For what it's worth, your father seemed like a good man. I only spoke with him for a few minutes, but that was long enough to see that he was good. You were lucky to have a father like that. I'd trade this key for that father." "You shouldn't have to choose." "No, you shouldn't."

We sat there, not saying anything. I examined the pictures on his desk again. All of them were of Abby.

He said, "Why don't you come with me to the bank?" "You're nice, but no thank you." "Are you sure?" It's not that I wasn't curious. I was incredibly curious. It's that I was afraid of getting confused.

He said, "What is it?" "Nothing." "Are you all right?" I wanted to keep the tears in, but I couldn't. He said, "I'm so, so sorry."

"Can I tell you something that I've never told anyone else?"

"Of course."

"On that day, they let us out of school basically as soon as we got there. They didn't really tell us why, just that something bad had happened. We didn't get it, I guess. Or we didn't get that something bad could happen to us. A lot of parents came to pick up their kids, but since school is only five blocks from my apartment, I walked home. My friend told me he was going to call, so I went to the answering machine and the light was beeping. There were five messages. They were all from him." "Your friend?" "My dad."

He covered his mouth with his hand.

"He just kept saying that he was OK, and that everything would be fine, and that we shouldn't worry."

A tear went down his cheek and rested on his finger.

"But this is the thing that I've never told anyone. After I listened to the messages, the phone rang. It was 10:26. I looked at the caller ID and saw that it was his cell phone." "Oh, God." "Could you please put your hand on me so I can finish the rest?" "Of course," he said, and he scooted his chair around his desk and next to me.

"I couldn't pick up the phone. I just couldn't do it. It rang and rang, and I couldn't move. I wanted to pick it up, but I couldn't.

"The answering machine went on, and I heard my own voice."

Hi, you've reached the Schell residence. Here is today's fact of the day: It's so cold in Yukatia, which is in Siberia, that breath instantly freezes with a crackling noise that they call the whispering of the stars. On extremely cold days, the towns are covered in a fog caused by the breath of humans and animals. Please leave a message.

"There was a beep.
"Then I heard Dad's voice."

Are you there? Are you there? Are you there?

"He needed me, and I couldn't pick up. I just couldn't pick up. I just couldn't. *Are you there?* He asked eleven times. I know, because I've counted. It's one more than I can count on my fingers. Why did he keep asking? Was he waiting for someone to come home? And why didn't he say 'anyone'? *Is anyone there?* 'You' is just one person. Sometimes I think he knew I was there. Maybe he kept saying it to give me time to get brave enough to pick up. Also, there was so much space between the times he asked. There are fifteen seconds between the third and the fourth, which is the longest space. You can hear people in the background screaming and crying. And you can hear glass breaking, which is part of what makes me wonder if people were jumping.

Are you there? Are you there? Are you there? Are you there? Are you there? Are you there? Are you there? Are you there? Are you there? Are you there? Are you

"And then it cut off.

"I've timed the message, and it's one minute and twenty-seven seconds. Which means it ended at 10:28. Which was when the building came down. So maybe that's how he died."

"I'm so sorry," he said.

"I've never told that to anyone."

He squeezed me, almost like a hug, and I could feel him shaking his head.

I asked him, "Do you forgive me?"

"Do I forgive you?"

"Yeah."

"For not being able to pick up?"

"For not being able to tell anyone."

He said, "I do."

I took the string off my neck and put it around his neck.

"What about this other key?" he asked.

I told him, "That's to our apartment."

The renter was standing under the streetlamp when I got home. We met there every night to talk about the details of our plan, like what time we should leave, and what we would do if it was raining, or if a guard asked us what we were doing. We ran out of realistic details in just a few meetings, but for some reason we still weren't ready to go. So we made up unrealistic details to plan, like alternate driving routes in case the Fifty-ninth Street Bridge collapsed, and ways to get over the cemetery fence in case it was electrified, and how to outsmart the police if we were arrested. We had all sorts of maps and secret codes and tools. We probably would have gone on making plans forever if I hadn't met William Black that night, and learned what I'd learned.

The renter wrote, "You're late." I shrugged my shoulders, just like Dad used to. He wrote, "I got us a rope ladder, just in case." I nodded. "Where were you? I was worried." I told him, "I found the lock."

"You found it?" I nodded. "And?"

I didn't know what to say. I found it and now I can stop looking? I found it and it had nothing to do with Dad? I found it and now I'll wear heavy boots for the rest of my life?

"I wish I hadn't found it." "It wasn't what you were looking for?"

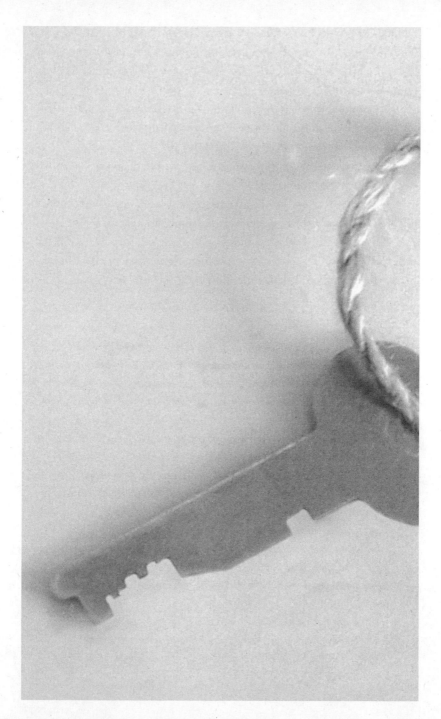

"That's not it." "Then what?" "I found it and now I can't look for it." I could tell he didn't understand me. "Looking for it let me stay close to him for a little while longer." "But won't you always be close to him?" I knew the truth. "No."

He nodded like he was thinking of something, or thinking about a lot of things, or thinking about everything, if that's even possible. He wrote, "Maybe it's time to do the thing we've been planning."

I opened my left hand, because I knew if I tried to say something I would just start crying again.

We agreed to go on Thursday night, which was the second anniversary of Dad's death, which seemed appropriate.

Before I walked into the building, he handed me a letter. "What is this?" He wrote, "Stan went to get coffee. He told me to give this to you in case he didn't get back in time." "What is it?" He shrugged his shoulders and went across the street.

> *Dear Oskar Schell,*
>
> *I've read every letter that you've sent me these past two years. In return, I've sent you many form letters, with the hope of one day being able to give you the proper response you deserve. But the more letters you wrote to me, and the more of yourself you gave, the more daunting my task became.*
>
> *I'm sitting beneath a pear tree as I dictate this to you, overlooking the orchards of a friend's estate. I've spent the past few days here, recovering from some medical treatment that has left me physically and emotionally depleted. As I moped about this morning, feeling sorry for myself, it occurred to me, like a simple solution to an impossible problem: today is the day I've been waiting for.*
>
> *You asked me in your first letter if you could be my protégé. I don't know about that, but I would be happy to have you join me in Cambridge for a few days. I could introduce you to my colleagues, treat you to the best curry outside India, and show you just how boring the life of an astrophysicist can be.*
>
> *You can have a bright future in the sciences, Oskar.*
> *I would be happy to do anything possible to facilitate such a path. It's wonderful to think what would happen if you put your imagination toward scientific ends.*

But Oskar, intelligent people write to me all the time. In your fifth letter you asked, "What if I never stop inventing?" That question has stuck with me.

I wish I were a poet. I've never confessed that to anyone, and I'm confessing it to you, because you've given me reason to feel that I can trust you. I've spent my life observing the universe, mostly in my mind's eye. It's been a tremendously rewarding life, a wonderful life. I've been able to explore the origins of time and space with some of the great living thinkers. But I wish I were a poet.

Albert Einstein, a hero of mine, once wrote, "Our situation is the following. We are standing in front of a closed box which we cannot open."

I'm sure I don't have to tell you that the vast majority of the universe is composed of dark matter. The fragile balance depends on things we'll never be able to see, hear, smell, taste, or touch. Life itself depends on them. What's real? What isn't real? Maybe those aren't the right questions to be asking. What does life depend on?

I wish I had made things for life to depend on.

What if you never stop inventing?

Maybe you're not inventing at all.

I'm being called in for breakfast, so I'll have to end this letter here. There's more I want to tell you, and more I want to hear from you. It's a shame we live on different continents. One shame of many.

It's so beautiful at this hour. The sun is low, the shadows are long, the air is cold and clean. You won't be awake for another five hours, but I can't help feeling that we're sharing this clear and beautiful morning.

> *Your friend,*
> *Stephen Hawking*

MY FEELINGS

A knocking woke me up in the middle of the night.

I had been dreaming about where I came from.

I put on my robe and went to the door.

Who could it be?   Why didn't the doorman ring up?   A neighbor? But why?

More knocking.   I looked through the peephole.   It was your grandfather.

Come in.   Where were you?   Are you OK?

The bottoms of his pants were covered in dirt.

Are you OK?

He nodded.

Come in.   Let me clean you off.   What happened?

He shrugged his shoulders.

Did someone hurt you?

He showed me his right hand.

Are you hurt?

We went to the kitchen table and sat down.   Next to each other.   The windows were black.   He put his hands on his knees.

I slid closer to him until our sides touched.   I put my head on his shoulder.   I wanted as much of us to touch as possible.

I told him, You have to tell me what happened for me to be able to help.

He took a pen from his shirt pocket but there was nothing to write on.

I gave him my open hand.

He wrote, I want to get you some magazines.

In my dream, all of the collapsed ceilings re-formed above us.   The fire went back into the bombs, which rose up and into the bellies of planes whose propellers turned backward, like the second hands of the clocks across Dresden, only faster.

I wanted to slap him with his words.

I wanted to shout, It isn't fair, and bang my fists against the table like a child.

Anything special? he asked on my arm.

Everything special, I said.

Art magazines?

Yes.

Nature magazines?

Yes.

Politics?

Yes.

Celebrities?

Yes.

I told him to bring a suitcase so he could come back with one of everything.

I wanted him to be able to take his things with him.

In my dream, spring came after summer, came after fall, came after winter, came after spring.

I made him breakfast.   I tried to make it delicious.   I wanted him to have good memories, so that maybe he would come back again one day. Or at least miss me.

I wiped the rim of the plate before I gave it to him.   I spread his napkin on his lap.   He didn't say anything.

When the time came, I went downstairs with him.

There was nothing to write on, so he wrote on me.

I might not be back until late.

I told him I understood.

He wrote, I'm going to get you magazines.

I told him, I don't want any magazines.

Maybe not now, but you'll be grateful to have them.

My eyes are crummy.

Your eyes are perfect.

Promise me that you'll take care.

He wrote, I'm only going to get magazines.

Don't cry, I said, by putting my fingers on my face and pushing imaginary tears up my cheeks and back into my eyes.

I was angry because they were my tears.

I told him, You're only getting magazines.

He showed me his left hand.

I tried to notice everything, because I wanted to be able to remember it perfectly.   I've forgotten everything important in my life.

I can't remember what the front door of the house I grew up in looked like.   Or who stopped kissing first, me or my sister.   Or the view from any window but my own.   Some nights I lay awake for hours trying to remember my mother's face.

He turned around and walked away from me.

I went back up to the apartment and sat on the sofa waiting.   Waiting for what?

I can't remember the last thing my father said to me.

He was trapped under the ceiling.   The plaster that covered him was turning red.

He said, I can't feel everything.

I didn't know if he'd meant to say he couldn't feel anything.

He asked, Where is Mommy?

I didn't know if he was talking about my mother or his.

I tried to pull the ceiling off him.

He said, Can you find my glasses for me?

I told him I would look for them.   But everything had been buried.

I had never seen my father cry before.

He said, With my glasses I could be helpful.

I told him, Let me try to free you.

He said, Find my glasses.

They were shouting for everyone to get out.   The rest of the ceiling was about to collapse.

I wanted to stay with him.

But I knew he would want me to leave him.

I told him, Daddy, I have to leave you.

Then he said something.

JONATHAN SAFRAN FOER

It was the last thing he ever said to me.

I can't remember it.

In my dream, the tears went up his cheeks and back into his eyes.

I got up off the sofa and filled a suitcase with the typewriter and as much paper as would fit.

I wrote a note and taped it to the window.   I didn't know whom it was for.

I went from room to room turning off the lights.   I made sure none of the faucets were dripping.   I turned off the heat and unplugged the appliances.   I closed all the windows.

As the cab drove me away, I saw the note.   But I couldn't read it because my eyes are crummy.

In my dream, painters separated green into yellow and blue.

Brown into the rainbow.

Children pulled color from coloring books with crayons, and mothers who had lost children mended their black clothing with scissors.

I think about all of the things I've done, Oskar.   And all of the things I didn't do.   The mistakes I've made are dead to me.   But I can't take back the things I never did.

I found him in the international terminal.   He was sitting at a table with his hands on his knees.

I watched him all morning.

He asked people what time it was, and each person pointed at the clock on the wall.

I have been an expert at watching him.   It's been my life's work. From my bedroom window.   From behind trees.   From across the kitchen table.

I wanted to be with him.

Or anyone.

I don't know if I've ever loved your grandfather.

But I've loved not being alone.

I got very close to him.

I wanted to shout myself into his ear.

I touched his shoulder.

He lowered his head.

How could you?

He wouldn't show me his eyes.   I hate silence.

Say something.

He took his pen from his shirt pocket and the top napkin from the stack on the table.

He wrote, You were happy when I was away.

How could you think that?

We are lying to ourselves and to each other.

Lying about what?   I don't care if we're lying.

I am a bad person.

I don't care.   I don't care what you are.

I can't.

What's killing you?

He took another napkin from the stack.

He wrote, You're killing me.

And then I was silent.

He wrote, You remind me.

I put my hands on the table and told him, You have me.

He took another napkin and wrote, Anna was pregnant.

I told him, I know. She told me.

You know?

I didn't think you knew.   She said it was a secret.   I'm glad you know.

He wrote, I'm sorry I know.

It's better to lose than never to have had.

I lost something I never had.

You had everything.

When did she tell you?

We were in bed talking.

He pointed at, When.

Near the end.

What did she say?

She said, I'm going to have a baby.

Was she happy?

She was overjoyed.

Why didn't you say anything?

Why didn't you?

In my dream, people apologized for things that were about to happen, and lit candles by inhaling.

I have been seeing Oskar, he wrote.

I know.

You know?

Of course I know.

He flipped back to, Why didn't you say anything?

Why didn't you?

The alphabet went z, y, x, w . . .

The clocks went tock-tick, tock-tick . . .

He wrote, I was with him last night.   That's where I was.   I buried the letters.

What letters?

The letters I never sent.

Buried them where?

In the ground.   That's where I was.   I buried the key, too.

What key?

To your apartment.

Our apartment.

He put his hands on the table.

Lovers pulled up each other's underwear, buttoned each other's shirts, and dressed and dressed and dressed.

I told him, Say it.

When I saw Anna for the last time.

Say it.

When we.

Say it!

He put his hands on his knees.

I wanted to hit him.

I wanted to hold him.

I wanted to shout myself into his ear.

I asked, So what happens now?

I don't know.

Do you want to go home?

He flipped back to, I can't.

Then you'll go away?

He pointed at, I can't.

Then we are out of options.

We sat there.

Things were happening around us, but nothing was happening between us.

Above us, the screens said which flights were landing and which were taking off.

Madrid departing.

Rio arriving.

Stockholm departing.

Paris departing.

Milan arriving.

Everyone was coming or going.

People around the world were moving from one place to another.

No one was staying.

I said, What if we stay?

Stay?

Here.   What if we stay here at the airport?

He wrote, Is that another joke?

I shook my head no.

How could we stay here?

I told him, There are pay phones, so I could call Oskar and let him know I'm OK.   And there are paper stores where you could buy daybooks and pens.   There are places to eat.   And money machines. And bathrooms.   Even televisions.

Not coming or going.

Not something or nothing.

Not yes or no.

My dream went all the way back to the beginning.

The rain rose into the clouds, and the animals descended the ramp.

Two by two.

Two giraffes.

Two spiders.

Two goats.

Two lions.

Two mice.

Two monkeys.

Two snakes.

Two elephants.

The rain came after the rainbow.

As I type this, we are sitting across from each other at a table.   It's not big, but it's big enough for the two of us.   He has a cup of coffee and I am drinking tea.

When the pages are in the typewriter, I can't see his face.

In that way I am choosing you over him.

I don't need to see him.

I don't need to know if he is looking up at me.

It's not even that I trust him not to leave.

I know this won't last.

I'd rather be me than him.

The words are coming so easily.

The pages are coming easily.

At the end of my dream, Eve put the apple back on the branch.   The tree went back into the ground.   It became a sapling, which became a seed.

God brought together the land and the water, the sky and the water, the water and the water, evening and morning, something and nothing.

He said, Let there be light.

And there was darkness.

Oskar.

The night before I lost everything was like any other night.

Anna and I kept each other awake very late.   We laughed.   Young sisters in a bed under the roof of their childhood home.   Wind on the window.

How could anything less deserve to be destroyed?

I thought we would be awake all night.   Awake for the rest of our lives.

The spaces between our words grew.

It became difficult to tell when we were talking and when we were silent.

The hairs of our arms touched.

It was late, and we were tired.

We assumed there would be other nights.

Anna's breathing started to slow, but I still wanted to talk.

She rolled onto her side.

I said, I want to tell you something.

She said, You can tell me tomorrow.

I had never told her how much I loved her.

She was my sister.

We slept in the same bed.

There was never a right time to say it.

It was always unnecessary.

The books in my father's shed were sighing.

The sheets were rising and falling around me with Anna's breathing.

I thought about waking her.

But it was unnecessary.

There would be other nights.

And how can you say I love you to someone you love?

I rolled onto my side and fell asleep next to her.

Here is the point of everything I have been trying to tell you, Oskar.

It's always necessary.

I love you,

Grandma

BEAUTIFUL AND TRUE

Mom made spaghetti for dinner that night. Ron ate with us. I asked him if he was still interested in buying me a five-piece drum set with Zildjian cymbals. He said, "Yeah. I think that would be great." "How about a double bass pedal?" "I don't know what that is, but I bet we could arrange it." I asked him why he didn't have his own family. Mom said, "Oskar!" I said, *"What?"* Ron put down his knife and fork and said, "It's OK." He said, "I did have a family, Oskar. I had a wife and a daughter." "Did you get divorced?" He laughed and said, "No." "Then where are they?" Mom looked at her plate. Ron said, "They were in an accident." "What kind of accident?" "A car accident." "I didn't know that." "Your mom and I met in a group for people that have lost family. That's where we became friends." I didn't look at Mom, and she didn't look at me. Why hadn't she told me she was in a group?

"How come you didn't die in the accident?" Mom said, "That's enough, Oskar." Ron said, "I wasn't in the car." "Why weren't you in the car?" Mom looked out the window. Ron ran his finger around his plate and said, "I don't know." "What's weird," I said, "is that I've never seen you cry." He said, "I cry all the time."

My backpack was already packed, and I'd already gotten the other supplies together, like the altimeter and granola bars and the Swiss Army knife I'd dug up in Central Park, so there was nothing else to do. Mom tucked me in at 9:36.

"Do you want me to read to you?" "No thanks." "Is there anything you want to talk about?" If she wasn't going to say anything, I wasn't going to say anything, so I shook my head no. "I could make up a story?" "No thank you." "Or look for mistakes in the *Times*?" "Thanks,

Mom, but not really." "That was nice of Ron to tell you about his family." "I guess so." "Try to be nice to him. He's been such a good friend, and he needs help, too." "I'm tired."

I set my alarm for 11:50 P.M., even though I knew I wouldn't sleep.

While I lay there in bed, waiting for the time to come, I did a lot of inventing.

I invented a biodegradable car.

I invented a book that listed every word in every language. It wouldn't be a very useful book, but you could hold it and know that everything you could possibly say was in your hands.

What about a googolplex telephones?

What about safety nets everywhere?

At 11:50 P.M., I got up extremely quietly, took my things from under the bed, and opened the door one millimeter at a time, so it wouldn't make any noise. Bart, the night doorman, was asleep at the desk, which was lucky, because it meant I didn't have to tell any more lies. The renter was waiting for me under the streetlamp. We shook hands, which was weird. At exactly 12:00, Gerald pulled up in the limousine. He opened the door for us, and I told him, "I knew you'd be on time." He patted me on the back and said, "I wouldn't be late." It was my second time in a limousine ever.

As we drove, I imagined we were standing still and the world was coming toward us. The renter sat all the way on his side, not doing anything, and I saw the Trump Tower, which Dad thought was the ugliest building in America, and the United Nations, which Dad thought was incredibly beautiful. I rolled down the window and stuck my arm out. I curved my hand like an airplane wing. If my hand had been big enough, I could've made the limousine fly. What about enormous gloves?

Gerald smiled at me in the rearview mirror and asked if we wanted any music. I asked him if he had any kids. He said he had two daughters. "What do they like?" "What do they *like?*" "Yeah." "Lemme see. Kelly, my baby, likes Barbie and puppies and bead bracelets." "I'll make her a bead bracelet." "I'm sure she'd like that." "What else?" "If it's soft and pink, she likes it." "I like soft and pink things, too." He said, "Well, all

JONATHAN SAFRAN FOER

right." "And what about your other daughter?" "Janet? She likes sports. Her favorite is basketball, and I'll tell you, she can play. I don't mean for a girl, either. I mean she's *good*."

"Are they both special?" He cracked up and said, "Of course their pop is gonna say they're special." "But objectively." "What's that?" "Like, factually. Truthfully." "The truth is I'm their pop."

I stared out the window some more. We went over the part of the bridge that wasn't in any borough, and I turned around and watched the buildings get smaller. I figured out which button opened the sunroof, and I stood up with the top half of my body sticking out of the car. I took pictures of the stars with Grandpa's camera, and in my head I connected them to make words, whatever words I wanted. Whenever we were about to go under a bridge or into a tunnel, Gerald told me to get back into the car so I wouldn't be decapitated, which I know about but really, *really* wish I didn't. In my brain I made "shoe" and "inertia" and "invincible."

It was 12:56 A.M. when Gerald drove up onto the grass and pulled the limousine right next to the cemetery. I put on my backpack, and the renter got the shovel, and we climbed onto the roof of the limousine so we could get over the fence.

Gerald whispered, "You sure you want to do this?"

Through the fence I told him, "It probably won't take more than twenty minutes. Maybe thirty." He tossed over the renter's suitcases and said, "I'll be here."

Because it was so dark, we had to follow the beam of my flashlight. I pointed it at a lot of tombstones, looking for Dad's.

Mark Crawford
Diana Strait
Jason Barker, Jr.
Morris Cooper
May Goodman
Helen Stein
Gregory Robertson Judd
John Fielder
Susan Kidd

JONATHAN SAFRAN FOER

I kept thinking about how they were all the names of dead people, and how names are basically the only thing that dead people keep.

It was 1:22 when we found Dad's grave.

The renter offered me the shovel.

I said, "You go first."

He put it in my hand.

I pushed it into the dirt and stepped all of my weight onto it. I didn't even know how many pounds I was, because I'd been so busy trying to find Dad.

It was extremely hard work, and I was only strong enough to remove a little bit of dirt at a time. My arms got incredibly tired, but that was OK, because since we only had one shovel, we took turns.

The twenty minutes passed, and then another twenty minutes.

We kept digging, but we weren't getting anywhere.

Another twenty minutes passed.

Then the batteries in the flashlight ran out, and we couldn't see our hands in front of us. That wasn't part of our plan, and neither were replacement batteries, even though they obviously should have been. How could I have forgotten something so simple and important?

I called Gerald's cell phone and asked if he could go pick up some D batteries for us. He asked if everything was all right. It was so dark that it was even hard to hear. I said, "Yeah, we're OK, we just need some D batteries." He said the only store he remembered was about fifteen minutes away. I told him, "I'll pay you extra." He said, "It's not about paying me extra."

Fortunately, because what we were doing was digging up Dad's grave, we didn't need to see our hands in front of us. We only had to feel the shovel moving the dirt.

So we shoveled in the darkness and silence.

I thought about everything underground, like worms, and roots, and clay, and buried treasure.

We shoveled.

I wondered how many things had died since the first thing was born. A trillion? A googolplex?

We shoveled.

I wondered what the renter was thinking about.

After a while, my phone played "The Flight of the Bumblebee," so I looked at the caller ID. "Gerald." "Got 'em." "Can you bring them to us so we don't have to waste time going back to the limousine?" He didn't say anything for a few seconds. "I guess I could do that." I couldn't describe where we were to him, so I just kept calling his name, and he found my voice.

It felt much better to be able to see. Gerald said, "Doesn't look like you two have gotten very far." I told him, "We're not good shovelers." He put his driving gloves in his jacket pocket, kissed the cross that he wore around his neck, and took the shovel from me. Because he was so strong, he could move a lot of dirt quickly.

It was 2:56 when the shovel touched the coffin. We all heard the sound and looked at each other.

I told Gerald thanks.

He winked at me, then started walking back to the car, and then he disappeared in the darkness. "Oh yeah," I heard him say, even though I couldn't find him with my flashlight, "Janet, the older one, she loves cereal. She'd eat it three meals a day if we let her."

I told him, "I love cereal, too."

He said, "All right," and his footsteps got quieter and quieter.

I lowered myself into the hole and used my paintbrush to wipe away the dirt that was left.

One thing that surprised me was that the coffin was wet. I guess I wasn't expecting that, because how could so much water get underground?

Another thing that surprised me was that the coffin was cracked in a few places, probably from the weight of all that dirt. If Dad had been in there, ants and worms could have gotten in through the cracks and eaten him, or at least microscopic bacteria could have. I knew it shouldn't matter, because once you're dead, you don't feel anything. So why did it feel like it mattered?

Another thing that surprised me was how the coffin wasn't locked or even nailed shut. The lid just rested on top of it, so that anyone who wanted to could open it up. That didn't seem right. But on the other hand, who would want to open a coffin?

I opened the coffin.

I was surprised again, although again I shouldn't have been. I was surprised that Dad wasn't there. In my brain I knew he wouldn't be, obviously, but I guess my heart believed something else. Or maybe I was surprised by how incredibly empty it was. I felt like I was looking into the dictionary definition of emptiness.

I'd had the idea to dig up Dad's coffin the night after I met the renter. I was lying in bed and I had the revelation, like a simple solution to an impossible problem. The next morning I threw pebbles at the guest room window, like he wrote for me to in his note, but I'm not very accurate at throwing, so I had Stan do it. When the renter met me at the corner I told him my idea.

He wrote, "Why would you want to do that?" I told him, "Because it's the truth, and Dad loved the truth." "What truth?" "That he's dead."

After that, we met every afternoon and discussed the details, like we were planning a war. We talked about how we would get to the cemetery, and different ways of climbing fences, and where we would find a shovel, and all of the other necessary instruments, like a flashlight and wire cutters and juice boxes. We planned and planned, but for some reason we never talked about what we would actually do once we'd opened the coffin.

It wasn't until the day before we were going to go that the renter asked the obvious question.

I told him, "We'll fill it, obviously."

He asked another obvious question.

At first I suggested filling the coffin with things from Dad's life, like his red pens or his jeweler's magnifying glass, which is called a loupe, or even his tuxedo. I guess I got that idea from the Blacks who made museums of each other. But the more we discussed it, the less sense it made, because what good would that do, anyway? Dad wouldn't be able to use them, because he was dead, and the renter also pointed out that it would probably be nice to have things of his around.

"I could fill the coffin with jewelry, like they used to do with famous Egyptians, which I know about." "But he wasn't Egyptian." "And he didn't like jewelry." "He didn't like jewelry?"

"Maybe I could bury things I'm ashamed of," I suggested, and in my head I was thinking of the old telephone, and the sheet of stamps of Great American Inventors that I got mad at Grandma about, and the script of *Hamlet*, and the letters I had received from strangers, and the stupid card I'd made for myself, and my tambourine, and the unfinished scarf. But that didn't make any sense either, because the renter reminded me that just because you bury something, you don't really *bury* it. "Then what?" I asked.

"I have an idea," he wrote. "I'll show you tomorrow."

Why did I trust him so much?

The next night, when I met him on the corner at 11:50, he had two suitcases. I didn't ask him what was in them, because for some reason I thought I should wait until he told me, even though he was *my* dad, which made the coffin mine, too.

Three hours later, when I climbed into the hole, brushed away the dirt, and opened the lid, the renter opened the suitcases. They were filled with papers. I asked him what they were. He wrote, "I lost a son." "You did?" He showed me his left palm. "How did he die?" "I lost him before he died." "How?" "I went away." "Why?" He wrote, "I was afraid." "Afraid of what?" "Afraid of losing him." "Were you afraid of him dying?" "I was afraid of him living." "Why?" He wrote, "Life is scarier than death."

"So what's all that paper?"

He wrote, "Things I wasn't able to tell him. Letters."

To be honest, I don't know what I understood then.

I don't think I figured out that he was my grandpa, not even in the deep parts of my brain. I definitely didn't make the connection between the letters in his suitcases and the envelopes in Grandma's dresser, even if I should have.

But I must have understood something, I *must* have, because why else would I have opened my left hand?

When I got home it was 4:22 A.M. Mom was on the sofa by the door. I thought she would be incredibly angry at me, but she didn't say anything. She just kissed my head.

"Don't you want to know where I was?" She said, "I trust you."

"But aren't you curious?" She said, "I assume you'd tell me if you wanted me to know." "Are you going to tuck me in?" "I thought I'd stay here for a little while longer." "Are you mad at me?" She shook her head no. "Is Ron mad at me?" "No." "Are you sure?" "Yes."

I went to my room.

My hands were dirty, but I didn't wash them. I wanted them to stay dirty, at least until the next morning. I hoped some of the dirt would stay under my fingernails for a long time, and maybe some of the microscopic material would be there forever.

I turned off the lights.

I put my backpack on the floor, took off my clothes, and got into bed.

I stared at the fake stars.

What about windmills on the roof of every skyscraper?

What about a kite-string bracelet?

A fishing-line bracelet?

What if skyscrapers had roots?

What if you had to water skyscrapers, and play classical music to them, and know if they like sun or shade?

What about a teakettle?

I got out of bed and ran to the door in my undies.

Mom was still on the sofa. She wasn't reading, or listening to music, or doing anything.

She said, "You're awake."

I started crying.

She opened her arms and said, "What is it?"

I ran to her and said, "I don't want to be hospitalized."

She pulled me into her so my head was against the soft part of her shoulder, and she squeezed me. "You're not going to be hospitalized."

I told her, "I promise I'm going to be better soon."

She said, "There's nothing wrong with you."

"I'll be happy and normal."

She put her fingers around the back of my neck.

I told her, "I tried incredibly hard. I don't know how I could have tried harder."

She said, "Dad would have been very proud of you."

"Do you think so?"

"I know so."

I cried some more. I wanted to tell her all of the lies that I'd told her. And then I wanted her to tell me that it was OK, because sometimes you have to do something bad to do something good. And then I wanted to tell her about the phone. And then I wanted her to tell me that Dad still would have been proud of me.

She said, "Dad called me from the building that day."

I pulled away from her.

"What?"

"He called from the building."

"On your cell phone?"

She nodded yes, and it was the first time since Dad died that I'd seen her not try to stop her tears. Was she relieved? Was she depressed? Grateful? Exhausted?

"What did he say?"

"He told me he was on the street, that he'd gotten out of the building. He said he was walking home."

"But he wasn't."

"No."

Was I angry? Was I glad?

"He made it up so you wouldn't worry."

"That's right."

Frustrated? Panicky? Optimistic?

"But he knew you knew."

"He did."

I put my fingers around her neck, where her hair started.

I don't know how late it got.

I probably fell asleep, but I don't remember. I cried so much that everything blurred into everything else. At some point she was carrying me to my room. Then I was in bed. She was looking over me. I don't believe in God, but I believe that things are extremely complicated, and her looking over me was as complicated as anything ever could be. But it was also incredibly simple. In my only life, she was my mom, and I was her son.

I told her, "It's OK if you fall in love again."

She said, "I won't fall in love again."

I told her, "I want you to."

She kissed me and said, "I'll never fall in love again."

I told her, "You don't have to make it up so I won't worry."

She said, "I love you."

I rolled onto my side and listened to her walk back to the sofa.

I heard her crying. I imagined her wet sleeves. Her tired eyes.

One minute fifty-one seconds . . .

Four minutes thirty-eight seconds . . .

Seven minutes . . .

I felt in the space between the bed and the wall, and found *Stuff That Happened to Me*. It was completely full. I was going to have to start a new volume soon. I read that it was the paper that kept the towers burning. All of those notepads, and Xeroxes, and printed e-mails, and photographs of kids, and books, and dollar bills in wallets, and documents in files . . . all of them were fuel. Maybe if we lived in a paperless society, which lots of scientists say we'll probably live in one day soon, Dad would still be alive. Maybe I shouldn't start a new volume.

I grabbed the flashlight from my backpack and aimed it at the book. I saw maps and drawings, pictures from magazines and newspapers and the Internet, pictures I'd taken with Grandpa's camera. The whole world was in there. Finally, I found the pictures of the falling body.

Was it Dad?

Maybe.

Whoever it was, it was somebody.

I ripped the pages out of the book.

I reversed the order, so the last one was first, and the first was last.

When I flipped through them, it looked like the man was floating up through the sky.

And if I'd had more pictures, he would've flown through a window, back into the building, and the smoke would've poured into the hole that the plane was about to come out of.

Dad would've left his messages backward, until the machine was empty, and the plane would've flown backward away from him, all the way to Boston.

He would've taken the elevator to the street and pressed the button for the top floor.

He would've walked backward to the subway, and the subway would've gone backward through the tunnel, back to our stop.

Dad would've gone backward through the turnstile, then swiped his Metrocard backward, then walked home backward as he read the *New York Times* from right to left.

He would've spit coffee into his mug, unbrushed his teeth, and put hair on his face with a razor.

He would've gotten back into bed, the alarm would've rung backward, he would've dreamt backward.

Then he would've gotten up again at the end of the night before the worst day.

He would've walked backward to my room, whistling "I Am the Walrus" backward.

He would've gotten into bed with me.

We would've looked at the stars on my ceiling, which would've pulled back their light from our eyes.

I'd have said "Nothing" backward.

He'd have said "Yeah, buddy?" backward.

I'd have said "Dad?" backward, which would have sounded the same as "Dad" forward.

He would have told me the story of the Sixth Borough, from the voice in the can at the end to the beginning, from "I love you" to "Once upon a time . . ."

We would have been safe.

JONATHAN SAFRAN FOER

A portion of *Everything is Illuminated* previously appeared in *The New Yorker.* This is a work of fiction. Names, characters, and incidents are the product of the author's imagination, except in the case of historical figures and events, which are used fictitiously, and, of course, the case of JSF himself.

ACKNOWLEDGMENTS

At least once every day since I met her, I have felt blessed to know Nicole Aragi. She inspires me not only to write more ambitiously, but to smile more widely, and to have a fuller, better heart. I am so, so grateful. (*Atyab lee itha entee toukleha.*)

And it is my pleasure, and honor, to think of the wonderful people at Houghton Mifflin as family — Eric Chinski, in particular, whose advise, in literature and life, seems always to boil down to: feel more. Which is always the best advice.

Finally, to those who read earlier drafts of this: thank you.

•

Letters attributed to real people in *Extremely Loud and Incredibly Close* are entirely fictitious, even if they seem real.

ILLUSTRATIONS

Pages 283, 319, 343, 405, 424, 438, 502, 550, 551, 555, copyright © 2005 by Debra Meltzer; pages 285, 456–457, © Marianne Müller; pages 287, 393, copyright © 2005 by Christopher Moisan; page 344 © The Scotsman / Corbis Sygma; page 345, © Underwood & Underwood / Corbis; page 346, © Stephen Waits; page 347, © Peter Johnson / Corbis; page 348 © Alison Wright / Corbis; pages 349, 352, 495, 617–645 (right-hand pages), photo illustration based on a photograph by Lyle Owerko © 2001 / Polaris; pages 350, 351 © David Bell / Corbis; page 354, © Chang W. Lee / New York Times; page 355, © Randy Faris / Corbis; page 356, "Earliest Human Relatives (American Museum of Natural History)," © Hiroshi Sugimoto; page 357, © ESA / CNES / Corbis Sygma; page 379, © Alan Schein Photography / Corbis; pages 382, 579, © Kevin Fleming / Corbis, page 385 © Palani Mohan / Corbis; page 445, © Lester V. Bergman / Corbis; page 481, © Ralph Crane / Time & Life Pictures / Getty; page 531, video grab courtesy of WNYW Television / AFP / Getty; page 536 © James Leynse / Corbis; page 543, © Mario Tama / Getty Images North America / Getty; page 584, © Philip Harvey / Corbis; page 593, copyright © 2005 by Anne Chalmers; page 608, © Rob Matheson / Corbis.

ACKNOWLEDGMENTS

A major heartfelt thank you to everyone at Houghton Mifflin. You have encouraged me to be myself, even when that self would test a mother's patience. I feel lucky to be a part of your family.